LOVERS
AND LIARS

Sally Beauman

BANTAM BOOKS

LONDON · NEW YORK · TORONTO · SYDNEY · AUCKLAND

LOVERS AND LIARS
A BANTAM BOOK : 0 553 40727 9

Originally published in Great Britain by Bantam Press,
a division of Transworld Publishers Ltd

PRINTING HISTORY
Bantam Press edition published 1994
Bantam edition published 1995

Set in 10pt Linotype Plantin by
Chippendale Type Ltd, Otley, West Yorkshire.

Bantam Books are published by Transworld Publishers Ltd,
61–63 Uxbridge Road, Ealing, London W5 5SA,
in Australia by Transworld Publishers (Australia) Pty Ltd,
15–25 Helles Avenue, Moorebank, NSW 2170,
and in New Zealand by Transworld Publishers (NZ) Ltd,
3 William Pickering Drive, Albany, Auckland.

Reproduced, printed and bound in Great Britain by
Cox & Wyman Ltd, Reading, Berks.

Also by Sally Beauman

DESTINY
DARK ANGEL

To James; with my love and thanks also to my friends Carlos, Alexis, Howard, and that great games-player, Mr Mackenzie.

PROLOGUE
FOUR PARCELS

The main London office of ICD – Intercontinental Deliveries – is off St Mary Axe in the City. A century ago, there was a dank overcrowded cluster of houses around the courtyard site. They included a lodging-house for sailors, a brothel and a public house which sold gin at twopence a glass. But that was a century ago, before City land values rose to their present heights: ICD's head office was now on the fifteenth floor of an elegant temple of steel and glass.

From this office, true to the company name, five continents were linked. An expanding fleet of planes, trucks, vans and motor cycles ensured that urgent parcels and documents were delivered promptly, by uniformed courier, all over the world.

In the summer of 1993, a new employee was hired to adorn ICD's recently redecorated reception area. The position was advertised in *The Times*. The successful candidate was a twinset-and-pearls girl named Susannah. She had a diploma in flower arranging from a Swiss finishing-school, a generous dress allowance from her businessman father and an accent like the finest cut-glass.

Had Susannah's assets been purely decorative, subsequent events might have turned out very differently. But she proved to be intelligent, a fast efficient worker, with good word-processing skills. More important still Susannah had an excellent memory. Unlike most witnesses, her recall of events was unwavering and sharp.

This was to prove important, for it was Susannah, early in January the following year, who took delivery of the four identical parcels, and Susannah – returning to the office after the extended Christmas and New Year break – who at nine-thirty in the morning took their sender's odd and crucial first call.

It was a Tuesday morning. It was threatening snow outside, and the City was still quiet. Susannah expected business to be slack. The New Year's celebrations had fallen on a weekend, so yesterday, a Monday, had been a holiday too. An extra day's escape from office tedium. Susannah yawned and stretched. She was not complaining; the long weekend had given her an extra morning on the ski-slopes at Gstaad.

She made herself some coffee, greeted a few late arrivals who worked backstage in accounts, arranged the fresh flowers she always had on her desk, and in a desultory way flicked through the pages of December *Vogue*.

Her mind was still on the ski-slopes, and a certain stockbroker she had met, who took the worst of the black runs with fearless skill. He had been at Eton with her older brothers, and a fellow guest at her chalet. She wondered whether, as promised, he would call her to arrange lunch. When the telephone rang at nine-thirty, she felt a sense of pleased anticipation – but it was not her stockbroker. A woman's voice. Business, then. Susannah checked her watch, and logged the call.

Most ICD deliveries were requested by female secretaries, so there was nothing unusual about this call initially – except the caller's voice, which was low-pitched, English, harmonious, with an accent very similar to Susannah's own. Susannah would have denied fiercely that she was a snob, had anyone ever accused her of such a thing, but she was certainly aware, as is everyone English, of the subtle and tell-tale modulations of accent. She responded at once to the fact that her caller was one of her own peer group – and this was to prove useful. As a witness, and from the first, Susannah was alert.

There was, however, something odd about the caller's manner. It was exceptionally hesitant, even vague.

'I wonder,' said the voice, as if this were the most unlikely request to make to a courier company, 'if you could possibly arrange hand-delivery of four parcels?'

'Of course,' Susannah said. 'The destination of the parcels?'

'One must go to Paris,' said the voice, 'and one to New York—'

'City or state?' Susannah interrupted.

'Oh, city. Yes. Manhattan. Then one is within London, and the fourth must go to Venice . . . ' The voice sounded apologetic, doubtful, as if Venice were a village in Tibet, or some Arctic Circle settlement. There was a breathy pause. 'Will that be possible?'

'Absolutely. No problem.'

'How wonderful.' The voice sounded greatly relieved. 'How clever. The thing is . . . the four parcels must be delivered tomorrow morning, without fail.'

Susannah's manner became a little less warm. She began to suspect that this female caller was putting her on. 'I can guarantee that,' she replied crisply, 'providing we take delivery before four this afternoon.'

'Oh, they'll definitely be with you this morning.'

'Would you like me to arrange a pick-up?'

'Pick-up?' There was a hesitation, then a low laugh. 'No. That won't be necessary. I'll bring them over to your office myself. They'll be with you by eleven . . . '

By now, Susannah found the woman's approach distinctly odd. Urgency mixed with such vagueness was unusual. The woman sounded spaced-out, or perhaps under some terrible pressure. Susannah began to run down the details on her despatch programme, at which point – or so she would later claim – the woman became evasive.

'Size of parcels?' Susannah said.

'I'm sorry?'

'Size. You see, if they're especially large or heavy, I need to make special arrangements.'

'Oh, they're not *large*.' The woman sounded reproachful. 'They're light. Quite light. Not heavy at all . . . '

'Contents?'

'I don't understand . . . '

'We need to attach customs declaration forms for the three going abroad,' Susannah explained. 'Because of narcotics regulations, mainly. So I need an indication as to contents.'

'Oh I *see*.' The voice sounded amused. 'Well, I'm not sending cocaine, and I don't *think* I'd use a courier company if I were . . . Still, I do see the problem. Contents . . . yes. Could you put "Gifts"?'

'I'd need to be more specific, I'm afraid . . . '

'Of course. Birthday gifts?'

Susannah set her lips. 'More specific still. Confectionery. Books. Toys – something like that.'

'Oh, that's easy then. Birthday gifts – articles of clothing. Put that, please.'

'On all those going abroad?'

'Yes.' There was a pleasant laugh. 'Odd, isn't it? All my closest friends seem to be Capricorns . . . '

Susannah made a face at her computer. She began flashing up details of flights and courier runs. Watching figures and times, she began to run down the remaining queries: address of sender, addresses of recipients, preferred method of billing. The voice interrupted.

'Oh, that can all be dealt with when I bring the parcels in . . . '

'Fine. But will you want to pay by cheque or credit card? I can take the details now—'

'Cash,' the voice interrupted, suddenly firm. 'I'll settle the account in cash. When I come in.'

Cash settlement was very unusual; it was at this point that Susannah's doubts really began. She said, 'Fine. If I could just take a name and contact number—'

'I have to go now,' said the voice. 'Thank you *so* much. You've been tremendously helpful.' Then, without further clarification, this odd woman hung up the phone.

Susannah was left feeling irritated. She suspected she had heard the last of this transaction. She did not expect the woman caller to materialize. She did not expect ever to set eyes on these four parcels. A time-waster, she decided. But she was wrong.

*   *   *

At 11 a.m. precisely the lobby doors swung back, and one of the most beautiful women Susannah had ever seen walked into reception. Susannah was at once certain that she must be a model although she did not recognize her. She managed not to stare, but so exquisite was this woman, so perfect and so costly every detail of her dress, that Susannah was transfixed. She was, later, able to furnish an exact description – as perhaps had been the intention all along.

The woman was at least five feet ten inches tall, and enviably slender. Her hair, cut short, was that compendium of gold and silver achieved only when nature has been aided by an expensive hairdresser. She needed, and wore, no make-up. Her skin was tanned, her eyes sapphire blue, her teeth perfect, and her smile warm.

Around her wrist, just visible, was a gold Cartier tank watch on a green crocodile strap, which Susannah at once coveted. She was wearing the most beautiful fur coat Susannah had ever seen in her life, a coat which made Susannah revise all her pious beliefs about protecting small furry animals: this coat, full length and luxuriant, was sable.

Beneath the coat the woman wore Chanel head to foot. On this point Susannah was later adamant. It was a suit of soft beige tweed, featured in the very issue of *Vogue* now on her desk. Susannah could point to the page on which it was modelled, and she could explain that all the accessories were identical too, from the classic impractical two-tone sling-back Chanel shoes, to the double strand of real matched pearls. There they were around this amazing woman's throat – and there they were on the page of the magazine, with a caption detailing their source (Bulgari) and their cost (a quarter million).

Under her arm, the woman carried four small parcels of identical size and shape, packed in an identical way, but of varying weight. The hand-over was swift. The details were lodged on Susannah's computer and could later be re-called. This was the information they gave:

Name and address of sender:

Mrs J. A. Hamilton
132 Eaton Place
London SW1
Telephone – 071 750 0007

Names and addresses of recipients:

1) M. Pascal Lamartine
Atelier 5
13, rue du Bac
PARIS 56742

2) Mr Johnny Appleyard
Apt 15, 31 Gramercy Park
New York 10003
NY

3) Signor James McMullen
6, Palazzo Ossorio
Calle Streta
Campiello Albrizzi
VENICE 2361

4) Ms Genevieve Hunter
Flat 1, 56 Gibson Square
London N1

The total delivery charge was £175.50. The required notes
were peeled from a brand-new Vuitton wallet; the fifty-
pence piece was taken from a brand-new Vuitton purse.
With polite low-voiced thanks, the sender left the ICD
office ten minutes after she arrived.

Later, when it emerged that this transaction was not
all it seemed – one of the recipients was already dead,
and none of the recipients had birthdays in January –
Susannah was not surprised. There had been, she said,
a number of odd inconsistencies.

In the first place, the woman in the sable coat had claimed to be Mrs J. A. Hamilton but she had worn no wedding ring. In the second, she claimed to be the person who had telephoned earlier and this was patently absurd. The woman on the telephone had been English, very English indeed; the beauty in the sable coat had been American.

'Which was strange,' Susannah said, frowning. She turned away from her two questioners to look out of her window; her gaze rested on its view of City towers and spires.

'Why strange?' the first of her questioners prompted.

'Because the discrepancy was unnecessary,' Susannah replied. 'It was as if she knew . . . '

'Knew what?' the second questioner asked.

'Knew that I'd be asked about the transaction,' said Susannah. 'Don't you see? That amazing coat, those clothes. Two different women, claiming to be one and the same. Whoever she was, she wanted to make sure that I remembered . . . ' She paused. Her two questioners exchanged glances.

'Why would she want to do that?' Susannah asked.

PART ONE
FOUR DELIVERIES

I

PASCAL LAMARTINE

The package was delivered shortly after nine. Pascal Lamartine, running late for his meeting, signed for it, shook it, and put it down on the breakfast table. No urgency: he would open it later. Meanwhile, he was trying to do several things simultaneously – make coffee, pack, check his camera cases, and, most difficult of all, persuade his daughter Marianne to eat her breakfast egg.

Packages, to Pascal, came in two categories. If they were flat, they contained photographs and might be urgent; if they were not then they were usually something unimportant, promotional materials sent out by a PR firm. His daughter Marianne, aged seven, saw things differently. To her, parcels signified Christmas or birthdays; they signified pleasure. When Pascal had completed his packing, and made the coffee, he returned to the table to find Marianne had the parcel in her hand. The egg – unappetizing, Pascal had to admit, but then he could not cook the simplest things – was being ignored.

Marianne examined the parcel. She fingered its string. She fixed her father with an expectant gaze.

'A present,' she said. 'Look, Papa. Someone's sent you a present. You should open it at once.'

Pascal smiled. He concentrated on the task of mixing a perfect *café au lait*, Marianne-style. The drink had to be milky and sweet. It had to be served in the traditional French way, in the green pottery bowl his mother had given Marianne, a bowl she adored, which had an orange china rooster perched on its rim. The bowl then had to be positioned on the table so the rooster faced Marianne. His daughter had a passion for finicky detail which sometimes worried him. Pascal feared that it might be a by-product of his bitter divorce. He stirred in three sugar lumps, and passed the bowl across to her. He looked at it sadly. The bowl, three years old, slightly chipped, was a relic: his mother had been dead almost a year.

'I'm afraid it won't be a present, darling,' he said, sitting down. 'No-one sends me presents any more. No doubt it's because I'm so very, very old . . . ' He hunched his shoulders as he said this, and stooped his tall frame. He pulled a long melancholy face, and attempted to convey extreme decrepitude. Marianne laughed. 'How old are you?' she said, still fingering the parcel.

'Thirty-five.' Pascal resisted the temptation briefly, then lit a cigarette. He sighed. 'Thirty-six this spring. Ancient!'

Marianne assessed this. There was a tiny flicker in the eyes, a pursing of the lips. To her, Pascal realized, thirty-five must indeed sound very old. My father, Methuselah. He gave a small shrug: some shadow passed at the back of his mind. To Marianne, age was a fact, without corollaries or consequences. She was still too young to associate ageing with sickness or with death, even now.

'The egg's a failure, isn't it?' He smiled. 'Don't struggle with it. Eat the *tartine* instead.'

Marianne gave him a grateful look and took a bite of the crisp bread with its coating of strawberry jam. Jam at once adhered itself to chin, hand, tablecloth. Pascal reached across tenderly and transferred a morsel from her chin to the tip of her nose. Marianne giggled. She munched with a contented expression, then slid the parcel across to him.

'It might be a present,' she said seriously. 'A nice present. You never know. Open it, Papa, please. Before we go.'

Pascal glanced at his watch. He had one hour in which to deliver Marianne back to her mother in the suburbs, brave the rush-hour traffic back into the centre of Paris, get to the meeting with Françoise, and hand over the new batch of photographs. If he was not delayed, he could easily make it to de Gaulle airport for the noon flight to London. He hesitated: they should have left his apartment ten minutes ago . . .

On the other hand, Marianne's smart and pathetic suitcase, the suitcase he had bought for her himself, was already packed. The menagerie of teddy bears and rabbits, and the sad stuffed kangaroo without which she could not sleep were all ready and waiting in the hall. He hated to disappoint her, and he could see the expectation in her eyes.

'Very well,' he said. 'Let's see what I have here . . . ' He drew the parcel towards him. Now that he examined it more closely, it did look interesting – and unusual too, not the kind of package sent out by PRs. Brown paper, new, enclosing some kind of box. Light in weight. A neat parcel, about six inches square. The string binding had been knotted at intervals, the knots sealed with red wax. He had not seen, let alone received, such a parcel in years. His name and address, he saw, had been printed by hand in capitals with precise care. He looked more closely, and then realized that the precision could be explained – a stencil had been used.

He was careful to betray no reaction, but thinking back afterwards, he realized he had moved too quickly, scraping back his chair. Perhaps he paled – there must have been some hint of his reaction, and Marianne picked up on it. She had an only child's thin-skinned sensitivity to nuance, a sixth sense for trouble which had been honed by years of parental arguments behind closed doors. Now, as he casually picked up the parcel, and began to move away, her face clouded. She looked at him uncertainly.

'Papa, what's wrong?'

'Nothing, darling. Nothing.' He kept his voice level. 'I've just realized the time, that's all. Run and get your coat, will you?'

She sat for a moment, watching him. She watched him leave the cigarette burning in the ashtray. She watched him carry the parcel through into the kitchen, and place it on the stainless-steel draining-board. She watched him start to run the water in the sink. Then, suddenly obedient, she climbed down from her chair.

When he next looked round she had fetched her coat, and returned to the kitchen. She stood in the centre of the large room, watching him, the light from the tall windows striking her hair. On her face was an expression Pascal had not seen for months, an expression he had promised himself he would never provoke again once the divorce was over: a pinched expression of confusion and guilt. Leaving the package, Pascal returned to her. He kissed the top of her head, put his arm around her, and began to steer her gently towards the front door. She stopped just inside it, and looked up at him, her face pink with anxiety.

'Something's wrong,' she said again. 'Papa, what did I do?'

The question cut Pascal to the heart. He wondered if this was the fate of all children of divorced parents – to go through life blaming themselves for their parents' failings.

'Nothing, darling,' he replied, catching her against him. 'I told you – we're terribly late, and I just realized how late, that's all. Listen, Marianne . . . ' He opened the doorway onto the landing, and edged her gently outside. 'I'll open that stupid package later – when I get back from London. And if it's anything exciting, I'll phone and tell you, I promise. On with the coat, that's it. What have we here? One bear, one rabbit, one kangaroo – now, I have an idea. You run down to the ground floor and wait for me there, will you do that? Wait right by the door, don't go outside, and I'll be down in a second. Papa just has to find a few papers, his airline ticket . . . '

It was working. Marianne's face had cleared. 'Can I say hallo to Madame Lavalle, like I did last time?'

Pascal smiled. He silently blessed an amiable concierge, who was devoted to his daughter. 'Of course, darling. Introduce her to the animals, I bet she'd like that . . . '

Marianne nodded, and ran to the staircase. Pascal listened to the clatter of her shoes as she descended, the sound of a door opening, then Madame Lavalle's voice.

'My goodness, and what have we here today? A rabbit. A bear and – *mon Dieu*, what can this be? I never saw such an animal!'

'It's a kangaroo, Madame.' Marianne's high voice floated up the stairwell. 'And you see, look, she can keep her baby very close, safe in this little pouch here . . . '

Pascal closed the door. He wiped the sweat from his brow. He walked back into the kitchen and stood looking at that neat old-fashioned parcel, foursquare on the draining-board, the knots neatly sealed. It was five years since he had covered the PLO story, six since he had been in Northern Ireland. His work now might be very different, but the wariness – once necessarily acute – still remained.

Reaching across, he rested his hand on the parcel lightly. He ran his fingers across the surface of the paper, feeling for ridges, for the tell-tale presence of wire.

He could detect nothing. He turned the parcel so the edges of the wrapping paper faced him. The overlap was unsealed, but taut. He hesitated, then picked up his sharpest kitchen knife. He prised the seals loose first. He cut the string in four places and eased it off.

Nothing. He was already beginning to feel foolish, to see his suspicions as exaggerated. Yet why a stencilled address? He looked at the stains of developing fluid on his fingernails. He frowned at the parcel, and thought of the photographs packed in his briefcase, awaiting delivery.

To obtain those pictures he had donned camouflage clothing, and crawled five hundred yards through the outlying scrub of a Provençal estate. He had carried with him a 1200 mm telephoto lens that weighed more than twenty pounds, and a special low-level tripod, made to his specifications. Together these ensured that he could take clear, unblurred portraits at a range of three hundred yards from his unsuspecting quarry, while lying on his belly like a snake. Once upon a time, he had been a war photographer. The lessons and techniques learned then were now applied in other ways. What was he now? he thought, still looking at the parcel. A paparazzo – not a man worth injuring any more, not someone worth the damage a letter-bomb could inflict. He felt a second of self-loathing, a familiar shame. Then with a quick movement he unfolded the brown wrapping paper, and eased the lid from the box.

What he found inside, cushioned in new tissue-paper, was curious and made little sense to him then. Inside the foldings and interleavings of tissue there was no note, no accompanying card or message, just a crumpled black shape which he took at first to be a scrap of material.

He drew it out, and found to his surprise that the material was leather, the finest, softest, black kid, and the object was a woman's glove.

A left-handed glove, and brand-new – unworn, he thought at first. Then he noticed the faint creases across the palm, as if a hand *had* worn this glove, if briefly, and that hand had been tightly clenched. He examined it more closely. It was narrowly cut, made to fit a delicate hand. An evening glove. Against a woman's arm, he estimated, this glove would encase from elbow to finger-tips.

He stared at it, trying to decipher its message. Was it meant to be seductive or threatening? Was it a clue or a prank? He was about to toss it back in its box when a lingering curiosity made him examine it more closely. He pressed it against the back of his hand and felt it slip easily against his skin as if it had been oiled. Then he raised it to his face, and sniffed.

The glove had a pungent and disturbing scent. He could detect the odour of a woman's perfume, and beneath that, imperfectly masked by ambergris, civet and damask, another earthier smell. Fish, blood – something like that. Suddenly the supple glove disgusted him.

He threw it down. *Late*, he thought, checking his watch one more time; that damned parcel had delayed him. He grabbed his briefcase, his camera cases and the small battered valise of inexpertly packed clothes. As he opened the studio door, his daughter's voice floated up to him. A week until the next access day. He felt a surge of love and protectiveness so painfully sharp that, for an instant, it immobilized him.

He stood there on the landing, staring out unseeingly at a view of roofscapes, a pale, drab, leaden sky. Rain today, rain yesterday, rain the day before that: endless winter. Spring, he thought with a sudden and passionate longing; and there, for a brief second, he glimpsed it, even sensed it on his skin, all the springtimes of his boyhood, the optimism and elation that accompanied them. He could see and smell the fields, the vineyards, the oak woods of his childhood. Across the endless gold of the long afternoon he heard his mother call to him, and watched the river coil through the valley below as the light paled to silver.

Now that house was sold and his mother was dead. It was years since the coming of spring had brought him any sense of hope or renewal.

Nostalgia was weak. He slammed the door on it. From below, his daughter called to him. Shouldering his cases, Pascal turned and ran down the stairs.

II

JOHNNY APPLEYARD

The building Johnny Appleyard lived in lay on the south-west corner of Gramercy Park. It was tall, turreted, Gothic. Julio Severas, the ICD courier for that area of New York, arrived there shortly before 10 a.m.

It was a clear cold day, and had snowed during the night. The sidewalk outside Appleyard's building was well swept; Julio paused to admire the building's massive portico, its gleaming marble steps. Julio liked his job – it gave him the opportunity to see how the other half lived. He looked around him with interest as he entered the lobby: dark panelling, a stained-glass window – weird, he thought, like some kind of church.

The porter, a Greek, showed no inclination to talk. He escorted Julio into a lift – more panelling, a little leather-covered seat. The lift was hand-operated. Julio stared in astonishment as the porter hauled expertly on a rope. There was the sound of machinery, of counter-weights. With a surprising efficiency, the lift glided up.

'Some system,' Julio said. 'No electrics, right?'

The porter pointed to a brightly polished brass plate. It said *Otis Elevators 1908*. 'Original,' he said. 'Hand-operated. One hundred per cent reliable. In New York City – unique.'

'Regular antique, huh?' said Julio, and stored this piece of information away for his wife. She too was fascinated by details of how the rich chose to live. 'Expensive building, I guess. Exclusive,' he ventured, as the Greek brought them to a halt.

The Greek gave him a look of contempt. He ushered him out onto polished parquet, facing a tall mahogany

26

door. He rang the bell and stood there with Julio, shoulder to shoulder. From behind the door came the roar of rock music.

Julio sighed and tried again. 'You get a lot of celebrities here, maybe? Rock stars? Actors? Art-world types?'

The porter gave him a withering look. 'Listen,' he said, 'I told you downstairs already. Mr Appleyard, he's not here. No reply, OK? Now, you want to leave that package with me?'

'No,' said Julio, getting his own back. 'I don't.'

The porter lifted his hand to try the bell again, but before he could ring, the door suddenly opened. A strong scent of rose bath oil eddied out. An exquisite girl stood in the doorway, swathed from shoulder to ankle in a white towelling bath-robe. When she saw the two men, her face fell.

'Oh. I thought it was Johnny . . . ' she began, in a low, husky voice. The rest of the sentence trailed away.

Julio blinked. He looked more closely and realized his mistake. Not a young woman, a young man: a young man with clear olive skin, hyacinth blue eyes and long thick waving blond hair. The hair brushed his shoulders; one damp tendril clung to the damp skin of his throat. He was wearing a gold ear-ring in his right earlobe, and a narrow gold bracelet on his right wrist. He was around twenty years old, tall, slender and devastating. Only the pitch of his voice declared his sex. If Julio had encountered him elsewhere, just passed him by on the sidewalk, he'd never have guessed. *Jesus*; Julio felt himself blushing. He averted his gaze and stared hard at the boy's bare feet.

'Parcel for Mr Appleyard,' the Greek announced in an insolent tone. He jerked a thumb at Julio. 'I told him already. He's out, right? Haven't seen him in days.'

The remark sounded oddly like a jibe. The boy blushed. Looking up, Julio saw he was fighting back tears.

'He's out *now*,' he replied, in a defensive way, 'but I expect him back real soon. This afternoon, maybe later this morning . . . ' He held out one slender hand for the

27

parcel. 'I'll take that. I'll give it to Johnny the minute he gets back. You need me to sign?'

Julio handed the parcel across. The kid had a rural accent, slow, with a kind of hick twang. Out west someplace, Julio thought. The boy was examining the package in a childlike way, turning it this way and that. He gave it a little shake, frowned at the customs slip. '*Articles of clothing. Birthday gift,*' he read out. 'Birthday gift?' The boy looked confused. 'Johnny's birthday's in July. He's a Leo, like me. Someone's six months early. That's weird . . . '

He gave the parcel another little shake. There was a faint rustle. Julio glanced at the porter.

'He lives here?'

'Sure he lives here. Stevey's Mr Appleyard's room-mate, right Stevey?' He grinned. 'Been here three years now, maybe four. Looks after Mr Appleyard real nice. Looks after his apartment when he's away . . . '

Julio felt sorry for the boy. The insinuation in the porter's tone was obvious; insolence now veered towards the rude. The porter rocked on his heels, still grinning, looking the boy up and down. Julio waited for Stevey to come back at him, put him down. What was the guy, after all? Just hired help.

To his surprise the boy made no comeback. He looked at the Greek in a wide-eyed hesitant way, as if hoping the remark might be a compliment. Julio gave the Greek a glance of dislike. He proffered his clipboard and a pen; the boy hesitated then signed an illegible scrawl.

'Have a nice day now,' Julio said, trying to make amends for the porter. The boy nodded, smiling shyly and closed the door on a gust of rose-scented air.

'Fucking faggots,' said the Greek succinctly, then gave Julio a malicious grin. 'Poor little Stevey. What's he gonna do now that Mr Appleyard's not so keen any more? The kid's getting anxious. You saw? Jesus, he was nearly in tears. Mr Appleyard, he ain't set foot in the building in over a week. Got himself a new toy boy, I guess. Still, who the fuck cares?'

He waddled out into the lobby. Julio followed, more slowly. He still felt a lingering sympathy for the boy. He was rehearsing in his mind how he'd relate all this to his wife later that evening, what he'd leave out, what he'd put in. This was the aspect of his job he liked best. It was like a movie: little clips from other people's lives.

'So, this Appleyard guy . . . ' He was in the doorway now; he gave it one last try. 'The name's kind of familiar. I've heard of him, maybe? A singer? Musician?'

'Works for the newspapers. Hangs out with the stars. A tight-wad. Likes pretty boys. Lots of them.'

'Each to his own, right?' Julio said uneasily. The porter rolled his eyes. 'And this Appleyard, he's older, I guess?'

'Forty years old and a prize ass-hole. The prince of shits.' The Greek gave one last malevolent grin, and slammed the door.

III

JAMES McMULLEN

Giovanni Carona was the ICD courier in Venice. It was
not a full-time job. Giovanni, newly married, living still
with his parents and saving up for an apartment, fitted it
in when the calls came. Come summer, come the tourists,
he did well enough, ferrying Americans and Japanese up
the Grand Canal and out onto the lagoon. Come winter,
he took whatever work he could get.

The package was due in at the airport at nine o'clock.
At eight, on a bitterly cold morning, Giovanni was out on
the tiny canal behind his father's house, coaxing the engine
of his father's old launch into life. By eight-thirty he was
easing his way through a maze of narrow waterways. A
greyish mist lingered over the canals. The city was just
coming to life.

Out past the cemetery isle of St Michele – Giovanni
crossed himself as he passed – and into the channel which
led to the airport. The boat chugged between the black
piles that marked the route. The mist was denser here,
clammy against the skin. Up ahead, where the industrial
sector of Mestre was situated beyond the airport, the fog
was yellowish, bunched like thunder clouds, dense.

Fog delayed the London flight by an hour. It was
almost eleven by the time the hand-over formalities were
completed, and Giovanni was making his way back. He
took a different route this time, approaching the city by
the Grand Canal, then turning into the snaking maze of
waterways on its southern flank.

This was a part of Venice few tourists penetrated, but
it was Giovanni's home ground. He relaxed; he felt no
sense of urgency. A thin sun was coming out, warming

and dissipating the mist. By the time he drew alongside the Palazzo Ossorio, it was nearly noon. He tied up, and surveyed the building, hands on hip. The place might once have been magnificent, but now it was a wreck.

Giovanni's eyes scanned the palazzo's sagging façade. Its lowest storey had been abandoned long ago; the cracked ochre of its stucco was stained a seaweedy green. The palazzo's windows, dark, closed and unwelcoming, were twisted out of true by subsidence. Half its shutters were missing and its graceful balconies, and tall pilastered entrance gates were in a ruinous condition. The entire building looked unsafe.

Giovanni glanced down at his package. *McMullen*: a foreigner – English? Irish? American? In his experience, most foreigners avoided places such as this. McMullen must be eccentric, someone who found decay picturesque. Giovanni had no patience with such indulgences. He clambered ashore, and made for the palazzo's entrance courtyard. As he entered it, he heard a scuttle of movement, but did not glimpse the rat.

There was no sign of a concierge or porter, no sign of any inhabitants, come to that. All the windows overlooking this interior courtyard had their shutters clamped.

In the corner of the courtyard was a wide flight of stone stairs. Apartment six, this McMullen's apartment, would be on the top floor; a peeling painted arrow directed him up. Giovanni heard and saw no-one on his ascent. Dead leaves rustled in the corners of stairs; the doors he passed looked long closed up. He began to think he must be in the wrong place – but no, this was the Palazzo Ossorio and here, on the top floor, was a door clearly numbered 'six'.

Giovanni peered at the door. The landing was ill-lit; he could see no bell, no knocker. He hammered against the thick door panels, listened, then hammered again. No footsteps; no response.

There was a note, faded and fly-spotted, pinned to the door. Giovanni's English was sufficient: *If I'm out, try later*, it read.

An English name on the parcel, an English note on the door – it was the right place. Giovanni hammered a third time. He called a few *holas* through the panels. Then he drew back, wrinkling his nose in distaste. This place was not only dirty and decaying, it stank.

A musty and ammoniac smell, as if people used the stairway as a urinal – but beyond that scent, something even more unpleasant, like rotting meat. Giovanni felt a sense of irritation.

He heard a mewing sound. Glancing down he saw a thin ginger cat, sidling along the walls, inching its way warily towards him. It looked half-starved. Giovanni bent towards it. The cat arched its back, bared its teeth, and spat.

Giovanni aimed a clumsy kick in its direction, which missed. He considered the package, and the note on the door. It was strictly against ICD rules to leave a parcel unsigned for. On the other hand, no-one was likely to steal it from here. McMullen's receipt signature could always be forged; no-one ever checked . . . Giovanni hesitated. He was tempted. It was past noon now, he was hungry and he'd already wasted a whole morning on this. Coming to a decision, he bent, rested the package against the door, and left: the hell with this.

Later that afternoon, he got anxious: he'd been lazy, he'd broken the rules. He needed this job, and now he'd put his job at risk. He debated with his wife what to do; at her urging, he returned later that evening to the Palazzo Ossorio.

His wife accompanied him. The plan was, they'd just check the parcel was safely received, then they'd go for an evening stroll, stop for a glass of wine in a café someplace.

Just as before, the building was deserted. There was still no reply from McMullen's apartment. The parcel, though, had disappeared, and beside the door there was now a saucer of milk for the cat. Presumably the package had been received therefore: but Giovanni still felt uneasy. He hammered several times on the door panels, then pressed his ear against them. He listened, and stiffened. He was certain he could hear someone inside; there were slow rustling movements behind the door, then the creak of a floorboard. Someone was there, moving about.

The light was failing. His wife plucked his sleeve. She gave a shiver, and glanced over her shoulder.

'Let's go, Giovanni,' she whispered. 'Let's leave. It's creepy here.'

Giovanni raised his finger to his lips. 'Listen,' he said in a low voice. 'There's someone in there. I can hear them . . . If he's in there, why doesn't he answer the door?'

'I can't hear anything. It's just the wind.' His wife, too, had pressed her ear to the door. Now she recoiled sharply. 'Giovanni, what's that horrible smell? It's foul . . . '

'Drains, I guess. It certainly stinks. Worse than this morning.'

He drew back with a puzzled frown. He hammered one last time on the door. Silence this time, complete silence.

'Please let's go, Giovanni. *Please*. You're imagining things.'

'OK, OK. God, it's cold. You're shivering. We'll go . . . '

They walked around the corner to a small café in the square, and drank a glass of red wine apiece. Giovanni tried asking the café owner a few questions – whether he knew this Signor McMullen, whether the Palazzo Ossorio was occupied – but he got nowhere. The café owner, a taciturn man, shrugged. That place? One mad old grandmother, he thought, with around fifty stray cats. No-one else. It would fall down into the canal any day now, through sheer neglect . . .

Whether the café owner knew it or not, this information was incorrect. As Giovanni and his wife passed the palazzo one last time on their way home, Giovanni looked up. The window of apartment six was on the top floor, in the corner of the building. All the windows in the palazzo were dark, except that one.

Giovanni stood looking up at it; no, he was not mistaken, and he had been right earlier, too. Someone was in that apartment then and was there now. The shutters were closed but between them he could see a band of faint light.

34

IV

GENEVIEVE HUNTER

Genevieve Hunter lived in the basement flat of a tall, terraced, early-Victorian house overlooking one of Islington's prettiest squares. When the ICD courier arrived it was shortly after nine in the morning and she was already resigned to the fact that she would be late for her newspaper office that day. She was upstairs in the rooms occupied by her elderly neighbour when she heard the knocking from the basement area below. Opening the window, she leaned out and saw a uniformed man below, cradling a package and a clipboard.

'Hold on – I'll be right down,' she called. The man looked up at her, shivered, stamped his feet, and nodded.

Genevieve closed the window, and carefully locked it. She looked around the meagre bedroom in which her upstairs neighbour, Mrs Henshaw, had spent five years of widowhood and nearly forty years of married life. Linoleum covered the floor; the only furniture was a massive wardrobe and an ancient, equally massive bed. The only heating was provided by a gas fire. Genevieve checked the gas was off, then shouldered Mrs Henshaw's two large suitcases and made for the stairs.

Her neighbour, who was one of the few remaining residents from the days when this area was run-down, and who could still remember what Islington had been like before it was discovered and 'gentrified', was due to spend ten days with her married daughter in Devon. She was sixty-eight now, and unused to travelling. She had packed enough clothes, judging by the weight of these cases, for a stay of two months.

Gini smiled to herself, and manœuvred the cases down

35

the narrow stairs. When Gini had first purchased her basement flat, with its central heating, its modern kitchen and bathroom, Mrs Henshaw had regarded her with some suspicion and alarm: a tall, thin American girl, unmarried, working for a London newspaper. 'I like to keep myself to myself,' Mrs Henshaw had said, eyeing her round the crack of her front door when Genevieve came up to introduce herself. Then, gradually, this suspicion had worn off: Mrs Henshaw discovered that this young American kept a cat – a magnificent marmalade cat, called Napoleon – and Mrs Henshaw was very fond of cats. This forged the first bond; then Mrs Henshaw found to her surprise that this eager boyishly dressed young woman, who seemed to work such long hours, could always spare the time to fetch her groceries when her arthritis was bad, and was even prepared, over a cup of strong tea, to listen to Mrs Henshaw's memories of the area, to look through her old faded photograph albums, to hear the stories of hard times past, and the six children Mrs Henshaw had brought up in this place.

Mrs Henshaw, resigned to being chivvied and dismissed as an elderly bore, lonely since her children had married and moved away, responded to this. 'That Genevieve – she's like a daughter to me,' she would now claim, in Mr Patel's grocery shop.

As Gini made her way down the stairs, she found Mrs Henshaw waiting anxiously in the hall below. She was wearing zip-up furry bootees, three cardigans, an overcoat, a new woolly scarf Genevieve had bought her, and her best hat. She was trembling with nerves. As Genevieve descended, she was checking the contents of her handbag for the third time, and muttering to herself. Tickets, spectacles, hanky, purse, pension-book, keys: Genevieve put down the suitcases, and put an arm gently around her shoulders. It was hard, she thought, to make the simplest journey when you were old, and poor, and alone and unused to travelling further than the corner shop. The important thing was not to rush her neighbour, or to show the least sign of impatience.

'Mrs H.,' she said, 'that is one incredible hat. You look great.'

Mrs Henshaw flushed pink. The flurry and anxiety diminished a fraction. She peered at her reflection in the small hall mirror, and then smiled.

'It's my best. I last wore it for my Doreen's youngest's christening, and that's eight years back. My Doreen always did like it, so I thought . . .'

From the basement below came the sound of renewed knocking; the noise put Mrs Henshaw into a new panic at once.

'Oh, Gini, love – all that banging, I can't think straight. Did I put the gas off? What about the milk? I forgot to cancel the milk . . .'

Genevieve edged to the front door, opened it, called down again to the delivery man in the area below, and then began the complicated process of persuading Mrs Henshaw out of her house. She tried not to think of how late this was making her for the *News* offices, and tried to keep up a soothing refrain. Yes, the gas was off, she had checked in every room; yes, the milk delivery was cancelled, and all the windows shut and locked. Yes, Mrs Henshaw's daughter would meet her at the station the other end, and at this end, the cab driver would help her onto the train, even carry her cases on for her – it was all fixed.

Genevieve helped Mrs Henshaw out of the doorway, and down the front steps to the street. Her neighbour had a new plastic hip, but her pace was still unsteady and slow. When her attention was diverted, Genevieve gave the cab driver a hefty tip.

'You'll see her onto the train? You'll take care of her bags? Oh – and please don't hurry her. It gets her in a state . . .'

The young cab driver looked her up and down and grinned.

'Your gran, is it, love?'

'No. Just a friend. But she's not used to travelling. She doesn't go out much.'

37

'Don't you worry. I'll see she's all right.' He bent his head into the cab, and grinned at Mrs Henshaw. 'All comfortable? Right, you sit back now and relax. By the way – I like the hat.'

'It's my best.' Mrs Henshaw quivered, and Genevieve felt a surge of pity for her. She leaned into the cab, and planted a kiss on her whiskery cheek. A squeeze of her hand, another check through the handbag to make sure the tickets were there, and Mrs Henshaw was off. Genevieve stood watching her disappear into the distance. She lifted her face to the damp grey air as the cab rounded the corner. She sighed and turned back to the basement steps.

The uniformed courier was now mounting them. In his hand he was carrying a neat package. Gini saw that it was tied with string and sealed with red wax.

The courier looked this Genevieve Hunter up and down. When she had opened the window above, and called down to him, he had at first taken her for a young man; now, on closer inspection, he could see some of the reasons for that mistake. She was tall and slender, and dressed in a mannish way: black trousers, black polo-neck sweater, flat boots. Her long fair hair was tucked back beneath a battered khaki baseball cap, and she wore an odd military-style trenchcoat which reached to mid-calf and was adorned with innumerable flaps and pockets and epaulettes. Now that he could see her properly, however, there was no mistaking her sex: this young woman had a grave, clear-eyed and rather beautiful face.

'Sorry I kept you waiting,' Genevieve said. She signed for the package, and was about to stuff it, unopened, into her bag, when she stopped and looked at it more closely. She might be in a hurry to reach the *News* offices, but this parcel was unusual, to say the least.

'How strange,' she said. 'Can you believe it? Look . . . ' She held the package out to the courier. 'Someone's stencilled the address.'

She shook the package, as the courier bent forward to

38

inspect it. There was a small rattling noise. Genevieve frowned, and the courier shook his head.

'Maybe it's meant to be a surprise,' he said, in an encouraging tone. 'So you can't recognize the handwriting, won't know who sent it until you open it up. Boyfriend, maybe?' He gave her a shrewd glance. 'A surprise present from the boyfriend, something like that?'

Genevieve smiled; there *was* no boyfriend, at the moment, and the last possible candidate for that title had left to edit an Australian newspaper a month back. Genevieve did not miss him greatly, and he was, in any case, not the kind of man to send surprise parcels. She felt a momentary unease, gave the package another tentative shake. The courier, who seemed as curious as she was, produced a pocket-knife.

'Here.' He handed it to her with a smile. 'You never know these days, love – it could be a bad idea, carrying that around. Maybe you ought to open it up.'

Genevieve did so. Carefully, she cut the string and removed the brown wrapping paper. Inside, there was a plain cardboard box. Inside the box there were sheaves of new tissue-paper. Inside this was a pair of handcuffs. They were made of heavy steel. A small key was inserted in their lock.

Genevieve drew them out with a cry of surprise. The sense of unease deepened. She felt around inside the tissue, but the handcuffs came with no accompanying message, or note. Her mouth tightened in anger, and her cheeks flushed.

'Great. No note.' She looked at the courier, who was shaking his head in disbelief. 'I'm getting a pretty strong message all the same. What kind of a creep would send me this?'

She frowned down at the handcuffs, trying to think of candidates: who might find such an anonymous gift appealing? Who might want to play this kind of sick joke?

She could think of no-one. She had enemies as well as friends at her office, of course, and there were people she had alienated as a result of past articles, certainly, but she could think of no-one who would retaliate in this particular underhand way. With an angry shrug, she began to fold up the wrapping paper.

'Chuck them away, love – I would,' the courier said, on a defensive note. He gestured to a dustbin up the street.

'No way.' She set her lips. 'I need them. I'm going to find out who sent me this . . . '

She began to push the handcuffs into her bag. The courier hesitated.

'I could make a few enquiries if you like,' he began. 'At my office. They were sent out from our City branch – I know that much. I could call in there after work – ask around . . . ' Genevieve gave him a grateful smile.

'Would you? I'd check myself, but I'm tied up all day.' She handed him her card. 'Those are my numbers – work and home. I should be back here around six. Will you call me if you discover anything? I'd be very grateful.'

The courier promised he would do so; he said that his name was George, and he would call her at home, without fail, after six. He then left, for his next delivery, and Genevieve stood for a while on the pavement, watching his van disappear. It was cold, and beginning to rain. She turned up the collar of her coat, and gave a small shiver. Handcuffs. Did that mean that she had an unknown enemy? Or was this anonymous package meant to convey something else?

She walked across to her car, and drove off. The rush-hour traffic was heavy, and delayed her further still, but she drove the whole way to her newspaper's docklands offices unaware of the passing time, considering her anonymous present. Halfway there, she finally made the obvious deduction: the sender of these handcuffs was likely to be male – and at that her residual sense of sick unease increased.

PART TWO
AN INVESTIGATION

V

It was typical of his ex-wife, Pascal thought, turning into
the smart estate where she lived, to elect to live here,
in Paris and yet not in Paris, in surroundings which
could scarcely be less French. His former wife, born
with a gift for languages, fluent in French, German and
Italian, remained English to the core. She retained a
thin-lipped disdain for foreigners, an unshakeable belief
in their inferiority. 'Paris?' Helen had said, at the time of
the divorce. 'Live *in* Paris? Are you insane? I only stay
in France on sufferance, for Marianne's sake. I've already
found the perfect house. It's on the outskirts. It costs five
million francs. We can build it in to the settlement. I
hope you're not going to quibble, Pascal. It's cheap at
the price.'

The five-million-franc house lay ahead of him now,
just up the street. It was what Helen called an 'executive'
house. It had seven bedrooms, all expensively furnished
and five of them unused. It had seven bathrooms, a
kitchen like an operating theatre, a four-car garage, and
a view of desolate immaculate turf. It was a house which
could have been built in any expensive suburb in the
world. Pascal had seen others just like it, equally vulgar,
in Brussels, London, Bonn, Detroit. Its bricks were an
aggressive scarlet. He had loathed it on sight.

This morning, there was a change in the routine.
Normally, by tacit agreement, Pascal and Helen never
met. At the end of an access weekend, Pascal would
pull up outside the house. Helen, watching from the
picture windows, would rush to the doorway, and hold
out her arms. Marianne would run inside, the door would
close, and Pascal would drive off.

This morning was to be different, it seemed. Helen

43

was waiting in the driveway, looking thin, elegant and irritable. She kissed Marianne in a perfunctory way, and the child ran inside. Pascal wound down the window of his car.

In English, Helen said: 'You're late.'

'I know. I'm sorry. The traffic was bad.'

She raised her eyebrows in a small arc of reproachful disbelief. 'Really? Well, it hardly matters. I have nothing else to do except wait around, as I'm sure you know. Could you come in for a moment? I'd like us to talk.'

'I can't. I have an appointment in Paris in twenty minutes and I have to catch the flight to London at noon.'

'When don't you have a flight to catch?' She turned away, faint colour rising in her cheeks. 'Nothing changes, it seems. Well, if you can't spare me ten minutes of your time, I'll do it through the lawyers. Slower, and more expensive, of course – but it's your choice.'

At the word 'lawyers', Pascal switched off the engine. He climbed out, slammed the car door, and strode ahead of her into the house. In the kitchen, he picked up the telephone and started dialling. He observed the cafetière filled with fresh coffee, the plate of biscuits on the white marble kitchen worktop, the two white cups and saucers, the two plates.

Helen came into the kitchen and closed the door, a tiny smile of triumph on her lips. She frowned when she saw him at the telephone.

'Who are you calling?'

'The magazine. I told you, I have an appointment. I'm now going to be late.'

She ignored this. While Pascal completed the call, she filled the two cups with coffee and carried them over to the table by the window. She placed a porcelain jug of milk and a porcelain sugar bowl in the centre of its white, empty expanse.

'Do sit down,' she said, as Pascal replaced the telephone. 'Try not to glower. I shall keep this brief.'

Pascal eyed the coffee, the two waiting cups, this

evidence of his ex-wife's assumption that no matter how reluctant, he would eventually toe the line. He shrugged and sat down. 'If you would be brief I'd be grateful.' His tone was polite. 'It's important I catch this flight.'

'Oh, I'm sure.' She smiled. 'It always was. When I look back on our marriage – something I try to do as little as possible, I might add – you know what I find the single most significant fact? *You were never there.* Whenever I or Marianne might have needed you, where were you? At an airport. In the middle of a war zone. In some flea-bitten hotel in the back of beyond, where the switchboard didn't work. And if the switchboard *did* work . . . ' she picked up a biscuit and bit into it delicately, 'you were never in your room. Odd, that.'

Pascal looked away. Keeping his voice level, he said: 'That's all ancient history. We've agreed not to go over it again. You knew when you married me—'

'When I married you I knew nothing at all.' Her voice became bitter. She composed herself almost at once. 'However, as you say – ancient history. So I'll come to the point. I want us to be civilized about this. You should know, I've sold the house.'

There was a silence. Pascal looked at her carefully. His stomach lurched. 'This house?'

'Well, of course, this house. It is the only one I have. And I find . . . I find it doesn't suit.'

'Doesn't *suit*? You chose it. It cost five million francs. You've lived in it less than three years and you find it doesn't *suit*?'

'I have *endured* this house for three years.' Her colour had risen. 'And you will please keep your voice down. I don't want Marianne to hear, or the nanny, come to that. I don't want any more resignations. Marianne needs continuity, and these girls don't like scenes.'

'Scenes? *Scenes?*' Pascal stood up. 'Considering the wages I pay her, she could stand the odd scene, I'd think.'

'That was uncalled for. And uncouth.' Helen also rose.

She had flushed scarlet. 'I try to talk to you, in a reasonable manner, for five minutes . . . And this happens . . . '

She was shaking, Pascal saw. He looked at her for a long slow moment. His former wife was virtually unchanged from the day he'd first met her, outside the Unesco offices in Paris, where she worked as a translator. She had loved Paris then, or claimed to. A slender girl, with sleek dark hair, and a nervous intense thin face, she had been wearing a dark coat, a scarlet scarf: he could still see her, standing on the pavement the day he met her. Their affair had been brief and fraught. They argued continually. Yet after the marriage, there had been contentment as well as incompatibility, surely? The birth of Marianne, for instance. He said, surprising them both: 'I loved you once.'

'Thanks for the past tense.'

She turned away. Pascal looked at her narrow back, at the strain in her shoulders. He had not meant to be cruel. The remark had sprung of its own accord to his lips. Then and now: the woman he had once loved stood three feet in front of him and yet did not exist.

'I'm sorry.' He started on a clumsy apology, then stopped. 'You're right. It's better if we keep all this—'

'Businesslike?' She swung around with a scornful look. 'I do so agree. That was exactly my point. So. I've sold the house. Shall we take it from there?'

Pascal stared at her. The announcement had taken him by surprise, and now he sensed that pain was about to be inflicted. His previous remark had probably ensured the pain would be lingering. Helen's face became set; her gaze slid away from his face.

'I've decided to return to England. Daddy's promised to help find me a place. Somewhere in Surrey, we thought. Not too far from home. With the slump in the market over there, Daddy thinks we can pick up a bargain. Something really nice. Somewhere with a paddock, so Marianne can have a pony of her own. She's mad about horses, did she tell you that?'

Pascal stared at his wife. There was perceptible triumph

46

at the back of her eyes. He said, 'You can't do that.'

'Oh, but I can. Daddy's talked to the lawyers. I've talked to the lawyers. We were married in England, Marianne was born in England . . . '

'You insisted on that . . . '

'She has dual nationality. I have custody. Daddy's man says I have virtual *carte blanche*. I can take her anywhere I like.'

'You agreed!' Pascal could hardly speak. 'You signed an agreement to bring her up here. You wanted to facilitate access, you *said* that. To me. To her grandmother—'

'Your mother's dead.'

'You signed an agreement. You gave me your *word*—'

'Agreements can be renegotiated. I'm renegotiating now. The lawyers say you can object, but it will be expensive, and you'll lose in the end. If it goes to a hearing, they'll bring up the work you do now – the *nature* of your work. They'll point out that you're never around anyway, whereas I am – day in, day out.'

'I'm *always* here,' he burst out. 'When I'm allowed to see her, I'm here. One evening a week. One weekend in four. In three years I've never missed one of those appointments, not one.'

'In fact,' she pressed on, her voice riding over the top of his, 'the lawyers say your access might well be reduced. It would have to take place in England, certainly. Maybe France for a few weeks in the summer, but—'

'Why are you doing this?'

The question angered her.

'Why? *Why?* Because I hate this country and I always did. I want to be back in my own country. I want to see my parents and friends. I want to work again—'

'You can work here. Translators can work anywhere. You always said that.'

'I want to work *there*! I want to be with people I know, people I grew up with . . . '

'*I want. I want* . . . ' He stepped back from her. 'That's all we have to consider, is it? What about Marianne? What about what she wants?'

47

'Marianne thinks it's a lovely idea. A house in the country, ponies . . .'

'You've already discussed it? Jesus Christ.'

'Yes, I have. And if you must know, I asked her not to mention it to you, not just yet, not until we'd had a chance to discuss it—'

'Discuss it? You call this discussing it?' He could feel the anger rising in him uncontrollably now, and he could see an answering delight in his wife's face. She relished her powers of provocation, he had always known that. He moved towards the door. If he stayed another five minutes in this terrible room, he knew he might hit Helen – perfect evidence in a court of law. She had never been able to accuse him of violence. Perhaps this, he thought, was her attempt to rectify that.

In the doorway he turned back. He said, 'I'll fight you over this. No matter how long it takes. No matter what it costs. I'll fight you inch by inch.'

'Your choice.' She turned away with a shrug.

'Helen, think. Just think.' He risked one last appeal, made an awkward gesture of the hand to her.

'I'm her *father*. Don't you want me to see her? Are you trying to exclude me?'

'Exclude you? Of course not. If you agree to my proposals the access arrangements can remain the same. One evening a week. One weekend a month.'

'An *evening*? In England? In *Surrey*? What am I supposed to do, travel three hours every week to spend two hours with my daughter, then travel three hours back?'

Helen smiled. With beautiful politeness, she said, 'But you *love* air travel, Pascal. You spend half your life on planes. Why not spend a little more?'

In the seventh-floor executive offices at *Paris Jour*, senior editor Françoise Leduc spread Pascal's photographs across her conference table. Monochrome prints to the left, colour to the right: a damning tableau. Pascal, whom she had known for many years, whose career she had launched fifteen years before, stood watching her. Françoise, who had in her younger days been painfully in love with him, was puzzled by his manner. He had just presented her with a magazine sensation, a news-stand sell-out, yet he showed little interest. His manner was abstracted and tense.

'You're smoking too much, Pascal,' she said, in the mothering tone she had adopted years before as the safest device to defuse the attraction she felt.

'I know. You're right.'

He gave a half-shrug and extinguished this, his second cigarette in ten minutes. He moved towards the window, and looked out at a wintry sky.

Françoise could see the tension in his back. She hesitated. They were good friends and colleagues now, she and Pascal, and Françoise valued that. It was a triumph she had earned by virtue of iron control. For five, six, seven years – maybe more – she had hidden her feelings for this man absolutely, never betraying them by the least gesture or inflection. No-one had ever suspected, least of all Pascal himself. A handsome man, he was without vanity – a rare gift. Perhaps also a little lacking in imagination. Françoise smiled to herself. Pascal, always absorbed, dedicated to his work, had a priestlike quality. If he ever noticed the reaction he provoked in women, he ignored it; but Françoise suspected he noticed nothing, was curiously blind to his own often dramatic effect.

Her sacrifice had been worth it. Françoise was a pragmatic woman. At fifty, she valued the long-term benefits of friendship to any short-term gains that might have accrued from an affair. She had hidden her feelings and her reward was Pascal's trust.

She glanced down at his photographs, then looked back at Pascal, a slight frown of puzzlement on her face. She could still remember vividly the first time she had encountered him, an unknown twenty-year-old photographer, newly returned from his first trip to Beirut, standing here in this same office, talking, gesturing, spilling photographs across her desk. She had seen him as a favour to a mutual friend, and assigned him ten minutes in her packed schedule. The ten minutes had expanded to half an hour; the half-hour, after some last-minute cancellations, had expanded into lunch. When this extraordinary young man finally left her some four hours later, she sat in the restaurant, shaken: this was unprecedented. Why had she done this?

Because his photographs were exceptionally good? That was true, certainly, and she'd run the pictures over six pages the following week – so, yes, there were professional reasons. But there were other reasons too – powerful reasons, and not sexual ones either, for Françoise was too disciplined a professional for that.

The only explanation she could find at the time was something she had seen in his face: innocence, youth, passion, dedication. An unswerving conviction expressed in a whirl of sentences, confirmed by blazing eyes in a pale intent face, that he was presenting Françoise with a gift beyond price – not just any photographs but documentation, evidence, truth.

He had been very young, very naïve, very inexperienced and very gifted. The combination cut Françoise to the quick. As he talked about Beirut, and the violence he had seen there, Françoise was forced to look at herself. She saw all the compromises, the adjustments she made in the day-to-day course of her work; she saw the creeping nature of her own professional cynicism. What had she said to her secretary, before Pascal arrived? *How boring. It won't take five minutes. Just some kid with more bomb pictures. Who gives a damn? The last thing we need is more sob stuff from Beirut . . .*

Then this young man had burst into her office, waving a banner, crying out for a crusade, waging some personal war against injustice, lies and deceit. Françoise had listened and been chastened. She might be the more worldly of the two, but this twenty-year-old made her feel cheap.

Fifteen years ago. Outwardly, Pascal was little changed since then. Tall, narrow-hipped, wide-shouldered, quick of movement, elegant yet somewhat scruffily dressed. Françoise smiled: the clothes he wore today were, as usual, good and, as usual, unpressed. She doubted Pascal possessed an iron, or would know how to use one. He could no more sew on a button than he could make an omelette or compliment a woman on her dress. He was sublimely impractical, sublimely indifferent to such things – yet put a camera in his hands, and he was transformed at once.

With cameras, with a story in view, Pascal was unstoppable: indifferent to obstacles, privation, physical danger or difficulties. In pursuit of a story, Pascal became a man possessed.

Except . . . Françoise, who had been about to speak, stopped herself. She looked down at the photographs on the table. Once Pascal Lamartine had been one of the best war photographers in the world. He had covered every major conflict, bringing back photographs which broke people's hearts, which provoked passionate debate. What had he brought her now? Adultery: sneak shots of a man in the act of cheating on his wife.

In the pictures before her, the French Cabinet Minister and his American movie-star mistress were very clearly identifiable. Françoise could see the shape of the swimming-pool behind them, the title of the book the minister's bodyguard was reading. She could see the minister's wedding ring as his hand caressed the movie-star's legendary breasts. The pictures did not surprise Françoise. The minister concerned was an aggressive apostle of family values, and had a reputation for absolute rectitude: so the world went.

But that Pascal should take these photographs – that did surprise her. That he should take on work of this kind once, twice perhaps, at the time of his divorce – yes, she could even understand that: lawyers were expensive. But that he should continue to do so now, three years later, when the divorce settlement was long finalized, the alimony long agreed, the child maintenance fixed . . . that she could not understand. Pascal himself never discussed his ex-wife's demands, and this kind of work certainly paid far better than pictures of wars. But if this was the price Helen Lamartine was demanding, it was extortionate.

Françoise picked up one of the photographs, then put it down. Professional, circulation-boosting: she would publish them, of course. Yet she hated them. The photographs had a double venality: they were the evidence that a man she much admired was destroying himself.

'OK.' She swept the pictures into a pile. 'We'll run them. Next week. Three spreads plus the cover. We'll deny we've even got them, obviously, maybe prepare another dummy lead. Even so, it's bound to leak.'

Pascal shrugged. 'You think he'll bring an injunction?'

'Maybe. And sue once we've published, under the privacy laws. He keeps three lawyers permanently on their toes.' She smiled. 'The man's a fool. In bed with Sonia Swan? Every red-blooded male in France will vote for him after this. He could be the next President of the Republic – maybe. I'll be doing him a favour. But I don't expect him to see it like that.' She paused. Pascal was paying little attention. 'Provided the pictures run first in England and the States, we're covered anyway,' she continued. 'No invasion of privacy once the privacy's invaded elsewhere. Then it becomes a legitimate news story – just about. Anyway, he's a sanctimonious son of a bitch. *Petit Fascist*. It's worth the risk.'

'You don't have to worry,' Pascal turned. 'Those deals are sewn up. The pictures will be on the news-stands in London and New York by the end of the week.'

'I know.' Françoise began returning the prints to their folders. 'Nicky Jenkins called from London this morning. So suave. I could hear him licking his lips.'

Pascal, who disliked Nicholas Jenkins, editor of the London *Daily News*, as much as she did, betrayed no reaction. He was already moving to the door, checking his watch.

'Françoise, I'm sorry. I have to go. I'm meeting Nicholas for lunch. With luck I might still make the noon flight.'

'Call me when you get back. Some friends are coming

52

over for dinner Wednesday night. It would be nice if you could join us.'

She knew from his expression that the invitation would be refused: Pascal was turning into a loner. Most invitations were now refused, unless they assisted his work.

'I might not be back. Nicholas has some new lead. Something he wants me to work on.'

'More scandals?'

'So he said.'

'Bigger than this?' She gestured at the photographs.

'Much bigger. Very hush-hush. But then Nicholas exaggerates.'

'If it's good, tell him I want a tie-in. I don't want it going to *Paris Match*.' Françoise hesitated. Pascal's cool grey eyes had met hers.

'Just listen to us both,' he said. He made the remark drily, looking away. When he turned back the irony had left his face. He looked desperately tired – or tiredly desperate, she could not have said which.

'Pascal,' she began awkwardly, 'we're friends. We know each other. I hope we trust one another. Once upon a time, your work was so . . . Pascal, why do you do this?'

She looked down at the photographs as she spoke. Pascal's eyes followed her gaze. He pushed back one lock of dark hair which fell across his forehead – an irritable careless gesture, one Françoise had seen him make a thousand times before. He was greying a little at the temples now, she saw; there were lines she did not remember, from nose to mouth. For a moment she thought she had angered him. His eyes glinted. She waited for the impetuous reply he would once have given, but none came. He turned to the door, and Françoise thought he intended to leave her question unanswered. Yet at the door he turned, then shrugged.

'Françoise, I work for the money,' he said. 'What else?'

'That wasn't always the case.'

'No. Once I worked for . . . ' He broke off. His expression became closed. 'Circumstances change,' he said in a flat tone. It was his final remark, one that told her nothing, and he closed the door on it.

Outside, in the car-park below, Pascal climbed into his car, switched on its engine, then switched it off. Françoise's final question had gone unerringly to the heart of the matter, he knew that. For an instant, staring straight ahead of him, seeing no cars, no traffic beyond, no passers-by, he looked down into it, this emptiness now central to his life. No optimism, no self-respect, a great deal of self-hate. He felt a sensation of vertiginous despair, then anger with himself.

There was no point in dwelling on this. Self-hate was perilously close to self-pity – and that he refused to indulge. Besides, there was a cure for despair; not drink, not drugs, not women – those exits led to dead ends.

Work, he said to himself, and fired the engine. He slammed the car into reverse, turned, accelerated fast, and made for the airport via the *périphérique*. Work, speed, haste, an accumulation of detail, these were the cures he now relied upon. They had one supreme benefit: properly manipulated they left no time in which to think. Racing for the plane, Pascal congratulated himself dourly: the past three years had made him an expert in this.

VI

Genevieve was working on a new story about telephone sex. It was Nicholas Jenkins's idea. Most of his feature proposals concerned sex in one form or another. In the year he had been editor, the *News*'s circulation had increased by a hundred thousand, so presumably – by that yardstick anyway – Jenkins's editorial instincts were correct.

It was not, however, a policy Genevieve liked. She found it both sly and cheap. The *News* was a middle-market paper, not a tabloid, and Jenkins's new editorial policy involved a balancing act. The saucy expressions of pin-up girls were not for the *News*, so the titillation of a typical Jenkins story had to be disguised. An 'exposé' was the form that disguise usually took. Thus could titillation become a crusade. Jenkins was in the process of elevating scurrility to an art-form. Genevieve could have put up with the scurrility a whole lot better, she often thought, had it not come so larded with cant.

Her initial research on this new story consisted of calling a representative sample of telephone sex lines, widely and excitably advertised by one of the *News*'s most sensationalistic competitors. By noon, seated at her desk in the Features department, she had been engaged in this activity for more than two hours; her spirits felt leaden, and her head ached.

Nicholas Jenkins's theory was that somewhere in England there was the Mister Big of telephone sex. Genevieve's crusading task was to find this man, and expose his activities. According to Jenkins the man was – or might be – a well-known international entrepreneur, whose more legitimate business interests ranged from American modelling agencies to rock-star management . . . or so

Johnny Appleyard had suggested to Jenkins, and Jenkins placed great faith in Appleyard's tips.

Genevieve placed less faith in them. In her book, Appleyard was an intrusive ubiquitous busy-body with an expensive nasal hobby, a man whose transatlantic tip-offs were one per cent hot and ninety-nine per cent myth.

With a sigh, she replaced the telephone on a breathy South London girl (*French Governess Corrects Your Mistakes*). She closed her eyes, buried her aching head in her hands, and considered for the hundredth time, just how pleasant it would be to tell Nicholas Jenkins to stick this job. Before his advent at the *News*, she'd taken pride in the work she did. In the ten years she'd worked in England in journalism, she'd fought hard to establish herself. No fashion coverage, no women's page fluff, no soft-focus human-interest stories: she had wanted to cover hard news, to start out the way her journalist father had. Her ambition – never confessed to her father, whom she rarely saw, and who would have scoffed – was to move up through investigative journalism to foreign reporting. Sam Hunter had covered wars – indeed, had won a Pulitzer for his Vietnam dispatches. Why should she not take a similar course? So she had served her apprenticeship, but kept that goal ahead of her. One day, she would be truly out in the field, she too would be there, at the front.

Wars drew her like a magnet, she knew this. To bring back the truth from a war zone seemed to her a tremendous thing. If she could ever do that, she felt she would prove something to herself – and perhaps also prove something to her father, although this aspect of her plan made her uneasy, and she ignored it as much as she could.

And she had come so close to her goal – so very close. All the hard work of her apprenticeship, her years first on a provincial paper, then on the *Guardian*, then on *The Times*, finally at the *News* in its previous more sober incarnation, had finally paid off. Nicholas Jenkins's predecessor, a man Genevieve had admired very much, had given her assignments with teeth. The last story she had covered for him, an investigation into police corruption in the north-east, had won the paper two awards. Her reward, so long sought, was to have been a three-month posting to Yugoslavia. The day before it was confirmed, that editor was fired and Nicholas Jenkins took his place.

'Yugoslavia?' he had said, in the six and a half minutes he finally spared her. 'Sarajevo? My dear Genevieve, I think not.'

'Why not?' Genevieve asked, although she knew the answer, which had nothing to do with her capabilities and everything to do with her sex.

'Because I need you here,' Jenkins replied. 'I've got some big stories lining up. I'm not ruling out foreign stories – don't think that. We'll review the situation in six months . . . '

Six months later, there had been another excuse; a third was proffered three months after that. Now a year had gone by, she was no nearer her goal, she no longer trusted Jenkins's temporizings, and what was she now stuck with? Telephone sex; a Johnny Appleyard tip. Genevieve glared at the lurid advertisements in front of her. She punched the next number. She would give this charade, she told herself, just one more month. If the assignments did not improve by then, if she was still being fobbed off with this trivial stuff, then she would confront the slippery Jenkins. Some tougher assignments – or, Nicholas, dear, you can shove this job.

Meanwhile, she was through to the next sex line (*Big Blondes*) and another girl was launched on an all too familiar spiel.

'Oooh,' moaned a bored and breathy voice. 'I'm all alone tonight. I'm going to unhook my bra now. I know I shouldn't, but the weather's sooo hot. By the way, did I mention it's a 42D cup . . . ?'

Genevieve groaned and looked out of the office window. Outside the sky was grey. It was beginning to sleet.

'Hot weather?' she muttered. 'Lucky for you, sweetheart. Not here, it's not.'

The recording continued. There was a rustling sound

as the girl turned the pages of her script. 'I think I'm going to tell you what I'm doing. Oooh yes. I'm undoing my bra now. Oooh that's better. I'm just *easing* it off. It's black lace, did I mention that?'

'No, you didn't, moron, get on with it,' Genevieve snapped.

'It's wired underneath,' breathed the girl. She giggled mirthlessly. 'Well, it has to be, you see, because I'm a *big* girl, and it carries a lot of weight . . . '

'Dammit,' said Genevieve. 'What is this – an engineering manual? Get to the point.'

She knew she was wasting her breath. Apart from the fact that the recording could not hear her, delay was the whole purpose of these tapes. The longer the poor sucker kept listening, the greater the profits. There seemed to be hours of this anodyne build-up. The scripts were risible, their delivery amateurish. Genevieve could imagine only too well the kind of businessmen behind them: small-time wide boys making a few bucks on the side from a back room someplace. The more she listened the less she placed any credence in Appleyard's tip.

She yawned, hung up on *Big Blondes*, and tried *Swedish Au Pair*. Such a feast of stereotypes. *Swedish Au Pair* also had a South London accent. She sounded dyslexic. Two-syllable words were giving her problems. When desperate, she whirred a vibrator. She was describing her panties, at length.

'Give me a *break*,' Gini moaned.

'You're the wrong sex for this story.' One of the men from the news desk leaned over her shoulder, and pressed his ear to the receiver. 'Why didn't Nicholas give it to me? Good God, who *is* this?'

'It's number thirty-five. *Swedish Au Pair*.'

'She sounds as if she comes from Neasden, not Stockholm.'

'They all sound like that.'

'Bloody hell. What's that?'

'Her vibrator. Again. She lets it buzz for thirty seconds. They all do. I timed them.'

'Nicky wants you. Now. In his office.' The news-desk man was already bored. 'He says drop everything, something's come up.'

'He should write these scripts. He has the perfect style.' Genevieve replaced the receiver.

'It's lunch,' said the newsman, drifting away. 'He says if you've made arrangements, cancel them. You have to meet some photographer and it must be important. I overheard his secretary making the arrangements. Editor's dining-room stuff.'

Genevieve groaned. She stood up. 'That's the afternoon blown. You're sure he said me? Since when did you become his messenger?'

The news-desk man gave her a languid salute. 'Aren't we all?' He turned and threaded his way down the room, through the ranked word processors, the ranked desks.

When God summoned, you went. Gini took the lift to the fifteenth floor. She stepped out onto thick Wilton carpeting. From here the large windows overlooked dock-lands: there was a grey view of cranes, girders, the river and Thames mud.

She made her way through the outer office, through the inner office. As she approached the sanctum itself, the door was thrown back and Nicholas Jenkins emerged looking powerful, pink, complacent and svelte.

'Ah, there you are at last, Gini,' he said. 'Come in, come in. Charlotte, get Gini a drink.'

Charlotte, his senior secretary, made one of her rude minion faces behind his back. She moved between Gini and the open doorway. Gini remained rooted to the spot. She was staring into the office beyond, where a tall dark-haired man stood by Nicholas Jenkins's desk. The office became silent; the air moved, flickered, became excessively bright.

'Come in, come in.' Nicholas bustled around her. He drew her through the door. He was leading her across to the man, who had turned and was regarding her equably.

'Gini, I want you to meet Pascal Lamartine. You'll have heard of him, of course . . . '

59

Gini took the hand that was being held out to her. She could feel the blood draining from her face. She shook Lamartine's hand, and released it quickly. She had to say something – Nicholas was staring.

'Yes,' she said, 'I've heard of him. More than that – we've met.'

'A long time ago,' Lamartine put in, in a polite neutral tone. His accent was unchanged. Gini could still feel Jenkins's eyes resting curiously on her face.

'Years ago,' she said rapidly, taking her tone from Lamartine. 'I was still at school. Pascal is an old friend of my father's.'

'Oh, I see,' said Jenkins – and to Gini's relief lost interest at once.

Years ago, in Beirut. And he had never been a friend of her father's – quite the reverse. Her father might have won that Pulitzer for his Vietnam work, but by that time fame and bourbon had made him soft.

'An old warhorse,' he would say, easing himself into the first highball of the day, holding court in the palm bar at Beirut's four-star Hotel Ledoyen, surrounded by cronies, surrounded by sycophants quick to prompt. There was her father, sluicing bourbon and anecdotes, and there she was, silent, ignored and embarrassed, averting her eyes from the spectacle, watching the ceiling fans as they rotated above his head.

An old warhorse, an old news hound, a forty-six-year-old boozer. Her father, a living legend, the great Sam Hunter – worshipped by the rest of the press corps. These days he relied on stringers, helpers. Once a week he took a taxi to what he called the front.

And there, on the edge of the group, was a young photographer. He was French, introduced by an Australian reporter, flanked by the man from UPI. Pascal Lamartine, aged twenty-three and already on his third Beirut trip. She had seen his photographs, and admired them. Sam Hunter had also seen them and dismissed them at once.

'Pictures? Who gives a damn?' It was one of his favourite refrains. 'Spare me the Leica leeches, please God. One story's worth a thousand pictures, I'll tell you that. This stuff – today it rates an easy tear, tomorrow it's wrapping trash. But words – they stick. They lodge in the goddamn reader's goddamn brain. Genevieve, remember that.'

The contempt was mutual, she had known that at once. The Frenchman was introduced; he made some polite remark. He stood on the edge of the group. Some sycophant made some sycophantic joke, and her father was launched.

The Frenchman watched him quietly. He never spoke once, but Gini could feel the eddies of Lamartine's dislike. She was young and naïve, and she loved her father very much. The ceiling fans revolved; on and on her father talked, and Gini's heart shrivelled inside her. The young Frenchman stood there, silent and stony-faced. He made no effort to disguise his contempt.

Gini could feel Beirut on her skin now, in a newspaper dining-room. She could smell Beirut – honey and pastries, arak and coffee grounds, cordite and mortar dust – while the English waiter served them an English lunch. Nicholas Jenkins was speaking, but over and above and through his words came a richer sound – the clamour of the Beirut streets.

Machine-gun fire and the cries of street vendors; the liquid voices of the bar girls; the creak of louvred shutters, the sudden drum of summer rain, the Western songs seeping out from the dancehalls, the thunderclap of bombs and wail of Arab ululations. She could feel it now, that new foreign land, that dry rasping heat.

Pascal Lamartine had lived in a room by the harbour. It was next door to a bar, over a cheap dancehall: twelve feet square, bare as a monk's cell, all his pictures filed in boxes. There was a mattress on the floor, two chairs and one table. When she went to the room, she found that the dancehall music from below filtered up. It made the air move and the floor vibrate like the deck of a ship. Several times, in the evenings, she'd stood at his window and watched night fall. When darkness came, the fishing boats left the harbour beyond, and the dancers below began their routines. She could hear the murmurs of their male audience, soft as distant thunder, a million miles beneath.

She'd imagine then, waiting, how it would be if Pascal did not come back. She'd hear the bomb, see the sniper, live his deaths. She would count the seconds, the clink of glasses from the bar, the passers-by in the streets, whispers in foreign tongues. And then the door would open, and Pascal would come back. *Quick, my darling*, he would say, or she would say, *please be quick*.

Smoky twilights; neon seeping through the shutters. She could smell his skin now, recollect the detail of his gaze, feel the touch of his hand. She closed her eyes, and thought, Dear God, will I never forget?

Years ago, another place, another life. She had encountered Pascal just once since.

She looked up, tried to push the past back where it belonged, in the deadzone. She sipped a glass of water. A modish newspaper dining-room deconstructed then reassembled itself. The lunch provided was elaborate, unusually so – as if Jenkins intended to impress. In front of her on a white plate was a tiny bird of some kind, its glazed skin impaled with grapes. Jenkins was talking, and she had not heard a single word he'd said. Sense was fragmenting: Pascal sat three feet away from her as polite as a stranger. There was still a pair of handcuffs in her bag; this room was a very normal and a very crazy place.

Jenkins was drinking Meursault. He drained his glass and continued speaking. Beirut receded: this was some briefing, a new assignment. For the first time Gini began to listen to what he said.

' . . . total confidentiality.' He smiled. Nicholas Jenkins, thirty-five, pink-cheeked, baby-faced, growing plump. He wore rimless nuclear-physicist-style spectacles. His *bonhomie* never quite disguised the fact that Jenkins was on the make.

'No leaks,' he continued, stabbing the air with his knife. 'Anything you discover, we check it once, we check it twice. Make doubly sure. We can't afford any errors. This story will be big.'

He looked from Gini to Pascal. He pushed his quail aside, half-eaten. 'I'm using you, Pascal, because I want pictures. Pictures equal proof. And I'm using you, Gini, because you have certain contacts.' He paused, and gave a tight secretive smile. 'You'll understand when I give you a name. Then you keep that name to yourselves. You don't tout it at dinner tables. You don't leave it in a notebook in the office. You don't stick it up on a computer screen. You don't use it on the office phones. You don't trot it out to wives, girlfriends, boyfriends, favourite dogs – you've both got that? Radio silence.'

He gave them both an impressive glance. 'You work together on this. You start today, and you report to me – to me and no-one else, under any circumstances. Understood?'

'Understood, Nicholas,' Gini replied, thinking what a self-dramatist he was.

She caught an answering glint of mockery in Pascal's eyes. Then Jenkins came out with the name – and the glint of amusement vanished. Pascal's face became alert. Like Gini, he started to pay attention, and at once.

'John Hawthorne.'

Jenkins leaned back in his chair watching them. When he was sure they were suitably surprised and intrigued, he continued. A smile played around his lips.

'John Symonds Hawthorne – and the fabled Lise Courtney Hawthorne, his wife. Or, to put it another way, his Excellency the United States Ambassador to the Court of St James. The American ambassador, and his wife.' He lifted his glass in a mock toast.

'The perfect couple, or so we're always told. Except, as I know, and you know, my dears, there's no such thing as the perfect couple.'

Gini registered the name, and the implication – and was

shocked. She began to concentrate. She had a reporter's memory, and so did Pascal. As the filing cards in her mind started to flick, she saw his expression also become intent. Names, dates, connections, rumours, new and old hints. She saw her own mental process mirrored, checking and re-checking, in his eyes.

Nicholas Jenkins would have liked a more dramatic reaction. He liked to stage-manage his own effects. Now, as if deciding to keep his revelations in reserve, to make them wait, he leaned forward, suddenly businesslike.

'Tell me what you know,' he said. 'Then I'll tell you what I've heard. Pascal, you first.'

Gini watched Pascal closely. The Pascal she once knew did not care much for ambassadors and their society wives – but this Pascal apparently did.

'Very well,' Pascal began. 'Politics in the blood. Three generations of public service at least. The Hawthorne money comes from steel and shipyards originally. The younger brother – Prescott – runs the companies now. They were ranked sixth in America on the last Forbes list. John Hawthorne is aged around forty-six, forty-seven—'

'Forty-seven,' Jenkins put in. 'He'll be forty-eight in a couple of weeks.'

'Educated at Groton, then Yale. Went through Yale law school.' Pascal paused. 'He served in Vietnam, which for a man of his background makes him unusual, maybe unique.'

'*Not* a draft-dodger. Unlike others we could all mention . . .'

'Indeed.' Pascal frowned. 'What else? There's his father, of course. Stanhope Symonds Hawthorne, known to his enemies as SS. A not inappropriate nickname, either, given his political views. Stanhope's still alive though he must be eighty at least. The legendary wheeler-dealer, the man at the heart of the political machine. He's semi-paralysed now, I gather, from the last stroke. In a wheelchair. But he still lords it over that vast place they have in New York State.'

'S. S. Hawthorne,' Jenkins chuckled. 'Old SS. Kind of

a cross between King Lear and a Nazi. Not the easiest of parents. What about the mother?'

'Long dead.' Pascal shrugged and lit a cigarette. 'She was killed in a car crash years back, when Hawthorne was still a child, aged about eight. The father never remarried. He ruled the dynasty single-handed from then on.'

'And the wife? John Hawthorne's wife?' Jenkins put in silkily.

'The famous Lise? She's very beautiful, of course. Related to Hawthorne, I think, but distantly. Second cousins, third perhaps – I'd have to check. They married a decade ago. People say S. S. Hawthorne handpicked his son's bride, but I don't know about that. John Hawthorne was said to be besotted with her. Anyway, it was a notorious wedding. One-thousand-plus guests . . . ' A glint of amusement returned to his eyes. 'As I recall, the bride wore a thirty-thousand-dollar St Laurent dress.'

'Did you cover the wedding?' Jenkins asked.

Gini flinched.

Pascal gave him a cold look. 'No,' he replied. 'I told you, it was ten years ago. I was in Mozambique at the time. I didn't cover society weddings then.'

'Yes, yes, of course.' Jenkins sounded impatient, un-concerned at his own lack of tact. Other people's pasts held no interest for him, unless they had direct bearing on a story. 'So, anything else, Pascal? You hear rumours – it's your job to hear rumours. Any scandal about the Hawthornes? Any ripples, hints?'

'Nothing at all,' Pascal replied evenly. 'But then it's some time since I was last in the States. I've been working in Europe this past year. Something could have come up in that time. All I hear is that the Hawthornes are unfashionably happy. Two children, both boys. Marital devotion . . . ' A hard note had entered his voice. He shrugged. 'Good works and public service. Husband and wife – everywhere seen, everywhere admired. In short, the perfect couple. Just as you said.'

Nicholas Jenkins gave Pascal a sharp glance. Gini felt that he might have liked to make some jibe, and then

. Pascal Lamartine's temper was well
.... kins obviously decided to watch his tongue.
.......ed back in his chair looking secretive and smug.
...ow he loved information, Gini thought. Jenkins nursing
a story was like a miser hoarding gold. He turned to her.

'Your turn, Gini. There's plenty to add.'

'There certainly is.' She hesitated. 'I should say that
I've met John Hawthorne, of course.'

The second the words were said, she regretted them.
The 'of course' had slipped past her guard. Across the
table Pascal picked up on it at once.

'Of course?' he said. 'Is Hawthorne another friend of
your father's?'

There was a nasty little silence. Jenkins, who always
enjoyed tensions between others, gave a smirk. Gini
looked away. The tone in which Pascal had spoken, lazily
disguising what she knew to be a reprimand of sorts, hurt
her. She waited a second, then Jenkins intervened.

'Am I missing something here?' he said in an arch voice.
'Is there some little mystery, Gini? Does your father know
him?'

'He may well have run into him.' She gave a quick
dismissive shrug. 'No, that's not the link. As I'm sure
you know, Nicholas, there are other contacts.'

'*Thought* so.' Jenkins beamed. 'Go on.'

'There's very little to say. I've met Hawthorne precisely
twice. Once, years ago, when he was first a senator. This
was before he married, when I was still at school. I was
about thirteen, and I talked to him for about ten minutes
– less.'

'This was in England? He was making a trip to England?'
Jenkins said.

'That's right. The second time was last year, when he
first arrived at the embassy here. I went to one of the
parties given to welcome him. Again, I spoke to him very
briefly. He was busy. There were about two hundred
guests.'

'Busy?'

'He was working the room, Nicholas.'

'Efficiently?'

'Oh, very efficiently.'

'And the lovely Lise, she was there too?'

'Yes. But I never had a chance to speak to her. She was surrounded by admirers all night.'

'Interesting. Interesting . . . ' Jenkins leaned back in his chair. Pascal said nothing, merely sat and watched her in a thoughtful way. Gini could feel something emanating from that cool watchful regard. It could have been hostility, it could have been dislike. It made her nervous, and self-conscious, and also determined. Let him remain silent; she refused to let him put her off.

'Wake up, Gini.' Jenkins had leaned forward again. 'I'm longing to know . . . Impressions?'

'Of Hawthorne? Very little. The obvious things. He's exceptionally good-looking. He's as charming as most people say. I've heard he can be both kind and generous. He works a room ruthlessly, but then a lot of politicians do.'

'Fine. Fine.' Jenkins shifted in his seat. 'Background, then. Is there anything you want to add to what Pascal's just said?'

She paused once more, and glanced across at Pascal. His rundown on Hawthorne had puzzled her. Accurate it might be, but it had skirted the most important facts. Could Pascal's new work have made him obsessed with trivia – with society weddings, and designer gowns? She could not believe that. Possibly he had been mocking Jenkins's pomposity. She could not tell. The fact remained that Pascal, whose journalistic instincts had once been so sharp, had ignored the most important and most curious aspect of John Hawthorne's meteoric career. Now, why should he do that?

'I'll stick to politics, I think,' she said. 'We ought to start with a puzzle, a mystery, if you like. OK, so John Hawthorne is now the US ambassador here. Fine. But let's remember that in his terms, that's a demotion. Five years ago, John Hawthorne was one of the best known senators in the country and he seemed poised for greater power still. Back in 1989, 1990, all the forecasters agreed: Hawthorne was all set to be the next Democratic candidate for the Presidency.'

'Precisely.' Jenkins smiled broadly. 'And given his clout, his wealth and his charisma, he might even have made it to the White House. If, that is, he could be persuaded to run. And no-one anticipated any difficulties about *that*. Fascinating, isn't it?'

Jenkins waited in silence, savouring the implications while he performed an elaborate ritual of cigar lighting.

'Fine,' he said finally. 'John Hawthorne might have been the 1992 Democratic candidate for the Presidency. He might even have made it to the Oval Office. But he didn't. Gini, go on.'

'John Hawthorne's part of a machine,' Gini began. 'A family machine. There are parallels with the Kennedys obviously, though in Hawthorne's case, no Irish connections. His descent is Catholic Scots. He was the third generation to make it to the Senate. He was groomed by his father for political office from his earliest childhood. Law school, a serving officer in Vietnam, congressman, senator – it was a smooth, perfect, unimpeded ascent. He's rich, smart, charismatic, driven. Master of the sound bite. Perfect on TV. Almost unnatural good looks. A tough campaign record . . . In a word, perfect modern presidential material. Hawthorne as the Democratic candidate in 1992 – that was the prediction . . . ' She paused. 'Only something went wrong. Hawthorne never announced his candidacy. He resigned from the Senate early in 1991. He disappeared off the political map for an entire year to much rejoicing in Arkansas. Clinton had a clean run.'

'Reasons?' Jenkins said.

'It was never explained. That's what's so curious. Why resign from the Senate? He had powerful backers in the Democratic party – why disappoint them? Count the column inches on that. And the answer? No-one knows. There was no scandal, no hint of skeletons in the closet, no smoking bimbos, no bribes, no unfortunate connections with organized crime. Nothing. Just, one day he was there – the next he was gone—'

'There were reasons given,' Pascal interrupted. 'He put out a statement. One of the children, the younger son, had been seriously ill.'

'Oh, sure. And Hawthorne wanted to spend more time with his family as a result. Don't tell me you swallowed that.'

'Possibly not.'

'If you did, Pascal, you're in a minority of one.'

'Children, children, please. Do I detect a note of hostility here?' Jenkins, who loved to detect such tensions, his guiding principle being divide and rule, made a calming gesture. 'Let's stick to the point,' he said. 'Fast forward – we haven't got all day. Hawthorne resigns from the Senate, as you say. He stays well clear of the subsequent presidential election. One month after the inauguration, what do we find? John Hawthorne kissing hands with the Queen. His Excellency the Ambassador. A *very* unexpected appointment, Gini, don't you agree? Run that one past me. Explain *that* as a career move.'

Gini shrugged. 'I can understand why the Clinton administration might offer him the job – I can see them in the Oval Office saying, How do we get rid of Hawthorne, how do you bury America's crown prince? I can see that. But for Hawthorne to accept the posting to London? All his life this man's been like a heat-seeking missile, straight on target to the White House—'

'And then he veers off,' Jenkins cut in. 'Of course, one could say that being ambassador to Britain is a prestigious post. Other people even saw it as an effective launch-pad to the presidency – Joseph Kennedy, for one.'

'Maybe so. But that was over fifty years ago. Times change. Now ambassadorships go to yesterday's mèn, or women. As a reward for services rendered. In American terms right now, Hawthorne's invisible. Ambassadors don't make headlines. All this posting does for him is delay any political comeback. It cuts him off from the power centre. I'd say he has to have accepted that.

69

He knows it's over. Maybe he wants it to be over. Politically, Hawthorne's all washed up.'

There was a pause. Jenkins savoured the moment, then seemed to decide he had held out long enough. He leaned forward, wafting cigar smoke at them both.

'Suppose I told you that Hawthorne wasn't washed up? Suppose I told you that Hawthorne was having second thoughts, that he now wished he'd never abandoned that golden career?'

'I'd say he's left it too late.'

'Are you sure?' Jenkins smiled. 'After all, make the calculations: let's suppose Clinton enjoys office for two full terms. That takes us to the year 2000. By which time John Hawthorne will be in his mid-fifties. He's a man, in any case, who looks a good ten years younger than his age. Would you rule him out of the presidential running then – a man of his looks and abilities, a man with his connections? If you would, I'm not sure I'd agree.'

'OK,' Gini said. 'I agree. Up to a point. It's feasible Hawthorne could make a comeback further down the road. But not without re-establishing his American base. Not if he remains here too long. If he does that, he's dead in the water.' She paused. Jenkins was watching her, smiling. Gini, who knew his techniques, realized that she had been given, and missed, a clue.

'*Connections,*' she said, leaning forward. 'Oh, I see, Nicholas. You mean it might not just be a question of Hawthorne's own ambitions? You mean there are other people promoting Hawthorne's political future as well?'

'Well, my dear Gini, I'd say so, wouldn't you? His father, for one. That goes without saying, and old SS should never be underestimated, wheelchair or no. I've heard other names mentioned as well, powerful names representing powerful vested interests. Still—'

He broke off, and leaned back in his chair, drawing on his cigar. 'We don't need to concentrate on those details, not for now. I didn't bring you both here today to discuss them. John Hawthorne may or may not have an illustrious political future. Right now, he's one of his country's most senior ambassadors, a man with an unblemished reputation. And – unlike you – I have been hearing stories about him. Very interesting stories. Revelatory, you might say. Your job will be to discover if they're true. If they are, then Hawthorne will have no political future at all.'

He paused, looking from Pascal to Gini. The end of his cigar glowed. Gini hesitated, puzzled by Pascal's silence. She glanced across at him, then turned back to Jenkins.

'You mean Hawthorne has an enemy?'

'Oh, very much so.'

'That doesn't necessarily mean much. Men in Hawthorne's position breed enemies.'

'I do so agree,' Jenkins said smoothly. 'An enemy means nothing – unless that enemy could come up with something John Hawthorne hoped to keep well buried. Something never rumoured, never whispered about before. Now, if an enemy could do that—'

'They'd go straight to an American newspaper.' It was Pascal who cut in, making Gini jump. He was watching Jenkins closely.

'They'd go straight to the *New York Times*, Nicholas, or the *Washington Post*. Their approach might be indirect, devious. But that's where they'd go. Not a British newspaper. You know that.'

'True. Very true.' Jenkins remained unruffled. 'I agree. That's precisely what they'd do. Unless they happened to be in England at the time. Unless it just so happened that they had an English contact, someone whom they had reason to trust.'

There was another silence. Jenkins continued to sit there, smiling at them both. He had every intention, Gini could see, of spinning this out. Silently, she cursed him for this characteristic and labyrinthine approach. Jenkins parted with information as reluctantly as a glutton parted with food. The story, she saw, would have to be prised out.

'OK,' she said, 'let me get this straight, Nicholas. You've heard rumours about Hawthorne, yes? There's something he wants to hide. Fiscal? Some tax scam?'

'No.'

'Influences then. Friends in the wrong places? Electoral bribes? Some link-up with organized crime?'

'Nothing like that. Not a hint. In that respect, Hawthorne's unusual. The original Mr Clean.'

'Come on, Nicholas. I'm getting sick of guessing games.'

'One more try.'

'All right. Sex. It's something sexual he wants to hide.'

'Getting warmer. Go on.'

'Well, if it's sexual, it's predictable . . .'

'The best stories often are.'

'A mistress? An illegitimate child? Call-girls? Unwise moments with blondes . . .'

'You're right about the blondes.' Jenkins's smile broadened. 'They *have* to be blondes, or so I hear . . .'

He broke off while they sat in silence, Jenkins enjoying their suspense. He continued to puff at his cigar, pink, plump and magisterial, like a benign Buddha enthroned on a chair.

Finally, Gini said, '*Have* to be blondes? That's an odd way of putting it.'

'Oh no. It's precise.' Jenkins beamed. 'When their services are arranged, he stipulates blondes. He has other requirements as well. Hawthorne's *extremely* specific, or so I hear.'

'Get to the point, Nicholas.'

'Of course, Pascal. Blondes. Hawthorne needs blondes. But the ways in which he needs them are unusual to say the least. Even to me, and I've heard it all. *First*,' he held up one finger, 'he requires a blonde, a hired blonde, with absolute regularity. One a month, always on the same day. Always on a Sunday, as it happens – the third Sunday of any calendar month.

'*Second*,' he went on, 'the blonde must remain silent at all times. During the . . . sessions they have together, she must not speak or cry out while in his presence. In view of what happens, that must present difficulties, but those are the rules.

'*Thirdly*, the meetings last for exactly two hours and a

costume is provided for the girl. Much of that costume will be removed. Except for one item. The girl is provided with long black leather gloves, and the gloves must be worn at all times. The girl is never permitted to touch Hawthorne, except with a gloved hand.'

'*Gloves?*' Pascal said, and Gini caught his reaction.

Jenkins, launched now, did not; he pressed on. '*Fourth,* generally speaking, the girl is there to obey Hawthorne's commands. Some of those commands are . . . unusual, shall we say? Though each to his own, of course. Occasionally the girls have required medical attention afterwards. It's partly for that reason, I imagine, that they're so well paid. The going rate was twenty thousand dollars a session in America. It's ten thousand pounds here. No girl is ever used twice.'

'Twenty thousand dollars?' Gini stared at him in disbelief.

'Generous, isn't it?' Jenkins smiled. 'Maybe that accounts for the fact that none of these girls has gone running to the tabloids. There is another reason, of course. In view of what's happened. They're too scared.'

There was a silence. Nicholas Jenkins looked well pleased. He leaned back in his chair. 'Fascinating, don't you find? The patterns of obsessive behaviour. And Hawthorne a man with so much to lose . . . '

'It's ridiculous,' Gini began a second before Pascal. 'It's trash. Garbage. Colourful, sure – and beyond that, Nicholas, I have to say I don't believe a word.'

'Nor do I.' Pascal rose. 'This is a total waste of time. Once a month, every month? For God's sake, Nicholas, the man's an ambassador. He used to be a US senator. To arrange something like that, other people would have to be involved. Aides, bodyguards certainly. A man like Hawthorne is protected, rarely alone. There's no way on earth you could keep that kind of thing under wraps. Two months, three at most – and the story's all over town.'

'I know.' Jenkins's smile became complacent. 'Yet I hear it's been going on for years. Four years at least – that's a great many blondes.'

'You must have taken leave of your senses.' Pascal now made no attempt to disguise his impatience. 'You flew me to London for this? I might as well go now.'

'Oh, I wouldn't do that. You haven't heard it all. Just listen. Consider – my reaction was exactly the same as yours. The first time it was put to me, well, I wouldn't have given it a second's credence. And I certainly wouldn't have flown you in, not at your rates.' Pascal flushed; Jenkins waved him back to his chair. 'Sit down – there's a good fellow. And let me explain. There's one very obvious question, isn't there? Who was my source?'

'OK. Five minutes.' Pascal sat down. 'Who *was* your source? One of the girls?'

'Certainly not.' Jenkins looked offended. 'You think I'd react this way to some story from a two-bit tart? My source is right in there, close to the ambassador.'

'You've talked to this source yourself?'

For the first time, some of Jenkins's ebullience diminished. He shifted his gaze slightly. 'No,' he admitted in a grudging way, 'I haven't. Not yet. My information was filtered, if you like. It came through a third party.'

'Who?'

'The name's not likely to mean anything to you, or Gini. It's a man. James McMullen. I was at school with him, as it happens. I've known him for years.'

'McMullen?' Pascal glanced across at Gini, who shook her head. 'And who is he, this school-friend of yours?'

'Nobody much,' Jenkins replied, and there were signs his confidence was returning. 'Well-connected. Clever – up to a point – in fact, he was an Oxford scholar. But a bit weak maybe – vacillating, no drive. Left Oxford without a degree, spent some years as an army officer, then resigned. Took a few jobs in the City. Became a bit of a drifter – a handsome, charming drifter. Goodhearted. Honest. A bit of a throw-back – not in touch with the modern world. He first approached me about three months ago. Out of the blue. I hadn't laid eyes on him in years.'

'He told you the story about the blondes?' Gini asked,

watching him closely. 'Was he selling it? How much did he want?'

'Nothing. My friend James doesn't operate that way. He's a gentleman, one of a dying breed. I doubt he even knows newspapers pay for information, and if he did, he'd be appalled. No. He didn't want money. He wanted something more subtle. He wanted the truth about Hawthorne to come out.'

There was another silence. Gini could see Pascal thinking, calculating. His impatience had gone.

'All right,' he said, when Jenkins volunteered nothing further. 'Your friend McMullen was an intermediary, bringing you information on someone else's behalf. How close is that person to the ambassador?'

'Oh very close indeed.'

'And you can substantiate McMullen's link with that source?'

'Pascal, *please*, of course. That was my opening request. That groundwork's done. It was arranged for me to witness McMullen lunching with his source. There's no doubt they know each other. They're old friends. And then . . . ' He paused, smiling. 'Then – also at my suggestion – James recorded a telephone conversation between them, with equipment I provided. The tape's being copied now. I'll let you have it tomorrow. When you hear it, you'll see. James wasn't lying. And he's very close to his source.'

Pascal shrugged. 'Very well,' he said. 'Let's take that as read for now. McMullen is close to this source, and the source is close to Hawthorne. How close? Someone employed in the household, or at the embassy? A maid? A driver? One of his aides? Some security man?'

'Closer than that.'

'Someone in Hawthorne's family? His brother? One of that tribe of cousins?' Gini suggested, then shook her head. 'No. I can't believe that. A united front. No-one in that family would talk.'

Jenkins was not listening. His gaze was now directed towards the windows, and the fading light of a winter

75

afternoon. Gini could see how much he was relishing this, and she had an intuition: Jenkins loved scoops, he loved the *coup de grâce*. He would have saved the best, and the nastiest twist, for last.

'In a way,' he began slowly, in a meditative tone, 'you could say that the source is almost the ambassador himself. Because there's another aspect to those monthly rituals – one I didn't mention before. It seems that when Hawthorne returns from one of his sessions, he likes to go over its details, chapter and verse. Blow-by-blow descriptions, as you might appropriately say . . . It's the conclusion to the night's entertainments, apparently. And from what I gather, for Hawthorne it's the most satisfying part of all.'

'You mean he *tells* someone all this?' Gini stared at him in astonishment. 'That can't be true. You mean he comes back, sits down by the fireside, and *describes* what he's done? Nicholas . . . '

'Not by the fireside, I hear.' Jenkins's smile was now one of malicious delight. 'In bed is the favoured location, or so I'm told.'

'In bed? You mean . . . ?'

'I mean, my dears, that our source is the ambassador's *wife*. Lise Hawthorne herself. She told McMullen, her old friend, confidant and self-appointed protector, and eventually McMullen told me. Rather trusting, as I'm sure you'll agree, handing a stick of dynamite to an editor – but then my friend James *is* trusting, and so I'm beginning to suspect is the ambassador's wife. Trusting, frightened, trapped and increasingly desperate . . . And such a beautiful woman, too.'

Jenkins had finally obtained his hoped-for reaction. He bathed a few minutes in the glow of their astonishment, then rose to his feet.

'Mrs Hawthorne wants this story to come out,' he continued, more briskly. 'Since she's a devout Catholic, a divorce is ruled out. Now a divorce court, of course, would bring the truth to light – but since she hasn't that option, she's turned to the Press. To us.' He paused. 'On one condition. We have to substantiate this story without any apparent assistance from her. She cannot be revealed as its source—'

'You mean we can't talk to her?' Gini interrupted. 'We can't approach the main source directly?'

'My dear Gini, absolutely *not*. Under no circumstances. That's the first rule, the first condition McMullen laid down. No interviews with the lovely Lise.' Jenkins favoured both of them with a benign, and possibly gloating, smile. 'Leg-work, my dears. No cosy phone calls to the ambassadorial residence. No cosy tête-à-têtes with Lise. No enquiries to staff that get back to the ambassador three seconds after you hang up the phone.'

'Damn.' Gini had opened her diary meanwhile. She was flicking through its pages. 'I was just checking how the Sundays fall. It's eleven days to the third Sunday this month.'

'I know,' Jenkins replied. 'And you'll need every one of those days. There's a lot to check out. And, annoyingly, there were gaps in my friend James's narrative. We know *when* these meetings allegedly take place—'

'But not where,' Gini finished for him.

'This shouldn't be too much of a problem.' Pascal rose. He looked at Jenkins thoughtfully. 'After all, McMullen's told you everything else. He's been a very obliging kind of source. Location shouldn't be a difficulty. Where is your friend Mr McMullen, Nicholas? How do we contact him?'

Pascal's tone had been sarcastic. Jenkins seemed pleased to have riled him.

'Ah, tiny problem,' he said cheerily. 'I should have mentioned it before. McMullen's disappeared. Gone to ground. We were due to meet just before Christmas. McMullen had promised to provide the next assignation address. Unfortunately McMullen never showed. He's not been in his London flat for over two weeks. None of his friends has clapped eyes on him. He hasn't written, hasn't telephoned . . . Most mysterious. As if he's dead . . . Still, I'm sure you'll both track him down.'

He gave them both a jovial salute. Gini felt that for some reason he now chose to forestall further questions. 'Must rush. Late for my own editorial meeting. Here, Gini.'

He slid a card and a photograph across the table. The picture must have been taken some years before, Gini noted, for in it McMullen wore uniform. A good-looking fair-haired man, wearing combat fatigues. It was not a very good photograph, nor a very clear likeness.

'That's his address, and the only picture I could get hold of. Just to give you both a start. Pascal, talk to my girl Charlotte. I know she's booked you a room somewhere comfortable. Check back with me in a couple of days, when you've got some results. Be ingenious, my dears. Have fun. *Ciao.*'

VII

'Is Jenkins always like that?' Pascal asked, some time later as they left the *News* building.

Gini shrugged, and pulled her coat tighter around her. It was almost dark now, at three-thirty in the afternoon. It was cold; rain alternated with sleet. 'You've met Nicholas before. You should know. And yes, he is.'

'He's a shit,' Pascal said in a gloomy way. 'I always thought that, and now I'm sure. He gloats.'

'Sure. He enjoys other people's misfortunes. He's not alone in that.'

'It's a wild-goose chase.' Pascal glanced at the yellowish sky, and turned up the collar of his jacket. 'None of this will stand up. It's too far-fetched.'

'Maybe. I'm not so sure of that. Nicholas knows a good story when he hears one. Think about it – from his point of view it could work two ways. If the allegations about Hawthorne are true, that's headline stuff. If they turn out to be untrue, there's still a story: Lise Hawthorne, peddling lies about her husband to the Press.'

'Maybe. Maybe so.'

There was a small awkward silence. She could feel Pascal's gaze, and averted her face. She looked around her. The *News* offices, in former years after the move from Fleet Street, had been under siege to union pickets. They were a grim place. 'Fortress Docklands' they'd been nicknamed, and the tag was apt. From where they stood, just outside the brutalist office building itself, they were ringed by fifteen-foot walls, barbed-wire fencing, and electronic security-manned gates. A few blocks beyond, through a maze of grim council estates and converted warehouses, was the River Thames. The proximity of the river and its low-tide mud flats made the air dank. *I work in a prison*, Gini sometimes thought.

'Genevieve?'

Pascal had turned to her. He touched the sleeve of her coat, then quickly withdrew his hand. His use of her full name, and the French manner in which he pronounced it, brought the past roaring back. For one brief and painful instant Gini remembered how it had once been in that little room by the harbour. She remembered how the dancehall music made the floor pulse, how the lights of the fishing boats glittered across the water at night, how it felt when Pascal took her in his arms.

She averted her face, and kept her eyes fixed firmly on the security gates.

'I'm sorry.' Pascal hesitated. His manner was awkward.

'I wasn't told I would be working with you. I promise you, Gini, until just before you walked into that room, Jenkins had said nothing. I had no idea.'

Gini turned to look at him. 'If you had known in advance would you have agreed to work with me or refused?'

A shadow passed across his face, but the Pascal she remembered had always been honest, and he gave her an honest answer now. 'If it had happened a few years ago – yes, I'd have refused. I was trying to make my marriage work. There was Marianne – my daughter.' He paused, looked towards her, then away. He thrust his hands into his jacket pockets, half-shrugged. 'So – yes, if this had happened a few years back, I would have refused. You know why, I think.'

'Too many memories?'

'Partly. And too much risk.'

There was a little silence. Gini stared hard at the gates. Eventually, she said, 'Risk?'

'We quarrelled once. I had no wish to do so again.'

It was not the answer Gini had hoped for. She began to move across the yard in the direction of her car. She pushed her wet hair back from her face. Pascal came after her, and touched her sleeve. She came to a halt.

'Why do you ask?' he said, in an agitated way. 'You don't want to work with me now, is that it?'

Gini turned to look at him. His face was pale and drawn, his hair wet from the rain. She could both feel his tension, and see it written on his features.

'If that's the case, just say so, Gini, I'll understand. I'll tell Jenkins I'm pulling out. It doesn't matter. There's plenty of other work. I'll do that, Gini. I'll tell him right now. If you want.'

Gini hesitated. The sleety rain was cold against her cheeks. Tiny wet particles clung to her eyelids and lashes. She blinked.

'No,' she said eventually. 'No, don't do that . . . After all, it's a good story. It could be a major story. There's no reason why we can't work together as a team. I might have found it hard too, a few years back. But not now. Now it's fine. I'm over all that . . . '

'I see.'

'It was a long time ago, Pascal. Twelve years.'

He touched her shoulder, and made her face him. He looked down at her intently, then with a half-smile, tilted up the brim of her cap.

'Why the disguise, Gini? A boy's cap, a man's overcoat, your lovely hair all tied back? Trousers, boots. Are you trying to change your sex?'

'No, no, of course not.' She gave a quick protective irritable gesture. 'I just don't like to look too female, that's all. Not when I work. I work with men all the time, and . . . I find it's simpler, that's all.'

'Your eyes haven't changed, you know that?'

'Pascal, don't.'

She drew back from him sharply, and looked away. She could feel his gaze rest upon her face. The sleet fell. Across the yard, a car engine started up. She tried to fight down all the memories that surged forward when she heard that tone, amused, half-tender, in his voice. She said to herself: *I will not let this happen to me again; I won't.*

Pascal moved a few paces off. He made an odd gesture of

the hand, as if relinquishing something. He said, 'You're right. Of course.'

'Friends,' Gini began in a rush. 'We can work together as friends, surely? We always said that was how it would be – if we met again. No bitterness. No recriminations.'

'Is that what we said?'

'It was. You know it was. More or less.'

'Maybe. I remember it rather differently.' It was his turn to look away. He frowned up at the sky, then turned back with a shrug. 'Still. Friends. I'm sure you're right. Reporters. Colleagues. *Tout à fait, les professionels, toi et moi.*'

'Pascal, please don't speak French.'

'You used to speak it once.' He smiled. 'Bad grammar, the accent not so good – but you still spoke it. I can still hear the sound of your voice. Gini—'

'No. Don't do this. I won't work with you if you do this.' She had raised her voice. It echoed around the courtyard. Pascal seemed about to argue, then reconsidered. Gini thought: *He has changed; he would have argued once.* She glanced toward him; there was a tired grey resignation on his face.

'It throws me,' he said simply. 'It throws me badly, meeting you like this.'

'I know.' She set her lips. 'Me too. We'll get over that.'

There was defiance in her tone; Pascal ignored it. He made no comment. Turning, he began to walk back towards the gates. Gini fell into step beside him. Behind them, from the *News* offices, a cold fluorescence spilled into the dusk. As they reached her small Volkswagen Beetle, Pascal said, 'I'm divorced now.'

'I know. I heard. Someone in the office mentioned it. I thought of writing to you to say how sorry I was. I am sorry, Pascal.'

'It happens.' His tone was flat. Then his face lightened. 'I still see my daughter, of course. Marianne. She's seven now. She lives with my wife, but I see her every week. In the holidays . . . ' He paused. 'You never married, then?'

'No. I never married. I live alone. Maybe I'm not the marrying type. You know how it is.'

There was another silence. How awkward we are, Gini thought, and how bleak we sound. She opened her bag, and began to rummage inside it for her car keys.

'I used to think of you,' Pascal said, in a sudden abrupt way. 'I'd see articles you wrote. I could see you were doing well. I was glad. I always wanted you to succeed. To be happy. I hope you know that was the case—'

'I am happy,' Gini replied quickly. 'I'm fine. Everything's worked out very well. Listen, I should go, Pascal. We've got work to do. I think I'll go over to the Press Association, go through the clippings on the Hawthornes. And you'll want to check in at your hotel. Can I give you a lift?'

'No, no. There's a cab pulling in. I'll take that.'

He signalled to the taxi-driver. Gini still fumbled for her keys in her overflowing bag. Her fingers touched wrapping paper, a box, the cold metal of a pair of handcuffs. She had almost forgotten this parcel. She fumbled again, and found the keys at last. When she looked up, she found Pascal was still watching her, a slight frown on his face.

'Your father? How is he?' he asked. 'Well, I hope.'

'My father's at the Washington bureau now. Drinking just a little bit more. I rarely see him. You don't have to be polite.'

'And your stepmother? She lives in the country still?'

'No. In London. She remarried some years ago. Very happily. Her husband died last year. So it's been hard for her. But she's fighting back. She's like that.' She paused. 'You'd like her, I think. You should meet her anyway.'

'I should?' He looked surprised.

'Oh yes. She might help us. She's the reason Jenkins put me on this story. She's the "contact" Jenkins mentioned.'

'Your stepmother?'

'Yes. Mary's known the Hawthorne family for forty years at least. They're old old friends. She and Hawthorne are very close. It was through Mary that I met him. At her house, at her party.'

A look she could not quite interpret crossed Pascal's face. 'Oh, of course,' he said. 'All those family connections of yours. Instant entrée.'

'I don't advertise them, Pascal.'

'I'm sure you don't.'

'Mary's nothing like my father, in any case. And my father . . . ' She broke off. 'Pascal. You shouldn't have blamed him.'

'I didn't blame him.' He spoke sharply. 'I blamed myself.' Across the yard, the taxi-driver leaned on his horn. 'Damn.' Pascal glanced over his shoulder. 'He's getting impatient, I'd better go. And you'd better hurry, if you want to go through the clippings on Hawthorne. The files will be a foot thick. So . . . ' He turned to glance at her. 'What shall we do? Would you like to meet later? Shall we have dinner tonight?'

'No, not tonight. I'm going out tonight. Let's make a start in the morning. Call me then. You've got the number?'

She stopped. Another memory had come back. For an instant she felt on her skin the heat of a Beirut summer. Sometimes, when he was working, Pascal would be away all night. If he was, he always called her hotel first thing in the morning. He always called at eight. She always picked up on the first ring. That was their ritual. *Darling, can you come over now? I got the pictures. It's all right. I'm safe.* She turned away. These memories hurt.

Pascal hesitated, as if about to say more, then moved off to the waiting cab. Over his shoulder, from a few yards off, he said, 'I'll call in the morning. I'll call at eight.'

Inside her little Beetle it was cold. The seats felt damp. Gini switched on the windscreen wipers. She watched the cab pull away, then disappear through the gates. She switched off the car engine. Water rattled against the car roof. The windscreen became a blur. She slumped against the steering wheel, and covered her face.

She felt tense with the effort of concealment. If she had known she was to meet him, then she would have coped

84

so much better, she thought. It was hard to be greeted by him as an acquaintance, a virtual stranger, yet if she had had time she could have prepared for that.

She straightened, started the engine once more and looked out across this prison-yard place. It was twelve years since Beirut, and five since the last occasion, the only other occasion, when they had met. Sitting outside a café on a wide Paris boulevard on the left bank. It had been a day of bright sunshine, the light dazzled in the street. And she had not been alone, she had been with another journalist, an Englishman much older than herself. Her affair with him had been uneasy and quarrelsome from the first; the visit to Paris had not improved things. They had spent much of the previous night arguing, and all of the morning. As she sat outside the café, she was trying to blot out the stream of accusations that came from her left. She had been thinking: *In a moment, I'll just stand up and leave. Then I'll never need to see him again.* And she looked away, up the boulevard, with its plane trees, watching the passing people, and her eyes focused on a single family group.

They were walking towards her at a leisurely pace, a tall dark-haired man, a dark-haired woman, and their child. The man had his arms around the woman's shoulders; the woman was pushing a buggy with a little girl in it. The child was laughing, and waving her fists. She looked about two years old, Gini thought. It was their ease, their evident contentment, which drew her eye. She watched them approach, the little girl was wearing a bright blue frock, a little pinafore – and then she realized. It was Pascal who was laughing at something this woman had just said to him. It was Pascal who took one of her hands, and swung it, and increased his pace. It was Pascal, who stopped just a few yards away, turned to her, said something, and kissed her upturned face.

The shock was acute. She had known that he was married; she had heard he had a child; until that moment she had not understood what she had lost.

She had looked away quickly, and bent her head. She

85

told herself that he would not notice her, and that if he did, he would walk on by, but he did not. He stopped, hesitated, and then he spoke.

She did not want to remember the scene after that. The stiff introductions, the meaningless exchanges, the fixed and glassy smiles. The air eddied with undercurrents. Pascal's wife's face became tight. The little girl began to cry. Eventually, the family group moved off. Beside her, her companion knocked back his drink.

'Well, well, well,' he said. 'Pascal Lamartine, no less. So tell me, when did you screw *him* – and don't bother denying it, Gini. It was written all over your face. And his.'

She had not said one word. She simply rose and walked away. As she did so, she felt the headiest relief. She ran back to their hotel, packed her bags, and left. The man was completely unimportant. Now, still sitting in her car, she could scarcely remember his name, let alone his face.

But that glimpse of marital happiness – she could remember that only too clearly. Looking across the wet yard, she watched it, gesture by gesture, Pascal's other life. When, just a few minutes earlier, he had mentioned his daughter, he had made no reference to the incident. Perhaps he had forgotten it, forgotten she had ever seen his wife or Marianne.

It was likely, to be expected. Releasing the brake, she drove forward, and out of the gates.

Pascal's hotel turned out to be in Park Lane. It was large, efficient, international and anonymous. He had been assigned a business suite with two telephones and a fax machine. His life was now lived in similar hotel rooms. He felt he could move around them blindfolded. It took him two seconds to unpack.

He checked his cameras, dialled room service, and told them to bring some food at eight. He showered, changed, inspected the crumpled garments in the closets, and resolved to reform. Would Gini want to work with a man who looked as if he'd slept the night before in a hedge? No, she would not. He rang the valet service, and feeling proud of himself, gestured grandly at the closets.

'Take them away,' he said. 'All of them. I want them all cleaned and pressed. Oh, and the shirts laundered. Can you do that?'

The valet smiled and said he could. He made no comment when he opened the closet doors to find it contained three ancient shirts, three pairs of blue jeans, and innumerable pairs of odd socks.

'The leather jacket as well, would it be, sir?'

Pascal ran his hands through his hair, so it stood on end. 'No. Maybe not the jacket. It's cold. I'll need this.'

'Replace the missing buttons on the shirts, sir?'

'That is possible? Superb.'

'If you'll be staying with us some while, sir, I could make a suggestion . . . '

'One week. Two weeks. Maybe more. What?'

'There is a very good shop in the hotel arcade, sir. It sells excellent gentlemen's clothing . . . '

'Suits?' Pascal said, on a suspicious note.

'More your actual informal wear, sir. I think you'd find it to your taste. It stays open until eight.'

'Excellent.' Pascal gave the man a very generous tip. He went downstairs at once. He inspected the shop in question warily, since clothes did not interest him in the least, and he bought them rarely, only when the previous garments gave up the ghost. Steeling himself, he went inside and began grabbing things from shelves.

'These,' he said, 'and these. And three of these. And those over there . . . '

The pile on the counter mounted. The assistant watched him, straight-faced. 'They're all black, sir. You're sure you—'

'Yes, yes, black,' said Pascal, proffering plastic. He was already bored with this. 'Everything black. It's simpler like that.'

The assistant knew a pushover when he saw one: customers in a hurry were usually the best. Besides, this customer would be a pleasure to advise: he was tall, lean, rangy. He deserved to be well dressed.

'If I might make a few suggestions, sir? To complement these purchases. A classic white shirt, perhaps? We have Turnbull and Asser in stock. And a nice tie to go with it. Knitted silk is back . . . '

Pascal was not aware that knitted silk had ever been away. He gave the man a blank look. 'Ties? Ties? I never wear ties . . . '

'For a dinner engagement, sir? Or a business meeting, perhaps?'

Pascal hesitated. He had a sudden vision of Gini seated next to him at a candlelit table. He and Gini were drinking champagne and eating wonderful food. Gini looked rapturously happy. Women liked to be taken to restaurants, he thought vaguely. He frowned.

'A tie,' he said in a meditative tone. 'A tie. Yes, maybe you are right.'

'And then, sir, we have the new Armani jackets just in. The unstructured look, with just a *fraction* more tailoring than last year. Now this one here . . . ' He produced a jacket. Unfortunately Pascal looked at the price tag. An expression of pure horror came upon his face.

'Ah no. Here I draw the line. Impossible. Unthinkable. Indefensible. I have a leather jacket upstairs.'

'Ah yes. But for that dinner engagement, sir? Would the leather really be suitable? This is cashmere, of course.'

Pascal still looked shaken, and unconvinced. Inspiration came to the assistant.

'And then it would last, sir, there's always that. Classic styling, superb fabric. Ten years from now, you could still be wearing it.'

Pascal was less naïve than he seemed. He knew an astute sales pitch when he heard one, and he smiled at this. He made a quick calculation: perhaps it could be justified, this once. He added the white shirt, the knitted tie and the jacket to the pile.

'*Ça suffit.* Not a sock, not a belt, not an item more. Enough.'

Returning to his hotel room, Pascal made an effort. He actually hung up the new clothes. Then they made him feel guilty, and despondent – restaurant, what restaurant? He'd probably never even take Gini to a restaurant. They would work together during the day, and then in the evenings she'd go out with whoever was the new man in her life. He glowered at the foolish clothes and shut the door on them at once.

Work, he said to himself, and he set himself to work. He could feel the memories, just there at the edge of his consciousness, and he wanted them no closer. Work would keep them at bay. He opened his heavy address book and began to run down the names of contacts. Forget Beirut, forget that small square bare room above the harbour, forget everything that happened there. That was in another country, in another life.

He closed his eyes briefly. For an instant he saw Gini, the Gini he had known then. She was standing, quietly, near the window. It was dawn, the shutters were closed, and the pale outline of her naked body was striped with the pinkish light from the louvres. She was watching him, silently, a little sadly, as he slept. Waking, seeing her, he at once ached to hold her. He lifted his hand to her.

'Darling. Don't worry. Don't be sad. We'll find a solution. I love you. Come back to bed.'

He swore under his breath, closed the address book, opened it again. The memory faded, eased away, but he knew it would come back. Names, contacts, he said to himself. Somewhere in this address book there would be someone who could help with the Hawthorne story. Someone – but who? Of all these numbers – which?

Pascal's contacts were his life blood. They had to be better than those of his competitors: his contacts, as much as his camera skills, kept him ahead of the pack. These connections spanned the social scale: at one end were the hostesses, the party-givers, the jet-set pleasure-seekers; at the other end were those who serviced the needs of the first – the private plane pilots, the chauffeurs, the hotel clerks, the ski-instructors, the security operatives, the maids, nannies and gardeners – all those who quietly, efficiently and invisibly served the whims and caprices of the rich.

The night-club owners, the croupiers, the swimming-pool servicers, the golf pros, the tennis coaches, the *vendeuses*, the call-girls: it was a huge and useful under-class. Pascal had experienced the pulse of their resentment. Their banked hostility to their employers no longer surprised him. Like them, he had learned from proximity. He had little sympathy for the hypocrisies of the privileged and powerful, little sympathy for the sublime carelessness of the rich.

He paid well and promptly for information received. Sometimes the advantage this gave him amused him, and sometimes it disgusted him. His mother, tough, forthright and uncompromising, had attacked him for this work, right up to and including the day of her death.

'Once your work meant something,' she said. 'Now what are you? A jackal, a hyena, *une espèce de parasite*.'

Pascal had not replied. He was adding bills in his head. French lawyers. English lawyers. A house in the suburbs that cost five million francs he didn't have. A house – or so the French lawyer believed, so Helen had said – which would make his ex-wife happy and keep her in France. Keep Marianne in France, near by, near him, at a French school, speaking French.

This had mattered to him once, passionately. Now even that achievement, that attempt to rescue some security for his child from the wreckage of the marriage, even that might be lost.

Pascal flicked through the pages of his address book, closed it again.

'If there was no wrong-doing, *Maman*, I would have no story . . . ' He had said that once, twenty times. 'People lie, *Maman*. They cheat. They double-cross. My photographs show them doing that. They show the truth.'

His mother had not deigned to answer him, and Pascal, shamed, had turned away. Better not to try to justify this work, although it could be justified, perhaps. He needed money and this paid better than wars or deprivation. There was an inexhaustible appetite for these stories. He was in tune with his society's values: let that be his excuse.

He stood up, and switched on the television. On the news programme were reports from several Middle Eastern countries. The previous week, Israeli troops had opened up on a village in the occupied territories: sixteen Arabs had died, two of them possible terrorists, and five of them children. The incident had occurred while the latest round of US–Israeli talks was proceeding. Increased US aid to Israel, and a boost in US arms supplies were widely rumoured to be part of the new package. The anti-US demonstrations had begun in Egypt, in Syria, now in Iraq and Iran: outside the US embassies, outside the premises of US businesses. Pascal watched his past in his present: the processions, the placards, the slogans, the burial of the dead.

In London, the latest IRA bombing campaign was continuing. A bomb had been defused in a van outside Victoria Station. In Brussels, EEC ministers had met to . . . In the West Country, severe flooding had . . . Pascal rose and switched off the set. He spent some time on the telephone to various contacts of his, including one – formerly the *madame* of an exquisite brothel in the sixteenth *arrondissement* of Paris, who might know where a powerful man would go, once a month, to hire blondes for a liaison with sado-masochistic overtones. The results of the calls might prove helpful, but for the moment were inconclusive. Pascal stood, and stared at the wall of his hotel room. He thought of Genevieve; he heard the music of that small room above a dance hall in Beirut.

At seven, needing air, feeling trapped, he left the hotel and walked the streets for a while. He passed through a silent Mayfair and skirted the brilliant empty shops of Oxford Street. He thought he walked at random, without purpose or direction, but this was not the case.

His footsteps led him to Grosvenor Square, and to the US embassy there.

He halted, and watched the building from across the street. Rain now fell heavily, in a thick curtain. Lights still blazed from the office windows with their protective bomb-blast curtaining. Outside the main doorway, at the head of the steps, two Marines stood on guard. This was unusual; Pascal stared. He could see the startling white of their puttees, the glint of their cap badges. The front of the building was floodlit. Pascal's eyes moved up to where the bronze eagle, wings outspread, soared along the roof-line.

Protective in its attitude, yet predatory: Pascal regarded it with distrust. Eagles, hammers, sickles – he disliked the icons of imperialism. He shifted his eyes higher to the flagpole, with its stars and stripes.

The Marines alerted him. He heard the stamp of their feet as they came to attention. As he lowered his gaze, the doors were already swinging back.

A cluster of men in dark coats was moving rapidly down the steps. At the foot of those steps, a long black limousine had drawn up, engine running, doors open. Two operatives were already in position, one at the front of the car, one at the back, their practised eyes raking the square.

Still the cluster of men came down the steps. Then, just by the car, as if at a hidden signal, the group parted and drew aside. One of the bodyguards raised his arm and spoke into his wrist-mike. For half a second – no more – one man stood alone on the brink of the car. Light caught his pale hair. Then he ducked and was inside the car, the door was closed, and the limousine was pulling away from the pavement.

Fast, discreet, one back-up car, no outriders. From across the square, Pascal had that half-second to glimpse the ambassador's face.

Pure chance – but he had glimpsed his quarry. Pascal turned, and retraced his steps.

VIII

'Is that Miss Hunter? Miss Genevieve Hunter?' said the telephone voice.

The line was bad. The voice was interrupted by a series of clicks. Genevieve shook the receiver. She had been back in her flat less than five minutes. Her cat was demanding food. She still had her coat on. She didn't recognize the voice.

'What? Yes. Yes, that's me . . . '

'It's George, Miss Hunter.'

'Who? George who?'

'George from ICD. The courier service.' He sounded reproachful. 'You told me to call.'

'Oh, *that* George. I'm sorry.' Gini struggled out of her coat. Tucking the receiver under her chin, she negotiated her living-room. It was not tidy. Books and papers had spilled over on to the chairs; more piles of papers lay in wait underfoot. She made it to the tiny kitchen, Napoleon – a demanding cat – rubbing against her legs. 'I've only just got in. I wasn't thinking. Can you hear that racket? It's my cat. Demanding food. Go on talking. Ignore him. I'm listening, I'm just trying to find a tin-opener. And a tin.'

'Well, I made my enquiries.' George sounded conspiratorial. He was, Gini thought, enjoying this. She found a tin of cat food, attempted to open it one-handed, and gave a cry.

'What's the matter?'

'Nothing. I just cut myself on this damn can, that's all. Go on.'

'The parcel went out from the City office, like I said. It was one of a batch of four, apparently.'

'*Four?*'

'That's right. All identical,' the supervisor said. 'Same wrapping, all used sealing-wax. He remembered that.'

'There were *four*? That's odd.' Gini spooned the catfood into Napoleon's bowl, and set it down by the sink. Napoleon stopped mewing and began in a fastidious but determined way to eat.

'Four.' Gini smiled. 'You think they were all hand-cuffs?'

'Articles of clothing, that's what the form said. The other three all went abroad. I couldn't find out much more than that.'

'You couldn't get addresses?'

'No. That side of things is confidential and I didn't like to ask too much. You could, maybe. Talk to the girl upstairs, in despatch.'

'I might just do that. In the morning. Thank you, George.'

'You get any problems, you can always give me a ring. I might be able to find out a bit more . . . ' He paused. 'It's not nice, getting sent something like that anonymously. It's a shock.'

'You're right, George, it is.' Gini felt a sudden pity for the man: she could hear loneliness, and recognize it, she thought wryly, since she was often lonely herself.

She took his number, scribbled it on the back of an insurance bill she should have paid the previous week, and rang off. Napoleon had finished his supper. He looked pointedly at the meaty chunks remaining in the tin. When the tin was replaced in the refrigerator, he gave her one reproachful glance, then set about his toilette.

'Oh, Napoleon, Napoleon.' Gini kissed his head. 'Hand-cuffs. And I'd almost forgotten them. Was someone trying to frighten me – or threaten me? Or just play a dumb joke? What do you think?'

Gini despised herself for this habit of talking to her cat but continued to indulge it. Napoleon took it well. When she returned to her living-room, he glided behind her, leapt up into the only chair not piled with papers, and composed himself for sleep.

Gini, who was not planning on going out – why had she said that? – made a brief and half-hearted attempt to tidy her flat. She transferred some of the papers from the floor to her desk. She lit the gas fire which made the somewhat shabby room more welcoming. She kicked off her shoes, padded into the bedroom, surveyed encroaching chaos, shoved some of it into cupboards, straightened the duvet and thus made the bed.

She found a whole heap of washing she'd forgotten for days, in which several pairs of tights were inextricably entwined in an octopus grip. She pushed the whole sorry lot into the machine, switched it on, and checked the fridge. It contained one orange, a piece of elderly cheese, the half-tin of cat-food, a clove of garlic, two limp lettuce leaves, and one tuna-fish sandwich wrapped in clingfilm which she'd forgotten, and which now smelled off.

She tipped the sandwich into the bin, and slammed the fridge door. She briefly considered going out again, and walking three blocks to Mr Patel's grocery store, the only one for miles which stayed open till eight o'clock. She phoned for a pizza instead.

On an impulse, waiting for the pizza to arrive, and feeling furtive and guilty, she rifled through the drawers of her desk. She despised sentimentality, just as she despised pathetic people who talked to their cats, but even so, here at the back of a drawer, carefully hidden so she would be reminded as little as possible, was a shoebox. In the box were relics. Yes, relics, she said sternly to herself.

Sitting by the fire, she took them out one by one. They were poor things, she thought: junk to most people, of significance only to herself. A card listing the hours of room service in the Hotel Ledoyen, Beirut; on the back of it, in pencil, Pascal had written his address. A yellowing paperback copy of a novel in French: *L'Etranger* by Camus, bought because Pascal had once said he admired it, and because she had sworn to herself that she would read it the second she improved her French. A one-page letter from Pascal in French. A flower from a courtyard near his house, which he had picked for her once: it was unidentifiable now, a dry brittle thing, scattering its few remaining petals at her touch. A bullet casing Pascal had once brought her for luck, when the bullet in question had ricocheted and missed him by less than a foot. One ear-ring, tiny, gold, of the kind made for and worn by Arab children. Pascal, a romantic, had talked the jewellery merchant into selling them by instalments: this one now, for her birthday, its pair for Christmas. Christmas was then four months away. But by Christmas, they had parted. Pascal was in Beirut still, but she had left.

She took the little ear-ring out of the box, and held it in the palm of her hand. Its purchase had been an extended transaction. She could see the dim interior of the merchant's shop, the glitter of gold and silver, the scales the merchant used to determine cost by weight. She and Pascal sat on upright chairs; a boy brought them sweet mint tea. The smallest, simplest purchase, she was learning, had its rituals in Beirut. The jewellery merchant spoke to Pascal in a mixture of French and Arabic. He was explaining, Pascal said to her with a smile, that such a gift, from a young man to a young woman, was a sacred affair. 'He will be disappointed if we choose quickly,' Pascal said, in English. 'Sip the tea slowly. This has to last half an hour at least.'

She had sipped the tea. She could taste, now, the sugar and mint. She could hear the murmur and rasp of French and Arabic. She had stared at the floor, and told herself that now, now, was the moment to confess. She must explain to Pascal now, before the purchase was made, that she had lied about her age. The sentence was simple enough: *Pascal, I am not eighteen, I'm fifteen.* She stared at the floor. Gold glittered. The simple sentence refused to be said. Pascal was showing her a ring, then a bracelet. She shook her head. She swallowed: perhaps there was a softer way of putting it? If she explained that her forthcoming birthday would be her sixteenth, would that sound better? After all, back in Britain, sixteen was the official age of consent.

She averted her gaze. It made no difference: no matter

how she put it, the fact remained that she had misled him, and if he discovered the truth, she knew how he would react. He would be angry, guilty – perhaps contrite. However he reacted, it would be over, she was certain of that. So she had said nothing, not one word. The heat in the shadowy room intensified. She sat there, flushed and miserable, in an agony of deceit. Later, back in his bare white room, Pascal clipped the little gold ear-ring into place. He kissed her earlobe, then looked at her anxiously. 'You like it? You're sure you like it? It looks so tiny . . . '

'I like it. I love it. I love you.' She flung her arms around him, and hid her hot face against his neck. Age did not really matter, the lie was not an important one, she told herself: one day she would explain to him, but not yet, not yet. Midday heat shimmered; reflections of waves moved on the white walls. Closing the shutters, she took his hand, and drew him towards the bed. They lay down, and the lie no longer mattered. Time passed: hours, days, a week more together – until the break finally came, that one little truth was never expressed.

Let the past rest. She took the little ear-ring, and hooked it into place. An indulgence, perhaps, bringing with it the ghost of an old happiness. Then the ordinary present reasserted itself. The pizza arrived. She removed the ear-ring, packed it carefully away with the other relics, pushed all of them into the box, and back into the desk drawer. She was stern with herself. No more relics, no more nostalgia, she told herself. She unpacked the newspaper clippings she had photocopied and spread them out on her desk.

John Hawthorne's and Lise Hawthorne's features stared back at her. She forced herself to concentrate. The Hawthornes, that perfect couple, looked famous, familiar and unreadable. She sighed, and sank her head in her hands: behind this public façade was there a secret life?

When she had been working for over an hour, she took a break, made coffee, returned to her desk. She felt a sense of frustration. Here were all the staging-posts of a glittering career, here were the same anecdotes, the same quotes, endlessly repeated. Here was Hawthorne at twenty, at thirty, at forty – yet what had she actually learned? It was as if what she was reading were an authorized version, formulated years before, perhaps by an astute PR advisor, perhaps by Hawthorne's father, or by Hawthorne himself. It was all too perfect, all too pat. Most of the interviews recycled material first given by Hawthorne long before, a phenomenon she was familiar with. It meant either that the journalists concerned had been lazy, content to write from clippings, or that Hawthorne himself refused to depart from a set script. No-one here seemed to have reached below his guard: even those journalists obviously hostile to him wrote articles that lacked sting.

Unlike his notoriously right-wing father, John Hawthorne had an impeccable civil rights record. Sure, he had fought in Vietnam in the late-Sixties and had been decorated three times for valour; but before he was drafted he had marched in Selma and Birmingham and been befriended by Martin Luther King. His political stance now was hard to define: pro-Israel, markedly so. In favour of massive aid to the Russians but an early advocate of intervention in Bosnia. Strong on law-enforcement, a hard-liner on capital punishment, a supporter of the NRA and anti gun-law reform, yet a liberal when it came to abortion and women's rights.

Not a unique balancing act in American politics, perhaps, but one Hawthorne performed with exceptional skill, none the less. Was this the result of conviction, or opportunism? It was impossible to judge. She had only her instincts to guide her and her initial reaction was suspicion: Hawthorne looked too good and smelled too clean. He was too adroit, too careful, too perfect – a verdict that applied equally to his political and to his personal life.

The coverage here of that personal life was extensive, the price Hawthorne paid for a famous name, a privileged background, and exceptional good looks. Here, before her, was Hawthorne the devoted husband, Hawthorne the proud father, and – old clippings these – Hawthorne the golden youth.

Here he was as an eighteen-year-old, flanked by his younger brother Prescott, by all three sisters, and by the patriarch, S. S. Hawthorne himself. They stood outside the Hawthornes' country house overlooking the Hudson. John Hawthorne smiled fixedly at the camera, his father's arm around his shoulders; two spaniels lay panting at their feet.

The resemblance between father and son was strong. Both were tall, strong-featured, strikingly blond. Both conveyed a certain arrogance in their stance, Gini thought – or was that something she read into the photograph, a prejudice of her own, a reaction to the wide lawns, the expensive sports cars parked in the drive, and the towering façade of the house itself? She looked at the picture more closely. Thirty years old, a blurred copy of blurred newsprint. On closer examination, she decided John Hawthorne looked ill at ease and constrained, as if he endured with reluctance that fatherly embrace.

She pushed that picture aside, and turned to others. A young Hawthorne with numerous well-connected girl-friends – but then the young Hawthorne had a reputation as a Lothario. There seemed to be a new girlfriend each month. Hawthorne at Yale, with a group of friends – John sprawled in a chair while two unidentified women knelt in worshipful attitudes, at his feet. Pictures of him in uniform; pictures of him as a young congressman, then as a senator. The first photograph of Hawthorne with Lise, snatched for a gossip column, as they left a Washington restaurant together. They were indeed, as Pascal had suggested, related. Third cousins, Gini saw, friendly since early childhood, part of the immense tribe of inter-linked Hawthornes and Courtneys who seemed to spend the endless summers of their youth in a round of parties at one another's estates. Long Island, Nantucket, Tuscany; a stud-farm on the west coast of Ireland; an English manor house in Wiltshire; a castle, belonging to the Scottish branch of the family, in Perthshire –

they moved around the globe, the golden members of this tribe, always to an aunt's, an uncle's, a cousin's place, always to a place where there were servants, tennis courts, swimming-pools, horses, abundant acres. They journeyed, Gini thought, and yet they remained cocooned in that citadel peculiar to the rich.

John Hawthorne and his distant cousin Lise had re-encountered each other, she saw, some eleven years before. Lise, who had had some training in art history, had been away working for old family friends in Italy, cataloguing their art collection. It was some five or six years since she and her senator cousin had met. Their re-meeting was staged by Hawthorne's father – or so the gossip columns claimed – and it took place at the Southampton estate of another distant cousin, Lord Kilmartin, a diplomat then assigned to the UN.

Hawthorne was then thirty-six, and known as one of Washington's most eligible bachelors; Lise was twenty-eight, though she looked much younger; she was in mourning for her parents, killed in an air-crash some six months before. According to the newspapers, the attraction had been immediate, the courtship swift. Certainly the engagement was brief.

Within a year, the celebrated wedding. Gini scanned the photocopies in front of her. Again, she saw, Pascal had been correct. There was Lise, radiant, legendarily lovely, encased from neck to ankles in a nun-like, virginal, Yves St Laurent dress. Her black hair was worn loose; a white lace veil framed her beautiful face. The train, of heavy silk, was fifteen yards long requiring four diminutive pages and six tiny bridesmaids, in processional behind the bride, to keep the train in place.

The wedding of the decade, the headlines screamed. And a decade later, here were all the details: the name of the Catholic bishop who officiated at the wedding mass; the special flights and trains laid on for the thousand-plus guests. S. S. Hawthorne had piloted his own helicopter to the ceremony. In the photographs, formal and informal, he was ubiquitous, resplendent in morning dress.

Fireworks had lit the sky – a Hawthorne family tradition. The dancing began at midnight and continued to dawn. The roster of guests' names was an illustrious one – statesmen, politicians, a clutch of Euro-titles; the Hollywood contingent, the authors, the diplomats, the opera diva, the English royal duchess.

There were many famous names here, and some infamous ones, since S. S. Hawthorne, less circumspect than his son, had contacts going back decades which might have surprised, even alarmed, some of the other wedding guests. A Middle Eastern arms dealer, for instance; a Sicilian–American rumoured to own a tranch of Las Vegas clubs . . . If such guests were cold-shouldered by his son, S. S. Hawthorne, Gini saw, had made up for any neglect. There he was with the arms dealer, here with the Sicilian. Robust, huge, unquenchable, indestructible, radiating purpose and energy even from faded newsprint: S. S. Hawthorne, networking, pressing the flesh.

And here, finally, were the formal photographs, the posed wedding-group pictures, taken by Lord Lichfield. They had an idyllic and yet a mysterious quality. Perfectly posed, perfectly lit, they were designed to convey perfection – and yet Gini felt they suggested something beneath and beyond: there was an inner story here, she sensed, of which Lichfield conveyed hints.

In all the official wedding pictures, John Hawthorne seemed at ease with himself. Tall, debonair, astonishingly blond, his cool blue gaze rested unerringly on the heart of the photographer's lens. He appeared, throughout, to be slightly amused by this circus; in every photograph there was a curious, almost disdainful, half-smile on his lips.

His bride, then little used to such publicity, looked as lovely as legend claimed, but also a little nervous, a little stiff. Later, as Gini knew, Lise Hawthorne would master the art of the photo opportunity, but here, at the very beginning of her public career, her inexperience showed. She clung to her new husband's arm as if in need of support; her eyes were either modestly lowered or fixed in anxious devotion on her new husband's face. There was a startled, almost sacrificial quality about her, Gini decided. Her wide dark eyes stared out of newsprint a decade old, and they seemed to carry a plea – as if Lise, encountering fame in its raw form for the first time, were silently praying to escape.

Interesting, Gini thought – and interesting too how quickly Lise adapted, how adept she soon became at dealing with photographers, with public appearances, with the campaign trail, with the Press. Now, only a decade after that wedding, Lise had carefully forged a very public identity for herself. She was celebrated for her charity work, for her skills as a hostess, and – on a thousand magazine covers – for her continuing, unrelenting, chic. No sign, in recent photographs, of any strain or unease. Lise now greeted photographers with a radiant calm. Gini might find Lise's present image a somewhat cloying one but this, she knew, was a minority view. The popular conception of Lise Hawthorne was that she was beautiful, good-hearted and devout. She was an exemplary wife, an exemplary mother. Her friends, constantly quoted in profiles, spoke with one voice: Lise might not be her husband's intellectual equal, indeed intellect was not Lise's strongest point, but what did that matter? Lise was that great rarity – a beautiful woman with a good heart. 'The thing you have to understand about Lise,' said the friends, 'is that she's just terribly, *terribly* nice . . . '

Was she? Gini frowned. Personally, she found niceness hard to equate with a taste for thirty-thousand-dollar Yves St Laurent dresses. But perhaps that was unfair, churlish, puritan even – another example of her own prejudice. Vanity was a pardonable weakness, perhaps, in a woman as lovely as Lise. All the evidence here told the same story. Lise worked hard for her pet charities; she adored her husband and children; she lived an upright, blameless life.

Gini sighed, and pushed the bundle of newsprint to one side. She turned to the last item, not culled from the press archive, but bought at a news-stand that evening. It was the latest issue of the magazine *Hello!*, that bland periodical chronicling the home lives of the famous and rich. There on the cover, and inside across six pages, the pictures in brilliant colour, were the Hawthornes *en famille*. They had been photographed in Winfield House, the newly decorated ambassadorial residence in Regent's Park.

Lise was famous for her taste; the re-vamped house looked as perfect as a stage set: not so much as a newspaper marred its serenity; every chair, vase, cushion was in exact alignment; every colour used was harmonious. Lise, readers of the magazine were informed, had selected the chintz used to curtain the room because it blended so well with the Picasso that hung above the fireplace. Gini suppressed a smile. The rose-period Picasso, she noted, was flanked by an equally pinkish Matisse.

All the photographs had this roseate glow. They must have been taken the previous summer, for here were the Hawthornes in the large garden behind the house; here they walked along a path framed with pink roses; here they sat in a huge bower of pink roses, flanked by their two angelic-faced sons. The two boys, Gini saw, were aged six and eight. Both the elder, Robert, and the younger, Adam, bore a marked resemblance to their father. Both, like him, had startlingly blond hair, and blue eyes. The eight-year-old seemed the more outgoing of the two. He met the camera lens with a mischievous grin, and in several of the garden pictures, swung from his proud father's arms like an agile little monkey. Adam, the younger, was the child who had been so seriously ill, some four years back. According to his mother, he had made a near-miraculous recovery from the meningitis which had threatened his life. In contrast to his brother, Adam seemed nervous and subdued, ill at ease with the cameras. In several pictures he averted his eyes, and clung closely to his mother. 'Adam's just fine now,' his father was quoted as saying. 'All he needs now is some toughening-up.'

An interesting remark, Gini thought, given John Hawthorne's own rigorous upbringing. She closed the magazine, but its images of roseate domesticity remained.

She rubbed her eyes tiredly, and thought of the story Nicholas Jenkins had recounted earlier with such malicious delight. Either he had been misinformed, or these photographs lied. Which was the true version – her editor's or this?

She thought back, trying to recall every small detail, to those two occasions on which she had encountered Hawthorne herself. The second, the previous year at Mary's party, told her nothing beyond the fact that Hawthorne was now an accomplished, experienced, politician. But the previous occasion – what about that?

She could remember it vividly. The meeting had taken place at the house Mary then lived in, in Kent. It was the end of the Easter holidays and Gini was due back at her boarding-school that afternoon. A friend from school had been staying, and the two of them were taking the train back together.

John Hawthorne was due to arrive for a brief stay that afternoon, and both the girls had been excited by that. Gini might never have met Hawthorne, but she knew of him from Mary's stories; she had seen photographs of him – and had showed them to her friend. They were both thirteen at the time, and had agreed, with much giggling, that this young, handsome, and then unmarried American was, as her friend put it, a *dish*.

'How old is he?' said Gini's friend, whose name was Rosie.

'Too old for us. He's thirty something.'

'Great. I like older men.'

'Don't be a moron. He won't even notice we're there. Two stupid schoolgirls . . . '

Rosie had given her a sideways look.

'Oh, I don't know. You look older. You look pretty good. I wish I had long blond hair. Still – you wait. When I'm introduced, I'm going to give him my *look*. Then I'm going to lick my lips.'

They both gurgled with laughter.

'Lick your lips? Why?'

'I read it in this magazine. You have to look them right

in the eye when you do it. It drives men *wild*, totally crazy with lust, the magazine said.'

'OK. I dare you.'

And, of course, that was all bravado and silliness. The actual meeting had been nothing like that. John Hawthorne was late arriving. She and Rosie grew bored with waiting. They went into the garden and played tennis on Mary's old cracked court. It was a very hot sunny day, and Gini said she'd go back to the house for some lemonade. She ran back, across the terrace, in through the french windows at the back of the house, carrying a pink cardigan which she threw down onto a chair, and paused in the doorway, out of breath, to refasten one of the buttons on her short white tennis dress. She started across the cool of the room, and then stopped dead.

He was here. John Hawthorne was actually here. He was alone in the room – Mary must have gone to fetch tea – and he was standing there, looking at her, a slight smile on his face.

He was, at that point, quite simply the most handsome man she had ever seen in her young life. Much more handsome than he appeared in photographs. Photographs might convey the colour of his hair, his tan, the extra- ordinary sharp blue of his eyes, but they could not convey his vitality, his force. He could only have been American: he radiated a peculiarly American fitness and health. Gini stared at him, and then to her fury, started to blush. It was a habit she was trying to cure. She had thought she had almost succeeded, but now she could feel the colour sweep up from the scooped neckline of her dress, to her neck, to her face. If only he would stop staring, she thought to herself. It was that intent stare, now unsmiling, though still amused, considering, which was making her blush. At which point, when with a thirteen-year-old's passion she was telling herself it would be better to die, right now, he held out his hand to her, and spoke.

'And you must be Genevieve,' he said. 'Nice to meet you at last, Genevieve.'

He shook her hand. He looked her up and down:

the scuffed tennis shoes worn with no socks; her long legs, her old mended tennis dress; her hair which was in a mess, tumbled and falling about her shoulders. Her hair was damp from her exertions on the court; blond tendrils clung to her forehead. To her total astonishment, he lifted his hand, and with one finger he pushed one of these damp curls back. He looked so deeply into her eyes that Gini told herself she was going to faint. Then he stepped back, and laughed.

'Well, it was obviously some game of tennis. Did you win?'

At that moment Mary returned with the tea tray, and started in on train timetables. Gini fled back to the garden, and Rosie, who was lying on the grass, flat on her back.

'Oh my God.' Rosie sat up. 'He's *there*, isn't he? I can tell from your face. Why didn't you call me, you pig? What's he like?'

'*Devastating*,' said Gini – it was that year's word.

'What did he do?'

'Shook hands. Then he lifted this little bit of hair off my face—'

'No! Were you looking like a beetroot then? You look like one now. Quick, let's go back . . . '

They went back. Rosie was impressed. She was so impressed she forgot to give him the *look*, or lick her lips. Like Gini, she stared at the floor and went red.

They talked over this major, this significant event the whole way back to school. They boasted about the meeting shamelessly in the dormitory at night. They cut out pictures of John Hawthorne from *Time*, and pinned them up next to their beds. The infatuation was heady, intense. It lasted about two months, perhaps three, and then – in the ways of things – they gradually forgot this young American god, and the infatuation wore off.

So, yes, Gini could remember that meeting well, and she had no intention of describing the details of her own foolishness to anyone, least of all Pascal. Looking back at it now, she could see it for the unremarkable thing it was. It was her own emotions at the time which magnified it. Once she analysed what had happened, she could see that Hawthorne probably guessed what was going on and was amused.

He had been, in the half-hour before she and Rosie finally left, polite, considerate, urbane – and utterly the other side of that barrier between the young and the grown-up. Mary had probably shared his amusement – Gini could recall their exchanging wry looks as she and Rosie stammered their way through blushing, inarticulate replies to Hawthorne's questions about their school, and the subjects they had been studying.

Gini sighed now, and stood up. She pushed this unhelpful memory to one side, and gathered up the press clippings. What she needed now was more direct testimony, she decided: an update on the Hawthornes, as seen by someone who knew them well.

It was eight-thirty. There was still time this evening. She dialled her stepmother's number, hoping that for once Mary would be in. Mary was fighting a characteristically tough battle against the loneliness and grief of her widowhood. She saw friends, and went out, as often as she could.

Mary answered on the third ring. On hearing Gini's voice, she gave a laugh of delight.

'Oh, it's *you*, darling. How lovely. What? No – absolutely nothing. Sitting curled up on the sofa, watching that new American soap – the one that's so bad it's good . . . I'd love to see you, darling. I'll make us some sandwiches . . . What? Half a pizza? *Again?* Gini, when will you learn? Wonderful, darling. Come at once . . . '

'I *suspect*,' Mary said, ushering Gini into the large untidy room which had once been her artist grandfather's studio, 'I *suspect* that the third wife is going to murder the second wife because they've both been having a *huge* affair with the husband's son by his *first* wife . . . '

She moved across to the television, where the credits for the soap opera were now rolling. She switched it off.

'On the other hand,' she went on, 'it could be that the

107

son's the real villain. He could be setting up wife number three, because although he's been having this mad affair with her, he's actually gay and loathes all women . . . '

'It sounds complicated, Mary.'

'Terribly.' Mary gave her a smile of pure delight. 'Complicated tosh – just the kind I like. In the end it will all resolve itself, it always does. Then I'll know – who was really bad, and who was really good. I like to keep that clear. None of this modern muddying of the waters . . . Now, what will you have to drink?'

'Coffee would be fine.'

'You drink too much coffee. You eat too many take-away meals. It's good to have a chance to feed you once in a while. You sit by the fire, and I'll just finish making those sandwiches. Then we can sin. There's a chocolate mousse.'

Gini smiled. She knew better than to argue, she knew better than to bother Mary in her kitchen. She sat down by the huge fire, as commanded, and looked around the familiar room with pleasure. Just to be here, as always, brought a sense of contentment, of safety. At Mary's she could always relax.

Gini could not remember her own mother, who had died when Gini was little more than a baby. She could – just – remember the succession of nannies and friends who had been roped in by her father to look after her when she was a small child. It was not a period she liked to recall. But she could remember, with great clarity, the advent of Mary in her life.

Gini had been five, and one day Sam had arrived home with this impulsive untidy plain-spoken young Englishwoman. It had been a whirlwind romance – and this, he announced to Gini, was his new wife. Gini had liked Mary then; she had come to love her rapidly, for Sam was always away and it was the first time any one person had stayed long enough to *be* loved; she had loved, and trusted Mary, ever since.

Five years after that marriage, Mary finally decided that Sam's infidelities, his long absences abroad, and his increasingly heavy drinking, could not be tolerated any longer. She had made this clear to Sam, without rancour, and they had duly – and quite amiably in the circumstances – divorced. Gini had spent the next year in Washington; of that year, her father was abroad for nine months. A new succession of friends and nannies were left to manage – and when Mary discovered this, she had told Sam in her clear firm way that this would not do. Since he could not cope, Gini would go to England to live. She would attend Mary's old school. She would live with Mary who then, years prior to her second marriage, lived alone in reduced financial circumstances, in the country, in Kent. Sam was supposed to visit regularly, and did – for the first year. Then his good intentions slipped away; the excuses began. Mary would nag and cajole and argue, and Sam would say: 'Sure, sure. Give me a break, will you? I'll visit on my way back.'

Then he would take off, to the Middle East, or the Far East, or Afghanistan or wherever, and sometimes he would remember to visit, and sometimes he would forget.

But Mary, always, was there. When Gini thought of her now, she felt none of the muddle and pain associated with her love for her father: her feelings for Mary were simple and calm; they had remained so throughout the period of Mary's second marriage, which occurred when Gini was seventeen (and just beginning work), and they remained unaltered now, though intensified, at this time of Mary's widowhood. For Mary she felt love, and also an absolute trust. On only one occasion in her past life had she ever kept anything from Mary: she had never told Mary what had happened to her that summer when, caught up in the confusion and striving of adolescence, she had run off to Beirut.

My one secret, Gini thought now, looking around her. She felt a little anxiety at that, but it swiftly passed. This room calmed her, even lulled her: Mary had the gift of imparting happiness, and this room was very like Mary herself.

It was attached to the side of Mary's tall rambling

Kensington house; it was where Mary now opted to spend most of her time. It was here that she held her frequent and famous parties, with their catholic mix of guests. It was here that Mary devoured her favourite crime novels, or worked on the water-colours she liked to call her 'daubs' or her 'mistakes'.

The room was spacious, generous, shabby and without pretension. It spoke of Mary's past, of her strong affection for family and friends. Mary's greatest quality was her loyalty, Gini thought: warmly and undeviatingly loyal to her living friends, she was equally loyal and loving towards the dead.

The room was filled with mementoes from Mary's childhood and with her grandfather's huge Victorian oils, her diplomat father's books. Somehow they had been crammed in beside the magpie spoils of Mary's own life – the Italian ceramics, the Moroccan rugs, the little rickety brass tables brought back from the Far East. Mary was an inveterate traveller, with a keen eye for a bargain. 'What I cannot resist,' she would sometimes wail, 'is junk.' So, here, cheek by jowl with inherited Chippendale, was a terrible vase, picked up in some bazaar; here, too, was a fat pink china cat of unparalleled ugliness bought by Gini for Mary's birthday – a long ago birthday in Washington DC, when Mary and Sam were still married, and Gini, already devoted to her new English stepmother, was aged six.

Here, too, was more evidence that for Mary love and affection were of far greater importance than taste: a ghastly and vulgar piece of Steuben glass, presented by Sam to compensate for one of his 'flings', as he called them. Here, more happily, was all the impedimenta of Mary's second marriage: bits of fishing-rods and reels, a mounted stag's head, with the date on which Sir Richard shot it engraved on a plaque beneath. Here were Richard's books, Richard's pipes, his chess set, all the objects he and Mary had acquired abroad on his various diplomatic postings. 'Don't they make you sad?' Gini had asked a few months after his death, and Mary had been astonished by the question.

'Sad? Of course not, darling. How could they? They bring him back.'

Gini sighed, feeling guilty. She had not done enough to help Mary through her first year of widowhood, she felt sometimes. She saw Mary as often as she could, when work did not take her away from London, but it was as if Mary needed some comfort Gini herself could not give; as if her own ability to show love were constrained, even with Mary, to whom she had been so close for most of her life. Sometimes Gini would ask herself when she had first become wary of showing emotion. Was it since Beirut, or in Beirut that she had become guarded – or did the damage begin much further back?

From the small kitchen beyond the studio came the rattle of plates. Impetuously, suddenly angry with herself, Gini rose to her feet. She went out to the kitchen, put her arms around Mary, and gave her a kiss. Mary returned her hug, then laughed.

'That's a nice surprise, darling. What brought that on?'

'Nothing. I'm very fond of you. Just occasionally, I guess it's time to remind you of that.'

'And a very good thing too. Now, you take this tray. We'll eat by the fire, would that be nice? No, Dog, you damn well can't have a sandwich.'

She bent and gave Dog, an ancient and malodorous Labrador, a shove. Dog, who had a winning disposition, did not budge. Once trained to the gun, and Sir Richard's favourite gun-dog, he had in latter years grown soft. Since the demise of his sister – known equally succinctly as Bitch – he had lorded it over Mary's heart and house. He continued, now, to sit under her feet, his eyes fixed on hers with liquid adoration. Mary sniffed.

'Cupboard love,' she said to him sternly, then – as Gini could have predicted – relented at once.

'Oh, very well.' She sighed. 'One digestive biscuit – and that's it.'

Gini smiled, and carried the tray back into the studio. Mary followed, Dog padding behind her. Pacified by the biscuit, Dog lowered himself with arthritic care onto the hearthrug, closed his eyes, and pretended to go to sleep.

Mary curled up on the sofa opposite Gini. She gave Dog a fond look. 'Poor old thing. I shouldn't weaken – he's like me, getting old and fat.'

'Plump,' Gini corrected her, passing the sandwiches across. 'And that's good. It suits you.'

'Maybe. I'm not sure. You know, after Richard died, I said to myself – right, now I'm going to give in to all my worst tendencies. I'm going to go to bed late, stay in bed all morning, read novels, eat chocolates, stop tinting my hair, and get fat if I feel like it . . . ' Mary paused. 'Oh, and stop entertaining endless strangers, that too. Forget I was ever a diplomat's daughter or a diplomat's wife. From now on, I said to myself, I shall never have more than four people to dinner, and they won't get in the door unless they're people I really like . . . '

'I see.' Gini smiled. 'So what went wrong?'

'Training.' Mary gave a comfortable sigh. 'Habit. I found I couldn't give it all up. And then it's good to keep busy – and people were very kind. They kept asking me out, so I had to ask them back . . . Still, ' she grinned, 'I kept some of my resolutions. Just look at me. White hair. A whole stone heavier. A perfect fright . . . '

Gini glanced across at her stepmother. The description was incorrect. True, Mary's hair was now an uncompromising white, and she was undeniably plumper, but to Gini's eyes Mary had, and had always had, the best and most lasting kind of beauty. Her skin was clear, her blue eyes astute, and her kindness could be read in her face.

'Not true,' Gini said drily. 'And I hope you know that.'

'Good of you to say so.' Mary reached unrepentantly for another sandwich. 'I lack self-discipline. Always did. I saw Lise this afternoon – I took her a box of those wonderful Belgian chocolates to cheer her up. And what happened? Lise nibbled at one, the way she does, and I scoffed five of them. Five! The shame of it! And after a huge tea, at that.'

'I expect she forgave you.' Gini poured herself some coffee. There was her opening, she thought – as easily as that. 'Cheer her up?' She went on, in a casual tone. 'Why was that?'

'Oh, I don't know, darling. Lise takes these dips occasionally. She was feeling pretty low, I think. She just got back today from their country place – they'd been down there over Christmas and New Year, as you know, and apparently Lise had some bug. Flu or a vile cold, something like that. Actually, she seemed fine. By the time I left, she'd perked up. I think the truth is, she worries about John much more than she'll admit . . . '

'Worries about John?'

'Oh, you know, darling. Security. With all this current Middle Eastern business – threats to embassies and so on. She sees terrorists behind every bush. I've told her a thousand times, John's perfectly safe. Everywhere he goes, he's surrounded by these terrifying thugs . . . Well, maybe I shouldn't call them that. But they are ex-Marines, most of them, average height six foot six, so they give a thuggish impression, though actually when you talk to them, they're really very nice . . . '

Mary's voice tailed away vaguely. One of Mary's weaknesses as a witness, Gini thought, was her inherent good nature. Although no fool, Mary erred on the side of charity; in her book, most people – until conclusively proved otherwise – were 'nice'.

'I've been reading about the Hawthornes,' Gini said, still in a casual tone. 'Tonight – a huge feature on them at home. In *Hello!* magazine—'

'Oh, I saw that!' Mary's face brightened. 'Didn't the children look sweet? So like John. I can remember him, you know, when he was their age. In fact, that was when I first met him – when my father was posted to Washington. Old SS rather courted Daddy for a bit – I forget why, but I expect he thought Daddy could be useful to him. Anyway, we went to stay at their country place, you remember, I told you, overlooking the Hudson. I was about twenty and terribly impressed . . . ' She hesitated.

'No, not impressed, that's the wrong word. Awed. It was so fearfully grand, quite terrifying. Millions of flunkeys and maids, and these tremendous formal feasts . . . I hadn't been in America very long then, and back in England, well, there was still this grey post-war make-do sort of world. So I couldn't quite believe people still lived like that. And SS was such a grandee, such a martinet.'

'Did you like him?'

'What, old SS?' Mary wrinkled her nose thoughtfully. 'No. I didn't. And neither did my father, I can remember that. He thought he wasn't to be trusted – but then everyone knew that. I thought he was a bully – much too used to getting his own way. And rather crude, in an odd way. I mean, he had perfect manners, when he wanted, and the kind of charm that turns on and off like a tap. But he thought everyone had his price. He thought he could buy anyone or anything. Unfortunately, he was usually right. But I didn't like that.'

'Interesting . . . And a martinet too?'

'Darling – and how!' Mary reached for the chocolate mousse. 'The whole house was run by a stop-watch. Drinks at seven-thirty, dinner at eight, everyone in place, to the second, and woe betide anyone who was late. And those poor children! So regimented, private classes in this, that and everything. They never had a second's peace. And then, of course, they had to excel at absolutely everything, they could never be second-best . . . Mmmm. This mousse is absolutely delicious. Are you sure you won't have some?'

Gini shook her head. She leaned forward to give a now somnolent Dog a stroke. Dog made appreciative whiffling noises. Gini straightened. She knew that Mary, once launched on the past, would need only a small prompt.

'All the children?' she said. 'Boys as well as girls? John too?'

'Oh *yes*.' Mary frowned. 'Maybe, when his mother was still alive, she managed to intervene – though I doubt it. But when I went there that time, she was quite recently dead. Maybe that made SS harsher with the children for some reason, I don't know. But it could be very ugly. He'd cross-question them, in front of guests, and put them down in this terrible biting way he had. The second boy, Prescott, was absolutely terrified of him. He had a very bad stammer then, and his father would make fun of him – and the poor boy, you could see he was utterly crushed. He'd stand there, scarlet in the face, physically shaking . . . It was really horrible. It made me feel sick.'

'Didn't any of them stand up to him?'

'Well, darling, they were so young – John was the eldest, of course, but he was only about ten. There was one time . . . ' Mary hesitated, then broke off.

'Yes?' Gini said.

Mary's face became troubled. 'I'll tell you, darling, but you have to promise, it's between us. I'd never mention it to John, I expect he thinks I've forgotten and if he knew I'd told anyone, he'd be terribly upset.'

'Of course. Between us . . . '

'Well,' Mary leaned forward, and lowered her voice, 'it was quite extraordinary, really. It was the third day of our visit and old SS knew I rode. I think he wanted to show off a bit – he had some fine horses, very grand stables, that sort of thing. Anyway, we went out for a ride, my father and I, S. S. Hawthorne, and the two boys, Prescott and John. I knew straight away that poor Prescott hated horses – he was afraid of them, you can always tell. So I couldn't understand – when we arrived at the stables, one of the grooms brought out a pony for Prescott, a sweet little mare, very quiet, and just as he was helping the boy into the saddle, S. S. Hawthorne stopped him. He told him to change the boy's mount . . . ' Mary frowned. 'I think Prescott knew what was happening. He went white as a sheet. John said something, the groom said something, but SS just started shouting and blustering the way he always did, and in the end, they gave in. They saddled up this other horse – it was far too big for a six-year-old boy, and it was even giving the stable-hands problems, jerking and kicking, and rolling its eyes . . . Anyway, to cut a long story short, poor Prescott had to ride it, and half a mile from the house, the horse threw him. He wasn't hurt, but he was badly shaken. He was crying, and he had a cut on his face. John was with him by then. He'd dismounted, and he was helping his brother up – and then this extraordinary thing happened, well two extraordinary things, really. S. S. Hawthorne had dismounted as well. He strode across to the two boys, and I thought he was going to comfort Prescott, take him back to the house. But he didn't. He just stood there, looking down at them, and then in this horrible voice, this really icy voice, he told Prescott to remount.'

'A six-year-old boy?'

'That's right. I couldn't believe my eyes. By this time Prescott's horse was frothing and sweating. SS could scarcely hold it, it was almost ready to bolt. But he just stood there, looking down at Prescott, and he said: "Get back on the horse." '

'And did he?'

Mary gave a sigh. 'Darling, I don't think he could have done. He was terrified, paralysed with fear. So he just stood there, I think he was trying to say something, but he couldn't, no words would come out. And then John did this astonishing thing . . . '

'He intervened?'

'More than that. He moved, so he was standing right in front of his father, with Prescott cowering behind him, and he just looked at his father with this white set face, and then he said: "He's not getting back on that horse. I won't let him. It's not safe . . . " I'm not sure quite what happened next, it was very very fast, but his father started to say something, and made some move – to push John aside, something like that. And John hit him. He hit him really hard. He was tall for his age, and he just sort of reached up with his riding-crop and hit his father, across the face.'

There was a small silence. Mary gave a shiver.

'Aged ten?' Gini said.

'Aged ten. It was quite extraordinary. So very deliberate. It wasn't as if John had lost his temper – nothing like that. He was absolutely calm, a bit pale maybe – but his expression was almost blank. And he hit SS hard – there was this red weal right across his cheek . . . '

'So what did S. S. Hawthorne do? Hit him back?'

'No. Not at all. He just stood there, looking down at John, not saying a word, and then he started to laugh – really laugh. There was this huge eruption of laughter. He threw his head back, his whole body shook, and you could see . . . He wasn't angry, or embarrassed or shocked. He was delighted. Exultant. Then he threw his arms around John in a huge bear-hug, lifted him off the ground, kissed his cheeks . . . '

'And that was it?'

'That was it. Drama over. Prescott was reprieved, John never said a word, Daddy and I rode back to the house. Daddy was terribly, terribly angry. In fact, he cut short our visit. We left that afternoon. But S. S. Hawthorne didn't give a damn. He just boasted about how one of his children had stood up to him for once. How at least one of his sons was a true man and not a milksop. It was ghastly – in front of all the children, all the house-guests. It went on right through lunch.'

Mary's gaze met Gini's. Her kind face had set, and her eyes were anxious, as if something were troubling her. She sighed, and shook her head. 'So, there you are. A little vignette.' She made an attempt at a smile. 'The home life of the Hawthornes. It explains a lot about John, I think, that incident. It shows you how brave he was, even then. And sometimes, now, when I look back . . . ' She allowed the sentence to trail away.

'Yes?' Gini prompted, but for some reason Mary chose not to be drawn.

'Oh nothing,' she said, more briskly. 'Just that John isn't an easy person to know, that's all, not even when you've been friends with him as long as I have. He . . . still, never mind that. You didn't come here to reminisce about the Hawthornes. I must be boring you to death.'

Mary had risen. From a cigarette box she took the one cigarette she permitted herself per day, and lit it. Something was still troubling her, Gini could tell, and she watched Mary almost physically push the thought away. She gave herself a little shake, then turned back to Gini with a smile.

'Anyway, I'd love you to meet John properly. And Lise, of course. It's so maddening. Every time I try and get you two together, you're out of town, or he's out of town. I don't suppose you're free this Saturday, are you?'

'This Saturday? Yes, I am.'

'Well, why don't you come over then? It's Lise's birthday.' Mary smiled. 'I thought I'd have a party, a sort of mixture of duty and fun. There's a lot of rather boring people I owe invitations to, so the actual dinner will probably be a bit grim. You know what diplomats are like. Protocol and placements. But John and Lise will be there . . . ' She hesitated, then her face brightened. 'I know. Why don't you join us for drinks afterwards? Much more fun. All the bores will have left by then.'

'Will the Hawthornes stay on?'

'Of course.' Mary laughed. 'John always stays late. Hits form at midnight. Like me—'

She broke off. The front-door bell had just rung. Mary gave an exclamation of annoyance.

'What on earth? It's way past ten – who the devil could that be?' From the hearthrug, Dog lifted his huge head. He turned his gaze towards the door. He raised his hackles and gave a faint growl. The bell rang again. Mary glanced toward Gini.

'How absurd. You know I despise myself for this, but since Richard died, I get nervous sometimes, being alone at night in such a big house. Too stupid – but Dog's perfectly useless. All bark and no bite . . . '

'I'll go.'

Gini crossed the room, and went into the hall, Mary hovering behind her in the open studio doorway. She felt a second's angry concern for her stepmother. Why had it never occurred to her that Mary could be nervous?

Then she noticed that, typically, Mary's front door was unprotected. It had a flimsy lock and an old, inefficient bolt; no chain, no spy-hole. Making a mental note to get that changed, she opened the door and looked out into the night.

There was an odd sound, a faint crackle, like radio static. It was raining, and the street was ill-lit. She peered out into the darkness, trying to accustom her eyes to the thin light. She made out the dark gleam of a car, then a shadow moved at the foot of the steps. Light suddenly caught pale hair, the sleeve of a man's dark overcoat, then the man swung around.

'Mary?' he said. 'I thought you must be out. I brought that book you wanted. I . . . '

He broke off, staring at Gini. There was a brief silence, an odd taut second in which Gini felt sure that though this visitor enacted surprise, he experienced none on seeing her. Then, as he moved towards the door and up the steps, Mary moved too, rushing forward, arms outstretched.

'John!' she said. 'What a lovely surprise. This is Gini – Genevieve. You remember? Come in, come in . . . '

Hawthorne's opening remark was that he would stay five minutes. He stayed ten. He had, he explained, been at meetings all evening, and had just picked up his two sons from friends. His sons, he said with a wry smile, had just had their first experience of an English Christmas pantomime.

'They couldn't make head nor tail of it,' he said. 'Men dressed as women, women dressed as men, dancing horses, fairies and demons . . . When I picked them up, they were wildly overexcited. And now the inevitable has happened. They're both asleep in the back of the car. No, no, they're fine, Frank is with them, but I mustn't stay. Lise will be waiting for us. I have to get back.'

'Well, it's very sweet of you . . . ' Mary was clutching her new book. 'But you needn't have bothered.'

'Nonsense. You said you couldn't wait to read it. And these friends live right around the corner, so I thought

I'd drop it in. It was no trouble at all. You have – if you'll forgive my saying so, Mary – the most lurid taste in books.' He flicked the cover. 'Murders. Serial killers on the loose. You'll be awake half the night.'

'I know.' Mary looked guilty but unrepentant. 'But I adore them. I always have. It's very kind of you, John. Thank you very much.'

He turned back to the watching Gini with an easy smile. 'How about you, Genevieve? Do you share Mary's taste for blood and gore?'

'Not really. No.'

'Me neither. And I never seem to have the time to read any more, anyway. Not for pleasure . . . No, Mary, really. I mustn't stay, much as I'd like to – and no, I won't have a drink.'

'Just a little one?' Mary waved a whisky bottle.

Hawthorne laughed. 'A little one? You never poured a small drink in your life. You make the stiffest drinks I ever encountered – and I don't dare take the risk. I really do have to get back.'

He began to move towards the door.

'Genevieve,' he took her hand briefly in a firm grip, then released it. 'It's good to see you again. One of these days perhaps we'll have a chance to meet properly. Mary talks about you so much, I feel I know you already – and Lise has been longing to meet you . . . What?' He swung around as Mary interjected, then smiled warmly. 'This Saturday? Well, that would be great . . . '

He moved out towards the hall, Mary following him. From the studio, Gini watched them. She saw him put his arm around her stepmother's shoulders. He made some enquiry as to Mary's welfare, which Gini could only half catch. Mary laughed, and gave him a push.

'Of course. I'm absolutely fine,' she heard. 'You fuss too much, John. It's very good of you, but you don't need to worry. One gets used to it – truly. I just take it one day at a time.'

They passed out of sight. In the doorway, they paused, and Gini heard Hawthorne make some low-voiced remark;

Mary hooted with laughter. The door opened; Gini heard Hawthorne's feet descend the steps.

'Gini . . . ' Mary called to her. 'Gini, come and look at this. Aren't they adorable? Look . . . '

Gini reached the front door just as Hawthorne climbed into the waiting black limousine. In the back of it, just visible next to the bulk of a large security man, were two angelic blond children, both fast asleep. Hawthorne lifted his hand; the car moved away. Gini and Mary moved back into the studio. Mary gave her a small triumphant sideways glance.

'Well,' she said. 'You, Gini, made a hit.'

'I did?'

'You most certainly did. Are your ears burning?'

'No, why? What did he say?'

'Never mind, but it was complimentary.'

'I can't think why. I hardly opened my mouth.'

'Then it can't be what you said that impressed him,' Mary replied smartly, with an arch look. She moved across the room, picked up her new book, then put it down. 'So, anyway, you promise you'll come on Saturday? Just say you will – and then I'm going to shoo you out. I need my sleep.'

'Rubbish. You just can't wait to read that book . . . '

'All right,' Mary smiled, 'I admit it – but just promise me you'll come.'

'Sure. I'd love to. There's just one thing . . . '

'Yes?'

'Would you mind if I brought someone with me? Just a friend from France. He's staying in London at the moment, and . . . '

At this, Mary rapidly lost interest in her new book, and Gini's heart sank. She knew what was coming next.

'A friend?' Mary, who was a bad actress, attempted a casual tone. 'Is he anyone I know?'

'I don't think so, no. He's called Pascal Lamartine.'

'Have you known him long?'

Gini considered. She averted her gaze. She could say she had known Pascal twelve years; she could say she had known Pascal for those three weeks in Beirut. Both statements were true. She said, 'No. Not really. He's working for the *News* right now, that's all—'

'Single?'

'Mary, give me a break, will you? Yes. Sort of. He's divorced.'

Mary considered this. Her concentration, Gini saw, was now intense. 'A journalist, darling? An editor, perhaps?'

'A photographer. He used to be a war photographer – a very good one. Now he's a – well, I guess paparazzi would be the right term.'

She seized on this description with a sense of relief. She might still find it hard to think of Pascal in that way, but the term had its uses. It would surely put Mary off.

To her despair, she realized it had quite the opposite effect. Mary gave a squeak of delight. A match-making look came upon her features; it was a look Gini had learned to dread.

'*Paparazzi!*' she said. 'No! How absolutely splendid. I've *always* wanted to meet one of those. Such daredevils – roaring around on motor bikes, wearing dark glasses at midnight, what was that film?'

'*La Dolce Vita*, Mary. Fellini. And it was motor scooters, not motor bikes—'

'Same difference! I remember it terribly well. Is he like that, your Pascal?'

'He drives a car, as far as I know,' Gini said patiently. 'And he's not "my" Pascal.'

She said this with extreme firmness. Mary took no notice at all. She made a noise indicating derision, and continued her cross-examination. She was still babbling about Fellini and cameras and exciting young men on motor bikes some fifteen minutes later, when Gini finally managed her escape.

'Motor bikes,' she called after Gini, down the steps. 'I'm perfectly *certain* it was motor bikes. I shall ask him on Saturday – your Pascal . . . '

IX

Pascal telephoned at eight the next morning. Gini, who had been awake since six, was careful. Sitting a foot from the receiver she picked it up on the fifth ring. Pascal made no comment on this, but said, 'It's me. I've hired a motor bike. I'll pick you up at ten.'

'You've done what?'

'I've hired a motor bike. It's black, German. A BMW. Very fast.'

'Pascal, I have a car. You saw my car yesterday.'

'Precisely. I saw your car. That's why I hired the bike.'

'Is there something wrong with my car?'

'There are many things wrong with your car. It is old. It is slow. It is painted bright yellow. Once seen, never forgotten, your car. It won't do at all.' He paused. 'Besides, we may need to split up – and if we don't, you can ride pillion. I'll bring a spare helmet, yes?'

'Pascal . . .'

'At ten. I have somewhere else to go first, then I'm with you. *Au revoir*.'

Gini replaced the receiver and sat staring into space. After some consideration, she removed the skirt she had put on, and replaced it with jeans.

'My stepmother Mary has second-sight, did you know that, Napoleon?' she remarked.

She picked him up, and kissed him between his ears. Napoleon resisted such intimacies. He struggled, kneaded her lap, settled himself, and then purred.

She had thought she remembered Pascal so well – yet she had forgotten one of his most marked characteristics: his energy. Pascal in pursuit of a story was totally single-minded. He worked hard and he worked fast: he forgot about sleep or such minor inconveniences as eating. He left those working with him gasping for air.

At ten the motor bike roared to a halt outside her flat. At one minute past ten, Pascal was in her living-room, two helmets under his arm. He was wearing black jeans, a black sweater, a black leather jacket and no sun-glasses. *Thanks, Fellini*, Gini thought. As he closed the door, papers fluttered, the air whirled.

'Very well,' he began, striding into the centre of the room, which immediately felt too small. 'I have found out two things. One last night, one this morning.'

'Have some coffee,' said Gini, passing him a pottery mug. 'And sit down. You're too tall for this room. You're making me nervous. I've made some progress as well.'

'You have?'

Pascal took the coffee, and drank half of it without appearing to notice that it was in his hand. He put the mug down on the mantelpiece, sat down on the sofa, and stretched out his very long legs. 'May I smoke?'

'Yes.'

'Thank you. So, tell me.'

Gini explained. She recounted her visit to Mary, and the meeting with Hawthorne. Pascal listened intently. When she had finished, he frowned.

'I don't understand. He seemed surprised to see you there, but you felt he was acting? Why?'

'I don't know. It was just an instinct I had. Something to do with his timing, the way he spoke. He did a kind of double take . . .'

'So? If he was expecting Mary to open the door, he would do—'

'No. You're wrong. First of all, it was too well done, just like an actor. Second, although he performed it well enough, the timing was off. He must have been able to see me perfectly. I was standing in full light in an open doorway. He must have seen it wasn't Mary right away, but he carried on acting surprised. Why do that?'

Pascal shrugged. 'You probably imagined it. What are

you saying, that he already knew you were there? He was expecting to see you?'

'Something like that. And I wasn't imagining it.'

'Could he have known you were there?'

'I don't see how. I'd only called Mary an hour before. The meeting wasn't pre-arranged.'

'Do you see her every Wednesday?'

'No. We see each other often, but not on regular days.' Gini hesitated. She felt a sense of disappointment. Pascal was clearly not impressed by this story, and indeed, now that she recounted it, she felt it was lame. What was she describing after all? An odd coincidence, an instinctual reaction of her own – nothing more.

'Let's forget it,' she said. 'It's probably not important – you're right. But it's good that we'll get to meet them, isn't it?'

'On Saturday? If we're careful. Sure. Hawthorne mustn't suspect any interest in him on our part. If he does we're blown.'

Gini said nothing. She felt a brief resentment that Pascal should dismiss so easily what she'd done, but this quickly passed. Pascal took a small package from his jacket pocket, and opened it. Gini gave an exclamation of excitement.

'That's the tape McMullen recorded?'

'Yes. Jenkins sent it over to the hotel this morning by messenger.' Pascal smiled. 'It virtually came under armed guard. We can play it in a moment. But first, let me tell you what I've found out.'

He placed the tape on the coffee table in front of him, and leaned forward, intent now. 'James McMullen. Our source. Where is he? Why did he disappear? I checked back with Jenkins yesterday. The last time Jenkins saw McMullen was when he handed over that tape. That was two weeks before Christmas. They were due to meet the following week, but McMullen never showed. It seems to me that's our first lead. We have to find McMullen. And that may not be so easy. Jenkins is right – he isn't at his flat for a start . . . '

'You're sure? How do you know that?'

'Because I went there first thing this morning. I spoke to the porter, and also to a cleaning woman. Both of them last saw him sometime before Christmas, they couldn't say for certain when.'

'I see.'

'I guessed that would be the case, so last night I called a friend of mine who works at Heathrow. He checked the flight records for me for the past three weeks. No McMullen, not at Heathrow, Gatwick, Stansted or the new City airport. So, either McMullen left the country by boat or train, or—'

'Your friend checked the flight records?' Gini stared at him. '*All* the flight records?'

'But of course.' Pascal showed signs of slight impatience. 'They are computerized. If you have a name, you can run a computer search. It doesn't take very long.'

'What a useful friend to have,' Gini said drily.

Pascal smiled. 'I have a lot of useful friends. In fact it doesn't help very much. He could fly from a provincial airport, use a friend's passport, even obtain a visitors' passport in another name. Over Christmas, when there are so many passengers, they don't check very closely. So, then I tried the taxi firms, the mini-cabs, those.'

'The mini-cab firms?' Gini gave him a look of disbelief. 'There are about three thousand in central London alone.'

Pascal brushed this detail aside. 'Of course. But McMullen lives in an apartment, yes? In one of those converted warehouses not far from the *News* offices. In apartment blocks, residents tend to use the same taxi services, sometimes the porter will recommend a firm. So, I asked the porter in McMullen's building. He gave me three cards. The second was a firm in Wapping, three blocks from McMullen's flat. They knew him well, often drove him. It was on their records, the last time he used them. They picked him up at eight in the evening, and drove him to Victoria Station. That was on December twenty-first, last year. The day before he was due to meet Jenkins.'

There was a silence.

'The boat-trains to Europe go from Victoria,' Gini said.

'Exactly what I thought. And they keep no record of passengers, unless they book a sleeping compartment on the overnight trains. McMullen didn't. I checked. On the other hand, two trains left for Dover/Calais that evening. One at five minutes to nine and one at eleven-ten. He could have been on either train.'

'Or neither. Or any other that left Victoria that night. Or he might not have left from Victoria at all. It could be a false trail.'

Pascal looked pleased at this. Gini had the impression that it would have disappointed him had their task been easier. He smiled. 'Exactly. Maybe something. Maybe nothing. So, this morning we have to get into his apartment. It shouldn't be difficult.'

'It shouldn't?'

'No, very easy, I think. I have a plan.' He glanced at his watch. 'We'll aim to get there around midday. But first, we should listen to that tape. And maybe we could have some more coffee?'

Gini sighed. Along with the other aspects of Pascal's character which she had forgotten, there was his addiction to caffeine. She stood up.

'Nothing easier. It comes in a jar. You spoon out the granules, add hot water, and *voilà*.'

'That is not coffee.' Pascal also rose. Suddenly he was very tall and very close. He looked down at her in a gentle and somewhat melancholy way. 'Next time I'll bring you some coffee-beans, Colombian coffee-beans. I cannot cook, but I make excellent coffee.'

He moved away quickly in the direction of the kitchen, at exactly the moment Gini had thought he was about to touch her, or take her hand. There was the sound of the electric kettle being filled, and a few muttered French swear words.

She felt weak, and sat down. After some time, Pascal returned with two mugs. He made a grimace.

'Nescafé. An abomination. Never mind. It will do.'

*　　*　　*

Gini placed her tape recorder on a table between them. She inserted the tape. Pascal leaned forward attentively. She pressed 'Play'. There was a crackle, some hissing, then the voices began:

— Hallo? Hallo? Am I through to Adelaide?
— No. This is Sydney.
— Oh, *James*. Thank God. I'm always afraid someone else will be using your phone-booth, and they'll pick up . . .
— Don't worry, darling. I always get here a half-hour in advance. Where are you? Is it safe?
— I think so. I'm having lunch with my friend Mary. We're at The Ivy. I said I was going to the ladies' room. Frank checked the dining-room five minutes ago. He'll check it again in about ten minutes. He's back outside with the driver now. I mustn't be long. Oh God, it's so good to hear your voice . . .
— Darling, don't get upset. Don't cry. You mustn't. Try to be brave. My friend will help us. I know he will . . .
— I know. I know. James, you're the best friend in the world. If it wasn't for you . . . If we couldn't talk. It's like being in prison. All the time I feel watched. You know, I saw him last night on television, being interviewed. He was so good, so convincing, and I thought – all those people watching out there, if only they knew . . .

At this point, there was interference on the phone line, and a tiny jump in the tape. Gini pressed the 'Pause' button. She looked at Pascal. 'The tape's been edited – at least it sounds as if it has.'

Pascal nodded. 'I think so too.'

'She sounds terrified.' Gini frowned.

'Like a little girl, a frightened child.' He glanced towards Gini. 'Is it Lise Hawthorne? Or could it be a fake? What would you say?'

'I'm certain it's her. I may not have spoken to her at

that party of Mary's, but I was standing close to her. I've seen her interviewed, on television. She has a very distinctive voice – breathy, childlike. I can check if she did have lunch with Mary at The Ivy – meantime, I'm sure it's her.'

'Jenkins is certainly convinced. He had some voice-print experts match part of this tape to a radio interview she gave last year. They were one hundred per cent certain. Or so he says.'

'Let's go on . . . '

'OK. Turn the volume up.'

Gini did so. After the tiny blip on the tape came a sound between a sigh and a moan, then McMullen's voice, speaking urgently.

— Darling, darling. Please don't. I can't bear to hear you cry . . .

— I know. I know. I'm sorry, it's just . . . I can never forget, you see. It's with me all the time. I think about the last Sunday, and then just when I've nearly managed to forget it, wipe it out of my mind, there's another Sunday coming closer and closer . . . James, it's torture, he's made my life a torture. I think that's why he plans it this way, torment then a space, then more torment again. I look at him, and sometimes I want to die . . .

— Darling, don't – please don't. Listen. Remember what I said – the next time – can't you go away then? What if you went away on your own, to friends, for the weekend . . .

— I can't. I can't. Don't ask me. You don't under-stand. He'd punish me if I did that. He'd never let me leave. I tried – once I tried. It was terrible. I'll never do that again. Can you imagine what it's like – being watched all the time? James – if it wasn't for you. And my children. I saw that doctor last week – you remember? The one your sister told you about?

— Darling, that's good. Well done. You see? It's easy when you make up your mind. You'll see. It's all falling into place now. They'll work – all our plans . . .

Gini stopped the tape again. She looked at Pascal.

'Odd, isn't it? What does that sequence mean?'

Pascal shook his head, frowning. 'I'm not sure. There was a sense-jump – something I couldn't follow. Play that again.'

Gini rewound the tape. There was a blur, a babble of sound. She found the correct place, and they listened to the sequence again, then she pressed the 'Pause' button. Pascal was still frowning.

'OK. McMullen's sister recommended some doctor. Lise made an appointment to see him – McMullen congratulates her—'

'That makes sense. If he was worried about her health. She sounds close to breakdown . . . '

'Sure, sure. But the sense-jump is after that. Why should her seeing that doctor make McMullen say everything's falling into place? Just what are their plans?'

'I don't know. Us, I imagine. Going to Jenkins, approaching the Press. I have to admit, I don't see where the doctor fits in.'

'Maybe he doesn't. It just sounds that way. People who know one another well tend to speak in a kind of shorthand. Never mind for now. Let's go on.'

They listened to the remainder of the tape in silence. When it was over, Gini looked at Pascal. 'Well. I don't know what you think, but it seems to confirm the story McMullen told Jenkins.'

'The Sunday references?'

'Sure. Beyond that, I'm certain it's Lise Hawthorne, and I'm certain she's terrified.'

'Oh, I agree. Either that, or she's a very good actress.'

'It doesn't sound like acting to me, Pascal.'

'Nor to me.'

'In which case . . . ' Gini felt a pulse of excitement. 'In which case, it just might be true . . . '

'I know. I know. I can't believe it either. No wonder

Nicholas Jenkins reacted the way he did. If we make this story stand up – can you imagine the reaction? Here? In America?'

'Only too well.'

'Still . . . ' Pascal lifted his hand. 'We mustn't jump to conclusions. We have to take this one step at a time. There're things on that tape I don't understand. It's elliptic. Odd. Play that section at the end again – where she and McMullen plan to meet . . . '

'Wait. Before we do that, take a look at this.' Gini rummaged among the photocopied press clippings on her desk. She produced one, a small item from the *Daily Mail*'s gossip column. 'You see? The details in the tape's last section check out. Lise *does* see an osteopath in Harley Street, pretty regularly. Some back problem. She took a bad fall, apparently, years ago, out hunting. It still causes her pain.'

Pascal scanned the clipping, then looked up. 'OK. That checks out. Apparently. Play that end section again. Then we should go.'

Gini fast-forwarded the tape. The whole conversation lasted six minutes; most of it consisted of McMullen calming Lise down. The section concerning the osteopath came immediately before the conversation's abrupt end:

— I have that hospital charity committee in the morning. That's no good. But next week, Tuesday . . . He's in Brussels all day. I have to go for my back treatment in the afternoon. At three. I always drive myself there . . .

— Darling, the one we used before? Yes – but what about Frank?

— It's all right. It's his off-duty day. His replacement – I'll get rid of him. Send him on a shopping errand . . .

— Darling, really? A shopping errand? What for? New clothes?

— He can't refuse. Not if I insist. Maybe I'll send

him somewhere with the boys. If you wait in that mews . . .

— You mustn't take risks. Not now.

— It's all right. It's safe. I can slip out the back way. I'll leave my car parked in Harley Street. If they check, they'll see it. They'll assume I'm still inside. James, please – it's almost Christmas. He'll make me go to the country. We won't have another chance for weeks . . .

— It's all right, don't get upset, I'll be there. You know I'd cross the world to spend five minutes at your side . . .

— We can have more than five minutes. If we're careful . . .

— Oh, darling. You have the wickedest laugh. It's so good to hear you laugh . . .

— It makes me happy – just to know I'll see you, that's all. If you wait in the mews, the way you did before – I'll wear a headscarf. We can go to that . . . Oh, I'm sorry. Someone wants to use the phone. Well, if that's agreeable to the rest of the committee? Of course. Very good. I'll see you at the next meeting then. Excellent. Goodbye.

Gini switched off the tape. Pascal rose and picked up the two motor cycle helmets. He made no comment as they left the flat, but seemed abstracted, puzzled, as if there were something on that tape he did not understand.

'It's odd.' He came to a halt by a huge gleaming black motor bike. He turned to look at Gini, his gaze intent. 'Are they lovers, Lise Hawthorne and McMullen? What would you say?'

'I don't know. I was trying to decide the same thing.' Gini glanced away, trying not to remember certain telephone calls of her own.

'Case unproven,' she said at last. 'I think that's all you can say. It's certainly not a normal lovers' conversation – but then, given the circumstances . . .'

Pascal stood still, frowning into the middle distance.

'Of course. They are being careful . . . Yet he [obscured] "darling" – not once or twice, but again and again.'

'And she only speaks of friendship. She calls him her friend.'

'Exactly. He is in love with her, I would say . . . ' Pascal glanced at Gini.

'And his love isn't returned?'

'Not to the same degree.'

This seemed to worry him. He considered it a moment more, then shrugged it aside with a sudden impatience. 'Still. Never mind that now.' He held out a large, shiny helmet with a black visor. 'Put this on, hold tight. Lean when I lean, the same way as me. It's eleven fifteen now. We should be inside McMullen's apartment around noon.'

'Oh yes? And you've worked out how we do that?'

'Of course.' He gave her a reproachful look. 'We burgle it. It should be easy. The whole building's alarmed.'

X

McMullen's apartment building was a nineteenth-century spice warehouse, directly fronting the Thames. It was huge and fortress-like, and had been expensively and painstakingly converted at the height of the Thatcher boom-years, about seven years before.

Pascal parked his bike, and led Gini through winding cobbled streets lined with Range Rovers, Jaguars and expensive German cars. He guided her away from the street approach to the building – a large courtyard modishly decorated with clipped box in tubs, and with treillage. 'Not the main entrance, not yet.'

Taking her hand, he ducked down the side of the building, where a narrow stone alleyway, overshadowed by the twelve-storey warehouses on either side of it, led to steps and to the Thames.

It was still low tide. As Gini stepped out onto sandy mud and shingle, she gasped. Here was a new London, a London she worked near yet had never seen. Before her curved the grey expanse of the river. To her left was the glittering white pinnacle of Canary Wharf; to her right, up river, was the bridge and the crouching stone castellations of the Tower. A police launch passed, and a barge. Pascal ignored them. He was staring up at McMullen's apartment building, ranked with large arched windows.

'That's McMullen's.' He gestured. 'There, in the middle, on the top floor.'

Gini looked upwards. The drop from the apartment was vertiginous: a wall of brick sixty feet high, with a sheer fall to a landing wharf and the water below. Up the face of the building snaked a black iron fire-escape. Pascal turned to her, and smiled.

'Right. Now do exactly what I told you. Talk to the porter. He doubles as a security man. Distract his attention for five minutes. I'm sure you can do that.' His smile broadened. 'Normally I work alone. I find it has its uses, working with such a beautiful blonde.'

Gini ignored this. She said, 'And then?'

'You'll hear the alarm. Stay a few minutes more, then leave. The building has a coffee-shop, American style. It's just to the right of the main entrance. I'll meet you there.'

'Pascal, is this going to work? There're security cameras – I saw them in the courtyard.'

'Of course there are security cameras. If they actually have film in them, and if they're in operation, they scan the entrance, the lobbies, the lifts and the corridors. Also the fire-escape. As I said, it's good you're blonde.'

Gini gave in. She left him by the side of the water and retraced her steps. She stopped, and applied some lipstick, reserved for occasions such as this one. She crossed the courtyard and entered the lobby. In the corner was the porter's desk. It was flanked with an impressive array of technology, several telephones, an intercom system, a switchboard, and – behind him – just visible from where she stood looking plaintive, an array of video-screens. One showed a grainy picture of a fire-escape – an empty fire-escape. The porter was aged about thirty, outfitted in a blue uniform. Gini greeted him warmly. Strengthening her American accent, she launched herself on her spiel.

Afterwards she could scarcely remember what she had said: some convoluted story about a friend who'd rented an apartment here, and recommended it, followed up by a lengthy enquiry as to whether any apartments were available right now, and if so, who were the rental agents . . . The porter threw himself into her predicament. Gini did not dare glance at the video-screens behind him. The porter was in the act of finding the agents' telephone number, when the alarm went off.

Gini jumped: a buzzer sounded behind the desk; a series of red lights began to flash; in the distance, muffled by the size of the building, she could just hear the jangle of the alarm itself.

The porter reacted unexpectedly. He swore, and then apologized. 'Sorry, miss. It's this new system they've just fitted. High-tech. Given us nothing but trouble, it has. Hang on just a second . . . '

He turned. Gini fixed her eyes on the central video-screen: it still showed a fire-escape – an empty fire-escape.

The porter consulted a clipboard, then the flashing control-board. 'Apartment 12. Mr McMullen again. Would you believe it? It's the second time this week. And we're short-staffed. Here's that address you need, miss. The police will be here in a minute. But I have to go straight up and check—'

'The police?' Gini said.

'Direct transmission to the station – they're just up the street. A waste of their time and a waste of mine. You know what sets them off half the time? The heat.'

'Heat?'

'Heat and insects, blasted things. It's all those magic eyes – body-heat and movement detectors. All the flats have them. And the insects just love them – they're always warm, see? Flies, spiders, little earwig things. They crawl in, make a nice little nest, and before you know where you are . . . Still, I'd better go up. Might not be insects. Might be Raffles, yes?' He grinned. Gini thanked him and left.

In the coffee-shop, which was deserted, Muzak was playing. Outside there was an empty terrace, where dripping plastic chairs and tables were stacked. Pascal had positioned himself so he could see out through the room's plate-glass windows front and back. He was reading a newspaper, and smoking a cigarette. Two cups of coffee were on the table. In the far corner a bored waitress leaned on a counter reading a book. Gini sat down.

'Pascal,' she began, in a low voice, 'the police are coming. It might be kind of a good idea if we left.'

Pascal glanced at his watch. 'But of course the police are coming. That is the whole point. Sit still. We wait.'

'Act naturally?'

'Something like that.'

'Do you realize just how recognizable you are, Pascal? You're six feet four inches tall. You've got a ridiculous French accent—'

'My accent is not ridiculous. I resent that.'

'It's *memorable*, dammit. You stick out. People will remember you. The porter. That waitress over there. They'll remember me . . . '

'So what if they do? I have no criminal record. Do you?'

'It's a miracle you *don't* have a criminal record, the stunts you pull. Creeping into people's private estates, holing up in their shrubberies, burgling people's flats . . . ' She broke off. Pascal was paying not the slightest attention. 'In which context,' she said, leaning forward, 'it may interest you to know – it could be we're not the only people anxious to get into McMullen's apartment. This is the second time his alarm's gone off this week.'

'You're sure? How do you know?'

'The porter mentioned it. Presumably there were no visible signs of a break-in. The porter put it down to mechanical failure. He didn't seem worried at all.'

'*Tais-toi*.' Pascal rested his hand over hers. 'Here's the police – look.'

A white car had pulled up by the courtyard. Two uniformed constables climbed out. They did not appear to treat this as a matter of great urgency, but strolled, almost sauntered through the gates.

'Five minutes,' Pascal said. 'Ten at the very outside. Wait.'

He was correct in his second estimate. Some ten minutes later, the policemen departed. Five minutes after that, Pascal rose to his feet.

He took her arm, paid for the coffees, exchanged a few pleasantries with the waitress, and led Gini outside, where he drew her back along the alleyway to the Thames, skirted the water whose level seemed much higher than before, and came to a halt at the foot of the fire-escape steps.

'Right. Now we go up. Fast. And we hope for the best. If this works we've got half an hour in McMullen's apartment – no more.'

'Only half an hour?'

'After that, the tide will be in. It comes in at four feet a minute, which is fast. And dangerous. We'd have to sit on the fire-escape and wait for the ebb. Not the best idea. OK, you first.' He gave her a gallant look. 'You don't suffer from vertigo, I hope?'

Gini mounted the fire-escape fast, Pascal at her back. She tried not to think about video-screens, or the apartment windows which overlooked these steps.

Halfway up, it began to rain without warning, and with considerable force. Pascal cursed. By the time they reached McMullen's windows, Gini's hair was drenched, and water ran down her face.

Pascal ignored these conditions. From his pocket he produced a heavy clasp knife. 'Now,' he said, 'either we force the window and nothing happens, or we force the window and the alarm goes off. It's a gamble.'

'What are the odds?'

'About fifty-fifty, I think. Usually, with these alarms, when they've been triggered, they have to be re-set . . . '

'Did you trigger it? How?'

'Easy. Look.' He pointed to two small black boxes on the inside of the window frame. 'These are contact alarms. If you hit the window frame hard, they go off. Luckily, these are over-sensitive; they need adjustment. Sometimes you really have to slam into them. These went off easily. A gentle touch . . . ' He grinned.

Gini said, 'You sound very knowledgeable. I guess you've done this before?'

'Of course.' He inserted the blade of the knife between the upper and lower frame of the window. 'As sytems go this is medium good, medium price. I've dealt with better than this. And worse.'

138

He grunted, pushed harder, levered the knife back and forth. Inside, the catch slid back, and Pascal gave a sigh of satisfaction. He eased the window frame up, and held out his hand to her to help her up.

Gini ignored the hand. She hauled herself up onto the window ledge and peered into the huge room beyond. 'What about those magic eye things? The porter said they had them.'

Pascal showed signs of impatience. 'I told you. It's all right. The system's off. If it was on it would have gone off the minute I inserted the knife. Listen, when an alarm system's been triggered, it has to be re-set by an engineer. There was just a possibility the porter had the codes but I thought he wouldn't – too great a security risk. He'll be downstairs now, calling the alarm company, telling them no, he's checked, the police checked, there was no sign of forced entry, so it must be a mechanical fault. They'll come out to re-set, but not immediately – at least I hope not immediately. Sometime this afternoon, I expect. Meanwhile we have half an hour before the tide rises so hurry up.'

'A common criminal.' Gini looked at him with admiring disgust. 'I'm working with a common criminal. Great.'

'Get a move on,' Pascal said, charmingly. 'I'll take the bedroom. You check the desk.'

'What am I looking for?'

'Anything. Diary. Address book. Letters. Telephone messages. Something, anything, that tells us where McMullen's gone to ground.'

The apartment was the nearest thing Gini had seen in London to a New York loft. The living-room was enormous, its ceiling double-height. Looking around her, Gini revised her ideas of James McMullen. It had not occurred to her that McMullen the drifter could be rich.

Yet rich he must undoubtedly be. He could afford floor space that dwarfed most London flats. He could afford, or had perhaps inherited, some fine antiques. The room gave her clues to the man: he liked both old and modern furniture. McMullen was not only well-off, he had taste. He liked listening to music – there was a large collection of CDs, most of them works by Mozart. He was a reader – one wall contained floor-to-ceiling bookshelves. There must have been at least two thousand books, many of them works of history, many of them in languages Gini could not read. She stood frowning in front of these, revising her opinion of the man again. A former Oxford scholar after all, she reminded herself. She checked the kitchen – well-equipped, the refrigerator empty – then made for the desk.

An expanse of well-polished mahogany. Some books, one blotting-pad – unmarked; one container for pens, and one photograph – the only one she had seen in the flat. She turned its heavy silver frame to the light. Lise Hawthorne smiled up at her. It was a studio photograph, taken some time before evidently, for Lise looked no more than twenty. She was radiant in a débutante's white evening dress.

Gini turned her attention to the desk drawers. There were six of them, all unlocked. Empty too: she stared at them in astonishment. No stationery, no files, no letters, no diaries, no address books, nothing – not so much as a paper clip. The desk had been cleaned out. Gini gave a low whistle. She felt around the back of the drawers. Nothing.

Moving quickly now, she re-checked the room. Examining it more closely, she could see that it too had been stripped. Yes, there was furniture, rugs, paintings, books – but the details of McMullen's existence had gone. There were no papers, no letters, no bills: she opened every drawer, including those in the kitchen, but there was nothing to be found, not one single scrap of paper.

She looked around her with a sense of frustration. Who could have done this? McMullen himself – or someone else? From the bedroom beyond she could hear the sound of Pascal, opening doors and drawers. Gini frowned, and returned to the desk.

A blotting-pad, a container for pens, that pile of well-worn books, the photograph of Lise Hawthorne.

Leaning across, she picked up the books and shook them, half-hoping some hidden communication from McMullen might flutter out. There was nothing concealed in them, just three books: *The Oxford Book of Modern Verse*, a copy of Milton's *Paradise Lost*, and a battered paperback of a Carson McCullers novel *The Ballad of the Sad Café*. The second book had McMullen's name written on the fly-leaf, and beneath it the words: *Christ Church, Oxford – 1968*.

This helped a little – it identified the Oxford college McMullen had attended, and the year he was there, but nothing more. Gini replaced the books. She stared fixedly at the desk. There must be something – she was certain of it. After all, McMullen had initiated this whole story: if he had had to disappear, if he had chosen to disappear, would he not try to ensure he could be traced?

The blotter? Carefully, she removed the paper, but there was nothing concealed beneath. She lifted the photograph of Lise, and gently undid the frame fastenings on its back. At first she thought there was nothing there either, just a backing of cardboard and paper between the picture and the back of the frame – and then she saw it. On one of the sheets of paper used as padding, a series of numbers, written in pencil, arranged like this:

3
6/2/6
2/1/6

It could have been something; it could have been nothing at all. If it was a code of some kind, or a reference, there was no time to decipher it now. Quickly she folded the piece of paper, and put it in her pocket. She pushed the glass, picture and frame back together, and closed it up. She turned, about to tell Pascal what she had found, when from the bedroom beyond came a low exclamation and Pascal called to her. 'Gini, Gini, quickly. Look at this.'

Gini gave a small involuntary shiver. It unsettled her, it felt creepy and illicit, doing this.

She crossed to the bedroom. It was unmistakably a man's room, austere, well-ordered. One wall was flanked with cupboards. Their opened doors revealed row upon row of conservative jackets, conservative suits.

Pascal stood in the centre of the room, by the large double bed. Next to him was a chest of drawers. Several of its drawers had been opened. Gini gestured towards them.

'Did you do this?'

'What – open the closets and drawers? Yes. Why?'

'Because the desk is totally empty. It's been cleared. I was trying to figure out who did that. McMullen – or the person who set off the alarm, earlier in the week?'

'Someone's been through the desk?'

'That's right. Plus every single other drawer in the place. There's not one single scrap of paper – except this.'

She held out the piece of paper she had found. Pascal examined it closely.

'It means nothing to me.'

'Nor me. But it was inside the frame of Lise Hawthorne's photograph on his desk.'

'Keep it. We'll look at it later.' Pascal lowered his voice, and caught her by the arm. 'Now I'll show you what I found. Something very curious indeed. Look at this.' He gestured towards one of the drawers. Gini looked inside it, frowning.

'Shirts,' she said. 'I see shirts. Umpteen identical white shirts – all very neat, back from a laundry, still in their cellophane sleeves. So what?'

'So this McMullen – he's a well-organized, a methodical man, yes? He keeps white shirts in this drawer, blue shirts in the next. Here, in this top drawer on the right, handkerchiefs – also just back from the laundry. And here, in this top drawer on the left – what would you expect to find there?'

'Oh God, I don't know . . . ' Gini glanced over her shoulder. Outside it was still raining heavily. The light was grey and thick. The silence was unnerving.

'Look, Pascal – let's go. I don't like this. We shouldn't be here, searching through someone's personal belongings. It doesn't feel right.'

Pascal ignored her. His face was now pale and intent. 'Just tell me what you'd expect to find in this top drawer.'

'Oh, very well. Underwear. Socks, maybe. Something like that.'

'Exactly.' Pascal gave a small tight triumphant smile. 'You were right the second time. Socks. That's what you might expect to find – and so, when you did, you might not investigate too closely. If you were in a hurry, you'd move on, look somewhere else . . .'

'You mean you think this apartment *was* searched?'

'I'm not sure. I think McMullen expected it to be searched, so he cleared it out – with military precision – before he left. Only, as it happens, he left something behind. Look.'

Pascal opened the top left-hand drawer. Inside it, as Gini had predicted, were pile upon pile of socks: dark grey socks, black socks, socks that matched the conservative suits and the image she was building of a conservative ex-army man.

Pascal reached into the drawer, and took something from it, a scrap of black material. He held it out to her; Gini stared at it blankly. It was a glove, a woman's glove, made to be worn in the evening, for it was long and would reach from elbow to fingertips. It was made of the finest black kid.

'So it's a glove,' she began. 'A woman's glove. Some girlfriend probably left it behind. Maybe it's Lise's glove, and he kept it, for sentimental reasons, and . . .' She broke off, as the memory came back to her. *The girl is provided with a costume, with long black leather gloves . . . She is never permitted to touch Hawthorne, except with a gloved hand . . .*

'Oh my God, Pascal . . .'

'Precisely.' Pascal's face was now pale with excitement. 'But there's more than that. This is a very special kind of glove. Highly memorable. Look closely. Smell . . .'

He held the glove close to her face. Gini recoiled. The glove smelled of a heavy musky perfume, but also something else. She could not be certain, but it might have been blood. She took a step backwards.

'It smells foul . . . '

'I know. Not a smell you'd forget. Also, if you touch it,' he guided her hand to the soft leather. 'You see? As if it had been oiled.'

Gini gave a small shiver. She glanced over her shoulder. Somewhere on this floor, muffled by thick walls and corridors, a door closed. She touched Pascal's arm.

'Pascal, I don't like this. We've been here more than half an hour now. Let's go.'

'Fine. I agree. There's nothing else here anyway. I've been through everything. We'll go. But this . . . ' he held up the glove, then pushed it into the pocket of his jacket, 'this, we take with us.'

'One right-handed glove? Why? It doesn't prove anything, not for sure—'

'It tells me something. Something I don't understand . . . Come on.' He gripped her arm firmly, and led her back towards the fire-escape window. Gini was about to argue, then, looking down, she saw the waters of the rising tide gushing below. She climbed out of the window. The wind gusted; a squall of rain washed against her face.

They descended the fire-escape, negotiated the now fast-flowing water, and regained the safety of the alleyway steps. Gini turned to him.

'OK,' she said, 'explain. What does that glove tell you? I want to know, Pascal. I want to know now.'

'It tells me there are connections here – connections I don't understand.'

He looked down at the grey of the Thames. The water sucked at the shingle. His face was troubled. Gini caught at his arm. 'I have the pair to this glove,' he went on, frowning. 'Identical in every way. The same smell, the same texture, the same faint creases on the palm . . . '

'*You* have its pair?' Gini stared at him in astonishment. 'But how can that be?'

144

'It was sent to me – anonymously.' Pascal's voice was suddenly grim. 'It arrived yesterday, in Paris, by special courier. In a neat brown-paper parcel. The address was stencilled. It was fastened with string, and – what's the matter?'

'Just one little question.' Gini's skin had gone cold. She raised her eyes to his. 'Did the sender use sealing-wax – red sealing-wax?'

XI

'Damn,' Gini said. 'Damn, damn, *damn* . . . '

She slammed down the telephone receiver. From across her living-room, Pascal watched her. He was holding the pair of handcuffs she had been sent. In a thoughtful way he weighed them from hand to hand.

'They won't co-operate?'

'Won't or can't. The woman who took delivery of the parcels isn't there this afternoon. Her mother's ill apparently – so they let her go home. She'll be back first thing tomorrow morning. Her name's Susannah. We can talk to her then.'

'Can't someone else help? It must all be on computer—'

'Of course it's on computer. ICD is a huge firm. But this Susannah has to give her authorization, apparently. All transactions are confidential . . . We'll have to go down there, Pascal. Tomorrow. I can tell we'll get precisely nowhere on the phone.'

'That's OK. I'll go down there, first thing—'

'*We'll* go down there,' Gini said, a little sharply. 'We'll both go. I want to talk to this Susannah as well.'

'Sure.' Pascal hesitated, then glanced away; Gini frowned.

They had returned here, to Islington, straight from McMullen's apartment. It was now past three in the afternoon, and the wintry light was fading. Gini's clothes were still soaked, but she couldn't be bothered to change them. She could still feel it, that adrenalin rush, the sensation that one more phone call might bring a vital lead they needed and she couldn't understand Pascal's reaction: surely he felt this too?

He gave no sign of it. Indeed, from the moment she showed him the handcuffs, she could sense a change in him, a withdrawal, a slowing-down.

She looked at him uncertainly. There was something he was keeping back from her, she felt sure of it. He was still standing, holding the handcuffs. All the energy and drive of the morning seemed to have left him. For the past hour, while she explained, and telephoned, he had remained silent and thoughtful. Now he looked up, with a frown.

'You should change your clothes, Gini – take a warm shower. You're soaked through. There's nothing more we can usefully do now anyway. We'll just have to wait. And that's no bad thing. It gives us time to talk this over, think it through . . . '

'Pascal, is something wrong?'

'Wrong? Wrong?' He gave her an odd glance. 'Oh no, there's nothing wrong. Someone sends you a pair of handcuffs. It's the most normal thing in the world . . . '

'So? They sent you a glove. There's a direct link to McMullen. It has to be some kind of signal, some kind of clue. Four parcels were sent out altogether, the courier told me. One to you, one to me – and two others, which both went abroad. Don't you see, Pascal – if we can just find out who sent them, where the other two went . . . ? It has to be a lead. It just has to . . . '

'Oh, I agree. We've been handed it on a plate. And I don't like that at all.'

'So it's too convenient, too pat – who cares? We still have to check it out. As soon as we can—'

'Who cares? *I* care . . . ' He gave her an angry glance. 'And if you thought for a second, instead of flying off the handle like this, you'd care too. Do you usually work like this – it's your method, is it? – to act first and think afterwards? Well, it isn't mine. Just slow down.'

Gini started on some quick sharp reply, then stopped herself. The accusation stung, particularly coming from Pascal. Also, there was some truth in it, as she knew. She could be impetuous when she worked; sometimes that had paid dividends, but not always: it could lead to errors, to trouble, as well.

Her father had always said that the secret of journalism was detail, a passion for detail: 'I check,' he used to say, 'then cross-check, then cross-check again. I put the pieces of the puzzle together very slowly and very carefully. Then, when I've got every piece in place – *every* piece, mind you, not just some of them . . . Well, then I'm home and dry. That's the good part.' He grinned. 'That's when I nail the lying bastards to the wall.'

She felt herself colour, and looked away. Both her father, and Pascal, were right. In a careful voice, avoiding Pascal's eyes, she said, 'Sure. Maybe you're right. I can rush at things. Go too fast. I do know that . . .'

Pascal seemed to ignore the implicit apology. He shrugged. 'When we're starting out,' he said, 'we all do . . .'

Gini swung around to look at him. There was a small loaded silence.

'Starting out?' she began. 'I'm not starting out, Pascal. I know I haven't reached your exalted heights, but I have been a reporter for nearly ten years. I've worked on some big stories. I'm not a schoolgirl now. For God's sake . . .' She felt a sudden spurt of anger. 'I'm not some kid out of journalism school, Pascal. I'm twenty-seven years old.'

'It's not likely I'd forget your age.' His face too, had become set. 'I've every reason to remember it, given past circumstances.'

'I don't believe this . . .' Gini rose angrily to her feet. 'Do you have to bring that up now?'

'I didn't bring it up,' he snapped. 'You did. And in any case, you misunderstood. When I said "starting out", I wasn't suggesting you lacked experience. I meant starting out on a new story, that's all.'

'The hell you did. Don't lie. You were patronizing me. You were putting me down.'

'I damn well was not . . .' His eyes glinted with anger. 'You're jumping to conclusions again. You're getting things wrong. Look, Gini, if we're going to work together—'

'If? If?' She took a step towards him. 'I was damn well *assigned* to this story. No "ifs" and no "buts". If you don't like that, Pascal, too bad because—'

'Jesus Christ . . . '

Pascal began to swear, at length, and in French. They were now only a few feet apart. The warm air in the room felt acrid with sudden anger. Gini felt flushed and hot, almost blinded by resentment, and a horrible weakening distress. She never wept – it was years since she had wept – but she could feel now that tears were close.

She was about to launch herself on some new angry reply, when something in his eyes stopped her. The anger fell away. She gave a small resigned gesture, and to her surprise Pascal suddenly took her hand, and drew her towards him. He, too, was no longer angry, she saw. There was sadness and bewilderment in his face.

'I'm sorry,' he said. 'We're arguing about the past, aren't we, Gini? Not this story at all. We're fighting about something that happened twelve years ago.'

Gini gave a sigh, and looked away. 'Yes. You're right. I guess we are.'

'We mustn't do that. Gini . . . ' His hand tightened its grip. 'Look at me. If we let that happen . . . We mustn't make that mistake . . . '

'I know that. I know that. It's just sometimes . . . Pascal, it's not so easy to put it aside, to forget . . . '

'I know that too. It spills over, and then . . . ' His tone was gentle now. 'Listen, Gini. You're right – that time, it was my fault. I expressed myself badly. I'm not used to working with anyone else, I expect. I've been a loner too long. I get irritable and impatient. But there is a reason, Gini, can't you see that? You're a woman – no, listen to me. You're a woman, living alone, and someone's sent you an anonymous gift. A pair of handcuffs. Now, that may not alarm you, but it alarms me.'

He looked down at Gini, as he said this. He watched as colour came and went in her face, and he watched her expression change, as if within her a short and painful struggle took place.

'I'm not used to that,' she answered at last, in an odd stiff voice. He could hear pride and pain in her tone. 'I'm not used to someone's being protective, maybe it's that. I usually work alone, and I live alone, there's no reason for anyone to care where I go, what I do, what time I get back. I expect I've made a fetish of that. And then . . . ' She broke off.

'Tell me,' Pascal said.

She raised her head to look at him. An odd pinched expression had come over her face.

'Oh nothing . . . ' She made an attempt to sound dismissive. 'My father always said a woman couldn't be independent, the way a man could. I used to think I'd prove him wrong. Maybe I have proved him wrong. I'm different, Pascal – I'm not the girl you used to know.'

'I'm not so sure of that.'

'I am. I was so weak then, so stupid. I rushed into things. I let my heart rule my head . . . '

'That's not always a sin, is it?'

'Maybe not. Just a part of growing up. Anyway,' she released his hand, and stepped back, 'I'm different now, Pascal. I can take care of myself. I find any protectiveness from a man hard to deal with.'

'You do?' Pascal looked at her curiously. 'Why is that?'

Gini smiled suddenly. 'Oh, I guess because I'm afraid I'll get to like it. Depend on it—'

'And that would be a bad thing?'

'Judging from past experience, yes.'

'I see.' Pascal frowned, then he too smiled. 'Well, if it helps, think of it as a weakness on my part. My French upbringing, an irresistible impulse to be gallant. I'd be protective to any woman, in these circumstances. It's my age – it's a sort of generalized complaint I suffer from.'

There was a silence. Gini, looking back at Pascal, saw an expression she could not interpret cross his face. Abruptly, he moved away from her. When he next spoke, his voice was much more brisk.

'So,' he said, 'that's cleared the air, I hope? Maybe if we make a few rules? No references to the past. If my protectiveness gets out of hand, you rein me in . . . I still think you should change those wet clothes. While you do that, I'll make us some coffee. Then we'll sit by the fire, and talk this story through, yes?'

'That sounds reasonable.'

'Fine. Meanwhile, think this over. There's one peculiar thing, something that especially puzzles me.'

'Yes?'

'Take a look at the timing on this. We were assigned to the Hawthorne story yesterday morning. The same morning we received the parcels. Who knew we'd be working on the story?'

'Nicholas Jenkins.'

'Who else?'

'No-one. Until I went into his office, even I didn't know. And neither did you.'

'Yet someone else *did* know, don't you see that, Gini?' Pascal frowned. 'They must have known. They sent out those parcels twenty-four hours before we were even briefed. They laid out a trail for us, before we even started work. It can't be coincidence. Someone else *knew* we'd be working together on this. Can you explain that? Because I certainly can't.'

When the door closed behind Gini, Pascal knew he could stop acting. He ran his hands through his hair. He began to pace the room. He told himself that he had at least managed to disguise it, but his agitation was intense. It had been a mistake to touch Gini. He should never have allowed himself to take her hands. He should not have lost his temper, that was the worst mistake: that made it all short-circuit, brought the past roaring back. Three weeks in a war zone twelve years before, but the time-gap was immaterial. He had wanted Gini now; he had wanted her then. The need was unchanged, still as sharp as ever. It was as immediate, as fierce.

Yesterday, yesterday, he told himself; yesterday, he'd felt safe. He'd been watching her, carefully, right through the lunch with Nicholas Jenkins, and he'd been able to tell himself that he was, thank God, invulnerable now. This was a new Gini, a stranger: of course he could work with this woman – when he looked at her he felt nothing at all.

'The thing is,' Jenkins had said, before Gini arrived, 'she's a good reporter. She's quick, she's got an instinct for leads. She does her homework. You could make a good team . . . ' Pascal could hear the 'but' coming; he waited. Jenkins grinned. 'But – and it's a big "but" – she can be difficult to work with. Like a lot of the ladies now . . . You know, the feminist thing . . . '

Jenkins made a face. '*Plus*, she has one helluva chip on her shoulder about her father. Every fucking story she works on – it has to be bloody perfect. Daddy might read it, you see – not that Daddy ever does, I suspect, because Daddy doesn't give a damn, by all accounts. But she can't see that. She's trying to prove something, and when she writes an article, she's writing it for him.'

'I've met her father,' Pascal interjected. He gave Jenkins a quick glance, but there was no reaction. Again Jenkins grinned.

'You have? Well then, you'll know. Just stay off the subject of Sam Hunter and his fucking Pulitzer prize. She'll sing his praises for an entire evening. Believe me, I know.' A note of more personal resentment entered his voice as he made this remark. An overture rejected?

'Anything else?' Pascal said.

'Yes. She's pushy. Sharp. Very good-looking, of course, but a bit short in the female charm department.'

'Meaning?'

'Put it this way. She can freeze a man's balls at five paces. So don't try making a pass.'

'That's OK.' Pascal gave him a cold look. 'I'm here to work with her.'

Jenkins laughed. 'Pascal, *please* – so very PC. Just wait till you see her . . . ' He sketched a female outline with his hands. 'You may just change your mind.'

And then Gini had come into the room; for a moment Pascal did not recognize her. He stared at this tall, thin young woman. She had a cool manner, a slightly combative air. He looked at her with dismay and regret. He thought:

My lovely Gini; and then he thought: *all that beauty, and it's gone.*

All through lunch, he felt the same. He could see that she disliked Jenkins, and was containing her hostility to him with some difficulty – that was fine; his own reaction was much the same. But it was more than that: she gave off an almost palpable chill. She sat opposite him, and she never once smiled. It seemed to him, as time passed, that there was something false, something forced in her behaviour, as if she chose to act a part. Such pains, to play the professional, to emphasize the information on Hawthorne she possessed. And then, she couldn't resist capping the remarks Pascal himself made, remarks to which she had listened with a tight set face.

'*Your turn, Gini, there's plenty to add,*' Jenkins had said.

'*There certainly is,*' she had replied, with a dismissive glance in Pascal's direction. '*I'll stick to politics, I think . . .* '

It was a put-down, and it startled him. Watching her, he thought: *How changed she is – she's hard as nails.*

She showed no emotion as the story about Hawthorne emerged: there was no sign of shock, or sympathy, just that cold alert dispassionate appraisal. Pascal had watched it, listened to it, and it seemed to him deeply unfeminine. By the end of the lunch, he was hideously depressed. He had known that Gini must be altered; it had not occurred to him she would become a woman he disliked.

When they left the building, he was arguing with himself; he was telling himself that with dislike came relief. He could work with this woman: there was no entanglement here. The girl he remembered, he told himself, was dead. She was a ghost, a phantom, alive only in his memory; how strange. For twelve years he had been thinking about her, and now that he'd met her again, she did not exist.

And then something happened – something he could not explain. A little magic, a trick of the light, some accidental angle of the head, some shadow that passed across her eyes. She had been silent in the half-dusk, staring towards the security gates across the yard, and then, suddenly, a transformation took place. Suddenly he could see the girl in the woman she had become: he glimpsed vulnerability beneath that new combative façade. He saw the ghost of the girl in the shape of her eyes, in the curve of her cheek. He rested his eyes on her face, and he saw again that she was lovely. Recognition flooded through him; a sudden and astonishing joy swept through him. Before he could stop himself, he greeted her. He said her name, in the old way, in the old accents. She swung around, startled, colour ebbing from her cheeks, and before she could disguise it, it was there, still there, absolutely unaltered, that quality he had once loved, transparent in her face.

Nothing he could define: gravity, honesty, the courage to give joy – in the past he had used these poor terms, and others equally inexact to explain the inexplicable, what it was that he found delightful in her face. He had tried many times in Beirut to capture it on film. He had, of course, failed. Film could not capture her resonance any more than words could: film froze the instant; it could not convey the touch of her hand, or the tone of her voice. This reductiveness became a challenge. Pascal told himself that the camera could and did convey so much: it could convey anger, happiness, desolation, vanity, grief . . . His determination to capture her on film became an obsession with him, a quest. 'Stand here,' he would say. 'Turn your face to the light. Look at me. Yes. Yes. That's right . . . '

But what he saw with his eyes was not what his lenses recorded. When he looked at the printed images, they were effective but dead. He kept them, nevertheless, and one of them in particular, just a small black-and-white shot, he kept still. Sitting in Gini's London room now, he drew it out.

He had taken it late one afternoon, close by the harbour. From a technical point of view, it was a failure, he knew that. The light had been difficult, the shutter speed, possibly the aperture, incorrect. It was over-exposed:

her face was given a translucent hazy quality, the fault of reflected light. Even so, it was his favourite picture. Looking at it in the past, even looking at it now, he knew why he had kept it, why he had allowed it to become such a talisman.

It was a young girl, just a girl, someone who had lied about her age and who was, in fact, much younger than he had realized when he took this shot. Her pale hair blew across her forehead; she was wearing only one ear-ring and a loose ordinary open-necked shirt. She had a wide-set, level-eyed gaze; she was half-frowning, half-smiling. It was an unremarkable picture in every way, it belied his professional gifts; it was, to most eyes, just a pretty girl, with the movement of waves behind her, a typical holiday snap – but to Pascal it was of crucial importance. To look at this, was to look at his own truth, a truth which would never alter or erode.

Whatever love meant, however much, later, he came to doubt its deceptions and seductions, there was still this. The day he took this picture, his camera had been lucky – for once it had captured joy. That still had the capacity to astonish him: he was so used, by then, to capturing death.

It happened, he told himself now. It happened, and this picture had been his proof. Then, not half an hour ago, he had seen far greater proof than this. He had seen the past as he remembered and hoped it had been: he had seen it written in Gini's eyes and face. Let go, he thought; he had no further need for photographs.

Bending, on a sudden impulse, he touched the picture to the flames of the fire, and watched it catch. It burned instantly, in a flare of chemicals, and he brushed the tell-tale ashes underfoot. Rituals had their uses; to ac-knowledge once and for all that it had happened, but it was over, helped.

Hearing movement from the room beyond, he went out to the kitchen and made coffee. Colleagues, friends, professionals, a working team: he said this to himself.

'What we will do,' he said cheerfully, when Gini

returned, 'is go out for dinner, yes? Have some good red wine, some food, discuss the case.'

He broke off. Gini was watching him quietly. She agreed, in a subdued way, that this was a good course.

Pascal was careful; he kept up this note of camaraderie until, a while later, they were about to leave her flat. Then, although he knew it was wise to leave the past interred, because that way it retained its perfection and its power, and it remained untainted by the mess he had made of the rest of his life, he asked a foolish question, one he had resolved not to ask.

'That ear-ring,' he said, as they were moving towards the door. 'You remember? The one we chose together? Did you keep it? Do you ever wear it?'

A bad question. Gini crimsoned. 'The ear-ring? No – I don't wear it. In fact, I don't know if I still have it. The last time I moved apartments I lost it, I think.' She unlatched the chain on her door, and held it open for her cat, who marched ahead of them, tail waving, intent on exploring the streets.

'Come on, Pascal . . . ' she said. 'The reservation's for eight. We'll be late.'

The restaurant Gini had chosen was a few streets from her flat; it was a small, unpretentious, neighbourhood place, run by a local Italian family. Midweek, it was quiet and it served simple good food.

They were given an alcove table, to the rear of the restaurant. One side of them, there were photographs of Italian film actors and Italian football stars; the walls were painted white; the ceiling was strung with Chianti bottles and plastic vines. Pascal looked at these decorations and smiled.

'A little Italy in North London. It's nice, Gini.'

'It's quiet. The pasta's good. We can talk.'

When the waiter had brought them their spaghetti and salads, and Pascal had poured out the wine, he drew out a notebook.

'Now,' he said. 'Let's make a start.'

'List the possible leads? Sure.'

'First there's the courier company, obviously. We find out where the other two parcels went, and who sent them. That may indicate *why* they were sent, whether or not it's a deliberate trail . . . '

'Then there's McMullen himself . . . ' Gini leaned forward. 'We ought to trace his family, and his friends. Check out his past – Oxford, that army career. It could help us to find him.'

'Jenkins gave me some contacts – names and phone numbers. He sent them with the tape . . . ' Pascal tapped the notebook thoughtfully. 'There's that sister of his, for instance, the one mentioned on the tape. An ex-actress, apparently. It would be worth talking to her.'

'She lives in London?'

'Yes. Near Sloane Square. The parents are still alive too – apparently the father's an art historian. Distinguished, according to Jenkins.'

'London?'

'No. Shropshire, unfortunately. Miles away – and I'd rather not approach them by phone. Not initially anyway. The sister first then, and some of the friends.'

'Are there many?'

'Not according to Jenkins. McMullen seems to be something of a loner.'

'And then there's Hawthorne himself,' Gini said. 'We could try checking out parts of McMullen's story. After all, if Hawthorne requires these blondes, every month, there must be some source of supply. How do you hire a blonde, Pascal?'

Pascal shrugged. 'Escort agencies, call-girl networks. Talk to the head porter in any top London hotel—'

'Hawthorne's not exactly likely to do that, is he?'

'No, but the point is, it's not difficult. If a man has the money, the women are available.'

'I can't believe he'd go through some agency.' Gini shook her head. 'It's too public, too risky.'

'I would say so too. On the other hand, he would use a false name, obviously.'

'But he's so well known, Pascal. He'd be recognized . . . '

'So? He wouldn't be the first – or the last – famous man to hire call-girls. You can buy discretion – and co-operation – if you know where to go.'

'You sound very knowledgeable.'

'I am very knowledgeable. I've been down this particular route before.'

'Call-girls? Prostitutes?'

'Models. Massage parlours. Madames. Sure. Come on, Gini,' he tapped the notebook impatiently, 'whom do you imagine I get leads from? Bank presidents? You know the kind of work I do.'

'Yes. Yes. I know.' Gini looked away. There was a silence, while Pascal continued to make notes, and she toyed with her food. She found she had lost her appetite. The question of Pascal's present mode of working, of the kind of stories he now chose to cover lay between them, a territory she would have liked to explore. She would have liked to ask him why he had embarked on this work, and whether he saw it as a betrayal of himself and his gifts. But the question was one she instinctively shied away from. Let it wait until she had been working with him longer, until he perhaps had more reason to trust her than he did now. For he did not trust her now, not entirely; she could sense that. Perhaps he trusted no-one. Any mention of his wife, his child, or his work and the shutters came down.

A shadow had passed across his face when he made his last remark about his sources. As he concentrated on his notes, however, that momentary darkening passed. She watched him as he jotted words and phrases, his concentration absolute. His dark hair, now greying a little at the temples, fell forward across his forehead. His eyes were lowered to the notebook in front of him. She could watch him with impunity and with a secret pleasure too.

Pascal, who was altered and unaltered. There was, on his left cheek-bone, a tiny scar, the mark of some childhood accident, some fall. Once upon a time, lying in darkness while the music from the dancehall below moved the air in his room, she had traced that scar with her fingers as he slept beside her. She had read all the details of his face with her fingers, the dear geography of eyes, nose, chin, throat, hair. She could remember with absolute precision the particular scent of his skin, the shape and grip of his hands, the ways, words and hows of physical intimacy. She could remember little shafts of detail: ways he moved, inflections he used. It pained her, that these recollections were so sharp, for there was now, of course, one component missing, the component which gave vitality to all the rest. Once, when they looked at each other, there had been such interaction of the eyes. But then lovers did not need words, because a glance spoke a better language.

'Is something wrong?' Pascal looked up, suddenly.

'No. Nothing.' She snapped back to the lesser present. 'Why?'

'You looked sad, that's all.'

'Not sad, concentrated. I was just thinking about this story . . . ' She gestured towards the waiter. 'Shall we get some coffee?'

He nodded, lit a cigarette.

'We have one other lead,' she went on, speaking rapidly. 'That piece of paper I found in McMullen's apartment, we mustn't forget that. It might mean something – and it might mean nothing at all.'

She took out the piece of paper as she said this, and passed it across. Pascal frowned, holding it up to the candlelight. 'Three sets of numbers – they're not dates. They could be anything. A set of measurements, some combination . . . they could be old, or recent . . . '

'They're carefully written, Pascal.'

'Even so. It could just be something someone jotted down. Then they needed a piece of paper, to pad out that photograph frame, so they used this. It might not even be McMullen's writing.'

'That's true.' Gini took the piece of paper back from him and scanned it. 'It's just . . . the way McMullen disappeared. Why contact Jenkins, then disappear?'

'Something happened, obviously between the meeting when he delivered that tape, and December twenty-first last year. Maybe he thought he was in danger.'

'But then surely he'd want to make contact? The story was reaching a crucial stage. He was about to provide that assignation address. If he had to disappear for any reason, surely he'd try to make contact of some kind?'

'Leave a trail, you mean? Possibly.' Pascal looked across at the paper. 'But if that's some kind of coded message, I can't crack it, can you?'

'No. I can't. But then codes aren't my strong point. Never were. We could try the obvious things, I guess, substituting letters for numbers. Try that, Pascal.'

'With the letter "A" as number one? OK . . . ' He scribbled in the notebook, then grinned. 'Not too helpful. Look.' He passed the page across. It now read like this:

3	C
6/2/6	F/B/F
2/1/6	B/A/F

'Gibberish. Damn.' Gini frowned. 'Let's try it with "B" as number one, or "C". "C" is the third letter of the alphabet, Pascal – maybe that's what the number three at the top means . . . Try that.'

They tried this and other combinations for some time. None of the combinations produced anything resembling a message, not even a clear word.

'Hopeless.' Pascal was the first to grow impatient. He pushed the paper to one side. 'I think we're wasting our time.'

'One last try. Think, Pascal. It was the only scrap of writing in the whole flat. It was inside Lise Hawthorne's photograph. That suggests something, surely?'

'Maybe, maybe . . . ' Pascal smiled. 'I can see it's tempting. OK. Perhaps you missed something. Maybe you can't make this work on its own. Maybe it has to be matched, to something else. Tell me again, how you found it.'

'I went through the desk twice. There was a leather blotter . . . '

'Clean blotting-paper?'

'Pristine. Unused. I checked under it – nothing there. Then there was a pile of books, but there were books everywhere, on the shelves, on the coffee table, piled on the floor, by his bed – you saw.'

'You checked inside the books?'

'Obviously. Nothing. Oh, one of them had his name, his Oxford college and a date written – nineteen sixty-eight. I'll check, but I imagine it's the date he was there.'

'Nothing underlined in the book texts, written in the margin?'

'Nothing I could see. I was looking quickly. They were well read, but clean.'

'What books were they?'

'A poetry anthology, Milton's *Paradise Lost*, a Carson McCullers novel.'

'Eclectic.'

'Sure, but the bookshelves were the same. Novels, political works, poetry, history. Masses of history, maybe that was his subject at Oxford. Oh, and books in foreign languages, German, French, Italian . . . '

'A well-educated army officer. Interesting . . . ' Pascal sighed. 'It doesn't seem to help, however. Go on.'

'That was it. The books, the blotter, the photograph of Lise – not a recent photograph by the way – and a leather container for pens and pencils. Nothing more.'

Pascal shook his head. 'Then I don't see it. It's a blind alley.' He smiled. 'You don't know any friendly neighbourhood code-crackers, by any chance?'

'Unfortunately, no. Not my line. Except – wait a minute. There *is* someone who might help. A friend of Mary's – erstwhile Cambridge don. He worked in military intelligence in the war – at least, I think he did. He compiles crosswords now, fiendish crosswords for *The Times*.'

She broke off. Pascal, she saw, was watching her closely, his expression absorbed, gentle, slightly sad.

'Is something wrong?'

'No, nothing.' He smiled. 'I like it when you concentrate, that's all. There's a certain expression that comes into your face then. You push your hair back, behind your ears, and you . . . It's nothing. Just the way the light was falling on your skin. My photographer's eye.'

Gini looked at him uncertainly. Pascal rose abruptly to his feet.

'I'll get the bill,' he said. 'And then I'll walk you home.'

When they were back in her flat, Pascal showed no inclination to leave. While Gini made coffee, he prowled about the room. He checked the doors, the windows, the pictures, the bookshelves, in a way that made her nervous. She sat down by the fire, stroking Napoleon, while Pascal peered at prints of art exhibitions. Eventually, she could stand it no longer.

'Just what are you doing, Pascal?'

'What?' He swung around, and gave her an absent-minded look, as if his concentration were elsewhere.

'It's a very ordinary apartment,' Gini said patiently. 'Ordinary posters, pretty obvious books. You appear to be casing it. I just wondered why.'

'I'd like to know you, perhaps.' He gave a shrug.

'You do know me.'

'Maybe. You've changed. I'm not so sure.'

'So what does your investigation tell you?'

'Oh, a number of things. We like the same painters. We've even been to some of the same art exhibitions. This one, for instance – in Paris.' He gestured at the poster. 'You were there. I was there.'

'Yes, and so were roughly twenty-five thousand other people, Pascal. It was a very successful exhibition.'

'Even so.' He gave her a sharp glance. 'It was in Paris. I live in Paris. That exhibition was last year.' He paused.

'Did you go to it on your own?'

'Yes, I did, as it happens.'

'No boyfriend?'

162

'I was probably between boyfriends. I quite often am.'

'I also went to this exhibition on my own . . . ' He hesitated again. 'You never thought of calling me then, when you were in Paris?'

'No, I didn't. Pascal, it was years since we met. You had a wife, a family, I—'

'Not last year. No wife. I was divorced three years ago. You knew that.'

'Did I?'

'That's what you said yesterday. You said you'd heard . . . '

Gini looked away quickly. This deception was hard. She wondered what Pascal's reaction would be if she told him the truth: that she could never go to Paris, or anywhere else in France for that matter, without every street, every café, singing his name. She remembered the times, the many times in the past, when she had walked the Paris boulevards, sat in Paris cafés, and seen his features in the air, in the reflections on the Seine. 'What about London?' She turned back to look at him. 'You must have been to London, hundreds of times. You never called me, Pascal. You never wrote. There was just that one accidental meeting in Paris.'

It was Pascal's turn to look away. He wondered what Gini's reaction would be if he told her the truth: that he *had* called her, that he *had* spoken to her – many, many times, in his own mind. Could you explain to someone that despite absence and the passing of time, it was perfectly possible to maintain an imagined dialogue with her, that those exchanges could take on vitality, a life of their own? No, you could not explain, he decided grimly, any more than you could explain how their influence remained with you, how it entered into you and stained you, and how sometimes, with a particularly painful trickery, it would surface in dreams.

He stared at the curtains of Gini's room, and for a brief instant saw his own home in Paris, the home he had then shared with Helen, five years before. Mid-afternoon, spring sunshine; his daughter was asleep in the next room;

Helen had gone shopping. He picked up the telephone, put it down; he did this three times, then finally he dialled.

He had seen Gini outside that café just a few hours before. All that time, the impulse had been mounting. Now, guiltily, he gave into it. During that brief glacial embarrassed conversation, she had mentioned the name of her hotel. Such was his perturbation he was incapable of thinking. All he knew was that he had to speak to her, hear the sound of her voice. So he dialled, spoke to the receptionist, waited; his pulse accelerated. The room number rang three times, four, five . . . Then a man's voice answered. Pascal froze. He should have foreseen this, it was so obvious, she had made the situation perfectly clear . . . He was about to hang up, and then found he was unable to do so:

'*Je peux parler à Mademoiselle Hunter?*'

'*Non. Je regrette . . .* ' The Englishman's French was good, almost unaccented. There was a slight pause. '*Elle est partie.*'

'*Quand?*'

'*Cet après-midi – une demi-heure . . . Vous voulez laisser un message?*'

'*Non. Ce n'est pas important. Merci. Au revoir . . .* '

He knew, as he replaced the receiver, that Helen had returned. He could feel her presence, through his shoulder-blades. He swung around.

'No luck?' She gave a small tight smile. 'What a disappointment for you. I wondered when you'd call.' She gave a quick glance down at her watch. 'Two and a half hours. I'm surprised you waited that long. But then of course you couldn't call earlier, could you? I was here.'

She placed her shopping-bag on the table, and began calmly to unpack it: bread, wine, vegetables, cheese. 'Never mind, Pascal. Try her next time you're in England. She'll be delighted to hear from you. She made that *very* clear.'

'She's a friend,' Pascal began, hopelessly. 'I told you—'

'Oh, I know what you told me – and you lie terribly

badly. You always did. I thought that particularly interesting. After all – why lie? Why should I care? It was years before you met me. Just another of your foreign affairs. Why pretend otherwise? Unless, of course, it was a very special affair. Was it special, Pascal?'

'I won't discuss this. You're wrong. You wouldn't understand—'

'Wrong?' She met his eyes coldly. 'Oh no, I don't think so. Not at all. I find it quite remarkable – that you've never once mentioned her name, not in all the years I've known you. So secretive. Her hands were shaking – did you notice?'

'No, I damn well didn't.'

'Well, they were.'

'Look, can we just forget this?'

'Oh, I can. Probably.' Her gaze became coolly speculative. 'The question is, can you?' She folded up the grocery bag, very deliberately. 'Unfinished business, I'd say. I can always tell. My advice would be to go to London, finish it off, and when you've got it out of your system, come home.'

'Helen . . .'

'Why not? It's much the best way. Go to bed with her. You obviously still want to. Why else phone?'

'For Christ's sake, that's the only reason to phone a woman, is it? Because you want to go to bed with her?'

'No. Of course not. But it's the reason in your case, whether you know it or not.'

'That's not true.'

'Do you know, I really don't care? I don't care any more where you go, what you do, or who you screw.' She paused, gave him a considering look. 'Have you been faithful? Are you faithful?'

'As a matter of fact, yes. I am. With difficulty.'

As always, anger and retaliation pleased her. She gave another chill smile. 'Well, don't fight it any more on my account, Pascal. If you loved me, I might feel differently. But since you don't, it really makes no difference. Feel free. Fuck around.'

She turned away, still quite calmly, opened the fridge, and began to put away the groceries. Pascal lost his temper. He lost his temper with his wife, with the room, with the air. He smashed his hand down hard on the kitchen table.

'*Why?*' he shouted. '*Why* do you do this? *Why* do you say that? I married you, after all.'

'Ah yes. You married me.' She turned around, and looked at him. 'And you said that you loved me. I even believed you – for a while.'

'*I* believed it, damn you.' He hit the table again, and knocked over the wine. 'I wouldn't have said it otherwise.'

Helen righted the bottle expertly. She gave him a cool glance. 'Ah, but *did* you believe it, Pascal? I could see you tried – but did you really believe it, in your heart?'

There was a silence, a long silence. Pascal turned away and Helen sighed.

'Precisely,' she said, and this time the bitterness came through in her voice. 'Maybe that's why I never felt like your wife even with your ring on my hand. Face facts, Pascal. You married me because I very unwisely let you get me pregnant. You married me because it was the decent thing to do, and you can be a decent man. Very sweet, very touching – only then, unfortunately, I lost the child.'

Her voice had risen. It hit a high strained note. Pascal swung around.

'Why?' he said. He could scarcely speak. 'Why, in God's name do you do this?'

'Because it's the truth. Do you think I'm totally blind? After my miscarriage I knew exactly what you were thinking. You were thinking you needn't have married me, after all.'

'How can you say that?' He advanced on her, white-faced. 'I was here. I did everything possible. I found us this apartment – you said you wanted this apartment. I gave up job after job – for six months, longer, I scarcely left your side. My mother tried to help.'

'Oh don't bring your bloody boring mother into this. Your mother thinks like a French peasant. She thinks childbirth's nothing. She expects a woman to give birth easily, like some bloody animal in a farmyard. What does she understand?'

Pascal bit back an angry reply. His mother had come up to Paris, had stayed several months. She had tried hard to help Helen after the miscarriage: she had shopped for her, cooked for her – and been insulted for her pains. He looked at his wife, and his face hardened.

'Forget that then,' he said. 'Distort everything. There's one thing even you can't forget. We had Marianne.'

A tiny spasm of pain tightened her face. She made a shaky gesture of the hand, then regained control. 'Ah yes. We had Marianne. I finally gave you a reason to stay with me. Thanks, Pascal.'

She turned away and began to lay the table for Marianne's tea. She shook out a tablecloth, found a bib, a child's plate, Marianne's special spoon. Pascal felt a sense of pain and bewilderment. Some of these charges were old, some new and they left him wary. He had been down this particular road so often before. He could go to Helen, and hold her; she would cry. Later, a day later, two days later, it would begin all over again.

Perhaps she had been expecting him to make just such an overture, because when he did not, it angered her. Two patches of colour rose in her cheeks. She stopped laying the table, looked up at him.

'I always knew,' she said, on a tight, shrill note of control. 'Right from the very beginning. Before you married me – I knew then. I knew there was someone else, at the back of your mind. Well, at least she has a face now. I'm glad I've seen her. And she has an interesting face, I'll say that much. A lover in tow, of course, but I'm sure that won't worry you. He was so much older than she was, and your little Genevieve didn't seem very keen.'

Her use of Genevieve's name made him flinch. His face became pale with anger. He turned, and moved towards the door. 'That's enough.' He could not bring himself to look at her. 'I'm going out. I'm not listening to this any more.'

'Just tell me, was it really an accidental meeting, Pascal? Or did you know she was in Paris? Was it planned?'

'No, it damn well wasn't planned. I told you. I had no idea she was here. I haven't seen her in years.'

'I'm sure you'll make up for lost time.' She smiled. 'Take my advice. Pursue her to London. Maybe then you'll learn the lesson I've learned, the hard way . . . '

Pascal was in the doorway. He stopped. 'Lesson? What lesson?'

'Perfection doesn't exist, Pascal. And if it does, it doesn't last. So fuck around in London. Have your affair. Then you'll find out how it feels.'

'I do not understand. I do not damn well understand . . . '

'You will. Because you'll find out she's not the person you imagined, just the way you weren't the person I imagined. Try it, Pascal.' She gave a thin tight laugh. 'Find out how it feels to fuck a dream.'

He could still hear the words, their precise intonation. They repeated themselves, and again repeated themselves. They invaded Gini's living-room. Pascal looked around him blankly. He had been asked a question, and he had not answered it. Gini was still watching him expectantly. In the interval how many centuries, how many seconds, had passed? Helen's advice had never been taken, and one of the many reasons for that was a residual fear, still with him, that her final remark might be true.

He turned back to face Gini. She continued to stroke her cat; Napoleon purred. Gini bent to him affectionately; one gold strand of her hair mingled with his marmalade fur. Pascal thought: *She does not look like a dream, or an invention; she looks as I remember her: actual, exact, real.* 'London?' he said. Gini smiled; the time-gap then must have been short between question and reply. How odd, the distortions of the mind.

'Yes, London,' she replied. 'You must have come here, very often. You never called.'

'I know.' He gave an awkward gesture. 'Superstition, maybe.'

'Not anger?'

'No, not anger. Never that. I was angry when you left Beirut. Not afterwards.'

'Truly?'

'Truly.'

She gave a sigh. 'I'm glad.'

There was a silence. Outside the rain still fell, and Gini listened to the rain. It was lulling, peaceful; she could feel a new contentment, creeping up on her. She closed her eyes, then opened them. Pascal was still standing, watching her, his manner awkward.

'You're tired,' he said. 'It's late. I ought to go . . . ' But he hesitated. 'You'll lock the door after me? Bolt it? You promise me?'

'Of course.'

'Gini, I mean it. I don't like to leave you alone, in a basement flat.'

'Pascal, I'll be perfectly fine. I told you. I've never had a break-in, and—'

'And you've never been sent a pair of handcuffs before,' he said. 'Gini, take this seriously. This story on Hawthorne. It's a story about sadism. With women as the victims.'

'We don't even know if the story is true . . . '

'Maybe not. But someone knows where you live. Whoever sent those handcuffs knows where you live. If they know that much, they probably also know you live alone.'

'Pascal, don't.' She rose and crossed to him. 'You're adding two and two and making ten.'

'Oh no.' He looked down at her gently, touched her face, then drew away. 'I have an instinct for trouble. And I can feel it coming. I know.'

There was an obvious concern in his voice and his eyes, and Gini was touched by it. Looking up at him, she said, 'No-one's safe, not these days, Pascal. Not me, not you . . . '

Something flickered in his eyes, some glint of amusement or irony. 'Oh I know that,' he replied. 'Believe me, I know.' There was a tiny pause, a beat, as if he waited for her to pick up some meaning in this remark, then Pascal turned to the door. 'I'll call you in the morning, at eight?'

'Eight would be fine.'

'I'll pick you up around eight-thirty. We can be down at that courier office by nine.'

Still he lingered. Gini, who wanted him to linger, stared at the floor.

Eventually, still awkwardly, he touched her hand. 'Good night,' he said.

'Good night, Pascal.'

She closed the door behind him, and bolted it, as promised. Then she stood for a long while, looking at her own warm, familiar room. Something about it puzzled her, and it took her some time to understand what it was. Then she realized. It was the same room but depleted. It lacked Pascal's presence. It felt a thousand times emptier than it had ever felt before.

XII

The next morning, they were at the ICD offices in the City at nine. Susannah quickly gave them the information they needed.

'Handcuffs?' She looked first at the woman journalist, then at her photographer companion. Both looked pale and strained, as if they had slept little the night before. The woman worked for the *News* and this little episode was not the kind of publicity ICD needed.

'I'm most awfully sorry,' she began. 'Obviously, if I'd had any idea . . . And she seemed such a nice woman, as well. Anything I can do, in the circumstances . . . of course. I remember her very well. And I have the details on computer, right here.'

The meeting lasted half an hour. Pascal and Gini were in Belgravia shortly after ten. It was raining again. Pascal parked the motor bike. They walked the length of Eaton Place twice before they admitted the obvious. The beautiful blonde claiming to be Mrs J. A. Hamilton had given a plausible, but false address. There was no 132 Eaton Place. They tried Eaton Square and Eaton Terrace without success. They returned once more to Eaton Place. The rain stopped, then started again.

'*Merde*,' Pascal said, looking along the line of discreet expensive white-stuccoed houses. '*Merde*. We might have known it. I'll check the phone number that Hamilton woman gave – if her name *was* Hamilton, which I doubt. You try knocking on doors. Describe her, mention the coat. It's worth a try. She could live in the neighbourhood. Something might jog people's memory.'

There was a telephone box across the street. Pascal made for that. Gini walked slowly along the road. She examined the houses to right and left. Their white façades were immaculate, their iron railings perfectly preserved. There were window-boxes here, expensive curtains and blinds, an atmosphere of affluence. A few minutes' walk from the fashionable shops of Sloane Street, a brief taxi-ride to Harrods or Harvey Nichols, it was the perfect address, no doubt carefully selected, for a woman delivering parcels dressed like a fashion-plate in *Vogue*.

An idea was coming to her, a route she could explore next. Meantime, she would try knocking on doors. She could see Pascal down the street, on the telephone, gesturing. When he had arrived at her flat that morning, he had looked tense and exhausted, and she had wondered if he, as she had, had spent a wakeful night. Now, even at a distance, she could see the familiar energy returning. He seemed to be arguing with someone; she saw him slam down the receiver and re-dial. She smiled to herself, and turned into the gate of the end house. Like its neighbours, its paint was new, its curtains smart.

Its owner finally answered on the third ring: a slender well-dressed woman with short dark hair. 'If it's about the jumble sale,' she said rapidly, 'you're too late. I did ring and explain. We spent *weeks* waiting for you to collect them. Now I've taken them to Oxfam. *Including* the Ozbek evening dress which is really the most awful waste—'

'It's not about the jumble sale,' Gini began.

'Oh God, it's not religious, I hope?' The woman looked harassed. 'If you're one of those Mormons, or those Witness people, I'm afraid it's no good. We're all C. of E. here.'

Gini explained. The woman looked inclined to close the door, but grew more interested as Gini described the coat.

'Sable? Good Lord . . . Tall – and blonde?'

'Very recognizable.' Gini smiled. 'We roomed together in college. She always was vague. Such an idiot, giving me the wrong address . . .'

The woman frowned. 'Well, it could be one of the other

172

Eatons, I suppose. There's quite a few. Eaton Square, Eaton Terrace—'

'I know. I already tried them. No luck.'

'Well, we've lived here three years, and there's certainly no-one like your friend in this street. Actually, most of the neighbours are getting on – or foreign. You know how it is – oh, sorry I don't mean American.' She smiled. 'Arab. Quite a lot of Japanese. That sort of thing.'

'Could she have stayed here some time – or visited . . . ?'

'Well, of course, it's always possible. Hamilton, Hamilton – no, I'm sure there's no-one of that name that I've met. Why don't you try Lady Knowles across the street? She knows everyone. She's lived here yonks . . . '

'Yonks' turned out to be thirty years, and Lady Knowles knew no resident by the name of Hamilton either. The description evoked no response. Gini tried five other houses, then returned to the bike. Pascal was astride it, the helmet under his arm. He looked gloomily up at the sky.

'Does it ever stop raining in this country?' he said.

'Not in January. No.'

'No luck?'

'None. A total blank, just as we expected. You?'

'Nothing. The number she gave doesn't exist. No listing for any J. A. Hamilton, male or female, anywhere in London. So. That's that.'

'Never mind. That girl at ICD was very useful. We've got an address for McMullen now.'

'In Venice.' Pascal sighed. 'That's three hours away, minimum – and I'll bet he's not there.'

'And Johnny Appleyard. I told you, I *know* Appleyard. I can always get hold of him.'

'He's a gossip columnist?'

'No. Not really. A tipster for gossip columns, among other things. The kind who keeps in touch with Hollywood gynaecologists, so he can tell the *National Inquirer* a movie-star's pregnant about one hour before she gets the results of her tests.' Gini made a face. 'He's ubiquitous. A creep.'

'Appleyard. Appleyard.' Pascal frowned. 'Why send a parcel to him?'

'I don't know. But I can call and ask him. He knows me. Jenkins is always using his stuff. I've talked to him on the phone several times. I've met him once – no, twice.'

'And McMullen? In Venice? In January? Why would he go there when Lise Hawthorne was so anxious to keep him in London?'

'He might have connections in Venice. Besides, it's a quiet place in winter. A good enough hiding-place, if he wanted to disappear.'

'He hasn't disappeared.' Pascal met her eyes. 'Or not effectively enough. Someone knows where he is. And sent him a parcel. Just like us.' He ran his hands through his hair. The worried look returned to his face. 'Who's the puppet-master?' he said. 'I would like to know who's pulling the strings. Someone is.'

'Who's jerking us around, you mean?' Gini smiled. 'No-one perhaps. It could all be coincidence.'

'I think not. I feel manœuvred.' Pascal glanced away. Further along the street, a black car pulled into the curb. Its engine was left running; no driver or passenger emerged.

'I feel watched.' Pascal frowned.

Gini shivered, and drew her greatcoat tighter around her. She glanced towards the black car; she could just make out two occupants, a man and a woman. As she watched them, the man took the woman in his arms.

'We shouldn't be paranoid,' she said, turning back to Pascal. 'It's an occupational disease. Let's concentrate on what we do next.'

'I think I know what we're *supposed* to do,' Pascal began. 'Go chasing off to Venice, the same way we came chasing over here. I get the feeling that someone's trying to delay us, or waste our time. Now, we could go to Venice – except it's Friday today, and we're supposed to be meeting the Hawthornes tomorrow at your stepmother's house. I don't want to miss that.'

'Neither do I. I want you to meet Hawthorne. In the flesh.'

'So, first I'll check if this Palazzo Ossorio has a telephone. I have a friend who works for the Italian phone company.'

'And at least we do know the Palazzo Ossorio exists,' Gini put in. 'Unlike Mrs Hamilton and her house here. It must be a real place, it must *be* there – that parcel was delivered, after all.'

'Exactly.' Pascal frowned. 'I suppose we *could* go to Venice today. But if we did, we'd be very tight on time. I suppose it's just possible we could go to the palazzo and find McMullen there – but I doubt it. It's too simple by far. And if he *isn't* there, we'd have no time to make enquiries, we'd have to get back. One problem with the flight – fog, delays – and we miss Hawthorne. No. It's not worth it.' He paused. 'Better to go the day after, Sunday morning, we could take an early flight, stay over in Venice, return Monday . . . '

His expression altered; a shadow passed across his face. 'If we did that,' he went on, 'I'd have to return via Paris. It's my visiting day. I cannot miss that. I see Marianne then.'

There was a silence. Gini looked away up the street. She was tempted to question him; she would have liked to offer consolation, even if it was only the opportunity to talk. She had tried that the previous evening, on their way to the restaurant: it had been a mistake. All personal questions met a wall of silence. Eventually, sensing bitterness and pain, she had stayed away from the subject. Pascal's defences were formidable: she could see he preferred them unbreached.

'All right,' she said at last, turning back. 'Let's plan on that. Venice on Sunday, why not?' She hesitated. 'Meanwhile, I think we should split up. I want to go back to the office. I want to check out Appleyard, plus one or two other things . . . '

'What other things?'

'Nothing. Just an idea I had.'

175

Pascal looked reluctant to accept this. He argued against it for a while, then eventually, with an air of resignation, gave in.

'Very well. Maybe you're right. We save time that way. I'll go back to my hotel. Make some telephone calls. Try to fix up a meeting with McMullen's sister. Then I'll meet you back at your place. Around three?'

Gini glanced at her watch. 'Better say four. If you get there before me, you can let yourself in, unless you feel like burgling me, of course—'

Pascal gave her a cool glance. 'It wouldn't be exactly difficult. I've looked at your windows and doors. You know how long it would take me to break in? Five seconds flat.'

'Well, you won't need to,' Gini said sweetly, 'because there's a spare key. I keep it there for my upstairs neighbour. Sometimes she pops down to feed Napoleon. It's under the third flowerpot from the left.'

'And I suppose it was there all last night?'

'Yes, it was. I forgot. Anyway, it doesn't matter. You can't open a door with a key when the person inside has shot the bolt.'

'Impossible,' Pascal said.

He paused, about to put on his helmet. He looked into her face. He lifted his hand. With one finger, gently, he wiped the rain from her cheeks.

'Impossible,' he said. 'Headstrong. Obstinate. I thought that the very first day I met you. Twelve years later, and what do I discover? You're unchanged, Gini. And I was right.'

He put on the helmet. Gini confronted a black glass visor, an invisible face. He lifted his hand in a half-wave, then kicked the starter pedal. The engine fired; he wheeled and roared off down the street.

Gini waited until he was out of sight. She watched him round the corner, and for a moment his absence was intense in the street. Gini stood there for a while in the rain, waiting for the sensation of loss to abate. When she was sure she had it under control, she took the tube to Baker Street. From there, she walked north to Regent's Park, entering it at its south-western corner, through Hanover Gate.

The park was ringed by an outer circle road. She stood there, looking to right and left. To her right was a terrace of serene and beautiful Nash houses; to her immediate left were the buildings of the London Central Mosque. Beyond its pale stone, and the copper gleam of its dome, the road curved. On the opposite side of that road, actually within the park itself, was Winfield House, official London residence of the US Ambassador. It was no more than seventy yards to her left, shrouded from the road by a thick belt of shrubbery: John Hawthorne's home.

Crossing the street, she entered the park. She wanted to take a closer look at that residence, but she approached it discreetly, by a circuitous route. She wound her way through Regent's Park first, passing the boating lake and making for the bandstand where, in summer, military bands sometimes played. The rain fell heavily; the park was almost deserted; only a few stalwarts walked their dogs. The gaily painted bandstand, and the Guards' band playing in it, had been an IRA target once, years before. Several men had died here. She walked on.

She approached the ambassador's residence from the rear, where its large gardens bellied out into the park. From here too, the house was almost invisible. She could glimpse only its roofs and chimneys through the trees and evergreen shrubs which had been planted inside its tall spiked perimeter fence.

She circled the gardens, then returned to the road. She walked along the pavement directly in front of the house. There were two entrances, she saw, one barred off with reinforced gates, an entrance which looked unused. The other, to the north of the house itself, was flanked by a low lodge-type building. Aerials bristled from its roof; security cameras were trained onto gates and driveway; a window of greenish bullet-proof glass confronted anyone seeking admission to the house.

She was beginning to feel conspicuous. There were the watching cameras, and there were also security men. She glimpsed them to the side of the entrance lodge, in the driveway. They were wearing dark suits, and dark mackintoshes. There were two – no, three – leaning up against a black limousine, ostentatiously ignoring her as she passed.

At her desk in the Features department, walled in by word processors, and by the babble of other people's work, she telephoned. Mary first.

Her stepmother seemed surprised to hear from her again; she was rushing out to see friends, but she did have time to confirm that, yes, The Ivy was certainly a restaurant she'd recommend.

'Oh yes, darling,' she said, 'do take your friends there. I'm sure they'd love it. Try those little tomato tart things they do. Scrumptious.'

'I know it's always full in the evenings . . . ' Gini pushed a little harder. 'What's it like for lunch?'

'Oh I love it, I often go there before matinées. It's always full of actors, writers – lots of chums . . . '

There was a pause. Gini said nothing. Sometimes it was better not to prompt. 'When was I last there at lunch-time?' Mary went on. 'Let me think . . . I know! I took Lise there, that's right. It was just before Christmas. I remember, because she was going down to the country the following week. She'd never been there, for some reason, and she adored it – so it has her recommendation too. I knew it would be her kind of place. Not John's perhaps, but – what, darling? Your other line? Fine. I'll see you and your Pascal tomorrow night.'

Gini hung up. This she had expected, but it was as well to check. Appleyard next.

She flicked the cards on her Rolodex. Appleyard. There were two numbers, she remembered, two lines to his Gramercy Park apartment. She tried the first. She let it ring for a long time. Just as she was about to disconnect, the receiver was lifted.

The answering voice was wary. It was male, and sounded young. 'Yes?' it said. 'Who is it?'

'Hi. This is Gini Hunter. I'm calling from the *News*. Is Johnny in?'

There was a pause, a scrabbling sound. Then the voice said, 'Could you spell that, ma'am? The *News*? Which *News* is that? I'm just writing that down . . .'

Gini could hear the broad accent now. Midwest, she thought. She spelled her name, and explained she was calling from London. For the boy to take this down took an age. He sounded so pathetically anxious to be efficient that Gini was patient.

'I guess Johnny's out, then?' she said finally. 'Do you work for him? Do you know when he'll be back?'

'Oh, no. I don't work for him. Not exactly. I mean, I get to take messages, that kind of thing. I'm Stevey. Stevey with a "y". I'm Johnny's room-mate, his friend. I guess we haven't spoken before, but I've been living here a real long time.'

Of course: it came back to her then, some malicious reference Jenkins had made to Johnny Appleyard's current toy boy, encountered on Jenkins's last New York visit: *A face like a young Rudi Nureyev, my dears. Semi-literate, and oh-so-anxious to please. He spent an entire evening telling me about pig-breeding – sorry, breeding hawgs. Tedious? It was fucking tedious. Johnny picked him up at Penn Station, yes, straight off the train. Couldn't resist his bum, apparently. I said, Johnny give me a break. He's straight out of a Steinbeck novel. He's still got straw in his hair.*

Gini hesitated. She said: 'Stevey? Of course. That's right, I remember now. The last time I saw Johnny, on his last London trip, someone mentioned your name.'

'They did?' The boy seemed pleased by this. 'That would be the trip Johnny made last fall, I guess . . . I nearly came along on that trip.'

'You did, Stevey?'

'Sure. I was real excited. I've never been overseas. We had it all planned out, but I guess – well, it's pretty expensive. Johnny changed his mind . . .'

Indeed, Gini thought, given Appleyard's rumoured behaviour on trips to London, a devoted farm-boy might have cramped his style. She felt a shaft of pity for the boy.

'So, tell me, Stevey, when do you expect Johnny back? I need to talk to him urgently.'

'Well, that's kind of difficult to say . . . ' He hesitated, and his voice took a dip. 'You see – I don't know where he is right now. He just took off real suddenly – and since then, he hasn't phoned.'

'Oh I see.' Gini could hear unhappiness and anxiety in Stevey's voice. Gently, she said, 'He just took off, Stevey? You mean he's been gone – what? A couple of days?'

'More than that, ma'am. He left December twenty-seventh. I was expecting him back that evening. He's been gone now ten, eleven days . . . '

Gini wrote down the date; she tensed. It seemed an unusually long time. An absence of a few nights might be understandable enough, given Appleyard's predilections, but ten days? 'That's quite a while, Stevey,' she said, keeping her voice casual. 'I guess you must be getting pretty anxious. Maybe some story came up . . . '

'I don't reckon so, ma'am,' he said cautiously. 'He'd have told me, he always does. And then, he'd have phoned. He always phones to collect his messages. Even when he's out of town.'

'You mean you've no idea where he is, Stevey? I really do need to get hold of him. You've no idea at all?'

There was a long silence. Eventually the boy said, in a reluctant way, 'Well, he did send me a fax. But that was five days ago. And it was a weird kind of fax, too.'

'Weird in what way, Stevey?'

'He didn't tell me where he was – just said he'd be in touch. It was typed and Johnny always writes his faxes by hand. Also, he spelled my name wrong. He put "ie" on the end, not "ey". Johnny would never do that.'

Gini frowned, and made a note of these details. She said quickly, 'Well, I expect there's an explanation, Stevey.

Maybe he was in a hurry, and got some secretary to send the fax . . . '

'Maybe. I guess so.'

'Do you know where the fax was sent from, Stevey?'

'No. There was just a whole lot of numbers along the top. When I read it, with my name wrong and all, I figured someone else sent it. Maybe someone Johnny was with, you know . . . '

Gini could hear the misery in his voice clearly now. Stevey feared he had been ditched – and that was always possible, of course. A new lover was one explanation for ten days' absence – but it was not the only explanation. 'I imagine some new story's come up,' she said carefully.

'I'll bet that's it, Stevey. You'll see. Something big – some exclusive, and he had to follow it up, drop everything, rush off. You know how it is.'

'I guess so. Now I think about it, he did say . . . You could be right . . . '

The attempt at cheerfulness seemed to have worked. Stevey now sounded less miserable.

'Next thing you know, he'll be walking in the door,' Gini went on, in an encouraging voice. 'Meantime, Stevey, if I can't speak to Johnny, you might be able to help. You've been at home all this week?'

'I sure have.'

'Was Johnny sent a parcel? It would have arrived Wednesday morning, by courier. Sent from England. A neat-looking package, brown paper, string, sealed with red wax?'

'A package? Yes, he did. Wednesday – yes, Wednesday, that's right. I took delivery . . . ' He broke off. 'How d'you know about that? Was it you who sent it? Why? That wasn't a funny thing to do. No way! It was sick. I—'

'Hold on a second, Stevey.' His voice had risen angrily. 'I didn't send that parcel and I don't know who did. But I was sent one too, exactly the same, special delivery. And mine wasn't amusing either.'

'It wasn't?' he said, in an uncertain way.

Gini hesitated; sometimes, to acquire information, you had to provide some yourself. 'Stevey. They sent me a pair of handcuffs, no message. I live alone. I wasn't laughing either, when I opened it up. That's why I'm calling Johnny now, because I've had a big fight with the courier company, and they said he was sent a parcel too . . . ' She paused, but the boy made no response. 'I wanted to find out what they sent Johnny. Whether he had any idea – who was playing games . . . ' She paused again. Still silence. 'Stevey,' she said, gently again, 'I really want to find out who did this, and why. Tell me something. Johnny's package, did you open it for him, by any chance?'

Another long silence, then the boy finally replied. 'I did open it,' he began, in a hesitant way. 'I guess – well, I was anxious about Johnny. And on the form with it – it said "Birthday Gift". Johnny's birthday isn't in January, it's in July. So I looked at it, and I looked at it – and Johnny still didn't call. I left it a whole day. Then I opened it. I thought it might explain where Johnny was.'

'Stevey . . . ' Gini paused. This would have to be coaxed out of him, she could tell. 'Will you tell me what the parcel contained? It could help me . . . '

'I can't do that, ma'am.'

'Well, was there a message with it, Stevey?'

'No. No card. No message. I looked.'

'Was it handcuffs – the same as mine, or something else?'

'Something else.'

'Something similar, Stevey? Something with unpleasant implications, maybe? Something that might have made Johnny upset?'

'I don't know. It might have made Johnny mad – he might have laughed. I . . . ' He hesitated. 'It's kind of embarrassing, ma'am—'

'Stevey, stop calling me ma'am. It's Gini, all right? And I can promise you, I won't be embarrassed. I'm a reporter. I don't embarrass easily. Please, Stevey. I really need to know. I want to nail them – the people who did this.'

'OK – Gini. If you put it like that . . . ' He paused,

and then lowered his voice; Gini could almost hear the blush.

'It was underwear. Ladies underwear. You know – with frills, black lace. Panties, ma'am. The kind they advertise in the little ads in the back of magazines. Or you can send off for them, out of a catalogue, because they wouldn't sell them, not in any decent store—'

It was years since Gini had encountered Midwest prudery. She was amused, and touched. That any boy exposed to Johnny Appleyard's world could remain this naïve and unsullied was remarkable. Quickly, she cut him off.

'It's OK, Stevey. I'm getting the picture. Do you have sisters, Stevey?'

'I do, ma'am.'

'And these weren't the kind of underwear your sisters would wear, right?'

'My sisters?' His voice rose in indignation. 'No way, ma'am. These were whorehouse stuff, fancy, slit all the way up the front, and . . . ' He broke off. There was a ringing noise in the background, then a pause, then Stevey came back on line. 'I'm sorry, ma'am. That's someone at the door. I'll have to go now.'

'Fine. One last thing, Stevey. I still need to talk to Johnny, urgently. When you next see him or speak to him, will you ask him to contact me? This is my home phone number, and my fax . . . '

It took a painfully long time for these numbers to be taken down. Gini could hear a doorbell continuing to peal in the distance.

'I'll be right there,' Stevey shouted. He read the numbers back.

'That's great,' Gini said. 'Thank you, Stevey, for all your help.'

'You're welcome, ma – Gini,' he said, and hung up.

Gini sat for a while, considering this information. A ten-day silence from Appleyard; whorehouse panties. What, if anything, could she deduce from that?

*   *   *

183

Her next call was the Fashion department. Someone there could surely help with an aspect of this story which had been bothering her ever since the interview with Susannah. Why had the mysterious woman delivering the parcels been so memorably and so identifiably dressed?

On her way to the Fashion department, she passed the picture editor's office. Its door was open, and the room beyond was crowded with men. Half the Art department were in there, together with a large and raucous contingent of sub-editors. Men spilled over into the corridor, blocking her path. Something was being passed from hand to hand. There were whispers, cat-calls and whoops.

Gini stopped. One of the men, slightly sheepishly, handed her some photographs.

'Lamartine.' He grinned. 'We're finalizing the lay-out. Jenkins has just given the OK. We're running them tomorrow. What d'you think?'

'Come on, Gini,' someone shouted from beyond. 'Give us the woman's viewpoint. Hot or not?'

There was more laughter. Gini looked down at the pictures. Sonia Swan was instantly recognizable, and so was the well-known French Cabinet Minister in her embrace. The movie-star's platinum hair was tousled. Her lips, newly injected with silicone according to the latest gossip-column reports, were parted. Her throat was arched back. She was naked to the waist; the Cabinet Minister was cupping her right breast to his mouth; his tongue lapped her nipple.

'This one we can't run on the front,' said the picture editor, emerging from his office, and peering at the picture over Gini's shoulder, an assessing look on his face. 'Alas. Inside, *maybe*. Jenkins is in two minds. He thinks it's a bit hot. We're running them over six pages. Dynamite, yes?'

'Pascal Lamartine took these?' Gini said, feeling sick.

'Who else? The whole place was guarded. Guards, fucking Dobermanns, would you believe? God knows how he got in there, but he did.'

'Well, the frog can kiss goodbye to the Presidency

after this.' The picture editor grinned. 'Serves him right, arrogant little shit. Hey, hey, there might be a headline there . . . ' He turned to his companions. 'Sonia Swan – and the minister is a write-off. *Swan Song*, how about that?'

Groans greeted this attempt. The crowd of men ebbed back into the picture editor's office. Gini handed the pictures back to a lingering assistant editor. She offered no comment, but made her way down the corridor to the lift. When its doors opened, she found herself face to face with Nicholas Jenkins. Jenkins radiated importance: his senior minion, a Glaswegian by the name of Daiches, stood next to him, adoring and taking notes.

'It's OK,' Gini said, 'I'm waiting to go down.'

'No, you're not.' Jenkins beckoned. 'Up. In my office. Five minutes. Daiches, tell them I need that quote from the Elysée in the next fifteen minutes. Is the minister's position secure, yes or no? They've had all fucking day. If they can't get a statement, then fucking well invent one. Just say "spokesman", but make it convincing. Who does frogspeak?'

'Holmes can do the Elysée style. Or Mitchell.'

Daiches, widely known in the offices as Jenkins's representative on earth, was mild of manner. This was deceptive. He was Jenkins's eyes and ears. When Jenkins decided to dispense with a journalist's services, a not uncommon occurrence, it was Daiches who did the firing. His pale eyes fixed on Gini as she entered the lift. He had never liked her, and she detested him. He acknowledged her presence with a slight inclination of the head.

'Mitchell,' Jenkins said. 'Put Mitchell on to it.'

Daiches nodded, and made a note. They had reached the fifteenth floor. Jenkins strode across the Wilton. Through the outer office, through the inner office, where a number of waiting hacks leaped to their feet.

'Not now. Not now. No time. Daiches, deal with this.' Jenkins brushed them aside. He strode ahead into the sanctum, Gini at his heels. One of his telephones was ringing. Jenkins snatched it up. With exquisite politeness, he said, 'No fucking calls for the next fucking five minutes, all right, Charlotte?' and slammed the receiver back in place.

He sat. Gini stood at the other side of the desk. Jenkins acted power energetically for another minute or two, consulting papers on his desk. Then he looked up.

'Progress?' he said.

'Yes. Quite a bit.'

'You've found McMullen?'

'Maybe. We have another address. I—'

'No time. Never mind the details. Check back with me Monday when all hell isn't breaking loose.' He moved a piece of paper half an inch. 'What about telephone sex?'

Gini hesitated. 'I've put that to one side, for the moment. I thought you wanted me to concentrate on the Hawthorne story. You said—'

'Jesus. You can walk and chew gum at the same time, can't you?'

'Sure, Nicholas.'

'Then do it. Work on them both.' He looked down at his desk in an irritable way. 'Anything else?'

It was characteristic of Jenkins when in this mood, to summon employees, then behave as if they had sought him. Gini, who knew this, ignored his tone.

'There is one thing,' she said. 'Who else here knew about the Hawthorne story, Nicholas? Anyone?'

'I told you. You, me, Pascal. That's it.'

'Daiches doesn't know, for instance?'

'How many times do I have to say it? No, he does not. This was my lead, and it's my story. I've nursed it along, and I've kept it under wraps . . . What are you smiling at?'

'Nothing, Nicholas. I just thought it might be my story too. And Pascal's, of course.'

'So it is. So it is. So just don't fucking well cock-up on it, that's all I ask.' He paused. 'And tell Pascal to watch his fucking expenses, this is a newspaper, not the Royal Mint.'

'Sure. I'll tell him that, Nicholas.'

She began to move towards the door. Jenkins gave her a sharp look.

'You and Pascal? You're getting along all right? Good chemistry?'

'Fine so far. Yes.'

'Well, just keep it that way. I need teamwork on this. You could learn a lot from Pascal.'

'I'm sure I could.'

'You've seen the Sonia Swan pictures?' He gave her a sudden smile of entirely fake benevolence.

'I saw them just now.'

'Great, aren't they?' He rose to his feet, crossed the carpet, and put his arm around her shoulders. 'Give Pascal a message from me, will you? Tell him I'm increasing the print-run tomorrow by another hundred thousand. That Sonia Swan – we've got her going down on that minister, you know, right in front of his bodyguard. Can you believe that? Pascal got the whole thing. We can't run those pictures, obviously, but we can hint . . . ' He patted Gini's shoulder. 'Meantime, word's out. The *Mail* and the *Express* are pissing gallstones. Tell Pascal. Another hundred thousand on the print-run. Tomorrow, we wipe those ass-holes off the streets.'

The Fashion department was in chaos, as usual. They were arranging a big shoot.

'Ball-gowns in Siberia?' Gini said.

'Not quite.' Her friend Lindsay, the fashion editor, smiled. 'Bondage clothing, couture-style. In Martinique.'

'Lindsay, listen. I need a favour. Would you call Chanel for me? They know you. They'll talk to you. Chanel, and a couple of other places. There're some details I need checking on a sable coat—'

'A *sable* coat? Bloody hell.' Lindsay grinned. 'You do know there're virtually no furriers left in London, do you? Not even Harrods sells fur coats now.'

'There must be some, Lindsay.'

'Yes. One or two. What else?'

'Nothing difficult. Chanel accessories. A Chanel suit. *This* Chanel suit, and these accessories.'

Gini produced the relevant page from December *Vogue*. Lindsay looked at it.

'Oh, I remember that. It's lovely. Classic stuff.'

'Yes. Well, I want to know who bought it. Ditto the coat. And I can give you a pretty exact date.' Gini explained the details. When she had finished, Lindsay gave her a speculative look.

'Why?' she said.

'Never mind why, Lindsay. Just help me out. Please. If I try they'll clam up. If you try it'll take you ten minutes. Less.'

'Oh, very well. Since it's you . . . ' She paused. 'Hey, I hear you're working with Pascal Lamartine, is that true?'

'Who said that?'

'I can't remember. Someone. I thought – Gini gets all the luck. Tall, dark, handsome, smouldering. *Deeply* sexy.'

'Cut it out, Lindsay. He's not my type.'

'I'd load his film for him any time.' Lindsay laughed. 'D'you think I could persuade him to do a fashion shoot?'

'No, Lindsay, I don't.'

'Pity. It could be interesting. Seriously. It's erotic. Snatched photographs, the paparazzi approach . . . '

'Secrets are erotic, that's why . . . '

'*And* how. Have you seen his Sonia Swan stuff? Unbelievable. Can you imagine, lying in the undergrowth, shooting that? D'you think he gets turned on by it?'

'I haven't the slightest idea.'

'Defensive, defensive . . . OK, OK. I'll say no more. I know when to back off. I thought you said he wasn't your type?'

'Lindsay . . . '

Lindsay gave Gini a close look, then made a gesture of mock-surrender. 'Not another word. I swear. Your secret's safe with me.'

'Lindsay, just call those stores for me, would you?'

'Right, right. I'm doing it now. Don't bite my head off.'

Lindsay began to work the phones. While she did so, Gini began to leaf through the directories of fashion models. Susannah at ICD was a good witness, she thought, an exceptionally good witness – and what had been her first reaction when the woman delivering the parcels walked into reception? That she might have been a model. Gini frowned: the woman wasn't Mrs J. A. Hamilton. Susannah's instincts might have been correct.

The pile of directories was thick: *Models One*, *Storm*, *Elite*. Face after beautiful face. She stared down at the pictures. The ease with which these women could transform themselves was unnerving; here was Evangelista as a blonde, a redhead, a brunette . . .

After a half-hour, Lindsay completed her calls. She crossed to Gini, and handed her a sheaf of notes. She was looking pleased with herself.

Gini read down the notes with astonishment, and with mounting excitement. She made no comment. When she had finished, she said: 'You're totally certain about this?'

Lindsay nodded. 'One hundred per cent. I know the manager at Chanel well. I spoke to him personally. There's no mistake.'

'Would they often make an arrangement like that?'

'For a famous customer? A good customer? Sure, what do you think?' She looked at Gini closely. 'You look excited, Gini – and I know that look. Is this important? Something big?'

'No, not really . . . ' Gini said hastily. 'Just background. Thank you, Lindsay. Oh, and don't mention to anyone that I was asking, all right?'

'Not a word, I promise.'

Lindsay began to turn away. She yawned and stretched, and looked at the chaos of this office. She had hours of work yet. She glanced back at Gini, who was now gathering up her various belongings. She frowned: she could see that there really was something wrong, for

189

Gini's features wore a tight, closed, angry expression, as if she were concentrating on her work, yes – but also fighting something else. It was unusual for Gini to be irritable, she thought: they were good friends, in fact Gini was her closest friend at the *News*, and she could rarely remember seeing Gini this tense.

As Gini reached out for her coat, Lindsay stopped her. 'Hey, slow down,' she said. 'Gini, are you OK?'

'No. Not really. No. I'm not.' Gini gave her a quick look then shrugged. 'You know how it is. This damn place . . . '

'Coffee?' Lindsay looked at her closely. She and Gini were used to speaking in a kind of female shorthand in which the offer of coffee was also the offer to talk.

Gini hesitated. 'I shouldn't . . . maybe ten minutes . . . '

'I could use a break myself. Come into my office. It's less like bedlam in there.'

'All right. Thanks, Lindsay. I forgot about lunch. Coffee would be good. But ten minutes only, then I must rush.'

Lindsay smiled. 'You rush too much,' she said. 'One of your problems, Gini. What are you afraid of? Actually having some time to think?'

As soon as they were in Lindsay's office, and the door was closed, Gini began to pace. She had just put on her overcoat. Now she took it off again, and threw it down on a chair. It was followed by the scarf she had been wearing, by the overflowing bag she always carried, by a pair of scarlet gloves. Lindsay watched this divesting take place, and put the kettle on to boil. In the cruel fluorescent office lighting, Gini's fair hair took on a silver tinge; the light sharpened the planes of her face.

'*Christ*, Lindsay,' she said, still pacing. 'I can't stand it much longer. This place, the *men* who work in this place . . . '

Lindsay said nothing. Gini appeared oblivious to her in any case, and she had never, on any occasion in the past, seen Gini behave like this. Normally, Gini kept herself on the tightest of reins. Lindsay had often wondered how much that cost her. Well, now she saw, she thought.

'How can you bear it, Lindsay?' Gini swung around to look at her, then began pacing again. 'The endless looks, the sniggers, the language, the innuendo, the little pats when you're at the Xerox machine, the taking orders from men like Nicholas Jenkins, and all the time, you can never ever say what you truly think, because you're a *woman*, and so you have to tread so damn carefully, can't lose your temper, can't speak your mind, because if you did, *if* you did – then that would just prove all their points?'

She swung around again. 'Don't you think you'd like to speak the truth, just occasionally, tell them what you really think of them and not care that then they'll put you down as hysterical, or having your period – or being a ball-breaker. Oh, Lindsay, don't you ever wish you could stop acting, acting, just for once?'

There was a silence. Lindsay made the coffee. She put it on her desk. Gini continued pacing. With a sudden angry gesture, she undid the band tying back her hair, so it fell across her shoulders and across her face. Lindsay watched her toss that hair back, and continue to pace, as if this office were a cage. She looked a little crazy and a little magnificent, Lindsay thought, like a maenad, like some wonderful and anarchic embodiment of female force.

'I have my own domain, Gini,' she said eventually. 'It's a female domain, so I'm safe. They don't trespass in here and if they do I can tell them to fuck off. They don't mind. Fashion doesn't threaten them.'

'Oh God, oh God.' Gini suddenly banged her hands down hard on the desk. 'Sometimes I'd like to blow it all up, this entire place.'

'What brought this on? Come on, Gini, if you're so keen to speak your mind, do it for once.'

'What brought it on? Jenkins brought it on. I loathe and detest and despise him. And I loathe and detest and despise myself for working for him. I should have walked out, months ago, and I didn't. I should never have listened to all those lies and promises of his. Next month, Gini, maybe then we'll send you overseas . . . ' She did a vicious and accurate impression of Jenkins. 'Meantime, Gini, if you'd just get on with this really key story. It's about telephone sex lines, for God's sake . . . '

'OK.' Lindsay lit a cigarette. She could not quite believe this was happening, that Gini – quiet, cool, controlled Gini, who so rarely so much as lost her temper – was acting like this. 'OK,' she said. 'What else?'

'What else? What else? Those damn voyeurs, for a start, passing those Sonia Swan pictures around. "Hey, Gini, hot or not?" They make me sick. Sick. Not one of them has the nerve to stand up to Jenkins and say, Why the hell are we running this stuff? Who cares if Sonia Swan screws the entire French Cabinet, so what?' She drew in a deep breath, and swung around to look at Lindsay once more.

'*They* don't have the courage – and neither do I, do you see? I could have said that to Jenkins. I had the perfect chance up there in his office, and did I? No. I kept my mouth shut. Why? Because I'm frightened of him?' She paused, and then shook her head. 'No. It isn't even that. Because I'm working on something right now that I actually want to work on. And I didn't want to risk losing it. So I toed the line yet again. Yes, Nicholas. No, Nicholas. I hate myself.'

'And?' Lindsay said.

Gini met her eyes. She hesitated. Lindsay watched her fight herself, watched some angry internal struggle take place.

'All right,' she said finally. 'All right. It's Pascal Lamartine. Him above all. He took those Sonia Swan photographs, and I *mind*. I mind passionately about that.'

'Why?' Lindsay said, although she already knew the answer. It flared in Gini's eyes, it sprang from every feature of her face.

'Why? Because he's better than that. Much better. You know the kind of work he used to do. You know the kind of pictures he used to take. And now he does *this*. And he hates himself for doing it – I can see that he does,

192

Lindsay. It's destroying him. It's his own very special way of committing suicide, and I can't bear to watch it.'

She pressed her hands to her heart as she said this. Then she made a wild and angry gesture, as if she was relinquishing something, or giving up. She moved her head, and that astonishing hair flared with a bluish-white fluorescence. Lindsay waited, one beat, then two. Gini's gaze met hers, then faltered. She looked away.

Lindsay gave a sigh. She hesitated, then said, 'OK, Gini. Tell me. When?'

She was expecting Gini to say nothing at all. Or, if she admitted it, something like, last year, or six months ago. She did not.

'Twelve years ago,' she said, and began pacing again.

'Twelve *years*?' Lindsay stared at her. She could not remember Gini's having mentioned Pascal Lamartine's name, ever.

'Twelve years? You mean you were *fifteen*?'

'Yes. But he didn't know that. I lied about my age to him.'

'Where was this?'

'In Beirut.'

'How long, Gini?'

'Three weeks.'

'That's all?'

Gini swung around angrily. 'It was enough. Believe me, it makes no difference. He's still here.' She pressed her hands against her chest. 'He's in my heart and in my head. I can't get him out. I never could.'

Lindsay hesitated. She herself was ten years older than Gini; she suddenly felt that the age gap was much greater than that.

'So what happened, Gini?' she said, more gently, and thought: *How can I explain? How do you talk someone down from this?*

'What happened? My father happened. He found out.' Another turn, another wild gesture of the hand, another swirl of hair.

'And that was it?' Lindsay said. 'Nothing afterwards?'

193

'Just silence,' Gini said. 'Silence. I met him once, by accident, in Paris. But that was all. Just silence until I met him again this week.'

'The kind of silence that talks?'

'On my side. Not on his. He married. He had a child. He divorced—'

'Did he contact you then?'

'No.'

'Did you hope he would?'

'When I let myself. Yes.'

Pride flared in her face. She turned away. There was a long silence. The lights flickered. Outside the rain lashed the windows. Several storeys below a truck passed. In the outside office a telephone rang. 'Three weeks then twelve years of silence?' Lindsay said slowly. 'Gini, do you want to get hurt? Again?'

'No. I want God to intervene and make everything wrong come right.' Her voice dipped then rose more strongly. 'Failing that – if it comes to a choice, something happening and getting hurt, or nothing happening and I stay safe – then I'd risk getting hurt. I'd even *rather* get hurt. I wouldn't care.'

'That's not very sensible.'

'Sensible?' She turned and stared at Lindsay. Her face contracted for an instant. 'I don't even know what that means any more. It isn't part of the equation. I can't go through this inch by inch, measuring this, accounting for that.'

'So tell him then,' Lindsay said, a little sharply.

'No. No. I can't do that. That's the one thing I can't do. You don't know what he's like. He's just been through a horrible divorce. The last thing he needs is more problems.'

'Rubbish.' Quite suddenly Lindsay lost sympathy and patience. 'He sounds like a first-class bastard to me, Gini.'

There was absolute silence. Gini's face went white.

'Why do you say that? Why?'

'Oh come on, Gini. *Grow up*. Three weeks in a war zone

and a twelve-year silence? That sounds like indifference to me. Exploitation and then indifference.'

'You're wrong. Totally wrong. It wasn't like that. He was never like that. He isn't like that now.'

'You're sure?' Lindsay said more kindly. 'Or is that you, Gini, writing his script?'

There was another silence, briefer this time. Then Gini whirled about. She began putting on her coat, her gloves, her scarf. She picked up her bag. Lindsay said nothing. Gini had not touched her coffee, and was now hesitating by the door, a stricken look on her face.

'Lindsay . . .'

'Yes?'

'I'm sorry. I shouldn't have hit you with all this. It's – it's not something I've ever talked about before.'

'I can see that.'

'You won't tell anyone else? You promise me?'

'Come on, Gini. You know I won't.'

Gini did know that; she hesitated again, then made a little half-pleading gesture of the hand. 'Lindsay, what you said about indifference – is that really what you think?'

Lindsay sighed. She rose, and they hugged each other. 'Come on, Gini,' she said. 'You know I can't judge. Outsiders never can. But just reading the *facts* – no, they don't look good. I'd be lying if I said they did.'

'I suppose you're right.' Gini's face took on a closed, blank look. 'I mean, I always knew, in a way. Twelve years of silence. I had been dealing with it. Really, Lindsay, I'd almost put the whole thing right out of my mind. It's just meeting him again, so unexpectedly. It brought all the past back.'

'Just so long as you remember it *is* the past, Gini.'

'Yes. Except we *are* our pasts. He is a part of me . . .'

Lindsay began to protest, and Gini gave herself a shake. She smiled. 'No. No. You're right. Grow up. That's just what I should do. Thank you, Lindsay. Have a wonderful time in Martinique.'

A few minutes later, Gini left. She took with her the

directories for the model agencies. She crammed them into a carrier-bag, and hurried out of the offices.

It was past four o'clock. Rain was falling heavily, sluicing the streets. If she was quick, she could make it easily to the City and the ICD offices before Susannah left. Perhaps the woman who had delivered those parcels had indeed been a model, just as Susannah had assumed, a model hired to do an unusual job. Perhaps, if Susannah went through these directories, she would recognize the woman's face.

It was a long shot, but worth trying. Then, when she returned home to Pascal, she would have made more progress still. Another part of this puzzle would have slotted into place.

She stopped abruptly, in the middle of the street. Home to Pascal – why had she allowed herself to think that? She would be going home, to her flat, and Pascal might be there, but she was not returning home to *him*: it was vital she remember that.

She stood for a moment, the rain beating down on her head. Throughout the conversation with Lindsay she had known that Lindsay was correct in all she said, that she gave sensible and good advice. Her mind did not doubt that, but her heart did. *I loved him*, she said to herself. She let the words repeat, and repeat, until they were just a refrain, utterly meaningless, a fifteen-year-old girl's delusion, a delusion she should have had the strength to discard years ago.

When she was certain she saw that delusion for the foolish thing it was, she began to walk onwards. There were no taxis. All the buses were full. She walked the whole way back to the City, and she discarded the illusion, tossed it aside like a physical thing, into the grey water of the Thames, as she passed by Tower Bridge. She felt light, unburdened, and empty, insubstantial. She felt a quick furtive sense of betrayal, then walked on. The pain was intense.

XIII

James McMullen's sister was called Katherine, or, as she always insisted, Kate. She lived in a small three-storey house in Chester Row, Belgravia, leased at enormous expense from the Westminster estate. Modest enough from the outside, but in a prime residential area, the house was an extravagance. The lease had been purchased some twelve years before, when Kate had been younger, prettier, and still in demand as an actress. She had then been a household name, thanks to her twice-weekly appearances in a prime-time, highly popular TV soap.

Then, not six months after she'd signed the lease, that bastard of a producer had walked out on her, and two months after that her character started slurping pills and within a month – a little month, Kate thought vengefully – well, what do you know? Her character was dead.

And so was her career. This idea, not a pleasant one, recurred now and then. Kate pushed it to one side, or drowned it in a vodka tonic, whenever it popped up. The truth was, TV chewed you up and spat you out, but she refused to give up. She still found work occasionally. Any day now, in the very next post, the perfect script, the perfect part might plop onto the mat.

Meantime, she thought grimly, returning to Chester Row after an unsuccessful audition for a TV detergent ad, meantime this sweet little doll's house cost too much. But it helped to keep up appearances, and appearances mattered in this business. She'd taken great care with her appearance today, but had she got the job? No, she had not. And now, to add insult to injury, it was raining again. She paused to glare at the sky, then quickened her pace – her house was in sight now – and then stopped.

A man was standing on her doorstep, an extremely

handsome man, an utterly gorgeous man, just the kind of man she liked. He was tall, with black hair worn rather long, designer stubble; long legs, narrow hips, tight black jeans, a black sweater, a black leather jacket. He looked moody and dangerous like a French movie-star. He looked like the kind of man who made love magnificently, then smoked a Gauloise in bed. He looked like trouble with a capital 'T' – and he was ringing her doorbell. She increased her pace rapidly. Things were definitely, but definitely, looking up.

She arrived at her doorstep out of breath. The man looked down at her. He had wonderful smoky-grey eyes, and an astonishing smile. When he spoke, the accent was the kind that made her knees weak.

'You must be Katherine,' he said. 'I'm a friend of your brother, James.'

Kate didn't give a damn who he was. He could have been James's sworn enemy for all she cared.

'My name's François,' Pascal said. 'François Leduc.'

'Oh, of *course* . . . ' The name meant nothing to Kate. She gave him a radiant smile. 'James is always talking about you. God, this rain! Come in, come in and have a drink.'

'So, François,' Kate McMullen said, 'there's vodka and then there's vodka. Is vodka all right?'

Pascal inclined his head politely. '*Merveilleux*,' he said. He looked around him. The drawing-room was dated, cluttered, and not very clean. There were dirty glasses everywhere. Paisley shawls were draped across the sofa, scripts were piled on the coffee table, the room smelled of joss-sticks or possibly marijuana. *Chelsea*, he thought, circa *1968*.

He was surprised to find himself inside it so easily, but Katherine McMullen seemed unconcerned. She was rummaging around for clean glasses: a tall woman, slightly over-weight, once attractive perhaps, but now in her mid-forties aging badly. She had long thick hair, heavily hennaed and tied around with a hippie-ish scarf. A great many bangles on her arms; she was wearing too much make-up and a voluminous multi-layered dress. Over this she wore an embroidered Afghan coat; it was a get-up some twenty years out of date, and Katherine McMullen very nearly carried it off. She gave a grand gesture of the hand – chipped nail polish – and waved the vodka bottle.

'Sit down, sit down. Oh, Christ, I'm out of tonic. D'you mind it straight?'

Pascal said straight would be fine. He said, 'Thank you, Katherine.'

'Kate,' she cried dramatically, removing her coat. 'Please. Kate.'

'I am not inconveniencing you, I hope?'

'Christ, no. Quite the contrary. I've had a bitch of a day. I was auditioning. I need cheering up.'

'Ah yes. Of course. James told me you were an actress.'

'For this TV ad. This stupid, pathetic, feeble detergent ad. Two tarts in a kitchen. That's what they call them, those ads. And this little creep from the agency, five feet nothing, covered in pimples, aged approximately *fifteen*, can you imagine? He says I don't look right. He says I have the wrong accent. The wrong accent!' She made a violent gesture.

'So I told him – "Listen, darling, any accent you need, I can do. I'm an actress, remember? You want Scots, I'll do you Scots. I can do Irish, I can do Liverpool, London, Manchester. I can do American. I can do Australian. If you really twist my arm, I can do you bloody Welsh." ' She plonked a very full glass of neat vodka down on the table in front of him. Pascal smiled encouragingly, waited for her to sit down, then sat down himself.

Interesting, he thought, the question of accents in this case: an English voice on the telephone to ICD, then an American delivering the parcels. It was something he must mention to Gini, Kate McMullen's boast.

'You must forgive me,' he said with studied politeness, as she reached for a cigarette. 'Turning up on your doorstep like this. But I was hoping to see James while I was in London, and I thought perhaps you could point me in his direction. I've tried several friends. None of them seemed to know where he was.'

'Oh, James . . . ' She gave him a slightly sullen look, as if this explanation bored her. 'Wouldn't we all like to know? I'm entirely pissed off with him, actually. He swore blind to me that he'd try to get back for Christmas. We always go home to the aged parents then – you know how it is. Well, bloody James never turned up. Guess who had to help stuff the turkey, and walk the damn dogs? Shropshire in December is not exactly my idea of fun.'

'Swore blind?' Pascal leaned forward to light her cigarette. 'You've seen him recently then?'

'Seen him? You must be joking. No such luck. I haven't seen James since last summer. He's far too busy to bother with me. Always rushing around, doing God knows what. No, he telephoned. Said he was going off skiing with some bloody boring friend of his. And *that* wasn't even true either, because I ran into the bloody boring friend at a party two nights later, and he hadn't even *heard* from James, not for months.'

'How odd. Maybe he changed his plans – went with some other friend . . . '

'Some other friend?' She gave him a wry look. 'You can't know James too well. James hardly has any friends. Not these days. He's turning into a bloody recluse.'

'But he did telephone you? When was this?'

'Oh God, I don't know – when was it? Before Christmas, obviously, but not very long before, because when he said he was going skiing, I told him he was cutting it a bit fine.' She made a face. 'That's when he swore he'd get back. Said he was only going for a few days. It must have been around December the nineteenth, twentieth, something like that. No, the twentieth, that's it. I remember, because it was the day my sodding agent actually bought me lunch. When James phoned, I'd just got back . . . '

She paused, looking at Pascal in a way that made him feel slightly alarmed. She leaned forward, revealing a considerable amount of cleavage. 'More voddie?' she said. 'No? Well, I'll just top mine up a bit.'

'So,' Pascal said, as she sashayed back to the drinks table, 'he never made it for the Christmas celebrations . . . ?'

'No. Nor the New Year. Not even a phone call. Daddy was *not* over-pleased. Mummy wept into the pudding and brandy butter. I had a lot of the thankless-child bit. Actually, I think Daddy's given up on James. When he was in the Army, it was OK – but since he left . . . '

'That's how I know him,' Pascal said firmly. 'Through the Army. That's how we first met. On a NATO exercise . . . ' He did a rapid calculation, then remembered the date on the photograph Jenkins had given them. 'Around nineteen eighty-eight, something like that . . . '

He wondered if McMullen's sister knew that a Frenchman was unlikely to be involved in a NATO exercise, but the anxiety was unnecessary. Clearly, the circumstances under which he had known her brother did not interest her in the least. She was the kind of woman, he began to realize, who became bored when the conversation did not concern herself.

'Oh really?' she said, pouring vodka. 'Well, of course James left the Army around then. Back then he was still the golden boy, apple of Daddy's eye, Sword of Honour at Sandhurst, all set to be a general, all that boring bit. Personally, I think it's all balls – Queen and country, all that antique stuff. Still, James always lapped it up. He'd have been just fine, when we still had an Empire. Still, enough of him . . . Tell me about yourself.'

She weaved her way back to the chair opposite. Pascal took a discreet look at his watch. It was almost three, and already dark outside. He would have to speed this up. He took another minute sip of the neat vodka.

'So,' he said, 'do you think James actually did go skiing? If he did, could he still be away? It's just—'

The return to the subject of her brother did not please her. She gave a shrug. 'Oh God knows. He probably did. Changed his plans at the last moment, went with some other people, joined a chalet party. It's possible. If he did, he'll have gone to Italy, that's for sure. That's where he usually skis, the Italian Alps. If so, he could be gone weeks. He's mad about Italy, always was. Especially out of season, when it isn't crawling with tourists. He could be anywhere – Florence, Venice, Rome, Sienna . . . Memory lane – James loves that. We spent half our youth trailing round bloody museums in Italy. That's how we spent our school holidays, staring at sodding paintings, while Daddy researched another book. Shit!' She had spilled vodka on the front of her dress. She mopped at it ineffectively, then gave Pascal an odd look. 'Daddy the art historian. The Titian-bloody-Tintoretto expert. Surely James mentioned that?'

The gear-change from amiability to hostility was swift. Pascal, who had encountered heavy drinkers many times, and was used to such sudden swerves, made a placatory gesture. 'Of course. The art historian. Yes.'

'So that's where he probably is.' She made a face. 'Either skiing, or sopping up culture. Take your pick. Why should he worry? James got Granny's trust fund. He doesn't need to suck up to sickening little ad men. He doesn't need to work for a living like the rest of us. James is rich.'

'Ah well, in that case . . . ' Pascal rose to his feet. 'I'll miss him, I guess. I'm not in London long . . . '

'You're not?' She gave him an unfocused look, then laughed. She tossed back another gulp of vodka. 'Oh well. I might have known. Too bad. *Salut.*'

Pascal edged towards the door. There he paused. 'I wonder,' he said. 'There's no-one else you can think of, who might know where he is?'

'Who have you tried?'

'A couple of people.' He mentioned names Jenkins had given him, whom he had called earlier that day. Kate McMullen gave a shrug; more vodka spilled.

'Christ. What persistence. That's about it. Who else? Oh, well, there's a guy called Nicholas Jenkins, and a loathsome toad he is. He was at school with James. He might still see him. I wouldn't think so.'

'Nicholas Jenkins,' Pascal said solemnly.

'Works at the *News*. Oh, and there's Jeremy Prior-Kent. They went to prep school together, they were at Christ Church together. He's an ass-hole too. Makes TV commercials, for Christ's sake. Not that he's ever seen fit to cast *me* in one of them, but—'

'I have his name. He's out of town . . . ' Pascal paused. He gave McMullen's sister a careful look. Her words were now noticeably slurred: it was worth the risk. 'And then, I think he mentioned once, there was a close woman friend, yes? American . . . '

'What, Lise? The beloved, you mean?' She rose and gave a harsh laugh. 'Oh sure, try Lise Hawthorne. I wish you luck.'

'I'm sorry?'

'Lise Hawthorne is a fucking stupid bitch. In my opinion. But then I don't know her very well. I'm allergic to super-sweet women. They screw men up. Try calling her, by all means, if you can get past the thirty-five secretaries. She may even know where James is, though for his sake, I hope not.'

'Why do you say that?' Pascal asked and he knew at once, it was a question too far, one enquiry too much. Kate McMullen swayed on her feet. She put down her glass with deliberate care, then gave him a narrow-eyed look.

'What is this? Who are you, anyway?'

'I told you. I'm a friend of your brother's. I was in London, so I thought I'd look him up.'

'The fuck you are . . . What is this? Questions, questions, James this, James that . . . What's going on? What the hell is this?'

'Look, I'd better leave, yes?' Pascal opened the door.

'Army. You said you were in the Army – you met James on exercise – is that what you said? You don't look like a soldier to me. You don't look like an officer. Your hair's too bloody long. Oh, shit.'

'Nevertheless,' Pascal gave a polite half-bow, 'Second Parachute Regiment, Captain Leduc. Since retired, like your brother.'

Kate McMullen was not listening. She lurched forward,

then stopped. 'That's what the other one said. Now I come to think of it. He said he was an army friend too. Jesus Christ, is this some kind of joke? Bring on the whole bloody platoon, why don't you? First an American officer, now a French officer . . . Who's next? Christ, send in the Khmer Rouge, send in the Foreign Legion . . . What is this? Why's James so bloody popular all of a sudden?'

Pascal turned back. 'An American?' he said. 'He was looking for your brother? When was this?'

'Christmas bloody Eve. Just when I was leaving for Shropshire.' She drew in a deep breath, then abruptly sat down. 'Oh fuck it,' she said. 'It's not funny. Just sod off.'

Pascal hesitated. He said, 'I regret, but—'

Kate McMullen threw her vodka glass across the room. It missed his head by half an inch. 'Piss off.' She gave him a venomous look. 'Who cooked this up? It's a joke, right? At my expense? Well, I don't fucking well find it funny, I can tell you that. Oh – hang on – I get it . . . ' She rose unsteadily to her feet. 'It's a *bet*. Between brother officers. Well, fuck you. Who wins? Just tell me that . . . '

Pascal began on some reply; Kate McMullen cut him off.

'Don't bother lying. I can imagine. The winner's the first one to score, right? You bastards. Wait till James hears about this.'

She broke off, fumbled her way back to the drinks, and slopped more vodka into a glass, then turned around. 'Still there? I told you. Piss off. Screw you . . . ' She gave him one last vicious glance. 'I preferred the American. He looked like hell but at least he took me out for a drink.'

The traffic was heavy, and the wet air thick with exhaust fumes. Pascal mounted his motor bike, and weaved his way between buses and trucks, heading north-east. Stopping at a traffic light as he approached King's Cross Station, he checked his watch. It was four now. He would be at Gini's flat within ten minutes. He had a lot to tell her, he was impatient to see her. By now, she would surely be back.

As he reached the station, however, all traffic stopped. Suddenly, there were police everywhere; the air was shrill with sirens, lit with flashing blue lights. An accident, another IRA bomb scare or an actual bombing? Pascal felt his heart contract. What if they had bombed an underground station again? What if Gini had taken the tube home?

He peered ahead of him, through the swell of traffic. People were spilling out of the station concourse, and being herded along the pavements by police. His anxiety redoubled; at the next intersection, inching his way forward, he turned off into a side-street. He roared down it – just in time. Glancing back, he saw barricades being set up. He headed north, approaching Islington through a hinterland of decaying back streets. He accelerated, just missed an incautious pedestrian, swerved, swore, and picked up speed again. At four-twenty he reached Gibson Square, and slammed on his brakes.

There were no lights on in Gini's flat. Anxiety tightened his throat. He ran down the steps to the basement area. In the darkness he scrabbled around the flowerpots, found the key, inserted it, and threw the front door back.

He ran into the living-room, switching on the lights, and calling her name, just in case she had returned. Then his eyes took in the room, and he stopped dead.

He stared around him, with fear, then anger, then disbelief. Gini had had visitors. And they had left a calling-card of a kind, a large one, an unusual one. There it was, four-square, neatly centred, on the top of her desk.

When Gini emerged from the Angel tube station, it was six. The pavements were crowded with office workers going home; she could hear the wail of sirens in the distance. Two ambulances passed, shooting the intersection's red lights. She could not wait to be home, to tell Pascal of her success. She began to run as she got closer to Gibson Square. When she reached it, the first thing she saw was Pascal's motor bike. Her heart lifted. She ran down the steps. The curtains were drawn, but the lights in her flat were on. It was good, she thought, to see that. She was so used to returning to dark rooms and silence.

She was calling Pascal's name before the door was half-open. The sentence she had been storing all this way home was already on her lips.

'Pascal, Pascal,' she called. 'I've found her – the woman who delivered those parcels. I know who she is . . . '

She crossed the tiny lobby, opened the door to the living-room, and stopped dead. She gave a little cry, staring around her in disbelief. Her flat had been rifled. More than that, it had been wrecked.

In the midst of the wreckage stood Pascal. He swung around as she entered, white-faced. The tension in the room was like a force-field. Gini felt herself collide with it. The next second Pascal was across the room. His arms tightened around her. He pressed her against him.

'Gini, Gini . . . ' he said. 'Oh, thank Christ . . . '

He was still wearing his jacket, and it was wet. Gini felt the slickness of wet leather against her face. Through the thickness of the leather, she could feel his heart beat. She closed her eyes, clung to him, and just for an instant let the past come swooping back. Pascal was touching her. She felt his hands against her wet hair, cradling her head. He began to kiss her hair, her forehead, then abruptly he drew back.

He held her a long time, at arm's length, still gripping her hands. He touched her face, and to her astonishment she realized his hand was shaking.

'There was another bomb,' he said. 'At King's Cross. I saw the police clearing the station. I just heard it on the radio. I thought – you could have come back that way. But you didn't. You're safe . . . '

She could see him, fighting down the emotion in his voice. Releasing her hands, he gave a sudden almost angry gesture. 'I'm sorry. It's a legacy from the war years. Bombs. Snipers. You see someone at breakfast. You find out they're dead that night. The suddenness of death. The fact that it's arbitrary, no-one's safe. Ever. I can't forget . . . '

'Pascal, it's all right. I remember too. I didn't come that way. I came straight home from the City. I . . . ' She stopped and looked away. Chaos surrounded them: possessions tossed in heaps. She saw herself stand and wait, all those years before: a square, bare room, hours passing, people passing, bombs in the distance, the rattle of machine-guns, all those Beirut hours when she feared for him. She hesitated, fought to remain steady, looked around the room. She said: 'Who would do this? Why? There's nothing here worth stealing.'

'I don't think theft was the point.'

He spoke flatly, and Gini knew there was something in his tone, some warning, but her mind couldn't catch it. Events were too fast, too sharp. Her home felt invaded; she felt invaded. She gave a little shiver, gazing around her with mute distress. This hurt: it hurt to think of strangers rifling her cupboards, going through her desk. On the floor, scattered, were all the bits and pieces that made a life: letters, postcards, tapes, books, photographs, diaries. Had they read her diaries, read her letters? She hesitated, then looked back at Pascal's white intent face. He was watching her closely, carefully, and she felt an instant's sudden panic, a sensation of defencelessness. She looked away: was that due to the break-in, or Pascal's momentary closeness, his embrace?

She took a few steps forward. In a flat voice, she said, 'I suppose I'd better call the police.'

'No.' Pascal moved, so he stood between her and her desk. 'No. Don't do that. I wouldn't call the police.'

'Why not?'

'Because this isn't an ordinary break-in, Gini. There's no sign of forced entry, for one thing. No broken glass, no broken locks.'

Gini stared at him. Her mind seemed to be working very slowly. 'You mean they used the key?'

'I think so, yes. If so, they were good enough to replace it. But Gini, it's more than that.' His face was troubled. He hesitated. 'In a minute, I'll show you. They've been everywhere. In the kitchen. The bathroom—'

'My bedroom?' She swallowed; she began to feel sick.

'Yes. There too.' He paused. 'But before we go in there . . . There's something else you have to look at. These were unusual thieves, Gini. Thieves don't usually leave gifts.'

'Gifts? I don't understand . . . '

'They left you something, Gini. They left you this.'

He moved slightly to the side as he spoke, and she saw it then, on the desk behind him. Another parcel, larger than the first. As before, it was neatly wrapped in brown paper; as before, the string was sealed with scarlet wax.

Pascal cut the string with a knife. Inside the wrapping paper, there was a box. Inside the box were sheaves of black tissue-paper. Inside the nest of paper was a shoe: one shoe, a woman's, made to fit the left foot. It was black patent leather; it had a four-inch stiletto heel. Inside the shoe was a stocking, also black, very sheer. She laid it out on the desk in front of them, her hands trembling slightly. There was a sharp intake of breath from Pascal. Gini stared down at the stocking, puzzled. It had a pretty lace-edged top. At first she thought it had been looped together in some odd way. Then she realized what Pascal had already discovered: the black stocking was tied in a noose.

She gave a low exclamation. Pascal's face became set. He picked up the shoe, then the stocking, and examined them closely. Both appeared new. The sole of the shoe was leather, and unmarked. Neither shoe nor stocking bore any maker's name.

Pascal turned to look at her. 'I know what you're thinking,' he said grimly. 'I'm thinking the same thing. You'd better try it on.'

Gini removed her own shoe. She inserted her foot into the black patent leather. It pained her instep, for she never wore heels this high. Even so, it was at once apparent to them both: this shoe might have been made for her. Cinderella's slipper. Gini looked down. She hated this shoe, she loathed this shoe, but she couldn't deny it was a perfect fit.

'I feared this,' Pascal said. 'I feared this . . . '

Gini kicked the shoe off. She bent, replaced her own, then straightened. 'They're trying to frighten me, Pascal. They want to frighten me off. Well, I won't let them do that. I know what they thought – they planned it very carefully. They thought I'd be alone, that I'd come home, alone, in the dark, and find this . . . ' She hesitated; an expression she did not understand crossed his face. Impulsively, she reached for his hands. 'Don't you see, Pascal? That's how they planned it? And they were wrong. I'm *not* alone. You're here, and—'

'Oh no, Gini. I'm afraid you're wrong. I think they knew I'd be here. This message is for both of us.'

'They can't have known that. How? It's not possible.'

'I don't know how they knew, but they did. Gini.' He hesitated. 'Come into the bedroom. You'll understand then . . . '

The bedroom, like the living-room, was in a hideous mess. All the wardrobe doors, all the drawers, had been opened. There were clothes tossed everywhere. There was a trail, from door to window, of all her most personal belongings: her underclothes, her nightdresses, make-up, jewellery, all tossed down in a heap. On the top of the pile, near the door, were the two photographs she kept by her bed. A picture of Mary, a picture of her father: their silver frames were buckled, their glass was smashed as if someone had stamped on them, and ground them underfoot.

Pascal, beside her, put his arm around her gently. 'Gini,' he said, 'Gini, try not to be upset. They like to smash things, to hurt. So far, so predictable, in an ordinary break-in, you might expect to find this. But look over here.'

He hesitated as if unwilling to continue, then gestured towards the bed. 'You see? It's random destruction, apparently. But there's nothing random about this . . . '

Gini followed his gaze. She gave a low cry. She felt the blood drain from her face.

They had arranged the display on the bed very carefully,

as an artist might arrange a still-life. There, laid out across the duvet, was a white nightdress, the nightdress she had slept in the previous night. Around it and upon it were her relics, those sad little secret mementoes of her past life. A dried flower, Pascal's one-page letter, a bullet-casing, the room-service menu from a Beirut hotel, a copy of *L'Etranger* by Camus. In the centre of the nightdress, carefully placed, was one small gold ear-ring. She took a step forward; the ear-ring glittered, struck the light.

She gave a small incoherent gesture, took another step forward, reached out her hand. Suddenly, almost harshly, Pascal jerked her back.

'Don't,' he said sharply. 'Don't touch the nightdress. Don't, Gini. I'll deal with it . . . '

'What? Why? I don't understand . . . '

He put his arms around her, and drew her away. 'It was a man who did this. At a certain point . . . it excited him, Gini. He's used your nightdress. Please, don't look. Come out of here, now.'

Gini broke away from him, she backed into the doorway. Her skin felt icy, then clammy and hot. She felt the room sway, start to shift. Pascal gave an exclamation of concern, and tried to take her hand, but she pushed him aside.

'Don't touch me,' she said. 'Please, just don't touch me!'

She ran away from him, into the bathroom, slammed the door and locked it. Then she knelt on the white tiles, surrounded by more detritus, broken scent bottles, shards of glass. She could hear Pascal outside, calling her name, hammering on the door. She knelt there shivering; the glass cut her hand, this space was cold and white and hideously shameful. After a while, Pascal stopped hammering on the door. There was a long, long corridor of silence, then she was violently sick.

She had forgotten how kind Pascal could be; she had forgotten, or not allowed herself to remember, how his kindness conveyed immense strength. When she finally emerged from the bathroom, he took her in his arms like

210

a child. He bathed her hands and her face. He took her back to the living-room, and made a space for her by the fire. He wrapped a blanket around her, and made her sit still. He fetched her sweet tea, and then a little weak whisky to drink.

'Sit there,' he said. 'Just sit there quietly, Gini. You're in shock. I'll come back in a minute. There's just some things I need to clear up.'

She listened to his footsteps as he moved around her bedroom, then the kitchen. She heard the backdoor open, the clang of the dustbin lid. Cold air eddied through into the room. Pascal returned. He was carrying Napoleon.

'Here, Gini.' He stroked Napoleon, then placed him on her lap. 'One cat. One wet, bedraggled, forlorn cat. He must have been outside in the yard all this time. Shall I get him some milk?'

Gini nodded. She held Napoleon close. He bristled his fur, and watched her warily with his huge topaz eyes. Then he curled beside her, and began to lick his wet fur into place. Pascal returned with a saucer of milk, which he placed near the sofa. Then he knelt down, so he was directly in front of her, and took her hand in his.

'Now,' he began, his voice gentle but firm, 'I want you to listen to me, Gini. Promise? You won't interrupt?'

Gini nodded.

'Where did you keep those things – those things from Beirut? Were they in your bedroom?'

'No.' Gini swallowed. She lowered her gaze. 'I kept them in here. In a box. In my desk.'

'Darling, don't. Don't. Don't cry.' He leant forward, and drew her against him. He stroked her hair, and waited while she wept. When the little storm of tears was over, he drew back from her gently. Gini couldn't tell whether he regretted that endearment or not. Perhaps it had been instinctual, accidental, just meant to be soothing. It was not repeated.

'Listen to me, Gini.' He clasped her hands. 'You understand what this means? Someone – whoever came here, or whoever sent them – that person knows a great deal. I think they knew about that key. They certainly know your shoe size. And they know how to hurt you, and me.' He paused, 'Gini, they know about Beirut.'

'That's not possible. *No-one* knows.' Her throat felt dry, and it was hard to speak. 'You. My father. Me. No-one else . . .'

'Does Mary know?'

'No. No. I never told her.'

'Would your father have told her?'

'No. He swore to me he wouldn't. He promised he wouldn't tell anyone. If he had told Mary . . . Pascal, Mary's so honest, so direct. If she knew, I'd have guessed.'

Pascal frowned. 'Then I don't understand. I've never discussed this. Not with anyone. Not even my wife. Gini, think. You're sure? No-one?'

Gini hesitated. She looked down. 'I told a friend today. At work. That I'd known you before. But that was the first time, ever. Truly, Pascal. And that can't have any bearing on this. I only saw her this afternoon. Late. It was past three o'clock.'

'That doesn't account for it. I was back here just after four. Damn it. It has to be your father, Gini. He must have told someone – it has to be. Unless . . .'

She saw him break off, hesitate, look around the flat, at the phone, at her desk.

'Unless what, Pascal?'

'Nothing. Never mind that now.' He turned back to her.

'There's something more important. Never mind how they knew for the moment. Take this.'

He held out to her some tiny thing, in his palm. When Gini looked down, she saw it was a small gold ear-ring.

'Put it on. Will you do that?'

'Now?'

'Yes.'

He watched intently while she fastened the little ring, then he reached across, and smoothed her hair back, took her hand in his.

'Did you really think you'd lost it?'

'No. I lied. I knew I had it.'

'Why lie, Gini?' There was consternation in his eyes. 'Why lie, to me of all people, about that?'

'I don't *know* why . . . ' She glanced away. 'Except, it looks sentimental. Foolish. I thought you'd despise me if you knew.'

'Despise you? You can't have thought that.'

'Well, I did.'

'Listen, Gini. I want you to understand something. The person who came here today . . . ' His voice hardened. 'So stupid. So crass. They think they can come in here, and smash something up. Cause pain by doing it. Well, they should learn there are some things you cannot smash. What you remember, what I remember – they can't alter that. They can't touch *us*, Gini – don't you see? Not unless we let them. And I don't plan on doing that.'

'You mean – they can't alter what we felt?' Gini raised her eyes to his. There was a long silence. As soon she said the words, she regretted their caution, that past tense. A glint of sudden amusement came into his eyes. Leaning forward, he kissed her brow, then quickly rose.

'Of course,' he said, in a dry tone. 'That's exactly what I meant. And now,' he gestured around him to the detritus, the chaos, 'now. I'll get rid of them. Exorcise them. I'll clean this up.'

They tidied the flat together. They replaced everything, books, tapes, clothes, china. Nothing was missing that Gini could see, but that did not surprise her. Pascal had been right: the reason for this break-in was not theft.

A residual feeling of sick distress remained with her as she packed away her possessions. She tried not to think forward to how it would be, later, when Pascal left for his hotel, and she was alone here. Looking around her when the rooms were restored to their original state, she found them altered. She felt none of the confidence of yesterday. Her home now looked fragile, easily violated, unsafe.

She would have liked to stay in, and eat at home, but

Pascal was curiously adamant, insisting they go out to a restaurant, a different restaurant.

They selected, at random, a Chinese one in the high street near by. This Friday evening, as always on Fridays, the place was noisy and crowded. When they were finally seated, Gini said, 'Didn't you like the other restaurant, Pascal? The Italian one?'

He gave her a cool glance. 'No, no. I liked it. It was fine. It just might be a good idea to avoid repetitive patterns of behaviour, that's all. I also think we should be careful what we say in your apartment.'

Gini stared at him. 'You can't mean that.'

'Oh, but certainly, I can. Someone is very well informed about us. It won't hurt to make their lives a little more difficult, yes?'

'Are you telling me there's a wire-tap on my phone, Pascal?'

'Gini,' he leaned forward, 'how much do you know about modern listening devices?'

'Not very much.'

'Well, forget all the films you've seen. Forget little bugs behind pictures, inside phones, under table-tops. They can still be used, obviously. But there are other devices too. With the right laser equipment someone could be in a car outside your house. They could be in a room across the square. And they could pick up your words as clearly as if they were standing three feet from you. Less. Even when you're alone, when you're not speaking, you're not safe. They can tell which room you're in. They can hear you pour a drink. They can hear the tap of your word-processor keys. They can hear you yawn. They can listen to your breathing when you're asleep . . . '

Gini shivered.

'You're beginning to believe it, aren't you?' she said slowly. 'You're beginning to believe that story about Hawthorne . . . '

'I certainly believe there *is* a story. Which may or may not be the story we were told. I also believe that we're being helped, and hindered. Both at the same time.' He paused. 'One thing I'm quite sure of. We're not the only people anxious to find James McMullen. There are others on his trail.'

He told her, then, about his meeting with McMullen's sister, and conversations with his friends.

Gini listened intently. When he had finished, she said, 'How strange. "The beloved" – that's what she said?' She frowned. 'Listen, Pascal. Two other parcels were sent, besides the two we received. And *both* those recipients are now missing.'

'Both?'

'Yes. Appleyard also. He's been missing for ten days.' She explained her conversation with Stevey. Pascal listened carefully, interjecting a question now and then. 'And there's more, Pascal, much more. I was trying to tell you earlier, when I came home . . . ' She leaned forward, her face now flushed and excited. 'I know who it was who delivered those parcels. Susannah identified her this afternoon.'

'Identified her? How?'

'From a photograph, a photograph in a directory of fashion models. I borrowed the directories from the office this afternoon. Susannah picked her out easily. She *is* American. She works for an agency in New York called *Models East* – it's one of the most successful firms. I called them, there and then, from the ICD offices. She's new, Pascal, just starting out. Her name's Lorna Munro.'

'You're sure?'

'Totally sure. Susannah was certain.'

'Did you get a number for her?'

'Yes. But it's maddening. She's in Italy, doing some work in Milan. I have a hotel number.'

'Have you tried it?'

'Yes. But she was out. So I left messages everywhere. With her booking agent in New York, at the hotel, with the magazine she was modelling for. She'll call back, Pascal, I'm sure.'

'And?' Pascal was smiling.

'And?' Gini replied.

'I can tell, there's more.' He gave a little shrug. 'The way your eyes light, the colour in your cheeks. Very tough, very tenacious, this reporter I'm working with. I'm not so sure I'd like her on my trail . . . '

'I don't like to give up.' Gini looked at him a little uncertainly. 'And neither do you, Pascal.'

'True.' He made no further comment. 'So what else did you find out?'

Gini hesitated. She drew out the notes Lindsay had taken down that afternoon. She glanced down at them, then frowned. 'Something I don't understand,' she began. 'It's a lead, but I don't understand it at all. That Chanel suit—'

'The one this Lorna Munro wore when she delivered the parcels?'

'Yes. I thought someone must have purchased it, but I was wrong. It was lent on approval, Pascal. It was out of the Bond Street shop for almost four days. It was collected on the afternoon of Friday December thirty-first and returned to the shop on the afternoon of Tuesday January fourth, after the long New Year weekend.'

He frowned. 'That's unusual?'

'Not necessarily. It's something they would only do for a very good customer. What *is* strange – very strange indeed – is who that customer was.' Gini leaned forward. '*Lise Hawthorne* requested the suit, Pascal!'

'Lise Hawthorne?' He stared at her in astonishment. 'You're sure of that?'

'As sure as I can be. The manager at Chanel knows Lise well. According to him, it was the ambassador's wife. She telephoned on the Friday morning. He spoke to her himself.'

When they left the restaurant, Pascal was thoughtful. He took her arm, and they began to walk back to her flat. It was still raining; the streets gleamed; as cars passed, their tyres hissed. Their footsteps echoed on the wet pavement. Gini could feel a little dread, inching its way towards her. She tried not to imagine how it would be, alone in her flat, after Pascal left.

At Pascal's insistence, they took a roundabout route. Halfway back to Gibson Square, in a deserted side-street, he paused.

'Your house, Gini,' he began. 'I've been thinking. Who lives upstairs?'

'My neighbour. Her name's Mrs Henshaw. She's one of the few original Islington tenants left. Back in the Sixties and early Seventies, this was still a poor area.' She gestured around them. 'Then it was discovered. Gentrified. Most of the original occupants left – or were persuaded to leave.'

'Bribed, threatened, you mean?' Pascal glanced at her.

'Oh, sure. Inadequately bribed. Or found their water was cut off, that they had no gas or electricity. It's not a pleasant story, what happened around here. Mrs Henshaw was luckier. They converted the basement flat, and then left her alone. But these houses are worth a lot of money now, so the landlord tried, a few years back, to get her out. She's lived in the house all her life. Her children were born there. Her husband died there . . . ' Gini's voice became angry. 'I did try pointing that out to the landlord. It cut no ice.'

'So what happened?'

'I found her a good lawyer. She has a protected tenancy. She's safe there, for life.'

'I see.'

They walked on a little further. Pascal said, 'So, this elderly neighbour, living alone upstairs, is she there at the moment? I've heard nothing, seen no-one.'

'No, she's gone to stay with one of her daughters.'

'But you have a key?'

'Yes, I do. Sometimes, you know, I do her shopping for her, pop in and see her. It's easier that way.'

'Fine.' Pascal glanced over his shoulder and quickened their pace. 'Give it to me, will you, when we get home? I'd just like to make a few checks.'

When they reached her flat, she silently handed Pascal the key. He left the room, and she heard him outside, mounting the steps to Mrs Henshaw's door. A creak of floorboards above her head, then absolute silence. She turned to the television set and watched part of the news bulletin. Anti-US demonstrations were spreading throughout the Middle East; at King's Cross the IRA bomb had detonated near a news-stand, spraying the concourse with shrapnel and broken glass. Forty-five people had been injured. Two – a woman and a four-year-old child – had been killed.

In comparison, her own fears seemed selfish and feeble. She switched off the set, angry with herself. She waited. There was silence from upstairs. She made herself walk into her bedroom, and she tried to pretend to herself that it was still, as always, her own familiar room. There were clean sheets on her bed, a clean nightdress was on her pillow. Pascal had disposed of the other nightdress. She told herself not to be foolish: it was gone.

She could still sense the presence though of the man who had been here. He had been through all her things, touched her clothes: he still tainted the air.

She backed out of the room, and across the small dividing hallway. She heard movement in the living-room behind her, and swung around.

It was Pascal. She stared at him. He was placing a blanket on her sofa, and some cushions in a pile at one end. Napoleon, who had taken to him, was rubbing against his legs. Once the blanket was in place, Napoleon jumped up onto it, kneaded, circled, and lay down. Pascal had not realized she was watching him. He smiled at her cat, reached forward, and replaced him on the ground.

'*Mais non* . . . ' he said, firmly. 'No, Napoleon. That's not the idea at all.'

'Pascal,' Gini said, walking forward. 'What are you doing?'

'Doing? I was checking upstairs. I found nothing and now . . . ' He gave her a sidelong glance in which there was a certain amusement he tried to disguise. 'Now I am making up a bed – *evidemment*.'

'Oh I *see*.' She hesitated. 'It's kind of you, Pascal – but really, I'll sleep in my own room. I have to go back there sooner or later. I'd better start now.'

'This bed is not for you. It's for me. You see? It fits me perfectly.'

He lay down on the sofa by way of demonstration. The sofa, a relatively short one, was not made to accommodate a prone man of six feet four.

'Pascal,' Gini said, trying to repress her laughter, 'it does *not* fit you. You don't look comfortable at all.'

'You're wrong.' He rose. 'I can sleep anywhere. On this. On the floor. It makes no difference to me. And don't argue. I'm staying here. I won't leave you alone.'

'You don't have to do this. I'm fine now. Sooner or later, I'm going to have to cope with this, and—'

'No.' Pascal had moved, and was now beside her. His expression was absolutely serious, and his voice, so amused a moment before, had gone cold.

'No,' he said again, and for the first time since Gini had met him again she felt the full force of his will. 'No,' he continued. 'You will *not* cope with this. You will not be alone. While we work on this story, I stay here. Those are my terms. Either that, or I call Jenkins right now, and get this story killed.'

Gini stared at him. The transformation in him startled her. He spoke in a new hard tone: there was no negotiation possible. Another aspect of Pascal she had forgotten, she thought, or suppressed, and as she gazed at him, other memories returned, she heard the old whispers in her mind.

'Would you do that?'

'Yes. I'd certainly make Jenkins pull you off the story. It wouldn't be difficult. He needs me, and he needs my pictures. He'd do exactly what I told him to do.'

'You mean you'd continue to work on it? Without me?'

'After this?' He gestured around the room. 'Of course.'

Gini looked away. She heard in her head all the old gossip, all the old rumours, in the press bar in Beirut. How Lamartine would do anything, anything to get a story. How he was conscience-less, a driven man. How he was a loner, not a true member of the pack. Stay away from Lamartine – that was the consensus, even among those journalists who liked him. Lamartine never shared his leads, never gossiped, allowed nothing and no-one to stand in his way.

She looked at him uncertainly. 'If you did that,' she began slowly, 'I'd fight back. I can talk to Jenkins, too.'

'But I'd win.'

He made the statement in a flat uncompromising way. Gini knew it was correct. She hesitated, then shrugged.

'Very well. Then I'd rather you stayed, obviously. I'm not giving up on this now.'

She broke off. It was not a very gracious acquiescence in the circumstances, and she realized she had hurt him. His mouth tightened.

'Fine,' he said, and turned away.

'No, wait, Pascal,' she said quickly. 'I *was* afraid to be alone, after this. I'd feel safer with you here – I can admit that . . . '

Pascal turned. He gave her a long considering look. It was appraising, and without warmth.

'If you thought I'd leave you tonight,' he said finally, in a quiet voice, 'you can't know me at all.'

XIV

Pascal lay in the darkness, on the sofa. The street outside
was silent. An hour passed, then another hour; he could
not sleep.

His thoughts went round and round the same treadmill.
He tried to force them back to work, to the Hawthorne
story, but they refused to remain there. They returned to
the past, to the present; they made him watch, with the
sickening despair of sleeplessness, the mess he had made
of his life.

At two he fell into a thin, jagged and insubstantial
sleep. He dreamed of his English lawyer, to whom he
had spoken briefly that morning, and then of his French
lawyer, who was dressed in the black gown he wore in
court. Their identities converged, merged: insubstantial
black forces pursued him. They followed him to Lebanon,
then to Africa; he saw a street he knew well in Maputo,
Mozambique. All around him, people lay dead. Those
still living reached out to him with thin hands from dark
doorways. *Shoot me*, cried a shape from one of those
doorways, but when Pascal raised his camera and focused,
this man too fell dead. He walked along the street, bending
over the bodies. The smell of blood was intense. He knelt
beside a small child, wearing a familiar dress. She was
lying face-down, and when he tried to turn her over,
he saw the child was Marianne.

He woke sweating, sure he had shouted out. The flat
was silent. Napoleon lay curled next to his feet. Pascal
knew these dreams, they were his old familiars; when
he slept, he was always close to deaths. He knew there
was no cure for them except activity. He knew that if
he tried to sleep again, they would return. They were
pitiless; they always came back.

He switched on the lamp, and waited. He watched the room, and reality, re-assert. He loathed and feared this free-fall of the mind in sleep; the way in which the past could rewrite itself, change shape. Sometimes dreams made nightmares of past events, as they had done tonight. At other times – and this he also feared – they took the actual sadnesses, and made them sweet.

They let him, sometimes, glimpse the might-have-beens of life. This Pascal hated most of all. At least, tonight, he had been spared that trickery. He rose, and began to pace the room. He made coffee, drank it, lit a cigarette. Work, sometimes, could divert him, and he tried that next. Quietly, fearing to disturb Gini, he played and then replayed McMullen's tape. He considered the interview with McMullen's sister. He read and reread the Hawthorne clippings. Opening the model agency directory Gini had showed him, he examined Lorna Munro's face.

Finally, with the persistence of exhaustion, he returned to that slip of paper found in a picture frame on McMullen's desk. He examined and re-examined the numbers and their pattern on the page. For a while he was sustained by a wild conviction that if he could just see them this way, turn them that way, he would decode their message, reveal their sense. An hour passed. A car swished by in the street. He tossed the paper aside, and admitted the truth: he could discern no pattern in these numbers, and no pattern in this story. If there was a way through, it was there in the interstices, some tiny pointer he had missed.

He returned to the sofa, and lit another cigarette. He lay back staring at the ceiling. He watched the smoke curl. After a while, as he had half-hoped, half-feared, the details of the Hawthorne story began to slip away. Cross-fade: he watched his own past shadow his mind, focus and take shape. A film twelve years old: there it was, frame by frame – a press bar in a five-star hotel, a box of a room by a harbour, a once-beautiful city. Lebanon, Beirut.

*   *   *

He was twenty-three years old, and this was his third Beirut trip. He had a growing reputation, and very little money. Two writers he had worked with in the past were now dead, so he preferred to work alone. On the day he met Gini, he had been back in Beirut two months. Two months of mayhem, lit by the cries of the dying. Two months of constant unrelenting heat. Two months without alcohol, or sex. When he was working he never drank and he never slept with women. This code, this puritanism, was mocked by friends and enemies alike. It made him conspicuous, but he did not care. It was *his* code.

It was 1981, July 1981 and one morning a friend took him to the press bar at the Hotel Ledoyen. The great Sam Hunter would be there, this friend said, and if Pascal minded his manners just for once, the friend – who had known Hunter in Vietnam – would ensure Pascal was introduced. Pascal shrugged and agreed. He stood on the edge of the group, ordered a mineral water, and watched Hunter perform. A thick-set aggressive American with a Harvard Yard accent. He was wearing Brooks Brothers clothes, smoking heavily, drinking bourbon on the rocks. It was eleven o'clock in the morning. Pascal watched Hunter contemptuously. He loathed the man on sight.

Eventually, the introduction was made. Hunter was gracious but dismissive. 'Sure, sure,' he said. 'I've seen your pictures. Who hasn't? Amazing stuff. But you want to watch it – that adrenalin sickness. One of these days you'll get too close. You'll get yourself shot.'

That was it. Hunter's attention span for others was short. He snapped his gaze away; the cronies joked and the sycophants prompted; Sam Hunter held court. This great Pulitzer prize-winner, Pascal thought, had gone soft. Men who had made their reputations, he implied, were not like ordinary mortals. There was always time for yet another bourbon on the rocks. If anything of any significance happened, one of his stringers, one of his street-boy network, would get in touch. Meantime, Lebanon was a small affair, an historical footnote. Sooner or later, the fighting would peter out. He'd filed a couple of reports, sure, but he was planning on leaving. Hunter had covered bigger wars than this one; he could coast.

Over in the corner, ignored, silent, the only female in a group of twenty men, was a girl – Hunter's daughter, someone negligently said. She was a daughter, Pascal noted, that Hunter did not bother to introduce.

Pascal edged past the man from UPI; he avoided two sweating Reuters men, a reporter from the Sydney *Morning Herald*, an Englishman from *The Times*. He positioned himself between his friend from *Le Monde* and a gloomy Russian, who spoke poor English, the representative from TASS. He took a closer look at the girl, and his French friend, following his gaze, gave a grin. There was more to this kid than met the eye, he said. Hadn't Pascal heard the story? Where the hell had he been this last week? Everyone else in the bar had. She'd been at some fancy English boarding-school, this friend said. One day, she'd just cut hockey or lacrosse or whatever damn game it was girls played at schools like that. She walked out, and turned up at six in the morning, unannounced, in Beirut.

Hunter had been regaling all and sundry with this story for the past few days: how he'd been roused by the hotel manager, how he'd come downstairs with a massive hangover, to find this kid in the lobby clutching her suitcase. Hunter, apparently, hadn't recognized her at first. He hadn't laid eyes on her in three years – the girl lived in England with his ex-wife – and in those three years, the girl had grown up, filled out . . . Here, Pascal's friend winked.

When he realized it was his only child, Hunter had not been pleased. He'd been all for putting the girl on the next plane back. The kid had dissuaded him, stood her ground – and Hunter changed his mind. He was like that. Her presence had amused him for a couple of days, he'd treated her like a lucky charm, a mascot. But now he was finding the girl's constant presence an irritant: the amusement was rapidly wearing off.

It was an interesting story, Pascal thought. Not too many teenage girls would fly out to Beirut in the middle of the night, get themselves from the airport through the city – through this dangerous city – and arrive in a strange hotel at dawn. His friend moved away to the bar, and Pascal turned back to study the girl again.

She was sitting to one side of her father in silence; since Pascal's arrival, she had not spoken once. She was tall, slender and boyishly dressed; Pascal put her age at seventeen, eighteen perhaps. She sat quietly, with an unconscious grace; her skin was tanned, and her somewhat untidy hair was sun-bleached. She wore it caught back carelessly at the nape of her neck; she was wearing khaki shorts, and an ordinary white T-shirt. On her feet was a pair of battered tennis shoes. From time to time, she would shift in her seat, glance towards the windows, glance back at her father, stretch. It seemed to Pascal that she longed to be outside, away from this crowded smoky room. Glancing towards the windows, her face became wistful; she crossed then uncrossed her long legs. She appeared not to notice that when she did so, she riveted the gaze of every man in the place.

Pascal moved a fraction closer, so he had a better view of her face. She had fine eyes, widely spaced. It was, he decided, a not unattractive face, but it wore an obstinate expression, as if there were elements in this room she disliked, but she was determined to ignore them, for her father's sake. Whenever she looked at Hunter, it was with a painful devotion. As Pascal watched, her father launched himself on yet another long wandering anecdote. The girl seemed embarrassed. She coloured, then stared at her feet.

Pascal's friend, returning, and seeing he was still watching her, grinned. Pathetic, wasn't it, how the girl worshipped that old windbag, her father? A little firebrand, too. She'd told Hunter apparently, in no uncertain terms, that nothing would make her go back to England. She intended to stay here and learn. Pascal's friend made

225

a face. Lowering his voice, half-laughing, he said, *'Pauvre petite fille. Elle veut être journaliste.'*

Pascal lost interest. The girl's ambitions were nothing to him. If she wanted to be a journalist, fine; it made a change from a model, or actress, or movie-star. He felt a sudden angry impatience; he was wasting time in this place.

He finished his drink, put down his glass, and left the bar. In the lobby of the hotel he paused, looking out into the white midday heat. From the distance, somewhere in the direction of West Beirut, came the chatter of machine-gun fire, then the muffled roar of an explosion. Another car-bomb.

The girl was at his elbow: Hunter's daughter was at his elbow. He had not realized this until, half-turning, about to leave, he found himself confronting accusing eyes, a pale fierce face.

'I saw you watching my father,' she said; no preliminaries. 'I know what you thought. You arrogant French bastard. How dare you look at him like that?'

In those days, Pascal's temperament was volatile. He could lose his temper very rapidly; he lost it then, at once. He looked at this stupid teenage girl, straight off the plane, a girl straight from some stupid boarding-school, a girl whose father he'd disliked on sight.

'You want to know why?' he answered her in English. 'Fine. I'll show you. Come with me.'

She hadn't expected this reaction, no doubt. It took her by surprise, so when he gripped her arm, and pulled her out of the hotel, she did not struggle or protest.

Pascal let go of her almost at once. He slung his camera bag over his shoulder, and strode off up the street. The girl followed him. He increased his pace. He already regretted this action, and would have shaken her off if he could, but the girl wasn't having that. She broke into a run, she was out of breath in the heat, but she kept pace.

Her tenacity angered him, as did his own foolishness. Even then, when the conflict was still localized, the streets of Beirut were not the place for teenage American girls.

He stopped; he said: 'Go back. Forget what I said. This isn't safe.'

'The hell with that.' She glared at him. 'Do what you said you'd do. You're not getting rid of me. I'm not going back.'

Pascal was tired. He had spent weeks under stress, with little sleep. Confronted with this fierce female obstinacy, his temper snapped again.

'OK. Have it your way.' He turned. 'Take a look at your father's unimportant little war. You won't find it in an hotel bar, any more than he will. It's just down this street.'

He turned the corner, and she followed him. As they rounded the corner, the dust was beginning to settle. The remnants of a car were skewed across the street. Huge chunks of masonry lay across their path; half a house tilted crazily against the skyline; there was a pile of rubble twenty feet high from which protruded a child's feet.

A water-main had burst: water gushed and pumped across the street. People were gathering: Pascal scarcely heard the screams and wails, he had learned to block them out, but the girl did.

Pascal had his cameras out. He worked with two – colour film in the Leica, the Olympus for monochrome. He had his eye to the viewfinder, on the attitudes of grief. Behind him, dimly, he was aware that the girl was still in the same place. Lowering his camera, glancing back, he saw her face register horror in slow motion. In slow motion she covered her ears, then her eyes, then her mouth.

There was a child-sized plastic sandal on the ground in front of her. It was red, cheap, thonged – almost all the Arab children wore them. She bent, and picked it up. Some men pushed past her. A woman dressed in black sank to her knees by the rubble, and raised her hands to the sky. The space became confused: people ran, pushed, shoved, began to claw at the rubble. Pascal could see the girl, then he could not see the girl. Masonry dust billowed. Pascal turned, became frantic, appalled by what he had done.

He ran in this direction, then that. People pressed.

He found her, finally, where the lamentation was loudest, where they were lifting what remained of a man onto a sheet of tin roofing, an improvised stretcher. She was helping them to lift the body, and getting in the way. A woman screamed at her in Arabic, then spat. The girl stepped back, her face rigid. She had blood on her hands, blood on her face.

When Pascal touched her, she did not speak. He put his arms around her, and pressed her tight against his chest. The tumult and confusion intensified. Her whole body was shaking. Her arms locked around his neck.

He could still hear the noise when he led her away. It pursued them down the streets. She stumbled, and he led on, walking blindly: when they were three blocks, four, five, from the scene of the car-bomb, he could still hear the turmoil in his head.

His room was over a bar, not far from the harbour. Outside, Pascal hesitated, uncertain, confused. The girl was clasping his arm. It was painfully hot in the street. He led her into the shade of the doorway: something was happening, and he could not tell what it was. Uncertainly he touched her face, then her throat. She looked at him. He helped her to the stairs. She stumbled as they went up.

When they were in his room, it seemed very silent, very empty, very white. The louvres were closed, and their shadows striped the floor. The air felt urgent. He pressed her back against the door, and kissed her mouth. She caught at his hands in a frantic way and drew them under her shirt, against her bare breasts. Neither of them spoke. He had never felt desire so intense.

Her hands were fumbling at his jeans, trying to unfasten them. She moaned a little. Lifting her shirt, he bent his head and kissed her breasts. She clasped his hand tight and drew it down inside her shorts; her cunt was wet.

She pulled him down to the floor, still kissing him. Her hair spread out across the floorboards. They fucked on the floor, still half-dressed. He came with his mouth on her mouth, his hands on her breasts. She gave a cry which sounded triumphant. He kissed her, then held her, then kissed her again. Her eyes were astonishing, the room was astonishing, the world was astonishing. Pascal, who never slept with women while in a war zone, looked at his changed life.

Back in France, between wars, there was a long trail of women; he liked women, who sometimes accused him of using them, and he liked sex. Like most people, he had experienced good sex, bad sex, memorable sex, indifferent sex – but this, he had never experienced this.

He stared down at the girl in bewilderment. From the distance came the rattle of machine-gun fire. The air in the room was stifling; both their bodies were slick with sweat. He looked down at her. He felt exultant, on the edge of some danger. He could feel the patterns of the world moving, altering, aligning themselves. They began to make perfect sense, perfect shape.

This and this and this and this. The long slow attitudes of love-making. He bent his head and kissed her breasts. He hardened inside her, and without withdrawing, began to fuck again. He felt a determination, an absolute determination, to make her come. She was not, he thought, very experienced but Pascal was; he was moved by her clumsiness, her awkward timing, her innocence of technique.

'Like this,' he said. 'Like this. No, more slowly. Don't fight me. Yes, yes . . . '

And slowly, stroke after stroke, it became sweet. Pascal forgot the tricks of pleasure, and the ways in which the correct touch, or word, or rhythm could make that pleasure increase. He pushed into some oblivion, a dark place, and she went with him. It was frantic, then calm; first a kind of war, then a kind of peace. He reached across, found a pillow, raised her up on it, thrust deeper. When she came, she shuddered against him. Pascal was close to climax himself, but he forced himself to wait. He watched her abandonment move like waves of light across her face. She closed those astonishing eyes, and arched her throat. He put his arm under her neck, and brought her mouth up to his. He could feel her cunt pulse, and when he came he felt he came for ever. Lying beside her, becoming calmer, he thought: *I do not know her name*. He began to stroke her hair, he clasped her hands. He kissed and licked the salt on her thighs, and her belly, and her breasts. There was blood on her thighs. She tasted of iron, and sweat and sex. He kissed her thighs, touched her, then drew her up. He held her close, and met her eyes. It felt like drowning. He could feel the waters closing in above his head. He showed her his hand, which was sticky and wet with blood.

'You should have told me,' he said. 'I didn't understand it was the first time.'

'Would it have made a difference?'

'No.' He hesitated, then admitted the truth. 'Nothing would have made any difference. Not once we were in this room.'

'Before that,' she said. 'On the stairs. I knew then. I knew in the street . . . '

'So did I.'

'I'm glad.' There was a triumphant candour in her face. 'Today you showed me two things. Death and this. I'm glad, glad, glad you did that . . . ' She broke off, then frowned. 'I thought I hated you,' she went on. 'At the hotel. I thought I hated you then. But I didn't. Just the opposite.' She raised her eyes to his with a childlike directness. 'Is it always like that? Like this?'

'Never, in my experience,' Pascal said.

Later, considerably later, they left the hot little room, and went out into the cool of evening streets. They walked by the harbour, and watched the fishermen prepare their nets. They ate dinner by the harbour, and watched darkness fall, and the city behind them become a place of shadows and moving lights. They talked. Pascal could remember, afterwards, how they talked, but never what they said. He felt a sense of absolute communication; he sat watching her and wanting her across the table. He thought: *How strange, so this is how it happens –*

without warning. This is how love feels, this is what it's like.

They had to touch each other, across the table, by the harbour, walking back through the streets. He had to clasp her hand, stroke her arm; in the dark, at a street corner, desire mounting, he had to kiss her mouth, open her blouse, kiss her breasts.

They fucked again then, with a desperate urgency, in the darkness against the wall of an Arab tenement, her legs locked around his waist. They went back to his room, and still he wanted her. At three in the morning, he took her back to the Hotel Ledoyen, and he still could not leave her. He went up to her room. They talked, made love, talked: they had to be careful, she said, they had to be quiet. It was an expensive hotel, but the partition walls were thin.

He remembered her father then, but her father was quickly dismissed.

'Don't worry, don't worry,' she said, and a shadow passed across her face. She clasped Pascal's hand tightly. 'He never cares where I go or what I do. Anyway, I'm eighteen now. It has nothing to do with him.'

And so it went on, day after day, night after night. It never once occurred to Pascal that she might have lied, or misled him. It was impossible: when he looked at her, when he touched her, he doubted nothing. Her eyes mirrored the love and need in his. When he looked into them, he saw only truth, a perfect mirror image of the love he himself felt. It filled him with desire, and with a measureless contentment.

Day after day, night after night, week after week. They had no sense of time, time now could expand or contract. A day together passed in a second, an hour apart felt like a century. When Pascal held her he felt he held the future: there was the rest of their lives, in his arms. Sometimes, he could see, she looked ahead and feared; sometimes she would share his blithe optimism, but at other times she would doubt. The summer was passing. Her father would not let her remain in Beirut for ever. He was already planning his own return to the States.

'He'll make me go back to England,' she said.

Pascal clasped her in his arms. That was out of the question, he replied. 'No,' he said. 'We'll go back to France. We can be married in France. I want you to meet my mother, my friends. I want you to see my village. It's very beautiful. It's in the South, in the hills. My father is buried there, in the little graveyard by the church. We could marry in the church, then drink wine in the cafés, dance in the square. Darling, I want you to see my home, to see Provence . . . '

He could see all these events and these places as he spoke of them, and he thought she could see them too. They would light her eyes and transfigure her face. But then, a few hours later, or a few days later, he would see that belief drain away, and a curious sadness return to her face.

Once or twice he wondered if there could be some difficulty, or some doubt which she refused to express, but whenever he questioned her, she would deny this. He could not understand how she could seem to hesitate, or fear, when for him their future was so vivid and so inevitable. Perhaps, he thought, she doubted him, doubted his love for her? He found that idea unbearable. Waking once, seeing her standing by the shutters, her lovely body striped with dawn light, her face sad and thoughtful, he felt his heart contract. He must have used the wrong words – words were the problem: they were too small, too inexact.

'Darling, don't be sad. We'll find a way,' he said, and drew her back to bed. When she was there, in his arms, he spelled it out for her as exactly as he could. He told her again that he loved her and always would.

'This cannot change.' He caught her to him. 'If it could then nothing has any meaning, nothing.' He touched the tiny ear-ring she wore, then bent and kissed it. 'You should have let me buy the ring,' he said. 'I wanted to buy the ring. I wanted you to wear it. I don't care about ceremonies, pieces of paper, priests. When we marry it will alter nothing. You are already my wife.'

She believed him then, he was certain. He could see belief, blinding, in her face. That blindness, of joy and desire, and love, they both shared – later he came to understand that. It made the rest of the world recede. It never occurred to him, nor – he thought – to her, that others were less blind, that they might talk. Talk, however, they did. And one night, when Gini was at her hotel, and he was returning late, around three in the morning, from seeing Arab contacts he used in West Beirut, he returned to that small room by the harbour, and found Sam Hunter sitting on a chair behind the door. Pascal did not see him at first. He was staring into the room beyond. The room had been trashed.

There were very few possessions in the room, and there was very little furniture, but what there was had been smashed. The shutters were open, and in the moonlight, in that strange eerie cold white light, Pascal could see how effectively someone had done this work.

The single lamp, a chair, a table, lay broken in pieces. Film coiled across the floor. Pascal's spare cameras lay smashed in fragments. His photographs, his precious photographs, covered the floor like fallen leaves. They were crumpled, slashed, ripped. In the centre of the room, the bed had been stripped. The sheets, stained with the evidence of the previous night's love-making, had been laid out on the floor, as if made ready for some inspection by the police.

As Pascal entered the room, and stopped, staring at this destruction, Hunter rose out of the darkness by the door and lurched to his feet.

He reeked of liquor. Pascal could smell the bourbon at four feet. Hunter wasted no time on preliminaries. He swung a punch at Pascal's head, missed, almost fell over, then righted himself. He propped himself against the wall. The moonlight caught his face, a wet blur of rage.

'You fucking bastard,' he said. 'You goddamned fucking sonovabitch. You've been screwing my daughter. She's

233

fifteen fucking years old. She's still at fucking school. Jesus Christ, you bastard. I'll kill you for this.'

He came at Pascal again, fists windmilling. Pascal stood absolutely still. He thought – *Fifteen* – and one of the random blows connected. Hunter was a big man, a heavy man, and though he was drunk, there was force behind the blow. It connected with the side of Pascal's head, and Pascal reeled back.

The anger then, swelled by sudden pain, made his mind blank. He looked at the sheets, and the torn photographs, this desecration both of Gini and of his work. It took thirty seconds, if that, then he swung around and hit Hunter back.

It was, after that, an unequal contest. Hunter was the heavier of the two, and the slower. Pascal was lithe, strong, young, and fit. Hunter had once boxed for Harvard, but Pascal had grown up in a small village, where no-one used the Queensberry Rules. He smashed his fist blindly into Hunter's face, punched him low in the stomach. Hunter attempted to grapple with him. He grunted, made a grab, lurched against Pascal with his full weight. Pascal hit him again; Hunter grabbed his throat. Pascal punched him hard in the neck, then kicked him in the ribs. Hunter made a choking noise, and slumped. He fell to his knees and crouched there, breathing heavily. Blood was smeared across his face. He levered himself slowly to his feet, then lurched to the door. He stood there, breathing heavily, dripping blood on his Brooks Brothers shirt.

'You piece of shit,' he said at last. 'You mother-fucker. Just wait. I'll get you for this.'

And, of course, he did. Pascal saw Gini just one more time, the following morning, at the Hotel Ledoyen. Her father was present throughout the interview, and the circumstances of that interview Pascal had no wish to recall even now, twelve years later.

It lasted half an hour. By noon Gini was on a plane, under escort from Hunter, leaving Beirut.

A day later, his commissions began to dry up. The *New York Times* called, then the *Washington Post*, then

Time. For two years after that, Pascal sold not one single photograph to any major outlet in America. He neither forgot, nor forgave Hunter for this. He felt, for Hunter and for those Hunter could influence, the deepest and most bitter contempt. It was from this period in his life, as he knew, that he truly began to take risks. Adrenalin sickness, perhaps, but Pascal believed the condition went deeper than that. In war zones, it was easier to take good pictures if you did not care whether you died or lived. It was from that date that the myths about him really began: that Pascal was indifferent to danger, and its possible outcome, was something his friends and rivals refused to accept. They glamourized his ennui, Pascal thought. While he endured two years, three, of this withering state, they claimed – wrongly – that it was excitement which motivated him, a death wish.

Pascal knew that to be untrue. During this period, there was a void at the heart of both his personal and his professional life. Both the seductions of work, and of women, left him cold. He used women to provide brief sexual satisfaction; he used men, women and children ruthlessly to get the pictures he needed. He moved on, to the next assignment, the next woman, untouched.

He felt neither love nor compassion; he was distanced, alienated and cold. It was, he thought sometimes, a kind of living death, and it brought only one benefit: his new cold eye, his disregard for danger, gave his pictures a distinctive edge.

His friends, not understanding that he was dying inside, that he could feel death in his brain, heart and bloodstream, claimed he sought death out, courted it, made love to it. Pascal didn't bother to argue with them, or correct their mistake – let them weave their myths. He knew: why would he court death when he had already possessed it? He and death were intimates, lovers: death was beside him while he worked; death sat down at the table when he ate and drank; death watched him when he had sex; death greeted him every morning on waking, and waited for him faithfully every night when he slept.

That period of his life was not something he liked to recall now. It had, in due course, become less grim. He had almost persuaded himself that it was possible to escape from that prison cell. He had married, believing this. He had tried hard to hide the darkness that clouded the edge of his vision from his wife. When she was expecting their first child, he allowed himself to hope – and he continued to cling to hope even after the miscarriage. Later, there was Marianne, and he saw her, his living child, as a great gift. Amid the tumult and wreckage of a dying marriage, Marianne was music: by her very existence, through the passionate and protective love he felt for her, she sounded a sweet, pure and enduring note.

She gave him his heart back; in his capacity as her father, if in no other, he could know death receded and he lived. Marianne was his comfort, the one person who could give meaning to his life. Yet now he could not be with her, except by appointment, by permission, and so even this last hope was marred by grief.

It was now four in the morning, still dark outside, the deadest time of night. With a sudden desperation, Pascal rose to his feet. He walked back and forth in the room. With despair he examined and re-examined these incidents, these states of mind, this plot that was his life. It seemed to him then, momentarily, that all the wrong turnings he had taken linked back to the same time, and the same place. That little room by the harbour, in a once beautiful city. How different might things be now, if he had acted differently then?

He stopped pacing, crossed the room, and stood silently by a door. Beyond that door, Gini slept. For an instant he felt a wild and heady conviction that if he opened that door now, even if he spoke to her only, and did nothing else, he could perhaps undo time, mend, amend, the course of his past life.

He actually allowed himself to touch the handle of the door, and to turn it. Then he stepped back. The conviction fell away, and he saw it for what it was: a by-product of fatigue, a delusion fed by despair and lack of sleep. He was, he thought, no longer that impetuous young man he had been in Beirut. These days he placed greater value on friendship than on love. Friendship was less combustible, but endured longer. Love affairs, for the most part, had painful, messy conclusions. He believed now that their corollary was parting, just as the corollary of marriage was disillusion, hurt children, the broken heart and the divorce.

He returned to the sofa and lay down. He extinguished the light. For the rest of the hours remaining before dawn, he forced himself to think only of work, and of the Hawthornes, that perfect couple who might or might not have achieved that rare thing, a perfect marriage. His mind dwelt in their story, their space. The hours passed; he did not sleep.

In the room beyond, Gini also lay awake. She heard Pascal's footsteps approach her door, then turn back. She almost called out to him, then remained silent instead. Shortly afterwards, the band of light beneath her door disappeared. Gini lay in the dark, and tried to will herself to sleep. When sleep finally came, she dreamed vividly. She was searching a war-torn city, despairing and frantic. The object of her search was uncertain, and the details of the dream shadowy. Sometimes the city resembled London, and sometimes Beirut.

She woke exhausted. Grey light filtered through her curtains. From beyond came the sound of rain beating down on the small enclosed yard behind the house. When she went out into the living-room, Pascal was standing by her desk. His back was towards her; the air was rich with the smell of coffee brewing. There was a faint hum of machinery. When Pascal turned, she could detect no signs of strain, or sleeplessness. His face was concentrated and alert. *My colleague*, Gini thought. He held out to her a fax.

'The story continues,' he said. 'It's speeding up. Apple-yard has just surfaced, look. He's flying into London this morning, he says. He's proposing a meeting – and we can fit it in, just. We can see him, then go on to your stepmother's house. Meet the Hawthornes as planned.' He paused, half-smiled.

Gini said nothing. Her dream was still with her. She was not certain of the year, she felt, let alone the day of the week.

She took the fax from Pascal. It was brief, typed, but otherwise characteristic of Appleyard. Assuming availability, he was proposing they meet for dinner at a Mayfair restaurant, at eight o'clock that night.

XV

That Saturday morning, Mary rose early: there were twenty people coming to dinner, she could no longer afford staff, and twenty people to feed meant hours of work. Mary did not mind this: from her childhood, it had always given her pleasure to cook. Sometimes, it was true, she would look back with a certain wry nostalgia to her embassy days. She would think of her father's and mother's perfectionism, and then of her husband's and her own: such a retinue of cooks and secretaries and butlers and helpers. All she had had to do was fuss about *placements* and precedence and how she would dress. All those years spent carefully entertaining a succession of strangers – she looked back and found she did not regret them one jot.

Meanwhile, she had to make up her mind on the menu for tonight. She was half-decided, almost decided, but there was a certain anxiety at the back of her mind, an anxiety that had nothing to do with this food or the dinner itself, and that anxiety was distracting her. It made her flurried, and indecisive. She opened her larder, examined the contents of her fridge. When distracted, she cooked badly. Concentrate, she told herself, stick to your original menu and don't vacillate; vacillation made things worse.

They would begin with the smoked salmon as planned, she decided, then move on to a dish which was always a success, pheasants cooked with apples and Calvados. Finally, the dessert. Mary had a great weakness for puddings, and even if that weakness was not shared by guests such as Lise, she intended to provide a choice: pears baked in red wine and cinnamon would look beautiful, the colour of rubies, and then – even more wicked, even more calorie-laden – her chocolate mousse.

She tied on her apron, and humming to herself, began her preparation, already feeling less anxious. The dinner, she told herself, would be a success. It had the virtue of simplicity – and, for her, the menu brought back happy memories of Richard. Odd how tastes could remind you of contentment and of love. And then, apart from this menu, she had chosen her guests well. Some were undeniably boring, it was true, but they would be useful to John Hawthorne – indeed had been invited at John's request.

'You devious man,' she had said to him, laughing, when he mentioned their names.

'But of course,' he had replied. 'I'm a diplomat now and deviousness comes with the territory, Mary. You know that.'

'You were born devious,' she had countered stoutly. 'One of nature's Machiavellis – Richard always said that.'

'It takes one to know one,' he replied in his dry way. 'Besides, in my position . . . ' he gave a shrug, 'you learn early, to watch your back.'

Indeed, Mary thought now. A well-developed sense of self-protection was necessary for any man or woman in public life. Her father might have made the same comment; so might her husband. A little streak of ruthlessness was indispensable.

Feeling pleased with herself, she began to grate the chocolate for the mousse, absent-mindedly nibbling at tiny chunks. She found the cream and the eggs; a little zest of orange peel, she thought contentedly, that always gave it a lift. She separated the eggs, began to whip the egg-whites, and let her mind drift back to happier days.

This recipe had been given her by one of Richard's aunts, an eccentric woman, who had lived for forty years as an expatriate, in Provence. She had had the most wonderful house, halfway up the side of a hill, the approach road flanked by huge bushes of rosemary and lavender. Richard had picked a sprig of lavender for her, crushed it slightly, then held it out to her. She had inhaled deeply; a hot dry aromatic scent. Richard said: 'To me, that's the smell of France, the South of France . . . '

Mary stopped. She put down the whisk. The anxiety had returned, sharply and abruptly. This very evening, just a few hours from now, this Pascal Lamartine would be here, in her house.

The prospect filled her with alarm. There was no point in ignoring it any longer, she thought; she would have to confront it, deal with it, decide what to do. Should she or should she not make it clear to this Frenchman that she knew about his past conduct? Should she tell him she knew exactly who, and what, he was?

Unnerved, Mary made herself some coffee, and broke an inviolable rule – she lit a morning cigarette. She sat at her kitchen table, and stared unseeingly into the middle distance, unhappy and perplexed.

She was certain that when, out of the blue, Gini had mentioned Lamartine's name, her own reaction had been quick. She was sure she had covered up well, and disguised from Gini the confusion and shock she immediately felt. Mary felt quite proud of herself for this. She knew that she was not the world's most accomplished actress, and that Gini was astute. Even so, Mary had been both a diplomat's daughter and a diplomat's wife. In emergencies she could summon up a repertoire of social deceit. She might not like to do so, for it was not in her nature to lie, especially to Gini, whom she loved; nevertheless, she had been schooled to conceal boredom or dislike, and she could disguise anxiety just as well. She had learned the techniques of the white lie, the polite evasion, the digression, from her childhood. She had employed them in the past at a hundred embassy receptions; last Wednesday, when Gini dropped the bombshell of Lamartine's name, those techniques had come to her aid. No, Gini had suspected nothing – she was certain of that. Her comments about the paparazzi had been idiotic, she knew, and in the circumstances, her match-making tone had been ill-advised. But they had achieved their objective, and they had bought her time. Now, unfortunately, time was running out. She had to decide what to do when she finally met Lamartine tonight.

After Gini had left her last Wednesday, Mary had not slept. She had tossed and turned half the night. On the Thursday evening she had been at a party at the French embassy, and John Hawthorne, who was there without his wife, had given her a lift home. He had come in with her, accepted a drink, seen that she was worried, questioned her gently . . . She had resisted for a while, then the whole story had poured out.

Well, she did not regret that, she thought now. John had never betrayed a confidence in his life. She had never discussed this with anyone, for Gini's sake, yet when she began her story, she had felt the greatest relief. One of the worst and most painful aspects of widowhood, she had decided, was the loneliness of decision-making. She missed acutely Richard's capacity for listening, his support, his quiet and almost infallibly wise advice.

That gap in her life was increasingly filled by John Hawthorne, and she was grateful to him for that. A harder man than her husband had ever been – though Richard could be tough – John Hawthorne shared many of her husband's qualities, none the less. His capacity for listening was famous, of course; those who liked him said it was the source of his charm, and those who disliked him said it accounted for his success. Beyond that, as she had discovered this past year, John Hawthorne was kind, generous and acute. He did not mince his words; he did not flatter or falsely console. He gave straight advice, in a straight manner, even when that advice was not what Mary always wanted to hear, and she would see, later, that the advice he gave was subtle. A reserved man, she thought now, a clever man; a man who, this past year, had gradually revealed to her hidden depths. How fortunate, to have such a man as a friend; how fortunate, to know she could rely on his protection and his trust.

'You mean – Gini knew this man before?' he had said, frowning.

'More than that. Much worse. Oh God, John, what am I going to do? If Sam finds out, he'll be furious . . . '

John, who had known her ex-husband in the past, gave a dry smile. 'And Sam in one of his rages is quite a sight. To be avoided at all costs, I'd say. Go on.'

'Oh John, I don't know where to begin. Gini has no idea I know what happened. It was all so ghastly. Sam and this Lamartine man had a fight – really, a physical fight. Sam had a cut eye, and a cracked rib. Gini – poor Gini, she was in such a state of *misery* for months and months. I was absolutely terrified she was pregnant – but of course, she wasn't, thank God. I kept telling myself she'd confide in me, and then she never did, never – not to this day, that's how deep it went. And now this bloody man has turned up again – and I just *know* she still feels something for him, John, I could see it in her face. What am I to do? Should I say nothing or intervene? Should I tell Sam this Lamartine's re-emerged – I always promised him I would, but that was twelve years ago. It seems foolish now, after all, Gini's grown up. There's nothing either of us could do, except advise her. Well, I did think, perhaps if I said something to Lamartine, on Saturday, he might back off. That is, if he's still interested in Gini, and he's probably not . . . '

She stopped, out of breath, and turned to him. 'You see my one concern is Gini. She's much more vulnerable than she looks. I can't bear to see her hurt again. He hurt her so badly before, John – and it was obvious, he couldn't have cared less. Why are some men like that? Why?'

'I don't know, Mary,' Hawthorne replied. He shot her an amused, affectionate glance. 'I might give you a better answer if you slowed down, and told me the story from the beginning. I'm not clear. Are we talking about a seduction, or a romance?'

'A seduction, of course.' Mary gave him an indignant look.

'John, it was twelve years ago. Gini was just fifteen years old . . . '

At that, his amusement vanished, and his expression became intent. He leaned forward, and he listened with

243

absolute attention. It was a long story, as Mary told it, and he scarcely interrupted once.

'It was that horrible summer,' Mary began. 'The summer of nineteen eighty-one. It was the worst year of my life – one of the worst years. I hadn't seen Sam in ages, and he had gone out to Beirut . . . '

She went through it all then – the icy telephone call from Gini's headmistress, the ghastliness of contacting the police, the relief when late that night Gini telephoned from the Hotel Ledoyen and explained where she was. The conversation with Sam that same night, when Sam had been slightly drunk, at the three-bourbon stage, Mary would have judged. Sam's careless reassurances that, of course, Gini would be fine, that he'd keep an eye on her, and Mary's anxiety: Beirut was a dangerous place, and Sam Hunter had never kept an eye on Gini in his life.

'Oh stop fussing, Mary,' Sam had said. 'She's here and she may as well stay for a while. Maybe it'll knock some sense into her. You know what she's saying now? She wants to be a journalist, for God's sake.'

'She's been saying that for the last five years, Sam. If you listened once in a while, on the rare occasions when you see her, you'd know that.'

'Mary, listen . . . This is a *child* we're talking about here. A sixteen-year-old kid—'

'Fifteen, Sam. She isn't sixteen for another four weeks.'

'Fifteen, sixteen, what difference does it make?' His voice had faded into a crackle of interference on the line. 'Journalist!' Mary made out, as it cleared. 'For Christ's sake. Well, let her find out what reporting really means. I guarantee it – she'll be out of here in a week.'

Looking into the fire, Mary paused, frowned, then continued her story. Sam, of course, had not been right. Two weeks went by, three. Mary herself would try to telephone, but Sam never took her calls, and Gini always seemed to be out, even when she called quite late.

Mary described the mounting anxiety and impotence she had felt. She described how she had scanned, every

244

day, the Beirut stories in the newspapers. And she described the day when Sam and Gini suddenly arrived back on her doorstep, unannounced. It was ten in the morning; there had been problems with their flights. She had heard the taxi pulling up outside the house in Kent. She had rushed out, full of questions, seen their faces, felt the thunder and tension in the air, and stopped.

Gini's face was white and streaked with tears. Sam was sweating, cursing, belligerent. He had a swollen jaw, ten stitches in a jagged cut above his eye, and he was walking with a limp. He half-pulled, half-pushed Gini into the hall.

'All right,' he said. 'You go to your room now, and you goddamn well stay in it. You come out when I say so and not before. Jesus Christ, Mary. I've been up all goddamn night. Fix me a drink, will you? A large drink.'

Gini ran up the stairs without a backward glance. Her bedroom was in the attic; in the distance a door slammed. Sam and Mary moved into the drawing-room. Sam shut the door behind him. Mary stared at him in consternation, white-faced. He drank three inches of bourbon straight down, then he came to the point.

'You want to know what's wrong? You want to know what's happened? Fine, I'll tell you. A man's happened. His name's Pascal Lamartine. A fucking Frenchman. A photographer. One of the Leica leeches. That's who's happened. Get a hold of yourself, Mary. He's been screwing Gini. He's been screwing Gini day and night for weeks . . . ' He stopped.

'Great. I mean just great, yes?' He poured another bourbon. 'I meet my daughter for the first time in three years, and what do I discover? She's a goddamned little liar. She's a goddamned little slut. You want to know what happened? I'll tell you. He got her into bed the day they met. Then they stayed there. For three weeks. They've been at it, morning, noon and fucking night. She couldn't get enough of it. My daughter. Jesus Christ!'

He swallowed down the bourbon in one gulp, then mopped his face. 'You know what's next? Pregnancy,

245

that's what's next. She'll have gotten herself fucking pregnant, I know it – she's goddamned stupid enough. Fifteen and pregnant. Do I deserve this? Well, if she has, I'll pay for the abortion, then that's it. From now on I wash my hands of her. The hell with her. The hell with that goddamned fancy school you chose for her, and the hell with their goddamned fucking fees. I hope they expel her. And I hope *you* understand, Mary. *You* look after her. *You* live with her. I blame you for this.'

And so it went on, for several hours. The bluster, the excuses, the accusations, the obscenities, the abuse. Mary listened quietly, until she had the story straight – or Sam's version of it anyway.

Lamartine was thirty; he had a bad reputation; he and Sam had had a fight. Sam had half-killed him, and didn't understand now why he hadn't gone the whole way, finished off the job. The story looped, looped back. For a second, a third time, she heard about the harbour room, its bed, its sheets.

'Sam,' she said finally, 'he knew how old Gini was? You're sure of that?'

'Sure? Of course I'm goddamn sure.'

'Did he admit as much?'

'Not to me, no – you think he would? He's not a fool. Gini tried to cover up, said she'd lied to him. Lied to *him*! She's a goddamned little liar through and through. He knew well enough. He'd been fucking *boasting*, Mary, in the bars, in the restaurants. How he seduced *my* fucking daughter. How he got her into bed the day they met. How she was fifteen years old, but under-age girls were best. He told everyone. *Everyone*. Jesus Christ. The whole press corps, the barman, the fucking waiters. They *all* knew. I was a laughing stock . . . He told them everything. Described it. What he'd taught her. What they did . . . '

'What did they do?' Hawthorne had said.

The question startled Mary. She looked up, then sighed and shook her head. 'I'm sorry, John. I was miles away. I can still see it so vividly. How I felt, what Sam said . . . What was your question?'

'Nothing. It doesn't matter.' He had been leaning forward, but now straightened up.

She had risen then, and made them both some coffee. Over the coffee, she had told Hawthorne the rest of it rapidly. How she had decided to say nothing, and allow Gini to believe that Sam had kept his promise to remain silent. If the privacy of this matter was so important to her, then that seemed the best course. Mary would pretend, and had pretended, that she accepted as truth some foolish incident – staying out late, coming home drunk – as the reason for their return from Beirut. Then, when Gini was ready to confide in her, when she needed Mary's help, when she was ready to give her own version of these events, Mary would be there, could help.

'And that moment never came?' Hawthorne had said, and Mary had had an intuition that his attention was now wandering, that this aspect of the story interested him less. She nodded.

'Fine.' Hawthorne leaned across, and touched her hand. 'I understand. Now I'll give you my advice . . .'

Then he had done so. The advice, as usual, had been sensible. 'Do nothing,' he had said.

Mary rose now, and looked around the chaos of her kitchen. She was running behind; she must get a move on, finish preparing the mousse, begin on the pheasants . . . She began again in a half-hearted way, to whisk the eggs. She measured out the cream, and the doubts crept back. Was it the best advice? Was it the right course? She had been sure at the time, when he spoke, but then John was so persuasive, so cogent, so cool and unemotional – and a little hard too, she had felt that.

'First,' he had said, 'this Lamartine's bad news – that's obvious enough. The name's familiar – I'll run some checks, let you know what I come up with . . .' He paused. 'Second, Gini has to discover for herself what Lamartine is. You can't do that for her, and you shouldn't try. She's a grown woman, not a child, Mary. She's an intelligent woman, judging from how she writes. Not a woman it would be easy to deceive.' He looked at Mary intently. 'Am I right?'

'I suppose so.'

'Then let her find out for herself what he is. Don't interfere. And above all, don't involve Sam. Sam can be guaranteed to make matters a whole lot worse.'

'Third,' he continued, after a pause, and it was this part of his advice that surprised her, 'don't make up your mind in advance. You're prejudiced against Lamartine . . . '

'Prejudiced?' Mary stared at him. 'I don't think I'm prejudiced. It's obvious what he did. He exploited Gini, and then waltzed off to the next woman. It was cruel and it was inexcusable.'

'Are you sure about that?' Something in his tone as he asked the question struck her as curious. It was almost as if he sympathized with Lamartine, she realized – and that was the last reaction she would have expected from him, for he could be old-fashioned, even censorious, when it came to matters of sexual morality. The Catholic in him, she had always thought.

'*Are* you sure, Mary?' he said again. 'Think. You've only heard one side of the story. In my experience . . . ' He looked away, frowning. 'In my experience, that can be very misleading. It distorts. Maybe there were mitigating circumstances.'

'What nonsense.' Mary felt angry. 'The facts speak for themselves—'

'No, they don't.' He interrupted her curtly. 'Facts rarely do that. You're *interpreting* those facts you happen to have heard. People do that all the time.' His voice had become almost bitter. 'I've been on the receiving end of that process. I should know.'

'All right, all right . . . ' Mary replied. 'I'll bide my time. Postpone judgement – is that what you're saying?'

'Yes. I am.' His tone was firm. It had a finality Mary did not like, and found difficult to accept.

'Don't rush to judgement,' he continued. 'Wait. See what you think when you actually meet the man. Meantime . . . ' He paused, and a glint of amusement entered his eyes. 'Meantime, Mary, loosen up. Be a little less strait-laced. Try considering it from Lamartine's point of view. Think of the temptations involved. He's under pressure, working in a war zone. It's a dangerous place, it's a dangerous time. Suddenly he meets a stranger, who happens to be a very beautiful blond-haired stranger. Come on, Mary. You can understand the dynamics of a situation like that. It has a certain eroticism, you know.'

'And that excuses his conduct? Not to me, it doesn't.'

'Not excuses it, but explains it, perhaps? Be realistic, Mary.' His voice hardened, became almost impatient. 'Fifteen-year-old girls can be very provocative sexually – you know that as well as I do. They're more than capable of leading a man on. They like to test their own sexual powers. It's an open invitation, Mary, or it can be. And you can't always blame the man when he responds.'

'You're blaming Gini,' Mary burst out hotly. 'Shame on you, John!'

'I'm doing nothing of the kind,' he said sharply. 'I'm saying it's a possibility, that's all. For a seduction to be effective, Mary, two people have to be involved.'

She had stared at him then, with incomprehension, and a sense of remorse. Suddenly, they were very close to quarrelling. She saw that realization in his face as well, and his reaction was swift.

'Don't answer that. I'm sorry, Mary. It's late and I should go. Meantime, I'm not putting this too well . . . ' He rose, and put his arm around her shoulders. 'All I'm trying to make you understand is the difference between men and women. All right, for Gini, it was just the way you describe – a love affair. I'm sure you're right. I'm sure it was. But from the man's point of view – just accept this, Mary, you have to admit it – the temptation was probably very strong. Men like sex, Mary. They like straightforward sex with no emotional strings. If it's on offer, they'll grab it . . . And don't pretend you don't know that as well as I do. Or pretend that you condemn

249

it out of hand. You can't. I know too much about your past.'

Mary hesitated, then, feeling grateful that a quarrel had been avoided, she smiled. 'Oh, very well. Very well. You've persuaded me, though why you should want to play devil's advocate, I don't know. All right. I'll try to keep an open mind.'

'You know how often men think about sex in the course of a day?' He was smiling now, and moving towards the door. 'I read some statistics, just the other week. Every two minutes, Mary. Or was it every three?'

'You liar.' Mary laughed. 'You're making that up.'

'Not so. It's true. I even tested it out on myself, to make sure I measured up.'

He flashed his boyish, appealing smile and said, 'And now it's late. Very late. And I'd better go home.'

He had done so, and Mary had congratulated herself. There had been a moment of tension, but that happened in close friendships, and fortunately they had both realized the danger in time. When he had left, there had been the usual easy and relaxed banter between them, and the friendship was unimpaired.

But had John's advice been correct? Now, two days later, with Lamartine's appearance imminent, she was less sure. Do nothing, or do something? She felt another flurry of indecision. Wait and see what she felt when she actually met Lamartine, she decided. Play it by ear. She began to whisk the eggs again. Just as they were reaching perfection, there was a ring at the door.

It was John Hawthorne. He was wearing informal weekend clothes, and was flanked by a new security man, one she did not recognize. The security man was loaded down with flowers, boxes and boxes of flowers.

'For you,' John said. 'For the party tonight. Malone, take them inside, would you? Yes. The kitchen, that's fine.'

Mary looked at the flowers and could have cried, they were so beautiful. Daffodils, hyacinths, irises, tulips. Spring flowers, out-of-season flowers, the kind of flowers she could not afford any more. For a moment her vision blurred.

'You're very good to me, John.' She reached for his hand. If he saw the tears, he had the wit and the discretion not to comment upon them. He pressed her hand in return.

'We'll see you later tonight. I have to run now.' He glanced into the house beyond her, made sure the new security man was not in earshot, and then held out to her a large manila envelope.

'Those details I promised you, on Lamartine. I put two people on it. They came up with a good deal.'

'Heavens above, John . . . ' Mary felt the weight of the envelope. 'Whatever's in here? It weighs a ton.'

'All the press clippings. Details of his past work, and his current exploits. Some things from a few less obvious sources as well.'

He turned, and began to descend the steps. Two security shadows instantly materialized, one at either end of his car.

'Dinner smells delicious.' He smiled back at her. 'I can smell wine, cinnamon – very good indeed. Lise sends her love. Enjoy your read.'

Later that afternoon, Mary opened that manila envelope. When she saw its contents, she gave a gasp. It was not the information *per se* which astonished her, but the extent of it. Of course she knew, vaguely, that with modern technology, such checks were easily made. She knew that for a man in John Hawthorne's position to run such checks was easier still. But the speed with which he had done this, and the breadth of information obtained still astonished her – and shocked her.

Here before her were the details of Pascal Lamartine's birth and parentage, his schooling, his career, his marriage, his divorce, his bank accounts, his earnings, his debts, his tax returns. She could follow his mortgage payments, and where he used his credit cards. She could learn what items he purchased from which shops, which countries he visited, when he flew, by which airline, on which flight, and what hotels he used. She knew the address of his Paris studio, and the name of his concierge. She knew whom he called long-distance from that studio, for it lay before her, a long list of numbers, a computer print-out of his calls.

Mary stared down at these papers. She then returned them – for the most part unread – to the envelope. She was aware that she was trembling. She felt deeply ashamed.

She burned the envelope and its contents there and then. It made her feel unclean, shabby, like a voyeur or a spy.

XVI

The restaurant Johnny Appleyard had selected for their meeting was called Stiltskins. It was the last restaurant in London that Gini would ever have chosen, a place much patronized by tourists, by out-of-town businessmen, and by the kind of women that Mary still quaintly referred to as *filles de joie*.

It was located on the edge of Mayfair, in Shepherd Market. They drove there in Gini's Beetle, parked a few blocks away, and began to walk through the rain. This had always been a red-light district, and call-girls still operated in the area, though they did so discreetly, by appointment and from upstairs rooms. They passed several male clients, who averted their faces.

The noise emanating from Stiltskins could be heard two streets away. When they reached the restaurant, a party of Japanese businessmen, Western girlfriends in tow, was spilling out onto the pavement. The interior was dark and cavernous, a sequence of hot, red, smoky rooms. A Tom Jones medley was playing full-blast; there were bad jokes in frames on the walls.

A reservation, it seemed, had been made by Appleyard, and the head waiter became deferential at the mere mention of his name. He ushered them through to a rear room, and a table set for four. There was no sign of Appleyard. They sat down. Pascal ordered some wine. Gini sighed.

'I'm afraid we're in for a wait,' she said. 'Appleyard's notoriously unpunctual.'

'Oh great.' Pascal looked around him gloomily. 'Well, I hope he turns up soon. I can't stand this place too long.'

'He won't. He'll keep us waiting – twenty minutes at least. He thinks being late indicates status.'

Pascal groaned. Raucous laughter came from the table behind them where a noisy party was ordering magnums of champagne. Pascal twisted around to survey a new group of people, just entering.

'He's not one of those? What does he look like?'

'No, afraid not. And very recognizable – you won't be able to miss him. Last time I ran into him he was having lunch with Jenkins. He was wearing a white suit, a mauve shirt, and a pink tie. He's not always that flamboyant, but he's a snappy dresser. Medium height, slight build, fair hair. Heavy on the peppermint breath-spray. Been known to wear a carnation. Thinks he's Oscar Wilde.'

'And he isn't?' Pascal was smiling.

'His scripts let him down. Also,' Gini hesitated, 'he's not a nice person. Malicious. Always screwing around.'

'Poor Stevey in New York, you mean?'

'Yes. He sounded very unhappy, poor Stevey.' Gini looked away as she spoke. Pascal saw her eyes scanning the other tables. He frowned.

He and Gini had worked from his hotel room that day, because he distrusted her phone. He had concentrated on James McMullen, Gini on Lorna Munro and the question of her clothes. At the end of the afternoon, they had returned to Gini's flat, so that Gini could change. In honour of Mary's party later that evening, she was wearing a new dress. It had been a Christmas present from Mary, and it was the first time she had worn it, she had said. It made her a little nervous, she had explained, because she so rarely wore dresses of this kind, but she would wear it for Mary, who would be pleased. Pascal had said nothing. He might have liked it, he thought, had Gini said she was wearing the dress to please him, but he pushed this idea aside quickly. It struck him as petty.

It was a very beautiful dress, a narrow column of black silk crêpe, which left her throat and shoulders bare. It fastened on the shoulders with two slender straps as narrow as knife-blades. Against the folds of the silk crêpe, her skin looked pale. There were two bluish shadows, just above her collar-bone. She looked delicate, Pascal thought, fragile, very young, and very pure.

He rested his eyes on the oval of her face. She had drawn back her pale gold hair. She was wearing only one small gold ear-ring, his ear-ring. Gold and ivory and a dress like shadows. He had a sudden image of that pale hair, loosened, spread out beneath him across the floor. The image burned in the recesses of his mind, and he looked quickly away. He had said nothing to Gini, but it troubled him deeply that the story they were working on centred on appointments with blond-haired women, and presumably an obsession with such women. He thought of the shoe she had been sent, and the black silk stocking, and the handcuffs and for an instant he wished, devoutly wished, that Gini had dark hair.

He pushed that thought away, and glanced around the room. Time was passing and there was still no sign of Appleyard. Gini had taken her notebook from her bag, and was turning its pages, head bent, unconscious of his gaze. He looked at the smooth coil of her hair. It was twisted, then fastened in some invisible and ingenious way. Pascal felt he would have liked to reach across the table, remove that fastening, and watch that hair uncoil. It struck him suddenly that here was the scene he had envisaged four days before. They were in a restaurant, and even if it was one he would never have chosen, it had candles, it had wine. He, also in honour of Mary's party, was wearing that jacket he had bought at the hotel, that white shirt, that damn tie. Here, more or less precisely, was the scene he had imagined, and what was Gini doing? She was reading a notebook. She was working. Did she ever *stop* working? Pascal gave a sigh.

Gini looked up, and smiled. 'I'm sorry, Pascal. He'll turn up soon. Any minute now. I just thought – while we're waiting . . . ' She tapped the notebook. 'Would you mind if I went over some of these details? I think I'm reading them correctly, but I might have missed something.'

Pascal lit a cigarette. He said, 'Now? Why not? Sure.'

His reply was terse. Gini looked at him uncertainly.

'Would you rather talk about McMullen?' she asked.

'No, no. We can go over that tomorrow on the plane to Venice. We're seeing the Hawthornes soon. Let's concentrate on them – or on Lise anyway.' He refilled her wineglass.

'I'll come to Lise in a minute. I found out something very interesting there . . . ' Gini flicked back through the pages of the notebook. 'First, this Lorna Munro—'

'She still hasn't called back?'

'No, she hasn't. And she's moved on, from Milan to Rome. She's doing a try-out for Italian *Vogue*, apparently. I have her new hotel number. I've left more messages there . . . ' She paused, frowning. 'The more I think about this, Pascal, the more certain I feel – Lorna Munro isn't closely involved. I think she was just hired by someone. Come to London, wear these clothes, deliver these parcels – like a modelling job, an unusual modelling job.'

'It's possible, I suppose. Presumably we'll find out when we finally speak to her. Go on . . . '

'Well, having drawn a blank there, I moved back to the clothes.' Gini sighed. 'Someone once said to me that the secret of journalism was detail – check and then cross-check again.' She paused. 'So, I tried. I went back to all the people Lindsay spoke to yesterday. I tried a more indirect approach – not that it got me that far. You want a summary?'

'Sure. Why not?' Pascal glanced over his shoulder. Still no sign of that damn Appleyard. He was over half an hour late now.

'I tried every major furrier in London. There are so few now, I'm glad to say. I despise furs. No luck. Not one would discuss client purchases, not with Lindsay yesterday, not with me today. The same with Bulgari. But they implied that the pearl necklace featured in *Vogue* had been sold.'

Pascal shrugged. 'Was Lorna Munro even wearing that particular necklace? One string of pearls looks much like another, doesn't it? Real, fake, cultured – they all look the same.'

Gini smiled. 'To a man perhaps. Those Bulgari pearls were real, perfectly matched, and they had a very distinctive clasp. Gold, with a cabochon ruby, designed to be worn at the front of the throat. Susannah at ICD was adamant that it was the necklace Lorna Munro was wearing.' She turned a page of the notebook. 'I gave up on Bulgari. Then I tried Cartier – you remember, Susannah said the woman was wearing one of their tank watches, with a green crocodile strap? Hopeless! I tried, but the Bond Street shop alone sold fifteen like that in the week before Christmas. That's just one outlet – hundreds of other jewellers up and down the country sell Cartier tank watches. So, nothing there either.'

She paused, and looked up from her notebook. An expression came onto her face that Pascal was beginning to recognize. Its eagerness touched him and he smiled.

'I can guess,' he said. 'You drew a blank, but then you made a breakthrough?'

'Not a breakthrough, exactly. But I did find out several interesting things. First of all – that Chanel suit. Something about that story puzzled me. I wasn't surprised that Lise was in the habit of having clothes sent on approval – lots of famous women, rich women, prefer not to try on clothes in public. But *French* clothes, Pascal? Lise is the American Ambassador's wife. I checked back through the magazine profiles, and I was right. Lise is careful. On public occasions, she flies the flag – American clothes, American designers: Oscar de la Renta, Calvin Klein, Donna Karan . . . '

Pascal was beginning to look bored. He lit a cigarette. 'Clothes?' he said. 'Is this important?'

'Yes, Pascal, it is. Try and understand.' Gini gave him a patient look. 'Clothes may not interest you, but they're important to Lise. They're a fundamental part of her image, her identity even—'

'More fool her.'

'*Listen*, Pascal. Why is Lise Hawthorne so famous?

Three reasons. One, she's beautiful. Two, she's astonishingly chic. Three, she's auditioning to be a saint.'

'You've left one out. *Four*, she's John Hawthorne's wife.' Pascal gave her a sharp look. 'If it wasn't for her husband, she wouldn't be famous at all.'

Gini hesitated, then shrugged. 'Yes. You're right. She'd certainly be a very great deal less famous. I wonder if she minds that? I would.'

'You would?' Pascal was watching her closely.

'Of course,' Gini replied. 'What woman wants her identity to depend on her husband? What woman wants to be seen as . . . a kind of appendage to her husband? An accessory, like his car?'

'Plenty of women,' he said, somewhat sharply. 'I'm not agreeing with that attitude, Gini, or disagreeing with it. But it exists, it's commonplace.'

'I know, I know.' Gini looked away. There was a moment of tension which she could sense in the air. More raucous laughter came from the table behind them. Pascal glanced down at his watch, then swore.

'Damn Appleyard. This is getting ridiculous. We've been here an hour. What do you think, shall we order? We may as well eat here.'

Gini agreed. They consulted the menus, which were discouraging.

'Steaks?' Pascal caught her eye, and smiled. 'Presumably they can't go too wrong with steaks and salads. Even here.'

'Fine.'

Pascal called the waiter over, and ordered. When he turned back to Gini, his manner was slightly awkward, slightly sad. 'I'm sorry,' he said, and rested his hand briefly over hers. 'I'm not being very receptive. It's not your fault. I'm thinking about meeting the Hawthornes. This place is getting on my nerves.' He hesitated. 'Take no notice. I'm tired as well, I think. I didn't sleep too well.'

'I did warn you about that sofa,' Gini began, then stopped. She looked more closely at the expression in his eyes. 'It wasn't just that?' she asked, more quietly.

'It was more than that? Pascal, I wish you'd tell me. I wish you'd *talk* to me.'

He looked away. She saw reticence mask his features. He gave a dismissive gesture of the hand. 'Yes, well. It's not your concern. There are certain problems at the moment – residues of my divorce. I had to talk to my lawyers here yesterday. Anyway, I often sleep badly . . . ' He shrugged. 'I dream of war.'

There was a brief silence. Gini wondered if he ever let anyone past these defences of his. She hoped, for his sake, that he did. She leaned forward.

'Why are you using lawyers in England?' she said gently.

'My wife has sold her house in Paris. She wants to return to live in England, with Marianne. I would prefer it if she did not do that . . . ' He left the rest of the explanation unfinished, and Gini, who could finish it in any case and who could now read quite clearly the pain at the back of his eyes, did not prompt him further.

'I see,' she said, just as the waiter arrived, bearing their food. It was ill-cooked. Pascal looked down at their plates with a very French expression of mingled outrage and despair.

'Shall I send it back?'

'No, leave it. It's not worth it.'

'You're right. The hell with it. We'll eat it and go . . . ' He glanced down at his watch. 'An hour and a half. You think Appleyard intends to keep this appointment?'

'It's still possible,' she replied, in a placatory tone. 'With Appleyard, you never know . . . '

They ate for a while in silence, then, by silent mutual consent, pushed their plates to one side. Pascal ordered coffee, and lit a cigarette. The period of silence seemed to have restored his temper. He gave her a wry glance.

'All right. Now I'll listen. All my attention. You were telling me about Lise and her clothes. Go on.'

'Very well.' Gini opened her notebook again. 'The question of Lise's clothes bothered me – why Chanel?

So I rang an old acquaintance of mine, who works for the *Washington Post*, on the Style Section. What she told me was interesting. Very interesting. I wish I'd spoken to her earlier.' Gini leaned forward. 'First, the minor things. The clothes. Apparently, Lise Hawthorne always used to wear French couture—'

'The wedding dress?'

'Precisely. Then, two years into their marriage, Lise had a change of heart. According to Washington gossip, John Hawthorne read her the riot act. He said French couture was just fine for the Ivana Trumps of this world but not for a senator's wife – or a future Democratic candidate's wife, for that matter. From then onwards Lise Hawthorne toed the line. On public occasions, that is. In private, at home, she continued to wear the clothes she preferred. French, Italian, whatever. Couture was too public, so she made do with ready-to-wear. For the last three or four years, her pet designer's been Karl Lagerfeld – his collections for Chanel.' Gini paused. 'It's a very minor deception, not important at all – except there are other ways in which Lise Hawthorne may not be quite the woman she seems. There *has* been gossip about the Hawthornes, Pascal. So far, it's been confined to Washington dinner parties, and a lot of it is pure supposition.'

'Gossip about Hawthorne himself, you mean?' Pascal said quickly. 'Not the monthly appointments, surely? Damn, damn . . . '

'No. Relax. Nothing like that. According to my friend – and she's not the most reliable source in the world – people have been saying Lise is ill. Apparently it started some time back. After the younger child, Adam, had meningitis. Around the same time – the word is Lise had a miscarriage—' She stopped and looked at him curiously. 'Pascal, is something wrong?'

'No. No.' He passed his hand across his face. 'Nothing. It's very noisy in here. Go on.'

'Well, after the miscarriage, Lise came close to a nervous breakdown. This was around four years ago.'

'Four years?' Pascal's expression was now intent. 'Exactly when those Sunday appointments began – according to Jenkins, that is.'

'Exactly.' Gini tapped the notebook. 'So, you can imagine. I started listening very closely indeed. I prompted – discreetly. It wasn't difficult. My friend's a great gossip. She said it was the talk of Georgetown, for a while. Then it quietened down. But apparently, Lise refused to sleep with Hawthorne after the miscarriage. Totally refused, and went on refusing. Separate bedrooms. One of the maids told another maid – and you know how it is.'

'I do.' Pascal grinned.

'But – and this is interesting – Hawthorne accepted it. Or so people say. Apparently, once the word got out, there were plenty of women hell-bent on consoling him. Well, you'd expect that. He's powerful, influential – and he's an exceptionally handsome man.'

'So you've said. Several times.'

'Well, he *is*, Pascal! You can't ignore that. It's a factor . . . Anyway, the women were disappointed, according to my friend. They made their offers and Hawthorne turned them down.'

Pascal gave an impatient gesture. 'You mean he's supposed to have been celibate? For four *years*? Come on, Gini.'

'Well, it may be gossip, but I suppose it is *just* possible,' she replied. 'Male celibacy isn't exactly unknown. There are monks, priests, for instance . . . '

Pascal smiled. Reaching across the table, he touched her hair. One strand had become loose. He smoothed it back into place. 'Gini, Gini . . . ' he said, in a kind tone. 'Think a little. Priests take a vow. That's rather different, you know. Most men – four years is a long time. Four *months* would be quite a long time.'

Gini crimsoned. She looked away. In a flat voice, she said, 'I suppose so. I do *know* that. It's just . . . '

'Gini,' Pascal took her hand. 'I'm not making fun of you. But we look at this from two different perspectives, you and I. That's inevitable. I'm a man, you're a woman. To me,' he hesitated, 'to me, that's an interesting story, but it's absurd. I don't believe it for a second. If that's what Lise Hawthorne did, then sooner or later, Hawthorne would have gone to another woman. Not for love necessarily. Just for sex. Men find it easy to make that distinction. Believe me. I know.'

Gini pulled her hand away. 'I know it too,' she began quickly. 'And you're wrong. Women can do precisely the same. They can make that – distinction, as you call it.'

'They can?' Pascal continued to watch her closely. 'I'm not sure I agree with you, but there's no point in arguing about it. And this story you heard . . . ' He frowned. 'It's rumour, but it's a very suggestive rumour from our point of view. Maybe these Sunday meetings were Hawthorne's solution. It could be.'

He turned away to scan the room, then checked his watch. 'It's nearly ten,' he said. 'Let's get out of here, give up on Appleyard.'

Gini looked back down at her notebook. She felt safer when she looked at the notebook. Words and phrases she had written down jumped out at her. *Miscarriage*; *separate bedrooms*; then a direct quote from her friend: *Darling, the word is – no sex, for four years.*

Suddenly she felt disgusted with herself, with her own questions: was this the journalism she had foreseen for herself, this prying into someone's marriage, this spying on another person's most private emotions, actions and thoughts? Quickly she turned the page, then looked up at Pascal. 'No,' she said. 'Let's wait. Give Appleyard ten more minutes. We have time. There's just one last thing I found out today. This isn't rumour or gossip. It's fact.' She paused. 'You know those faxes that came through to my apartment this evening?'

'Yes?'

'They were from another friend. He works out of Oxford now, for the *Oxford Mail*. The Hawthornes' country house is less than fifteen miles from Oxford . . . '

'So?'

'So, look at the timing on this. That suit was requested

from Chanel, by telephone, on the morning of Friday, December thirty-first, right?'

'Yes. According to the manager.'

'And the manager was convinced it was Lise herself calling. He's met her, knows her voice. All right, she has a very distinctive voice. But as Katherine McMullen said to you, voices can be changed, accents can be changed. Now, maybe it *was* Lise calling. On the other hand, maybe it was someone imitating her, and doing it very well. Think, Pascal – the manager at Chanel said that Lise told him she needed that suit because *if* she liked it, she was going to wear it the following day – New Year's Day. She intended to wear it to a very special luncheon. At Chequers. The Prime Minister's country home.'

'I begin to see . . . ' Pascal leaned forward. 'Naturally, the manager was delighted . . . '

'Over the moon. But, Pascal, it was a lie, and a very stupid lie, too.' She tapped her notebook. 'There's one advantage to working on a story about well-known people. It's easy to check their movements. So I did. I checked where Lise and John Hawthorne were for that four-day period. Friday, Saturday, Sunday and Bank Holiday Monday.'

'They weren't invited to luncheon at Chequers?'

'Well, if they were ever invited, they didn't go. Lise was in Oxfordshire, at their country house. Don't you remember, she mentions on McMullen's tape that she's going there the following week? She did. She went down there two days before Christmas, and she stayed there until the Wednesday *after* the New Year. She had tea in London with Mary that afternoon when she returned. Mary mentioned it to me.'

She paused. 'Pascal, take a look at the faxes when we get home. Lise's movements were extensively documented in the local Press the entire New Year weekend. On Friday evening she and Hawthorne went to a local New Year's Eve ball given by their Oxfordshire MP. On Saturday, Lise went hunting – she rides with the Vale of the White Horse hunt. On Sunday she and Hawthorne attended a special mass at their local church – they donated the funds for its new roof. On Monday she held a massive party at their home, and on Tuesday—'

'The day Lorna Munro delivered those parcels—'

'Precisely. On *that* day Lise was still in Oxfordshire. She visited a children's home in the morning, and a hospice for cancer victims that afternoon.' Gini paused. 'Pascal, she wasn't in London at all. She wasn't at Chequers. And I don't think that was Lise on the telephone either. Someone else called Chanel.'

Pascal frowned. 'It's not conclusive,' he began.

'I know it's not conclusive! But there's just one more interesting fact. Lise may have been in Oxfordshire throughout those four days. But her husband wasn't.'

'He was in London some of the time?'

'You bet he was in London. It's an hour's drive from Oxfordshire, that's all. He was here, and at highly significant times. He was in London on Friday, because he spoke at some industry lunch. And he was back in London on Tuesday, when those parcels were delivered. Another luncheon appointment. With the Prime Minister. At Number Ten.'

'You're certain?'

'Certain. It was a large luncheon, for a visiting head of state. The guest list was reprinted in full in *The Times*.'

Pascal gave her a sharp glance. 'Were wives included?'

'Yes, they were.'

'And yet Lise Hawthorne chose not to attend? How very interesting . . . ' He paused, frowning. 'I don't understand, Gini – I don't understand any of this. Let's rule Lise out – just as a working hypothesis. Let's say she knew nothing about these parcels.' He paused. 'But then why should John Hawthorne have anything to do with them either? Don't you see, it makes no sense. Why do something designed to lend credence to that story about the blondes? It's the *last* thing he'd do.'

'I agree. But he was in London at the key times.'

Pascal gave a sigh, and rose. 'Never mind,' he said. 'You've done well. Everything helps, Gini. Every tiny bit of information we can find. We're still not close enough. We're still too much in the dark.' He drew back her chair for her, and Gini rose.

'So, we're giving up on Appleyard?' she asked.

'Yes. We can't waste any more time.' He took her arm. 'Let's go and see the Hawthornes for ourselves.'

He steered her past the crowded tables. Just beyond the alcove where they had been seated was a particularly boisterous group of Americans: four dark-suited men and a bevy of redheads and blondes. As they passed, one of the men lurched to his feet, almost knocking Gini over.

'Where's the john?' he was demanding loudly. 'Just direct me to the goddamn john . . . '

Pascal gave him a look of distaste, and moved between them to allow Gini through. They found their waiter finally, paid the bill, and began to make their way through the maze of little rooms to the exit. There, the head waiter stopped them.

'Mr Lamartine? Mr Appleyard sends his apologies. He's been unavoidably delayed.'

'It's a pity you didn't inform us of that earlier,' Pascal began, then he stopped. Gini felt him tense. 'My name was mentioned?' He turned back to the head waiter. 'The meeting was arranged with Ms Hunter here . . . '

'Lamartine was the name I was given, sir. Mr Appleyard's assistant only just phoned . . . Oh, and he said you'd be needing this, sir. He sent it round by cab for you. It just came.'

He handed Pascal a small package. Pascal drew Gini outside. He walked a little way along the street, and then opened it. Inside it was an audio cassette. Pascal held it up to the light from a street-lamp. Across the road, a man entered a doorway, hesitated, then rang one of its bells. In an upstairs room above him, a light came on. A buzzer sounded; the man entered, and the door closed.

Pascal said, 'This isn't an ordinary tape, Gini. Look. It's too short . . . Damn. Damn.'

'We've been set up, haven't we?' Gini began slowly. 'I don't think Appleyard sent that fax.'

'Neither do I. And I don't think he's sent this either.' He glanced down at her. 'We've just done something very stupid. We've sat in a restaurant of someone else's choosing for over two hours. We've spent two hours going over this story. What we do know, what we don't know . . . *How* could I have been so stupid? Damn, damn!' With a furious gesture, he began to walk rapidly away. Gini hurried after him.

'Slow down,' she said. 'Pascal, slow down. You're tired. I'm tired – all right, we made a mistake. But think – it was very noisy back there. It would have been hard to pick up our conversation, surely.'

'Maybe, maybe. It's too late now anyway.' They had reached her car. Pascal waited impatiently while she unlocked it. Before she had got into her seat he had inserted the cassette in the tape-deck.

'Get in,' he said. 'Hurry up. Close the door.'

As soon as she had done so, Pascal pressed 'Play'. They sat there in silence. The tape hissed. There was silence on it for several seconds, then the breathing began. First heavy breathing, then pants, then groans. Gini's skin went cold. Beside her, Pascal gave a low exclamation, glanced at her, and reached for the tape-deck.

'No.' Gini stopped him. 'We've been sent a message. Let's hear what it is.'

'I can already hear what it is,' he began angrily.

'So can I, Pascal.'

'Is he alone?'

'If he isn't, he has a silent partner.'

'They *are* silent,' Pascal said in a grim voice. 'That's the rule. As we know.'

The tape lasted seven minutes. The man achieved climax, without words, after five. There was then a silence. At six and a half minutes, just before the tape ended, a woman screamed. Pascal reached forward, removed the tape. He glanced at Gini.

'You're all right?'

Gini was not all right, but she had no intention of saying so. She let in the brake, and pulled away. 'I told you before,' she said, when they were several streets away, 'someone's trying to frighten us off. The hell with that. We'll carry on, the way we planned. We'll go to this party. You concentrate on Lise, I'll talk to Hawthorne. We'll switch over if there's time.'

She could feel his tension and unease. It was a while before he replied.

'Just be careful,' he said finally. 'Be very careful what you say.' He glanced towards her. 'That break-in, the parcels, this missed appointment, this tape. Someone is two steps ahead of us, all the time.'

'Hawthorne?' She glanced across; Pascal's face was turned to the window. He was staring out into the wet darkness beyond.

'Maybe,' he replied eventually. 'Maybe. Whoever they are, we know one thing about them. They enjoy playing games. Nasty games.'

XVII

The dinner had gone well. The pheasants had been excellent, the pears and the chocolate mousse delicious. It was now ten-fifteen, Gini would be here soon, and Mary was in the process of weeding out the bores, a process at which she was skilled. Two were now departing; two more remained in the drawing-room, but she could see that John Hawthorne, as adept as she was in this respect, was manœuvring them towards the hall. In the hall a dour Bulgarian first secretary and his wife were being helped into their coats by the American security man stationed there. *The new thug*, Mary thought to herself; Malone – yes, that was his name – was proving highly useful. The Bulgarian shook her hand.

'Lady Pemberton,' he said, 'such a very excellent evening.' His English was good; his wife's less so.

'The pheasant birds,' she said. 'These I will have enjoyed.'

'A most interesting conversation with Ambassador Hawthorne,' the Bulgarian went on. 'He was fully cognizant of our latest export figures. A most well-informed man.'

'*Isn't* he?' Mary said with animation, edging him towards the door. The Bulgarian was one of the guests invited at John's behest. During the requisite ten minutes she had spent in conversation with him, he had explained, at length, Bulgaria's iron ore industries. Mary opened the door.

'*Such* a pity you can't stay. So *very* nice to have met your wife. Of course. Of course. *Absolutely!* Goodbye . . .'

Mary closed the door and raised her eyes heavenwards. Beyond her, this new man, Malone, gave a smile.

'Two more to weed out, ma'am?' He nodded towards the drawing-room.

Mary gave this new thug an appraising glance. Thug, she decided, was in this case most definitely not the appropriate word. Though Malone was six feet five, crew-cut, and huge, he appeared to have a sense of humour. This was unprecedented. She looked at the broad shoulders, at the regulation dark suit. She wondered in passing, if these men of John's were actually armed. What did the bulge of a shoulder holster really look like? Could you detect it? Or, if they carried weapons, did they conceal them elsewhere? *In their trouser waistbands, perhaps*, she thought vaguely. *Too ridiculous*, she decided, and smiled.

'I haven't thanked you, Mr Malone, for bringing in all those lovely flowers for me.'

'My pleasure, ma'am.'

'You're new, aren't you? I know I haven't seen you before . . . '

'I am, ma'am. I flew in from Washington two days ago.'

Mary looked at him in astonishment. In her experience these men never volunteered any information whatsoever. They spoke in two-word sentences. They said, 'no, ma'am' and 'yes, ma'am'.

'Usually, when John comes here, Frank is with him . . . '

Mary looked at the man hopefully. Since he actually spoke fully formed sentences, a fishing expedition was justified. She would have liked to know just how serious this current security alert was, and whether Frank's absence and Malone's arrival signified anything. John Hawthorne would certainly never tell her. And *something* was going on, she could sense it. All evening its effects upon Lise had been only too obvious. She glanced into the drawing-room; Lise was standing by the fire, alone. Lise never drank alcohol. Now she was holding an empty mineral water glass. She was staring into space turning the glass round and round in her hands.

Malone, Mary realized, had not replied. She turned back to him. One more try. 'Still, even you have to take a break sometimes. I expect Frank was due some leave?'

'Yes, ma'am. He's not on duty this weekend.'

'How nice for him . . . '

'Yes, ma'am.'

'I always think it must be so exhausting for you,' Mary continued, with a vague and incoherent gesture of the hand. 'Always on the alert. Ever watchful . . . '

'Yes, ma'am.'

'Rather like Cerberus, you know . . . ' She broke off. This was not the most tactful comparison – the dog Cerberus, eternally standing guard over the gates of hell. She attempted to cover her confusion, told herself that Malone was unlikely to be well versed in Greek mythology, had probably never even *heard* of Cerberus . . . and then realized that he had. She saw amusement way back in his eyes, then the bland blank look they all assumed.

'Yes, ma'am.'

'You wouldn't like a drink or anything, Mr Malone? Some Perrier, perhaps?'

'No thank you, ma'am.'

He had moved away a few steps. He was doing another thing they all did, something at which they were all skilled. He was making himself invisible. He was fading into the wall.

'Well, yes, of course, indeed,' Mary said, feeling flustered, feeling she had just made an idiot of herself. She glanced down at her watch. Ten-thirty: Gini and that Lamartine man would be here any minute. She felt suddenly very anxious, but her instincts as a hostess came to the fore. Going back into her large drawing-room, she edged past her other guests, around the backs of the two remaining bores, and crossed to the fireplace. Lise was still standing there alone.

'No Dog?' she asked, as Mary bent and put another log on the fire. Lise held out her hands to the flames. Mary saw that Lise was shivering, although she was three feet from the fire and the room was warm.

'No. He's been banished upstairs.' Mary smiled. 'He

will beg for tit-bits. Besides, I have to face facts. I may adore him, but he's old and he smells.'

'He's sweet,' Lise said without great conviction. Lise had never liked dogs. 'Terribly sweet. So . . .'

She stopped. Apparently she could think of no appropriate compliment. Her eyes met Mary's, in mute distress, then Lise looked away.

Mary took her arm. 'Lise,' she said firmly, 'is something wrong?'

'Wrong? No, of course not. I'm having a perfectly lovely time.'

Mary regarded Lise carefully. She looked very beautiful tonight in a white dress which, like all Lise's clothes, was austere in design. It was long-sleeved, high-necked, plain. As the right frame sets off a painting, so this dress, by its simplicity, by its exquisite cut, emphasized Lise's loveliness. She wore the necklace which had been her birthday present from John, and very little other jewellery; her black hair, worn loose, framed her face. That face, with its large dark blue eyes, now wore an anxious expression, like that of an apprehensive child. Today was Lise's thirty-eighth birthday. She was approaching forty, had admitted to Mary on numerous occasions that this watershed filled her with dread, and she looked, Mary thought, no more than twenty-five.

Except . . . she was looking strained. She was becoming painfully thin, and her long beautiful hands, adorned only by her wedding ring, were still clasping that glass tightly. Her knuckles were white. As Mary looked at her, she shivered again.

'Come on, Lise. Don't pretend, not to me.' Mary patted her arm. 'You've been on edge all evening. I know there's something wrong.'

Lise bit her lip like a little girl, lowered her eyes, then gave Mary a sidelong glance. 'Oh, Mary. All right. I'll admit it. I know it's very stupid, but I worry so about John. All this horrible Middle East business. I just know they're on a high-security alert, though, of course, John will never admit that. There was a bomb, you know, outside our embassy in Paris. They defused it tonight.'

'I hadn't heard that. It wasn't on the news.'

'It will be tomorrow. John told me this evening, when we were getting dressed to come here. There's a news black-out, I think. But you see, if the Paris embassy, why not here?'

'You mustn't think like that, you know, Lise. I'm sure John's perfectly safe.' Mary gave her an encouraging smile. 'Look at his security! Men everywhere – that nice Mr Malone outside in the hall . . . '

'Is he nice?' Lise gave her an odd look. 'I don't think he's nice, not at all. They're all so grim and silent. I hate them. Especially Frank. He's the worst of all.'

'I thought you liked Frank?' Mary looked at her in surprise. 'Don't you remember, Lise, when we had lunch before Christmas? You said then how much you liked him. You said he was very efficient and polite.'

'Did I say that? I don't remember.' Lise shivered again. 'Well, if I did, I've changed my mind. He's *too* efficient. It's like some horrible shadow, always following me around.'

'Well, you don't have to worry about him, anyway,' Mary said in a comfortable way. 'It's his weekend off, I gather, so—'

'It is?' Lise swung around to look at her. 'Who told you that? John? Where's Frank gone?'

'Lise, how would I know?' Mary stared at her in surprise. 'That Malone man mentioned it just now. I don't know where they take off to – I can't imagine. Maybe they get drunk for two days. Chase girls. Ring up their aged mothers in Omaha. God knows.' Mary smiled. 'What do ex-Marines do with their free time? Parachuting? Target practice? Fifty-mile runs?'

'Ex-Marines? Frank isn't an ex-Marine. What made you think that?'

The question was sharply put, but Mary was distracted. Across the room, there were some new arrivals, she saw – the more entertaining guests, who always started to arrive around this hour. She made out the features of a well-known poet; there was someone else with him. Really, she must get some glasses . . . But no, it was not Gini, or that Lamartine man. A couple of actor friends, and – yes – that amusing little journalist man, editor of one of London's more scurrilous magazines. She must remember to keep him well away from John.

'I'm sorry?' She turned back to Lise. 'I was just looking for Gini. What did you say, Lise?'

'Nothing. It doesn't matter.'

'No, what was it?'

'Oh, just Frank. He isn't a Marine. He was never a Marine.'

'Oh. I thought they all were . . . ' Mary looked back across the room. The two remaining bores were now by the hall. Time to detach them . . .

'Frank used to work for John's father. Didn't you know that?' Lise was now staring at her in a fixed, almost suspicious way, as if she thought Mary was hiding something from her.

'No. No, I didn't,' Mary said, frowning.

'Oh.' Lise shivered again. 'Well, he did. John's father wasn't satisfied with the security arrangements when John took this post. You know how he is.'

'I do indeed.'

'He insisted the official security people be supplemen-ted. Frank was one of the ones who came over.' She stopped, and looked directly into Mary's eyes. 'John never mentioned that to you?'

'No, Lise. He didn't.'

Lise gave a tremulous sigh. Her gaze fell. 'Oh. I just wondered. It's just – you and John are such good friends. You see each other all the time.'

Mary stared at her in astonishment. For a moment, she had sounded almost jealous. 'Lise,' she said firmly, 'I've known John since he was ten years old. I'm a fat frumpy old widow, and John's been very kind to me since Richard died. When he comes to see me, he does it to cheer me up. Which he's very good at, incidentally. We don't sit here

273

talking about his security people. Why on earth should we?'

Lise sensed the reproach at once. She gave Mary a shy smile, and took her arm. 'Oh, Mary, Mary, I'm being such an idiot tonight. I didn't mean – I'm so glad you *are* John's friend. He gets very tense, and he needs someone to talk to . . . '

'He has you to talk to, Lise.'

Lise did not reply. Her dark eyes met Mary's and for one appalling moment Mary thought she was about to cry. Mary watched her fight back the tears, then Lise moved away with an odd defensive gesture of the hand. She was carrying a small evening bag under her arm. She opened it, and began to fumble inside. 'Actually,' she said. 'Actually, I think I have one of my headaches coming on. Those hideous migraine things . . . '

'Are you sure you're all right? Would you like to go home? Let me have a word with John—'

'No. No. Don't do that.' For a second Lise looked terrified; she almost dropped the bag. 'No. He'd be so cross. I know he's looking forward to meeting Gini properly. And, of course, so am I. I have these wonderful little pills. My miracle pills . . . Ah, here they are. Truly, Mary. One of these and a glass of water, and I'll be just fine . . . '

Her manner had grown hectic, and her hands were shaking. Quietly, feeling troubled, Mary fetched her some water. She glanced back towards the hall, checked the room as she did so. The last bores, thank heaven, had left – and without saying goodbye. *Bores*, and *bad-mannered*, she thought. John was talking to the two actors; she heard the words *Academy Awards*. Everyone was occupied, had a drink; someone else was just arriving now.

She handed Lise the glass of Malvern water. Lise appeared calmer now. She swallowed the small white pill, and gave Mary a grateful glance. She too looked across the room.

'Is that Gini?' she said. 'Oh yes, it must be – how pretty

she is, Mary. What a lovely dress. And who's that man with her?'

Mary sighed. 'He's a photographer, I gather,' she said. 'He's French. His name's Pascal Lamartine.'

'How nice. I love France. I must talk to him later.' Lise was now moving off, towards the editor of the scurrilous magazine. Mary took her firmly by the arm and redirected her towards the poet.

'You remember,' she said. 'You've met before, Lise. *Stephen*. He has a new collection of poems just out . . . '

'He has? What's it called?' Lise said, and Mary smiled. Lise was already recovering, her instincts reasserting themselves.

'*Reflections*.'

'Thanks.' Lise gave her a sudden amused glance, a sidelong smile. She approached the poet, and held out her hand.

'*Stephen*,' Mary heard. 'How lovely. I was hoping you'd be here. *Reflections* is wonderful. John and I both love it. No, really, we were reading it together, this evening. Yes, before we came here . . . '

'So, tell me, M. Lamartine, are you staying in London long?'

'I'm not sure. Maybe a few more days only. Maybe a few weeks . . . '

Pascal looked down at Mary, this stepmother of Gini's. She was not, somehow, what he had expected. For no very good reason, he had imagined that any woman previously married to Sam Hunter would be tall, elegant and forceful. This woman was none of these things. She was short, no more than five feet four, and she was far from elegant. She was plump, and rather badly dressed in a very English way, in that she was wearing an unflattering dress of some pale material which needed ironing. She had white hair which stood up around her face in a fierce tufty halo. She had a superb English complexion, was wearing no make-up, and she was smiling at him. The smile, as yet, did not reach her eyes, which were a clear blue and had been fixed upon him since he'd entered the room not two minutes before. Pascal's immediate impression had been of vagueness and slight eccentricity. That impression was now being revised. She had greeted Gini and himself with warm affection and a blizzard of words. There had been a flurry of hand gestures. Nevertheless, he noted, Gini had somehow been detached from him with speedy efficiency, and was now talking to John Hawthorne. He himself, he realized, had also been detached, and was now backed into a corner by the fireplace. To his right was the fire, to his left was a huge, ancient, sagging chintz-covered armchair, and in front of him, cutting off all possible means of escape, was this fierce plump little woman. Pascal looked down at her, puzzled. Then he began to understand. She reminded him, suddenly, of his mother, and he had seen just that expression on his mother's face in times past. It was how she had looked – *exactly* how she had looked – whenever as a young man he'd brought girls home. Pascal smiled.

Mary looked up at him. It was, she thought, a disarming smile, but she had no intention of being disarmed. True, this Frenchman was not what she had envisioned – not at all. For a start he didn't look right. Mary had a vivid imagination, and she had had twelve years in which to summon up this man in her mind's eye. She had not examined the material John Hawthorne had given her at all closely, and so the image of Lamartine conjured up at the time of Beirut was unimpaired. A French womanizer, Mary had decided twelve years before; she knew the type only too well. Good-looking, smarmy, with ghastly come-to-bed eyes. Mary had never actually met a Frenchman like that, but she was perfectly certain that's how they were. Apart from the fact that he was good-looking, very good-looking – though he could have done with a haircut and a much closer shave – this Lamartine was none of these things. His manner was, if anything, slightly cool and distanced. His behaviour to Gini as they entered had been charming and correct. He had entered at her side, one hand at her elbow, to help steer her past the crush of other guests. On being introduced to Mary, he had shaken her hand, bent his head slightly in that rather delightful way some Frenchmen had, and said politely, '*Madame.*'

Not smarmy, Mary decided. She blinked. And not in his forties either, which he would have been had Sam given her his correct age. He was considerably younger, in his mid-thirties, she judged. *Damn Sam*, she thought, *and damn my wretched eyesight*. She peered up at Lamartine. He did not look in the least like some cheap womanizer. He did not have ghastly come-to-bed eyes. In fact, now that she looked more closely, he had rather good eyes, of a smoky-grey colour. Their expression was ironic, quizzical, as if something was amusing him . . . With a start, Mary realized that she was inspecting him in a quite unforgivable way. She took a step backwards. Lamartine's smile broadened. He had, she thought, a really rather wonderful smile.

'I'm sorry,' she said, speaking with great rapidity, and waving her hands. 'It's just . . . You're not what I expected at all . . . '

'And you are not what I expected,' he replied.

'You see,' Mary continued, rushing on, and trying to avoid the conversational pits and traps which suddenly seemed to surround her on all sides. 'You see, that is, Gini told me you were one of those paparazzi—'

This did not please him. The smile disappeared. 'Oh? That was what she said?'

He glanced across the room to where Gini was now deep in conversation with John Hawthorne. Mary swallowed and thought fast.

'Maybe I've got that wrong. I expect so. I'm such a scatter-brain. I muddle up things all the time, and—'

'No. She was perfectly correct. That's exactly what I am.' This was said seriously, but with detectable edge. Mary took a large swallow of her wine.

'Well, there you are,' she went on idiotically. 'I'm sure it's *most* exciting. Rushing around the world, that

277

kind of thing . . . ' She pulled herself together. 'So tell me, have you known Gini long?'

Pascal hesitated. 'No,' he said carefully. 'We've met a few times.'

Mary paused. Here was her perfect opportunity. Now was the moment to draw herself up, give him a withering stare and say, Come, come, M. Lamartine. You once knew Gini very well, I think. In Beirut. Twelve years ago. Mary looked up at this man, and found the words would not come. She could not possibly say them. In the first place, he was quite formidable, and she simply didn't dare; in the second, she could see they would be an unpardonable intrusion, rude, wrong, and possibly unfair. I know *nothing* about what happened, she realized, nothing at all. All I know is what Sam told me.

She met Lamartine's eyes again. Every instinct she possessed told her that some aspects of Sam's story must be wrong. On the other hand, she was not always a good judge of character; people could take her in . . . *John was right, totally right*, she thought. *I shouldn't trespass. I should say and do nothing at all.* This decision brought with it an enormous relief. Suddenly she relaxed.

'And meanwhile, you're working for the *News* too, I think Gini said?'

'Just briefly. Yes, I am.'

'Well, you'd be doing me a great favour,' she continued, more warmly, 'if you could make Gini see she should leave. It's a perfectly horrible newspaper now, an absolute rag – well, I suppose not entirely, but I don't like its tone. And that ghastly new editor gives Gini the most pathetic stories. Before he came, she was doing so well. Did she tell you, a couple of years ago, she won two awards . . . ?'

'No. She didn't mention that.'

'How typical! Well, she did. She did a very fine series on police corruption in the north. The previous editor admired her work enormously. He'd agreed to send her abroad – to Yugoslavia, which was the kind of story she'd always wanted to cover, of course. And she'd done a great deal of work in preparation, then—'

'Yugoslavia?' He was frowning. 'You mean she wanted to cover the war?'

'Yes. She did. That's the kind of work she's always wanted to do. And she would have pulled it off. Gini is absolutely determined, and she's very brave, too.'

'I don't doubt that.' He glanced across the room once more. Gini was still in conversation with John Hawthorne; she said something inaudible, and Hawthorne laughed.

'The thing is,' Mary rushed on, she was on her favourite subject, 'Gini would never admit this, but she's very influenced by her father. Where he went, she's always been determined to follow. Her mother died, you see, when Gini was terribly young – two years old. She doesn't remember her at all. When I first knew Gini, she was only five, but she was very advanced for her age. She could read and write very well. She used to write these stories – well, all children do that, I suppose – but Gini used to lay them out in little books, like a newspaper. Then she'd show them to her father, only . . . well, unfortunately, he never took very much interest. But that just made her more determined. She's very single-minded. You can't rein her in. Do you know, when she was fifteen years old, she just walked out of school one day and went rushing off to . . . '

Mary stopped. She flushed crimson. She knew that when launched on the subject of Gini, she found it difficult to stop; but to have walked into that, to have been so incredibly stupid. She would never have done it, she realized, had Lamartine not been listening with such close attention to her proud boast. She would never have done it had he not seemed so very different from that imagined man in Beirut. However, she *had* done it. Now she had to extricate herself.

'Went rushing off to where?' Lamartine said in polite tones.

'Oh heavens,' Mary looked around her distractedly. 'Could you excuse me, just one second? That wretched poet friend of mine is monopolizing Lise. I must intervene . . . '

279

She darted away. Pascal watched her thoughtfully. He liked her, he thought, and he had learned a great deal from her, things Gini would never have told him herself. He had also learned, of course, that Gini had been wrong. Her stepmother knew very well what had happened in Beirut, and that meant Sam Hunter had not kept his word. He had told Mary about those events. Who, in her turn, might Mary have told?

He would have preferred Mary not to have heard that story from Hunter, and not to have been prejudiced against him, but there was nothing he could do about that now. It explained the way in which she had greeted him, that fierce protective inspection she had given him. Now she had obviously decided to risk no more *faux pas*, for she was returning, together with Lise Hawthorne.

She made the necessary introductions, then hastened away. Pascal looked down at the ambassador's wife. Her lovely face was tilted up to his; she radiated a tense almost febrile animation.

'I'm so pleased to meet you,' she was saying, in a low breathy voice, so he had to bend slightly to catch her words. She gave him an amused glance, which was more than a little flirtatious. 'I've seen your photographs,' she was saying. 'Those ones of Stephanie of Monaco. M. Lamartine . . . ' She wagged one long, beautifully manicured finger at him, with a kind of arch reproof. 'M. Lamartine, I was shocked. You have a very bad reputation, you know . . . '

'So tell me about your father,' John Hawthorne was saying to Gini. 'Give me an update. It's too long since we've seen him. It must be five or six years.'

'He's in Washington now,' Gini began.

'Washington. Of course. But didn't I hear some rumour – wasn't he planning a new book? Afghanistan – no, the Middle East?'

'Vietnam,' Gini replied.

She was almost certain Hawthorne knew this as well as she did, but for reasons of his own – perhaps to draw

280

her out – kept that knowledge concealed. 'Vietnam, Laos and Cambodia,' she went on. 'It's almost twenty-five years since he was there. He wants to go back and write about the changes since the war. I think he feels he did his finest work there.'

'He's wrong.' Hawthorne spoke abruptly. 'Obviously, the pieces he filed from Vietnam were outstanding – that Pulitzer was well deserved. But he's still in a class of his own. I followed everything he wrote during the Gulf War. I'm afraid I even poached some of his material for speeches.'

'I'm sure he wouldn't have minded. Flattered, I'd say.'

'Maybe. Maybe. Sam never had much time for politicians.' He smiled. 'The point was he could always uncover something new, something the military might have liked to conceal. They couldn't buy him, and they couldn't gag him. He should do his book on Vietnam. It needs writing. And if Sam did it, it'd sell . . . ' He paused. 'Here, your glass is empty. Let me get you a drink. White wine?'

He crossed to the drinks table, paused to speak to a group there. New guests were still arriving. The room was becoming crowded now. Gini, glancing about her, saw her stepmother leading Lise Hawthorne across to Pascal. They were introduced: Lise Hawthorne held out her hand.

Gini turned back to look at Hawthorne. The remarks about her father had pleased her, particularly the fact that in Hawthorne's opinion her father was still writing well. Had the comments been made for that reason, to please, to ingratiate?

Gini felt unsure. Hawthorne had no need, surely, to ingratiate himself with her. Why bother? His manner, certainly, had suggested nothing of the kind. On the contrary, it had been easy and direct; when he first mentioned her father – and he had done so almost immediately – he had spoken with an amused affection. 'Didn't you know?' he'd said. 'Your father kept me sane in Vietnam. He was an observer on two missions with my platoon. Sam and I were once holed up in a fox-hole together for three days; under fire. He ate my rations, and I drank the contents of his whisky flask. I was twenty-one years old and scared shitless. Your father never turned a hair. He taught me a lesson I've never forgotten. I'm not sure if it was courage or blind stupidity. Either way, Sam and I go back a long way.'

A disarming story, Gini thought. Flattering to her father, self-deprecatory, even the mild obscenity introduced as if to signal that Hawthorne was no prude, no stuffed shirt . . . Yes, it might have been calculated to win her over. Still, it had been recounted naturally, and with warmth.

Gini frowned; she was not a novice when it came to interviewing celebrated, powerful men; she had interviewed numerous politicians. Hawthorne resembled none of them. He did not monopolize the conversation, but turned it away from himself. He did not patronize. He did not glance away to check whether someone more important than Gini had just entered the room. He gave her his full attention. He listened when she spoke, and responded to her words. She could sense him assessing her as she spoke, even testing her. She had the impression that he was making a series of quick, decisive judgements. She also had the impression that whatever silent test was being set, she'd passed it. Had he judged her a fool, she was sure he would have wasted no more time, but turned on his heel.

This too was flattering, of course – and perhaps the source of Hawthorne's much-touted charisma and charm. That useful ability to make his interlocutor believe himself the only person of interest in a room: was it to that ability she was succumbing? For succumbing she was, and Gini knew it. She liked Hawthorne, and she had liked him almost from the first.

He was returning to her now, two drinks balanced in his hands. Gini regarded him carefully. Could this man be the husband Lise Hawthorne had described? Could this man be the subject of McMullen's revelations? She did not believe it for an instant, she decided.

'So tell me,' he began, handing Gini her drink, 'why are you working for the *News*? Nicholas Jenkins may be increasing circulation, but he's dragging the paper down-market. He'll lose his middle-class readership if he's not careful.'

'Oh, Jenkins knows that. It's a balancing act. Jenkins believes he can stay on the tightrope.'

'Jenkins believes he can walk on water.' He smiled. 'I'm not too sure of his ability to do either. We'll see. He can't be too popular at Buckingham Palace at the moment, that's certain. Or with the Elysée, to judge from this morning's paper. I see that French minister has resigned, incidentally – though that's no great loss to the world. Tell me, what are you working on right now?'

He sprang the question expertly. Gini knew she took a second too long to reply.

'What am I working on? Well, it's a typical Jenkins story. Telephone sex lines. You know, sex by phone.'

'I don't know, but I've heard.' He seemed amused. 'Are you enjoying the research?'

'No. Not at all.' Gini paused. This line of conversation, she saw, might be useful. She looked him directly in the eye. 'So far I've just been sampling the recordings. It's early days.'

'And do you find them entertaining?'

'No. Anodyne. The girls sound very bored. They describe their bodies, and their underwear . . .'

'Do they now?'

'Occasionally they buzz a vibrator. I have the feeling I could write a better script myself.'

'Really? What makes you think so?'

'Well, of course, I might be wrong. I'm a woman, and these calls are aimed at men. Perhaps I wouldn't understand what turns a man on.'

'Sure you would. You're not stupid.' His tone, which had veered on the bantering, became sharp.

For a moment Gini expected him to curtail the conversation, right there. He looked away from her, across the room to where his wife was now seated with Pascal; then, to her surprise, he turned back to her, and continued, his manner serious now.

'Any man who uses one of those phone lines is alone. I imagine he calls with a specific end in view, don't you? In order to achieve that – well, there have been numerous surveys of the male response to pornography, as I'm sure you know. Unlike women, who respond to words, men respond to pictures, to images. The job of the phone lines, therefore, is to make the man *see*. He must see what the woman describes. It doesn't need to be very original. Pornography is never original, that's its point. Beyond that,' he continued, frowning, 'I'd imagine the male callers experience two distinct types of arousal. In the first place, obviously, they are silent eavesdroppers – and that's akin to being a voyeur. In the second . . .' he shrugged, 'I imagine calling gives them an illusion of power. Of domination. They have chosen the number, and thus the girl. At any moment of their choosing, they can end the conversation, terminate the call. Satisfaction without repercussions or involvement. Sex on the man's terms. Sex with a total stranger . . .'

He gave an impatient and dismissive gesture. 'Many men would find that highly desirable. I guess these phone lines will flourish here, the same way they do back home. They surely won't fail.'

Gini lowered her eyes. An interesting speech, made in an impersonal way, as if he were addressing some seminar. The words accompanied by a hard, direct stare, and visible impatience towards the end – possibly with the subject, possibly with her.

'It's not the level of story you should be working on anyway.' He spoke abruptly, making her jump. 'Mary's said that often enough to me, and she's right. If that's the kind of feature Jenkins sends your way, then you'd do better elsewhere.'

'That has crossed my mind.'

'Good.' He smiled. 'Do you know Henry Melrose? You should talk to him about it. Make your preferences clear.'

Gini gave him a look of disbelief. Henry Melrose – Lord Melrose – was the proprietor of the *News*.

'No. I've never met Lord Melrose,' she replied in a dry way. 'Not too many reporters do. When he's actually in the building, which isn't that often, he stays up there on Olympus – the fifteenth floor.'

Hawthorne returned her smile. 'So, meet the man elsewhere. It's easily arranged. You'd like him. Henry Melrose is a very smart man. He's intelligent – which is more than you can say for most newspaper proprietors these days – and he actually takes an interest in what people write in his newspapers. He's not blind to ability, even if Jenkins is. And he happens to own more than one paper. Here and back home. In fact, if you're dissatisfied, why work in London at all? Why not go back to Washington, New York?'

'I've never worked there,' Gini replied. 'Except as a freelance. I've worked in England ever since I left school.'

'So make a change. Strike out. Sam could help, surely? He must have contacts to spare.'

'That's exactly the reason I don't want to work there. I don't want to hitch a ride on my father's reputation. That doesn't apply here.'

'I apologize.'

She had spoken with some sharpness, and she could feel him assessing her again. She sensed that having fallen in his regard a few minutes before – perhaps simply because she did not know Melrose, perhaps for timidity – she was now being restored to grace. Certainly his manner warmed.

'I can understand that,' he began. 'Sam can be goddamn impossible – we all know that. Maybe all fathers can. My own, for instance . . . ' He paused. 'I had a pretty difficult time with him when I was younger, and still do, from time to time. Too much ambition on my behalf.' He broke off. 'However, I was fortunate. I learned how to deal with him. And there was Lise, of course.'

He smiled, and took her arm. As he did so, and Gini felt the touch of his hand, just above her elbow, against

285

her bare arm, she saw him give the dress she was wearing a quick assessing glance.

'That's a beautiful dress, incidentally,' he said. 'Was that the famous Christmas present from Mary? She mentioned it to me.'

'Yes. It was.'

'She chose very well. It sets off your hair. Now, you must come meet Lise. I know she's longing to talk to you. Has Mary told you that story of hers – how she persuaded me to propose?' He made a rueful face. 'Nonsense, of course. My father claims the same thing. Actually, I made up my own mind but I never tell Mary that. It's more fun to indulge her.' He smiled. 'I'm very fond of your stepmother. Did you know that when I first met her, I was ten years old? She's been teasing me unmercifully ever since. That makes it nearly forty years . . .'

He began steering her gently in his wife's direction, still with his hand on her arm. His face was now turned away from her, as he looked across the room towards his wife. Lise was seated on the sofa, still talking with great animation to Pascal. Gini glanced towards Hawthorne, who like most of the men present, was wearing a dinner jacket and black tie. He looked blond, tanned, handsome and unreadable – exactly as he had looked when she entered the room, or when she had met him all those years before, as a child. She thought: *I have made no progress; I've discovered nothing at all.*

Then she realized Hawthorne was frowning, and followed his gaze. Seated next to one another, Lise and Pascal were deep in conversation. Pascal looked relaxed and at ease, more so than Gini had seen him look in days. His eyes were fixed on Lise's face, and his expression was unmistakably attentive.

'No,' Gini heard him say, in response to some breathy remark from Lise. 'No. *C'est impossible*. Women like to make these claims. And maybe some of them believe them. But not you . . .'

Lise laughed. She leaned forward, and began speaking again. Hawthorne had come to a halt. He stood for a moment watching his wife, then turned back to Gini.

'Maybe now is not the moment to interrupt. Lise is well launched on one of her favourite subjects, by the look of it . . . '

'And that is?'

'Oh, astrology. Tarot cards. Destiny. Fate . . . ' He gave her an amused glance. 'All that mumbo-jumbo. If your friend isn't careful – and he doesn't look as if he's being too careful – then in about, let's see . . . ' He checked his watch. 'In about three minutes' time, Lise will offer to read his palm.'

'She often does that?'

Gini looked at him uncertainly. Hawthorne seemed neither embarrassed nor annoyed. He had released her arm, and was now looking at her in a different, more intent way. She saw his eyes move to the neckline of her dress, then to her hair, then her mouth, her eyes. He gave her a dazzling smile, and it was as if he had decided to throw some switch, suddenly releasing upon her the full power of that legendary charisma and charm. *So that is his technique*, Gini thought, *when his wife flirts, he flirts as well*.

'Oh sure, very often,' he replied. 'Lise genuinely believes it all, I'm afraid. She and I share a birthday in January. When I first met her, she told me it was a sign . . . We were both children at the time.' He paused. 'And speaking of birthdays – it's mine in a couple of weeks. We're having a party at our place in Oxfordshire. Mary's coming. Henry Melrose will be there. You must come, Gini. Now that I've met you properly at last, we should make up for lost time. Ah, you see? Three minutes exactly . . . '

He gestured across the room. Lise was now holding Pascal's palm in her hand. She held it between them in a delicate and formal way and began to indicate lines. Pascal appeared to be taking it seriously. Gini averted her eyes.

'My father's coming over for it,' Hawthorne was continuing. 'And my brother Prescott, my sisters. A great gathering of the clan. So you must come. I'll mention it to Lise. It would do her good, you know, to have some younger friends in London . . . ' He touched her arm again, and began to steer her forward. 'All this official partying and hob-nobbing isn't really her style. Or mine. Unfortunately, I have to put up with it, and I don't have too much free time. Too many meetings, too many damn speeches. At the moment, of course, with all this Middle East business—'

'Don't you find that a strain?' Gini put in quickly. 'The security? You must feel you can never be alone . . . '

'On the contrary. It reminds you just how alone you are . . . ' He spoke, suddenly, with genuine feeling, in a very different tone. The next second his manner was as before: forceful, neutral, urbane.

'In any case, you get used to it. It comes with the territory.' They had reached Pascal and Lise at last. Pascal rose. Mary reappeared. Lise Hawthorne also rose; she greeted Gini warmly. She pressed her hand tightly, and gazed at her in a way Gini found disconcerting, even strange.

'Oh, I'm so glad to meet you properly at last,' she said in her soft breathy voice. 'I've heard so much about you from Mary, of course. And from John.'

Hawthorne smiled. 'Good Lord, Gini won't even remember that,' he said. 'It was a very long time ago. But we did meet once, Gini, in Kent, at Mary's house. One Easter. You were just going back to school . . . '

'I remember,' Gini said.

Lise let go of her hand. Just to the side of them, Mary was attempting to introduce John Hawthorne to Pascal. When she finally succeeded in gaining the ambassador's attention, he gave Pascal a hard look and a cursory handshake.

'Lamartine?' He frowned. 'Don't I know the name? Ah yes. Sure. From this morning's newspapers. Excuse me, will you?'

He was already turning away. Mary's face bore an odd, almost guilty expression. Lise was clutching her tiny evening bag, her knuckles white with strain.

'Lise,' her husband said over his shoulder, 'five minutes

only, I'm afraid, and then we must go. I'll just speak to Malone . . . '

And with this, with an abruptness that was knowingly rude, he turned on his heel.

Exactly five minutes later, the Hawthornes moved out to the hall. For Mary's sake, Gini might have stayed longer, but Pascal shook his head. He took her arm.

'No. Now,' he said in a low voice. 'I want to leave at the same time as they do.'

There was a crush of guests in the hallway. Mary was there, the Hawthornes were there, the two actors were also leaving; by the door was a huge, crew-cut security man. From outside came the crackle of radio static.

'Malone?' Hawthorne said.

The man nodded. He opened the door, said something inaudible, and closed it again.

Hawthorne was helping his wife into her coat. Gini froze and almost exclaimed, but Pascal tightened his warning grip on her arm. Lise stroked the coat, and turned back to Mary with a smile.

'Isn't it heavenly? It was John's birthday present. And the necklace, too.' She reached up, and gave her husband an affectionate kiss. 'I'm so spoiled.'

'Nonsense, darling.' He smiled down at her, then put his arm around her shoulders. 'It's no more than you deserve.'

The Hawthornes said their thanks and goodbyes to Mary. They shook hands with the two actors. There was a flurry of movement, then Malone opened the door and moved out fast. On the steps beyond two shadows moved. There was another crackle of static. Gini and Pascal waited and watched the Hawthornes, flanked by two of those shadows, descend the portico steps and enter their long black limousine. Malone remained at the top of the steps, his eyes scanning the street. As the car pulled away Malone lifted his wrist, and spoke inaudibly into his wrist-mike. The limousine disappeared. A second car followed it, the regulation twenty yards back. Malone ran down the steps with surprising agility for a man of his size. A third car had already moved forward. Malone jumped into it, and it too pulled away, fast.

'Don't say anything,' Pascal bent closely to her ear. 'Nothing, Gini. Wait until we're outside . . . '

As they left, Pascal took her arm. They walked at a fast pace in the opposite direction from the street where Gini had parked her car. When Pascal was certain there was no-one following them, he drew her into a deserted cul-de-sac. There he stopped. He turned to Gini, his face alert and pale in the lamplight.

'Gini, you saw?'

'The coat? Of course I saw the coat. You can't exactly miss full-length sable.'

'And the necklace? You saw the pearls?'

'No.'

'It's because she was wearing the clasp at the back. You could only see it from behind. I noticed it earlier. The clasp was gold, with a cabochon ruby. Both the pearls and the coat were a birthday present from her husband. It's her birthday today, Gini.'

'I know. Mary mentioned it . . . '

'Well now.' Pascal took out a cigarette and lit it. He leaned back against a garden wall and looked at her. 'Isn't her husband the ambassador a generous man? A pearl necklace. A sable coat. I wonder if he mentioned who had worn them before?'

'Pascal, wait. You're sure about the pearls?'

'Of course. And what's more, we were right when we listened to that phone-tape. She's afraid, and she's under strain. Even your stepmother noticed it. She came over twice to ask her if she still felt unwell.'

'She didn't look unwell to me.' Gini gave him a sharp glance. 'She looked perfectly fine when she was reading your palm.'

'How could you tell?' His comeback was equally sharp. 'You were so wrapped up in Hawthorne you wouldn't have noticed a damn thing.'

'Well, at least I wasn't flirting with Hawthorne, which can't be said of you and Lise—'

'Oh really? You weren't? You were listening to him pretty damn closely, hanging on his every word. I saw the way he looked at you. I saw the way he took your arm—'

'Don't be so bloody ridiculous! Of course I was listening to him. That's why I was there. To get some kind of impression of the man.'

'Fine. Excellent. And so what was that impression?'

'I liked him, if you must know. On the whole. He's autocratic, but you'd expect that. If you'd tried to talk to him yourself, instead of sitting there having your palm read, for God's sake, you might have liked him too.'

'Tried to talk to him? Jesus Christ, are you totally blind?' Pascal gave a gesture of exasperation. 'You saw what happened the second Mary introduced me. As soon as he heard my name, he was off, gone. And calling his wife to heel.'

'I wonder he didn't do that earlier,' Gini replied. 'I've never seen anything so pathetic. Sitting on a sofa, whispering to you—'

'She was not whispering. She just has a low voice, that's all.'

'Whispering. Taking your palm in front of a whole room of people. Well, I could see you were flattered, Pascal, and I hate to disillusion you, but apparently, she does that all the time—'

'Is that so?' Pascal's voice, angry a moment before became suddenly and dangerously cool.

'Yes, she damn well does,' Gini continued. 'Hawthorne told me. He heard what she was saying – all that tripe about horoscopes and astrology or whatever it was. And he told me that in three minutes she'd be reading your palm. He was right to the second, what's more.'

'Was he? How very clever of her.'

'Clever of *her*?' Gini stared at him. 'Why?'

'Because she did something he expected her to do –

and because of that, he stopped paying attention. Instead, he turned his attention to you.'

'Will you stop this? He did no such thing. It was just a normal, ordinary conversation. We talked about work. About my father. He knew my father in Vietnam . . .'

Pascal gave her an impatient glance. 'But of course. He set out to charm you – that was obvious from the second we walked in. So he talked about your father. He was flattering you, Gini. Can't you see that?'

'No, I can't. I'm telling you, I liked him. He seemed honest. Straight. Sharp. I liked him. End of story. That's it.'

'You're biased in his favour now, is that it? But you can't explain those pearls, or that coat—'

'No. I can't. And neither can you. In themselves they prove nothing . . .'

'They suggest quite a lot.'

'Look,' Gini sighed, 'all I'm doing is giving him the benefit of the doubt. Innocent until proven guilty. Unlike you. You took one of your instant dislikes. It was just the same as when you met my father—'

'I don't believe I'm hearing this!' Pascal turned away and began to pace up and down. 'Fine. Right.' He turned back to her. 'Let me just make sure I've got this right. You associate Hawthorne with your father now, is that it?'

'No, I damn well don't.' Gini rounded on him angrily. 'Did I say that? No. I said you made one of your instant decisions—'

'I do not make instant decisions.'

'Yes, you do. How about Lise? You took one look and instantly capitulated. Suddenly Lise is this poor frightened creature in need of protection. We don't *know* that, Pascal. Lise could have made up this whole thing. So could McMullen, for that matter. It could be one long lie from beginning to end.'

'You think I don't know that? Why do you think I was talking to the stupid woman for so long? Why was I listening to her so carefully? You think I actually enjoyed

292

it – hours of horoscope nonsense, little lectures on Fate? Dear God, don't you know me at *all*?'

'You didn't *look* bored, Pascal.'

'Will you stop this and listen?' He moved suddenly and took hold of her arm.

'No. I will not. I *saw* you, Pascal. I've never seen you behave that way in my life. I—'

She broke off. Pascal was now very close to her. He was looking down into her face.

'There's more you want to say, perhaps, Gini? Other things you want to add? Or are you going to be quiet, and *listen*?'

'No. I'm not. And I have plenty more to say.'

Pascal gave a sigh. 'Oh, very well,' he said. 'Then we'll do it this way. I'll *make* you be quiet.'

Then he kissed her. He moved so quickly that he took her by surprise. He caught her roughly against him, and kissed her mouth hard.

'Now,' he said, stepping back from her, 'you will listen to what I have to say, and you won't interrupt until I've finished. First, Lise Hawthorne *was* under strain, she was jumpy, odd – maybe even on pills of some kind. Second, there must be a major security alert, because that house was crawling with security men. There were two back-up cars outside, and two men on foot. Inside, there was that Malone man in the hall, and another man positioned at the far side of the drawing-room by the other door. That's very unusual, in fact it's something I've never seen at a private party. Third, Lise Hawthorne was worried by the man in the room, and the man in the hall. She kept glancing across at them, and then at her husband. It was as if she felt watched. Four, she *was* watched, certainly by Hawthorne. Most of the time you were talking to him, you had your back to us. But he kept his eye on us, the entire time. All of which, Gini, *all of which* makes it all the more remarkable what she did, when she read my palm and that damn husband of hers finally turned away. She gave me this, Gini, look . . . '

He held out to her in the lamplight a tiny piece of paper, no more than an inch square.

'*Now*,' he said, 'do you understand why this apparently stupid woman reads my palm? It was very well done, Gini. I noticed nothing until I felt the paper in my hand. It was done in a second. So. Shall we see why?'

Pascal drew her closer to the streetlight. He unfolded the tiny scrap of paper, and smoothed it flat. On it, typed, was the word *Sunday*, and beneath it an address.

There was a small silence. Gini shivered.

'McMullen failed to provide next Sunday's assignation address,' Pascal said. 'So she did. At some risk.'

Gini was looking closely at the address. 'One thing you should know,' she said. 'This address is five minutes from Regent's Park. Five minutes from the US Ambassador's residence, Pascal, from John Hawthorne's house. We can pass it on the way home.'

They drove north, skirted Regent's Park, and turned into Avenue Road. Large houses lined the street on either side of them.

'Some neighbourhood,' Pascal said, without enthusiasm. It reminded him of Helen's house, of her neighbourhood.

'A *rich* neighbourhood,' Gini corrected him. 'A *nouveau riche* neighbourhood. Especially this part here.'

They passed some large white-stucco Victorian villas, interspersed with oversized brick palaces of more recent date. Most had security lighting; almost all had ground-floor windows which were barred.

'People buy them for investment, I think,' Gini said. 'Half of them are empty except for staff. That's a well-known private abortion clinic – I interviewed its director once. I think it's the next turning on the right . . . ' She slowed. 'Damn. It's a cul-de-sac.'

'Never mind. Turn in, drive to the end, circle and go out again.'

There were six houses on the street, three on each side. The one to which Lise had directed them was at the far

294

end, and was the only period house. They glimpsed white stucco, a curious Gothic porch set to the side. The rest of the building was hidden behind high laurel hedges. It was unlit, as were the rest of the houses. Apart from one street-lamp, the turning was dark.

Gini pulled back out into the main road. They drove north back to Islington, saying little. In her flat, Pascal made up the sofa in silence, and in silence began to pack his bag. Gini watched him.

'Venice tomorrow,' she said.

'Yes. The flight leaves at nine. We'll have to leave here around seven. You'd better get some sleep.'

'Perhaps we'll find McMullen,' she said. 'Perhaps he'll explain . . . '

'Maybe.' Pascal straightened. He looked around the room, and then back at her. 'Not here,' he said.

Gini looked around her room, which might or might not be safe. She wanted to ask Pascal why he had kissed her, and whether he had felt as she had felt when he did, but she did not want to ask that question in a room with listening walls.

She thought she could see the answer in his face, and in the resolute way he continued his packing, but she could not be sure. At the door of her bedroom, she hesitated. Pascal stopped packing, straightened, and looked at her. The silence was very eloquent.

'Was it just to silence me?' she said finally.

'No.' He smiled. 'I'd been considering it for some time. *Depuis mercredi, tu sais. Depuis douze ans . . .* '

He returned to his packing. She went into her bedroom and closed the door.

Those two phrases sang in the air. She liked the grammar, the French construction; they made the words echo and re-echo. *Since Wednesday*, she thought. A translation. *Since twelve years.*

XVIII

The flight was delayed. Pascal and Gini stood in line. There were few passengers for Venice. Most of the other travellers were heading for the ski-slopes. A calm, bored voice kept up a constant refrain on the Tannoy: *Due to the current international situation, additional security measures are in operation. Please do not leave bags unattended. Please be patient and co-operate with security personnel . . .*

Their luggage was hand-searched twice. Pascal's cameras were minutely examined. Gini's tape recorder was opened, the tape removed, checked, replaced.

Their plane was half-empty. Pascal, who had kept a close eye on the other passengers in the departure lounge, ensured they were given seats well separated from the others. They had two empty rows behind them, and two in front.

'There,' he said, as the plane took off. 'It's the best I can do. It's not one hundred per cent, but at least we're not easily overheard.'

'You think we'll be followed?'

Pascal shrugged. 'It's possible. I *feel* followed, and listened to, all the time. But no doubt that's partly paranoia, as you say. I've taken some precautions. We won't go to the hotel I booked us into; we'll go to another I know. A small, quiet place.' He paused while the stewardess brought copies of the newspapers.

'One thing,' he said, when she had gone. 'If McMullen did leave England for Italy, he timed it very well. Another couple of weeks and they'd have been checking all passports very carefully.'

'They checked yours for long enough,' Gini said.

'Too many Middle East visas, they don't like that.'

'Look at this.' She held out the copy of *The Sunday*

Times. 'More anti-US demonstrations. In Syria. And in Iran.'

'It's spreading, and it's intensifying. That was inevitable.' Pascal shrugged. 'Look.' He turned the pages of his own newspaper, pointed to one item. 'Yesterday there was a bomb outside the US embassy in Paris, did you see that?'

'Yes. I did. I suppose it could explain why Lise Hawthorne was so nervous. Mary did say that Lise worried about her husband's safety.'

Pascal frowned and turned away to the window. 'No,' he said, 'it was something else, something *more.*'

'She could be worrying about McMullen,' Gini said. 'That's the most obvious deduction, surely? After all, McMullen seems to have been her one confidant. She was depending on his help and support. It's well over two weeks since McMullen disappeared.'

'Twenty days. It's twenty days.'

'Suppose she hasn't heard from him in that time, either. Suppose she doesn't know where he is – even if he's dead or alive. And meanwhile, there's another of those Sundays, coming closer and closer. The next is just one week away.' She glanced towards him. 'Absence, Pascal. Uncertainty. Just those factors alone would explain it. She's anxious, and she's afraid for *him.*'

'If they aren't in contact.' He frowned. 'Maybe. Except I can't believe McMullen *wouldn't* contact her. You heard him on that tape. "I'd cross the world to spend five minutes at your side." He'd move heaven and earth to remain in touch, to reassure her. You could hear it in his voice.'

He looked at her as he said this, hesitated, then looked away. The plane banked, then gained height. Beyond the window there was dense cloud, then brilliant light.

'Anyway.' He folded up the newspapers and put them away. His manner became businesslike. 'Let's concentrate. In two hours or so we'll be at this Palazzo Ossorio – we could be actually talking to the man. We'd better prepare ourselves. Do you have that picture Jenkins gave us?'

Gini produced the photograph and they examined it together. McMullen's army days: he was wearing camouflage combat dress; his Parachute Regiment badge was just visible on his beret. He had turned to look at the camera, and the details of his face were slightly blurred. A man of average height, with fair hair and handsome but unremarkable features. He was wearing a signet ring; it could just be glimpsed on the small finger of his left hand. On the back of the photograph, it said: *Wiesbaden, West Germany – NATO exercise 1988*.

Gini gave a sigh. 'It doesn't tell us very much,' she said. 'Still, why should it? Photographs rarely do.'

Pascal smiled. 'I hope you don't mean that . . . '

'I don't mean your kind of photographs – you know that perfectly well. But this is just a snapshot. It tells us very little, it seems to me.'

'Put it together with other information and it tells us more.' Pascal paused. 'First of all, what does he look like? He'll be in his forties now. Good-looking, a little unmemorable, wearing a signet ring. You remember those suits and shirts in his apartment? A conventional Englishman, yes? Exactly what you'd expect from a man of his background and class. An officer and a gentleman, all set to be a general eventually, that's what his very unconventional sister said to me.'

'Except he left the Army?'

'Indeed. But there's more. The choice of regiment, for instance. The Paras? Might you not expect such a man – ex-public school, ex-Oxford, Sword of Honour at Sandhurst – to choose a more conventional, a more élitist regiment, like the Guards?'

'Maybe. Maybe. I'm not too up on the British army.'

'Well, take my word for it. It's an unusual choice. Not without precedent, obviously, but unusual just the same. And when I started checking out the man—'

'Other unusual elements?'

'Sure. First, his Oxford career. You remember what

Jenkins told us? Well, he was right. McMullen went to Christ Church, to read Modern History, in 1968. He was a high-flyer, Gini – and yet, what happens? He never takes his degree. He leaves, after only one year.'

'You checked with the college?'

'Sure.'

'Did they give a reason? Was he ill? Was he sent down – expelled?'

'If any of these factors applied, they weren't about to tell me.' Pascal took the photograph. He looked at it closely, then put it down. 'What's more,' he continued, 'when you look into his army career, it's the same pattern. There's a gap of three years after Oxford. He joins the Army in 1972. He seems destined for higher things, just the way his sister said, and then what happens? He reaches the rank of captain only, which is average promotion for his age and length of service. Then, in 1989, he suddenly resigns his commission. He leaves.'

Gini frowned thoughtfully. 'Four years ago. That's interesting. A period of time that comes up elsewhere in this story. Four years ago, Hawthorne's younger son is seriously ill. As a result of that, Hawthorne then abandons his career in politics. Four years ago, if you can believe the Washington tittle-tattle, which you probably can't, Lise Hawthorne becomes ill and as a result her marriage is under strain. Four years. Could there be a connection?'

'It's possible. I wish I knew exactly when he and Lise first met, how they met and where. The sister could have told me, obviously, but you know what happened there.'

'Did none of the friends know anything?'

'Nothing. They were useless. Obviously not in close touch with him. But then his sister said he was becoming a recluse. One man had last seen him in August last year. They went grouse shooting together in Yorkshire. He described McMullen as a good chap . . . Hopeless. I mentioned Lise Hawthorne, and none of them reacted. They all said the same: well, I could always try her, if I was really anxious to get hold of him, but they'd never heard him mention her name.'

'What about the other friend? The one his sister mentioned?'

'Jeremy Prior-Kent? He's out of town. He makes TV commercials. He's due back in London on Monday or Tuesday. We can try him then, but I'm not optimistic.'

'What about people he worked with in the City? Jenkins said he was in the City, after he left the Army.'

'I tried them all.' Pascal shrugged. 'And they were useless too. His last job was with a firm of stockbrokers, arranged through a friend of his father's. It wasn't a senior post, and it didn't pan out. He resigned suddenly, in January last year. He hasn't worked since then, nor does he need to, if you can believe his sister's account.'

'January. A year ago.' Gini glanced at him. 'That's another coincidence, Pascal. It was around then that Hawthorne was appointed ambassador. McMullen left his job just as Lise came to London. You think there's a link?'

'I suppose it's possible.' Pascal was beginning to look disheartened. 'I'm getting damn sick of suppositions. I just wish we had a few more facts.'

He turned back and scowled at the window. The noise of the plane's engines altered pitch. A meal, and drinks, were served. Not long afterwards, the seat-belt sign flashed on. They were beginning their descent. Gini craned her neck, and peered out of the window. She had never been to Venice, and in her imagination, the city was a miraculous place. She had seen glimpses of it so many times, as everyone had; glimpses in paintings, in photographs, in novels. She wanted to catch sight now of islands, the lagoon, but she could see nothing.

Pascal was staring into the clouds that enveloped the plane as they descended through thick mist. His face was preoccupied and tense. It had puzzled her before, his lack of excitement as this key meeting came close. Now, suddenly she understood it.

She said in a quiet voice, 'You don't believe we are going to find him, do you, Pascal? You think McMullen's dead.'

He gave a wry look, then a shrug. 'It seems to me a possibility. A twenty-day silence?'

'*Death in Venice?*'

'That's a novel way of putting it.' He gave a brief smile. 'But I'm afraid so. Yes.'

It was raining in Venice. It rained upon the airport; it rained upon the transfer launch; it rained upon them as they negotiated the maze of narrow waterways that led to their hotel. Inside, their rooms were adjacent. Pascal followed her into her room. He watched her cross straight to the window, and throw the shutters back. She gave a low cry of delight.

'Look, Pascal, look. Oh, what an astonishing place. I'm glad it's raining. Look at the light.'

He moved to her side. Their view of the Grand Canal outside was oblique. Water vapour made the air luminous. Across the water, through rain, a palazzo could be glimpsed. Rain gave its stone a silvery sheen. Below it, laid out across the water, was its twin, its reflection. Haze and perspective tricked the eye: the reflection of the palace was as real, as substantial and as insubstantial, as the palace itself. As they watched, a *vaporetto* passed. The reflections stirred and dissipated. As the water stilled and grew calm again, the phantom palaces reformed upon its surface.

The sky was without colour: the light had that shifting and endless subtlety of tone in which silver merged to pearl, pearl to grey, and grey to black. As Pascal watched this luminescence his instinct was to reach for his camera. Then he stopped, looked again, thought again. A camera was the wrong instrument for this. He laid his hand quietly across Gini's shoulders, and she swung round to look at him, delight in her face.

'I cannot trust my own eyes,' she said. 'Look. The rain deceives them and the reflections and the light . . . '

'I trust your eyes,' Pascal said.

Some while later, he closed the window, and they left their hotel. Within twenty minutes, they were lost. It would take them over an hour to locate the Palazzo

Ossorio, even though it was close by, and Pascal, ever practical, had come armed with a map.

'This city is like a labyrinth,' Pascal said, coming to a halt.

'It's a very beautiful labyrinth.'

'Even so.' Pascal frowned at the map. 'It seems so clear. We walk along here, into a square, then first left on the far side.'

'We've done that twice. We're walking in circles.'

They retraced their steps. This time, believing they followed the same route, they found themselves in a different place, a narrow and dark *passagieta*. The canal beside them moved with the tide; the air smelled salty. A gondola and a boat rocked beside the quay. They turned into a passageway, through a low archway, and found themselves facing a solid wall. They were about to turn back, when Gini froze.

'Listen, Pascal.' She caught at his sleeve. 'Footsteps. Someone is following us. I thought so once or twice before.'

Pascal placed a finger against her lips. They stood there in silence. The footsteps approached the entrance to the *passagieta*, then stopped, then retreated. Pascal ran back out to the quay but there was no-one in sight. He stood, frowning, looking this way and that.

'Did you see anyone?' Gini said, as she rejoined him.

'No. No-one. But look at this place, Gini.' He gestured around them. 'So many little turnings and doorways and passageways . . . ' He shrugged. 'It was probably nothing. We'll be more careful from now on.'

They were, but the Palazzo Ossorio still proved elusive, and eventually Pascal's patience ran out.

'There should damn well be a bridge here.' He came to a halt. 'Where the hell is it?'

'We've taken another wrong turn, I think.'

'This is ridiculous. I never get lost. Let's look at this map again.'

Gini peered over his shoulder at the map. She traced a

web of minute intersections and crossings. 'We're *here*. I think.'

'Impossible. We can't be. We're *there*. We're going in totally the wrong direction. What we have to do is get to this intersection here – you see, where four streets meet? Then we go around the corner, into the square, and we're practically there. It isn't that far.'

They followed his directions. When they came to the key intersection, they found six narrow streets met there, not four.

'*Merde*.' Pascal began to swear in French, and continued to swear, at length.

Gini said, 'It seems simple to me. We just take this street, then we keep aiming to the right. It's very close.'

'It's very close and we're not going to get there by guesswork. Or instinct. Gini – wait . . . '

Gini had darted off along the passageway she had indicated. Pascal followed her. She disappeared very suddenly from sight. Pascal began to run. He found himself in a square with a small café. Gini was waiting for him. Rain had drenched her hair, rain ran down her face. Taking his hand, she pointed, and around the corner, down a tiny and almost invisible passageway, they found a canal, a quay, and the Palazzo Ossorio at last. They stood and looked at it in silence, this elusive building. It was a palace no longer, and its splendours were ruined. Now it was semi-derelict; timbers propped up its crumbling portico. It looked both uninhabited and unsafe.

'He can't be here. Surely he can't be here?' Gini stared up at the building. A rat scuttled from the building's courtyard and into the canal.

'Shall we go in and find out?' Pascal said.

McMullen's apartment was on the top floor; the rest of the building appeared abandoned. Outside McMullen's door, which had neither knocker nor bell, was an empty saucer. A thin ginger cat watched them, crouched on a window-ledge. There was a fly-blown note, tacked to the door, instructing them in English that if the occupant should be out, to come back.

Dead leaves rustled in the corners of the stairs. From the distance, perhaps from an adjacent building, came the sound of a door slamming. A woman shouted; a child screamed. Then there was silence. The cat watched them with narrowed green eyes. Pascal approached the door, and hammered hard on its panels. There was no response. Pascal paused, then hammered again. His blows echoed down the stairwell. The cat leapt to the ground and slunk past them. Tail vertical, its tip twitching, the cat descended the stairs, rounded a bend, and disappeared.

Gini said, 'This is a horrible place. It smells foul. Damp. Murky. Decaying. Pascal, let's go. He's obviously not here.'

Pascal was examining the door, which, though old, was heavy. He examined its one lock. He crossed to the window where the cat had been perched, opened it with difficulty, and leaned out. There was a sheer fifty-foot drop to the canal below. No ledges. No pipes.

Gini said, 'Pascal, I know what you're thinking. Don't. One break-in is one too many. Let's come back later. We can ask at that café in the square.'

Pascal pounded one last time on the door. He tested its strength against his weight. The door did not shift an inch. He stepped back with an air of resignation.

'Very well. You're probably right. We'll make some enquiries. And then we'll come back.'

The owner of the café, a taciturn man, eyed them and shrugged. Englishman? What Englishman? He knew of no such person – this wasn't a tourist area. The Palazzo Ossorio? Impossible. The place was empty. There had been some mad old grandmother holed up there, but even she had not been seen in weeks. Maybe she'd died, maybe she'd moved on. Who in their right mind would want to live in a place like that?

Its owner? He had no idea. Well, yes, since they mentioned it, they could try rental agencies, but not in this neighbourhood. They might find some on the other side of the Grand Canal, there were places there that rented accommodations to foreigners, sure – but in the winter most of them closed. There was one they might try, in the Calle Larga XXII Marzo, off the west side of St Mark's Square.

The café owner stood watching them depart. He coughed as they rounded the corner, and from the café's rear room a tall man, dressed in a dark overcoat, emerged. '*Grazie mille*,' he said. He handed back his empty cup of espresso, looked out at the sky, and made a few disparaging remarks about the weather in Italian. The café owner noted that his accent was good, his phrasing idiomatic – though he was certainly not a Venetian, not from around here. The man peeled off a few notes, and tossed them down. They came to considerably more thousand lire than the price of an espresso. Without further comment, or backward glance, the foreigner walked out into the rain.

On the far side of the canal, Pascal and Gini found four rental agencies, including the one in the Calle Larga, but all four were closed and shuttered. They enquired in numerous hotels: none had any single Englishmen registered, let alone one who fitted McMullen's description. Few cafés or restaurants were open out of season; of those that were, they tried the obvious ones first, then the less obvious ones, tucked away in backstreets. No-one recognized McMullen's photograph.

'Nothing,' Pascal said. They had returned to St Mark's Square, and were standing outside the glitter and glimmer of the cathedral's façade. 'This is a hopeless task. There are thousands of cafés, thousands of hotels . . . ' He stared angrily across the square. The light was failing. Water made the paving-stones of the piazza shine. Lights spilled out from the cafés in the arcades on either side.

Gini glanced over her shoulder. From the cathedral porch behind came the sound of voices. A few out-of-season tourists made their way in and out. English voices; American voices; other languages she could neither identify nor understand. Shapes of people, shadows. She turned back to Pascal, and so did not notice that one of those shadows was close behind them by the steps.

She felt a sudden despondency. All this way, for nothing. She shook herself, then chafed her hands together. Pascal saw the expression on her face.

'Don't despair.' He put his arms around her. 'You're cold, and you're tired. But we mustn't give in. We'll go to a café, get something to eat. Drink some hot coffee. Then we'll go back to that apartment.'

'What if there's still no reply?'

Pascal hesitated. He said gently, 'Gini, you know the answer to that. Somehow or other – legally or illegally – we get in.'

At five they returned to Palazzo Ossorio. It was dark, and the surrounding streets were ill-lit. The whole area seemed deserted: there were no passers-by on the streets, no sounds of voices, or radios or televisions. Above the dark water of the canal rose a thin greenish mist.

Pascal led her across to the silent building. He took her hand, and they felt their way across the courtyard. At the foot of the stone staircase he produced a flashlight. By its narrow beam, still hand in hand, they began to mount the stone steps.

Halfway up, Gini froze. She said, 'What's that?'

They stood listening. Pascal switched off the flashlight. The darkness was thick; she could see nothing, not even the outlines of the steps. She felt her skin chill, and the hair prickle at the back of her neck.

From somewhere, perhaps below, perhaps above them, came the sound of a low crooning. The sound rose in pitch, then diminished to a whisper, then stopped. She felt Pascal's body tense.

After a pause, the noise began again, a low liquid murmuring sound, like an incantation. Gini felt something brush her legs. She stifled a cry, and Pascal drew her close. He pressed his hand across her lips, and said, in a low voice, 'Someone lives here. This building isn't deserted at all.'

He listened, the crooning began, again stopped. Some-where below them there was a shuffling sound. A door opened and closed. Against one of the stairway walls, momentarily, they saw a band of light. It disappeared as the door closed and the murmuring recommenced. '*Cats*,' Pascal said suddenly in a low voice. 'It's all right, Gini. Someone lives here and lives here alone. Listen, it's a woman – an old woman – and she's talking to her cats . . . '

Gini listened: she knew at once he was right. She was trembling, and ashamed of trembling. Pascal's grip on her hand tightened; he switched on the flashlight, and moved towards the steps.

McMullen's apartment was two flights further up. From the landing outside his door, the crooning was inaudible. Gini leaned against the wall. Outside, the wind buffeted the building; the window creaked.

She heard Pascal give a low exclamation, and swung around.

'Gini,' he whispered. 'Gini, look at this.'

The door had been unlocked since their earlier visit. It stood open an inch.

Beyond the door was darkness, and silence. Pascal seemed to hesitate. Gini approached. By the open door, the smell of damp decay was sickeningly strong. She recoiled from the stench. Pascal's face hardened. He put his arm across the doorway.

'You wait here. Wait here on the landing. I'm going in.'

'You're not leaving me here. I'm coming too—'

'No! You stay right here.'

In the torchlight, she saw the pallor of his face, and the anxiety in his eyes. The smell made her want to vomit. She covered her mouth with her hand, walked away a few paces, and drew in a deep breath.

'Gini, please. I don't want you to come in here.'

'I'm afraid. I'm afraid, Pascal.' She grasped his arm. 'I'm too afraid to stay here on my own. Someone might be in there . . . '

'Oh, someone's certainly in there,' he replied, his face grim. 'And they're unlikely to harm us, I think . . . '

'Please, Pascal . . . '

'Very well.'

He switched off the beam of the flashlight. Leaning against the door with his arm, and keeping to the side, he eased it back. There was a shuffling sound at their feet; a few pieces of paper, faded bits of card, lifted against the passage of the door, then fell back. Pascal shone the flashlight on them, then again switched it off. He stepped forward into the dark, feeling ahead of him as he went. Gini, following close behind him, also fumbled in the darkness. On either side of her, she felt a wall: they were in a long narrow corridor. There were bare floorboards underfoot.

After twenty or thirty feet – in the darkness she lost all sense of distance – the walls either side gave out. There was no door, just an archway hung with a heavy curtain. Pascal eased the drapery aside. She heard the rattle of wooden rings on the rail above her head. She stopped, clutching her mouth.

Later, she would tell herself that she must have known what they would find. But at the time, her mind was working slowly: all she could think of was that this space, wherever they were, was terrible, filled with the sweetly sour smell of rotten meat.

Pascal, having worked in war zones, knew precisely what it was. He knew what they must inevitably find. He switched on the flashlight and directed its beam away from the centre of the room, towards the walls. He ran the beam along them, until it pin-pointed a light switch.

In a quiet voice, he said, 'Gini. I want you to turn away. I'm going to switch the light on. Don't look.'

She closed her eyes, and felt the light against her lids. Behind her somewhere, she could hear Pascal's footsteps, the creak of the floorboards. She heard him say something, under his breath. She turned, opened her eyes, and looked.

There were two bodies in the room. Their wrists and

their ankles had been bound tight with tape. They had been positioned in a macabre proximity, seated side by side, their backs propped up against a chest. Apart from a table and a chair, it was the only furniture in the room.

The body nearest her she could scarcely bear to look at. She saw the lividity, the discolouration in the face, and glanced away, then forced herself to look back.

This body was male, a middle-aged man, fair-haired and slightly built. He was well dressed, in casual but expensive clothes, the condition of his body in stark contrast to the elegant sports jacket, silk tie and button-down shirt. He wore jeans, loafers, and yellow socks. His body was bloated. Gini covered then uncovered her face.

The other body, also male, was virtually naked. It was golden-haired, and wore only a pair of blue briefs. There was a single gold ear-ring in its right ear. One of his hands was outstretched, frozen in some last convulsive gesture towards his partner in death. He lolled against his partner's shoulder in a parody of affection, his head slumped forward. At the base of his skull where his longish hair had fallen forward there was a neat hole the size of a quarter or a ten-pence piece.

There was very little blood, just a small encrustation around the wound. Averting her eyes, Gini saw that before he had been killed, this man had been made to undress. His clothes lay on the bare floorboards a few yards from his body. They had been neatly folded and stacked in a pile, the two discarded shoes balanced on top. The clothes outraged her. Had he been made to fold them and stack them, then made to sit down to be shot? Or did someone take the trouble to stack them, as if for a military inspection, after the man was dead?

Pascal was kneeling on the floor beside the men. He examined their wounds, both alike at the base of the head. He examined the inch-wide sticky tape which bound their wrists and ankles. He straightened. He turned to her with a white face. 'They were professionally killed. One shot each.'

'But they didn't die at the same time . . . '

'Oh no. This one has been dead a day, perhaps two. The other . . . ' He gave a gesture of anger. 'Longer. Considerably longer. It's cold in here, no heating . . . I'd say ten days. Maybe two weeks.' He bent to the clothed man's body, and examined his fair hair, the signet ring he wore on his left hand.

'McMullen,' he said. 'And he'd been dead for some time before the other man was shot. A pleasant way to kill someone, to make them sit down next to that.'

He frowned, as if an idea had just come to him, and looked around the room. 'The parcel,' he said. 'Where's the parcel? Don't you see, Gini? McMullen must have been dead before it was even sent. So where is it? Someone took it in . . . '

He moved quickly across the room, and opened a door at its far side. Gini could see into a small bedroom. Its only contents were a mattress and rugs on the bare floor. Pascal went into the room; she heard the sound of cupboard doors being opened and shut. She knelt down on the floor next to the two bodies. The smell made her retch. She examined the clothed man's signet ring, and forced herself to look at the distortions decay had made to his face. Easing back his sleeve, she saw he was wearing a gold bracelet, and that the naked man wore another, identical in design. She gave a low moan, and rose to her feet.

Pascal did not hear her reaction. He came back into the room, opened a cupboard door to reveal an electric kettle, some mouldering bread, a few cups and plates. He closed it again.

'Where is it?' he said urgently. 'The parcel was received all right – by someone. The wrapping is still on the floor in the bedroom. The box is empty.'

'I know what they sent him, Pascal,' she said in a low voice.

'It's there on the floor, just by those clothes. Whoever killed them made use of it. Look. They've *applied* it . . . ' Her voice was shaking. With a muttered exclamation, Pascal bent and retrieved a small gold object. He opened it, and held it up.

'A *lipstick*? They sent McMullen a lipstick?'

'I think so. Look. They've smeared that man's face with it. It's horrible, Pascal. Look.'

Pascal bent. Gently, he lifted the naked man's head. Someone had applied the lipstick, a bright scarlet one, to his lips. They had drawn a crude Cupid's bow around his mouth; they had used it to rouge his cheeks. It gave him a cruel femininity. His blue eyes were still open. Pascal swore under his breath. 'Who would do this? Who is he? If that's McMullen, who's this?'

'It's not McMullen.' Gini turned back. 'I know who they are. Both of them. The one wearing the clothes is Johnny Appleyard. I think the other one is his friend. Stevey.'

'Stevey? It can't be. You spoke to him two days ago – in New York.'

'I think it is him. Do you see – the tape half hides them, but they're both wearing bracelets. They're love-tokens, Pascal, look.' She turned away. 'They have their names on them, and two hearts pierced with an arrow. Johnny and Stevey, Stevey with a "y". It's him.'

Pascal's face grew hard. He said nothing. He examined the bracelets, straightened.

'We have to check this place,' he said. 'Thoroughly. McMullen could have been here . . . ' He paused. 'McMullen could have done this, come to that. Gini, won't you wait outside?'

'No.' Averting her eyes, she crossed the room. 'I'll check through here. There might be something you missed.'

There was nothing in the bedroom she could see, just that mattress, a few blankets. She lifted them to one side, but they concealed nothing. They smelled of decay, and damp. Beyond the bedroom there was a primitive bathroom: a lavatory, a leaking shower, a cracked washbasin. No towels, no soap.

She returned to the main room. Pascal was kneeling beside the dead Appleyard; she saw him reach inside his jacket, and extract a wallet. She averted her eyes; sickness rose in her stomach. She crossed to the cupboard Pascal had already opened. A kettle, some bread, cups and plates – Gini noticed they were all washed. There was a small sink, and above it two wooden shelves, with some battered containers.

She opened each one in turn: instant coffee, tea-bags, sugar, a packet of salt, some rice, some pasta. She stared at these objects, trying to read them. Someone must have meant to stay here for a while. If you were staying just a night or two, would you provide pasta, rice? Had McMullen meant to stay here, then changed his plans in a hurry? She moved the box of damp salt an inch or so, and then she saw that behind it was a paperback book.

She took it down, and stared at it. Milton's *Paradise Lost*. That book, that same book, had been one of those on the desk in his London flat.

Her hands trembling now, she began to turn the pages, but there was no piece of paper concealed inside the leaves of the book, nothing written there that she could see, no name, no markings of any kind.

'Gini.' Pascal called to her in a low voice. 'Come here. Look at this.' He had been kneeling by that neat pile of clothes. Now, he stood. 'Both their wallets are here, with money, credit cards, everything. I thought there was nothing else. Then I found this. It was under this pile of clothes. Look.'

He held out to her something small, which glinted. Gini saw it was a button, a brass button, possibly a regimental button, or one of the kind worn on blazers. It was decorated with a garland of leaves.

'Military?'

'Possibly. It's not from either of their jackets. It belongs to someone else. The man who shot them, perhaps.' He saw the book. 'What's that?'

She told him, but the instant he realized it contained no message he moved away from her, then bent to his camera bag.

'Go and stand in the corridor, Gini,' he said. 'Don't move. I'm sorry, but I have to do this.'

Gini did as he said. She leaned against the wall, and

clutched the book. She closed her eyes; the floor felt as if it moved; the heavy, decay-laden air was making her faint. Against her closed lids she saw light flash as Pascal took his photographs. She knew it had to be done, but the flashes made her want to be sick. Pascal was swift. Only minutes later he was back at her side.

'That's it,' he said. 'I have some proof. Now we leave. Gini, come on.'

Gini hung back. 'Leave?' she said. 'We can't just leave them. We have to do something. We have to call the police.'

'There's nothing we can do for them. They're dead. Doctors, ambulances, police – they're not going to make any difference to them.'

'We can't leave them! Not like this. It's horrible. It's obscene. Someone should stay here—'

Pascal began to push her towards the archway. He said, 'If we call the police, we're involved. They'll question us. We'll be stuck in Venice days – maybe weeks. How do we follow up this story then? Don't you want to find out who killed them, Gini? If we owe them anything, don't we owe them that?'

'Yes, but it's still not right – just to leave them alone here. Pascal, it's so cruel and so sad.'

'Out,' Pascal said. He switched off the light. He began half-pushing, half-pulling her down the corridor. In the doorway, he stopped.

'Don't you see, Gini? Think. We come here earlier – the door's closed and locked. We come back this evening, and it's been opened. While we were chasing around Venice half the afternoon, someone came back. Came back and opened the door. They left it open – for us. *Now* will you come with me? Or do you want to wait here till they come back again?'

They went down the stairs. They crossed the silent courtyard, and paused by the canal. Gini gave a low cry: somewhere in the distance, a fearsome wailing began.

The sound was magnified by water. A siren had started up. The wail rose in pitch. Peering into the darkness, they glimpsed approaching lights on the water, through the mist.

'Of course. Of *course*. I'm a fool . . . ' Pascal caught hold of her and drew her down a dark alleyway out of sight.

'Call the police, Gini?' he whispered. 'We don't need to call the police, don't you see? Someone's *already* called them. Someone with a very accurate sense of timing, too. They gave us just enough time to get into that apartment and do what we had to do. Then they gave us just enough time to get out. Look.'

The lights were drawing nearer, their brilliance made a haze by the mist. Closer, then closer; they heard shouts. Pascal held her pressed back against damp stone: she could just see the quay outside the Palazzo Ossorio, then, emerging from the mist, the white prow of a launch. Suddenly light dazzled her eyes. Pascal dragged her further back into the shadows. She heard the slither of ropes as the police-launch tied up. She heard the sound of booted feet running across the quay, then their echo on the flagstones of the courtyard. Boots rang on the stone staircase, then the sound became muffled and died away.

Pascal stood silently listening, an intent frown on his face. 'Now why should they time it that way?' he said, under his breath. Then suddenly his face cleared. 'Of course. Of course,' he muttered. 'They don't want us arrested or held for questioning. We're too useful to them. I understand, Gini. I begin to understand . . . '

There was silence then, the only sound the wind, the drip of the rain on stone, and the slap of water against the sides of the canal.

Gini closed her eyes. She let the rain wash her face.

Pascal took her back to her room. When Gini could not stop shivering, he wrapped the eiderdown around her like a cloak. He went downstairs, and persuaded the desk clerk to provide some brandy, and some food: soup and bread. He brought it back to the room, and locked the door. He went to close the interior shutters, but Gini said, 'No, leave them open. I want to watch the moon and the sky and the water. It helps.'

Pascal turned back to look at her. Only one dim lamp was illumined; it threw shadows and stripes against the ceiling. Moonlight patched the floor by the window. Gini's eyes were shadowed and her face white. She was still trembling. Gently, he crossed to her side; then, with some firmness he made her eat. He produced the brandy, poured a small glass and made her drink.

'That's better.' He crouched down in front of her, took her hands in his and chafed them. He looked anxiously into her face. 'Much better. You're still cold, but there's some colour in your cheeks.'

He hesitated, then drew her closer. 'This changes everything,' he began, in a quiet voice. 'You must understand that, Gini. Before it was ugly, threatening – all right. But now . . . ' His voice hardened. 'Now it's murder. Someone killed those two in cold blood. And we were intended to find them. I'm certain of that.' He paused, holding her gaze. 'Gini, I was right – someone *is* beside us, every step of the way. We're being *used*. Maybe they think we'll lead them to McMullen eventually. Well, *enough*. I won't let you continue to work on this. Tomorrow I'm going to talk to Jenkins, and I'm going to tell him just that.'

Gini lowered her eyes; she said nothing. It was better to let this pass, and besides, she could not think about tomorrow, or Jenkins, or a newspaper office. They had no reality: she could not see beyond the room they had just left.

'Who killed them, Pascal?' she asked. 'Who would do that in such a terrible way? Appleyard was just a gossip-column tipster, Stevey had nothing to do with this. What could anyone gain from their deaths?'

'Silence,' Pascal said. He released her hands, rose, and began to pace the room. 'I think someone wanted to assure their silence – it's as obvious and simple as that. Appleyard must have known something. Presumably they

315

thought there was a risk he'd told Stevey. So it was safer if both of them were dead . . . '

'But why like *that*?' Gini bent her head and covered her face. 'If they intended to kill Stevey, why lure him here to do it? Did they have to bring him here, make him sit next to the dead body of someone he loved? Did they have to paint his face? It's so cruel. It's monstrous, Pascal.'

'Cruelty is central to this case,' he said. He crossed back to her, and took her hands again. 'Gini, you *know* that, you've seen it. Humiliation, subjugation. Sex – and now death. Whoever is behind this enjoys inflicting pain. Did you doubt that when you saw what they'd done to your apartment? When you listened to the man on that tape? Did you doubt it tonight?'

'No,' Gini replied. 'I didn't doubt it, of course not. But when you actually see the evidence. To make that poor boy undress, to fold up his clothes like that. To *deface* him!'

'They made him look like a woman. Or like a parody of a woman.' Pascal's voice had gone ice-cold. He looked at her closely. 'Someone here hates homosexuals, hates women, and hates sex too – at the same time as desiring it. Gini, you know the answer. Who does that suggest?'

'Hawthorne?'

'I would say so, yes.'

She began to answer him, to argue, but Pascal cut her off.

'All right, all right,' he said impatiently. 'I *know* all that. Nothing proven, just allegations, sure. But just take a look at the logistics, Gini, if nothing else.' He rose and began to pace again.

'Someone is well informed, yes? They knew we'd be working on this story before we did. They knew when your apartment would be empty, and how to enter it easily. They knew we were coming to Venice, and they made sure we could get into that apartment when it suited them. We *are* being watched and followed and listened to, Gini. There's no doubt in my mind about that. Now, just who can organize that kind of operation? Who could employ an executioner, so he never needed to set foot in

Venice himself? Come on, Gini, who's the one person who could possibly *gain* from all this?'

Gini straightened. She took another sip of brandy and tried to think. She still felt as cold as ice.

'Hawthorne,' she said eventually. Then: 'But not *only* Hawthorne. We still don't know enough about McMullen. McMullen might have something to gain too. If he *is* obsessed with Lise, if he wanted to destroy her husband's future career, their marriage. It could be McMullen, Pascal. You said yourself – a military-style execution, two neat shots in the back of the head.'

'I accept that.' Pascal crossed and sat down next to her. 'Obviously, I've thought of that too. But if you're weighing the two possible candidates, you have to admit, Hawthorne has advantages McMullen can't possibly have. Would it be as easy for McMullen to organize surveillance? No, it would not. All right, McMullen could conceivably have a personal motivation for blackening Hawthorne's name. But can you really believe he'd take it as far as murder? I certainly can't. Concoct a sexual slander, smear the man, sure – but actually kill two people? No. I can't believe that.' He paused. 'Whereas Hawthorne – Hawthorne has a great deal at stake. Look at what he stands to lose. His marriage, his sons, his reputation, his career – his whole future . . . ' He broke off, and she could see there was something more, something he was reluctant to say to her.

'What is it, Pascal?' She looked at him closely. 'There's something else, isn't there?'

'Several things,' he said after a moment. 'McMullen's disappearance, for one. I think McMullen knew he was in danger, Gini – and that brings us back to the same question. A simple one. Who might have discovered McMullen's plans? Who could have known about his conversations with Lise, the fact that he'd gone to a newspaper? Who can easily employ surveillance? Who can intercept mail, or listen to phone calls, even phone calls made to an apparently safe call-box? Who can draw on that kind of *expertise*, Gini? Hawthorne can. Now

McMullen also has some expertise – he's an ex-Para, after all. So he got out fast, he covered his tracks. And I now think he was successful. McMullen isn't dead.'

'You've changed your mind? Why?'

'I told you, Gini. Because we're being used, you and I. They're still looking for McMullen, and we might lead them to him. While that possibility remains we're *useful*. The minute we stop being useful . . . ' He paused. 'That's when they dispense with us. The same way we saw tonight. We lead them to McMullen – and we're dead.'

'You can't mean that, Pascal.'

'This morning – no. This evening – yes.' He turned to her in a sudden angry way, and took her hands in his. 'Gini, it's easy. It doesn't have to be a shot in the back of the head. It can be subtler than that – a road accident, a fall from an underground train, a little contretemps with a lift-shaft.'

'It can't be true. It *can't* be true.' Gini gave a little cry and rose to her feet. She walked over to the window and looked out. Cloud and intermittent moon-shine: the water of the canal below was a sheet of silver one moment, black the next.

'I was talking to Hawthorne,' she swung around with a pleading look, 'I was talking to him only yesterday. All the time he was speaking I was watching his eyes, his face. There would have been some sign, some indication.'

Pascal gave an impatient gesture. 'You think evil is that obvious? You're wrong, Gini. It isn't. I've met many evil men, I've photographed them. Ex-Nazis, mafiosi, tin-pot generals in Africa, Arab despots, different races, different ages, different men – and they all had one thing in common. Every one of them had killed without compunction and would do so again. And not in one case – not in a single one, Gini – did it show in the face.'

'But that's *different*,' Gini burst out. 'Hawthorne isn't some general, some dictator. He's an American politician.'

'Oh sure, sure.' Pascal's voice had become sharp. 'And you met him in a nice drawing-room, with nice

318

civilized people all around, having nice civilized after-dinner drinks. But just think a little, Gini. Think about some of your American politicians, or their English counterparts, for that matter, or Italian, or French. Think about them, Gini.'

'I am thinking about them – and it's totally different. All right, they can make a ruthless decision, in wartime, say. They can authorize a bombing raid, they can authorize appalling things, they can lift a finger and a village gets wiped out before lunch. I know that, of course I know that. But that's a *political* decision. It's not a personal one. It's not killing someone, or harming someone, to save their own skin.'

'And you're sure, are you, that no American politician could ever do that?' He looked at her quietly, then with a shrug, turned away. 'Are they all so pure? Take a look at some of your more recent presidents, Gini, and those close to them. Then tell me you're so certain about that.'

There was a silence. Eventually Gini said, 'Very well, I accept that. And the same could be said of politicians, of powerful men, the world over. In Europe, in Africa, in South America, in the Far East . . . '

Pascal sighed. 'Of course. The braking systems in a democratic country may work more effectively than in others. But the point is, back a certain kind of politician into a corner – so he has everything to lose by doing nothing, and everything to gain if he acts – and he will lie and cheat and blackmail, and, yes, even in some circumstances kill. And the one thing you can be certain of is that none of that, *none* of that, will be apparent in his face.'

There was a long silence after that. Pascal sat quietly thinking, smoking a cigarette. Gini stood by the window, and watched the water move below. She thought about this story, and about aspects of it which, initially, had worried her. She had not been altogether sure, embarking upon it, that it was right to investigate a man's private, sexual activities. Could some boundary not be drawn between a man's private behaviour and his public life? How much did it matter if a politician who had, in many respects, a fine record, proved to be a liar, even a womanizer, when away from his work? Did the one not out-balance the other? Could a distinction not be drawn?

She was certain now that it could not. Lies and deceptions could not be partitioned off in that way: they were, she thought, like a disease, spreading from one limb to the rest of the body, tainting and corrupting an entire life. Also – and here she saw that room at the Ossorio again – two men were now dead. She remembered her telephone call with Stevey: *I've never been overseas*, he had said. He had finally made it, his first and his last overseas trip. And as she realized that, the anger and the outrage she felt made her oddly calm. Turning back, she looked at Pascal.

'Pascal,' she began, 'you have to understand one thing. I'm not giving up on this. Not now. Do whatever you like. Talk to Jenkins if you must. Get me taken off this story if you must. I'll still work on it – you can't stop me, and neither can he. I'll work on it with you, or without you. I'll go on working on it, until I find out the truth. If Hawthorne is responsible, I'll finish him.'

She made a small quick gesture of the hand. 'Choose, Pascal. With me or without me. Take your pick.'

Pascal looked at her in silence. He did not doubt for one moment that she meant what she said. She had spoken quietly, her face set and pale, her eyes never wavering from his face. This was neither bravado, nor histrionics, but a quality he could recognize for he had once shared it himself. A stubborn and insistent belief that truth could be revealed, and that it was the revelation of a truth which was the heart and purpose of their work.

In that moment, looking at Gini, he saw and heard his own younger self. He was reminded how it had been when the work he did gave meaning to his life. He felt both shamed and strengthened, though he knew he could not tell Gini that.

Rising, he crossed to her. The moonlight made her hair silvery white. Her eyes, looking up at him, were huge and dark in the pallor of her face. She was still trembling, he saw, and he knew that what she had seen earlier was still with her. Silently, he took her hand in his, and drew her closer. He allowed himself to rest his hand against her throat, to loosen her hair, and then lift it back and away from her face. She gave a sharp intake of breath as he touched her. He allowed himself to catch her against him sharply, and cradle her head against his chest, although he knew what would be the consequence if he did.

He held her close, feeling the warmth of his body pass to hers. The immediate and familiar rightness of this passed like a shock through his whole body, and he sensed from her the same response. It was as if they fit, mind to mind, heart to heart, limb to limb, and at once this fitting brought back the desire her closeness had always provoked. He had known, even in memory, how overwhelming that desire had been. But touching her now he understood that the memory, however intense, had been as nothing compared to this.

That she felt this also, he could sense in every line of her body. When she drew back, looked up at him, he could see it in her eyes and face. Switching off the lamp, taking her hand, he drew her across to the bed, and they lay down together. Pascal held her quietly in his arms; they lay in the semi-darkness watching the moonlight ebb and flow. Pascal stroked her hair. After a while, he began to speak.

He had meant to tell her about their twelve years apart, about those years when he had felt so close to death, about the circumstances of his marriage, and indeed he told her many of those things, Gini lying silently, close beside him. But then he found that he wanted to take her back with him, further back, through the windings of the past. He spoke of their time in Beirut, then he went further back still, and spoke of his childhood, his mother and his long-dead father, that little village in Provence.

Some of this story was new to Gini, other parts of it he had spoken of before, in Beirut, and he could feel that as he was calmed by these memories, she was also. They were both lulled away from the events of that evening;

the residual trembling in her body became still, her skin grew warm against his.

After a while, when he paused, she too began to speak. She took him with her, back into her past, her childhood. This she had never before discussed, and he began to see why their weeks in Beirut had ended as they did, long before she explained them herself, and went on, in the same level voice, to tell him how she had felt after leaving him, and how he had remained in her mind during the years since.

Pascal was deeply moved by this. As she spoke, he began to stroke her arm, to trace the vein that ran on the inside of her arm, from elbow to wrist.

Such a deep, feathered, opium calm, to touch her like this. She trembled, and they turned in each other's arms, so they were closer still, and Pascal could peer into her face. She looked back at him mutely; he traced the line of her hair, of her brows, her eyes and her mouth. Gently, he stroked her throat, then her breasts. She gave a low moan, and moved against him; pleasure made the muscles of her face lax. It became soft, then content. Pascal leaned over her, and rested his lips against hers. They lay very still, then her mouth opened under his.

Her mouth tasted of the brandy, a little; her skin and her hair tasted of salt and sea-winds and rain; they made love very slowly, feeling their way back to a past place. Pascal felt a multitude of tiny memories surface in the seas of his mind – this was her gesture, this her precise scent, feel and touch. Recognition flooded through him; when he entered her body, he felt he rediscovered not only a woman he had loved, but also himself.

Afterwards, as they lay together, and the intensity of the pleasure slowly abated Pascal thought about this act, which past poets, he had read, had described as a little death. On this occasion, the words were wrong, he felt. There was no sensation of dying; he felt as if he had fallen a great distance, travelled a great distance; it felt like a re-birth.

★　　★　　★

They talked, and made love, for much of the night. Waking in her arms the next morning, he felt an absolute quietude, then the bewilderment of intense joy. He felt he had been deafened and blinded during the night, but that he now heard, saw and touched with a new more intuitive precision. Much though he longed to remain this way, to let the hours slip past, he knew that now was not the moment to operate in such a state.

So he roused himself deliberately. He did all the routine things which, usually, would make him alert. He showered, dressed, drank coffee, drank more coffee, rang the desk, paced the room, ordered a taxi launch. He was determined, absolutely determined, that they would not miss the first flight out of this place. They left for the airport much earlier than they needed, the launch weaving between the black piles that marked their channel through open water, the morning light still thin and grey, the mainland beyond obscured by greenish mist.

It was Monday morning, and they reached Venice's small airport before eight. A few guards lolled about, holding guns. The girl on the check-in desk was yawning. Both flights, she said, were slightly delayed. They would have at least an hour's wait.

It was only when she said 'both flights' that Pascal remembered their plans, and the bookings he had made: for Gini, a direct flight back to London; for himself a flight via Paris, with the onward journey to London booked for the five o'clock Paris–London flight. It was his visiting afternoon. Marianne was still on holiday, and he was due to see her for three hours, at noon. How could he forget that? He began to swear, furious with himself, then he looked down at Gini, and he knew precisely why he'd forgotten.

'This is your fault,' he said, fighting down the happiness which would creep into his voice. 'Your fault, Gini. I don't know where I am, or what in hell I'm doing. I can't think . . .'

It seemed to him then that only one sensible course

of action was open to him. He must cancel the visit to Marianne. 'You're not going back to London alone,' he said. 'I won't have you alone in that apartment.'

It was Gini who took him through into the airport café, plied him with more coffee, and dissuaded him.

'You can't do that,' she said. 'You need to talk to your wife, Pascal. Marianne will be expecting to see you, looking forward to seeing you. It's three hours – that's all. You'll be back in London by early evening. I'll be perfectly all right.'

But Pascal could still see the room at the Palazzo Ossorio, and what they had found there. Gini could see that he was adamant, and that nothing would change his mind. No, no, no – he would not have her alone in that Islington flat.

It was Gini who came up with a compromise. Very well then, instead of going to Islington from the airport, she would go straight to Mary's, and remain with Mary until Pascal returned to London later that night.

'You can even pick me up,' she said, 'from Mary's. I'll wait for you there. I'll call her now, just to make sure she'll be in. You'll see – it will be perfectly all right.' She paused. 'And useful, too. There's a number of things I want to ask Mary about.' She looked round the empty departure lounge, the empty café. 'Well, you know what I might want to ask her, I think.'

Pascal groaned. He started arguing again. Gini cut those arguments off. She knew, from what he had told her the previous night, that this meeting was of importance to him. She found a call-box, and telephoned Mary. She got through easily. Mary, who always rose early, answered the phone on its second ring. She sounded pleased to hear from Gini, as always; she also, Gini thought, sounded slightly constrained, slightly anxious. Slightly odd?

'About midday?' she said. 'Well, Gini, I'd love to see you, darling, you know that. But I'm not sure if that will be possible. It's a little difficult. What, darling? I can't hear you very well, this is an awful line . . . Well, if you really need to talk to me, darling, of course. It's just that

I may have to go out later, I'm not sure. Maybe if I called you back in an hour or so . . . '

Gini had not said from where she was calling. She said quickly, 'No, Mary, don't do that. You won't be able to reach me. I'm rushing out now. I'm out and about all morning. What if I made it a little later, twelve-thirty, say, or one – or do you have to be somewhere for lunch?'

'No, no . . . It's not lunch. I can't explain now. I'll explain when I see you, darling. It's just – something rather horrid has come up, and . . . ' Her voice faded, then returned. 'I know, darling, there's a very simple solution. You remember, we did it once before. I'll leave my key with my next-door neighbour, you know, at number fifty-six. Then, if I do have to go out, you can let yourself in. I don't want you standing around on my doorstep in this filthy weather. Yes, that's the solution. I may well be here anyway, but if I'm not, darling, let yourself in, be nice to poor old Dog. I'll leave you some sandwiches.'

'Mary—'

'No, let's decide on that. If I do have to leave here, it won't be for long. And if I'm delayed, well at least I know where to reach you.' She paused. 'Gini, is something wrong, darling? It isn't . . . you aren't . . . ? You haven't had any problems with . . . ? It isn't a man, I hope, darling?'

Gini smiled to herself. 'Sort of,' she said. 'In a way, yes.'

'Oh, Gini . . . Not your Pascal, I hope? And I thought he seemed rather nice . . . No? What, darling? Fine, all right, that's our plan. I'll see you soon. Lots of love . . . '

Gini replaced the receiver thoughtfully. The details of this arrangement, she thought, were better not mentioned to Pascal. She frowned, still slightly puzzled, and returned to the café.

'Fine,' she said. 'It's all fixed. I'll go to Mary's, and then—' She stopped, suddenly, unable to continue. All this, the words, the arrangements, the hows and whens, seemed very unimportant, once she looked at Pascal. He rose now, and with a sudden urgent movement, took her in his arms. He kissed her hair, her upturned face.

'You know I don't want to be away from you one hour, one minute?' he said. 'You do know that?'

He drew her to one side, into a quiet alcove, away from the impassive gaze of the *carabinieri*. There they stayed, in a muddle of words and embraces. Pascal felt unease and anxiety as well as great happiness; he nearly changed his plans twice, saying he must come with her after all. He could never quite decide, even long afterwards, whether it would have turned out better, or worse, if he had.

It was only when her flight was finally called that he remembered, suddenly, the one thing he had not told her the previous night.

'Beirut,' he said. 'Damn, Gini, it's important you know this. You remember, when they broke into your apartment, what they did – and I told you, it must be someone who knew how to hurt us, someone who knew about Beirut—'

'No-one knows. Only my father. I told you—'

'Darling, you're wrong. Mary knows. She made that very obvious at her party the other night. No, never mind how, there isn't time. Just trust me. I'm right. She knows what happened, Gini, and I think she told someone else.'

'She wouldn't do that. Never. Not Mary.'

He saw the mask of obstinacy start to settle on her face, and he caught her to him. 'Darling, listen. Think. Not in a gossipy way – no, of course not. But if she was anxious – she might well confide in someone then. Ask their advice. Who's been her closest friend, Gini, apart from you, ever since her husband died? Who's been there, helping her through her widowhood, turning up with books, presents . . . ? Who does she depend on, Gini?'

'John Hawthorne.'

'Exactly.' He drew back from her, and looked down into her face, his eyes dark with concern. 'If I'm right, Gini, he sent someone to your apartment with the specific intention of doing the one thing he knew would cause you pain.'

He frowned. 'Darling, promise me you'll be careful. I don't want him to hurt you.'

Gini reached up and kissed him. 'I won't let him do that. I won't let anyone do that.' She started for the departure gate, then turned impulsively back to him.

'He doesn't know what happened in Beirut anyway,' she said. 'He may think he does, but he's wrong. He doesn't know, no-one can know. Except us.'

XIX

The room was warm and hushed. In the distance a clock ticked. The street outside Mary's house was quiet, with just the occasional swish of tyres. Through the window, Gini could see that rain had given way to sleet. She had arrived here later than she had estimated. Now, it was almost two. The light was already thick and yellowish. She leaned back in the armchair. She could feel sleep creeping up on her, but then she had scarcely slept at all the previous night. She fought to stay awake, to think, but somnolence crept through her veins. It made her limbs feel heavy, and her mind imprecise. What she would do, she decided, was wait for Mary, and then ask her more about the Hawthornes. She herself had just met them properly for the first time, after all: such questions need not seem odd or out of place. She would ask Mary why she thought Lise had seemed so tense. She might even risk the mention of McMullen's name. Mary might possibly know how and when his friendship with Lise began. She would lead Mary back down the winding paths of memory, of anecdote, and if there was a deception on her own part there, it was one which could be excused, she felt.

Dog, who had settled himself on the hearthrug, began to snore lightly and to dream. He scrabbled with his paws and woofed. Gini heard the clock outside strike the half-hour, then chime three. Her eyelids felt heavy. The fire was warm. She thought of Pascal, and of how each passing hour brought his return closer. By now he would be with Marianne, perhaps playing with her, or reading to her, or taking her out for a walk. Then he would be on his way to the airport, on the plane, and then . . . She sighed, tried to waken herself, failed, and drifted into sleep.

*　　*　　*

She woke, startled, from deep sleep. The room was dark. There was a horrible banging and ringing. For a moment, deceived by travel, and tiredness, and darkness, she could not think where she was. Then she remembered. She was at Mary's, of course, and that noise came from the front door, where someone was knocking, and ringing the bell. She stumbled to her feet, almost falling over Dog. Then she saw the fire had burned low, was almost out. How long had she slept? Where was Mary? She felt her way to the nearest table, and switched on a lamp. Dog was now alert, his head raised, his hackles up. A low growl came from his throat. It was dark outside. She looked at her watch, saw it was almost five, and felt a dart of alarm. Where was Mary, and why had she not called as she'd promised she would?

The knocking at the door had stopped. She crossed into the hallway, and listened. Had the person outside left, or was he still there? She felt a sudden fear. She was alone in this house; it was dark outside. For an instant she saw that room in Venice, two dead bodies. She saw Stevey's blank blue-eyed stare, that small wound at the back of his neck, all it took to end a life. And she heard Pascal's warning voice: *It can be subtler than that – a road accident, a fall from an underground train, a little contretemps with a lift-shaft* . . .

Fighting down the fear, and despising herself, she opened the door, gave a cry of alarm, and stepped back. There was a rustling, some electricity in the air, then that familiar crackle of radio static. A strange man, dressed in dark clothes, blocked the doorway. He was very tall, and powerfully built. He was wearing a dark overcoat, and black gloves.

Gini hesitated, began to say something, changed her mind, and made to close the door.

A large foot, in a black Oxford shoe, was inserted in the gap.

'Ms Hunter? One moment, please,' said an American voice, and the door was pushed back.

* * *

Pascal arrived at his ex-wife's home at twelve-fifteen. Helen opened the door herself.

'You're late.'

'Fifteen minutes, Helen. The flight was slightly delayed. I had to pick up my car.'

'It's not very convenient, never knowing what time you'll turn up.' She gave him a pinched look. 'I'm going out, it's the nanny's day off. You've delayed me. Well, as you're here, you'd better come in, I suppose. I can't think what you propose doing. The weather's foul, and Marianne's being difficult today – it unsettles her, these visits of yours.'

Pascal answered none of this. Helen had led him into what she called the television room. It contained numerous expensive overstuffed chairs and too much chintz. Marianne was sitting on the floor, in front of the television set. She was watching an American cartoon, a series of brightly coloured animals engaged in a noisy and violent fight.

She greeted Pascal, but did not go to him, or stand up. Pascal looked at her, and his heart ached. These afternoons were often strained. Three hours was not long enough to build bridges with his daughter. It was hard, week after week, to think of new expeditions they could make.

In the summer months, when he could take her for swimming lessons, or to parks, it was easier – but in the winter? He looked out of the window. It was cold outside, and windy, but not raining as yet.

'I thought you might like to go to the playground, Marianne,' he began, thinking of the small park near by. 'You like the swings there, and the roundabouts . . . '

Marianne rose obediently to her feet. 'Yes, Papa,' she said, without enthusiasm. 'That would be nice. I'll get my coat.'

She left the room, with a hesitant glance at her mother as she passed. Helen shrugged.

'What you imagine you're going to do in the park all afternoon, I can't think. It's freezing cold . . . '

'We'll go there, then I'll take her somewhere for tea—'
Pascal began. Helen cut him off.

'Well, if you want. It's your choice. I'd better give
you the key. I'll try and be back by three, but if I'm
delayed you can let yourselves in.'

'Delayed?'

'For heaven's sake, Pascal, I am entitled to go out
occasionally. As a matter of fact, I'm seeing friends for
lunch. I'll try to get back by three, obviously.' Her eyes
slid away from his face.

'Fine,' Pascal said. 'Perhaps you'd better let me have
their number?'

She gave the response he expected, a cold impatient
glance.

'I can't do that. We're going to a restaurant somewhere
– and no, I don't know which. Surely you can manage,
Pascal, for three hours. It's not asking so very much.'

Pascal was calculating the time in his head. If Helen
returned at three, he could catch the five o'clock flight
without problems. If she delayed him, however . . . He
hesitated. He was about to mention the plane, then
stopped himself. Knowing he needed to be somewhere
else urgently would probably ensure Helen was late.

'Here're the keys. Double lock the doors, won't you?
I'll see you around three. Goodbye, Marianne. Don't let
Daddy tire you out.'

At the playground, Marianne allowed Pascal to push her
on the swings for a while, but she seemed not to enjoy it
very much. She climbed onto the merry-go-round at his
suggestion, and sat there politely while Pascal set it in
motion. As soon as it slowed, though, she climbed off.
Hand in hand they walked down to the small lake at the
edge of the playground to watch the ducks. Pascal had
forgotten to bring any bread to feed them.

'It doesn't matter, Papa,' Marianne said. She let go of
his hand, walked across to a bench and sat down.

Pascal followed her and sat down also. He felt a sense
of despair. Only half an hour had passed. 'Is anything the

matter, darling?' he said gently. 'Is something wrong?'

'My ear hurts a bit. My throat's sore,' she replied, and rubbed it. 'I feel cold.'

Pascal examined her face. Her forehead and lips were pale, but her cheeks were flushed. She shivered as he looked at her. He touched her forehead. It felt warm.

'Does your ear ache, darling?'

'It hurts. And I can't hear very well.'

Pascal hesitated. He looked despondently around the park. No other children had ventured out.

'Perhaps it's just the cold,' he said, in a cheerful voice. 'We'd be better off inside on a day like this, don't you think, Marianne? I wonder, would you like to go to that café where we went before? Do you remember? The one with the excellent ice-cream?'

Marianne gave a wan smile. 'No, thank you, Papa. I'd rather go home.'

This was unprecedented. Pascal felt the stirrings of alarm. He felt her forehead again, then took her hand.

'That's a very good suggestion. We'll go home, and make some tea. We can watch television together – how would that be?'

This prospect seemed to please her. She brightened.

'I'd like that,' she said. 'I always watch television on my own.'

'Doesn't Mummy watch with you, darling? Or the nanny – the new nanny? What's her name?'

'Elizabeth. She's English. Yes, she watches sometimes. Mummy always says she will, then she's too busy.' She clasped his hand more tightly. 'On Monday afternoons, it's *Dangermouse*, I think. I like him.'

'Good, then *Dangermouse* it shall be,' Pascal said.

It was not a long walk, but Marianne's pace grew slower and slower. She began to lag behind. Pascal felt her forehead again. It now felt very hot. He carried her the rest of the way home.

Indoors, he tucked Marianne up on a couch in the television room, and put a rug around her knees. He switched on the television set, and lit Helen's coal-effect gas fire. He went in search of aspirin, or paracetemol, and found them eventually in the third bathroom he checked, Helen's own. It was an elaborate bathroom, fitted out in rose marble. A long shelf was cluttered with cosmetics, with anti-ageing skin creams and bottles of scent. The aspirin were in the medicine cabinet, along with the horseshoe-shaped box containing Helen's diaphragm, and several tubes of spermicidal jelly. The box was open, and the diaphragm gone.

Pascal closed the cabinet, feeling guilty at having seen this. He fetched a glass of water, and went back to Marianne. He had been away no more than five minutes, but in that time, to judge from her face, her temperature had risen. She was now scarlet, and very hot to the touch. The act of swallowing the aspirin caused her pain.

'Papa, my throat hurts,' she said.

Pascal stroked her hair. He put a cushion behind her head, and gently unbuttoned the fastening of her dress. Her chest and neck were covered with a mottled rash. Pascal rebuttoned the dress. It was still only one o'clock.

'What time does your nanny – does Elizabeth come home on her day off, Marianne?'

'In the evening. After tea. To give me my bath.'

'Doesn't Mummy do that on Elizabeth's day off?'

'No. Elizabeth always does it. Then she reads me a story, and puts me to bed . . . '

Pascal frowned. Careful to keep his voice calm he said, 'Listen, Marianne, I think maybe Papa should call a doctor. See if he can give you something for that throat of yours. OK? Now, would you like me to call my doctor, or the one you usually see?'

'Your doctor, Papa. Our doctor's horrid. He's old, and he's always in a hurry. He's cross.'

The doctor was on the other side of Paris, treating an emergency – cardiac arrest. He would come after that, but Pascal should not expect him for two hours at least.

Pascal returned to the television room. Marianne had fallen asleep. He sat by her side and watched her anxiously for a while. Her breathing was regular, and her skin felt a little cooler – the aspirin taking effect.

Pascal rose, and began to pace the room. He felt restless, worried, and unable to settle. He picked up one of Helen's fashion magazines, then tossed it aside. There was never anything worth reading in this house. He looked across at the telephone, and considered telephoning Gini. It was past two now. He looked at Marianne, still sleeping. He began to acknowledge to himself that he might not catch that five o'clock flight. Some time after two, still restless, he went out to the street. There was still no sign of the doctor's car.

He returned inside, and sat down opposite Marianne. To calm himself he tried to think of work, but that did not have a calming effect. He remembered the Palazzo Ossorio, and he felt torn between two fears – fear for Gini, fear for Marianne. From his pocket, he took out the small brass button he had found the previous evening, beneath the pile of Stevey's clothes. It had been lodged in a crack in the floorboards, almost invisible. Did it belong to the assassin? It certainly looked new, bright and untarnished. He turned it this way and that. The design was well-worked. Examining it more closely, he saw it represented the kind of garland made to adorn a hero's brow, or a victorious general's. Bay, oak – whichever leaf indicated triumph – that.

He peered at the tiny thing closely, then put it away. From his camera bag he took out the book Gini had found. An old, battered paperback, a Penguin edition, available in thousands of shops. On the cover was a portrait of a young John Milton; inside the pages were discoloured by age, and spotted with damp. *Paradise Lost*. The same book Gini had found on McMullen's desk. Did it indicate more than a taste for Milton, for epic poetry – or not? The likelihood, he supposed, was that it did belong to McMullen, which indicated that at some point, McMullen had been in Venice. But it told him no more than that.

He glanced across at Marianne, who still slept. For want

of anything else to do, he began to read, but he quickly found himself in difficulties. Pascal's spoken English was excellent – his father had taught languages in the village school, the village where Pascal grew up. His father had died when Pascal was ten, and his memories of him were blurred, but he could remember the evenings, long ago, when his father had read to him, little extracts of English, little samplings of greatness, some Shakespeare, yes, he could remember that, and some Dickens. Not Milton that he could remember. He turned the page. The extraordinary clotted syntax here was beyond him; good his English might be, but not good enough for this. He turned another page, stiffened, then held the book up to the light.

Along the side of the verse there was a faint pencil mark: no words, but one passage had been marked, singled out. Pascal traced the words carefully:

> For now the thought
> Both of lost happiness and lasting pain
> Torments him.

Pascal frowned. The words reverberated in his mind. He applied them, briefly, to his own life. Did they fit McMullen's also? He closed the book. Across the room, Marianne had begun to murmur. She pushed the rug aside restlessly. Pascal felt her forehead again. The aspirin must be wearing off; her skin was burning hot.

He ran out into the hallway, opened the front door. Still no sign of the doctor's car. Anguish and alarm gripped him. He returned to the room, removed the rug covering his daughter, turned off the fire, and opened the window a crack. He must reduce her temperature; somehow he must reduce her temperature.

He knelt down at his daughter's side, and began to stroke her forehead. He wondered if he dared to give her more aspirin yet. On the packet, it said the dose should be given at four-hour intervals. He looked at his watch. What time had he given her the aspirin? Around two, he thought. It was now nearly four, too soon to give her more, surely?

He felt an agonized indecision, realized he had now missed his flight, then forgot the flight at once. Marianne had woken. She asked him for some water. When he brought it, she sipped, but seemed unable to swallow. Pascal laid her down again, went through into another room, and called the doctor's once more, his voice unsteady with anger and alarm.

'Don't worry, M. Lamartine,' said the receptionist, in a soothing tone. 'I'm sure she will be fine. Children do develop these high fevers suddenly. Keep her cool. The doctor will be with you shortly. Don't alarm yourself. She will be perfectly all right.'

The receptionist was wrong. Marianne was not all right. At five-thirty, just as Pascal was getting ready to give her more aspirin, he heard the doctor's car pull up outside. He was in the act of moving across the room to open the front door, when he stopped. Marianne had made the tiniest of noises, a horrible dry sucking-in of breath.

He swung around. With a dreadful suddenness, Marianne's eyes opened, then rolled back. She gave a small preliminary tremor, then her whole body convulsed.

'Apologies for alarming you, ma'am.' This huge man was, Gini thought, very polite – very polite and very impassive. His face was as blank as a barn door. He was now holding a wallet out to her. He flipped it open. She saw a US embassy crest, a photograph, and a name: *Frank Romero*. He snapped it shut.

'Lady Pemberton is at the ambassador's residence now. She wasn't available to call you as planned, ma'am. The ambassador felt it might be simpler if you joined her there, ma'am. I have a car here. He apologizes for your wait.'

Gini hesitated, and the man picked up on the hesitation at once. He handed her a plain white card on which was printed a number.

'If you'd like to call that number, ma'am. You can confirm the arrangements.'

'Thank you,' Gini said. 'I need to get my things, in any case.'

Gini hesitated again, then shut the door. She ran back into the sitting-room, and placed the call. It rang three times, then John Hawthorne answered it. He sounded calm, absolutely as he always did.

'Gini?' he said. 'I'm sorry about all this. I'll just pass you over to Mary . . . '

Mary sounded anything but calm. She sounded exhausted and flustered, too. 'Gini, I'm so terribly sorry, darling. There's been a bit of a drama. No, I can't talk. If you could just come straight over . . . What's that, John?' There was a pause. 'Oh good. Gini – are you there? I gather John's sent one of the – security people. Frank. Yes, darling – what?'

'I don't understand. Why do you need me there, Mary?'

'Darling, I can't explain now. Yes, when I see you. Good – in about twenty minutes, then, half an hour.'

Gini hung up. She gathered her bag and her coat, kissed Dog, and walked out to the steps. It had stopped raining. Frank Romero was standing by the car. He was in the act of removing his dark overcoat, which he folded neatly and placed on the back seat. By the time she had descended the steps, he was on the pavement, at the ready, opening the rear passenger door. Gini looked at him intently, very intently. She could see that beneath the coat, he had been wearing clothes which might have been sharp informal wear, or possibly a kind of uniform. Black shoes, dark grey trousers with a knife-edge crease, and a double-breasted blazer in black. The blazer was fastened with a double row of brass buttons. She stumbled convincingly; Frank Romero put out an arm to steady her.

'Watch your step, ma'am. The pavement's slippery . . . '

Gini leaned on his arm, wriggled her unhurt ankle and grimaced. There were also brass buttons on the sleeve of his jacket, and she could see them clearly now. They were stamped with an interesting, a memorable device – a little garland of oak leaves. She straightened up, and gave him a smile.

'I'm fine. It's OK. I just twisted it a bit. I'll sit in the front.'

She sat beside him, and waited until they'd travelled one street, two streets. 'So tell me,' she said, 'have you worked for the ambassador long?'

'Yes, ma'am.'

'How long?'

He glanced towards her then fixed his eyes on the road ahead. 'Since he was appointed, ma'am.'

'I guess it must be a very interesting job . . . '

'Yes, ma'am.'

Damn and blast, Gini thought. She sat in silence, trying to decide the best approach. Frank Romero kept his eyes on the road ahead. It was rush hour and the traffic was heavy. Near Hyde Park Corner, they came to a halt.

'Would you mind if I asked you a question, Frank?'

He gave her another quick covert glance, then turned his impassive face back to the traffic. 'It's something I've always wanted to know. You security people – how do you train for work like this? You have police training, maybe, or a period in the military, or what?'

'In my case, ma'am . . . ' he kept his eyes on the road, 'I had a period in the military. I'm a Vietnam vet.'

'How interesting. You have something in common with Ambassador Hawthorne then. He was telling me about his time in Vietnam the other night.'

'Yes, ma'am?'

There was a long silence. Gini did not prompt. Eventually, as she had been silently hoping, her remark seemed to encourage him, he actually volunteered some information.

'I served under Ambassador Hawthorne, ma'am. Out in 'Nam. I was sergeant to his platoon.'

'Oh, I see,' Gini said. 'Then your connection with the family goes back a long way.'

'Yes, ma'am. It does.'

He volunteered nothing more, and Gini knew better than to prompt further. She kept the conversation to innocuous topics from then on: the weather, London traffic. They reached Regent's Park, and turned in at Hanover Gate. They passed the mosque on their left; on the right was the lodge entrance to Winfield House. They halted there briefly, then were waved on. Frank Romero parked the car outside the residence. He came around, and politely held open her door. As Gini climbed out, she looked closely at the buttons on his jacket. Six on the front, three on each sleeve, none missing.

John Hawthorne had appeared on the steps. 'Everything all right, Frank?'

'Yes, Mr Ambassador.'

'I'll be three minutes. Gini, come inside out of the cold.' He glanced up at the sky, then took her arm. 'I'm so sorry about this.' He drew her up the steps and into a large hall. 'A few alarums and excursions. Mary will explain. I have to leave you, I'm afraid. I'm late for a meeting at the Foreign Office as it is. Mary's through here. Lise will be joining you shortly.'

He led her into the pinkish drawing-room she had seen in the *Hello!* magazine photographs. The curtains were drawn, a fire was lit; above the fireplace was the rose-period Picasso, to the right of it the pinkish Matisse. Mary rose to her feet from a chair near the fire. Gini could see at once that she looked both exhausted and distressed.

John Hawthorne, who appeared neither, stayed only a few minutes, then left.

As soon as the door closed on him, Mary held out her arms, then hugged Gini tight. Her kind and honest eyes met Gini's; she gave a tired sigh.

'Gini, I'm so terribly sorry. I would have called if I could. But really . . . ' She gave a helpless gesture. 'It's been pandemonium here, absolutely dreadful. My head's splitting. They just brought me some tea – would you like some tea? I'd better explain before Lise comes down. Then with any luck we'll be able to leave. I can't stand much more of this . . . '

★   ★   ★

Gini moved across to the fire, and sat down opposite Mary. As Mary poured tea, she looked around this pinkish room. The table next to her was weighted down with photographs: official photographs, family photographs: a young John Hawthorne in army uniform; the Hawthornes with various past presidents and other heads of state, the Hawthornes *en famille*. Two beautiful blond-haired boys, a house she recognized as Hawthorne's childhood home in New York State. Robert and Adam Hawthorne stood outside it with their grandfather, S. S. Hawthorne. He was seated in a wheelchair, John Hawthorne standing to his side: Lise was not in the picture.

She looked back at Mary, who was passing her a cup. Her hand trembled and the silver teaspoon rattled. To Gini's astonishment, Mary leaned forward, opened a cigarette box on the table in front of her, and lit a cigarette. Meeting Gini's eyes, she gave a wan smile.

'I know, I know. But after what I've been through, I need one, Gini. That or a damn stiff drink . . . '

'What on earth's been going on, Mary? Why am I here? I don't understand a thing.'

'I'll come to you in a moment.' Mary sighed. 'And don't ask me how it all started, or exactly when, because I don't know. All I know is that on Saturday at my party, I could see Lise was terribly tense. She said she was worried about John's safety. I thought it seemed odd, to be *so* strung up, but by the time they left, she seemed fine. Well, you saw. Much better. Very animated – a little too animated, perhaps . . . Anyway, I thought no more about it. Then on Sunday evening – yesterday, that's right – John telephoned me. I talked to him for hours. He was terribly upset.'

'About Lise, you mean?'

'Well, yes, but more than that.' Mary gave her a helpless look. 'The thing is, John's so loyal and he has this terrible stiff-necked pride. He'll never admit he has problems. He bottles them up. And as for asking for help, even advice – well, forget it. He hasn't said a word to me, but obviously this has been building up for months.

Anyway, never mind that. On Sunday, I could hear, he was close to breaking-point, and finally, finally, it all came out. Apparently Lise really *isn't* well, Gini, and hasn't been for ages. Since last summer at least. She's seen doctor after doctor, but none of them seemed to be any help. Apparently, all day Sunday, there'd been the most dreadful scenes, weeping, hysteria.'

'Why? What provoked that?'

Mary's face became perplexed. She gave another sigh.

'Well, I think *John* did – though he didn't mean to, of course. You see, apparently, he's been getting more and more worried as the weeks went by, for Lise obviously, but also for the boys. You know what children are like, they pick up every little thing. Lise was getting so het up about all this security business. She was making their lives impossible, fussing over them, weeping, then losing her temper with them for no reason at all. And then I think . . . ' Mary paused. 'Well, John would never tell me this directly, but I think it had caused problems with him as well. There had been quarrels, I suspect – and the younger boy, Adam, overheard one quarrel. He's been very difficult to handle. He's so close to Lise, you see – so all her anxiety and tension spilled over onto him. He's become very solitary, John says, and his school work has fallen behind badly. His teachers are concerned . . . '

She drew in a deep breath. 'Anyway, to cut a long story short, John came to a decision. He decided that the best thing would be to send the boys back to the States for a few months, to stay with his brother, Prescott. Of course, Prescott has a whole tribe of children. John thought it would do the boys good, give them a break from all this anger and tension and anxiety. He thought it would do Lise good too – apparently she'd been having some wild fantasies that someone was going to kidnap the boys, that kind of thing. So John thought it would help her too. Then when this current security alert died down, and Lise was calmer again, the boys could come back.'

Mary stopped, her face troubled. Gini said nothing.

This was one explanation, and a plausible one at that. There were others, of course.

'Anyway,' Mary continued, 'John then did a very stupid thing in my opinion – and I told him so, straight out. It's very typical of John, he makes a decision and that's that. Instead of *consulting* Lise about all this, he just went right ahead and made the arrangements. He informed Lise yesterday morning. The boys were on a plane, with entourage obviously, last night.'

'Last night?' Gini stared. 'You mean he just went ahead and did it?'

'Darling, I know! But he can be curiously blind like that. He thought it was all for the best, so he just *assumed* Lise would think so too. Even if he'd known she was going to oppose it, he'd *still* have acted the same way. Once John's made what he thinks is the right decision, you can't budge him. That's that.'

'And Lise was distraught?'

Mary glanced over her shoulder. She lowered her voice. 'Darling, much more than that. All day yesterday, there was the most ghastly scene. Screaming and weeping, I gather, and smashing things. By the time John called me last night, they'd had to get a doctor, they'd given her sedatives. He was absolutely desperate, darling, I felt so terribly sorry for him. I think he was close to tears – I could hear them in his voice. He was so worried as to what would happen today. So I said, if he needed me, I'd come over. And as you know, I did.'

She gave a little shiver. 'Gini, I got here at ten in the morning. I've been here ever since. It's gone on all day. John had to cancel a whole series of appointments. He wouldn't leave her. He thought, if we both talked to her, quietly, she would calm down, and she did at first. She'd been given some tranquillizers first thing in the morning. About eleven o'clock, they wore off. Then it started . . . Gini – I was so shocked. It was absolutely horrible. She accused John of the most terrible things – ridiculous things—'

'What sort of things, Mary?'

342

'I'm not going to repeat them.' Mary blushed. 'Mistresses, other women – you can imagine the kind of thing. I mean – it's so absurd! John has never *looked* at another woman. He's the most utterly loyal and faithful man. Then it was the children, how he was trying to take them away from her. Then . . . oh, lots of terrible mad things – he was having her watched, he was opening her letters. It went on and on and on. John was so incredibly kind and patient. I tried, but nothing anyone said made the least difference. John got them to send for the doctor again, but Lise wouldn't see him, she said she'd kill herself if he set foot in her room. So in the end, John sent him away. We went upstairs again, and tried one more time – this must have been about three o'clock – and she calmed down for a while. She said she felt better, that she was going to take a nap. Then, quite suddenly, for no reason at all, it all began again. Only worse. John was trying to help her across the bedroom, into bed and she suddenly flew at him, and she *attacked* him, Gini. She started pulling his hair, ripping his clothes. It was so frightening, so completely horrible. He just stood there, trying to fend her off, with this terrible expression on his face. He looked dead, Gini, in utter despair. So . . . I stopped her.'

'You stopped her?'

'Yes, I did. She was hysterical. I slapped her face.' Mary gave a tiny unhappy shake of the head. 'And oddly, it seemed to do the trick. After that, she became much calmer. She kept talking very fast, but at least she wasn't screaming and weeping any more. That's when I said I had to get back, because you were waiting for me. And that's when she started on a new tack. How John never let her have any friends, how he kept her away from all her friends, how she'd wanted to talk to you the other night, but he'd prevented her . . . I don't know, Gini. It was just more nonsense. Then she asked to see you. She kept saying it. *I want to see Gini, now. I want to talk to Gini.* So, I stayed with her, and John sent the car over. It just seemed the easiest thing to do. She's supposed to be coming down in a minute. If she does, she'll probably have forgotten she even mentioned your name. Then, with luck, as I said, we can go. There's a nurse here now. John says he shouldn't be much more than an hour at the Foreign Office, then he'll come straight back. I feel sorry for him, Gini, but frankly, I've had enough.'

Gini said nothing. She drank her tea, and put the cup back on the tray. She looked around this elegant room. The house was silent; it was now just past six o'clock. Pascal intended to catch the five o'clock flight, Paris time; there was an hour's time difference in the winter months. That meant he would be reaching Heathrow Airport at around 7 p.m. London time. Allow an hour from the airport into London. Around 8 p.m. he would be arriving at Mary's house. She did not want to miss him, but she could see that the meeting with Lise might not be as cursory as Mary seemed to expect. There were many reasons she could think of, pressing reasons, why Lise might want to speak to her . . . But not here, surely? She looked at the room: would you wire a drawing-room for sound? In your own home? Four days ago, she would have dismissed that thought as absurd, as paranoid; not now.

At that moment, the door opened, and Lise entered. She was dressed from head to foot in exquisite pale beige cashmere: over a cashmere dress, she was wearing a cashmere coat. She looked radiant.

Crossing the room, she kissed Gini warmly on both cheeks. Mary stared at her in astonishment.

'Come on, Mary, Gini . . . ' She looked from one to the other. 'We're going out.'

'Out?' Mary rose to her feet. 'Lise, that's not a good idea, you know . . . '

'It's a very good idea. I'm sorry, Mary, for all I put you through, but I realize now, I was just being stupid and neurotic. I think I had a bad reaction to whatever that quack of a doctor gave me yesterday. Well, it's worn off, thank God. I feel absolutely fine now. I've had a bath, a little sleep. I feel like a new person. I've told them to bring the car around. We'll go out. I thought

I'd buy you both dinner. My treat, Mary, my way of thanking you for being so sweet.'

'No, Lise.' Mary spoke firmly. 'I promised John you'd rest. He'll be home soon.'

'Nonsense. He won't be back before eight at the earliest. I know! If you won't come to dinner will you let me take you out for a drink? Please say yes. I've been cooped up all weekend. I need a change of air. There's this marvellous new place, not far from you, Mary. A friend of a friend runs it. They serve those delicious tapas things – just for an hour, OK?'

Mary gave a sigh, and turned away. Lise looked at Gini intently. Silently, she mouthed the words: *Say yes.*

'I think that's a good idea, Mary,' Gini said quickly. 'Just for an hour. It might do Lise good . . . '

Lise smiled, and began to move towards the door. Mary gave Gini an exhausted look.

'Come on, Mary,' Gini said, in a low voice. 'It could do her good. You never know. She seems fine now. They'll drive her there, then drive her back.'

Mary gave her a puzzled glance, then shrugged.

'On your head be it,' she said.

The Kensington wine bar Lise had selected proved to be only two blocks from Mary's house. It was chic, fashionable, and packed. They were driven there by a uniformed driver, with the security man from Mary's party, Malone, in the other front seat.

He did not speak once. When they arrived outside the bar, he climbed from the car, and went in first. He was inside five minutes, and Lise began to show signs of irritation.

'Oh, heavens,' she said. 'How they do *fuss*. I wish he'd hurry up.'

Malone's time, it seemed, had not been wasted. When they entered the crowded wine bar a table had been made available for them, close to the fire-exit, Gini noted. Malone hovered for a few seconds, then disappeared. Lise gave a sigh.

'Thank God. He'll wait outside, and check I'm still here every ten minutes. You can set your watch by them.'

'Come on now, Lise,' Mary said in an encouraging tone. 'You shouldn't resent them. They're only doing their job.'

'Oh, I know, I know . . . ' Lise gave a tiny impatient gesture. 'Better him than Frank, anyway.' She turned to Gini with an enquiring look. 'Was it Frank who brought you, Gini?'

'Yes, it was.'

Lise made a face. 'Horrible man. He's had the whole weekend off, thank heaven. I like him the least. Always creeping around on those crêpe-soled shoes of his. Still, John won't hear a word against him. They go back a long way. He served with John in Vietnam, you know. He was sergeant in John's platoon. Then he worked for John's father for years and years.'

Her voice had risen slightly. Mary's face became uneasy.

'Now, Lise, come on. Forget about him. Forget about all of them.'

'You're right.' Lise smiled and held up the menu. 'Gini, look at all these amazing cocktails they have. Which would you like? Mary?'

Both Lise and Gini ordered mineral water; Mary, with a wry glance at Gini, ordered a double Scotch. The drinks arrived, the tapas were served. The noise was deafening: background music, conversation, laughter. Lise looked around her and gave a slow smile.

'How *nice*,' she said. 'I like this place. Excuse me . . . ' She stopped the waitress. 'Would you just remove these? We won't be needing them . . . '

She indicated a small vase of flowers, two containers for salt and pepper. The waitress stared at her, then removed them. The moment the table was clear, Lise seemed to relax. She chatted away for a while, then suddenly rose to her feet.

'I must pop into the ladies' room for a moment,' she said.

Gini watched her make her way through the press of

346

people by the bar. The cloakrooms, she noted from the signs, were next to the telephones. She remembered that tape she had listened to with Pascal, and a similar ploy used by Lise on a former occasion. Could she intend to telephone someone? And why remove the objects on the table – unless she suspected they were bugged? She met Mary's eyes. Mary sighed and took a hefty swallow of her drink.

'Don't say it, Gini, I know. You're going to think I was imagining the whole thing. She seems perfectly all right. Well, I just hope it lasts, that's all. If it doesn't, there'll be all hell to pay when John finds out.'

'I thought it was a good idea to humour her,' Gini said.

'Darling, I hope to God you're right . . . ' Mary broke off. 'Oh – I've just remembered. You wanted to see me – you wanted to talk. I'd completely forgotten. What was wrong, darling?'

'Nothing. I'm fine now. Really.'

'You certainly look fine. You're looking better than I've seen you look in months.' Mary gave her a narrow look. 'I wonder why? Any particular reason, darling? New job, new man, something like that?'

'Don't fish, Mary . . . ' Gini smiled.

'Would I?' Mary gave her a wide-eyed look of innocence. She took another sip of whisky. 'I meant to tell you,' she continued in an off-hand way, which did not deceive Gini in the least, 'I was pleasantly surprised by your photographer. Not that I spoke to him for very long. But he seemed rather nice. How old is he, Gini?'

'Thirty-five.'

'Really? Yes, well, I thought he had very nice *eyes*. A man's eyes are very important, and—'

'Who are you talking about?'

Lise had returned. She removed her coat, and slid into her seat.

'Gini's friend. Pascal Lamartine,' Mary replied.

Lise's face instantly lit. 'Oh yes, Gini, what a *very* nice man he is. So intelligent. So French.' She gave Gini

347

a teasing, almost mischievous look. 'You know I was reading his palm – I hope you didn't mind – my little party trick . . . Well, his was most interesting. A deep lifeline, a strong fate-line, one marriage, one very strong attachment, four children in all—'

'Four?'

'Well, I gather he has one already. So there are three still to come. Oh,' she paused, 'and some very significant event, mid-life – between thirty-five and forty, around then. It was quite clearly marked – a strong break in his fate-line. I told him it could be bad or good but it was a major alteration, some radical change.'

'Really?' Gini said, realizing with some self-disgust that she was listening intently to this.

'Oh, most definitely.' Lise nodded. 'I never make a mistake. I told John that this would be a very difficult year for him, even a dangerous one, and I was right.'

'It's January, Lise . . . ' Mary put in.

Lise dismissed this blithely. 'I know – and it's begun the way it means to go on. Have one of these tapas, Mary. They're delicious, don't you think?'

For twenty minutes, Lise continued to chat.

She ate nothing; taking one of the tapas now and then, and crumbling it on her plate. Apart from this she seemed calm and relaxed. Gini found herself wondering: was Lise a very good actress – and if so, had she been feigning hysteria earlier, or was she acting now? Which was her true self?

Mary, who seemed exhausted, took little part in this conversation. Lise told Gini about her work on the residence in London, the redecorations at her country house, the work John had organized in the gardens there – her husband was passionate about gardens, she said. She discussed her two sons, with no sign of distress; she spoke warmly of their uncle, Prescott, and how good it would be for the boys to spend some time back in the States. She described the party to be held shortly for her husband's forty-eighth birthday, and pressed Gini to attend, as her husband had done. Her conversation was lively, even amusing at times, and the only unusual feature of it that Gini noted was the frequency of her references to her husband. She quoted his views constantly. His name punctuated every sentence. John thinks, John says, John feels, John hopes . . .

Gini glanced covertly at her watch. She intended to leave soon, and before she did, it was time to give this conversation a little push.

'Tell me,' she said, 'when this posting to Britain is over, does your husband intend to return to political life?'

'Oh *yes*.' Lise glanced at Mary. 'Poor John. He only took this position for my sake. He thought it would give me a role, you see – and also that we would be able to see more of each other. He knew I hated living in Washington. Such a one-horse town, politics morning, noon and night.' She paused, and glanced at Mary again. 'I hope he's beginning to understand that he should never have done that. It was a sacrifice I never wanted him to make. I pleaded with him not to resign from the Senate. But John can be so immovable. I knew he would regret it, and he has. When you're born for high office, as John was, there's no escaping your fate.'

'Why did he resign?' Gini said. 'I've never understood that.'

'Oh Gini, no-one did.' Lise sighed. 'You'd have to know John terribly well to understand. I think, basically, he felt terribly *guilty*.' She gave Gini a quick glance. 'Our little boy Adam had been so ill, he nearly died, you know – it was the most terrible time. John felt he should have been with us more, that he'd failed in his responsibilities to us. So he just made the decision. He didn't even consult me. And that was that . . . ' She hesitated, and her lovely face clouded. 'Since then he's changed. I know he's not happy. Not fulfilled. Ambassador!' She gave a dismissive gesture. 'Anyone can be an ambassador. John was always destined for greater things than that.'

There was a silence. Mary raised her eyebrows but said nothing. Gini leaned forward.

'So, you think he'll return to full-time politics in due course?'

'Oh, more than that.' Lise's face took on an earnest look. She resembled a child repeating a well-learned lesson. 'John will run for the presidency eventually, just the way his father always planned, the way he always planned. And he'll be elected, of course.'

She said this with an air of absolute certainty, as if she could look into the future. There was no trace of boasting.

'I see.' Gini was shaken by her manner. 'And how would you feel about that?' she said carefully. 'What about your objections to Washington?'

'Washington?' Lise's face became blank.

'Well, that's where the White House was, the last time I visited.'

'Oh, I *see*.' Amusement lit her face. 'Well, I never really objected to Washington, not as such. John *thought* I did, but it was all in his mind . . .'

Gini frowned. 'But I thought you just said . . . when you lived there before, you found it limiting, a one-horse town . . .'

'Did I say that?' Lise looked genuinely surprised, despite the fact that it was less than five minutes since she had made the remark. She gave a small shrug, glanced down at her watch, then across at Mary. She sighed. 'Perhaps I've had some reservations in the past. I used to be so shy. It took me years to get used to such a public life. But now . . . well, I mustn't stand in John's way. That would be wrong of me, I think. Besides . . .' Her voice faltered. 'I could be an asset to John – he used to say that. It would be such a boost, for all my charities, and then I could redecorate the White House, restore it, the way Jackie Kennedy did. I'm quite good with houses, even John says that . . .'

She gave a sweet, childlike and slightly anxious smile. Then, lifting her hand, she made little waving gestures as if trying to attract their waitress's attention.

'Oh, what a *nuisance*,' she said. 'I can't catch that

wretched girl's eye. And I can see Mary's absolutely exhausted. No, Mary, you are, and it's entirely my fault. I'm talking on and on, and you're just longing to go home and have a rest. Dammit, she simply will *not* look this way.'

She half-rose to her feet, but Mary stopped her.

'No, don't be silly, Lise. You're squashed in there in the corner. I'll get her. Where is she?'

'She's over there, I think. Just beyond that crush at the bar. The one with the red frizzy hair, I think . . . '

Mary rose, and began to push her way through the throng of people. Gini looked around the room. The waitress who had served them, she noted, did not have red hair, and she was not over by the bar, she was standing at the opposite end of the long room. She turned back to look at Lise. The alteration in Lise's demeanour had been immediate. The expression of somewhat sugary rapture was wiped from her face. Her features were now tense and set; she had paled. She glanced quickly over her shoulder, leaned across the table, and grasped Gini's wrist.

'Oh my God, I'm sorry. I had to talk to you. Can you help me? Are you helping me?' she asked.

Gini began to reply, but Lise interrupted her, speaking fast in a very low voice.

'I had to do this. I had to speak to you somehow. I would have tried at Mary's the other night but he was watching me all the time. I didn't dare. I tried to help, did your friend tell you? John didn't realize what I did, but even so, he was so angry, so angry. I can't tell you what he's like when he's angry. He punishes me – that's why he sent my sons home the next day, to punish me. Please, please, you have to help me. You're my last hope.'

She had begun to tremble. Her grip tightened on Gini's wrist. 'Have you found James yet? Have you? You must have looked for him? Where is he? Do you know?'

'No,' Gini said.

'Oh God, oh God.' Her face had turned chalk white. 'You must find him. Frank was on leave this weekend. I have to know James is safe. I'm so afraid he's dead . . . '

Her grip on Gini's wrist had become painful. Suddenly, she released that grip, and began to fumble with the sleeve of her sweater.

'Look,' she said. 'Look.'

Her bared arm was painfully thin, and the bruise very large. Gini could see the imprint of fingers clearly, violet-black against her skin. Above the bruise were three round marks; Gini stared, then realized that they were burn marks, made with the tip of a cigarette.

'John did that yesterday. There are other marks. On my neck. On my back. That's why I broke down. I can't take it any more. Mary doesn't know. No-one knows. Listen, please find James. Before next Sunday – you understand? Next Sunday . . . ' Her voice died in her throat.

'I understand. Next Sunday is the third of the month.'

'Find James and go to that house. I gave your friend the address. I think he'll use it, it's his usual place – on Sunday, you understand? He's always watching me. Well, now it's his turn to be watched . . . '

She gave a shiver and again glanced over her shoulder. Again she gripped Gini's wrist. 'He's so clever, Gini – you have to understand that. He makes me see all these doctors, doctor after doctor. Then they give me these pills, and he makes me take them, injections too. He wants people to think I'm having a breakdown, losing my mind. That's why he got Mary there today, so she'd be a witness. Do you see?'

She trembled violently. 'And, of course, it works. I can see what people think. They think I'm a fool, a nervous wreck, a bad mother.' Tears filled her eyes. 'Sometimes I almost believe it all myself, all the lies he tells about me. I'm so desperate, Gini. You have to believe me. You have to help me. For my sake and my sons' sake. They need me so much. You see, he doesn't care what it takes . . . '

She made a choking sound, and the tears spilled over down her white cheeks.

'He hasn't loved me, Gini, not for years – if he ever did. He's such a cold man. He's just like his father. He wants me out of the way, so he can carry on with that glorious future of his. I knew, if he ever discovered I'd talked to James, if he found out James had gone to the Press, that would be the end. And he does know, I'm sure of it. That's why James left, and now . . . Oh God, oh God. Mary's coming back . . . '

She broke off, then pulled down her sleeve. She began to twist her wedding ring. 'Listen, quickly. You mustn't talk on your telephone. Be careful in your apartment. I'm watched. You're watched. Never let that man Frank near you. The others are all right, they're legitimate security men, but not Frank. Remember what I said . . . If you have to talk use a park, an open space, better still a crowded restaurant like this one, that's the safest of all. Dear God . . . '

She fixed Gini with her eyes. Her pupils were huge, dilated, black. She was shaking uncontrollably now, and was white to the lips.

'Mary's nearly here. I'll try to see you again. It may not be possible. Wednesday. I'll try then. Walk in the park, just behind my house. I used to meet James there then, on Wednesdays, about ten. You'll come, you promise me?'

'I'll be there,' Gini said.

'Thank you.' She grasped Gini's hand feverishly, and pressed it between her thin dry palms. 'In God's name thank you. I shall never forget this . . . '

Mary had finally reached their table. She looked down at Lise in consternation. Lise wiped her eyes with a handkerchief, and rose to her feet. She embraced Mary warmly, then kissed Gini.

'I'm sorry, Mary,' she said. 'The tears just started, and then I couldn't stop. I miss the boys so . . . I'll go home now with Malone. Thank you both. This has helped, really it has . . . '

Without another word, she picked up her coat, and began to walk through the restaurant. Mary hurried after her but by the time she reached the door, the car was pulling away with Lise and Malone in the back.

Mary stood watching the car disappear. When she

turned back to Gini, there were tears of sympathy in her eyes. She pressed Gini's hand.

'I fear for her,' she said. 'I'm afraid for her, Gini. Two such marvellous people – and now this. All that good work she does, all that love she's poured into her marriage – and now this. Life is cruel, Gini, don't you think?'

'People are,' Gini replied, but Mary did not hear her.

XX

Pascal had been speaking to Gini on the telephone in his wife's living-room. He put down the receiver, stared into the silence for a while, then returned to the kitchen. Helen was sitting where he had left her, at the table, her head slumped in her hands.

'I'll stay, Helen,' he said at last. 'It's all right, I won't leave you alone. I'll stay tonight and maybe tomorrow – until we're both sure she's better.'

Helen gave him a blank look. Her face was tear-stained. When Pascal sat down opposite her, he could still detect the faint lunch-time smell of wine on her breath. A clock was ticking. The room was as white, as hygienic, as an operating theatre. Upstairs, Marianne was now sleeping peacefully, her English nanny keeping watch. It was half-past eight, and it felt like a week since he'd arrived at the house.

'Scarlet fever,' Helen said, in a dull voice. 'I don't understand. No-one gets that. Not any more . . . '

'It's unusual, but it responds to penicillin. Helen, don't cry any more. The crisis is over. She'll be all right, the doctor said.'

'I wasn't here.' Helen looked away. 'I wasn't here – and I can't forgive myself for that.'

'Helen, you can't be here all the time. *I* was here. And I wasn't a great deal of use either . . . ' He gave a helpless shrug.

'I wouldn't say that.' She raised her eyes to look at him. 'You did your best. It's never happened before. I wouldn't have known what to do either. Sponge her down, give more aspirin sooner . . . I wouldn't have known that.' She hesitated. 'Would you make me some tea, Pascal? It might stop me feeling sick.'

Pascal made the tea. All the time he was doing so, he could feel her watching him.

Eventually, in a stiff way, she said, 'I haven't always been fair to you, Pascal. I do realize that. In my better moments.' She gave a shrug.

'I realize too.' Pascal passed her the tea. He produced a tired smile. 'In *my* better moments, I see where I went wrong. What I did.'

'Do you?' She sipped the tea, gave him a long considering look. 'Well, it's in the past now, Pascal, anyway. It's just . . . '

She hesitated. He watched her fight back the tears. Helen hated to show weakness.

When she had succeeded in controlling the tears, she said, 'I'm not good at showing affection any more. Even with Marianne. I've lost the knack.'

'I'm sure that's not true.'

'No, you're wrong. It is.' She paused, her colour deepening, then began speaking again, rushing past the words, as if she had to admit this, but hated to do so. 'It's because I'm afraid. That's why. I always think, if I show any love, sooner or later it will get thrown back in my face. No, don't say anything. It's not your fault. I was always like that. Long before I married you.'

Pascal looked at her wordlessly. After a moment, he reached across and took her hand. 'Helen,' he began. 'Why did you never tell me that? If we'd talked more, been more open with each other . . . '

'It wouldn't have made any difference. We were never right for each other. I know that. You know that. There it is.'

Pascal removed his hand. They looked at each other. Helen gave a sad smile.

'You see? We both know it's true. That's a kind of progress, at least. You see,' she looked away, 'I was hoping, Pascal, I have been hoping, that I could change. Learn actually to trust someone, perhaps. There's another reason why I want to go back to England.'

There was silence. Pascal counted the seconds. He said, 'I see. You've met someone else?'

'Yes, I have.' She hesitated. 'He's a good man. Very English, very reliable, very steady. Not as exciting as you were – but I don't want excitement any more. Not now. I want peace.'

'I can understand that.'

'You can?' She looked surprised. 'The thing is, I wouldn't rush into anything, I promise you. I'd be very sure this time before I committed myself.'

'He wants to marry you?'

'He says he does. I met him today, it's him I was meeting. We talked about it then. I told him he'd have to be patient. And he will be . . . ' A tiny flurry of emotion passed across her face. 'He's a kind man, Pascal. I think you'd like him. He'd be good to Marianne. He has children, too, he's a widower. He wouldn't try to replace you – nothing like that. He's sensitive and kind and a little bit dull and it would ease the money situation for you, and . . . Pascal. I'm only thirty-one. I have to have a life.'

'I know that.' Pascal stared down at the white table in front of him. He tried to tell himself that he had known this was inevitable.

'Do you mean that?'

Pascal looked up. He frowned. 'Yes, I do, oddly enough. Since I last saw you I've had time to think. So much bitterness – I never wanted it to be like that. It shouldn't be like that for Marianne's sake.'

'Ours too.' She looked at him closely. 'And we did like each other once. Almost loved each other. For a time. You were good to me, after the miscarriage. Under all the pain and the bitterness I felt, I did know that. And tonight, when I came back, when I saw your face . . . ' She broke off. 'I do know how much you love Marianne, Pascal. And I hope you know I love her too.'

She bent her head, and began to cry a little. Then she wiped her eyes, and straightened.

'I could talk to the lawyers,' she said, in a stiff way.

'I'd be prepared to do that. When I'm in England we could alter the custody arrangements to make it easier for you . . . '

Pascal hesitated. He looked at the table. He moved his teacup forward then back. 'If I were living in England,' he began slowly. 'If I made England my base, would you object to that?'

'England?' She looked astonished, then frowned. 'No, I suppose I wouldn't object. I don't want you next door, or in the next village, obviously.'

'You know I wouldn't do that.'

'Yes, I know.' She paused. 'Well, I suppose it might work out. Marianne would be pleased. You never know . . . ' She gave him a dry look. 'We might even end up friends, Pascal. Stranger things have happened. I must say I'm surprised though. England? You? Whatever draws you to England?'

'Oh, the past. The future,' Pascal hesitated, his face suddenly anxious. 'May I use your phone again?' he asked.

Gini returned to her flat at ten. There was a pile of mail on her mat. She stood in the centre of her living-room holding it. Outside, footsteps passed, then a car. She tried to tell herself that this was her home. But it did not feel like her home; it did not feel safe.

When Pascal telephoned to explain he could not return, he had tried to persuade her to stay at Mary's that night. She had refused, and when she did so, had felt a rebellious anger in herself. She would not be driven out of her own space by a break-in, by the fear of what she had seen in Venice the previous night. Let them send their sick parcels, and their sick audiotapes. Pascal had phoned back twice at Mary's to try to dissuade her, but she refused to back down. 'I will not be made a fugitive,' she had said. And that was fine, when Mary was near by, just through in the kitchen, clattering plates. It was less fine now she was alone, and it was night.

She locked and bolted both front and back doors. She checked that all the windows were securely fastened.

She drew the curtains and the blinds, moving swiftly from room to room, still in her overcoat. She lit the fire, switched on every lamp, tossed the pile of letters onto her desk, removed her overcoat, looked around her, and at once felt better. It might be foolish, but with the curtains drawn, she felt more secure; at least she knew she could not be watched.

Napoleon was sitting on the sofa watching these activities. When she crossed to him, he turned away his topaz eyes and flicked his tail. Cats could speak, Gini thought, in their way, and every line of Napoleon's body indicated reproach.

He did not like to be left; with her neighbour Mrs Henshaw absent too, he clearly felt doubly abandoned. Gini stroked him, and kissed his marmalade ears, but Napoleon refused to be mollified. He gave her a cold feline stare. Then, as if other priorities had just occurred to him, he leapt to the floor, and made his way to the kitchen at a dignified pace.

He had ignored the food she had left for him, but Gini, who had anticipated this, had brought an offering from Mary's. A little poached salmon, Napoleon's favourite dish. The instant he smelled it, he licked his lips. By the time he had eaten it, exited through the cat-flap to the yard beyond, explored the dank and malodorous dustbins in the lane beyond that, and returned, his humour was restored. He followed Gini back into the living-room, and leapt up onto her lap.

Gini yawned and stretched. She would just go through her mail, she decided – it was sure to be bills – and then have an early night. In the morning she intended to go to the *News* offices first thing: there was work to do, leads to follow, and there were certain questions she was eager – very eager – to ask Nicholas Jenkins. Such as, who else knew they were assigned to this story, because, quite obviously, he had lied and someone did.

She began to leaf through the letters. Circulars. Bills. There were a couple of invitations, a couple of postcards; the first, from that unmemorable man friend now in

Australia, she read quickly then tossed to one side. The second . . . She stared at the second. Who had sent her this?

On the front of it was a reproduction of a painting by Uccello. It showed, quaintly and with charm, a mounted St George slaying a dragon. Close by stood the maiden he was saving. She stood at the mouth of a cave, waiting calmly for the dragon's death. Fifteenth century, Florentine school. It was a famous painting, and one Gini knew well. The perspective and proportions were naïve: St George and the dragon were large, the lady small. Gini turned the postcard over; the message was brief and neatly written:

> *Do you remember those three books I lent you? Could you let me have them back when you're next in Oxford? Need them for revision – ugh! Thanks for the pasta the other week. You make a great bolognese – the best! See you soon. Don't work too hard. Take care.*
>
>

Lots of love,
Jacob

Gini stared at the card. She knew no-one named Jacob, she knew no-one studying at Oxford; she had borrowed no books from anyone recently, and it was at least a year since she had served anyone – it had been Lindsay in any case – spaghetti bolognese.

She turned the card this way and that. An Italian painting, though it was not identified as such on the card; *three* books. Could it be? Was this McMullen's way of contacting her? She looked at her other mail – the bills, the brochures. They showed no signs of being tampered with, but then they wouldn't, of course. If he had wanted to contact her, what could be more apparently innocuous than an open postcard, a postcard with a cheery inconsequential message from some friend, little different from that other postcard from Australia.

She looked at the postcard more closely, and then realized: of course – *Jacob*. And her mind slid back to her hated English boarding-school, to the Latin lessons, to the history lessons. The Latin form of the name 'James' was *Jacobus*. It had been used by English kings, James I, James II – *Jacobus rex*.

It was cunning, she thought – too cunning. If this was some form of coded message it was not one she understood. Which sentences carried hidden meanings, and which were there purely for decoration? She seemed to be being pointed towards Oxford, that was simple enough, and back yet again to those three books left out on McMullen's desk. But what did 'revision' mean? Were the references to Italian food important or unimportant?

Puzzled, she retrieved the piece of paper she had found in McMullen's apartment. She looked at the numbers, she considered the three books, she looked back at the postcard. It still made no sense. One of the books had been *The Oxford Book of Modern Verse*. Oxford again – and Milton twice, if she included the paperback found in Venice. Milton and Oxford, a Carson McCullers novel. Perhaps the first set of numbers were page references, she thought, and the second referred to words on those pages. If so, she was thwarted; to check, she needed those editions, those books. Surely it had to be simpler than that? She sat there for an hour, and she could feel her brain starting to lock.

Around midnight, she gave up. She left all the lights in the living-room on – it felt safer – and went to bed.

Even then, she could not sleep. She lay in the semi-darkness, light drifting through the doorway, Napoleon curled up on her feet. She stared at the ceiling, and the details of this story went round and round in her mind. She saw those brass buttons on Frank Romero's jacket, then Lise Hawthorne's anguished white face. She went back to that first conversation with Nicholas Jenkins, and remembered a phrase he had used then.

The patterns of obsessive behaviour, he had said. It was not a comforting phrase, Gini thought. She had interviewed some people in the past who might be described as obsessives, and she thought of them now. The man serving a life sentence in Broadmoor Prison for the Criminally Insane, for instance, who had lived alone with his dog in a North London flat, and who always photographed himself embracing his victims' bodies before he dismembered and disposed of them.

He had had his rules: all his boy victims were under twenty, all were white; they had to have dark hair, and he picked them up in the same bar, always on a Saturday night.

The woman who believed an eminent surgeon was passionately in love with her, when the man had encountered her on only two occasions, at a conference, but had unwisely replied to one of the woman's letters, explaining he was devoted to his children and his wife. That woman, too, had been an obsessive, and had approached Gini herself. She thought Gini should tell the world that this distinguished man was, in reality, a liar and a cheat. She had showed Gini, with cold indignation, the love-letters the surgeon had written her: they were in her own handwriting. Gini had half-pitied the woman, but the surgeon feared her. On one occasion she had broken into his home and slashed his suits to ribbons with a knife.

So, yes, Gini had some experience of the patterns of obsessive behaviour – and it was not the kind that induced peaceful sleep. Obsession unravelled reason, and blurred the edges of life. To talk to an obsessive was to step into the mirror and watch truth reverse. Every person she had ever encountered who fitted this category shared one characteristic. For the most part, the madness did not show. Until you knew the truth, these people were ordinary, no more alarming than the next person in the supermarket, or the bus. They lied with quiet conviction because they were truly convinced their lies and their inversions were the truth.

So, had Lise Hawthorne been lying that evening? Gini could not tell. Had Hawthorne himself, the previous Saturday, been acting and disguising his true self? Again she did not know. But there was one factor besides Pascal's arguments, besides the mounting evidence, which counted against Hawthorne, and it was this: famous and powerful men often seemed to court danger and the destruction of their careers. Every week newspaper stories gave evidence of this.

She and Pascal had discussed it, in a café in Venice. These days such instincts provided Pascal with much of his work. How else could you explain the long succession of eminent men who risked a career they'd spent a lifetime building, for a night with a call-girl, an affair with a gabby actress who ran straight from bed to the tabloids? How else could you explain a man who prosecuted corruption in public life, then cheated on his taxes, or accepted a kick-back?

She had asked this question, and Pascal had sighed. 'Because they enjoy the risk,' he said. 'They crave the danger – they must. Perhaps they can only value their achievements when they know that one word in the wrong quarter, and everything's lost. Maybe they simply get bored with the safety of success.' He paused. 'They *seek* self-destruction, Gini. I think it's that.'

It was a viable theory, Gini thought. It explained the phenomenon as well, and as little, as anything else. It might explain Hawthorne – perhaps.

She closed her eyes. The house was quiet. It was well past midnight now. She felt herself begin to drift at last towards sleep.

It was two in the morning when she woke. She sat up and listened. Something had woken her, and her cat. Napoleon lifted his head. He turned his green eyes in the direction of the bedroom window. Gini tensed. From the yard beyond, she heard the wood of the fence creak. A twig snapped outside. She sat rigid: she could hear footsteps now. Slowly and stealthily they approached her window, then stopped. They moved towards the rear kitchen door. There was a rustling sound, a small rattle, then silence.

Gini stifled a cry. Carefully and quietly, she pushed

the bedcovers aside, and stood up. She listened. The footsteps were retreating now. She heard their muffled progress across the yard; there was another creak from the fence. She clenched her hands to stop them trembling. Had he gone, or was he selecting an alternative route?

In bare feet, making no sound, she pressed herself against the wall, and edged towards the lights of the living-room. The curtains there were drawn well across. No-one could see in, surely no-one could see in? She listened. She heard the creak of the iron gate opening at the top of the area steps. She tensed. She crept silently to the front door, and pressed her ear against it. The footsteps were descending.

They came down slowly, then paused. She heard them move towards the window. She braced herself for the sound of breaking glass, or the catch being forced.

It did not come. There was a shuffling sound, then the footsteps approached the door where she stood. And stopped.

Whoever was there was as close to the door as she was. Two inches of flimsy wood separated them. Through the panels she could hear his breathing: a quiet inhalation and exhalation of breath.

Her limbs felt leaden with fear. She thought: *I should have switched off the lights, and now it's too late*. She thought: *I must decide, now, what to do when he comes in*. Her mind worked with a slow clarity; it was like watching a sixty-mile-an-hour car-smash slowly approach. She told herself: *I must move, so I'm behind the door when it opens*. She took one step, then another. The lights in the flat flickered, and went out.

She gave a low moan of terror. The darkness was thick, she could see nothing. She backed away from the door, and collided with a table behind her. A vase crashed to the floor and smashed. Outside, the footsteps hesitated, then moved off. They remounted the steps, crossed the pavement above in the direction of the square's central gardens. The footsteps were rapid now. They faded into the distance. The silence was intense.

She was flooded with relief. It coursed through her like blood. She inched forward, and broken glass cut her foot. Carefully, feeling for glass, she fumbled her way across the room. There was a flashlight in her desk. She could see nothing. She felt space, then the handle of a desk drawer. She opened the drawer, and felt around its contents. A leather glove brushed her hand. She felt the cold metal of the handcuffs. She scrabbled frantically at the back of the drawer: she could not bear this absence of light. She was crouching down, feeling in the drawer, when the telephone rang next to her face. The sound was sudden and loud; she started, and almost knocked the machine to the floor.

Who would call now, at this hour? She fumbled in the dark for the receiver, and as she did so relief flooded her body again. Pascal. She was sure it was Pascal. Her hand closed on the receiver and she eagerly snatched it up.

A man's voice, but not Pascal's, began to speak.

'Gini,' he said. 'Gini, is it you?'

Her skin went cold. The voice was low, unrecognizable, and thick.

'Gini, I know it's you. I got you out of bed. Listen, Gini, it's late – and it's time for us to talk . . . '

'Who is this?' Gini said. 'What do you want?'

The man continued speaking, right across her question. The voice was whispery, the line poor.

'Are you wearing your nightdress, Gini? I think you are. The white one, with the blue ribbon at the neck? I like it. It's pretty. The material's thin . . . '

'Listen, whoever you are,' Gini began. She heard the fear in her own voice. She *was* wearing a white nightdress; its ribbon was blue. It was made of fine thin cotton voile.

'Stand still,' said the voice, riding over her words again. 'That's right. Now I can see your breasts through the cotton. You have beautiful breasts, Gini. You know what they do to me? They make me hard . . . All the blood goes straight to my cock, Gini. It's stiff.'

Gini's hand had closed over the flashlight. She drew it

out, and switched it on. Light made her feel stronger. She held the receiver at arm's length, and heard the voice whisper on. She brought the receiver closer.

'Listen, you creep,' she said distinctly, 'do us both a favour. Go screw yourself, OK?'

She replaced the receiver on its cradle. As soon as the room was silent once more, she went to the bathroom and threw up.

She was pretty sure he'd call back again, whoever he was. When he did, fifteen minutes later precisely, she was ready for him – or as ready as she could make herself. With the aid of the flashlight and some candles, she had banished as much darkness as she could. On the desk, next to the telephone, she had placed her tape recorder. She had connected its microphone, and inserted a new tape.

This was not the best way to record a call, but it was the only method available. When the telephone rang, she picked it up, spoke briefly. As soon as the man began speaking, she pressed her microphone tight to the earpiece. She could not avoid hearing some of what he said. She tensed, listened. The same words, the same sentences, in exactly the same order as before . . .

This was no ordinary caller, no ordinary man. She was listening to a *tape*. That was why he spoke over her words as he did: because this call was pre-recorded. And with whom had she discussed pre-recorded telephone sex lines, not two days before? John Hawthorne. She listened, trying to block out the words and hear only the intonation of the voice.

It was not Hawthorne's, she felt, though she was uncertain. The voice was slow, and neither English nor American, but somewhere between the two. It sounded muffled, as if the man spoke through a piece of material, as if he had something pressed against his mouth. It was muffled, filtered, recorded – even so, the man was becoming aroused as he spoke. She could hear his breathing grow rougher as his script grew more direct.

'Let me suck your breasts,' he said, on and on in that

low whispery voice. 'Then I'll tie your hands behind your back. You got the handcuffs, Gini? I'll use those, I think. Then I want you to kneel down in front of me, like you're in church. I want you to watch me take it out . . . ' There was a deep sigh, a rustling sound, then the whispering went on.

'Then, then – I'll do all the things I like. I'll rub my cock on your hair, on your face, on your lips. Over your breasts, where the skin's soft. It's hard, and it's big, bitch – can you feel it yet? Open your mouth and suck me off. Then maybe I'll fuck you, like you've never been fucked . . . '

Gini could feel the anger begin. It was like something red in her mind. It drove out the fear and even the disgust. It was useful, this red anger: it felt good. Very carefully, she placed the receiver and microphone on the desk. She let him continue, and her tape run. She wouldn't listen, but she would record, tape to tape.

She let him continue for ten minutes. Standing at a distance of five feet, she couldn't hear the words, but she could hear the scratch of his voice. Ten minutes was enough.

She approached the desk again, and disconnected the microphone. The man was approaching climax on the tape; she was afraid to hear what came after that – another woman's scream, perhaps. She put the receiver down on the man's groans. She switched the machine to answer-mode. She went back to the bedroom, and held Napoleon close. The rest of the night seemed interminable. She scarcely slept. The man did not call again.

In the morning, she woke from a brief and exhausted sleep. All the lights were back on. When she went out to the kitchen, the rattling sound she had heard was explained. Her night-time visitor had left her a present, pushed through the cat-flap.

Same wrapping, same box, same shoe – to make a pair. No stocking this time.

Gini looked at the stiletto heel for a while. Then she unbolted the back door. It was raining again.

She hurled the black shoe the length of the yard. It hit the back fence, and fell among the shrubbery. Gini closed the door and bolted it again.

It was six-thirty, Tuesday morning. She showered and dressed. She fed Napoleon, and let him purr in slumbrous luxury for a while on her lap. He purred, and she planned. She would do this first, and then that. Before this week was out, before Sunday came, she would find McMullen, and wind this story up.

'I'm going to fix him,' she said to Napoleon. 'I'm going to fix the bastard who did all this.'

Napoleon narrowed his topaz eyes. He washed himself, then went to sleep.

At eight precisely, Pascal called, as she had hoped. 'Not on this line,' he said. 'Call me later – the way we agreed, yes?'

XXI

Gini left her house at eight-thirty. She headed south for the *News* offices, through heavy traffic, cursing the hold-ups and red lights. If she could reach the office around nine, she had a good chance of cornering Nicholas Jenkins before the crises that made up his editorial day barred her from entry. Jenkins, she was now certain, had been less than totally frank when originally briefing her and Pascal. He *must* have told someone else who would be assigned to the story. He might have told Daiches. She was also beginning to wonder if he could possibly have told Appleyard, even, indeed, if the first hint of the story had come from Appleyard, and not McMullen as Jenkins claimed. This made some sense: it was characteristic of Jenkins to snatch the credit entirely for himself; it was also characteristic of him to react strongly to one of Appleyard's hints. She knew the two had been in touch in recent months. Now that she considered it, she realized that both the Hawthorne story *and* the telephone sex story had come her way the same week.

Halting at red lights outside the Barbican, she had a brief, ugly and disturbing vision of Appleyard in that Venice room, two weeks dead. She closed her eyes. The driver behind her leaned on his horn. The lights were now green. Gini jerked the car into gear and drove off. A squall of rain smashed against her windscreen. She switched on her headlights. It was a dark, cold, wet morning; she could already foresee a day of perpetual twilight.

Appleyard, she thought. Appleyard, who had always been Jenkins's favourite tipster. Appleyard, who was a notorious gossip, though protective of his own leads.

There was some connection, some link, she felt certain – but what?

*　　*　　*

On the fifteenth floor, Charlotte, the senior secretary, together with her two assistants, was already at her desk. The door to Nicholas Jenkins's office was shut. And it would be likely to *stay* shut, Charlotte implied, with a weary glance. Jenkins was in conference with his witchy familiar Daiches; both had a meeting later that morning with their proprietor, Lord Melrose. In Charlotte's opinion, as Gini well knew, Melrose had inherited his father's newspaper empire, but not his father's aptitude: it was Charlotte who had to try to shield Jenkins when Melrose had one of his periodic flaps.

'Melrose is making waves again,' Charlotte said. 'Something blew up over the weekend, apparently – don't ask me what. You won't get near Nicholas all day, Gini, don't even *ask*, all right?' She paused, and gave a small secretive smile. 'Whatever it is you want, you can discuss it tonight.'

'Tonight?'

'This just came for you. By messenger.' She handed Gini a large vellum envelope. 'I know what it is already. I had Lord Melrose's personal assistant on the phone about it, at half-past eight.'

Gini opened the envelope. Inside was an engraved invitation to a dinner given by the Newspaper Publishers' Association that night. The chairman of the association was currently Lord Melrose; the dinner was at the Savoy, the guest of honour and main speaker was His Excellency the US Ambassador; and the subject of John Hawthorne's speech was to be *Privacy and the Press*. Written across the top of the card was her name, in exquisite italic script. Gini stared at this thoughtfully.

'Lord Melrose's office sent this?'

'Oh yes. At the behest of the great man himself.' Charlotte gave her a narrow look. 'So what have you been up to, Gini? I didn't know you hobnobbed with the great and the good.'

'I don't. Not often.'

Gini looked down at the card again. She knew precisely who had procured this invitation for her. John Hawthorne. Well, well, well: in the circumstances she would be interested to hear his views on privacy and the Press.

'Nicholas knows, by the way.' Charlotte grinned. 'And he was *beside* himself with curiosity. He says you can drive there and back in his car.' She made a face. '*Be there*. That was the gist of what he said. He'll pick you up at your flat at seven-thirty. Can I tell him that's fixed?'

'Sure,' Gini said.

The door to Jenkins's office opened; Daiches came out. He gave Gini a pale glance. Charlotte, who had her back to him, seemed to sense his presence through her shoulder-blades. She turned back to her word processor and began to type. Daiches made straight for Gini, a little smile on his face.

'Well, Gini,' he said, walking beside her towards the lift, 'I hear you're now a friend of Melrose, no less. Congratulations. This should do your future career here a *great* deal of good. Friends in the right places – the secret of every lady journalist's success.'

'Oh, fuck off, Daiches,' Gini said.

Daiches gave a little pout of delight. 'Gini, language, language! And you're usually so polite. You're going down? Me too. How nice.'

Daiches followed her into the lift. He was carrying a pile of papers. The floors flashed by. Daiches turned to her, and indicated the top-most fax.

'Johnny Appleyard's dead,' he said. 'Had you heard? This just came in from our stringer in Rome. Murder, Gini – how about that?'

Gini glanced down at the fax. It gave some details of the killing, and they were already inaccurate. She made no response.

'Appleyard *and* that weirdo he lived with. What was his name?'

'Stevey, I think.'

371

'Stevey, that's right. The farm-boy with the pretty face. Bound hand and foot, Gini. One of those queer killings by the sound of it. Heartbreaking, the prejudice in this wicked world of ours . . . '

'Give it a rest, Daiches.'

Daiches gave her a long, cold, pale look. 'Ah well,' he said, shuffling the pages. 'It *is* murder. Worth a couple of columns, don't you think?'

They had reached the Features floor. With relief Gini stepped out of the lift; Daiches held the doors open.

'Just one little thing, Gini – before you rush off.' His smile became sweet. 'Don't forget the telephone sex story, will you? Nicholas did mention it to you last Friday. I need it, and I need it soon.'

'When?'

'Not later than the end of the week.'

'That's not possible.'

'Then make it possible, dear,' he said, in his mildest and most dangerous voice. The lift doors began to close. 'Friday, 3 p.m. at the latest,' he called through them. 'On my desk, Gini. On my desk.'

Back in the Features department, Gini went through her notes. She took a pen and a fresh sheet of paper. *A list of priorities*, she told herself: *a shopping-list.* She wrote:

1) *Find McMullen. Call Oxford college. Try Jeremy Prior-Kent.*
2) *Trace/speak to Lorna Munro.*
3) *Where hire high-spec blondes? Escort agencies?*
4) *Appleyard. Any connection this & telephone sex?*
5) *Talk Mary's crossword friend re codes.*

The first two of these tasks were straightforward. She called Christ Church, and quickly discovered that McMullen's tutor there had been a history don whose name she knew well: Dr Anthony Knowles, a man with a maverick reputation who was something of a media star, a frequent television pundit, and a contributor to newspapers, as well as a very eminent historian. To her surprise, she was even able to speak briefly to Dr Knowles himself, and most amiable he was. He gave her considerably more information about McMullen's brief Oxford career. However, he proved no help at all when it came to the question of McMullen's whereabouts.

'My dear, I wish I could be of help. But alas, I cannot. James used to call on me occasionally, for old times' sake, if he was passing through Oxford. And I'm always delighted to see him – an excellent mind, one of my best undergraduates. But I'm afraid I've neither seen nor heard from James for at least a year. Let me see, whom might you try? There was a rather foolish young man who was at school with him, who came up the same year. They had rooms on the same staircase. I believe they remained in touch. Now what was his name? Jeremy something, I think . . . '

'Jeremy Prior-Kent?'

'That's it. Of course. And now, I'm afraid I must curtail this conversation.'

She tried the offices of Prior-Kent's film-production company in Soho. Unfortunately, his secretary said, he had changed plans; he would now not be returning to London until late Thursday night. He and his location manager were scouting locations in Cornwall, and so could not be reached.

The woman made Cornwall sound like the Sahara Desert. She made Prior-Kent sound like Cecil B. de Mille.

'Of course, should Mr Kent get in contact, I'll pass on your message. You're calling from the *News*? If it's urgent—'

'It is urgent. Very.'

'I expect I could find a *small* window for you on Friday. Let me just check his diary . . . '

'A window? Thanks.'

During the long pause that followed, Gini leafed through the office directory of film-production companies. Kent's company, Salamander Films, had a few listed credits for TV commercials and minor documentaries; no feature films as yet. *Windows*, Gini thought; *location scouting in Cornwall: pretentious idiots*. Why were all film people, especially the minor ones, like this?

'Twelve on Friday.' The girl came back on the line. 'It's his only gap. He could spare you an hour then. Then he has a big lunch. Shall we say the Groucho? It's right around the corner from here. It's convenient for him.'

'Thanks very much. Luckily, I can spare an hour on Friday too. I'll see him at the Groucho then.'

She hung up on the girl's wails about confirmation, and dialled the number of Lorna Munro's Rome hotel. This would be her sixth call to the model, and none had been returned. It was of no surprise to learn that, yet again, Lorna Munro had left. There was a contact number, though, for a French magazine. It took Gini fifteen minutes of toil, in rusty French, to discover that Lorna Munro was now in Paris. She called Pascal at once. It was ten, the time she had arranged to call him, but the telephone was answered by Helen Lamartine. It was a shock to hear her voice. To Gini's surprise she sounded almost friendly, if brisk.

'Marianne?' she said. 'Oh, she's much better this morning, thank you, on the road to recovery. We'll have to watch her carefully, just for the next twenty-four hours or so. But the penicillin seems to have done the trick. One moment, Pascal's in the other room . . . Pascal, it's London. Work.'

While she waited for Pascal to come on the line, Gini stared into space. That 'we' had hurt. All the old familiarity of a marriage, that was what she had heard in Helen's voice. Even if it had been an unhappy marriage, her own claims seemed, beside it, very tenuous, very frail. She felt an instant's foreboding, but it passed the second she heard Pascal's voice.

She told him quickly the news about Lorna Munro: that she was in Paris for just twenty-four hours; that she was doing a photo-session of Gaultier dresses for

Elle magazine – no, not in studio; the location was the left bank, outside the church of St Germain.

'That's fine,' Pascal said quickly. 'I can cover that. Marianne's much better today. She won't miss me for an hour or two.' He paused. 'Her temperature is still fluctuating. I ought to stay one more day here, Gini, just to make sure she's well again. I'll fly back tomorrow. Meanwhile,' his voice altered, 'I miss you, you know.'

'I miss you too.'

'Darling, tell me, you were all right last night?'

Gini hesitated. She would have liked to tell him that she had been far from all right; she would have liked to tell him about the strange postcard, the footsteps, the power cut, the darkness, and that horrible whispering obscene tape. But it was better to wait.

'I was fine,' she said quickly. 'I saw Lise, as I mentioned. Very strange. I have a lot to tell you. I'll explain all the details when I see you. Now I'm tying up a few loose ends. Tonight I have to go to some grand newspaper dinner. With Jenkins.'

'Well, you know what to ask *him* . . . '

'Yes. I do. Whether he'll answer is another matter. Meantime,' she paused, 'I'm going to work on the Appleyard connection . . . '

'Which is?'

'I don't know. But I know there is one. I think it has something to do with women – and the different ways in which you can hire them, for sex.'

When Appleyard had given Nicholas Jenkins the original idea for the story on telephone sex lines, he had produced the names of three companies whose primary business this was. The first two of these were just as Gini had imagined them: small hole-in-the-wall affairs. One operated from a backstreet in Hackney, the other, which doubled as a mini-cab firm, appeared to be a mother-and-daughter operation. It functioned out of one-room premises behind King's Cross Station, in the red-light district there. The mother, a hard-faced woman, said little. The daughter, a fat girl unwisely encased in Lycra leggings, explained in an antagonistic way that this work was easy money, that it was easy to find women to recruit.

'Look,' she said to Gini, 'which would you prefer? Sitting at home with a tape recorder and a script, or turning tricks with some fat slob in a car behind the gas-works up the street?' She gestured out of the window to the wasteland that covered several acres to the north of the station.

'Which would you rather?' The girl's voice took on a derisive note. 'Five quid for a hand-job up a back alley – or this? We look after our girls, Mum and me. And since you're asking – *I* write the scripts. All legal and above board. Now, piss off.'

Gini obeyed. She moved on to Appleyard's third company, and when she saw its premises, in a smart, bright terraced house in Fulham – Sloane Ranger territory – her hopes increased. If Appleyard's tip could be trusted at all, if there were some more large-scale operator behind these businesses, this was the kind of front for it she would expect.

And the kind of front-man she would anticipate too, she thought, when the door opened on a sharply dressed, gold-braceleted youth. His name was Bernie, and Bernie proved to be the perfect interviewee – garrulous, knowing, flattered to talk to a reporter, and unused to dealing with the Press.

It was lunch-time, and Bernie responded favourably to the suggestion that she buy him a drink.

'What have I got to lose, right?' He eyed her. 'I mean, the stories I could tell . . . And the beauty is, Gini, this is a one hundred per cent kosher operation. Like, who gets harmed, right? We have a licence for this.' He winked. 'A licence to print money – don't quote me on that.'

He led the way to a wine bar around the corner in the Fulham Road; it was filled with the kind of women who still wore velvet Alice bands and whose habitual tone of voice was a strangulated shriek. Gini ordered champagne and Kir at five pounds a glass – Bernie's choice. A few questions, just to kick-start him, and Bernie was off. He explained a few of the market-forces principles behind his work.

'The way I look at it, Gini, is this . . . What makes the world go round? Sex. What's the one commodity you can always flog? Sex. What's the new, nice, clean, guaranteed AIDS-free way to dispense it? Down the telephone line. This is a growth industry we're looking at here, Gini, and you *can* quote me on that . . . '

He talked on, and Gini listened with only half her attention. She had worked on stories before which took her into this twilight zone. The needs catered for there were intense, and the methods used to salve those needs were many: street girls, call-girls, escort agencies, models, magazines, strip-clubs, peep-shows, phone lines, books, videos. An empire for the unsatisfied to explore, an empire that could cater to every permutation of sexual taste. As Bernie was only too happy to explain, growth industries required dedication; some of the amateurs involved in the phone-line business failed to understand this.

'What you *need*, Gini,' he said, sipping his second champagne and Kir, 'what you need is market identification – and we've got that. You have to understand the punter's specialized taste. For instance, our company – we do rubber. We do bondage. Spanking – we've got three spanking lines, don't ask me why, but spanking's big. Black girls, Swedish girls, French maids. OK it's *predictable*, Gini, I'll say that before you do. But our callers don't want surprises. They want what triggers *them*, if you get my point. Blondes, brunettes, redheads. We do gay lines, obviously. We do virgins – or sluts. Sluts, well, they mouth off a lot, they verbalize, right? So they're always in demand. Plus, mentioning *mouths*, a lot of clients are what you might call anatomically demanding. So we do leg-lines and bum-lines. And then there's our number one bestseller—'

'Which is?'

'Breasts.' Bernie rolled his eyes. He made generous gestures with his hands. 'Big breasts.'

He sighed. The predictability of his clients' desires seemed to disappoint him.

Gini said, 'How many lines do you personally supervise, Bernie?'

'Me? Eighty-six. And it's rising each week.'

'That's impressive, Bernie. Let me get you another drink . . .'

As Gini had hoped, the third drink relaxed Bernie quite a lot. He grew more garrulous still. Gently Gini steered him in the direction she wanted: who was behind his company, and were there perhaps other aspects to their empire besides telephone sex? On the question of his employers, Bernie became cautious.

'No names. OK? Let's just say I work for one smart operator, yes?'

On the question of this operator's other activities, Bernie was more inclined to be drawn. Discretion fought a losing battle with the desire to boast. He first hinted, then confirmed, that telephone sex lines were just the tip of this iceberg, and that for an up-and-coming man – Bernie grinned – there were career opportunities here. Promotion beckoned. His company also had an escort agency arm – a high-class escort agency, he added hastily, top girls and credit-card facilities. Finally, a recent diversification this, there was the company's video arm. Not sleaze videos, he wouldn't want her to think that, but the new sex education videos, one hundred per cent legit, *very* explicit, fronted by doctors and therapists, on sale in the high street, on sale in ultra-respectable shops. His company's most recent offering, *Married Love II*, had sold seven hundred and fifty thousand copies within six weeks.

Gini looked suitably impressed. 'That's fascinating, Bernie,' she said. 'I'd really like to know more. Especially about the escort agency. Would they talk to me, d'you think?'

'Course they would. If I'm with you. Hazel runs it. She and me, we're like *that*.' He held up two fingers crossed. 'You want to go over now?'

'Can you spare the time, Bernie?'

'Sure I can. That's cool,' he said in a magnanimous way, and lurched to his feet.

Both the escort agency and the video film studio proved to be in Shepherd's Bush. The agency, *Elite Introductions*, was surprisingly swish. To the right of its entrance, another door, unmarked, led down to the video studio in the basement. Bernie jerked his thumb in its direction.

'The equipment they've got down there,' he said, 'you wouldn't believe. Three camera set-ups, top-of-the-range sound equipment, a revolve – three-quarters of a million at least. They're filming now, so it's off-limits. Pity. It's artistic. You'd be impressed.'

He opened the door to the escort agency, and led her in. Hazel, a tall, brassy redhead, was sitting flanked by filing cabinets, telephones and expensive flower arrangements. She was painting her nails at her desk. She was aged about thirty, with green eyes and a green dress. She was painting her nails cerise. She seemed pleased enough to see Bernie, who gave her a hug and a kiss.

'Ooh,' she said, 'Bernie, you really stink. You been at them champagne cocktails again? Fancy a coffee? I'm parched myself. You, Gini? It's no trouble.' She made a face. 'Tuesdays business is always a bit slack.'

Like Bernie, Hazel seemed unworried at talking to the Press; it turned out she was a regular reader of the *News*, and her main interest, initially, was the identities of famous people Gini had interviewed in the past.

Gini fed her a few names. Hazel, having dispensed coffee, settled again at her desk. She winked at Bernie.

'One or two of them are familiar to us, Bernie – yes? We get them all in here, you know, Gini. Movie-stars, Arab princes, top businessmen – well, I mustn't say more. We have to be discreet. Of course,' she went on, her eyes narrowing slightly, 'we're an *escort* agency, Gini. All above board. What you see is what you get. Our girls – and we have some very lovely girls – are there for company, light conversation, dinner on the town. No extra-curricular activities. We're strict about that.'

'Of course,' said Gini. 'What are your rates?'

'It depends on the girl. Eight till midnight, that's two hundred and fifty quid. After midnight, we charge by the hour. For our very special ladies, there's a premium. Our two top girls can make five hundred a night, easy.'

'That's a lot of money.'

'Eighty per cent to the girls, twenty to the agency . . .' She paused, and gave Bernie a glance. 'And then, if they're enjoying themselves, and they want to make a private agreement with the client – well, that's up to the girl concerned, right?'

Gini decided it was time to push. She said, 'What interests me is the clients. Bernie was telling me earlier, with the phone lines, how he has to cater to very specific tastes. I guess you find the same thing? Some men will always want a blonde, others a brunette – do you find that?'

'And how.' Hazel reached for a large directory on her desk. She flipped it open, and beckoned Gini to look. 'That's how we classify the girls, see? By hair colour. We've found it's the best. Sometimes we'll get a punter with more specific needs – remember that one, Bernie, who liked Irish girls? He was sweet. I liked him. Said it had to be Irish, he liked the lilt in the voice . . .'

Gini turned the pages of the directory in front of her. It resembled the model agency brochures she had borrowed from Lindsay, and many of the women pictured here might almost have made it as models. Neither Hazel nor Bernie had been exaggerating: the women pictured were all young and attractive; none looked in the least cheap. There was a section on blondes, on redheads, on brunettes. Beneath the photographs there were details of the women's height and vital statistics as well as their names – *noms de guerre* presumably. Most seemed to end in a 'y'. Among the blondes alone there were Nicky and Lucky and Vicky and Suzy. Suzy, in particular, had a beautiful face.

'I wonder,' Gini said, 'you have regular clients, I guess.

Do some of them like to see the girls on a regular basis? Every week, say, or every month?'

Bernie laughed. 'Every week? At our rates? You must be joking. Not too many of those, Hazel, right?'

'No. But plenty of once-a-monthers.' She made a face. 'Regular as the moon, some of them. Have to have their little monthly treat.'

'Maybe it's like a ritual for them,' Gini said. 'Do you ever feel like that? Like, they have to see a girl on a certain day of the week. Or at a certain time. Or in a certain place. That adds to the thrill, maybe?'

Hazel gave her a sharp look. 'Hey, you've got the right instincts, I'll say that. You want a job here?' She sighed. 'There's lots of them like that. There was one last year – I won't mention specifics, but he's a household name, put it like that. He had a thing about *red*. Every girl we sent, she had to wear a red dress. Then there was that Jap, Bernie, remember him? Had a thing about feet. Didn't care about the hair colour, the figure, the face – just the feet. One girl we sent over, she wore varnish on her toenails, and this guy, he threw a fit.' She raised her eyes heavenwards. '*Men*. They're really weird, I'll tell you that.'

This was not helpful. Gini persevered.

'What about days of the week,' she said. 'Do they ever insist on a certain day? Always on a Monday? Always a Sunday, anything like that?'

'Not that I recall.' Hazel shrugged. 'Maybe, if I went through and checked. It's feasible – like it's the one day a month their wife's out of town, something like that? Mind you,' she smiled, 'some of them, you wouldn't believe how brazen they are. Couldn't give a damn who knows what they're up to. You remember that one last year, Bernie – that yank who got his secretary to make the call? I felt so sorry for her, though I say it myself. You could tell she was nicely brought up, she had this really posh voice—'

'Really?' Gini leaned forward. 'She was English?'

'Oh yes. Very la-di-da, but nice with it. I mean, I could hear her blushing down the phone, poor kid. Three

times he made her go through that . . . I've got it here.'
She flipped the pages of the appointments book. 'There
you are, October, November and December. A once-
a-monther – and *specific*! I wonder he didn't send the
secretary round with a measuring tape. They had to be
blonde. They had to be at least five feet nine and no
more than five ten. Long legs, young – he liked them
young. Big tits . . . Well, nothing so unusual about *that*.
But can you credit it? Making some poor secretary spell
that out on the phone? That's why it sticks in my memory.
Usually, they're cagey. They always call themselves. What
a creep.'

'Extraordinary,' Gini said. 'So what happened?'

'Well, it was weird, actually.' Hazel lowered her voice
to a confidential tone. She began to flick the pages of her
appointments book. 'Let me just check back . . . Ah, here
we are. When she first calls, this poor girl, she says her
boss will be flying in from the States the next week, and
she has to set him up with a date. Then she goes through
all these specifics, the way I said, then she says she'll call
back, and then the next thing I know I have to send round
a whole lot of pictures. This guy's made a short-list, would
you believe? So, I send the pictures round to some hotel
off Albemarle Street. Three times I do this. October,
November, December. Christ knows why. He chose Suzy
every time. So the secretary calls back *again*, and makes
the booking and – oh, what do you know? How weird. He
booked a Sunday, now I come to look. I'd forgotten that.'

'He did?' Gini felt herself tense. She looked down at
the brochure in front of her. Suzy's pensive features
gazed back. She had thick blond hair which reached to
her shoulders, and a very young, somewhat vulnerable
face. She was wearing a white high-necked evening dress,
with long sleeves. She looked like a beautiful schoolgirl,
out on her first date.

'I'm not surprised at his choice,' she said carefully.
'She's very pretty. She looks terribly *young*, though . . . '

Hazel winked. 'Not as young, nor as innocent, as she
looks, our Suzy. But she is one of our top girls.' She

shrugged. 'Made no difference, anyway. He cancelled – or the secretary did, on his behalf. Said he'd altered his plans, something like that. All that fuss then three cancellations. Can you believe that?'

'He cancelled?' Gini stared at her. 'You're sure of that?'

'That's right.' Hazel closed the appointments book. 'Like I say – men are weird, right? Maybe just seeing the pictures gave him some kind of kick. Maybe he went to another agency, found a girl he liked better. Who knows?'

'You mean he never even met Suzy? Not once?'

'Not exactly.' Hazel smiled. 'But we reckon he saw her. Once.'

'What makes you think that?'

'Because the last time the secretary rang, in December, she said he wanted to take a look at her. On approval. I mean, bloody cheek! So Suzy has to go round to some plush West End hotel, sit in the lobby for half an hour, then leave. Which she did.'

'And he was in the lobby too, you mean? Checking her out?'

'You tell me.' Hazel shrugged. 'If he was, he never spoke to her – nothing like that. I thought, maybe he was so choosy, and when he saw her, she didn't come up to scratch. Anyway, the secretary rang back, poor kid, and cancelled again. Then I never heard another word. It cost him, mind you. Full fees for late cancellations, an extra fee for the hotel visit. The best part of two thousand quid. He must be loaded.'

'Credit card?' Gini said.

Hazel unscrewed the bottle of nail varnish and began to apply a second coat.

'Cash. By courier,' she said. 'The easiest money we ever made, right, Bernie? I wish all our customers were like that.'

On the pavement outside, Gini's mind raced. It had to be Hawthorne, surely, and it was the first possible outside corroboration of McMullen's story that she had.

An English secretary on the telephone, an English voice calling ICD about those parcels: there must be a connection. The coincidence was too great. She glanced back at the agency office, wishing she had been able to examine that appointments book for herself. But it would probably have told her little: Hawthorne would use an alias. Besides, there was another way to discover more about this.

She turned to Bernie, who lingered at her side, to thank him for his help. As she did so, the door to the basement video studio opened, and a group of people spilled out. Two, a good-looking young man with long dark curling hair and a very pretty young girl, might have been the stars of the sex instruction video. The others looked like technicians – cameramen, sound men, perhaps.

They were followed by a tall thin man in his mid-forties, with reddish hair drawn back in a pony-tail. He was resplendent, head to foot in mustard yellow Armani. At the sight of him, Bernie ducked aside, and drew her into a shop doorway until he had passed. He was clearly not anxious to be seen.

Gini said, 'Your boss, was it, Bernie?'

Bernie shuffled his feet. 'One of them. Put it like that. I'd better get back. Keep in touch, right?'

The Armani-clad man climbed into a brand-new black BMW. Bernie, looking shifty, sloped off in the opposite direction. Gini made for the tube, where she stood on the platform thinking hard. The next person to talk to was Suzy, obviously. She did not have Suzy's real name or her telephone number or her address. Further enquiries at *Elite Introductions* might cause suspicion. But Suzy's company could be hired by the evening. Gini might not be able to hire her – but Pascal certainly could.

XXII

At three that Tuesday afternoon, about the time Gini arrived at the escort agency, Pascal finally persuaded Lorna Munro to talk to him. Her photographic session over, he took her for a drink in the *Deux Magots* café on Boulevard St Germain, just across the street from the St Germain church.

This elusive American girl looked no more than eighteen. She was at least six feet tall, Pascal calculated, and could have weighed no more than one hundred pounds. She was still in the strong make-up she'd needed that afternoon for monochrome shots. Her short thick hair, on close inspection, was naturally blonde. She had wide-set sapphire blue eyes, a broad friendly smile, and an air of radiant health. She was wearing flat shoes, black leggings, a man's white shirt and a man's tweed overcoat. Despite this androgenous outfit every male in the café turned to stare when they walked in.

Lorna Munro seemed impervious, or indifferent to this. They were seated in the café's glass-enclosed pavement section, fronting the boulevard. Lorna Munro looked at him somewhat warily, then grinned.

'OK,' she said, 'I did my best. Tell your friend in England I'm sorry. Will you do that? I might have known you'd catch up with me one way or another . . . You mind if I order some food? I'm ravenous. It feels like a week since breakfast . . . ' She turned to the waiter with a dazzling smile. 'I'll have a large steak sandwich, *pommes frites* on the side, a green salad no dressing . . . Oh, and maybe some hot chocolate. It's freezing out there. My hands are numb. My feet are numb. My butt's numb, come to that.'

Pascal smiled. With the freakishness peculiar to fashion

magazines, Lorna Munro had been required to model Gaultier's summer collection on a January day, on a windswept pavement. Most of the dresses in which she'd posed had been sleeveless and backless; several had featured metallic conical breast-shields. Lorna Munro had been professional enough to ignore the crowds this attracted, and the gooseflesh it induced.

He said, 'Hot chocolate? A steak sandwich? And I thought all models were supposed to be anorexic.'

'No way. Not this baby. I eat like a horse, always have – and I never gain a pound. Life's unfair . . . ' She paused, took one of the cigarettes Pascal offered, then looked at him in an assessing way. 'Pascal Lamartine. I've heard of you. You took those Sonia Swan pictures, right? And those ones of Princess Stephanie, back last summer?' She made a face. 'Heck, if I'd known it was you chasing me, I'd really have run a mile.'

'This is rather different,' Pascal said quickly. 'Not necessarily a news story as such . . . '

'Oh, come on.' She grinned again. 'I'm not that dumb. That woman from the *News* in London – what's her name? Gini? – she must have left a zillion messages. She calls Milan, she calls Rome, she calls the agency. And I don't think she wants to arrange a modelling session, right?'

'No, she doesn't. And neither do I. We want to ask you about some parcels. Four parcels to be exact. You delivered them to a courier office in London, one week ago today.'

There was a silence. Lorna Munro drew on her cigarette. Her blue eyes fixed themselves on his face. She made no reply.

'You've been identified for us,' Pascal continued, 'by the woman at the courier office. I suspect you were meant to be identified. If you hadn't been, I think they'd have hired someone less memorable to deliver those parcels.'

'You think I'm memorable? That's nice.' She gave him a flirtatious glance.

Pascal responded with gallantry. He said, 'Very beautiful women usually are.'

Lorna Munro was not stupid. The compliment made her smile. 'Come on, you can do better than that. Don't pretend to be interested when you're not. I can always tell when a man's really interested. It takes me five seconds. I just look in their eyes . . . ' She frowned thoughtfully. 'So, you're not interested in me, but you are interested in those parcels? You came all the way here to Paris, just to ask me about those?'

'No, I didn't. I was in London, working with Gini. But I've been in Paris since yesterday. My daughter's ill.'

'Hey, I'm sorry.' She seemed genuinely concerned. 'What's wrong?'

'Scarlet fever, the doctor says. She's only seven. Yesterday she was in a bad way. Today – well, she's better. Picking up. I just left her now.'

'You have a picture? I like kids. I've got four sisters myself. The youngest's your daughter's age.'

Pascal drew out his wallet, and passed her a photograph. Lorna Munro smiled. 'Oh, she's cute. What a lovely face. She takes after her father, I can see that. What's her name?'

'Marianne.'

'Well, tell her from me to get better quickly, OK? Oh, here's the food at last.'

The waiter laid the food before her with silent admiration. Lorna Munro began to eat rapidly, and with evident enjoyment. Pascal sipped his black coffee, and waited. He could see she was assessing him, deciding what to say, perhaps deciding whether to lie.

'OK,' she said eventually. 'Tell me this first. Suppose I admit I delivered those packages – so what? Delivering packages isn't a crime.'

'No. It's not.' Pascal met her gaze. 'You don't have to answer my questions. But I hope you will. You see, one of those parcels was sent to me – as you'll know. Another went to Gini – as you'll also know. What you may *not* know is what was inside them.'

'Oh my God.' She stopped eating. 'Not drugs?'

387

'No. Nothing illegal. In my case, a glove. In Gini's case, a pair of handcuffs. No message. No note.'

'Handcuffs? To a woman?' She frowned. 'That's not nice.'

'Exactly.' Pascal paused. 'So, someone has been playing a little joke we think, Gini and I. We'd like to find out who that was . . . and why.'

There was another silence. Lorna Munro continued to eat her meal. When she had finished, she pushed her plate aside, and accepted another cigarette. She watched its smoke drift for a while, then turned back to Pascal, as if she had made up her mind.

'OK. For what it's worth, I'll tell you what I know. Handcuffs – that's not funny. I'm surprised. He seemed like such a regular guy . . . '

'Who did? It was a man who gave you these parcels?'

'Slow down.' She smiled. 'I'll start at the beginning, right? It starts in New York. You won't know him, I guess, but there's a man there I know, he's like some kind of tipster, for gossip columns. Name of Appleyard.'

'Johnny Appleyard?'

'Right. One of the parcels was addressed to him.' She gave him a sidelong glance. 'If you know this much I guess you know that too.'

'You're right.'

'OK. A few weeks back, before Christmas, I ran into Appleyard at a party in Soho. I'd met him once or twice before – I didn't know him exactly, just enough to say hallo. He's the kind of guy I avoid like the plague, usually, because he's on the look-out for scandal ninety-nine per cent of the time. And he's everywhere, you know? Restaurants, gallery openings, theatre first nights – you name it, Appleyard's there. He hangs around the agency, snoops on photo-sessions, gossips with the make-up artists. He gets a lot of stories, models, their private lives . . . ' She paused. Pascal said nothing. It was obvious to him Lorna Munro had no inkling that Appleyard was dead. 'So, as I say, I ran into him that night in Soho . . . '

'Can you remember the exact date?'

She frowned. 'Yes, I can. I was flying home for Christmas the next day, so it must have been the night of December the twenty-third.'

Two days after McMullen disappeared, Pascal thought. He said, 'Good. Go on.'

'Well, Appleyard came up to me at the party, said he'd heard I'd just been signed by *Models East*, congratulated me . . . I could tell he was leading up to something. Eventually, he came out with it. Would I be free to do a modelling job – an unusual one – in London? I'd need to be there just two days, Monday January the third, and Tuesday January the fourth. It was an easy job, and well paid . . . ' She hesitated. 'I almost said no. Any modelling job that came via Appleyard spelled trouble. Then he mentioned the money.'

'It was generous?'

'Oh, sure.' She gave him a glance. 'Twenty thousand dollars in cash, no percentage to the agency, no questions asked. *Plus* a first-class air ticket each way, overnight accommodation at Claridge's, no less—'

'Claridge's?'

Lorna Munro grinned. 'Funnily enough, that's what swung it as much as the money. I've never stayed in a place that grand – and I thought, This doesn't sound so sleazy. So I listened some more.'

'Did Appleyard explain what you'd have to do?'

'Sure. He said no photographs were involved. All I had to do was turn up in London, wear some classy clothes, and pay a visit to someone on the Tuesday morning. He said it was for a friend of his, a kind of elaborate practical joke this friend wanted to set up.'

'You believed him?'

'Not really, but in the end, I decided to give it a try. After all – twenty thousand dollars, that's a lot of money. I'm not averse to that. I can be a material girl.'

'You don't look it. You don't sound it . . . '

'Nice of you to say so.' Lorna Munro smiled. 'Let's say I'm realistic then. If I'm lucky and I work hard, I can make a good living at modelling for what – the next ten years? After that, you're starting to go over the hill. So you make what you can, when you can. I told you, I've got four sisters, a mother and a father getting harder up every year. I don't plan for us all to stay poor.'

Pascal's liking for Lorna Munro grew. He liked her directness, and he liked her smile. He lit another cigarette for her, then leaned back in his chair.

'All right,' he said, 'go on. You flew to London . . . '

'I flew to London. Went to Claridge's – and there was a suite reserved for me. How about that? Flowers, fruit, champagne in an ice-bucket. I thought, Whatever happens this joker friend of Appleyard's has style. I had a return airline ticket. I thought, So things go wrong, I can always just cut and run, no problem. As it happened, it couldn't have been easier. And nothing went wrong.'

'Who made contact with you in London?'

'An Englishman. He called Monday around noon. He came to the hotel later that afternoon. He brought a Chanel suit with him, shoes. I tried them on. That was the only problem. I'm so skinny, the suit was loose, too large.'

'Did the man give you a name? Can you describe him?'

'He said his name was John Hamilton. I didn't ask for ID. He was very English – kind of stiff upper lip, you know? About five ten, slim build, fair haired, well dressed, polite. Pretty formal in manner. Forty-something. As I said – a regular guy.'

'Was this the man?' Pascal had two photographs ready. One of McMullen and one of John Hawthorne. He passed across McMullen's photograph first. Lorna Munro examined it carefully.

'It looks like him. Yeah, I guess so. It's difficult to tell when he's dressed like that. He looks younger here . . . Yes, I'd say that was him.'

Pascal stared at her. 'You're certain?'

'Yeah. Now that I look at it closely. It's him.'

Pascal replaced the photographs in his pocket. This meant revising many of his previous ideas. He leaned forward. 'So, did he explain what he wanted you to do?'

'Yes.' She smiled. 'In detail. He went over and over it, where I had to go, what I should say. Like some goddamn military briefing . . . He gave me these names and addresses I had to learn. I said – if I'm posing as your wife, shouldn't I wear a wedding ring? He said no.'

'Did you believe it really was a practical joke?'

'It could have been. That's what he said. Frankly, I didn't much care. Anyway,' she paused, 'he came back the next morning, with the most incredible fur coat I ever saw in my life, and these unbelievable pearls. The coat was to hide the fact that the Chanel suit didn't fit too well – he had it all figured out. There's not much more to tell really. He had a cab waiting downstairs. He drove with me to that courier place, waited in the cab outside. I took the packages in, did my number . . . ' She grinned. 'Back to Claridge's, say farewell to the pearls and the coat, collect twenty thousand dollars, go home.'

'You sound as if you enjoyed it.'

'Sure. I did. I liked Hamilton. I thought it was fun. No harm done.' She paused.

'Was I wrong?'

'I'm afraid you were.'

'I thought so.' She gave him a shrewd glance. 'More than just sending some unwelcome handcuffs, right?'

'Yes, more than that.' Pascal hesitated. 'You haven't discussed this with anyone?'

'No. Only you. Hamilton said not to. So did Appleyard.' She glanced at him again. 'You look kind of grim, you know. Is this dangerous in some way? Am I in danger? Are you?'

Pascal signalled to the waiter to bring the bill. He was not sure of the answer to that question, but he was unwilling to say so.

Lorna Munro frowned. 'Great. I'm *not* all right in other words. And neither are you.'

'No, no.' Pascal rose, and paid for their meal. Lorna Munro also rose; together they walked out through the glass-enclosed forecourt of the café, onto the pavement of the Rue Bonaparte and into the rain.

Lorna Munro shivered, and wrapped her coat more tightly around her. The streetlights were on now, the rush hour just beginning; the daylight was starting to fail. The model braced herself against the wind, then smiled and turned back to Pascal.

'Well, it can't matter that much,' she said. 'All I did was deliver a few parcels. Still, I'll keep my mouth shut from now on.'

'It might be a good idea.'

'And avoid Appleyard.' She laughed. 'Well, I hope I was some kind of help. I have to get back to my hotel now. I fly back to New York tonight. Nice meeting you, Pascal.'

They shook hands. Lorna Munro turned away, then turned back. 'Hey, one last thing. When I'm famous, don't creep up and take pictures by my swimming-pool, OK?' She grinned. 'Let me know in advance. Come right in the front door . . . '

'I'll do that,' Pascal replied, and raised his hand in farewell.

Lorna Munro stepped off the pavement to the edge of the traffic streaming along the boulevard. She looked to right and left, saw the lights change at the St Germain intersection, and began to cross. Watching her, Pascal was certain she never saw the car.

It came out of the stream of traffic to his right, and accelerated fast. By the time it reached the red light and the intersection, it was travelling at around fifty miles an hour. A black Mercedes saloon, with tinted glass, it hit Lorna Munro sideways on, and tossed her body ten feet in the air. She landed across its bonnet, skewed, then was thrown to the ground.

A cacophony of horns filled the air. Pascal saw other passers-by on the pavement freeze as he froze, and stare. The Mercedes sped fast across the intersection, and disappeared down the boulevard with screeching tyres. Its driver never once touched its brakes; there was no time even to read the registration plates. One second it was there, the next it was gone.

Pascal began to run forwards into the boulevard. His limbs felt heavy and slow with shock. It seemed to take an immense time to travel twenty yards.

Lorna Munro must have been killed instantly, he knew that as soon as he reached her. Her neck had been broken, perhaps her spine. She lay on her back on the road, in a cluster of gathering people, her beautiful face unmarked, and her blue eyes gazing up at the sky.

A man checked for a pulse at her throat, then shook his head. Pascal hesitated, then turned aside, and pushed his way through the crowd. Other witnesses would have seen the car. He could be of no further use here. Police enquiries would hinder not help him. He stopped. He could still hear her voice, and the frank optimism with which she'd spoken of her future plans.

She'd had less than half an hour to live at the time. He leaned against a wall, and pressed his face against its grime. He looked at the question, and then looked at it again: if he had not contacted her, would Lorna Munro still be alive?

XXIII

'Who else knows about the Hawthorne story?' Gini said to Nicholas Jenkins.

They were in the back of Jenkins's chauffeur-driven Jaguar, the car being one of the perks of Jenkins's job. Speeding south to the Savoy through wet streets, Jenkins seemed distracted and on edge.

'Come on, Nicholas. Someone else knows. Who? Daiches?'

'Will you give me a break? How many times do I have to say it? You, Lamartine, me. That's it.' He stopped, then glanced at her sharply. 'Why?'

'Because I'm getting the strong feeling someone does know, Nicholas. They knew before you even assigned Pascal and me to this.'

'Crap. You're getting paranoid, Gini.'

'Look, Nicholas, just give me a straight answer, will you? Does Daiches know?'

'No, he bloody well does not. I know Daiches likes to imagine he's rather better informed than God, but I have news for him. He isn't.' He glanced at her again. 'Why, was he fishing?'

'Not exactly. He made a few remarks about this dinner with Hawthorne tonight.'

'So? I don't blame him. I made a few myself. Since when have you been so pally with our illustrious proprietor? Hand-delivered invitations—'

'Never mind that now, Nicholas. It's not important. This is. If Daiches doesn't know, did Johnny Appleyard? Had you heard any rumours about Hawthorne from Appleyard? Nicholas, did Appleyard give you this tip?'

'I don't believe I'm hearing this! How many times do I have to spell it out? This is *my* story, one hundred

394

per cent. It has nothing to do with fucking Appleyard, God rest his soul and all that. This was *my* lead, via *my* source, and it'll be *my* fucking exclusive if you and Pascal come up with the goods. *If* you actually make some progress. Are you making progress?'

'Yes, Nicholas, we are. I worked all damn weekend on this.'

'So? Big deal.'

'And what's more, it's a much bigger story than we originally thought.'

'It is?' Interest gleamed in his eyes, then he raised a finger to his lips. 'Save the details for later.' He glanced at the glass screen between them and his driver.

'After dinner, I'll drive you home. We can talk then.' He stared out of the window at the passing streets. Then he seemed to make an effort to improve his own mood; he turned back to her with a smile. 'This should be useful anyway,' he said. 'Gives you a chance to see Hawthorne's public persona . . . I must say, Gini, you're looking very pretty tonight. It makes a change to see you in a dress.'

He eyed her legs as he said this. Gini put another three inches of leather seat between them. The car was slowing. Jenkins peered through the window again.

'Oh, I don't believe it – what the fuck!'

Approaching Kingsway and Covent Garden, they came to an abrupt halt. Ahead of them through jammed traffic, Gini could see police cars and flashing lights. They inched their way towards the mêlée. Security barriers were being erected. All the traffic was being diverted. In the distance a siren wailed.

'Fucking IRA,' Jenkins said. He leaned forward, and opened the glass partition.

'Just step on it, will you, Chris? Cut through the Garden, and go down past the opera house.'

'That's just what I am doing, sir. So is everyone else.'

'Then use your ingenuity,' Jenkins snapped. 'That's what you're paid for. I don't intend to be late.'

*   *   *

The dinner at the Savoy was a large one. It was being held in the River Room, and Gini estimated there were three hundred guests.

The security was tight – because of the current round of bomb scares, Gini assumed at first. Jenkins corrected her on this.

'Nothing to do with the Dublin cowboys,' he said irritably. 'This was all laid on weeks ago, Melrose told me. We've John Hawthorne's presence to thank for this . . . '

He gestured towards the throng of people at the entrance to the River Room. Each person had to present a security pass; each pass was laboriously checked. When they finally reached the entrance, Gini's small evening bag was opened and searched.

'Perhaps you'd like me to turn out my pockets,' Jenkins said, in a blustering way.

'That won't be necessary, sir,' replied a polite American. 'Just run your hands under this scanner, front and back . . . Thank you, sir. Ma'am.'

Gini held her hands beneath a device the size of a portable phone. A bluish light scanned the backs of her hands, then her palms.

Nicholas took her arm, and they walked through a discreet scaffold device erected in the doorway. Jenkins had keys in his pocket which triggered an alarm. Politely but firmly, he was taken aside behind a screen. He emerged flushed, and spent the next half-hour boasting of his experiences there.

'The scanner?' he said jovially to right and left. 'The scanner's nothing. Believe me. *I* had the CIA grope. A testicular thrill. Best sex in years . . . '

The evening, as Gini had expected, was a high-powered affair. At the top table, some distance from where she and Jenkins were both seated, she counted four serving Cabinet Ministers, three press barons including Melrose, several well-known television news reporters, the head of the Independent Broadcasting Authority, and no less than four leading newspaper editors. When Jenkins observed these four, his expression became sour.

'Why's that pompous fart from *The Times* up there?' he said. 'And that Scots wanker. Great. Just great. Thanks a bunch, Melrose . . . '

He began to crumble his bread roll savagely. Turning his back on Gini, he launched into conversation with the woman seated his other side.

'Correct. Up a hundred thousand, and still rising . . . ' Gini heard.

She turned her attention back to the top table. John Hawthorne was seated at its centre, flanked by Lord Melrose and the Chairman of the BBC governors. There were no female faces, and Hawthorne was the youngest person there by at least a decade.

Compared to the powerful but ageing men who surrounded him, Hawthorne emanated youth and authority. The later speeches were to be televised, and the lights in the room were already strong. They blanched the skin, and gave several of Hawthorne's companions an appearance of fatigue. Not the ambassador, however. Hawthorne might have been wearing TV make-up – Gini was too far away to be sure. If so, it had been expertly applied. Hawthorne looked even more tanned and fit than usual; the tan emphasized the blue of his eyes, the white Hollywood perfection of his smile.

Where were the security men? Gini studied the room. She could see the toast-master, various waiters, a television crew just to the left of the dais, and another, more centrally placed, just below Hawthorne himself. A floor manager, with head-phones, two sound men . . . and then she saw them: that Malone man, immediately below the dais, and two more on either side. One was Frank Romero, the other a man she had not seen before.

As she looked she saw Romero turn, scan the room, glance back to the ambassador, then move across and speak to one of the waiters. The man nodded, and disappeared. Frank Romero made that movement which was now becoming familiar to her: he raised his arm, and appeared to mutter into his cuff. At a distance, the tiny wrist-mike was invisible. Romero lowered his arm, made another quick, hard inspection of the room, then crossed to one of the tables nearest the dais. He bent, and spoke into the ear of a white-haired man.

Gini stared. He was about forty feet from her, facing in her direction. He was unmistakable: it was the ambassador's father, S. S. Hawthorne. He listened intently to Romero, then said something. Romero walked swiftly away.

Gini frowned: Hawthorne had told her that his father was coming over for that forty-eighth birthday party – a party that was still more than a week away. She was certain that was how he had phrased it. He had given no indication that his father was arriving this soon.

Strange. She surveyed the other tables. It was difficult to be sure, but she thought Lise Hawthorne was not present this evening. So, the wife was absent, but the father was here: what could that mean?

She looked back at S. S. Hawthorne. She could now see that he was seated in a wheelchair. He was deep in conversation with the woman next to him. He looked much younger than his years. Like his son, he conveyed force and vitality. He had remained handsome; he looked vigorous. She would have put his age at little more than sixty-five, though she knew he was almost eighty.

'The Magus,' said the man seated to her left. He spoke suddenly, making Gini jump. Looking around, she saw that he had followed her gaze, and was also looking at S. S. Hawthorne. As she turned, he smiled. A short, grey-haired American, aged about fifty. He glanced down at the place card in front of her.

'Genevieve, it *is* you. Sam's daughter, right? I couldn't believe it when I saw you. Last time we met – well, I guess you were around four, five years old.' He held out his hand to her. 'You won't remember. I'm Jason Stein.'

'I'm afraid I don't remember meeting, but of course I know your name. *The New York Times*, yes?'

'Right. I'm head of the London bureau now. For my sins.' He grinned. 'Nice to meet you again. So tell me,' he lowered his voice, 'why the big interest in the Magus over there?' He nodded in S. S. Hawthorne's direction.

'That's what you call him, the Magus?'

Stein gave her a dry look. 'It's one of the terms. One of the more flattering ones, sure.'

Gini glanced back; S. S. Hawthorne lifted his head at that moment. Across the distance separating them he gave their table a hard, blue-eyed stare. Gini looked quickly away.

'No reason,' she said to Stein. 'I was intrigued, that's all. I've read enough about him, I just never saw him before.'

'I wonder what the heck brought him to London.' Stein had also averted his gaze from S. S. Hawthorne's table. 'These days he rarely leaves that palace of his in upstate New York. At least, that's what I always heard.'

'Maybe he's here to play the proud paterfamilias. John Hawthorne's the guest speaker, after all. It's a pretty big occasion . . .'

'This?' Stein gave a dismissive gesture. 'Hawthorne makes three speeches a week at equally prestigious gatherings. This is no big deal for him. Anyway,' he gave Gini a glance, 'you watch. Hawthorne's a good after-dinner speaker. He'll have them eating out of his hand.'

'This audience?' Gini looked around her doubtfully. 'So many journalists, so many media people? Not the easiest house to play.'

'Wait and see.' Stein paused while a waiter removed their first-course plates, and a second waiter moved between them to serve wine. He passed on around the table. Stein gestured to their wineglasses, and smiled. 'Call me cynical if you like, but one thing I've always noticed about any dinner where Hawthorne has to make a speech – you get very good wine. And plenty of it. Far more than usual. Try that claret, and you'll see what I mean.'

Gini did so. The claret was excellent. She smiled.

'Oh, come *on*. John Hawthorne isn't even the host tonight.'

'OK, you don't believe me? Watch this.' He picked up his claret glass. 'At most of these dinners – this many people, the waiters under pressure – they put the bottles on the table, right? So the guests can serve themselves. The standard ratio for a table like this – eight people – is four bottles initially, if you're very lucky, five.' Gini looked at the bottles flanking the flower arrangement in the centre of the table. There were eight of them. 'Now, watch this.' Stein drank the claret in his glass. He put the glass back on the table, but made no move towards the bottles. 'I give it thirty seconds,' he said in a dry way. 'I made a study of this a few years ago, when I followed Hawthorne on the campaign trail. I'm thinking of publishing it.' He smiled. 'A time-and-motion study. How to win friends and influence people . . . Ah.'

The wine waiter had materialized at his side. He refilled Stein's glass, and a couple of others at the table. He replaced the empty bottle with a full one.

'Right to the second,' Gini said.

'There you are. Now you know one of the reasons why John Hawthorne's speeches always go so well at these occasions. Attention to the tiny details.' He shrugged. 'But then that's the mark of the man.'

'So tell me,' Gini said, 'what's John Hawthorne like on the campaign trail? Which of his campaigns did you cover?'

'Two. I covered his first senatorial campaign – that's, what, around sixteen years ago. Then I covered his final one, when it looked like he'd be going for the Democratic candidacy in ninety-two. I put in the hours on the Learjet. And I can tell you – his methods hadn't changed. They're impressive – and so is the stamina. John Hawthorne can get by on three hours sleep a night – I swear it. I was punch-drunk after three days' of his schedule. But not him. Dawn at some god-forsaken airstrip someplace, and Hawthorne's there, fresh as a daisy, with the aides and the lists – all fired up and ready to go.'

Gini paused while the waiters served the second course. She glanced at Stein. 'Lists?' she said.

'Local worthies, factory officials, fund-raisers, women's groups, party workers, big wheels in the local police department . . . ' Stein shrugged. 'Whoever he's meeting that day. They're graded for him, by the aides. Level five get five minutes of his time, and—'

'And level one only gets one minute?'

Stein laughed. 'Sure, but a man like Hawthorne can do a whole lot of work in that time. He can clinch a vote in thirty seconds – that's what the aides liked to say. The right handshake, the right questions, little bursts of charm. Hawthorne's always briefed and always primed.'

'So what kind of questions would those be? It can't be that easy, surely . . . '

'Listen,' Stein said, 'Hawthorne never meets anyone of any use to him without knowing beforehand whether he's met them before, how many kids they have, which football team they support, whether they have a dog or a cat, hell – what brand of cereal they have at breakfast, for all I know. It's all printed out for him, by the aides. Hawthorne has an incredible memory. Best I've ever seen. He learns it on the way there, in the car or the plane. It works on red-necks and bank presidents. The aides call it CTC . . . '

'CTC?'

'Channelling the charm.'

There was a brief silence. Gini considered this. She ate a little of the food, which was excellent, and avoided the wine. Irrespective of other events, she was beginning to see that she had been wrong about her conversation with Hawthorne at Mary's, and Pascal right. *CTC*, she thought, *and I fell for it too*.

Jason Stein had turned to talk to the woman on the other side of him; Nicholas Jenkins continued to cold-shoulder her. She did not mind this isolation, which at least gave her time to think. When the waiters removed their plates, and began to serve dessert, Jason Stein turned back to her with a smile.

'So, you have a particular reason to be interested in Hawthorne?' he asked.

'No. No. Politicians interest me as a species, that's all. I like to work out how they operate, what makes them run.' She paused, looking at Stein, whom she knew to be an excellent journalist, well-informed, smart. 'You think he's really given up on US politics now?' she asked. 'You think he'll ever try for a come-back, further down the road?'

Stein shrugged. 'Hard to say. A year ago, when he accepted the posting here, I thought he'd thrown in the towel. God alone knows why – I mean, it was way out of character. But recently, I've heard a rumour or two, just straws in the wind. Hawthorne always had very powerful backers, you know, in the Democratic Party and elsewhere. There's a whole lot of very influential people, and pressure groups – and from what I hear, Hawthorne's still their favourite son.' He smiled. 'It depends. I don't have a crystal ball. But if you said to me, would I rule Hawthorne out as a future presidential candidate, even as President, I'd have to say, No.'

'I guess you're not going to elaborate on those rumours?' Gini gave him a sidelong glance.

Stein smiled. 'You're damn right. I'm not. Not to a reporter on the *News*, even if she is Sam Hunter's daughter. Look at it this way, Genevieve,' he gestured towards the top table, 'the man's forty-seven. He looks thirty-seven. He'll stay here in London how long? Maybe two, at most three years. I'd give it two. Then, before you know it, he's back in the States, rebuilding that political base of his. Meantime, in any case, he can rely on the Magus. I will tell you one thing. I hear – and I hear it from very good sources – that old SS *never* gave up. This is a blip, as far as he's concerned. Back home, he's busy wheeling and dealing the way he always was. He'll keep John Hawthorne's seat nice and warm.'

Gini glanced across at Hawthorne's father. He was speaking, she saw, to Frank Romero again. She turned to Stein.

'You see that guy over there, the man talking to Hawthorne's father?'

'I see him, sure.'

'He's one of Hawthorne's security people?'

'He's one of his *father's* security people, that I do know.' Stein's expression hardened. 'I forget his name, but I know him. He goes way back. He was always around, drafted in by the father, making sure that when John Hawthorne was campaigning, he stayed on the straight and narrow. Oh, and making sure he didn't get killed, of course. That too. SS knows how to protect his investments.'

'You mean that?' Gini stared at him. 'You mean the father hired the bodyguards.'

'And they doubled up as Daddy's spies?' Stein grinned. 'Sure. Way back, in the early days, before John Hawthorne became less tight-lipped than he is now, he used to talk about it. Joke about it even, late at night, after a day's campaigning, over a drink or two. His version was, the father was just a tad over-protective, like he wired his son's room at Yale, had his lady friends investigated, that kind of thing . . . '

'You're joking. Hawthorne himself talked about that?'

'Sure. I heard him myself, once or twice. Like I say, he'd pretend to be amused, tell the story in this dry, droll kind of way. Make light of it.' Stein shrugged, then gave a frown. 'He's an interesting man, Hawthorne. A complex man. What I said earlier – I didn't mean to belittle him. He's tough now, hard – that's inevitable. But I used to like him.'

'And you don't like him now?'

'I don't like his politics, that's for sure. Do you?' He gave her a sharp glance.

Gini said, 'You mean, all things to all men?'

'That's exactly what I mean. But that's what brings in the votes, Genevieve, *and* the donations . . . ' He began to count off items on his fingers. 'Pro-civil rights, so he brings in the black vote, and the Hispanics. Pro-Israel, a real Zionist – but a WASP at home. No Jewish friends. Hell.' Stein gave an almost angry shrug, and broke off. 'So, he's not a man of principle. He could have been, but he isn't. So, he's a politician. What's new?'

'Then it's not just his politics? You don't like the man?'

'I never met a politician I did like.' Stein grinned. 'Snakes in the grass, every goddamn one of them.'

He leaned back in his chair. Coffee was being served,

and liqueurs. Stein took one of the cigars being offered around the table, as did Jenkins. Through a haze of aromatic smoke, Gini saw the microphones being positioned. The full television lighting was switched on.

Lord Melrose stood, and began on his speech of introduction. It was elegant but overlong. He had not, Gini thought, made Hawthorne's task as main speaker any easier. The audience might be well-oiled, but there was restlessness in the room.

As John Hawthorne rose to his feet, the cameramen moved into position. Hawthorne waited until there was silence. Then he gave an easy smile, a Hollywood smile, and he threw the switch, Gini could sense him do it, just as he had done briefly at Mary's party. Whatever charisma was, that elusive, hard-to-define quality, Hawthorne had it. She could feel its force in the room.

'Privacy and the Press . . . ' Hawthorne looked around his audience. 'What an opportunity. Here I am, and I can give you my views, secure in the knowledge that when I get to the end, I won't have to take one single question . . . ' His tone had become dry. 'And let me tell you, when facing the British press corps, that's very good to know . . . '

It was perfectly judged, Gini thought. The delivery was good, the timing was good, the smile was good – and he got the response he wanted. There was a ripple of amusement from the audience, and a collective relaxation. The moment of tension that always precedes any speech had been quickly overcome. Having relaxed his audience, Hawthorne then proceeded to wind them in.

He spoke without notes, clearly and concisely. He kept his speech light initially, then turning to the central question – the freedom of the Press versus the protection of the individual – he began to take a tougher approach. He put the case for each side with scrupulous exactitude, like an attorney. Gini waited to see which side he would come down on: with this audience there could be no fudging of the issues. Would he take the liberal or the conservative line?

Pausing, Hawthorne fixed his audience with a cool blue stare. 'Several years ago now,' he continued, 'when I was still a United States senator, I made a long tour of Middle Eastern Arab states – something I guess I couldn't risk now. While I was out there, I learned at first-hand what it was like to live in a society where ordinary men and women had no access to the truth. Where newspapers and television had been corralled by the state. Where journalists like yourselves had to print and promulgate propaganda, or risk imprisonment and death.' His blue gaze raked the room.

'I'll say this – I was probably naïve. I had every reason to understand what those societies were like, and how they operated – I could read Western newspapers, after all. But to read those accounts, and actually to experience that kind of state propaganda were two very different things. I learned a lot from that trip, and one of the chief things I learned was fear. The techniques being used in those countries weren't new ones, you see. They'd been perfected at the time of the Third Reich, in Nazi Germany. Fifty years later, when the Cold War was ending, I could see propaganda methods first used by Joseph Goebbels. They had worked then – and they worked just as effectively, and just as damnably, right now.'

He paused, and gave his silent audience a long cool look. 'Now, of course, all of us here tonight are fortunate. I am, you are. We live in Western democracies. We have a free Press. We can look back over our own recent history, and we can point specifically to historic changes we owe to those freedoms. That isn't exaggeration. It isn't hyperbole. I'm thinking about events such as Watergate. I'm thinking, in particular, about the Vietnam War, and the journalists who risked their lives to bring back the truth from a war zone. Those men and women changed America. They turned a whole nation around. And in the final analysis, it was they, and their influence, that brought an end to that war.

'Now,' he paused again, and lightened his tone, 'I have to admit, all reporting isn't of that magnitude

– I feel that exposing the sexual peccadilloes of British Cabinet Ministers, or investigating the private lives of the monarchy, may not rank on quite the same scale as bringing home the truth about a war. When people say to me that kind of coverage is intrusive or morally wrong, I have to admit I have a certain sympathy with their view.' He smiled. 'I've suffered press investigations in the past, I've had those lenses trained on me and I know exactly how unpleasant it can feel . . . However,' his tone became serious again and the smile disappeared, 'I do believe this. Those of us who enjoy privilege, and those of us granted power – we *have* to remain accountable. For the public figure, there can be no truly private life. That is the price paid. Politicians, presidents, and – yes – even princes, have to face press scrutiny. After all, if they have nothing to hide, they have nothing to fear. That,' he stabbed the air, '*that* is how we preserve a free society – via that scrutiny. And if we don't like it, we can always go someplace where those in power are better protected.'

There was a ripple of response and Hawthorne cut it short. 'So,' he continued, and Gini could see he was winding down now, 'I believe we should all continue to fight for press freedom. We should oppose censorship. We should oppose other more insidious curbs. Press freedom ensures truth is revealed, and lies exposed. It is the bedrock of democratic society – even when, for those on the receiving end, it feels like a bed of nails.'

He lifted his glass. 'Lord Melrose, ladies and gentlemen, I give you a toast. The freedom of the Press. May the fourth estate continue to flourish, especially its many representatives here.'

The applause began and mounted. Hawthorne's audience cheered. At several tables, people rose to their feet. Others followed their example.

'The claque's here . . . ' Stein said irritably. 'They always are. Where they lead, others follow. Jesus Christ – Vietnam. Is there any string that man wouldn't pull?'

'Well, he did fight there,' Gini began.

'Precisely my point.' Stein gave her a hard look. 'While America was changing, he wasn't there. He was out in 'Nam, killing Vietcong. Take a look at his war record sometime, Gini. He was decorated three times – and it wasn't for winning hearts and minds. Hawthorne didn't speak out against that war until around nineteen eighty-five, long after it was safely over. He was a hawk right through the Seventies and beyond . . . '

'Well, maybe.' Gini hesitated. 'But it was a good speech, of its kind. I agreed with his arguments . . . '

'Sure. You're a reporter, like nearly everyone else here. He gave the right speech for this audience. Perfect pitch. Nazis, Goebbels? He didn't miss a trick . . . '

'That wasn't irrelevant. It's germane.'

'Sure. It's also emotive. I should know . . . ' Stein shrugged. 'Forget it, Gini. I guess I'm biased – but then I'm one of those Jews Hawthorne would never invite to dine.'

After the remaining toasts, guests began to circulate between tables. On the dais, Hawthorne and Lord Melrose stood in conversation. The evening's events were beginning to wind down. Gini looked around for Nicholas Jenkins, and saw he had moved across to another table. She lost sight of him. When she finally located him, he was deep in conversation with one of Melrose's assistants. A few minutes later, she saw Melrose himself join them. He drew Jenkins aside, into a lobby and out of sight.

John Hawthorne, she saw, had now made his way down from the dais into the throng. He was surrounded by well-wishers and by security men on all sides.

She sat down at the now-empty table to wait for Jenkins's return. She stared at the tablecloth, fiddled with the cutlery. She did not want to admit it to herself, but Hawthorne's speech had touched a nerve. Even now, after all Pascal's arguments, after all that had happened, she still felt a residual resistance to the idea of Hawthorne's involvement in these events. Earlier that day, at the escort agency, or when she had been speaking to his wife the previous evening, she had almost been able to accept the idea of his guilt. Now, again, it seemed so unlikely. A failure of imagination, perhaps, she told herself, but she could not imagine the man who had made tonight's speech making a series of appointments with hired blondes, or authorizing killings.

'Gini . . . it is Gini?'

She looked up to find Hawthorne and entourage had reached her table. He was now standing by her side. She rose, and took the hand he held out to her. His handshake was brisk and impersonal; people were milling around on all sides. Nevertheless, she could read something in his face, and something in his eyes. It might be wordless, but she could see that it was directed at her, and her alone, and it looked like an appeal.

'I wanted to thank you,' he said. 'Taking Lise out, yesterday evening. That was a very good idea of yours.'

Gini did not correct him. 'Lise is not here tonight?'

'No. No.' He hesitated slightly. 'She had a migraine.'

'I hope she feels better soon.'

'I'm sure she will. They don't usually last that long. I . . .'

He stopped, and Gini realized it was the first time she had seen him betray awkwardness; it was as if he were off-guard. Just for one passing instant, she saw that beneath the pace and energy, he looked desperately tired. He looked, she realized, as Mary had described, as if at heart he was in despair.

Already he was beginning to turn away, to the next table, the next group of admirers and friends.

'Give my love to Mary,' he said, and he was gone. Gini watched him leave the room, table by table. At the door, the security men bunched. She saw Frank Romero's burly figure, and that reminded her. She turned back, but she had missed the departure of Hawthorne's father. His table was now deserted, and S. S. Hawthorne had gone.

She went in search of Nicholas Jenkins, and found him eventually, on the far side of the room, still in conversation with Melrose. Jenkins was flushed, and sweating. As she glanced across, she saw him pull out a handkerchief, and mop his brow.

She was about to move quietly to one side, until this conversation was over, but Jenkins caught sight of her. He beckoned her over.

'Henry, here she is now. Gini, that was very good timing. We've been talking about you . . . '

'Among other things,' said Melrose, with a little smile.

Jenkins looked flustered at this. He performed the introductions clumsily, and his proprietor brushed them aside.

'I do know who Miss Hunter is, Nicholas.' He turned back to Gini. 'I've read her stories. And admired them too. I wonder . . . ' He drew Gini a little to one side. A tall man, aged about sixty, elegantly dressed; he had a courteous manner. 'I wonder,' he repeated, 'I give these luncheons occasionally, Gini – may I call you Gini? – for my writers, some of my editors, that kind of thing. Very informal. Just to toss ideas back and forth you know. What kind of stories we should be covering, how we cover them, whether the paper can be improved . . . '

He paused. Gini said nothing. She had heard of these lunches, and had never expected to attend one. More senior journalists than she lobbied hard to be invited, since they knew the lunches were the path to promotion. She knew Jenkins had attended in the past, and that the ambitious Daiches had never made the grade, though he continued to try. 'I generally try to have one a month, if I'm in London,' Melrose was continuing. 'And I have one planned for the *News* next week. I'd like you to attend. I'll ask my assistant to contact you shortly. You'll be free? Good, good. So glad to have met you . . . '

He wished Jenkins good-evening briefly, then drifted away. Jenkins, who had overheard this conversation, gave her an angry look. He was now clearly in a bad temper, and in no mood to disguise it.

'Bloody man,' he said, with some vehemence, once Melrose was well out of earshot. He took Gini's arm. 'Christ, what an evening. Let's go.'

* * *

In the Jaguar, driving north, Jenkins was preoccupied, speaking only to his driver, and then only to tell him curtly to take the quickest route.

When they reached Gini's flat, Jenkins saw her as far as the top of the steps. There he hesitated, then said, 'I'll come in if I may. Just for five minutes.'

In her living-room Jenkins did not sit down, or remove his coat. He stood in the centre of the room, looking ill at ease. He refused Gini's offer of coffee, or a drink.

'Look,' he said, in an abrupt way, 'I'd better get this over with. I'll come straight to the point. I'll talk to Lamartine in the morning, but you may as well know now. The Hawthorne story is off.'

There was a silence. Gini looked at him. 'The story's *off*?'

'That's right.' Jenkins shifted from foot to foot. 'It's dead. Killed. I'm killing it. You leave it alone from now on, both you and Pascal. You've got that?'

There was another silence. Gini let it run on. She removed her coat.

'You want to give me a reason, Nicholas?'

'I could give you several. One will do. I was misinformed. McMullen told me a pack of lies. We're not going to make this story stand up.' Jenkins shifted his eyes away from her face. His normally pink complexion became suffused with a dark flush. Gini looked at him for a long moment, measuring his discomfiture. It was considerable.

She sat down, and stared across the room. Of course: it was so obvious. Every little event of the evening replayed itself, the conversations she had seen between Hawthorne and Melrose; Melrose's subsequent conversation with Jenkins; she had been caught in the middle of a power play, she realized. Both the carrot and the stick were being used here, the classic approach.

She looked back at Jenkins. 'I see,' she said. 'Melrose told you to pull the story.'

'It's fucking well nothing to do with Melrose.' Jenkins

lost his temper at once. 'It's my decision. Just do what I fucking tell you, Gini, for once.'

'Give me a break, Nicholas.' Gini rose. She gave a furious gesture, and realized she was suddenly very angry. 'Do you think I'm some kind of idiot? Dear God – we sit there tonight, we listen to Hawthorne, and all that rhetoric about the freedom of the Press. I even damn well start to *believe* the rhetoric – and then what happens? Hawthorne has a quiet word with his old buddy Melrose, and the next thing is – the story's off. The hell with it, Nicholas. I thought the whole point of being an editor was that when someone leaned on you, you stayed standing up.'

Jenkins's face darkened further, 'Gini, I'm going to forget you said that. I'm telling you, Melrose has nothing to *do* with it. He doesn't even *know* about the Hawthorne story.'

'Come on, Nicholas. Don't give me that crap. Melrose knows. If you didn't tell him, his friend John Hawthorne did.'

'Listen,' Jenkins rushed on, paying no attention, 'I've been reconsidering our overall editorial policy. We have to watch all these sex-and-scandal stories, that's all. The *News* relies on its middle-class readership—'

'Don't tell me. We go too far and we alienate them. You know I've heard that same view very recently? And you know who from? The US ambassador, that's who. He fed it to me, he fed it to Melrose, and Melrose bought it. Plus, of course, he's delighted to intercede on his friend Hawthorne's behalf, so he leaned on you, and you promptly collapsed. Great. Do you usually alter your entire editorial policy, Nicholas, over dinner, during a fifteen-minute speech?'

'Just cut it out, all right?' Jenkins turned away, tight-lipped. 'Forgive me for saying so, but that's a woman's response – a typical woman's response. You see male conspiracies, Gini, everywhere you look.' He gave a curt gesture. 'Anyway. I might just remind you. I don't have to explain my editorial policy to my reporters. You don't like it, you know what you can do.'

'Resign, Nicholas? Oh, I don't think I should do that now, do you? After all, my damn proprietor has just invited me to one of his famous lunches. That's a big break for me, Nicholas – except I get the feeling there're a few *conditions* attached to that invitation. Like I agree to be a good little girl. Like I drop the Hawthorne story, and play ball. If I don't do that I suspect that lunch invitation might be cancelled rather suddenly. Who knows, I might even get fired. Dear God! The whole thing makes me sick—'

'Look, look. No-one's talking about firing anyone . . . ' Jenkins looked suddenly alarmed. He switched to a pacifying tone. 'We don't want to lose you, Gini. I don't want to lose you—'

'Oh sure. You'd just hate me to take this story else-where. Which, come to think of it, is one hell of a good idea.'

Jenkins opened his mouth to make some angry retort, then shut it again. If he had fired her, then and there, Gini would not have been surprised, so it was interesting – and revealing, she realized – that he continued, with some effort, to take a conciliatory tone.

'Listen,' he said, 'you're over-reacting. There's no need for this to be a resignation issue. You have to learn to face facts, Gini. All right, so this story didn't pan out. There are other stories, you know. You remember we talked about Yugoslavia? Well, now maybe we could take a look at that idea again, and . . . '

He talked on, in this vein while Gini watched him coldly, with increasing disgust. If he was prepared to go as far as discussing Yugoslavia again, he must really be desperate, both to get her off this story, and to prevent her from taking it elsewhere. She looked away from him, around the room, and suddenly remembered the possibility of its listening walls. In her anger, she had completely forgotten this factor, but now she saw it was one she could turn to her own advantage: if someone outside was listening in, why not tell them what they most wanted to hear? She let Nicholas Jenkins continue talking. When he finally finished she gave a shrug and a sigh.

'OK, OK,' she said carefully. 'Maybe you're right, Nicholas. I guess I was over-reacting. It was sudden, that's all.' She paused. 'You really mean that about Yugoslavia?'

'Sure, sure.' Jenkins beamed. 'Get it into your head, will you, Gini? I really value your work at the *News*. A woman's byline on reports from Bosnia, maybe a photograph of you – yes, it could work out very well.'

'Well, I guess if that was really a possibility . . . '

'It is a possibility. It's more than a possibility. Look, Gini, you've got that lunch with Melrose sewn up. You and I can talk new stories, next week maybe. This could all turn out well for you. Don't screw up now.'

'But I'd have to agree to drop the Hawthorne story?'

'Yes. And no more garbage about swanning off with it elsewhere.'

'OK.' She gave him a decisive smile. 'You've sold me on it, Nicholas.' She paused. 'Actually – I didn't want to say this before, but I wasn't making a whole lot of progress with it anyway. There were a lot of leads, then they all turned out to be dead-ends. I could have worked on this for months and got nowhere. Pascal feels the same. I don't want to do that – marking time. And if there was a serious possibility of Yugoslavia—'

'Gini, it's as good as fixed. Say no more.'

'The only thing is . . . ' She gave him a little glance. 'I'm pretty exhausted, Nicholas. The Hawthorne story really took it out of me. I don't want to go into details now, there's no point, but it was getting pretty scary. I could do with a break – just a short one. And I am owed some vacation time . . . '

'Take it. It's yours. You deserve it. A week, two weeks?'

'Two weeks would be amazing. You're sure, Nicholas?'

He thought he had won, and he now bubbled with benevolence. Crossing the room, he put his arm around her shoulders.

'Two weeks. Done. Go get some sun. Forget about work. Forget about the office. I don't want to see or hear from you, Gini . . . ' He smiled broadly. 'You know how you are. Well, this time, I want to forget I employ you,

OK? Then come back, with a good sun-tan, and we'll start lining up the work for you. Or maybe, fit in the Melrose lunch, then take off. It's up to you.'

'I think I will fit in the Melrose lunch. Then I'll fly off somewhere exotic. God, what a great idea. Sun, after all these months of rain . . . '

Jenkins patted her shoulder, then moved to the door. 'I knew you'd see it my way,' he said. 'Well done, Gini. Smart girl.'

When he had gone, Gini went to bed, and lay there turning the components of this story back and forth. She was tense, because she feared that her telephone might ring, that she might hear the whispering muffled male voice once more. But there were no calls that night. When she woke in the morning she wondered if it was her conversation with Jenkins which had won her that reprieve.

She hoped that, at eight, Pascal might telephone to let her know if he was returning to London, but Pascal did not call. This was a disappointment, but it probably meant only that he distrusted her phone. She would call him, she decided, from a pay phone, later that day. Meanwhile, she had that appointment with Lise Hawthorne in Regent's Park.

She sat for a while, preparing herself for this meeting, even though she thought Lise might be unable to keep the appointment. She stroked Napoleon, who was curled on her lap. He purred, and narrowed his eyes with pleasure. She traced the pink elegance of his paw-pads, and the delicate patterns of his marmalade fur.

Shortly before nine, she left her flat, and set off through the rain and the morning rush hour taking a roundabout route until she was reasonably certain that she was not followed. Then she headed south. She parked at some distance from her destination, continuing her journey on foot. Fifteen minutes ahead of the appointed time, she entered the gates of Regent's Park.

XXIV

The park was almost deserted. She could see a few determined joggers in the distance. She passed a few people, heads bent against the wind, walking their dogs. She followed the main path in the direction of the residence's gardens, then struck off onto the grass; mud squelched underfoot.

Lise Hawthorne had not been very exact in her directions. The residence gardens were large; they cut into the park itself in a deep horseshoe-shaped curve. For a time Gini patrolled this curve, back and forth. Then, although no-one seemed to be paying the least attention to her, she moved a little further off. She chose a well-positioned bench, fifty yards away, in the midst of open lawns. The minutes ticked by: ten, ten-fifteen, ten-thirty. She was becoming very cold, and she felt very conspicuous. It had not occurred to her at the time Lise made the arrangement, because she had been too shocked by the pallor and anguish in Lise's face, but now that she was actually here she saw the oddness of Lise's instructions. This was hardly a covert or discreet place to meet.

Could it really be true that she had, in the past, met McMullen here? Gini considered: perhaps she had been referring to a much earlier period, five or even six months earlier, some time before Hawthorne's suspicions were aroused. She wondered again, about the exact nature of the relationship between McMullen and Lise, and whether they had been lovers or not. Then, shivering, she rose to her feet.

She would give it one more try, she decided, one slow pass along the perimeter of that high horseshoe-shaped fence. Half an hour more: it was useful to remind herself, she thought, of what a citadel it was, this place where

Lise Hawthorne lived. Turning back to the north of the house, to the rear of the entrance lodge with its bristling aerials and cameras, she began to follow the fence around the deep curve of the gardens, to where it met the ring road to the south of the house.

This fence, completely encircling the rear gardens, was a formidable one. It was constructed of metal bars ten feet high, each with three curved spikes on the top. The bars themselves were shaped so as to make any purchase on them almost impossible; they were coated in anti-climb paint, and were narrowly spaced. There was no crossbar low enough to be used to wedge the feet. Through the bars, she could occasionally catch a glimpse of the house, and the wide lawns behind it, but for the most part the view was obscured by tall evergreen shrubs ten or twelve feet deep. This cover, Gini knew, would contain other less visible security devices: the care with which this boundary was protected was obvious – wherever the shrubbery gave insufficient cover, camouflage netting had been erected, yard upon yard of it, slung inside the bars of the perimeter fence.

The rain was easing off now. A jogger passed her, and a woman with a red umbrella walking a tiny delicate dog. Gini was approaching one of the park lakes; here two conduits ran off and formed an additional barrier, a moat which forced her some fifty yards away from the residence fence.

Ahead of her there were two small ornamental bridges, and a children's playground. A man and a woman stood on the further bridge, ignoring the rain and feeding bread to the ducks. Gini looked at them as she passed and they smiled, made a comment about the weather; both were sixty at least.

She walked on past the deserted playground. She was now on the southern side of the residence's gardens; they lay to her right, the circle road was straight ahead. In front of her, and just to her left on the far side of the road, was the large copper dome and the tall minaret of the London Central Mosque. She was struck, as she always was when passing it, by the unlikeliness of its placing. In this most English of parks, flanked by the Nash terraces at Hanover Gate, this Islamic exoticism was arresting. The minaret was just over a hundred feet high, an Arabian Nights' landmark visible for miles; the beautiful copper dome was crested with a sickle moon. Within an English park Arab territory and American territory were cheek by jowl. Less than one hundred yards separated Moslem devotions from the American Ambassador's private home.

Gini stood between the two buildings, beneath a grove of young chestnut trees. Their bare branches dripped; she saw that she was on a slight rise, a knoll, with the ground falling away to her right. From here she could walk down to her right and stand alongside that barred perimeter fence. She did so, and touched the bars with her hand. Beyond the camouflage netting, thick here, and the shrubbery, she could see nothing, but she could hear voices.

Men were working in the gardens beyond. She could hear the sound of spades, then the whine of a chain-saw. Some of the older trees on the edge of the gardens were being pruned. The noise of the saw stopped, and suddenly, to her astonishment, she heard Lise Hawthorne's voice. She was giving instructions to the workmen.

'No,' Gini heard. 'That branch there must go, and the large ones just above. It's casting too much shade, nothing will grow there as it is. Then that large sycamore must come out. It seeds itself everywhere, and my husband would like the small Himalayan birches in its place. Now, shall we take a look at the lavender walk? Or what's left of it after all this rain, which isn't a great deal . . . '

Her voice faded into the distance. The whine of the chain-saw recommenced.

Gini began to turn away, puzzled. She glanced back at the fencing, turned, then gave a gasp. The jogger who had passed her earlier was now standing two feet behind her. She had not heard him approach. He was wearing a black track suit; its hood was up, and she could scarcely see his face.

She took a quick step backwards, then stopped. The man looked threatening, but was making no move towards her. She looked at him more closely. He was breathing lightly. He lifted a hand to adjust his track-suit hood slightly; she saw he was wearing a signet ring on his left hand. He had fair hair.

'Are you looking for Jacob?' he asked.

He had an even, pleasant English voice. Gini hesitated. 'I came here to meet his friend,' she said. 'But I have been looking for Jacob, yes.'

As she stared at him, he lifted his head; the hood fell back just a little. He was older, obviously, but his features were imprinted on her memory. She had studied his photograph long enough. She gave a low exclamation: it was James McMullen.

She was about to speak, when he glanced over his shoulder, and lifted his finger to his lips. A man had just come into the park, through the ring road gate.

'The British Museum in an hour,' he said, in a low voice. 'Wait there. I'll meet you there. If it's safe.' The man was now walking towards them. McMullen raised his voice slightly. 'Can you give me directions?'

'Sure,' Gini replied. 'Across the park. Aim south. Then take a left . . . It's a pretty long way from here . . . '

'Thanks, I'll find it.'

Without a backward glance, he jogged off. He covered the ground very fast. Gini turned back to the ring road, passing the man, who was wearing a dark overcoat, but who was no-one she recognized. He did not even look at her. When she reached the road, she looked back. He was continuing along the path at a measured pace. He paused by the elderly couple on the bridge in the distance, the couple who were still feeding the ducks. Then he continued on. Some way beyond them, he lifted his hand towards his face.

It was too far away for Gini to be sure: it might have been an innocent gesture. He could have been consulting his watch; he could have been adjusting his tie; he could have been speaking into a wrist-mike. She began to walk rapidly away. The street was deserted. When she next looked back, she was passing the mosque, and the man in the park and James McMullen were both out of sight.

It took her ten minutes to get back to her car, twenty to get to the museum, and a further twenty to drive around it in circles to find a parking place.

She ran back to the museum, and ran up its deep flight of steps. She hurried into the entrance hall, where she was stopped by security guards, and her bag was searched. She hurried on, through a vast marble archway and into the huge ground-floor main hall. She stopped. It was years since she had been here, and she had forgotten the vast size of this place. The museum was a warren of galleries and ante-rooms. It was huge, labyrinthine. She might have been meant to come here, but where was she supposed to go next?

'I want Gini taken off this story,' Pascal said. He was in Nicholas Jenkins's fifteenth-floor sanctum, with its view of the new emerging docklands London. He could see towers and scaffolding through the plate glass behind Jenkins's head.

Jenkins was smiling, nodding, all amiability. It was 11 a.m. Pascal had come straight from the airport. He had been expecting a fight with Jenkins over this, yet Jenkins gave no indication of opposition. He continued to smile and nod, and give Pascal small devious looks.

Pascal tried to force out of his mind all memory of black Mercedes cars; he tried not to think of Lorna Munro's beautiful dead face. He had had all night to decide how to approach this, and exactly what lies to tell Jenkins, yet now he had the impression that Jenkins was several jumps ahead of him, and knew it. Pascal leaned across his desk.

'I'm getting through to you, am I, Nicholas? I won't work with Gini on this story. I want you to take her off it. You understand, yes?'

There was a small flicker of amusement behind the nuclear-physicist-style spectacles. Jenkins sighed.

'Oh dear,' he said, in a sweet-toned innocuous voice. 'What went wrong, Pascal? Bad chemistry? Or was it more dramatic than that?'

'Give it a rest, Nicholas. No, nothing like that. She's fine. She works hard, she's very thorough. But I work better on my own. I always have.'

'I did warn you.' Jenkins gave him a reproachful look. 'I told you she was good. I also told you she was a pain in the neck.'

'I didn't find that.' Pascal looked at him coldly. 'I don't need her any more – it's as simple as that. She was . . . ' he hesitated, 'slowing me down. Just let me carry on at my own pace. I can get this sewn up by the end of the week.'

'By Sunday, you mean?' Jenkins looked at him intently.

'If you're asking can I get the pictures then, the answer is yes. I think I can. And I'll do it a whole lot better and more efficiently on my own. This isn't a suitable story for a woman.'

Jenkins gave a little smile. 'I did wonder about that,' he said, 'when I heard Appleyard was dead.'

Pascal gave him a sharp glance. He was not about to be drawn, however: he had decided last night. He trusted no-one on this story, including Jenkins, and he had no intention of giving Jenkins any further details until it was over.

'Look,' he continued, 'I'm in a hurry, Nicholas. You give me a decision here and now. If you want those pictures, you take Gini off this story. It's as simple as that.' He gave a shrug. 'I did try to persuade her myself, and I got precisely nowhere. There's a chance she'll listen to you. Pull rank, Nicholas. Do whatever it takes.'

'Oh, but I already have.' Jenkins's smile was now broad and complacent. 'I did it last night. You just don't know how to handle her, Pascal. I had no problems at all. A piece of cake.'

There was a silence. Pascal stared at him.

'You took her off this story last night?'

'I most certainly did. And in the end, she agreed. She

argued first, of course – in fact, she was fucking rude to me, but never mind that.' Jenkins gave him a small gleaming look. 'Gini's never liked me, I'm afraid. She accused me of bowing to pressure from outside, from our dear proprietor Melrose, and Melrose's friend the ambassador.' He paused, eyeing Pascal. 'I told her I was killing this story, so I suppose she had some justification.'

'And are you killing this story?'

'No, Pascal. I'm not.'

He rose, moved across to the large plate-glass windows, looked out thoughtfully for a while, then turned back. The light winked against his spectacles. He gave Pascal a sharp look.

'Gini seems to think I'm a pushover. Some kind of poodle. Well, she'll learn in due course. You don't get where I've got by being weak. And you don't advance your career long-term by bowing and scraping when some boring old fart like Melrose snaps his fingers. What you do is, you smile, and you say *yes, Lord Melrose, of course, Lord Melrose* – and then you carry right on. Only take a more devious approach. Save the direct confrontation for when it really counts . . . ' He smiled. 'Like, about fifteen seconds before the presses start rolling. Or even later, when the papers actually hit the streets. That way, if the story's good enough, he doesn't dare to fire you. And if he does, you're still a hero, the fearless editor.' He grinned suddenly. 'Eat shit, Melrose, because I've got five other job offers. That's my general approach.'

There was a silence. Pascal extinguished one cigarette then lit another. He said slowly, 'I think you'd better bring me up to date. Obviously, a lot has been happening that I've missed.'

'Oh, a very great deal.' Jenkins gave a knowing smile, and returned to his desk. He sat down. He picked up one of the phones on his desk. 'Hold all calls for fifteen minutes, Charlotte. *All* calls, you've got that?' He replaced the receiver, and gave Pascal a long assessing look. 'When did you last get some sleep?' he said. 'You look like hell, do you know that?'

'Very probably.' Pascal shrugged. 'There are reasons for that.'

'I rather thought there might be. All right. Listen, Pascal, and listen carefully. I'm only going to say this once.' He paused. 'First of all, there's the question of who else knew you'd be working on this story. That question has been exercising Gini quite a lot. I'm afraid I wasn't straight with you before. I will be now. James McMullen knew. It was agreed between us last December, when he handed over that tape. Two weeks before he disappeared. He asked specifically that you work on it – which surprised me, but apparently he'd seen your war photographs as well as your recent work. Gini was my suggestion, agreed by him. Who else he told, I don't know, but there's one obvious candidate, though he claimed it was better she didn't know.'

'Lise Hawthorne?'

'Precisely. It's also possible,' Jenkins paused, frowning, 'it's possible our conversation was overheard. We were careful, obviously. I never went to his flat. He never set foot in this building. We met well away from other fucking journalists, and on that occasion, when your names were discussed, we met at the Army & Navy Club,' he said, then added, 'There're a few other things you should know, and they concern Johnny Appleyard. I thought his importance was tangential, and I was anxious to keep it like that. That's why I didn't mention it at first. I realized I was wrong when I heard that he was dead . . . Then we come to the really interesting part,' he said. 'We come to this last weekend, and to the dinner I attended with Gini last night.' He smiled. 'A concatenation of circumstances, Pascal. It's when I realized there had to be more to this than just a sex scandal.' His face took an expression of triumphant delight. 'That's when I realized that this story was *really* big.'

'Why?'

'Because I was *leaned* on, Pascal. Leaned on in a surprising way. Leaned on very heavily indeed. Always a good indicator, that.' He paused. 'How much do you know about Lord Melrose?'

'He's the proprietor of the *News*, obviously. He inherited his papers from his father. He has three others in this country, two in Australia, one in Canada, and one in the States. I gather he's a friend of Hawthorne's, or so Gini said.'

'Correct. But the most important thing about Melrose from our point of view now, is that he's an Establishment man, through and through. Friends in high places everywhere, including the Security Services, though Melrose tends to keep very quiet about that. We've had run-ins before, as a result. It happens like this: from time to time some nice discreet civil servant takes Melrose out to lunch at the Athenaeum, or Brooks's, it's usually somewhere like that. This man waits until they've served the coffee and the port, then he has a quiet word in Melrose's ear. If one of his papers is on to something a bit sensitive, the man steers Melrose off. Come on, old boy, national security and all that, time to call off the bloodhounds. Now, sometimes Melrose listens, and sometimes he remembers his nice liberal conscience and tells his friend to get lost. Last Friday, Melrose went to one of those lunches.'

'Last Friday?'

'That's right.' Jenkins gave a sly grin. 'Unfortunately, I'd kind of neglected to mention the Hawthorne investigation to Melrose – shockingly remiss of me, yes? So when Melrose found out, he wasn't pleased. In fact, he was mad as hell. What made it all rather worse was that this nice discreet faceless old Etonian was alarmingly well informed. Not only did he know we were working on the Hawthorne story, he knew the name of my source.'

'He mentioned McMullen by name?'

'To Melrose? Yes, he did. And he explained to Melrose that McMullen was *very* bad news. Not only had he been peddling a pack of lies to me about an eminent man, but – apparently – the old Etonian and his friends had had their eyes on McMullen for some time. As had their cousins across the pond. The British files on McMullen went back a long way – a *very* long way, Pascal. They hadn't looked at them in some time, but when they got them out and dusted them down – this was last summer – they found they were several inches thick.'

'Let me get this straight. According to Melrose McMullen had been investigated before? By British Security?'

'Yes, he had. Last summer, the Americans joined in the act. For which there's a simple explanation. They did so from last July onwards, at John Hawthorne's behest.' Jenkins tapped his fingers on the desk. 'Now, Melrose's reaction to all this was to panic,' Jenkins went on. 'He went into one of his flaps. He asked for the weekend to think it over, and his Etonian friend bought that. Then, on Sunday morning, at seven-thirty on Sunday morning, his friend John Hawthorne called him up personally. Then the shit *really* hit the fan.' Jenkins grinned. 'I was telephoned at home, summoned to château Melrose, and given a straight choice. Kill the Hawthorne story, or go in Monday morning and clear my desk.'

Pascal said nothing. He was thinking about the timing. Hawthorne called the morning *after* Mary's party. These manœuvres were taking place as he and Gini had left for Venice. He looked back at Jenkins.

'So – what did you do?' he said.

'I bought myself a little time – and I'm fucking good at that. I did a lot of injured outrage, banged on about censorship. I made Melrose feel like a fascist, and since he really fancies himself as a liberal, that did the trick. He gave me forty-eight hours to decide, on condition I published nothing in that time, obviously. And he agreed to go back to his Etonian friend, and get some more information. I said I wasn't being fobbed off with a whole lot of vague crap about McMullen being suspect. I wanted a few facts. The way Melrose was going on was ludicrous. McMullen could have been in the pay of Moscow, or he could have been late paying his taxes – it was as loose as that. So Melrose toddled back to the Athenaeum or wherever. I came in Monday morning, heard about

Appleyard's death and put our Italian stringer on to it that morning. I also ordered up every file on Hawthorne in existence. Mistake.'

'Why?'

'Because some fucking devious bastard told Melrose what I'd done.'

'Who told him?'

'I don't know. But when I find out, they're dead.' Jenkins paused. 'Finally Hawthorne had another go at Melrose, the next night. We were all at this bloody dinner. Hawthorne made this fucking sanctimonious speech about press freedom, then he took his old friend Melrose into a corner and really laid into him. Mentioned libel, criminal libel, a few things like that. Whereupon Melrose lost his nerve totally, and we were back to square one. Kill the story or else.'

'And you agreed? This was last night?'

'Of course I agreed. We bide our time, right? Gini's off the story, that looks good. That ought to help convince them I'm playing ball, and then—'

'You're not playing ball?'

Jenkins gave him a very sharp glance; his glasses flashed. 'You don't know me very well, Pascal. Genevieve-bloody-Hunter doesn't know me at all. Let's put it this way. I was a working-class boy once. A scholarship boy at a major public school. It left me a bit chippy, a bit sensitive about certain things. Like, I'm not too fucking keen on the old-boy network. I'm not too fucking keen on old Etonians who take other old Etonians out to lunch and lean on them. I'm not too fucking keen on WASPs like Hawthorne who preach one thing and do another – and when they *all* start to pressure me, I smell a rat. And I start thinking – if they're that worried, that keen, it has to be major. Maybe even more than we realized.'

He leaned across and unlocked a drawer of his desk. He extracted a large manila envelope, and passed it across the desk. 'Go on working on this,' he said. 'But cover your fucking tracks. I can't be involved. I don't even know what you're up to, all right? When you've got what we need, we can always rope Gini back in, if necessary. Get the pictures on Sunday and we're halfway there. Once we have pictures, Hawthorne's screwed. Even Melrose won't be able to protect his old friend then. Then we can *really* get to the bottom of this story. It's more than beating up on blonde call-girls once a month. It's more than a kink for expensive blow-jobs when the girl's wearing black gloves. There's something *more*, Pascal, I can smell it, and it's not recent, either, not a taste Hawthorne developed in the last four years, the way McMullen told me. It links back to earlier events. I may not know what they are – yet – but there's been a cover-up, and it goes back a long way. Take a look through this.'

He tapped the envelope. Pascal looked at it. It was sealed, and it was thick.

'What is that?'

'Details of John Hawthorne's exemplary military service. I got it faxed from a friend in Washington yesterday. Plus some details on my friend McMullen. Details *I* never bloody well knew.'

'Is he a security risk?'

'Difficult to say.' Jenkins made a balancing gesture of the hand. 'He was vetted for the Army, obviously. Some of this stuff came via Melrose's spooky friend, so it may or may not be reliable. It certainly doesn't look as if McMullen spent his entire army career in the Parachute Regiment. He's possibly more dangerous than I realized.' Jenkins paused. 'Most interesting of all, his links with John Hawthorne go back much further than he claimed to me.'

'Where to?' Pascal asked sharply.

'Oddly enough, to something Hawthorne touched on last night in his speech—'

'Where to, Nicholas?'

'To *Vietnam*,' Jenkins replied. 'Now how about that?'

Gini walked slowly along the huge marble-floored entrance hall of the museum. From here, she told herself, there were many places from which she could be watched. There were staircases, lobbies, pillars; innumerable places where, if he wished, James McMullen, could conceal himself. Presumably, she thought, as she turned and slowly retraced her steps, McMullen would wait, and approach her when it suited him. The roles of hunter and hunted were reversed.

Perhaps the best thing was simply to linger here. There were few other visitors to the museum on a wet mid-week January morning. There was a party of schoolchildren, being shepherded towards the museum shop; a group of dispirited Japanese with camcorders, one or two solitary figures, examining the classical heads and torsos on exhibition.

One more time, she walked slowly down the gallery, then returned. Nothing. A tomb-like somnolence hushed the air; her footsteps echoed; no-one approached.

After a while, she decided that this main hall was too open, and too public. She mounted one of the marble staircases which led to the first floor, and rapidly became lost. She lingered by large cases containing Roman coins and pottery. She turned into another room, and found herself in a glass-walled cul-de-sac lined with blind Grecian heads.

Down some stairs, along a corridor, up some stairs and she was in the Egyptian galleries. She watched her own reflection, a glacial ghost, as she passed along the cases filled with images of gods. Once, she thought she heard movement behind her, a light footfall, but when she turned, there was no-one there. She bent to the cases, examined the oil and grain jars, the papyrus scrolls, the tiny pottery grave relics, and the more gorgeous ornaments with which princes were lovingly sent on their journey into the afterlife. She looked at gods in the shape of hawks, and the shape of cats. Their painted stares met hers; on the glass she traced the ochre and black of their eyes. She listened intently. Nothing. She was still alone. She confronted line upon line of mummies, some standing, some lying, some still in their gilded and painted outer casings, some protected only by the swaddling of their bandages.

So many, so lovely, so various and so fearsome, these ways of death. She looked at a Pharaoh's son, laid to rest in garments of scarlet, lapis and indigo, painted calm on the painted likeness of his face. The air smelled dusty; in this, the older part of the galleries, the display cases made a second labyrinth within the outer one of the museum itself. She had to pass around, between, behind the dead. They cornered her, and she decided to wait elsewhere, in a more conspicuous place.

She returned to the main entrance, went outside, bought a newspaper, and returned to the museum again. In the café, where the schoolchildren were making a hubbub, she sat down. No-one approached.

The early edition of the *Evening Standard* led on John Hawthorne's speech the previous night. The headline was: *US Ambassador Slams 'Nazi' Arab States*. An incendiary description of Hawthorne's comments, she thought – and the comments seemed to have had an inflammatory effect. According to the *Stop Press*, demonstrations had begun outside the US Embassy in Grosvenor Square, and outside the London headquarters of several American banks. There had been clashes with the police.

Gini drank some coffee, waited fifteen minutes, then left. There were telephone booths near the entrance, and from there she telephoned first the number of Pascal's studio in Paris, then his wife's number; on both lines, an answering machine was the only response.

Perhaps he was returning, even now, as she called. This thought made her heart lift. She was still unwilling to give up on this museum. She had now been here an hour. One more try, she decided.

This time, she took the stairs which led down to the basement galleries. Here, the overall lighting was dim, and the individual sculptures, which included some of the museum's glories, were bathed in angled light. She passed along the Elgin Marbles, and a battle frieze which had once decorated the Parthenon. She looked at the great rearing marble haunches of the horses on the frieze, at the minutely observed weaponry, and at the frozen attitudes of dying men. Nothing; no-one; silence. She passed into a further gallery, and still another, and found herself in a part of the museum she had never penetrated before, in the Assyrian rooms.

Here, bathed in an angled light, were walls of massive stone reliefs. They were sombre, detailed and magnificent: she stood, listening, before a great procession of ten-feet kings and warriors and priests. They were carrying offerings, and Gini tried to concentrate on the bundles of corn, the bowls of wine, the sacrificial animals. The phalanx of men reminded her of that security phalanx that protected John Hawthorne wherever he went, though in the modern world, of course, their offerings were automatic weapons, and modern princes like Hawthorne were rarely accompanied by priests.

She bent to read the label which explained the symbols of these past events, and heard movement behind her – a single footfall, the brush of stone against cloth.

At last. She swung around sharply, and scanned the room. From the corner of her eye, in the shadows of the far entrance, she thought she saw darkness move. She turned, and it was gone. She ran across to the entrance, but the gallery beyond was empty. Massive reliefs rose up on either side of her. She stepped back, peering beyond them and dazzled by the lighting which now shone directly in her face. There was no-one there. There was no-one in the room behind her – but there were three other exits from this place. She checked each of them in turn, but each led to corridors and stairs, and if someone had been there, he was gone.

She came to a halt, and looked around her with a sense of angry frustration. Someone had been there, she was certain he had been there. Why was McMullen playing these cat-and-mouse tricks? She was now standing at the foot of a back staircase, in a small ill-lit lobby. From here she had a clear view back into the room where she had been when she first heard the noise. She could see the huge relief she had been studying, with its procession of warriors and priests. Just as she was about to turn away, a shadow moved across the face of the sculpture, and then a man came into sight.

He was wearing the same dark overcoat he had worn before, and he moved silently, on those soft-soled shoes described by Lise Hawthorne. Frank Romero. He stood in front of the relief, staring up at it for a moment. He touched it. He peered behind it, then bent to examine the floor in front of it. He began to move silently and stealthily around the room, examining each relief, each carving in turn, as if he were searching for something, some message left, perhaps.

Gini edged back into the shadows, and towards the stairs. A hand came out of the darkness, and clamped itself across her mouth. She felt a moment's pure fear. Before she could struggle, or even think, she felt a man pulling her closer against him, so his mouth was against her ear. She could feel his breath on her face.

'Don't scream, and don't speak,' he said in a low calm English voice. McMullen's voice. 'I'm going to give you a number. Call it tomorrow at noon. You understand? If you do, nod your head.' Gini nodded. 'Don't look round. Can you remember numbers?' Gini nodded again.

McMullen repeated the numbers, slowly and quietly. 'You've got that? Call it at noon tomorrow. Use a safe phone. Noon. Not five minutes before, not five afterwards. Now go up these stairs, turn right, then second left. You'll be in the main hall. Buy some postcards, as if this was a normal visit, then leave. No, don't look round. You've got that?'

He released her and Gini did as he said. She fled silently up the stairs, reciting the number to herself. Once she was safely back in her car, she took out a notebook and pencil and wrote it down, her hand shaking. The number had an 0865 prefix. An *Oxford* number.

A familiar Oxford number, too – at least she thought

it was, but she couldn't be certain, and she had left her address book at home in her flat.

She drove north as fast as she could, but the rain was still heavy, and street after street was grid-locked with traffic. She used every backstreet rat-run she knew, but even so it took her almost an hour to drive the five miles.

She parked in the square, and ran down the area steps, inserted her key in the lock. The address book was on her desk, just next to the telephone. She swung the living-room door open. As she closed it something soft brushed her face.

She continued a few paces on, towards the desk. Then the terrible wrongness of the room registered. She stopped. Sickness welled in the pit of her stomach. Something soft had brushed her face, as she closed the door. There was nothing there, there should be nothing there, to brush against her in that way. On the back of the door was an empty hook.

She turned, looked, and cried out. She ran across to the door, but it was too late – at least an hour too late.

Whoever had killed Napoleon had made a neat job. The black stocking sent her the previous week had been used to strangle him. They had wound the nylon around his throat, throttled him, and then left him to hang from the hook by this noose. His body was already stiffening. There was blood on his mouth and nostrils. There were scratch-marks on the door panels where he had scrabbled with his feet.

Gini thought: *How long did it take him to die?* She cradled his body, lifted him down, and held him close. She began to cry, and pressed him tight against her chest. His eyes were closed and her fingers fumbled to undo the stocking. She rocked him, and wept. Her fingers would not move too well, but in the end she unwound the noose. She sat down on the floor and crooned to Napoleon. She stroked his marmalade fur, and tried to believe that love could

431

resurrect. Napoleon lay inert in her arms. It cut her to the heart, the littleness of his body, in death.

She stroked his fur, and touched the beauties of his whiskers and his feet. After a long time, the wildness calmed and the tears stopped. She sat there, and made herself a final promise: no-one would stop her now, not after this.

She was still sitting there, holding Napoleon, when Pascal's motor bike drew up in the street. She did not hear the bike's engine, or his footsteps on pavement. She heard and saw nothing until he was in the room with her. Then she heard his closeness, and looked up. She saw his face change as he registered the stocking discarded on the floor and the bundle in her arms. He was angrier then than she had ever seen him, and she had a brief groping sensation of how formidable, in anger, he might be. Whoever made an enemy of Pascal made a mistake.

Then his face became gentle, an extraordinary tenderness lit in his eyes. With a few low words, he bent, and gathered her close.

He said, 'My darling, don't cry. We'll find them, I promise you, whoever did this.'

XXV

They buried Napoleon in the small garden behind the
house. The earth was soft from the rain, and the task
easy enough. They worked in silence, side by side, and
when it was over, Pascal said close to her ear, 'Not here.
Not here. Pack some clothes and come with me. We have
three days left. It's time to disappear.'

The journey was long and circuitous, though the distance
travelled was short. They went first to a small hotel
in St James's, where Pascal was known and a double
room had been booked. Pascal said the manager, an old
contact of his, would ensure the room appeared to be
occupied. Telephone calls would be made, and food sent
up.

'Our ghosts will occupy this room,' he said. 'But we'll
be somewhere else. For a day, maybe two, this will help.
Then, if necessary, we try something else.'

They moved on, setting off in one direction, then
doubling back. When Pascal was satisfied they were not
followed, he led them to their destination. It proved to be a
small cottage in Hampstead, near the summit of the heath.
It was situated in a maze of narrow cobbled alleyways
inaccessible by car. It had three entrances. Pascal parked
his motor bike in a shed to its rear.

'I came here earlier and checked the house,' he said.
'It's anonymous. It isn't overlooked at front or back, and
it has a number of other advantages, Gini. Look.'

He led her inside, and Gini went from room to room with
mounting astonishment. The house was well furnished
and equipped. The bed was made up. There was several
days' food in the fridge. The day's newspapers were
neatly stacked in its small sitting-room. All the windows

had thick wooden interior shutters. The exterior doors were reinforced with steel plates.

'Pascal,' she said, 'who lives here? What is this place?'

'It's a safe house – and no-one lives here as such. It belongs to a contact of mine. Once upon a time, she owned the most celebrated brothel in France. Then there was a little misunderstanding about tax. She retired to London, and invested the remains of her fortune in property. She's over seventy now. An extraordinary woman. She lets this place to former clients of hers, people who need somewhere secure and private, and clean in the electronic sense.'

'Are there many such people?'

'Oh yes. We can talk here, Gini. It has anti-electronic surveillance equipment, and it's regularly swept. It may not be one hundred per cent secure, nowhere is, but it's ninety-nine per cent.'

He drew her towards him, and took her hand. Her face was white, and still tear-stained. He kissed her brow gently.

'Now, listen, Gini,' he said. 'Go upstairs. Unpack. Have a bath. No – do as I say. It will make you feel better. While you do that, I'll make us something to eat. Then, later, when you feel stronger, we'll go over all this, piece by piece. We're close now, darling. I can feel it, it's starting to make sense.'

Gini drew back from him; she looked up at his face. 'You know you said you asked Jenkins to take me off the story. Why?'

Pascal smiled. 'I didn't know he'd already done so, obviously not.' He paused. 'I don't want anyone to know what we're up to, Gini, not even him. I don't trust him completely. I don't trust anyone. Apart from you, of course.'

'But you didn't mean what you said to him – Pascal, you promise me that?'

'No, I didn't mean it.' He hesitated. 'I'm afraid for you, yes. I'll protect us any way I can. I won't let what happened to Lorna Munro happen to you—' He broke

434

off. Gini's expression had become fixed. He told her, then, exactly what had happened, and how swiftly it had happened.

Gini gave a low cry. 'We killed her, Pascal. We did that. We as good as wrote her death certificate.'

'Don't.' He drew her close. 'Gini, I thought that at first. But it isn't true. It wasn't hard to trace her. Anyone could have done so. They could have killed her any time they liked. Don't you see, Gini, they waited until she had spoken to me, until I could actually witness her death. It was another of their warnings, like Napoleon, like Venice. So,' his face hardened, 'we pay attention to those warnings. We're much more careful from now on. We stay together, at all times. But we don't give up – either of us, no matter what Jenkins believes, or anyone else. We work *together* on this, and we *succeed*.' He paused, his expression now both sad and determined. 'What you said to me, in Venice – you remember? Believe me: I heard what you said.'

When Gini came downstairs, she felt stronger and refreshed. A delicious smell of cooking emanated from the kitchen. She found that Pascal had set the table there, and she was touched by what she saw: two places, laid in the French manner, two lighted candles, a checked cloth, and a small pot plant in the centre, removed from one of the rooms upstairs. Deep purple African violets. The candles were a little askew. Pascal gave this arrangement a proud look. He made a great play of opening oven doors and checking temperatures. He flourished dish-cloths a lot. Gini suppressed a smile. She knew perfectly well that Pascal could not cook. From the oven, he produced what turned out to be a very good *boeuf bourguignon*, which as they both knew, had come ready-cooked.

'Extraordinary,' he said with a smile as they ate. 'It's much easier than I realized, this cooking. You open the oven, put the thing in, and *voilà*.'

'It's a little bit more complicated, Pascal, if you're starting from scratch.'

'It is?' He looked at her with great seriousness. 'Could you make this?'

'From scratch? Yes, I could. It's not that difficult . . . '

'Excellent. I have a few French prejudices. It's nice if a woman can cook.'

'And if she can't?'

'No problem. If I love her enough. If I love her very much, I take lessons myself. Or we eat in a different restaurant every night. Or order in pizza. Or starve. So long as I'm with her, it won't matter in the least.' He rose to his feet. 'So, now I shall make us coffee. Then we can talk. Begin at the beginning, Gini. You first.'

And so Gini recounted to him, one by one, all the events of the past two days. She told him about Frank Romero, and the buttons on his jacket; about her meeting with Lise, and the things Mary had said; about the strange postcard signed 'Jacob' from McMullen, and about the circumstances of that long and frightening Monday night.

Pascal listened intently and quietly, smoking a cigarette. When she came to the question of the telephone call, of that whispering obscene male voice, his face paled with anger. 'You have that recording you made? Get it now.'

She left the room while he listened to it. When she returned, she had never seen him so coldly furious, she thought at first – and then she remembered; there had been another occasion, one other occasion: he had looked like this during that brief final interview with her and her father in the Hotel Ledoyen in Beirut. There was the same mixture of contained loathing and contempt in his eyes, and the same fury in his voice.

'Who is that man?' He slammed his hand down on the table. 'Who is it? Is it Hawthorne? I can't tell – can you recognize the voice?'

'No, I can't. I don't think it's Hawthorne. I'm not sure . . . '

'You should never have discussed that telephone sex story with him – never. What were you thinking of! *Why* did you do that?'

'Pascal, he asked me what I was working on. I couldn't say *him*, could I? I had to think fast. I just blurted it out. Then I thought it could be useful. To see how he'd react . . . '

'Oh for God's sake.' He gave a gesture of despair, then controlled the anger. 'Never mind, never mind. It's too late to undo it. If it isn't Hawthorne, then who is it? Romero? Could it be him?'

'I don't *know*, Pascal. But I'm sure Romero is involved. He was on leave the weekend we went to Venice. He could have been there. I'm sure the buttons on his blazer were identical to the one you found. He's worked for the Hawthorne family for years. He served under Hawthorne in Vietnam, and – what's the matter, Pascal?'

'Nothing. Wait. I'll explain later.' His face took on an odd and closed expression. 'Go on. Tell me what happened yesterday – up to and including the dinner for Hawthorne . . . '

Gini gave him her account of that day, of her conversation with McMullen's former tutor, Dr Anthony Knowles, of her discoveries at the escort agency, Jason Stein's remarks, the presence of S. S. Hawthorne at the dinner, and his son's speech on that occasion.

'And he mentioned Vietnam, during that speech? Jenkins told me. What did he say exactly?'

Gini told him. She gave Pascal a puzzled look. 'And so he said the reporting of that war helped to end it. He said it changed America . . . Pascal, what is this? Why are you harping on Vietnam? It's twenty years since the war ended, it can't have any relevance to this.'

'Maybe not.' Again his face took on that guarded expression. Gini did not prompt, but continued her story, stopping just short of her return to her flat, and her discovery of Napoleon. She did not want to re-experience that.

'And so,' she said finally, 'I'm sure it was McMullen in the park and in the museum. I think he had hoped to speak to me, but Frank Romero was there too. The number he gave me is an Oxford number. For a moment

I thought it was the number I called for Dr Knowles. But it wasn't. I checked this evening. Two different digits. I *wish* I could understand these messages he's been sending, the books, that postcard. But I can't. Still . . .' she paused, 'we can call that number tomorrow at noon. I'm sure we're close to finding McMullen, Pascal – or he's close to contacting us. That's progress, at least.'

Pascal frowned. 'Oh, you've made a lot of progress, I think. I'm beginning to see a pattern at last, in all this. Or perhaps two patterns, one the true one, and the other a reflection, designed to trick us, mislead us perhaps.' He rose and looked down at her thoughtfully, then held out his hand. 'Come upstairs,' he said. 'Let's sit by the fire there, and I'll tell you my side of things. It won't take long, and I don't want it to take long. You look exhausted. But if there's any chance that we really are close to McMullen at last – that we might actually get to speak to him, there're some things you should know first.'

'He isn't the man we took him for?'

Pascal shook his head. 'No,' he said slowly. 'No, I think not. Some of the information Jenkins obtained may be misinformation – it's hard to know. But one thing does seem clear. McMullen isn't just Lise Hawthorne's self-appointed protector. He lied to Jenkins – or lied by omission anyway. McMullen could be much more dangerous, and much more devious than we thought.'

Upstairs, Gini sat quietly and listened. Pascal spoke for several minutes. When he had finished, Gini gave a sigh.

'I begin to see,' she said. 'That fool Jenkins. Why wasn't he straight with us from the first?'

Pascal shrugged. 'Come on, Gini. You know what he's like. As a matter of fact, I revised my opinion of him this morning. I may not like him any more than I ever did, but he is tough, and he's not a fool either. Though I think he'd better watch his back.'

'All right, I was wrong. He's not the lackey I thought he was. But even so, why the hell couldn't he admit that it *was* Appleyard who first gave him the tip? I even

438

asked him, straight out and he *still* went on denying it.'

'Well, in his view, it wasn't an outright lie.' Pascal gave a dry smile. 'When he talked to Appleyard first, back in the autumn last year, all Appleyard had done was pick up on some of that Washington gossip. He'd heard Lise Hawthorne's health might be cracking up. He'd gone snooping around her London doctors and got nowhere—'

'That *isn't* all, Pascal,' Gini interrupted. 'James McMullen had actually contacted Appleyard. It was *Appleyard's* story. He was unwise enough to mention it to Jenkins, and Jenkins stole it. It was straightforward theft—'

'Of the kind that goes on in newspapers all the time.' Pascal's smile broadened. 'Come on, Gini. You know that. Anyway. Think. It wasn't as simple as that. All McMullen had done was tell Appleyard that he should stop chasing Lise's story, and take a good hard look at her husband. He'd hinted at infidelities, no more than that . . . '

'Fine. Maybe I'm missing the point here. It still sounds like theft to me. Tell me again.'

'Fine. This is the sequence. McMullen was playing Appleyard along. He must have heard about the enquiries to the doctors, so he *hinted* to Appleyard, but told him nothing specific. It's the first indication we have that McMullen isn't nearly as naïve as Jenkins thought. Then, unfortunately for Appleyard, he decided to pass the tip to Jenkins. And he mentioned the name of his source.'

'At which point, Jenkins licked his lips. Because he actually knew this man. So he saw right away that he could get to the story without Appleyard's help. In other words, he could ease Appleyard out.'

'True. But can you altogether blame him? Would you like to work on a really big story with Johnny Appleyard breathing down your neck?'

'No, I wouldn't. Especially if I were Jenkins. Jenkins would want two things – first, he'd want an exclusive, and second, if the story *was* strong, he'd want to syndicate – worldwide. Meanwhile, Appleyard would be on the phone busily selling it everywhere from Sydney to Toronto. That's how he worked. It made him rich.'

'Precisely. So Jenkins dispensed with his services. Apparently, it wasn't difficult. McMullen and Appleyard had spoken several times by then, and McMullen hadn't liked what he found. He was much happier to work with Jenkins, an Englishman, an ex-schoolfriend. So McMullen stopped returning Appleyard's calls – or so Jenkins thinks. We know differently. McMullen *must* have remained in touch with Appleyard. It was Appleyard who found Lorna Munro for him. And it was McMullen who organized the delivery of those first four parcels. So McMullen was playing some kind of double game from day one . . . ' He paused. 'What's more, I suspect Lise Hawthorne helped him, and is continuing to help him. Even now.'

Gini frowned. 'Now? That's not what she said to me. She said she hadn't spoken to him since he left London. She was in tears, Pascal. She was shaking. She said we had to find him, and she didn't even know if he was still alive or dead. I had the strong impression—'

'Yes?'

'I thought she was afraid he'd been killed. And that Romero might have been used to kill him, that very weekend. It was only an impression . . . '

'Then think about this.' Pascal leaned forward. 'Lise tells you she is *not* in contact with McMullen, yet she could have made a phone call from that wine bar, and she arranged to meet you this morning, in Regent's Park. She never showed but McMullen did. Doesn't that strike you as an odd coincidence? You think he's been running in the park behind her house for the past three weeks? I certainly don't. Come on, Gini. That meeting had to be set up.'

'Not necessarily. She said she always used to meet him there, at that time. He might have gone there in the hope of seeing her . . . '

'All right. Maybe. Not proven. But I know what I think. There's collusion here.'

'But we *know* that, Pascal – to some extent. We *know* Lise and McMullen are involved in this together. He's trying to help her. You heard that first tape.'

'Yes. McMullen the knight errant.' He gave her a cool glance. 'So the man is in love with her, obsessed with her, determined to free her from that sadist husband of hers. Well, maybe. I'm prepared to believe that. Except McMullen has conducted a campaign against Hawthorne before. A long time ago. A very very long time ago.' He rose. 'Do you have that postcard you were sent, Gini? The one signed "Jacob"? Let's just compare the handwriting, shall we, with these photocopied letters I have here.'

'Letters? What letters?'

Pascal had picked up the large manila envelope Jenkins had given him earlier that day. From it, he took a thick sheaf of papers, some of which, Gini could see, were press clippings. He extracted three single sheets of paper, and passed them across. Each was a copy of a neat, handwritten letter, sent from a London address. Gini stared at them. They were addressed to John Hawthorne, they were signed by James McMullen.

'The *dates*.' Gini looked up at him. 'Nineteen sixty-nine. Nineteen seventy. Nineteen seventy-two – that's the year Hawthorne was first elected to Congress. Pascal, what *is* this?'

'You can see for yourself. They're requests – markedly polite requests – for information about Hawthorne's period of military service in Vietnam. It's a matter of record anyway, and the letters were duly and politely replied to by one of Hawthorne's secretaries. I have copies of their answers here, too.'

'I don't understand, where did Jenkins get this?'

'From Melrose's security contact. Which means they could have come from anywhere – American Security, British Security, or even John Hawthorne himself. They could be forgeries, of course. But the match to the writing on your postcard is exact, isn't it?'

'Yes, yes, it is.' Gini stared at the postcard, then the letters. 'But I don't *understand*, Pascal. Why should he be making enquiries about that – and at that time? It's – when? After he left Oxford—'

'And before he joined the Army. Yes.'

'In that missing period you mentioned? How *strange*. But why? What possible connection can it have with this story now? Appointments with blonde call-girls and the Vietnam *War*? It doesn't make sense.'

'Not to us, perhaps, but I think it makes sense to McMullen. Look at this, Gini.' He passed her another sheaf of papers. 'Those are copies of letters McMullen sent to an American senator, in nineteen seventy-one. A Senator Melville – he's dead now. At the time, he was head of the Senate armed services committee. He was a well-known opponent of the Vietnam War, a dove from way back. McMullen bombarded him with letters and evidence. The letters mention enclosures, and none of the enclosures is here. Just the letters. He's trying to persuade the senator to launch an investigation into the conduct of the American military during the autumn of nineteen sixty-eight, in particular to the events that took place in a small village . . . ' Pascal hesitated, and again she saw that closed expression come into his face.

'The name of the village was My Nuc.'

'My Nuc?' Gini looked up, and frowned. 'That's familiar, but I can't remember why.'

'That's not surprising, Gini. You were two years old in nineteen sixty-eight. You were – what – seven or eight when the war ended? I was in my teens and when I saw this, the name meant nothing to me. But My Nuc was celebrated, briefly. It became one of the examples of American heroism. A platoon was cut off, and holed up under Vietcong fire, for nearly two weeks. One lieutenant particularly distinguished himself. He was decorated as a result of his actions there. His name was John Hawthorne.'

Again, Gini saw that closed expression come upon his face. She stared at him. When she saw the sympathy, and the hesitation in his eyes, she had a second's foreboding.

'I don't understand – how do you know all this, Pascal?'

'Because when McMullen started raising questions about what exactly had happened at My Nuc, when he started alleging that what actually happened there was very different from the official military accounts, the senator was able to give him a very straight and a very dismissive answer. The letter he wrote is there, Gini, in front of you. You see? It's an angry letter. No rape, no pillage, no murder – and how can the good senator be so sure?'

Pascal handed her a press clipping, a long article. 'He can be sure that the military's version was accurate because there was an independent witness, a journalist, who was with Hawthorne's platoon the entire time. The journalist wrote up the events afterwards. It wasn't the best of his despatches, nor one of his most famous ones, but along with many others written that year, it helped win him a Pulitzer prize.'

Gini stared at the papers in front of her. She closed her eyes. For a second, she heard Hawthorne's voice just a few nights before: *holed up in a fox-hole together for three days under fire; he ate my rations and I drank the contents of his whisky flask . . . I'm not sure if it was courage or blind stupidity . . .*

She looked up, white-faced, at Pascal. She watched this story loop, re-shape, and close in on herself. She saw the concern and the anxiety in Pascal's eyes. She threw the papers down on the floor.

'Then McMullen's a liar,' she said. 'I don't give a damn what he alleged then – and I'm not sure I give a damn any more what he's alleging now. He's suspect, Pascal. You said that yourself.'

'Darling, that *isn't* exactly what I said—'

'You just listen to me.' She had risen, and was now trembling with agitation, Pascal saw. 'If McMullen was suggesting my father would be party to any kind of cover-up in that war – he's wrong, that's all. I know you hate my father, I know what my father is. I don't have any illusions. I know he drinks too much, and he boasts, and he got lazy later on. But when he was younger, even now . . . He would never lie, Pascal. He would never distort the truth.' She hesitated. 'He may not have been a very good husband to Mary, or a very good father to me, but he *was* a fine reporter. The best – he was the best!'

There was a silence. She turned away, and Pascal could see her fight to regain control. Quietly, he bent and replaced the papers in their envelope. Then he put his arms around her. The one thing he intended to avoid now, at all costs, was any conflict about her father. He had made that mistake once, twelve years before, and he did not intend to make it again.

'Fine,' he said quietly. 'Then let's take it from there. If McMullen was deluded all those years ago about Hawthorne – and how he even came to be interested in those events I can't imagine – then he can be deluded again. Or deliberately smearing Hawthorne for some reason. Either way . . . '

'Yes?' She turned back to him with new hope in her face.

'Either way, it helps us when we finally meet him. Which I expect to do very soon.'

'Tomorrow?'

'I think so. Let's wait and see. Gini . . . ' He broke off, and looked down into her face. 'You do know how much I love you?'

'Yes. I do.'

'Then come to bed.'

At nine the next morning, Gini and Pascal were in the last of a sequence of taxi-cabs which they had used to transport themselves the short distance downhill from Hampstead to St John's Wood. At Pascal's request, the taxi cruised first one way up a street near Avenue Road, then another. Several of the large houses in this street had 'To Let' signboards outside, to which Pascal paid close attention.

The taxi-driver dropped them off near the Wellington army barracks. It was then nine-twenty. Minutes later, Pascal and Gini were in the company of an estate agent, viewing one of the houses they had passed earlier. It was a miniature St John's Wood palace, fully furnished and in very bad taste. Pascal looked at Gini, and repressed a smile. They had been upstairs, and were now back in the drawing-room.

'Decision time, darling,' he said. 'What do you think?'

Gini gave him a sidelong glance. She fingered the curtain-ring on her wedding finger, crossed to the rear window and looked out.

Beyond the ruched pink silk blinds she could see a terrace with bright white rococo garden chairs. There was a large built-in barbecue, a stretch of lawn, an unlikely white statue, and a fence. Beyond the fence, fifty feet away, were the white stucco walls, the Gothic porch and windows of the assignation house to which Lise Hawthorne had directed them. It was, as Pascal had quietly pointed out to her before they set foot in the agent's office, the perfect place for him to use that coming Sunday. The perfect place for photographs. From the rear windows the driveway and the Gothic porch were clearly visible. From here, anyone entering or leaving Hawthorne's house was in direct view.

'Darling, I'm not sure,' she replied in a dry voice. 'It's nice, but it's a bit over-looked at the back.'

Pascal gave her a repressive glance. He turned back to the agent, who was not looking hopeful, and who was avoiding the moment when he would have to mention the rent. 'I'm afraid my wife's a bit hard to please,' Pascal said. 'We must have looked at fifty houses this last week. This might be possible but we'd have to clear up all the formalities quickly. I'd want to be in here by Saturday morning. It's Thursday now. If that could be arranged . . .'

He left the sentence unfinished, and the agent blinked. This particular house had been vacant for eighteen months. The area was over-loaded with better houses than this, at a much more realistic rent. He began to talk, and talk fast.

'Well, of course, I'm sure that could be arranged. As you can see . . .' he waved a vague hand at oceans of pink brocade, 'the house comes very comprehensively equipped. Three months' rent in advance, naturally, and we would have to check references, of course, but that's just a formality. I can personally arrange for all the services to be switched back on, gas, electricity, telephone—'

'Banker's draft,' Pascal said. 'This morning. And I foresee no problem with references. What is the exact rent?'

The agent swallowed. He fixed his eyes on the pink blinds, and named the figure. He waited for the expostulations, the cries of disbelief. None came. Both husband and wife were now at the window, looking out at the garden at the back.

The agent studied this young couple, who had arrived at his office on foot. The woman, whom he judged attractive, was casually dressed. Her husband was wearing a black leather jacket and blue jeans. His hair was long by the agent's standards . . . The agent gave a little sigh. Once upon a time he had been able to assess his clients' income bracket from their dress. These days, as he had learned from bitter experience, it did not do to rely on such signals: the ones who looked like down-and-outs often turned out to work in movies or rock music, and to be annoyingly rich. Rock music, in this case, he decided. Too much money and no sense. They returned to his office, where a deal was swiftly struck. He ushered the couple to the door, all smiles. There, curious still, and a little envious, he asked, 'Rock music, would it be? I feel I know the face . . . '

The Frenchman gave a modest gesture. He smiled. He said, 'How did you guess?'

Half an hour later, the agent's telephone rang. On picking it up, he heard a man's voice, an American voice, 'Is Mr Lamartine still with you, by any chance?'

The agent explained that Mr Lamartine had just left.

'Oh. I was hoping to reach him there. This is his assistant . . . He said he'd call me if he decided to take the house so I could speed things up at the bank. I guess it slipped his mind. He has a stack of meetings all morning, too . . . '

'Well, he has decided,' the agent replied. 'I have the details here. I'm just processing the paperwork now.'

The assistant, who sounded efficient, then took all the rest of the details. 'Thanks for your help,' the American said.

They were back in the safe Hampstead cottage by eleven.

'One hour to go, then we telephone,' Gini said.

Pascal nodded. Gini could see that he too was tense. 'I'll make some coffee,' he said. 'I need to think.'

'Can you not think without the caffeine, Pascal?' She smiled.

'Sure I can. But I think a whole lot better with it. I'm going to make a list. Every actual *fact* we know about McMullen. No rumours, no suppositions, just the facts.'

He disappeared downstairs to the kitchen. Gini heard the whirr of the coffee-grinder. She sat down at the table in the sitting-room of the cottage, and made sure she had the telephone close. She took off her watch and put it next to the telephone; she watched the second-hand sweep.

On the way back to this cottage, she had stopped off at a bookshop in Hampstead, hoping to purchase the same three books, if not the same editions, as she had seen in McMullen's flat. She laid her purchases out on the table in front of her. She had been able to find *Paradise Lost*, and she put her own copy next to the identical edition found in Venice; next to that she put Carson McCullers' *The Ballad of the Sad Café*, and finally her last purchase. *The Oxford Book of Modern Verse* had not been in stock, but as an afterthought, she had bought a large British road atlas. In the back of it was a section with street plans for thirty major cities, Oxford among them. She took out the piece of paper with those numbers, found inside the frame of Lise Hawthorne's photograph, and the Uccello postcard from 'Jacob'. There was no time now to consult Mary's friend: she would make one last attempt at decoding this herself.

The page–word ploy did not seem to work, even with one component missing; one of the problems with this puzzle, she realized, was that there were so few numbers. The final message must be surely very short. She sat for a while with paper and pencil, making little headway. She flipped the pages of McMullen's copy of Milton's poem, until she found the place Pascal had said was marked. She could remember working on this poem at school. She could even remember, though vaguely, this particular passage. It came from Book One, and described the state of mind of Satan, after his fall from grace:

> For now the thought
> Both of lost happiness and lasting pain
> Torments him

Satan, by that point in the poem, had been expelled from paradise, and she could remember the description of his great fall. But this did not help her either. Feeling defeated, she bent over the road atlas, and traced the lines of Oxford's famous streets. Here was McMullen's college, Christ Church; here was the High Street, and the Carfax intersection and St Giles . . . And then she saw it, away to the south and west, on the edge of the central area of the city dominated by the colleges: Paradise Square, and Paradise Street.

Suddenly she understood McMullen's message: it did not refer to pages, but to book *titles*, and the reason it was brief was that it was an *address*, a brief address. Quickly she drew a page toward her, and began to write. As Pascal returned to the room with the coffee, she held up the page triumphantly.

'I've done it,' she said. 'Look, Pascal. He did leave a message for us in his apartment. He *did* refer me back to it on that postcard. It was much simpler than I thought! The number "3" at the top, refers to the three titles; the next line down, 6/2/6, refers to the number of words in each of the three titles. And the final line, 2/1/6, gives you the order of words to *extract* from the titles. *Oxford – Paradise Café* . . . you see?'

Pascal looked at the paper and frowned. 'If you think that's simple, I certainly don't. We don't know there's any such place anyway.'

'There's a Paradise Square. There's a Paradise Street. I'll bet you anything you like that in one or the other there's a Paradise Café as well. Watch . . . '

She picked up the telephone and dialled directory enquiries. She made one further short call; when she put the telephone down, she had a smile on her face.

'Don't tell me you're right?'

'You bet I'm right. Paradise Café, on the corner of Paradise Square . . . '

'He doesn't exactly believe in making things easy, does he?'

'If he made it *easy*,' Gini retorted, 'then someone else could have got there before us. As it is, he'd obviously decided it didn't work – hence the meeting in Regent's Park, and the noon telephone call . . . ' She broke off, and looked down at her watch. 'Twenty minutes to go, Pascal. Did you write your list?'

'Yes, I did. I put down all the information I obtained on McMullen from the Army, where he served and when. Then I put down all the things that don Anthony Knowles told you. The fact that McMullen was one of his best history students, that his studies were assisted by his gift for languages – he spoke fluent French and Italian, wasn't that what Knowles said?'

'That's right. The Italian as a result of the time he spent there as a child, with his family. The French, from school, I guess. Plus McMullen spent part of the nine-month gap before going up to Oxford and leaving school, doing courses at the Sorbonne in Paris. Knowles mentioned that. He gave it as an example of how dedicated McMullen was.'

'Fine. So McMullen was a keen student. A hard worker.' He paused. 'And the dates this took place?'

Gini shrugged. 'You know the dates, Pascal. We've looked at them before. McMullen went up to Christ Church in the Michaelmas term of nineteen sixty-eight, that's the fall of nineteen sixty-eight. He'd left school at the end of the previous year, after obtaining the scholarship to Oxford. He had a nine-month gap. He moved on to those

449

courses at the Sorbonne . . . Does this help, Pascal?' She glanced towards the telephone.

'Maybe. The spring of nineteen sixty-eight – that was a very significant time for a young man to be taking courses at the Sorbonne. *Les événements*, Gini – the protests and the street fighting, that whole outburst of radicalism. That took place in May, nineteen sixty-eight. I wonder if McMullen was drawn into those events, that's all. I'm trying to understand why a young man who leaves Oxford very suddenly the following year begins writing letters to American politicians about the Vietnam War. That war was a catalyst for his generation, sure. But it still seems so *odd* . . . '

He turned away, frowning, and began to pace the room. Gini drew the telephone towards her. It was now six minutes to twelve.

'I don't think we should think about that now,' she said. 'It's taking us away from the central issue here – and that's Hawthorne and the appointments with those blondes.'

Pascal gave her a quick glance. He knew why she said that, and he could tell she would resist any aspect of this story which curved back towards that war, and her own father's past.

'Maybe,' he said, in a thoughtful tone. 'Maybe, Gini. But there's a darkness here, right at the heart of this story. And I want to understand where that darkness begins.'

'Look, let's just get to *see* McMullen and talk to him first.'

'Very well.'

Pascal moved away, and sat down. He could sense the sudden tension between them, and it alarmed him. There was an issue between them, he knew; it had always been unresolved and remained unresolved still. It concerned her father's behaviour in Beirut, and Gini's willingness to obey him then, the excuses she continued to make for him, even now. For an instant, Pascal saw the figure of Sam Hunter as a continuing barrier between them. Even now, he thought unhappily, he and Gini would never agree about the nature of that man.

And now, just when Pascal had believed him safely distanced, back in Washington, with little day-to-day influence over Gini's life, Sam returned to haunt them. He emerged from the shadowy recesses of this story they were working on: Hawthorne, Romero, Hunter, McMullen. All their pasts intersected at one point: Vietnam. He passed his hand wearily across his brow. It was better to say nothing, to wait. Perhaps Gini was right, and that aspect of this story would prove marginal. He looked at his watch. The hands were moving to twelve.

'Now, Gini. Make the call,' he said.

Gini did so. It was answered on the first ring by a voice she recognized. She did not identify herself, and neither did he, but it was Dr Anthony Knowles. He came straight to the point.

'Thank you for calling,' he said. 'Jacob is anxious to meet you and your friend. He asks whether you know a restaurant here which would be suitable. He says he's *entitled* to ask. Do you know of one? Don't mention the name.'

'I do know of one,' Gini paused, and thought quickly. McMullen's clues had been more than a trail, she saw, they had also been an aptitude test.

'I selected it from a list of three,' she continued carefully. 'It's a rather *heavenly* place.'

'Fine.' Knowles sounded amused. 'Be there at six this evening. Wait outside, not inside. If there are any difficulties, call this number at nine tonight. After that, it will not be operable. You understand?'

'I understand.'

Without further words, Knowles hung up the phone.

Pascal was watching her intently. 'That was McMullen himself?'

'No. That ex-tutor of his, Knowles.'

'Interesting. So he has some kind of assistance. I thought so.' He paused. 'The Paradise Café? What time?'

'Six. We wait outside.'

'Good.' Pascal moved swiftly away. He began checking his camera bag. He picked up his thick address book, and

Gini could see that familiar return of energy, of speed. 'I need to make a few phone calls first, then we leave. On my bike we can be there in under an hour.'

'On that bike? Sixty miles? Pascal, do we have to? The meeting's not until six. We don't need to leave yet.'

'Yes, we do.' Pascal gave her a sharp glance. 'There are three things we know about McMullen for sure. One, he's devious. Two, he's clever. Three, he's commando trained. So I intend to check out the area before we meet him. I want to see this restaurant, and this Paradise Square, before it's dark.'

XXVI

When they reached Oxford, it was bitterly cold, and dampness pervaded the air. By the time they had completed their checks of the area, a low thin mist was rising from the river. As darkness fell, they took up their position in Paradise Square; the mist had thickened and was forming wisps and patches of a yellowish hue. It made the light from the few street-lamps a haze; it would clear momentarily, then descend again obscuring their view.

This area of the city, although close to the colleges, was run-down. Near by were the pens and yards of the cattle market, and to the north, just beyond the square, the high walls of Oxford prison. It was shabby and dispiriting, and almost deserted. Few cars and no pedestrians passed.

Most of the houses here were used as small offices; they were closed now and dark. The only source of light and cheer, were the steamed-up windows of the Paradise Café, just across from where they stood on the far side of the square.

At three minutes to six, Pascal gave her an encouraging glance, took her arm, and drew her across to the restaurant. It was small. The menu in the window showed it served primarily Greek-Cypriot food. Inside there were two waiters, and groups of students. Gini shivered. She looked to right and to left. No-one approached. The minutes ticked by.

She could sense Pascal's tension in every line of his body as she huddled against him for warmth. A chocolate-bar wrapper blew along the pavement in front of them, making a scuffling sound. The mist drifted; it felt clammy against her skin. At six-fifteen, Pascal began to show the signs of impatience she had known were inevitable. He swore.

453

'I've had enough. Don't tell me this is another damn wild-goose chase.'

'Wait, Pascal. Give it time.'

'It's goddamn freezing here.' He turned to look through the café windows. 'You think he could be inside?'

'He might be in the room at the back, I guess.' She peered through the glass. She could not see well through the steam and condensation, but all the customers looked far too young. 'Come on, Pascal.' She squeezed his arm. 'Think of something else. Stop counting seconds. That always makes it worse. Tell me some more of those famous facts of yours. You've been thinking of them all afternoon, I could tell.'

Pascal gave her an amused glance; she felt some of his tension subside. He turned back to peer through the window.

'Oh, very well. Learn to control this impatience of mine, yes? Fine. Well, I can tell you his postings – they're interesting. Three tours of duty in Northern Ireland, two stints in Germany. A spell in the Middle East. He served in Oman—'

'Yes, I did,' said a quiet voice behind them. 'In nineteen seventy-eight. Would you both get in the car?'

Pascal swore, and Gini swung around. The man who spoke had materialized silently from behind them. As before, he was wearing a black track suit and black running shoes. This time, the hood of the track suit was down.

The car he had indicated was parked across the square, a black mud-splattered Range Rover. Gini had noticed it, and it had been empty, as they passed.

'We can't talk here,' McMullen said. 'I haven't much time. Would you get in the car?'

It *was* McMullen. As he spoke, he turned slightly and lamplight gleamed palely against his fair hair. For an instant, she glimpsed his features. His face was stronger and more determined than it had appeared in the photograph. She felt Pascal hesitate; she turned and walked across to the car.

She sat in the rear, Pascal in the front. McMullen

negotiated Oxford's complex one-way system at speed.

He said, as they were leaving the outskirts of the city, 'It'll take about fifteen minutes to get there. It's not far.'

After that he did not speak, and Pascal did not prompt him. Gini guessed that, as she was, Pascal was concentrating on their route. In the dark, at speed, along a succession of winding, unlit country roads, this was not an easy task. Gini edged towards the window. At the next junction, when McMullen was forced to slow down, she caught one quick glimpse of a signpost in the headlights. She just had time to read the name of the next village.

It was enough. She kept her eyes on the route. She thought: *Of course – Oxford, Oxfordshire. The place where John Hawthorne has his country home.* The manor house he had bought had been extensively photographed; she had checked its precise location when they'd begun this story. Unless she was very much mistaken, it was his entrance gates they had just passed, and his estate wall now beside the road to their immediate left.

Wherever McMullen intended to take them, she was certain it would not be far.

She was correct. They followed the high stone wall that bordered the Hawthorne property for two miles, turned sharply right, then left onto a steep rough track. The going was rough, but the Range Rover's four-wheel drive coped with it easily. Three miles, she estimated, the track continuing to rise the whole way, and curving to the left. When McMullen stopped the car, they were in a clearing flanked by woods on three sides. In front of them was a small building, its windows unlit. To their left, and clear of the trees, the ground fell away in a deep bowl.

They climbed out of the car, and Gini moved towards the gap in the trees, Pascal close behind her. McMullen stood watching them both.

'There's no moon yet,' Gini said slowly, 'but I'm sure the view is spectacular from here. You must overlook John Hawthorne's land. Can you see his house, as well?'

'I can see the south terrace, with binoculars. Yes.'

McMullen spoke evenly. He unlocked a door behind them, waited until they were all inside and the door was closed behind them, then switched on the light.

They were standing in a small, sparsely furnished living-room. It seemed to be the only ground-floor room, except for a small lean-to kitchen at the back. An estate cottage once, Gini guessed, built to house a gamekeeper or forestry staff from one of the estates bordering Hawthorne's. There was a stone floor, a bare table, a few sticks of cheap furniture, a pile of newspapers in the corner. The windows were boarded up, and it was bitterly cold. McMullen crossed the room and lit a paraffin heater.

'I'm sorry – it's spartan,' he said. 'I like living that way.'

'You're living here now?' Gini said quickly.

McMullen sat back on his haunches. His face took on a guarded expression. He adjusted the flame of the heater. 'I stay here occasionally. From time to time.'

'Your London apartment isn't spartan,' Pascal said, watching him closely. 'Quite the opposite.'

McMullen gave a dour smile; he straightened. 'No. But then I'm very rarely there.' He paused. 'When exactly did you obtain entry there?'

'Last Wednesday. A week ago yesterday.'

McMullen gave a small quick nod, as if this satisfied him in some way. 'And Venice? You must have gone there.'

'Last Sunday.'

The question was put evenly; Pascal gave it an even reply. He volunteered nothing further; McMullen noted this, Gini saw, and appeared to approve. There was a brief silence. She watched the two men assessing each other, feeling their way.

'I intended originally to meet you in Venice.' McMullen spoke suddenly. 'That plan had to be changed. The reports of Appleyard's death there were in the papers yesterday. They don't make it clear when he died.'

He kept his eyes on Pascal, who replied, still evenly, 'Judging from the state of his body when we saw it, around ten days before.'

'I see.' There was a pause. 'And the other man with him?'

'He had died more recently. One or two days before.'

'Fine.' McMullen showed not a trace of emotion. He continued to ignore Gini, as if she were not even in the room.

'Fine?' she said now, sharply. 'It wasn't fine! It was unnecessarily cruel.'

'So I understand from the reports.' McMullen spoke crisply. He turned to look at her for the first time. It was a brief, cool inspection. He at once turned back to Pascal.

'I'll say this once to get the obvious question out of the way. I did not kill them. I met Appleyard only once, in October last year. I never even heard of his friend. If Appleyard had done as I told him, and stayed out of all this, he would still be alive. He meddled, and, as a result of that, he died.'

'That seems harsh,' Gini said quickly, stung by his tone.

'Very possibly. There's no point in pretending I feel any great sympathy. I disliked the man.'

'You *used* him,' Gini said, in a quieter tone. 'You also used Lorna Munro. Did you know she was dead too?'

There was a brief silence. McMullen looked from her to Pascal.

'Is that true?'

'Yes, it is.' Pascal paused. 'She was killed within a few minutes of speaking to me. In Paris. She was knocked down by a Mercedes.'

'Deliberately?'

'Oh yes. I witnessed it.'

For the first time, McMullen betrayed some emotion. There was a momentary concern in his face, then his mouth tightened.

'Yes, well. I regret that. Obviously I regret it. However, perhaps it proves to you what is at stake here, and exactly what I have been up against. Hawthorne tried to have me killed in December. It was then, of course,' his voice became dry, 'it was then it became urgent to disappear.'

457

'You know Hawthorne was behind the attempt?' Pascal said levelly. 'What method did he use?'

McMullen gave him a cool assessing glance. 'The man he employed was that henchman of his and his father's. Frank Romero. I think we can deduce he was acting on instructions, don't you? And the method was an obvious one, given I was in London then. It was at Bank tube station, in the rush hour. Romero attempted to push me under an oncoming train.' He paused. Neither Pascal nor Gini spoke. McMullen gave a small shrug. 'I've had training. He failed. Since then . . . I've had to be careful. Otherwise I would have found more direct ways of contacting you. And I would have done so before now.'

He stopped abruptly. He gave them both another of those blue measuring looks.

'I'm sorry. We should stop fencing around. I realize now I've overlooked something very obvious. You're journalists, and I'm not used to dealing with journalists. I'm assuming that when I tell you the truth, you'll believe me. I should know better. It's a mistake I've made before . . . '

He hesitated then, for the first time, and Gini realized that beneath his crisp questions and curt replies, McMullen was as tense as strung wire. He gave a sigh, and glanced around the grim, cold room.

'I'd set great store by this meeting,' he continued, his tone now much less calm. 'When I finally was able to meet you – what I should say, and do. I hadn't expected suspicion, or hostility. My mistake. Christ . . . ' He turned away with a sudden violent gesture. 'Christ! I should have known.'

The alteration in his demeanour had been very rapid: one minute, calm control; the next, strong emotion, which Gini could see he was fighting to subdue. She and Pascal exchanged looks. She made a quick covert calming gesture of the hand, and Pascal nodded.

'Look,' he said to McMullen in a more neutral tone, 'you must understand. The allegations you've made are very serious. If they became public they'd destroy a man's whole life and career. We're not hostile to you, we're trying to find out the truth, that's all.' He paused. 'Listen, it's very cold in here. Gini's freezing, and so am I. Could we have some tea, something warm to drink? Then we could sit down, and go through this carefully from beginning to end.'

McMullen looked at Pascal, then nodded. 'Very well.' He glanced down at his watch. 'But we must be quick. I don't have a great deal of time.'

He made his way out to the lean-to kitchen at the back. After another brief exchange of glances, Pascal followed him out there, and leaned in the doorway, blocking McMullen's view back into this room. Gini, who had known Pascal wanted to case the place as soon as he mentioned tea, began to move swiftly around the room. It told her a little, but not as much as she had hoped. The pile of newspapers dated back six months: some were local, some national. Flicking quickly through them she saw that several were open at reports of John Hawthorne's public activities, meetings and parties he had attended, or speeches he gave. The previous August, Hawthorne's Oxfordshire gardens had been opened to the public in aid of a hospital charity: the page reporting this event, with photographs of the gardens, had been cut out from that week's issue of the *Oxford Mail*.

In the corner of the room, near the door to the kitchen, was a green rucksack which might have been army-issue. It was laced tightly closed. Near the empty fireplace, on a shelf, was a half-full bottle of whisky and glasses. There was an ashtray with some unfiltered cigarette stubs in it. Next to that were two yellowing paperback novels, one by Frederick Forsyth, the other by Graham Greene. Nothing else: no pictures, no carpets, just furniture which looked as if it might have been abandoned with the house. The hiss of the heater, and the heavy oily smell of burning paraffin. Spartan, indeed.

There was one other door in the room. This she opened silently, easing up the latch, any noise she made drowned by the hiss of the gas stove in the kitchen beyond. It led, as she had expected, to a narrow flight of uncarpeted stairs. One room on the ground floor, and one above, presumably where McMullen slept.

She edged back to the warmth of the paraffin heater. How odd that McMullen should have chosen to bring them here, she thought. This was a place for a stake-out. But if McMullen actually *was* staking out Hawthorne, this was surely the last thing he would want them to know.

When Pascal and McMullen returned, McMullen's manner seemed to have thawed. He looked more at ease now, as if he had warmed to Pascal, if not to her. She watched him, as he adjusted the heater, then moved to a chair. He was several inches shorter than Pascal, with a slight but strong build. From his economy of movement, and his posture, she would have guessed at an army connection even had she not known his background. His training was evident in the way he spoke as well, and as he began speaking now, that impression deepened. He gave no sign of the brief emotion he had showed earlier. He began as if this were a military briefing which needed to be conducted with brevity and speed. He drew out a packet of strong unfiltered cigarettes, and lit one. He leaned forward.

'I'll make a suggestion. As I said, I'm not used to talking to journalists. If you agree, I'll tell you my side of this story, and we'll keep the questions until the end. It will save time. Then if you have questions, I'll do my best to answer them. Do you agree?'

The question was addressed to Pascal, who nodded.

McMullen drew on his cigarette. He watched its smoke curl upwards from his hand. After a pause, he began speaking again.

'First, the essential background. You may or may not know: I have been a close friend of Lise Hawthorne for many years. We first met shortly before I joined the Army, in nineteen seventy-two. This was long before her marriage, obviously. I spent a summer in Virginia with the Grenville family. At the time, I was recovering from an illness. The Grenvilles were old friends of my mother's, and distant cousins of Lise's. I needed a spell of rest and recuperation, at least my mother thought I did, and the Grenvilles very kindly took me in. Lise was seventeen then. It was her débutante year. That photograph in my flat – the one I used – was taken then. Lise and I liked one another immediately. We became, and remained, close friends.'

He paused, and glanced at Pascal.

'I should say this now. I want you to be perfectly clear. When I say friends, I mean friends. Lise and I have never been lovers. You understand?'

Pascal said nothing; he nodded. McMullen went on.

'It was and is a very deep friendship, however. I have always admired Lise. She is one of the few – the very few – genuinely good people I have ever known. She has shown me great kindness in the past, and I would do almost anything to return that kindness. Lise knew that. The opportunity finally came last summer.'

Gini glanced at Pascal as he said this, and McMullen, who was sharp-eyed, noticed at once.

'I should also make one other thing clear,' he continued. 'You may well feel I'm biased against Lise's husband – and perhaps I am. I don't believe that bias clouds my judgement, though you may. For what it's worth, I have never liked John Hawthorne, and I advised Lise against marrying him. I think he is a dangerous, cold, arrogant man – very like his father, in fact. I think he is manipulative, motivated by self-interest and ambition – a man utterly without principles, a politician of the worst sort. He is also highly intelligent, and gifted, which makes his behaviour far worse in my view. Lise used to claim . . . ' he hesitated fractionally, 'that I was mistaken. She would admit some of his faults – the arrogance, for instance – but she would say there were mitigating factors, his upbringing and so on. At the time she married him, she was passionately in love with him. At that time, I knew a great deal more about her future husband than Lise realized, and I had to decide whether to tell her what I knew, or remain silent. In the end, I decided to stay silent. Lise was so persuasive on his behalf, so full of his virtues, that it seemed cruel to speak out. In the first place, she would have refused to believe me. In the second, it would have brought our friendship to an end.' He paused, looking away from them.

'I convinced myself that Lise could be right, that Hawthorne might have changed. So I said nothing. I very much regret that now.'

There was a brief silence. McMullen extinguished his cigarette. He looked at Pascal.

'I'll come back to my reasons for distrusting Hawthorne later. I should like to leave those to the end. After all,' his voice became embittered, 'I know why you're here. I know why Nicholas Jenkins was so keen on this story in the first place. I may be unused to dealing with journalists, but even I know how fast they react to a hint of sexual scandal, to the idea of an eminent man leading a secret sexual life. Am I wrong?'

The question was sharply put. Gini said nothing, and allowed Pascal to reply. The bitterness in McMullen's tone interested her: it was as if, with a certain contempt, he was deciding to tell them what he believed they wanted to hear.

'No, you're not entirely wrong,' Pascal replied in even tones. 'I wouldn't say it was the only kind of story to which reporters reacted swiftly, but never mind that now. We can come back to that later, as you say. Go on.'

'Very well.' McMullen leaned back in his chair and began to speak more rapidly. 'During the years of her marriage I saw Lise less often than before. I was in the Army, she was in America, I had frequent postings abroad. We used to write to each other, from time to time. About four years ago, after I left the Army, I met her in Italy briefly, where she was staying, without her husband, with friends. I saw her on a few other occasions over the next three years, when she and Hawthorne were visiting London. I had dinner with them – and I noticed nothing amiss. Once Hawthorne was first posted here, I saw them more frequently. Lise invited me to various embassy dinners and parties, that kind of thing. I would meet Hawthorne, exchange a few words. He was always perfectly civil. Then, last July, I was invited for a long weekend at their country house here. And that was when I finally realized something was terribly wrong.

'I could see straight away that Lise was under strain. It was some weeks since I'd last seen her, and in that short time, it was as if she had wasted away. She'd become painfully thin, she scarcely ate, she seemed nervous around her husband, she had these sudden inexplicable changes of mood. It was very difficult to spend any time alone with her. The house was full of other guests; Hawthorne himself was there. On the second day, I managed to get her away. We went for a long walk in the grounds. Miles and miles. It started raining. Lise began crying. It was terrible. Finally, she broke down. She told me everything.' He broke off suddenly. His face had darkened, and he gave an angry gesture.

'What you have to understand is this, his treatment of Lise may have worsened, but it's been going on for years. A chain of other women, mistresses, secretaries. He slept with another woman the night before their marriage. He was faithful to his new wife for precisely five days. Lise knows that not because anyone gossiped, but because *he* chose to tell her. He's been systematically stripping Lise of any confidence she ever had, telling her she was stupid, inept, comparing her to the other women he had affairs with, boasting about his one-night stands . . . '

Again that violent emotion had surfaced. Gini watched as McMullen fought to get it back under control. He lit another cigarette, his hand shaking a little as he lifted the match, then abruptly he rose to his feet.

'I'm sorry. This isn't easy for me. I need a drink – and I hate to drink alone. You'll join me?'

The question, Gini noted, was directed solely at Pascal.

'Yes, we will,' Pascal said, and McMullen checked himself.

'I'm being rude,' he said, addressing Gini this time. 'I apologize. It wasn't intentional. I don't find it easy

463

to discuss any of these things, particularly in front of a woman.'

He poured three measures of whisky, added water. He handed their glasses to Gini and to Pascal, and then sat down. He glanced at his watch again.

Pascal said, 'Just how worried are you about the time? We do need to get this clear, you know.'

'Of course. It's all right,' McMullen said hastily. 'I'm coming to the point where you will already have quite a lot of information.' This time he made an effort to include Gini in his next question.

'You know there were rumours circulating in Washington, before they came over here? You know that Appleyard finally picked up on those rumours?'

'Yes,' Gini said, 'we do.'

'Fine.' He gave a curt nod. 'What you may not know is who started those rumours. It was John Hawthorne himself. It was part of a long campaign to undermine Lise.'

He stopped to light another cigarette, then continued. 'For years, the first six years of their marriage, Hawthorne believed his dominance over Lise was so strong that no matter what he did, he could get away with it. He knew Lise was too devout a Catholic ever to contemplate divorce. He knew how much she loved her children. He believed he could rely on that, and on her pride. Then there was a change. Around four years ago, Adam, their younger son, became ill.'

He paused, still trying to fight down emotion. 'He nearly died. I think something snapped in Lise then. She might have gone on enduring it all, the humiliations, the cruelty, the boasts – but after Adam's illness, she finally saw that she had to protect her children from this man. She began to see at last – at least this is what she tells me – that Hawthorne's influence on his children could ultimately be as harmful to them as *his* father's had been to him. So she gave Hawthorne an ultimatum. Either he changed his ways, or she would leave him and live apart with her children. She didn't threaten him with exposure – nothing like that. Just separation. And Hawthorne swore to her he would change.'

McMullen gave them both a cold glance. 'You can imagine how long that lasted. A few months. Hawthorne was panicked into resigning from the Senate – I think because he feared scandal, and for the first time in his life he was genuinely afraid of what Lise might do. But being a reformed man didn't suit him at all. He was drinking heavily; there were violent quarrels with Lise. Then, he stopped the drinking and took up with the women again. Only there was this new variation, an added twist. The mistresses and one-night stands weren't enough any more. That's when the monthly appointments with the blondes began. But he covered himself. He began on a new strategy. That's when the rumours about Lise's mental health began to circulate too . . .

'It was clever of him, you have to admit that.' McMullen looked at them closely. 'Lise was genuinely very near to breakdown then. Hawthorne told her, if she tried to leave him, he would get custody of the children. He would claim she was an unfit mother, mentally unstable. Both he and his father had a long interview with her, and they spelled it out very clearly. They showed her a list of witnesses who'd take the stand against her – servants, maids, secretaries, friends. Some of those Hawthorne and his father could bribe, others they simply leaned on – and they had years of experience in doing that. Hawthorne's father's proudest boast was that there was no-one he couldn't buy.

'Beyond that specific threat,' McMullen continued, 'the scheme was an effective one. Hawthorne was protecting himself in advance. If, in future, Lise ever did speak out against him, whether in a custody battle or just to friends, few people would believe her. Anything she said would be dismissed as paranoid, as deluded. And, of course, the saddest thing of all was that the more he pressured her in this way, the worse her health became. I personally believe that he and his father planned it that way: they were trying actually to drive her insane. After all, from John Hawthorne's own point of view, better an unstable wife in a mental institution than a smashed-up presidential career. That way Hawthorne got everyone's vote of sympathy – a sick wife could be turned to his advantage, do you see?'

'Up to a point.' Gini leaned forward. 'Except by then, Hawthorne's career was on hold. He'd resigned from the Senate. It was before he took up the posting here.'

'Hawthorne's career has *never* been on hold,' McMullen replied sharply. 'You have to understand that. It's fundamental to the man. He may have decided it was wise to take a back seat for a while, until he'd dealt with the question of Lise. He may have decided it was better to get her away from friends and relations in America, yes. But he has *never* abandoned his central ambition – and neither has his father. You can be quite certain that his father has been involved in all this, every step of the way. If Hawthorne ever did hesitate as to the wisdom of committing his wife, the mother of his sons, to a mental institution, you can be sure the father would be there at his shoulder, saying go right ahead, it's the best way.'

'Is that what you think?' Pascal leaned forward. 'You seriously think Hawthorne intended to have his wife committed?'

'I don't think it. I know. He threatened her with it several times. He's already selected the hospital. It's called Henley Grange. It's private and it's twenty miles outside London. Hawthorne gave them a sweetener – a donation of fifty thousand dollars, last year.'

'How do you know that?'

'Lise saw the cancelled cheque. Moreover, a doctor affiliated with Henley Grange has been treating Lise since last autumn. Hawthorne called him in personally. And you know when he did that? Two days after I first spoke to Appleyard. Which was also two days after Hawthorne started tapping my phone.'

He leaned forward, his face now strained and intent. 'Do you see? You have to understand the timing here. Last July, when Lise told me her story, I was appalled. I couldn't believe that any man would act in that way

– ritualizing his sexual encounters, then forcing his wife to listen to descriptions of them month after month. If anyone other than Lise had told me that story, I might not have believed it. But it *was* Lise – and Lise never lies. And, as it happened, it echoed other things I'd heard about Hawthorne long before. Hawthorne was always a sadist. He was a sadist as a very young man.'

He broke off, hesitated, then looked at Pascal. 'I want you to understand how desperate I was. That July, I tried so hard to persuade Lise to act, but she wouldn't, she was too afraid. I could see why Hawthorne was undermining her with that rumour campaign, and I was certain it would intensify. I was right. Last September the rumours finally filtered down to a journalist who was prepared to use them – Appleyard. That's when he started calling up Lise's doctors in London. When her doctors informed her, Lise knew she had to fight back, and fight back hard. So she and I began to plan. We were careful, but not careful enough. I think Hawthorne probably suspected that she had spoken to me in the summer. I'm sure that's when he began his surveillance, using Romero and others. There are three of them in London now who used to work for Hawthorne's father. Check them out some time.'

He took a deep swallow of his whisky, which seemed to steady him. 'Anyway. As soon as Hawthorne realized what was happening, that he was actually under threat of exposure, he acted fast. He had us both watched all the time. He made that donation, he called in those doctors, and they filled Lise up with Christ knows what – stimulants, sedatives, tranquillizers. Injections before breakfast, lunch and dinner, injections every night before bed. Pills, capsules; nurses in constant attendance. It was terrifying. I managed to get Lise to see a doctor I knew—'

'Ah yes,' Pascal said evenly. 'The one your sister recommended. It was mentioned on the tape you gave Jenkins.'

'Was it? I don't recall. He took blood tests. I wanted proof of what they were doing to Lise. He was horrified.

I have his name and number – I knew you'd need it. It's here.' He took a piece of paper from his jacket pocket, and passed it across. Pascal glanced at it, then put it away without comment.

'Go on,' he said.

'Obviously,' McMullen's manner became more hesitant now, 'it affected Lise's behaviour, that cocktail of drugs. I could see it affecting her as the weeks went by. It made her forgetful. Sometimes I'd talk to her, and she'd be nervous, febrile, very strung up, talking too fast. At other times, I could hardly get through to her at all. I would manage to meet her, and,' his face contracted, 'it would be like talking to an automaton. As if she were in a trance. I can't tell you how appalling that was. But there was nothing I could do. I had to wait. We had to be able to prove Hawthorne actually met those women every month, the way he said he did. I thought, maybe, if we could just trace one of those women, persuade her to talk, *pay* her to talk if necessary, that would be enough. But Nicholas Jenkins wouldn't agree. He said if we could get that testimony, fine – but it wasn't enough. If it came to a court case, and it could, that kind of witness was too unreliable; call-girls always went down badly with juries. The lawyers at the *News* wouldn't even pass the story for publication on that basis. There would have to be more. The meetings had to be documented, photographed . . . ' He paused, and looked at Pascal. 'That's when he suggested using you.'

'Really?' Pascal gave him a long, measured look. 'It was Jenkins who originally suggested my name?'

'I think so.' McMullen gave a quick dismissive gesture. 'I forget now exactly who mentioned you first. I knew of your work, in any case. When I was in the Army, I'd seen your war photographs. I'd admired them. I knew very vaguely of the kind of work you did now . . . '

He broke off. Pascal said nothing more. Gini watched McMullen closely. He had, she thought, just told his first lie. Up until then she had been convinced that everything he said he deeply believed to be true. Yet he lied about something minor, almost irrelevant: why?

468

McMullen looked at his watch again. He rose to his feet, adjusted the heater, replaced the whisky bottle on its shelf. He turned back to look at them.

'So,' he said, in a new brisk way, 'that brings you virtually up to date. I was waiting for Lise to discover the address of the house Hawthorne intended to use, next time. He said nothing in October, nothing in November. Oh, he discussed the women – what he liked to make them do, how he'd selected them, from where—'

'How did he do that?' Gini asked. She sprang the question, and McMullen fixed her again with that slow, blue stare.

'I thought you might have discovered that. By now.'

'Possibly. But I'd like to know your version.'

'He used agencies, and contacts of his own. He had them send round photographs. At least, that's what he told Lise. Neither she nor I know if that is true. He showed her some pictures once, of some of the girls. He asked her to select one of them for him.' His voice was ice-cold. 'That was fairly typical of the way he operated. He hit Lise when she refused.'

'Did he often do that?' Pascal asked coolly. 'Was physical violence often used?'

McMullen flushed scarlet. 'Yes, it damned well was. Do I have to spell out what he's put Lise through? It sickens me even to think of it. If you think I'm going to be cross-examined on that sort of detail . . . I won't be. It disgusts me. You understand?'

'It isn't irrelevant,' Gini said quietly. She glanced at Pascal, who nodded. 'Neither of us wants to press you on this. But you have to understand, all this is hearsay. All right, maybe that doctor can confirm that Lise was on a regimen of different drugs. But even that, in itself, isn't conclusive. You must see, the central difficulty here is lack of proof. Lise could have administered those drugs herself, quite willingly. We only have Lise's word for any of this – the former infidelities, Hawthorne's physical and mental cruelty, even the stories of his sexual encounters.' She paused. 'We've been working on this for just over a

469

week now, and we've put together a lot of evidence. But most of what we have is circumstantial. We still have no absolute proof that Hawthorne actually did make monthly appointments with these blondes.'

There was a long silence. McMullen was very angry, she could see, and fighting to control that anger. He gave her a cold, hostile look.

'I see. You're calling Lise a liar, in other words?'

'No. I'm not calling anyone a liar. I don't doubt for a moment the sincerity of what you say. But you must surely see—'

'No, I do not see,' he interrupted, his voice rising. 'You're here to provide the proof, to document those meetings. That's your damn job, not mine. Lise can do nothing. She's a virtual prisoner now. *I'm* a virtual prisoner. I can't stay in one place for any length of time. I have to keep moving on. I have a few friends to help me—' He broke off. 'Like the person you spoke to today. I cannot risk using a telephone. I have to watch my back all the time . . . I *tried* to contact you before – you do realize that, do you? Not the postcard I sent – I actually risked coming to your flat late at night.'

'Three days ago? That was you?'

'Yes. It was. I came to the front of your house. The lights were still on . . . ' He hesitated. 'And there was someone else there moving around at the rear of the house. I could hear them. I had to leave. I've tried my damnedest to help you both on this but there's a limit to what I can do. For Lise's sake, I have to stay alive.' His voice had now become heated; Pascal slid his next question in under this angry and indignant tirade.

'In that case,' he said, 'why come here, so close to Hawthorne's country home? Isn't that a little unwise?'

The questions brought McMullen up short. He gave them both a hard look. 'I'm careful. This suits my purposes. I have friends near by. Will you excuse me a moment?' He checked his watch again as he said this, and moved swiftly to the outside door. He went out, without further explanation, and closed it behind him.

In silence, Pascal and Gini looked at one another. She said, in a low voice, 'Do you believe him, Pascal?'

Pascal glanced towards the door. He was listening intently for sounds outside. He gave a noncommittal gesture, and said very quietly, 'I'm not sure.'

'He's very volatile.'

'Yes. And very tense. But that isn't surprising, in the circumstances.' He frowned. 'I'd like to know why he's so anxious about the time. What's he doing out there?'

'God knows. I can't hear a sound.'

'I can.' Pascal raised a finger to his lips. 'He's just outside the door now.' He lowered his voice to a whisper. 'Play it by ear, Gini. We know one thing. He hasn't finished. There's more.'

When McMullen returned to the room it was at once evident that he had calmed. His manner was now much as it had been when they'd first arrived – brisk, cold and impersonal. He made no further pretence of including Gini in any of his remarks. He ignored her completely, and addressed himself to Pascal.

'I'm sorry,' he said. 'There was something I had to check. I've had time to think, as well. I realize, I should have shown you this at once, before I began speaking about Lise.'

He crossed the room, bent, and deftly unlaced the army rucksack. From it, he took out a heavy folder. He straightened, and looked directly at Pascal.

'I should have realized,' he continued. 'I value discipline. I'm so used to military discipline that I can forget there are other kinds as well. Journalists have their own disciplines. You have them. I've seen the results in your case – and as I said, I admire them. I saw the pictures you took in the Falklands War, and you captured what it was like out there.' He paused, and gave an ironic gesture. 'You're very good at photographing hells . . . '

Pascal gave him a sharp glance. 'You served in the Falklands? With the Parachute Regiment?'

'I'm sure you'll have already checked that. Not with the Parachute Regiment, no.'

His jaw clenched, and they could both see that any further probings into McMullen's military career would go unanswered. He opened the folder. 'Because you're very good at that,' he continued, 'I'd like you to look at these pictures. They were taken in Vietnam twenty-five years ago. Before your time.'

He moved across to the table, and began taking a series of black-and-white photographs from the folder. He laid them neatly down on the table, like playing cards, with as little emotion as if he had been dealing cards. Pascal moved across. Gini half-rose, hesitated, then sat down again in her chair. Both men now had their backs to her.

'The name of this village was My Nuc,' McMullen continued in the same flat efficient tone. 'This is what was left of it after John Hawthorne's platoon withdrew. Before they arrived, fifty people lived in that village. All of them non-combatants. Most of them were women and children. There were some elderly men. This gives you an indication.'

He continued to slap down pictures on the table. 'One middle-aged woman and one twelve-year-old boy escaped and survived. The other forty-eight were all killed. The village huts were burned. Even the babies were killed. This girl here . . . ' He put down another picture.

'She was the sister of the woman who escaped. Before they did that to her,' he pointed down at the picture, 'she was raped fifteen times. Every man in the platoon took his turn. The sergeant was Frank Romero. He found a novel way of holding her down. He drove those pegs through her ankles and her hands. John Hawthorne stood next to her, and watched. He was the senior officer there, he was in command, so I imagine he could have gone first, had he wanted to do so. He didn't. He chose to go last. When it was over, she was half-dead anyway. You see how dusty the soil is? Well, that's what they used next. They filled her nose and her mouth with sand then they finished her off with a shot in the back of the neck. While they did that, John Hawthorne watched, the whole time.'

McMullen moved off a little way. Pascal continued to stare at the photographs. Gini did not move.

'I know you'll have witnessed similar obscenities,' McMullen continued, his voice still flat and quiet. 'They happen, in war. When they happen, there are disciplinary systems designed to deal with them. But in this case, no disciplinary action was taken. There was no court martial, nothing. But that's not surprising, because no accusations were ever made. Hawthorne's platoon was finally air-lifted out from a place three miles away. Those actually there were the only people who knew what had taken place at My Nuc – and as long as they remained silent, they were safe. If any evidence was ever discovered on the ground, it could always be blamed on the Vietcong. Originally, there were thirty-two men in that platoon, together with one journalist. But they'd been cut off, and under heavy fire for days. By the time they moved in on My Nuc, the journalist was still alive, and so were fifteen other men, including Hawthorne and Romero. The last two are still alive, obviously, and the journalist is too. But would you like to know what happened to those thirteen others? I'll tell you. Five of them were subsequently killed in action. That left eight. All eight returned to America in due course, and within a short time of their return, every one of them died. Some of them survived a few months back home, and a couple of them survived for over a year. But they all died eventually. An automobile accident in Louisiana, an overdose in Washington State, one died in a shooting incident in a gas station, another from a faulty blood transfusion, one drowned. Not a single one of them died from natural causes. They died in California, Missouri, New Jersey . . . You can check. All their details are in this file.'

He put the folder down on the table next to Pascal.

'What does that suggest to you? That Hawthorne and Romero both lived – and the rest all died? It suggests to me that Hawthorne and his ever protective father lived up to their reputation for efficiency, and that John

473

Hawthorne reaped the benefit. That I cannot prove. But this,' he gestured to the photographs, '*this* can be proved. Hawthorne's was the only unit in that area at the time. And the woman and the boy who escaped would testify. They saw this happen. They are still both alive.'

Pascal heard emotion begin to break through in McMullen's voice. He continued to look down at the pictures, which indeed were similar to others he had seen in the past, and to others which he himself had once taken: they were close, very close, to the images which rose up in his dreams. He felt a profound pity for McMullen then, to have nursed and pursued this all these years.

He looked across at him. 'Tell me,' he said quietly, 'what is your connection with this?' He gestured to the pictures. 'You can't have been more than twenty when this happened, and you can't have been in Vietnam.'

It was not the most honest of questions, given the information he already had, but McMullen seemed unaware of that. He was gazing away across the room.

'It was nineteen sixty-eight. I was eighteen,' he said. 'That year I was in Paris first, then Oxford. The raid on My Nuc actually happened while I was at Oxford. My first term.'

'And your connection? There must be one,' Pascal said gently.

McMullen's mouth tightened. He jerked his face away. 'I knew the woman in those photographs. The woman Romero killed. I had never met her sister – the one who escaped. But I was able to make contact with her, later, in later years.'

'Would you like to tell me how you knew the woman here?'

'No. I wouldn't. I don't want to discuss it any more.'

'All right. Then would you like to tell me who took these photographs?'

'His name is in that file. He is Vietnamese, obviously. It was his job to document that kind of atrocity. His unit

474

arrived there two days after Hawthorne's platoon pulled out. He's still alive also. He now lives in Ho Chi Minh City.'

'There were other witnesses?'

'To the aftermath? Yes. Their names are also there.'

'Have you made any attempt before to make this allegation public?'

'Yes, I have. I wrote to several American senators, towards the end of the war. When the war was over, I made one further attempt. I approached a newspaper.'

'And you weren't believed?'

'No. They didn't even make any investigation, except of the most cursory kind. They told me the pictures came from a suspect source – the former enemy in other words. Hawthorne was a congressman by then. No. I wasn't believed.'

'Anyone else?' It was Gini who spoke now. She rose. 'Why didn't you make contact with the journalist who was cut off with that platoon? He was a living witness, after all—'

'I did make contact with him.' McMullen met her gaze with a cold blue stare. 'I wrote to your father three times. You can ask him. He replied once, to the final letter. He informed me I was wrong. The next time I wrote, the reply came via his lawyers. I didn't write again.'

There was a silence. Pascal quietly began to gather up the pictures and return them to their envelope. Gini continued to look straight at McMullen.

'Why did you never mention this aspect of the story to Jenkins?'

'Because I knew what would happen if I did. I'd be dismissed as a lunatic, the way I was before. Who gives a damn about something that happened twenty-five years ago in some little village on the other side of the world?'

'Oh, I see. Whereas if you came to my paper with a sexual scandal about an eminent man, everyone would leap to attention – is that it?'

475

'Didn't you?' McMullen replied coldly. 'Didn't Jenkins? Didn't Appleyard?'

'Did you plan it that way?' Gini's voice had sharpened, and Pascal swung around.

'Gini . . . ' he began, on a warning note, and put a restraining hand on her arm.

'No. Let's just take a closer look at this . . . ' Gini pushed his hand aside and faced McMullen. 'You fed us precisely the kind of story designed to make us sit up and pay attention. It was lurid enough. You then lent credence to that story by organizing that whole parcels fiasco, on which Pascal and I wasted an immense amount of time, and as a direct result of which three people died. Why? What was the point of that if it wasn't just to wind us up further? You deliberately made it look as if Hawthorne might have sent those parcels—'

'Gini.' Pascal moved between her and McMullen. 'Not now.'

'This is pointless. And I don't have the time.' McMullen was already moving away.

Gini thrust herself between him and the door. 'Then you can damn well make the time,' she said. 'We've waited long enough for this meeting. Doesn't it occur to you that we might like to ask some questions? Or are we just supposed to accept all this because you tell us it's so? So far, you've produced the name of one doctor, and that's all. You've produced photographs that could have been taken anywhere in South-East Asia at any time—'

'That's *not* all I've produced.' McMullen had come to a halt in front of her, Pascal just to his side. 'You haven't even looked at the other evidence in there. There are statements, testimonies, eye-witness accounts.' His voice was choked with emotion. 'What does it take to convince you people of *anything*? You've witnessed what Hawthorne is. You've witnessed three deaths. Do you need any more?'

'Stop this.' Pascal moved swiftly between them. 'Can't you see? You're both wrong and you're both right. This achieves nothing—'

'No. Nothing at all,' McMullen interrupted. He attempted to push Pascal to one side, but Pascal held his ground. 'I realize now. I was a fool to believe either of you would help – least of all her.' He gestured angrily at Gini. 'You're like every other damn journalist I've ever met. Cynical. Blasé. You wouldn't recognize the truth if you saw it with your own eyes. I'm wasting my time. We're leaving. Now.'

'No. We are not leaving.' Pascal moved Gini to one side, and stood blocking the door. His voice was suddenly very cold. 'You can listen to me first, before we do. It's not our job to help you publish allegations. It's our job to discover the truth. And we've been trying to do that, for eight days. You have no right to speak to Gini, in that way. You know what she's been through this past week? Obscene phone calls at night, her apartment ransacked, and yesterday, when you had her chasing around the museum—'

'Don't, Pascal. Leave it. There's no point.'

'Oh, but there is.' Pascal swung back to look at McMullen, his eyes angry and his face set and pale. 'You think someone feels cynical, blasé, do you, when they're threatened in that way? Sent handcuffs anonymously. Then sent further identical parcels. Parcels that contain a pair of shoes that fits them exactly? Or a black silk stocking? Or has a man on the phone in the middle of the night when the lights have failed, talking filth, describing what she's wearing, at the exact moment he calls? You think Gini takes that in her stride, just dismisses it? Well, think again. And don't speak to her that way.'

There was silence. McMullen stepped back. He gave a gesture of bewilderment.

'Shoes? Stockings? What phone calls? I don't understand. What happened while we were at the museum yesterday?'

'Someone broke into my apartment, again.' Gini spoke flatly, and turned away. 'I have a cat. I had a cat. They strangled him. Then . . . they hung him up, on a hook on the back of the door. That's what they did. Someone did. And Pascal's right. When I found him, I didn't feel

477

blasé. You know what I felt?' She rounded on McMullen again. 'I felt angry. The same way I felt when I walked into that Venice apartment and saw the way two men had been killed. I could have backed off from this damn story any time I chose. So could Pascal. But neither of us did. Why in hell do you think we're here now? Because we do want to know the truth. And because neither of us intends to give up until we do.'

McMullen had moved further off as she spoke, though he listened intently. When she had finished, he hesitated, then turned away. He bent and re-laced the rucksack, moved across and turned off the heater.

'I'm sorry,' he said in a stiff way. 'I knew none of that. I had nothing to do with it. I sent the four parcels as an interim measure. A way of giving you a trail, a lead, a way of keeping you both on the story, until I could make contact with you. I had no idea what the repercussions would be, and I had no idea then that it would take this long to see you. I'm sorry, but I've told you all I know. There's nothing more I can add. I have no astonishing proof to produce. I give you my word that everything I've told you about John Hawthorne I believe to be true. And now I have no more time. I'll drive you both back to Oxford. I have to go.'

He spoke in a cold, clipped, final way. It was evident that further argument would be wasted. He moved across to the door, switched off the lights, then opened it. He had parked his car so it faced back down the slope of the track. When they were inside it, he slipped the gears into neutral and allowed the car to coast down to the road without lights. There, he switched them on, and started the engine. Only when they were beyond Hawthorne's village, and approaching the main road back into Oxford, did he speak again.

'You said you had questions,' he began. 'Ask them now.'

Gini was about to speak, and leaned forward to do so, but Pascal restrained her with a quick touch of the hand.

'I have a question. When Jenkins first suggested Gini for this story, did you know who her father was?'

'Not at first, no. I noticed the similarity in the name – but it's a common enough surname. Then, later on,' he glanced back at Gini, 'Jenkins mentioned that you had indirect links to the Hawthornes, through your stepmother. He said you were American. Finally he mentioned your father's name.' He paused. 'He was trying to sell me on the idea of using you. I was opposed to the idea of a woman working on it. I'd told him so.'

'And when you realized who Gini was, why didn't you block the idea? You must have known then that you intended to produce this evidence.' He indicated the folder, which McMullen had handed to him silently, as they walked out to the car. 'It must have worried you, that connection, surely? You must have known that Gini would react badly to the suggestion that her father was part of a cover-up?'

'Of course it occurred to me. But Jenkins said she never saw her father. He said they were estranged, that they hadn't been in contact for years. By the time he mentioned all this, events were moving fast. It was mid-December. I had to make a decision quickly. Besides, the writer seemed less important at that stage. What we had to do first was get the photographic proof of Hawthorne's activities. Once it was *proved* what kind of man he is, I thought any honest journalist would be prepared to investigate him and his family properly – expose it all, right back to those events in Vietnam. That's what I believed. Until tonight.' His voice hardened. 'Now, of course, I'm beginning to see that I was wrong.'

Gini leaned forward between the two seats.

'In that case,' she said quietly, 'I'll spell one thing out for you. If we ever prove your current allegations about John Hawthorne, if there proves to be any truth in this story about blondes, I won't stop there, and neither will Pascal. We'll go back and investigate everything. I'll take Hawthorne's past apart. Believe me or not – I don't give a damn. But this matters to me. Hawthorne is an American

479

politician. I'm an American. Born in the USA. I care.'

McMullen did not answer her. She saw his eyes flick up and fix on her in the rear-view mirror. He shifted gears fast, and took them up onto the dual carriageway into Oxford, a different route, Gini noted, from the one he had taken before. She watched him make these manœuvres. She could just see the side of his face, and his hands gripping the wheel.

'Meantime,' she continued, 'there are some questions I want to ask. Concerning the sending of those four original parcels. Let's assume, for the moment, that the further two sent were part of a campaign of intimidation. But about those four—'

'Do we have to go over this?' McMullen sounded irritable. 'Why? Is it that important? I already told you, it was a stop-gap, a ploy. Why don't you concentrate on Hawthorne? He's your story, not me.'

'Even so. I don't understand Appleyard's exact involvement. Why did you use him to contact Lorna Munro?'

'I had to be careful with Appleyard,' he replied. 'I'd tried to get him off the story, but he wouldn't leave it alone. Once Jenkins was involved, I had to find a way of keeping Appleyard quiet. I hoped to hold him off until Jenkins's story ran. All he knew was that John Hawthorne had a weakness for blond-haired women. Appleyard thought Lorna Munro would be meeting Hawthorne, and that I'd report to him on Hawthorne's reaction.' He paused. 'I think "honey-trap" was his term.'

'I see.' Gini waited, but McMullen said nothing more. 'So you decided to use the parcels ploy, as you call it. When exactly?'

'After I left London. I planned it then. I've already told you. I can see it was foolish. I regret it now.'

'Did you plan it on your own?'

'Yes, I did. Why?'

'It just seems – *feminine* in some ways. I wouldn't expect a man to get the details as right as you did. The clothes Lorna Munro wore, for instance . . . '

'Oh, that was simple. I happened to be visiting my sister

earlier that month. I'd glanced at her magazines. I'd seen that issue of *Vogue*.'

Gini said nothing. *Another lie*, she thought, *more definite this time*; his sister had told Pascal she had not seen McMullen since the summer of the previous year.

'But it must have been quite difficult to set up, surely,' she pressed on. 'To obtain that coat, the necklace, the Chanel suit—'

'It wasn't that difficult. Not at all.' His eyes flicked again to the rear-view mirror. He pulled out into the fast lane. Gini waited.

'In that case,' she said, 'who called Chanel?'

'I'm sorry? Wait just a minute, will you? We're coming up to the Headington roundabout. The traffic's heavy here . . . '

He accelerated onto the Oxford ring road at the roundabout, and then turned off and began weaving his way through a network of backstreets towards the centre of town. He still had not answered her question. Gini glanced at Pascal, whose silence now she found surprising. His gaze was fixed straight ahead. He gave no indication that he was even listening to this at all.

'Look . . . ' Gini leaned forward again. 'I'm sorry to press the point, but I need to know. You see, I—'

'Leave it, Gini.' Pascal turned around. He spoke lightly, but he caught hold of her hand, and pressed it hard against his seat-back, as if in warning. 'Leave it, there isn't time.' He glanced across at McMullen. 'These details concern us,' he went on, addressing him, 'because we spent a great deal of time checking them out. I am now sure that Gini and I have been under surveillance from day one. I think our phone calls and conversations have been listened to, much of the time. Now that may explain certain aspects of what's happened, but it doesn't explain it all. Why, for instance, if you intended us to follow that parcels trail, did you send a parcel addressed to Venice, to yourself?'

'I told you. Originally, I hoped to meet you both there. My main desire was to keep you on the story, to keep you occupied, and keep you keen.'

'All right. Then how did Appleyard know about that apartment in Venice? Who gave him the address? He went there before you even *sent* the parcels.'

'I don't know.' McMullen seemed glad to have moved away from the question of Lorna Munro's clothes. He gave every appearance now of trying genuinely to help them. 'I never gave him that address, though the apartment is mine. I've rented it for years. I can only think that someone tipped Appleyard off, told him he might find me there. He couldn't trace me in London, he wouldn't leave the story alone. So he went there – and got himself killed.'

'So who tipped him off? This would have been just after Christmas. John Hawthorne?'

'Not in person, obviously. He would have used one of his men – Frank Romero possibly. The Palazzo Ossorio address was in Lise's address book – I know that. She's written to me there in the past. Years ago. Also, I had been in Venice. I went there directly I left England. Possibly I was followed, or traced. I'm not sure. I knew it was not safe to stay there long. I was only there a day, maybe a day and a half. Then I moved on.'

'Would you like to tell us where?'

'No.'

'In that time – at any point between leaving London and now – were you able to make contact with Lise? You must have been very anxious to see her.'

'I was desperate to see her, but it was impossible. No.'

McMullen's manner had altered the instant Pascal mentioned Lise's name. He seemed agitated, and his driving became slightly erratic. He almost missed one stop sign; he took a corner too fast. He then slowed, and turned into the heart of Oxford.

'Is that all?' he said. 'Are there more of these questions? We're almost back at Paradise Square now. I'll drop you near there.'

'Yes, there is one,' Pascal said thoughtfully. 'You and Lise Hawthorne – you may not like this question . . . '

McMullen stiffened. 'I've already told you,' he began, 'Lise and I were never more than friends. If you knew Lise you would understand. Once she was married – she believes in the marriage vows. No matter what I might have felt – anything other than friendship was ruled out, was out of the question entirely. I—'

'That wasn't what I was asking, or implying,' Pascal answered quietly. 'But you mentioned the question of bias earlier. You don't have to be a woman's lover to love her, after all. On that tape of your phone conversation, you address Lise in a way a man doesn't usually address a friend.'

'I know.'

McMullen gave a sigh. He slowed the car and, turning into the deserted High Street, he drew up outside All Saints' church. In the city, the mist was much thicker than in the country beyond. Fog drifted, then cleared. McMullen switched off the engine. There was a silence, and Gini realized that his hands were trembling. He was gripping the wheel more tightly to hide this. His back and shoulders were rigid with tension.

'I love Lise. I have loved her for many years.' McMullen spoke suddenly, in a low voice, his face averted from them both. 'The love I feel for her has grown with time, despite our separation. I've never told her what I feel – well, I don't need to, of course. Lise must know. She can hear it in my voice. Read it in my eyes. I've only ever loved two women in my life, so it's not an inconsiderable thing. But there's been no . . . no impropriety, ever. If Lise could divorce, if it weren't for her religion – but she can't. That's out of the question. So if you're suggesting that I'm using all this as a means of freeing Lise from her husband – anything of that nature – the answer is no. I may hate Hawthorne but I would never invent lies about him in order to better my own chances with Lise. I *have* no chances, not while he's alive. Besides,' he turned to look at Pascal, 'although you don't know me, and have no reason to believe me, I would never harm Hawthorne for personal motives. I'm not that kind of man.'

Here, suddenly, was the McMullen that both Jenkins and McMullen's sister had described. Gini looked at him intently. It was less naïvety, she thought, than a simple, and an impressive, conviction. He spoke with quiet sincerity, and she did not for one second doubt him. Pascal was similarly convinced, she could see that. He looked at McMullen as if, for the first time, he both liked him and felt a kinship with him.

'As to what my motivations are . . . ' McMullen paused. He was frowning now, staring into the misty street in front of him. 'I've asked myself that question, many times. I asked it twenty-five years ago, and I still ask it. For the sake of my own self-respect, if nothing else, I had to be sure why I felt it right to expose Hawthorne for what he is. The answer is that I want to protect Lise, and her sons. But beyond that, I have this old-fashioned belief in truth. I don't like to see a man in his position get away with years of lies.'

Leaning behind him, as he spoke, he opened the rear door. It was evident the interview was over. McMullen waited until they were both out of the car, then wound down his window.

'I've almost forgotten the most important thing of all.' He gave an agitated gesture. 'Your leads, if you have them. What you intend to do—'

Gini began to reply, but Pascal interrupted her fast.

'We have the leads we need,' he said. 'As far as next Sunday is concerned, we know the details of Hawthorne's assignation. We know how and where he chose the woman concerned. We know the time and place of meeting. I shall take the necessary photographs.'

McMullen seemed surprised. Gini, who was astonished, kept quiet. Pascal could be impressive when he lied.

'You're sure?' McMullen stared at him. 'Why didn't you mention this earlier?'

'Maybe I trusted you less earlier.' Pascal gave a shrug.

McMullen hesitated, then glanced down at the clock on his dashboard. 'I have to go. I must go . . . ' He paused. 'We may be able to meet again. After Sunday . . . ' An odd, sad expression came into his face. 'When this is all over. I hope . . . I should like you to know how much I owe you. I must have seemed very ungrateful, rude, earlier . . . '

That's all right,' Pascal replied. 'When it's over, we can meet. If thanks are in order, you can thank us then.'

'Then?' McMullen looked at him blankly. The fog drifted between them. Then McMullen recovered. 'Ah, then. When it's over. Yes, of course. I must leave now. Goodbye . . . '

Without further words, he closed the window, started the engine, and pulled away. They stood watching his car disappear into the distance. Fog obscured its tail-lights. The noise of its engine faded. Pascal gave a sigh, and looked at Gini.

'What a strange man,' he said. 'What a very, very strange man.'

XXVII

Pascal had parked his motor bike in Holywell Street, not far away. When they reached it, Gini said, 'So, Pascal, do you want to explain?'

'Why I stopped you from pressing those endless questions, you mean?' He smiled.

'Sure, that. Also why you lied to him at the end.'

'Not yet. There isn't time. I want to give McMullen a slight lead, but not too much. Then I want to see where he went.'

'Back to that cottage?'

'Yes.' Pascal helped her onto the bike. 'But not immediately. I'm pretty certain of that.'

He climbed up in front of her; Gini gripped him around the waist. It was now very cold, and the speed at which Pascal drove made it colder still. He retraced, almost exactly, the route they had taken with McMullen. He stopped on the outskirts of Hawthorne's village, put his arm around her, and led her down a narrow and deserted lane towards the village church.

The mist here was less dense than in the city, and there was now some intermittent light from a pale and waning moon. Pascal led her carefully across the graveyard, skirting the tombstones. He stopped at an ivy-clad wall, overhung with leafless trees on the far side, mounted it, and hoisted her up.

'I thought so,' he said quietly, his mouth close to her ear. 'An English manor house is usually close to the church. That's Hawthorne's place. You see those gates down there?'

Gini peered down into the valley below them. As her eyes grew accustomed to the dark, she could just make out the bulk of a house, and the pale line of a driveway with tall iron gates fronting the road. She nodded.

'Very well. Now, watch.'

They sat in silence, watching, for ten minutes. A breeze rustled the bare branches of the trees, owls called to each other in the distance. Clouds scudded across the face of the moon. Behind them, the church clock struck.

It was ten, and exactly on the hour, when she saw the beam of headlights in the distance, breasting the hill beyond Hawthorne's house. They were startlingly powerful in the dark of the countryside, cutting a passage through the blackness: two cars. They must have radioed ahead, because as they drew level with the entrance to the drive, the gates swung back. Two large Lincoln cars passed through, at speed; the gates shut. Instantly, a single low-wattage light came on at the front of the house below. Dogs barked. The two cars came to a halt.

Their lights were extinguished. Car doors opened and shut. In what light remained, and it was not a great deal, Gini saw a dark forming cluster of men bunch around one of their party, and move fast up some steps. The light went out, the door closed.

'Hawthorne?'

'Yes. Minus his wife. Wait.'

Pascal was no longer looking at the house. He was scanning the fields on the other side of the valley. Gini also stared at these fields. She could see their grey outline, the darker line of hedges, stands of trees staining the outline of the hill, and at the top of it the blackness of woods.

Five minutes passed; ten. Gini shivered, and Pascal glanced down at his watch. Fifteen minutes after the door had closed on Hawthorne, Pascal tensed. In the distance, from the darkness opposite, came a tiny flare of light.

A split-second and it was gone. Gini was not even sure she had seen it: it was deceptive gazing at a monochrome landscape, where shadows took on substance, and moonlight tricked the eyes.

Pascal helped her down from the wall. Standing there in the graveyard, he said, 'Did you see that?'

'I saw something. I think. I'm not sure what it was.'

'It was the flare of a match. We were lucky to see that much. McMullen is a professional. He won't prowl around the woods up there with a flashlight. He won't advertise his presence with bare hands or a white face. He won't stumble over branches, or step on dry wood and set the dogs down there barking. But McMullen's nervous, as I'm sure you noticed, and he's a smoker. So cautious, and then at the last moment, so careless. He lit a cigarette.'

Gini glanced back over her shoulder. 'You mean he was up there all this time, watching?'

'Of course. He's staking Hawthorne out. He didn't trouble to hide that.'

'He was waiting for Hawthorne to arrive? That's why he kept checking his watch? But how would he know Hawthorne's movements, when to expect him?'

'It's an interesting question. And I think I know the answer.'

Pascal took her arm. They walked back down the lane to the bike. The village was silent, and many of the houses dark.

They stopped, and Gini said quietly, 'Pascal, explain. Why did you interrupt my questions about Lorna Munro's clothes?'

'Why?' Pascal gave an impatient gesture. 'Because he was lying to us, that's why. Maybe not before, maybe not after, but he was lying then.'

'What little he said wasn't convincing, I'll give you that.'

'It was ridiculous. The dates didn't fit. It could not possibly have been as simple as he claimed. But I didn't want McMullen to know we questioned it. Much better to lull him, I think.'

'Lull him?' Gini glanced at him sharply. 'And is that why you lied to him at the end? To lull him? "We know how he chose the woman concerned." I wish it were that simple. Pascal, why did you do that?'

Pascal took a while to reply. He stood, frowning, looking along the winding village street. 'Instinct. Self-preservation,' he said eventually, with a shrug. 'Mainly because I wanted to see how he'd react.'

'He reacted with surprise and relief,' Gini said. 'Intense relief. That was genuine. He wasn't acting, I'm sure.'

'Exactly. I agree. Yet it was odd . . . ' Pascal stood for a moment longer, as if trying to puzzle something out. Then he turned back to her. He took her hands. 'You're freezing,' he said. 'Come on. It's too late and too cold to go back to London tonight. We'll find somewhere to stay in Oxford. Get something to eat. Then we'll talk.'

'All right.' Gini moved to the motor bike, then stopped. 'Why odd, Pascal? Just tell me that.'

'Because that lie I told him about our leads ought to have been the most important thing we told him tonight. If it were true, it would mean Lise's ordeal was almost over, that McMullen had achieved everything he hoped. So important – and yet he didn't ask a single question. What were our sources? How did we discover the address of the meeting-place? All those were pretty key questions, wouldn't you think?'

'Sure.' Gini frowned. 'I noticed that. I also noticed he never asked the most obvious question of all: whether *we* had seen Lise Hawthorne. He never asked that.'

'Because he knew the answer,' Pascal said. 'I'm sure of it. He *knew* we had talked to Lise. He knew she had given us the address of that house. He knew when you would be in Regent's Park yesterday. He knew Hawthorne was expected here tonight – and I suspect that when he left us, went outside, it was to use that mobile phone he has in his car. Hawthorne's estimated time of arrival was given him then . . . Come on, Gini – how did he know all these things?'

'He *is* in touch with Lise? Still? Despite denying it?'

'I'm certain he is. Somehow. And that's why he started

lying when you asked him about the clothes as well. Because Lise was involved in the sending of those parcels, even if she was here at the time. She helped him organize it – so why won't he admit that?'

'Because he's protecting her?'

'Possibly.' Pascal gave her a quick glance. 'But just bear in mind, Gini, that there could be less innocent reasons as well.'

'Let's start with that house he took us to,' Pascal said. 'You tell me about the living-room, then I'll tell you about the kitchen.' He paused, and checked his watch. 'No, wait a second. We might just catch the end of the news.'

He switched on the television in the corner of the hotel room. It was the late-night bulletin; there were a few minor items of news, then the final headline recap. An IRA bomb had detonated in Piccadilly Circus, killing two; EEC ministers had been meeting in Brussels; the Labour Party was calling for a reduction in interest rates; there were allegations that Arab-financed hit squads were operating in London. The weather forecast began; Pascal switched the set off.

'London's turning into the terrorist capital of the world,' he said. 'You want some more coffee, Gini?' She shook her head. Pascal poured himself another cup. Under a false name, they had taken a room at the Randolph Hotel. It was anonymous, comfortable, quiet. Pascal sat down in the armchair opposite her, and stretched out his long legs. He drank his black coffee in one gulp, and lit a cigarette.

Gini said, 'Pascal, do you ever let up? Don't you ever feel you'd like a rest?'

'On a story?' He seemed surprised. 'Certainly not. We have too many things still to do. We must talk to that Suzy woman from the escort agency. We must talk to McMullen's friend Prior-Kent. Besides,' he smiled, 'I'm like Hawthorne perhaps. You remember what that *New York Times* journalist said to you? Three hours' sleep a night. I can manage on that too, for a while. On certain occasions, nothing to do with work as such, I can make do without sleep altogether – for nights at a time . . . '

'I've noticed that. Just recently . . . '

'Darling, come over here. Sit beside me.' He held his hand out to her.

Gini smiled. 'You're sure? It might not be such a good idea . . . '

'No. You're right. You're right.' He dropped his hand. 'We should think first. Work first, I know that. It's just – sometimes I can't wait for this story to be over. When it is, finally . . . ' He hesitated. 'Gini, would you come away with me then? Come somewhere with me where we could be alone together, somewhere quiet, somewhere where we can forget all these things?'

'You know I will. And do you know where I'd like to go?'

'Name it and we're there. India? South America? A Caribbean island? The middle of some wonderful desert? That would be good. We could just pitch our tent in the middle of the sand-dunes and stay there all day and all night. We'd have camels, obviously. Oh, and a well near by. Maybe a few palm trees. And at night, we'd come out of our tent, and look up, and there would be millions upon millions of stars. You see the best stars above the desert.'

'No. None of those places. Despite the stars. I want you to take me where you always promised to take me. To Provence, to your Provence.'

They looked at each other, and Pascal's face became gentle. 'Then that,' he said, 'is exactly what we'll do. I'll show you my old house, and the farm near by, and the little church. We'll drink red wine in the cafés, and then we'll dance all night in the square . . . '

'In winter?'

'Winter, summer, spring, autumn. I don't care . . . '

He held out his hand to her once more. Gini hesitated, then rose.

'Ten minutes . . . '

'Fifteen,' he replied. 'I just want to hold you. Fifteen, I swear.'

★ ★ ★

An hour later, Pascal rose. He poured himself more coffee, and took it across to the window. He drew the curtain aside.

'I hope this fog lifts,' he said. 'We need to get back to London first thing in the morning.'

'We will. Meanwhile, work. Where were we? I seem to have lost track there . . . '

Pascal smiled. He crossed the room, and sat down at some distance from her. He lit a cigarette.

'McMullen's house,' he said. 'That's where we'd got to. The living-room. What did you find there?'

Gini told him. Pascal listened intently.

'Did you have time to check the newspapers?'

'Yes. They date back to July last year. That chimes with what he said. He's been collecting them, and noting the reports on Hawthorne since Lise first told him her story. Which makes me wonder, among other things, when and why he moved into that house.'

'He's watching Hawthorne, obviously,' Pascal said thoughtfully. 'Sometimes here, sometimes in London. He claims he was in Venice. I wonder where else he went?'

'Wherever it was, I think Anthony Knowles must have known. Maybe he helped him disappear.'

'The rucksack . . . was it laced closed?'

'Unfortunately, yes.'

'You wouldn't have had time to look at it anyway. And McMullen was listening, all the time we were in the kitchen.'

'Was there anything significant there?'

'Only two things. There was a stick of camouflage cream by the sink – he would have put that on his face and hands when he was up there in the woods tonight. But it was half used, which suggests that night-time surveillance of Hawthorne's property is something he's done before.' He paused. 'Then there were some shelves by the back door. Canned foods, some plates and cups. Plus a small container of gun-oil.'

'Gun-oil?'

'It's used to lubricate the barrels of guns after cleaning them.'

'You think he had guns – a gun – there?'

'Yes. I do.' Pascal was frowning. 'Think, Gini. We haven't paid enough attention to something very obvious here. One of those friends I talked to, you remember? He mentioned joining a shooting party with McMullen last August. And what was one of the things Dr Knowles mentioned to you on the telephone, when he was detailing McMullen's intellectual and sporting prowess? Cricket, rowing – what else?'

'*Shooting*! Rifle shooting. Of course. He did mention that. Competition shooting. McMullen was outstanding, both at school and at Oxford. His shooting ability earned him a blue.'

'Meaning?'

'It means he was good enough to represent the University at the sport. Pascal—'

'I know. I know. Let's take this slowly.' Pascal rose, and began to pace as he spoke.

'First, this man is an ex-commando. Then there's the details of that army career, which still don't add up. You remember what he said about the Falklands?'

'Yes. He was there, but not with the Parachute Regiment. I didn't understand that.'

'I'm beginning to wonder if McMullen moved across, from the Paras, to something much more secretive. The SAS, for instance. You join the SAS by invitation only, they often recruit from the Paras, and a man of outstanding weapons ability would interest them.'

'If he *was* SAS, we won't be able to check. Nothing. A blank wall . . .'

'Not necessarily. If he was part of an SAS team in the Falklands – you heard. I worked out there. I covered that war. And I still have contacts from it, too. I could try . . . Anyway.' He frowned. 'Let's go back to where we were. McMullen is an ex-commando – that much is certain. He has been, and presumably still is, an outstanding shot. The presence of gun-oil in his kitchen, suggests he keeps a gun. Now that I should be able to check. Whatever kind of weapons he has – shotguns, rifles, handguns, they have to be licensed. Tomorrow, I'll check that. Meanwhile,' he turned back to look at Gini, his face now intent, 'if he does have a gun there – in a place which is quite obviously a stake-out – what does that suggest, Gini?'

Gini hesitated. 'It suggests there's another way of interpreting this story,' she said carefully. 'It suggests McMullen could be the hunter, and the ambassador the hunted, the quarry.'

'Let's turn this story inside out, look at it from a new point of view,' Pascal said. 'McMullen is a man with a grievance against Hawthorne that goes back twenty-five years, to Vietnam. McMullen loves the woman who becomes Hawthorne's wife. Let's say the marriage *is* an unhappy one – maybe there even are some infidelities on Hawthorne's side. So, together, Lise and McMullen plan a smear campaign. They invent the story about the blondes, because they know a newspaper will respond. They set up some circumstantial evidence to make it look as if that story could be true – they send out those four parcels, for instance, maybe even call that agency you went to. They remain in touch, even after McMullen has staged his disappearance, and Lise continues to give McMullen information. What *she* does not realize, meanwhile, is that McMullen's intentions go much further than a smear campaign. He does not intend merely to blacken Hawthorne's reputation – he intends to destroy the man. You remember what he said in the car tonight, Gini? How Lise would never contemplate divorce, how the only way she could ever be free to marry him would be if Hawthorne died?'

'McMullen plans to kill him, you mean? Some kind of half-assed assassination attempt?' Gini shook her head. 'I can't believe that, Pascal. Apart from anything else, you've seen Hawthorne's security. He wouldn't stand a chance.'

'Are you sure? No security is ever one hundred per cent. McMullen is a marksman, he's army trained. Northern

494

Ireland, the Falklands? Gini, it's very likely he's killed in the past. Could he not kill again? Both British and American security obviously consider him a risk – why? Because he's threatening Hawthorne's past reputation, or because he's actually a threat to Hawthorne's life? Think, Gini. Why, of all places, if he's in hiding, would he choose a place that close to Hawthorne's country home? Why all those newspapers? He could be building up a pattern of Hawthorne's movements.' Pascal gave a quick excited gesture. 'Maybe he thinks Hawthorne's security here is less good than in London. It's much more difficult to protect the ambassador in a house surrounded by open fields and woods. When he's in the country, Hawthorne attends mass every Sunday morning, the same small church. He throws open his splendid gardens to the public, and McMullen keeps a clipping on just that event.'

'You're over-reacting, Pascal.'

'No. I'm just putting forward a hypothesis – and it's one that makes more sense than I realized, that's all.'

'All right. It's a scenario. But it leaves too much un-explained, you know that. Are you suggesting McMullen killed Johnny Appleyard and Stevey? What about that button you found?'

'Lise gave it to him. McMullen planted it.'

'All right – I don't buy it, but still. Did he also kill Lorna Munro?'

'It's not impossible. Unlikely, I agree.'

'Who sent the other parcels, after the first four?'

'McMullen sent all of them. When you mentioned them tonight, he was just acting surprised.' Pascal broke off. 'It's all right, Gini – I don't believe it either. It's worth remembering how you can read all these events more than one way, it helps to stop us jumping to conclusions. But no, I don't believe McMullen was behind all those events. Besides . . . when he explained his motives, I believed him. I liked the man.'

Gini looked away. 'I almost liked him then – I certainly believed him. But I didn't like him earlier, at the cottage, when I confronted him on the question of Vietnam. He was so angry, so bitter and unrealistic. But everything I said was true. Those photographs he produced, they're no evidence at all . . . '

'You didn't look at them,' Pascal said.

'No. I could see he wanted to exclude me. I thought it was better to stay out of it, and let him talk to you. I don't really want to look at them, even now.' She paused, and turned to him. 'Were they conclusive evidence, Pascal?'

'On their own – no,' Pascal replied. 'But they explained the anger and the bitterness he showed. If you genuinely believed a crime of that magnitude had been committed, and no-one would listen to you, no-one would investigate it, if you got closed off by officialdom and corruption and laziness, wouldn't you be angry and bitter? I think you would.'

He had spoken quietly, but Gini could hear the gentle reproof in his voice. She looked away, then sighed.

'Very well. That's fair. You're right. But it was a strange story, Pascal, you have to admit that. What possible connection could there be between McMullen and that event? A young man at Oxford and a village in Vietnam? Even when you asked him directly what that connection was, how he came to know of the woman concerned, he wouldn't answer you.'

'It wasn't "know *of*". He *knew* her. Did you see his face, Gini?'

'No, not all the time. He turned away.'

'Well, I did,' he said quietly. 'Gini, I'm hardened to that kind of thing, but it was a terrible picture. That young woman – it was someone McMullen had known, and *loved*. I knew it the instant I looked at him. Even before, when he started talking, when he put those pictures down on the table like playing cards. He was trying to distance himself.' Pascal broke off. He crossed the room, knelt beside her and took her hand in his.

'Gini, listen. For the moment, whether what he told us is true or false, makes no difference. The point is, it's what McMullen *himself* believes. Passionately. Just as he now believes passionately the story of Lise's sufferings at

496

Hawthorne's hands. There are powerful emotions at work here, deeply powerful emotions. Love and anger; hatred and jealousy.'

'A desire for revenge?'

There was a brief silence; Pascal met her gaze, then sighed and rose to his feet. 'That too. Yes. I'm afraid so.'

He began to pace the room again. Gini sat in silence trying to force herself to be just. This was not easy, for she was no longer impartial, she knew that. Her impulse now was to discredit all that McMullen said; if she could prove to herself that McMullen was lying about Hawthorne's actions now, then the possibility that he had also been lying about Hawthorne's earlier actions strengthened. And she wanted to believe that he was lying, or at best mistaken, about those events in Vietnam: oh yes – she passionately wanted that.

After some time had passed, she looked up at Pascal. She knew he was waiting for her to speak.

'It's all right, Pascal,' she said. 'I believed McMullen too, for much of the time. This *can't* all be fabrication. Too much has happened – and McMullen can't possibly have been responsible for it all, I do know that. There has to be some truth in his allegations. This whole past week – Hawthorne has to be behind it. Unless his father is. Or that Romero man is working independently. McMullen wouldn't have made the telephone calls to me. He wouldn't have – couldn't have – broken into my apartment and carefully arranged all those things I kept from Beirut. He doesn't even *know* about Beirut – how could he? McMullen wouldn't do any of those things.' She paused. 'Put it this way, I didn't think he was cruel. I think he could kill, and I presume you're right, given his army record, that he *has* killed. But not torture an animal, for instance . . . He wouldn't have done that to Napoleon, I'm sure.'

Pascal hesitated. 'I thought of that too,' he said. 'I looked, Gini. No scratches on his hands. No scratches on his face or neck.'

'I know. I looked too.' Gini glanced away. 'Napoleon would have struggled. I hope he managed to inflict a little damage. I'd like to think he did.'

Pascal crossed to her then, and took her in his arms. He persuaded her that she should sleep, that they should both get some sleep. And so they did. But their sleep was not uninterrupted.

At four in the morning, the telephone rang. The telephone was on Gini's side of the bed. She reached sleepily for it, located it, and picked it up. Pascal heard her give a low cry. He was instantly awake. He took the receiver from her. He recognized it at once – that slow, scratchy, muffled voice. He put his hand over the mouthpiece, and looked at Gini. She was huddled, white-faced, against the pillows.

'How can he know where we are? We didn't use our names, Pascal. We didn't make any booking.'

Pascal turned away. He listened for a second or two. The man was describing what he wanted Gini to do to him, once she had put on the black gloves.

'All the way in,' he said. 'Swallow it. Now.'

Pascal was about to speak or to hang up, his mind had frozen and he could not decide which to do, when the man's tone suddenly altered.

'Remember our appointment Sunday,' he said. 'You know where to come. Be there, Gini. Come after dark. Oh, and be sure to wear that black dress . . . '

There was a click, then the dialling tone. Pascal stared across the shadows of the room, and fear for Gini rose up in him, he felt it clench around his heart. He replaced the receiver, and took her in his arms. Her body was stiff with tension and fear.

'What did he say? Pascal, what did he say?'

'Darling, nothing, very little.' He began to stroke her hair.

'The same as before?'

'Yes. And then he hung up. Darling, don't think about it. I'm here . . . ' And then, because he knew it always calmed her, he switched to his own language, all those

498

soothing phrases that he had used to her years before in Beirut — *soyez-calme, tu sais que je t'aime, reste tranquille.*

This gentle incantation worked for her: her breathing became regular and quiet as she became calmer and then slept. They did not work for Pascal. He lay awake, staring into the dark.

XXVIII

At eleven forty-five on Friday, Gini was sitting in the downstairs bar at the Groucho Club. At twelve, the first customers began arriving: a cluster of advertising people; one or two journalists she knew; an actor who was currently king of advertising voice-overs . . . but not the man she was here to see. Jeremy Prior-Kent, McMullen's close friend at school and at Oxford, was not a punctual man.

She ordered a mineral water, opened her newspaper, and flicked quickly through its pages. It led on the current round of IRA bombings; continuing royal scandals occupied pages three and four; on page five was a photograph of the US Ambassador's wife. Lise Hawthorne had visited Great Ormond Street Children's Hospital the previous day. She was currently chair of its fund-raising committee. There was a photograph of her looking radiant and concerned, with a group of young leukaemia victims.

Gini folded up the paper. A group of new arrivals had entered the bar, but none approached her table. It was now a quarter past twelve. Prior-Kent was already fifteen minutes late. She glanced down at the photograph of Lise once more, the woman McMullen had described as a latter-day saint. That morning, after returning from Oxford, she and Pascal had spent hours on the telephone at the Hampstead house, trying to check out the few details McMullen had let slip.

They had established that his claim to a connection with Lise Hawthorne's distant cousins, the Grenvilles, was true, but they had been unable to discover any more about the illness McMullen had mentioned, which had led to his stay with them in 1972. That 'illness' coming after his abrupt and unexplained departure from Oxford interested her: *why* had McMullen thrown up his studies so quickly? What had been the exact nature of that illness, and how long had it lasted? This, she hoped, was a question Prior-Kent might be able to answer – if he ever showed.

She glanced down at her watch. Pascal was due back here to collect her at around one-fifteen. While she was here, he was continuing his checks into McMullen's firearms licence, and his past army career. He would pick up the keys to the St John's Wood house before meeting her, and intended to move in there to set up his cameras the next morning. Gini felt a familiar sense of frustration. Sunday was now very close, and although she had not said this to Pascal, she was not optimistic that he would obtain the pictures they hoped for. Was it really likely that Hawthorne would turn up at the Gothic house, that he would conveniently stand there on the doorstep with the latest hired blonde? No, it seemed to her it was extremely *unlikely* – in which case they would be back to square one, still attempting to prove or disprove this story by other means.

Later that afternoon, they were meeting the woman Suzy from the escort agency and it was possible that she, or even Prior-Kent, would provide some sudden breakthrough, but if neither of them produced strong leads then she and Pascal were still thwarted: all this work, and still no absolute proof. She looked up as a new group of people entered the bar, but none was Jeremy Prior-Kent. It was another group of journalists, whose faces she knew. One of them was Lindsay. Her friend saw her at exactly the same moment, and quickly crossed to her side.

'Hi, Gini. D'you want to join us? We're just going in for lunch.'

'I can't I'm afraid. I'm meeting someone. How was Martinique?'

Lindsay made a face. 'Idyllic. Fraught. I got back yesterday – and all hell is breaking loose at the *News*. Have you heard?'

'No, I haven't been in the office for a couple of days.'

'Well, you should go.' Lindsay grinned. 'High drama. It's getting like some Jacobean play – heads rolling, murder and mayhem on the fifteenth floor—'

'Murder?'

'Not *literally*, just a sort of night of the long knives. You mean you really haven't heard?'

'Not a word. What's happened?'

'Well, first, *Daiches* was fired. By Jenkins himself.'

'No! *Daiches?* I can't believe it.'

'Well apparently they had some huge bust-up. Practically came to blows. Nicholas accused him of going behind his back to Melrose. According to Charlotte there's some big story Jenkins had been nursing along. Melrose told him to kill it, and Jenkins *pretended* to play ball. Then he went on with it, behind Melrose's back. And dear Daiches, like the loyal lieutenant he is, thought Melrose ought to be informed.'

Lindsay's smile was a perfect blend of joy and malice. 'Unfortunately, Nicholas had ordered up all these files or something, so Daiches could prove what he said was true. Anyway, the upshot was that Daiches was fired, and stayed fired for about three hours, then Melrose turned up, and stormed into Jenkins's office—'

'This was when?'

'Yesterday. Raised voices behind firmly closed doors. Shortly after Melrose finally left, Daiches was back in his office. Reinstated. The company Cassius. All smiles.'

'And Jenkins?'

'I don't *know*.' Lindsay grinned. 'We're all just going in to discuss it now over lunch – but the word is, Jenkins could be out of the building by the end of this afternoon. We're opening a book on it. You want to place a bet? We're giving odds on whether Jenkins will be fired, and who will succeed him.'

'What're the odds on Daiches?'

'Fifteen to one originally – now down to nine to one and shortening all the time.'

'Oh great. If Daiches gets the job, I'm unemployed.'

'Me too. We can resign together. Sign on together at the

Job Centre. On the other hand,' Lindsay gave her a dry glance, 'we could start putting out feelers elsewhere. I'm going to start hitting the phones after lunch. You should do the same.'

'I can't. Not today. No time.' She gave a shrug. 'Still, maybe this is good news in disguise. It concentrates the mind wonderfully. There's no way I'm staying at the *News* to work for Daiches.'

'Me neither.' Lindsay turned round to wave at her friends. 'I must go, Gini. See you soon. Oh, by the way,' she looked at Gini closely, 'did it resolve itself – that Pascal Lamartine business?'

'In a way. Yes.'

'I thought so.' Lindsay smiled, this time with genuine warmth. 'It shows, you know. Just a kind of light, in the eyes . . . See you, Gini.'

She turned away, and disappeared with her friends to the restaurant upstairs. Gini sat there quietly considering this news. Suppose Jenkins were fired? She began to run down a list in her mind of other newspapers or magazines she could approach with this story, should she need to do so. She was halfway through making this list when at twelve-thirty, some thirty minutes late, the door opened, and a man came into the bar. A tall man, a familiar man, not a man you would forget: he was thin, with reddish hair tied back in a pony-tail. As before, he was wearing a flamboyant mustard-yellow Armani suit. She saw him scan the tables, then begin to move across to her. So McMullen's old friend had not, it seemed, spent the last three days scouting for film locations in Cornwall. He had been otherwise engaged, directing a sex education video, over-seeing an escort agency, making sure Bernie dealt with eighty-six telephone sex lines.

Reaching her table, he gave her a long appraising look, then a broad smile. 'You must be Genevieve Hunter, yes?' he said. 'We meet at last. Sorry I'm late. So tell me – what have I done? Why the sudden interest from the *News*?'

* * *

Gini's first impression of the man was that he was – or intended to be – disarming. He seemed very relaxed; he ordered himself a Mexican beer, which he drank in a modish way, from the bottle with a twist of lime. He lit a cigarette, chatted away about nothing in particular, complained in a rueful way that he'd been at a party the night before, and was nursing the mother of all hangovers. He must have been in his forties, but looked younger. He had a soft, freckled, almost girlish face. His manner was mildly flirtatious, but he had alert greenish-blue eyes, and she suspected that beneath all his *badinage*, he was no fool.

That impression was rapidly confirmed the second she mentioned James McMullen's name. Kent was not ingenuous, as his employees Hazel and Bernie had been; she was scarcely into her preamble before he stopped her with a little lift of the hand.

'Hey, slow down just a second. Let me get this straight. That's why it was so urgent to see me? You want to ask about *James*? Why?'

Gini had anticipated this. 'Can this be confidential?' she asked.

'Sure. Sure. What fun. Go on.'

'Well, I can only give you an outline. James McMullen had been helping me with a story I'm working on, and—'

'What story would that be exactly?'

'It's an investigation. I'd prefer not to go into the details . . . '

'Oh dear.' He gave a small smile. 'I think you're going to have to. After all, James is a friend.'

'Very well. It's a story on British mercenary organizations. There are a number of them in existence. Their fortunes fluctuate. They've been especially active recently in Yugoslavia.'

'Sure. I've read that in the papers . . . '

'Most of those recruiting organizations are run by ex-army personnel. It's a secretive world, and it's not easy to get leads. James McMullen was one of my best sources. Then he disappeared, just before Christmas.'

'James did? Well, well, well.' He gave her an appraising look. 'Go on.'

'I want to find him again. Fast. His former regiment is no help at all. I've tried his sister and a number of friends – no luck. I thought you might know where I could track him down.'

'Is that all?' He smiled. 'And I thought it was me you were interested in. What a shame.' He took another swallow of beer. 'Can't help, I'm afraid. I haven't seen James in ages – not since last summer. James does take off, you know, for months at a time. He's done it before.'

'But you did see him last summer?'

'Sometime then. July, August – I can't remember. He rang up out of the blue. We had dinner together, a rather drunken dinner – on my side anyway. James doesn't drink much, as you may know. We went back to that apartment of his, down by the river – you've been there?'

'Yes, I have. It's a great apartment.'

'Isn't it just? Anyway, we went back there, talked for a while, I toddled off, late, around three in the morning, and I haven't seen him since.'

'Were you surprised to hear from him? Like that – out of the blue?'

He shrugged. 'Not really. James and I aren't that close any more. We see each other from time to time. Catch up on the news, what we've both been up to work-wise, woman-wise, that sort of thing.'

There was a pause. Gini considered the date of this meeting, which must have taken place around the time McMullen had been staying in Oxfordshire with the Hawthornes. She would have liked to date it more precisely, to know whether it took place before or after McMullen had heard the story of her marriage from Lise.

'So tell me,' she went on, 'when you had that meeting, did McMullen seem changed in any way? Did he discuss with you any major event that had happened to him recently?'

Kent considered, then shrugged. 'A major event?

Nothing I can remember. But then James doesn't really go in for confessionals – it's not his style. He'd thrown up that dreary banking job his father had foisted on him, but that was much earlier that year.' He gave her another of those rueful engaging smiles. 'I probably did most of the talking. Banged on about the films I was making, that kind of thing. Two drinks and I become a monomaniac.'

He glanced away towards the bar. Catching the eye of the voice-over king, he gave a little gesture of greeting. He took another long swallow of the Mexican beer. Gini hesitated. Prior-Kent was not the type of man she would expect to be behind an escort agency, or sex education videos, and she could foresee this interview dwindling away into amiable anecdotes that were no use to her at all. Thanks to his lateness, she was now running out of time. What she needed, she decided, was some leverage.

'So,' she began carefully, raising her eyes to his, 'when you had that conversation with James McMullen, and you were telling him about your work, did you mention your other activities, or just the ads you make for TV?'

There was a small silence. Kent put down his beer. 'Other activities?'

'Your less public activities. The ones you don't list for Salamander Films in the trade directories. The sex education videos you make, for instance. Or the escort agency your company runs from the same address. Or your telephone sex line operations. Did you tell James McMullen about those?'

The question had been risky, and the silence following it was long. Gini would not have been surprised had Kent ended the interview there and then, but he did not do so. He gave her a long, considering look; she saw amusement begin in his eyes; he smiled, and then he laughed.

'Oh *fuck*. Oh bloody *hell*.' He sighed. 'Mistake, Jeremy, my old son. Rule number one, never talk to reporters. Rule number two, be especially wary if they have blond hair and beautiful eyes and a sweet smile. I suppose I should have known. Ah well, I guess it had to happen sooner or later. What am I facing now, a full-scale exposé in the *News*? The porn-king revealed?'

He gave her a sidelong glance. 'I suppose there's no way to head you off? Think of my poor old white-haired mother, Genevieve, explaining this one to the neighbours. Think of my rather rich accountant trying to cope when the Revenue investigators start knocking on his door.' He smiled. 'Are you sure you have it in your heart to do this, Genevieve? It's all legal and above board, you know.'

He put his hand on his heart as he said this. He wrinkled his freckled nose, and gave her a look of mock pleading. 'Come on, Genevieve. Do you really want to leave me a broken man? Bloody hell – I don't think I can take this. On top of a screaming hangover too. Meeting my nemesis at the Groucho. It's too much. Maybe I'll have a gigantic gin and tonic. How about you?'

He rose to his feet as he said this, and ambled his way across to the bar. He returned with two very large gins and one small bottle of tonic. He slid into the seat opposite her, still with an air of contained amusement. He lit another cigarette, took a large swallow of neat gin, and shuddered.

'Fine. I feel *much* stronger now. Maybe I'll enjoy being notorious, you never know. I expect I'll learn to live with it. So tell me, where do we go from here?'

Despite herself, Gini was amused. She looked at Kent carefully. He gave her a nonchalant smile.

'Well,' she began, 'it may surprise you to hear this, but I do genuinely want to know about James McMullen.'

'You do?' He raised his eyebrows. 'But not for the reasons stated?'

'No. For other reasons. I need background. I need information. Now I could write a pretty good story about your business empire, but as you say, it is legal – just about. And it's not top of my list of priorities right now.'

'Ah, I begin to see.' His smile broadened. He began to look relieved. 'So you thought, to get that information, you'd pressure me just a little? Bad, Genevieve.

507

Bad . . . ' He shook a reproving finger at her. Gini smiled.

'Listen, I'd pressure you any way I can. Whatever it takes. I need this information, and I need it fast. If the only way to get it from you involves upsetting your poor white-haired old mother—'

'*And* my accountant. Let's not forget him.'

'*And* your accountant. If that's what it takes to get your assistance then too bad. On the other hand, if you were to co-operate . . . '

'Oh, I'll co-operate.' He leaned forward. 'Have dinner with me tonight, and I'll co-operate a whole lot more . . . No? Shame . . . ' He stretched, added a little tonic to the gin in his glass and sipped it. 'You needn't have gone to these lengths, you know,' he went on. 'I'll answer any questions you have about James. Why not? I don't know anything about him that reflects on him badly. James is terribly *upright*, you know. Not like me at all.'

'So you will answer my questions?'

'Can't wait.' He stretched. 'Give me the third degree. What a thrill.'

Gini took out her notebook.

'No tape recorder?' Kent smiled.

'It's too noisy in here. And I don't need it. I take shorthand.'

'You do? What a marvellous girl you are. Has anyone ever told you that your eyes . . . ' He broke off and laughed. 'OK. OK. Sorry. Go on.'

'Can we start with the meeting you had with James McMullen last summer? Can you date it more precisely? Was it July or August?'

'Now I think about it, it must have been August. Yes, that's right. James had just come back from some shooting party in Yorkshire – he's a very good shot, you know. Loves that kind of thing. Blasting birds out of the sky. The grouse season doesn't begin until August twelfth, so it must have been later that month. Yes.'

After the meeting with Lise, Gini thought. She tapped her notebook. 'At the meeting, did McMullen ask you specifically about your escort agency?'

'Let me think . . . ' Kent frowned. 'He knew abo
anyway, most of my friends do. I'm not its sole owner, by
the way – it's more of a sideline from my point of view.
It's the films that make the really big money. I know we
discussed those. The escort agency . . . You know, we *did*
discuss it, I remember now, because James was asking me
questions – what kind of men used it, that sort of thing.
And I was rather surprised. James is a pretty straight-laced
kind of guy, doesn't approve of that kind of thing.'

'So he knew about the agency, and questioned you
about it. Did he know its name and location?'

'Oh yes. Sure.'

'He didn't suggest he might ever make use of its
services?'

'James? Good God, not even as a joke. No way.'

'He didn't imply he knew of someone who might like
to make use of its services?'

'No. Definitely not. I told you, James disapproves of
anything like that. He has a very strict moral code.'

'Did he talk about his own personal life at all? He didn't
mention any emotional entanglement, any involvement
with a woman, for instance?'

'No.' He grinned. 'I banged on quite a lot about my
love life, which tends to be a bit operatic. In James's
case,' he frowned, 'I guess I've always rather assumed
there *wasn't* anyone. There never seemed to be. He's
not terribly good at dealing with women – can't talk
to them. A legacy from the Army, maybe, or school.
Except it didn't affect *me* that way – school, I mean. All
those years in a single-sex boarding-school. The minute
I left I made up for lost time.'

'All right,' Gini looked at him thoughtfully, 'fill me in
just a little. You were at school with James McMullen,
and you went up to Oxford, the same college, the same
year – autumn nineteen sixty-eight, is that right?'

'That's right. Sixty-eight.' He smiled. 'That glorious
year. I wasn't in James's league academically, needless
to say. He had a scholarship, I just scraped in. But I'd
known James for a very long time by then. We first met

when we were sent away to prep school. We boarded together aged eight onwards, you know. One of those English barbarities. All that regimentation. All that manly propaganda.'

'So can you tell me what happened once you went up to Oxford? If James McMullen was such a high-flier, how come he left?'

'Oh *that*. You didn't know?' He gave her a glance. 'Well, James was ill. He was whisked back home by that dire mother of his. Everyone thought it was just temporary. But it wasn't. He left, and he never returned.'

'So it was a serious illness? What kind of illness? Physical? Mental?'

'I'm not too sure.' He shrugged. 'James never discusses it. None of his family ever does, not even that sister of his.' He gave her a glance. 'The sister from hell. Have you met her?' He paused. 'No, the official line was James had one of those vague lingering things. Hepatitis? No. Rheumatic fever? I think that was it. I can't really remember the details. It was a long time ago.'

'If that was the official version, what was the true reason? Do you know?'

'No. Not for sure. I always suspected he had a breakdown of some kind. But if he did, they kept it very quiet. James was swept off to the depths of Shropshire. He wrote to me occasionally, but I didn't see him after he left Oxford. Not for two or three years.' He paused. 'If it *was* a breakdown, then it's all a bit odd. On the one hand it was serious enough to end his time at Oxford. On the other hand, it can't have been *that* serious. He was accepted by the Army at the end of nineteen seventy-two. And the British army isn't too keen on officer recruits who've put in time in a funny farm.'

'So what's your personal opinion?'

'I think he was badly stressed out. I think the parents coped, somehow, and presumably he got better. When the Army came to check his medical records, they must have been satisfied. And if they had any doubts, well, half James's family have heavy army connections. Grandfather, uncles, cousins: generals to the right of him, lieutenant-colonels to the left of him. They could always have pulled strings.'

'I see. That's interesting.' Gini looked at him thoughtfully. 'So, as a friend, how did you find him? Then and later. Would you have said he had a tendency to mental instability? Did you ever find him obsessional, say? Would you ever have described him as a fantasist, or a bit paranoid – anything like that?'

'No.' Kent did not even hesitate before he replied. 'No, not at all. Quite the reverse. James is frighteningly rational – he always was. I mean, we can all get a bit paranoid, can't we? I certainly do. But James isn't like that. In fact, if he has a weakness, it's that he doesn't understand grey areas. He likes everything to be clear, cut and dried, desperately *factual*. He does *have* an imagination, but I think he suppresses it. It alarms him. He was always like that, even at school. There's a wild side to James, a kind of passionate romantic crusading side to him. But he keeps it under very strict control.'

'So he is the kind of man who might be directed towards causes, for instance?'

'Oh sure. It's why he joined the Army. The Army gave him a sense of purpose. Something very simple with very definite honourable objectives. Defending his country, and so on. He clung to that idea.' He gave a smile. 'I was always rather touched by that. It seemed so old-fashioned. But by the time James was claiming to enjoy Sandhurst training, I was pounding the King's Road in sandals and Indian beads. Peace and love. Turn on, tune in and drop out. Flower power, Genevieve.' His smile broadened. 'Then time passed, of course. I discovered capitalism and commerce had some advantages after all.'

Kent gave her a little glance. He sighed. 'You don't remember, and why would you? You're far too young. And you're making me feel desperately old. But that's how it was, Genevieve. The wonderful world of the late Sixties and early Seventies. One long glorious trip. I took that voyage, but James didn't. Not at all.'

There was a silence. Gini scribbled a few notes. She looked at some of the paradoxes here: Kent, an ex-hippie now transformed into an Armani-clad high earner, boosting his income and staying just inside of the law; and McMullen, a rationalist, a self-disciplinarian, who saw joining the Army as a cause.

She turned a page of her notebook, and looked back at Kent, who was now checking his watch.

'You're making me late for my lunch,' he said, 'and I really don't care. What the hell. It's fun, remembering. You'd have really liked me then, Genevieve. I had a Che Guevara beard, and hair down to here . . . ' He gestured somewhere mid-chest.

Gini returned his smile. 'OK,' she said. 'Can we take a closer look at that period. Nineteen sixty-eight, the year you and McMullen went up to Oxford. He left the following year. You think he could have had some kind of nervous breakdown. Were there any signs of that, prior to his leaving Oxford? Did he seem under strain?'

'Not exactly. He was miserable, unhappy – that was obvious. He tried to throw himself into things – he worked desperately hard. But then he was expected to get a first, so he had to do that. He became a bit solitary, actually. You know – never went to parties, never took girls out, never got drunk. I should probably have made more effort to talk to him but you know how it is. I was too busy having a good time. Then, next thing I knew, he'd gone.'

'Right. Then can we look a little further back? If he seemed miserable at Oxford, was he before? Did he have moods, depressions, at school for instance?'

'At school? God no. Not at all.'

'So he changed in other words? Try to remember – when did that change begin? Did you see him at all between school and Oxford, for example? There's a nine-month period there, when he was in Paris, taking courses at the Sorbonne.'

'Oh, we were both in Paris then,' Kent said. 'Didn't you realize? We spent that time together. I went under protest, under persuasion from James, but it was really all his parents' idea. They were both culture-mad. Totally determined that James wouldn't fritter away the months before Oxford. So they fixed up for us to stay with this family in Paris, the Gravelliers. Marc Gravellier ran an art gallery on the left bank, so James's mother thought we'd be perfectly placed to soak up high culture, improve our French, et cetera. I went along because James talked me into it. And because I thought Paris was bound to be full of pretty girls.'

'I see. So you were there together. For how long?'

'About six months. January through to July. We had a whale of a time.' He leaned forward. 'James's mother hadn't done her homework thoroughly enough. She thought the Gravelliers were very *bon genre*. And so they were – up to a point. What she hadn't realized was that Madame, in particular, was this wonderful passionate Bohemian French intellectual. Lots of leftist friends. Parties until three a.m. Jean-Paul Sartre for supper. No house rules. No curfew. Can you imagine – after an English boarding-school? I went totally wild . . . In fact, looking back,' he grinned, 'that's when I probably started on the downward slope. I smelled freedom for the first time. No doubt very bad for the soul.'

'So you kicked over the traces? What about James? Did he do that as well?'

'Oh *James*.' He laughed. 'Well, he started off taking it all very seriously. Courses at the Sorbonne, for God's sake. I avoided all those like the plague.' He paused. 'I think he could scent it too, though, that other world. Well, you couldn't exactly miss it. By April, May, the whole of Paris – it felt like not just the city, but the whole world was ready to explode. James got caught up in that a bit, I think, the fervour, the excitement. He went on one or two marches with other students from the Sorbonne. But come May, of course, he had rather more pressing concerns.'

'Such as?'

'He fell in love.' Kent gave an amused shrug. 'And, being James, it hit him hard. The French have all the best terms for it – *un coup de foudre*, a thunderbolt. He was turned inside out and upside down. *Bouleversé*. But then you have to remember,' he glanced at her, 'we were two English schoolboys, brought up like monks. Both of us virgins, alas. And we were only eighteen years old.'

He broke off, and glanced toward the door. Pascal had just entered, and was making his way towards their table. Kent gave a sigh.

'Damn. A friend of yours. And I was just working up to that dinner invitation again. Pity. I don't think I'll mention it just now. I get the feeling it might not go down too well. Does he always frown that way, or only when men with pony-tails buy you large gins you don't drink? Oh, hi . . . ' He rose to his feet, was introduced, and sat down again. He looked at Pascal closely, as he drew up a chair.

'Well, well, well,' he said. 'Pascal Lamartine. Poor James. What on *earth* has he been up to? James doesn't chase movie-stars, as far as I know. I didn't realize you were working with the heavy brigade, Genevieve. If I had, I think I'd probably have fled.'

Pascal began to speak, and Gini kicked him hard under the table.

'Oh, Pascal's just a friend,' she said. 'We're having lunch, that's all. Nothing to do with this story or you.' She smiled at Kent. 'Really. He won't mind waiting a while, will you, Pascal?'

'Not at all.'

'It's just that you'd reached a very interesting part of your story. Won't you go on?'

'I'll get us a drink.' Pascal rose. 'Gin and tonic?'

Jeremy Prior-Kent hesitated, then shrugged. 'No. I'll switch back to beer, thanks. A Corona with lime. Cheers.'

Pascal withdrew. Kent lit another cigarette. He paused, looking at Gini, then smiled.

'I wonder why I'm getting the feeling that there's more going on here than meets the eye?'

'It's those paranoid tendencies of yours – you mentioned them, remember?'

'Maybe. Maybe. Still, what the hell? This isn't a state secret. You really want me to go on?'

'Yes. I do. Take it from where you left off. Paris nineteen sixty-eight. May nineteen sixty-eight. James McMullen fell head over heels in love. He embarked on his first love affair . . .'

'Slow down.' Kent lifted a hand to stop her. 'I said he fell in love. I never said he had an affair. *I* had affairs – lots of them. But not James. This was strictly platonic, as far as I know, and all the more intense as a result. James is a bit like that. He liked to put women up on a pedestal, and then worship them, serve them. A very parfit gentil knight. *Deeply* medieval, and rather dangerous in my opinion. It breeds all sorts of unhealthy illusions. But James, of course, wouldn't agree.'

'So who was this woman? How did he meet her?'

'Well the awful part is, I can't remember her name. I met her a couple of times. She was older than James, around twenty-two, or twenty-three. She was half-French and half-Vietnamese. Very beautiful, a tiny thing, very fragile-looking, with this astonishing long jet-black hair. She was Madame Gravellier's niece, and she didn't live in Paris. She was visiting, there was some conference thing going on, and her father was over for it, or her uncle . . . I can't remember the details. It's so long ago. And I don't see that it can be of any relevance now. I mean James never mentions her, ever. He's probably forgotten it ever happened.'

'She was half-Vietnamese?'

'That's right. Well, Vietnam was a former French colony and Madame Gravellier's family had connections there. A rubber plantation, I think – something like that. Madame Gravellier grew up in Indo-China, and came back to France eventually. But one of her sisters stayed on out there, and went native. Married a Vietnamese. I'm pretty sure that was the connection. Anyway, the point is, this girl turned up one day at one of the Gravelliers' crazy evenings, when there were about three thousand people milling about, students and artists and actors and writers and café intellectuals, and Christ knows what, and I was introduced to her and James was introduced to her – and the next time I looked round, I realized he was still sitting in the corner talking to her. And they'd been there for four hours.'

'That was how they met?'

'Yes. She didn't speak a word of English, but they were both fluent in French. So there they were, talking away. She was wearing this white jacket thing which buttoned all the way up to the neck, and one of those sort of sarong skirts. Her hair was loose. She was very tiny, very quiet, very self-contained. Well, I was curious. James wasn't very good with women. He was shy. Usually he wouldn't speak to them at all. So I was curious what line he was taking. I stood there, sort of hovered around – I don't think either of them even saw me. My French wasn't too good, so it took me a while to understand what in hell they were discussing . . . '

He stopped, and grinned. 'You know what it was? Politics. Can you *believe* it? This really amazing-looking woman, and what's James discussing? The thoughts of Ho Chi Minh.'

He broke off as Pascal quietly rejoined them, then shrugged. 'So, end of story. James went on seeing her, I know that much. She was in Paris around two months. Then she left, went back home. James and I split up then, around July, August. I didn't see him again until we went up to Christ Church that October.'

'And he never mentioned her then?'

'No. Not one word.'

'Could he have remained in contact with her?'

'I guess so.'

'Did it ever occur to you that the change that came over him then, at Oxford, might have been connected to her?'

'Not really. To be perfectly honest, I'd almost forgotten her. You know, it was amusing, watching James in the throes, in Paris. But that was months earlier. I assumed he'd come to his senses. I mean, we were eighteen. She was just another girl.'

He took a large swallow of his beer, glanced at the silent Pascal somewhat warily, then tapped his watch. 'Look, I'm sorry, but I have to go now. I'd better put in an appearance at this lunch of mine, at least.' He rose, and looked down at Gini in an uncertain way. 'James is OK, is he? I mean – he's not in trouble of any kind? I'm fond of James. We go back a long way . . . ' He glanced at Pascal. 'You're not hounding him, I hope?'

'Not hounding him, no.'

'Well, if you really do need to find him, I've thought of someone you could try.'

'Yes?'

'Her name's Lise Hawthorne. You know, the American Ambassador's wife. I met her with him once – ran into them in some dimly lit restaurant. She might know. They're very close friends . . . ' He smiled.

'When was this?'

'Last spring some time.'

'Did James McMullen say they were friends?'

'Yes. Subsequently . . . So he claimed. That wasn't *exactly* the impression I had at the time . . . ' Kent paused. He had been turning away. He stopped, looked back, gave Gini a meaningful look, and then grinned.

'Put it this way. They were holding hands under the table at the time. At least, to be charitable they were holding hands. She was looking flushed. James wasn't pleased to see me. *Very* bad timing on my part. But there you are – if people will carry on that way in a public place, what can one do?' He lifted a hand. 'Nice to meet you both. Remember my white-haired mother, Genevieve. Bye.'

The door to the bar swung closed behind him. There was a brief silence. Pascal and Gini looked at each other.

'Well, well, well,' Pascal said. 'So. Are they friends, the way McMullen claimed – or are they lovers?'

'I know what Jeremy Kent was implying and so do you. Lovers. Yet Kent spent most of the past hour explaining how straight-laced McMullen was in that respect.'

'That kind always fall the hardest. When they fall.'

517

'Indeed. What's more, Kent isn't just McMullen's old school-friend. I recognized him, Pascal, the second he walked in. He runs that escort agency I went to, he's one of its owners.'

'He admitted that?'

'Yes. And, furthermore, James McMullen knew about that agency. He questioned Kent about it within a month of his July meeting with Lise.'

'So you think McMullen could have been planning to use that escort agency? As a way of setting up Hawthorne?'

'It is a possibility, Pascal.' Gini closed her notebook. 'If Lise and McMullen *are* lovers, it does mean we have to look at this differently. Just for a start, it means they've both lied.'

'I do realize that.' Pascal rose. 'Come on, Gini. We have an appointment with that Suzy woman, remember. We meet her at three. I have the bike outside. Let's hear the call-girl's side of the story.'

'You think that's what she is? A call-girl?'

'Gini, this is a story about sex, yes?' He took her arm. 'Other things too – love, maybe. War, maybe. Lies, certainly. But sex, definitely. Of course I think she's a call-girl, don't you?'

XXIX

Pascal had booked a room in a large, discreet Knightsbridge hotel. It overlooked Hyde Park to the rear. They arrived there after taking their now-usual circuitous and time-consuming route, with some forty-five minutes to spare. Pascal had coffee brought up. He lit the first of several cigarettes, and began in his habitual way to pace the room.

'And so,' he said, 'I collected the keys for the St John's Wood house. We can move in, and I can start setting up my cameras tomorrow. If this damn meeting of Hawthorne's actually does take place, it could be at any point from midnight Saturday on. I want to have everything ready well before. I want to be certain that no-one can enter or leave without my seeing them, even after dark.'

He broke off, and shrugged. 'After that, I spent an age checking those gun licences and that was not straightforward at all. In the end, with the aid of someone from the firearms division at the Metropolitan police, I finally traced it. McMullen's guns are registered as being held at his London flat – and that's surprising. The regulations are very strict now. Guns have to be kept in a locked gun cabinet and the police check that they are. McMullen has no gun cabinet at that flat – we'd have seen it. But that's where the guns are registered. Two shotguns, and one rifle. The shotguns for sporting use, the rifle because he's a registered member of a gun club. According to the records, it's outside Oxford. He regularly uses its range.'

He stopped and turned back to Gini. 'So, there you are. No progress on his army career. I drew a blank there. So that's the sum of my achievements. Then I came to collect you. I thought that man Kent would be long gone by then. And I'm afraid I interrupted you at a bad moment, yes?'

'A bit. It was all right. He finished his story finally. And it looks as if you were right, Pascal. There really is a link between McMullen and a woman in Vietnam.' Quickly, she told him the details of her conversation with Kent. Pascal listened intently.

'I see. I see,' he said, when she had finished speaking. 'That could be possible if McMullen was living there with an ex-colonial family. Also there were always strong links between the left in France and Vietnam. And all the peace negotiations between the Americans and the North Vietnamese took place in Paris. Nineteen sixty-eight was a crucial year – it was the year Lyndon Johnson called a halt to the bombing of North Vietnam. It was the year of the Tet offensive. I think it was the year the final peace negotiations began – though they dragged on for years afterwards. I'd have to check that . . . ' He glanced at Gini. 'Kent mentioned a conference? He said that was why the woman was there?'

'He did. He didn't mention *what* conference. He was vague in some ways, specific in others. He could remember how she looked, this woman, but not her name.'

'How did he describe her?'

'As tiny. Very fragile. Quiet. She spoke fluent French. When he met her she wore white. She had long black hair.' Gini hesitated. 'It did cross my mind, Pascal—'

'What?'

'Well, the way in which types of women seem to recur on this story. First there are the blondes – all the women Hawthorne allegedly meets. Then Lorna Munro. Now Suzy. Then, suddenly, their very opposite: two women, poles apart in many respects, and yet they both share the same colouring, the same dark hair . . . '

'Maybe. Maybe.' Pascal shrugged. 'I'd say it was just a coincidence. Lots of women have dark hair.'

'Of course. But don't you remember? In the car in Oxford, McMullen said he'd only loved two women in his life, so what he felt for Lise was not an inconsiderable thing. Don't you see, Pascal, he might *associate* Lise in some ways with this other woman. And if he did it might explain a great deal. If she died – even if she didn't die in the way he believes – he could have transferred all the feelings he had for her to Lise. It would intensify his commitment to Lise.'

'Possibly.' Pascal made an impatient gesture. 'But I'm fed up with all this speculation. That's where we end up, again and again. With speculation. I want some facts. Some nice simple straightforward facts. Like, for instance, are McMullen and Lise Hawthorne lovers? Yes or no. What are you doing?'

He turned around. Gini had just picked up the telephone.

'I'm calling Mary. I agree with you. There're a few details I'd like to know as well.'

'Mary? Gini, I'm not sure that's a good idea.'

'Why not?'

'Darling, she's in constant touch with John Hawthorne, for one thing. This woman Suzy's arriving any second, for another.'

'No, she isn't. She's not due for another ten minutes. I just have time, Pascal. And I won't tell Mary where I am, obviously. I can make it just seem like a casual enquiry. I haven't spoken to her in days. She can't get hold of me at my apartment . . . Quite apart from anything else she'll start getting worried if she doesn't hear from me. I just want to find out what *she* knows about James McMullen – whether she ever met him at any of Lise's embassy parties, whether Lise ever discussed him. She could have, Pascal, and if she did, I want to know.'

She began dialling the number. Pascal hesitated, then shrugged. 'Oh, very well, very well – but for God's sake keep it casual. Talk about something else first. Then say you ran into McMullen or something and he mentioned Lise's name. Don't make it obvious, Gini. I don't like you calling her now. It's almost Sunday. For all you know, John Hawthorne could be with her. I—'

He broke off, as Gini began speaking. She had hardly

begun on her first sentence, before she was interrupted. She stopped, and stood listening in silence. Pascal could just hear the sound of Mary speaking rapidly.

'Oh, I see,' Gini said. 'I didn't realize. I've been out a lot. When? Oh, Mary, I'm not sure. I . . . It's rather short notice.'

Pascal moved a little closer to her. Gini had paled, he saw, and on her face was an expression he knew of old, a closed, blank, defensive look. She moved so her back was towards him, and began to twist the cord of the phone. Her answers became monosyllabic. He could hear and see that she was attempting to resist something, and then giving ground.

Finally she replaced the phone, and turned back to him. The alteration in her demeanour was startling. A confident young woman now looked like a nervous child. Only one person produced that effect on Gini. Gently, Pascal took her hand.

'Your father,' he said. 'You were speaking to your father, weren't you?'

'That's right. Mary passed him the phone.' She turned her face away. 'He's in London, passing through. Seeing some publisher about his Vietnam book. He's been trying to get hold of me for two days. He wants to see me at Mary's. Tonight. Not for long – they're going out somewhere. Just for an hour or so.'

There was a brief silence. Pascal watched her face. He said quietly, 'Gini, when did you last see him?'

'Oh, I don't know. Two years ago. Two and a half.'

'Does he call you? Does he write?'

'No.'

'But now he's passing through, so you have to drop everything and go running.'

'He said it was urgent, Pascal. Important. I'll have to go.'

'Oh, I'll bet it was important. And urgent. He knows you're working on the Hawthorne story, Gini. It's just more pressure. Hawthorne's roped him in.'

'He never mentioned Hawthorne.'

'Come on, Gini! He and Hawthorne go back a long way. You know perfectly well what your father wants to talk about. He's going to tell you to stay off Hawthorne's private life, and for God's sake don't start digging up anything to do with a certain incident in Vietnam—'

'Oh you think so?' She swung around to face him. 'Fine, well, shall we just wait and see before we decide that? It might be nothing to do with this story at all. You're pre-judging him, Pascal, the way you always do. It could be anything. He could be ill—'

'Oh for God's sake, Gini.' Pascal waved his hand in exasperation. 'He turns you into a child again and he always damn well did. You talk to him for five seconds, and suddenly you have no mind of your own.'

'That's not true! It's not fair!'

'Darling, he can twist you around his little finger. One word of praise and you'd die for him. One threat and you toe the line. He knows that – and I've no doubt that by now Hawthorne knows it as well . . . Gini?' He tried to put his arm around her, but Gini pushed him away. Pascal stepped back. He sighed and gave a helpless shrug. 'You agreed to go?'

'Yes. I did. I had to. Just for an hour, no more than two—'

'Fine. OK. I'll come with you.'

'No, you won't.' She rounded on him. 'Pascal, stop this, will you? Can you imagine what would happen if you came with me? He'd go totally mad.'

'So let him. Are you frightened of that? Why? Let him shout and bluster. You don't have to listen now. You're not fifteen any more.'

'It isn't a *question* of that. And I'm not frightened of him. I simply want to hear whatever it is he has to say, and then go. Mary will be there. Please, Pascal, don't fight me on this. I have to see him. Don't make it any harder than it is already.'

She held out her hand to him as she said this. Pascal took it. He looked down into her face with an expression of angry concern.

523

'Darling, *why*?' he said, and caught her in his arms. 'Why? I still don't understand. Why do you let him do this to you?'

Gini bent her head. She let him lock his arms around her, but she did not reply. Pascal held her close. She could feel the tension in his body; she could feel the beating of his heart.

Then the telephone rang. With a muttered exclamation Pascal went to answer it. Suzy was punctual, it seemed, and was now waiting at the front desk. In the three minutes it took her to reach their room, Gini had time to answer Pascal's final question – though she did so silently, and to herself.

Why? Because her father indeed made her feel like a child again – and a few other things besides, such as unloved, in the way, irritating, a nuisance, a bore . . . Maybe this time, she thought, maybe this time it will be different – and then she turned away sadly. For that hope, of course, was the source of his power over her, no matter how many times she had hoped, and been disappointed, before.

Suzy, when she entered, looked young and nervous. She was dressed as if for a job interview, in a neat cream suit with carefully matching accessories. Her fair hair was newly washed, her make-up minimal. It was only on closer inspection that the wariness in her eyes became apparent, and only when she spoke that the illusion of youth and innocence was destroyed.

She came into the room with a few light remarks about the hotel, and a slow measuring glance at Pascal. Then she saw Gini, and her whole manner altered. She stopped two feet inside the door. Her face hardened.

She said, in a sharp voice, 'What is this? I don't do threesomes. Not for this money. Fuck you.'

It took nearly ten minutes to persuade her to stay. In the end, after lengthy explanations and assurances, she seemed to hesitate. She gave Gini a long hard look, then gestured at Pascal.

'OK,' she said. 'I'll talk to you, but not with him here. On our own, all right?'

Pascal, at a sign from Gini, left the room. He did not seem pleased to do so. Suzy waited until the door closed, then crossed to a chair opposite Gini. She sat down, and lit a cigarette.

'I don't like men,' she said in a matter of fact way. 'I don't trust men. I screw them, but I don't trust them. How about you?'

'I trust some of them. Occasionally.'

'It's your funeral.' She shrugged. 'I'd rather talk to a woman any day. Before we talk, let's get one thing straight. I'm older than I look. I've got two kids to support. OK, so I'm not in a pension plan, but I can make good money doing what I do. It's a service industry, as far as I'm concerned. The clients buy my services – not me.'

'Fine. I understand.' Gini hesitated. 'I can't explain why I'm asking these questions, but they are important. Part of a much larger story.'

'That's OK.' Suzy exhaled a cloud of bluish smoke. 'I don't care. You're paying for my time. I don't mind telling you what happened. Bloody swine . . . Send the photographs on approval. Sit in a hotel lobby on approval.' She spoke with sudden vehemence; her eyes glittered with resentment. 'I mean, this was the third time this guy had booked me, right? And he'd already cancelled twice.'

Gini leaned forward. 'What happened that third time?' she asked. 'You didn't just sit in that hotel lobby for half an hour, did you?'

'No way. That's what he told the agency he wanted me to do. That's what I told them I had done. But it wasn't like that at all.'

She hesitated, drawing on her cigarette. 'Look,' she went on, 'let me tell it from the beginning, then maybe you'll understand. This was back in December last year. I was sitting there in the lobby, just the way he asked, all right? For fifteen, maybe twenty minutes. I was wearing this suit – I keep this for my work. I was sort of curious, you know? I get all kinds of requests, but this one was something new. I was trying to work out which of the men in the lobby was my client – and there were a lot of candidates. It was a busy time. Scores of blokes going through. Then I saw this woman, standing by the front desk. Staring at me. Watching me . . . '

'A woman? Can you describe her?'

'About thirty. Very attractive. She had long fair hair, cut a bit like mine. She was wearing beautiful clothes – ever such beautiful clothes. A dark navy suit, a cream silk shirt, pearls, expensive shoes – oh, and one of those famous handbags, like that movie-star used to carry . . . '

'A Grace Kelly bag? Hermès?'

'That's it. In crocodile. Two thousand quid a throw. Plus, she was wearing dark glasses and I thought that was odd. It was December, for God's sake. OK, it was a fine day outside, but indoors she still kept them on. She kept them on all the time . . . '

'Did she approach you? Talk to you?'

'Yes. She did. She came over, and she said she knew I must be Suzy because she'd called the agency herself. She said there'd been a change of plan. My client did still want to see me, but in his room. Would I mind going upstairs with her.'

'And you agreed?'

'Sure.' Suzy gave her a sharp glance. 'I thought, maybe the guy had been in the lobby earlier to check me out. I thought, maybe it turned him on, he wants to screw . . . ' She hesitated. 'I thought if he did, keep mum, no need to pay the agency commission. Why give them twenty per cent? They need never know. Besides, it was a ritzy place. I'd never been there before. I wanted to see the rooms.'

'So you went upstairs with the woman?'

'Right. First, she says she'll just show me the way. Then, when we get there, she comes in too. It was a suite. Really glamorous. Lovely thick carpets, silk covers on the chairs, huge great vases of flowers . . . Then I noticed something weird. It was mid-morning and all the curtains were closed.'

'You didn't notice that right away?'

'No. Too busy pricing the furniture maybe.' She gave a tight smile. 'Hotel rooms are often dark. And there were table lights switched on. Only part of the room was dark . . . ' She paused. 'This woman, she sits me down, next to a lamp. And then I realize: we aren't alone. There's this man, sitting over in the corner. In the shadows. Just sitting there. He doesn't speak. He doesn't move. Legs crossed, watching me. And the whole time I'm in there, the bastard never says one word.'

'Can you describe him, Suzy?'

'No. Not too well. I'm short-sighted. He was sitting in shadow. Well-dressed – a black overcoat, unbuttoned; a dark suit. Fortyish maybe. Tallish. Fair hair.'

'Handsome? Tanned? Blue eyes? Brown eyes?'

'I couldn't say.'

'OK. What about the woman? She was still there? Did she say anything?'

'Oh, she was still there all right.' Suzy's tone hardened. 'And gestures speak louder than words, right? You know what she did? She opened that handbag of hers and inside, it was full of money. She held it out, so I could see. She lets me look at it for a bit, then very slowly, she starts taking it out. It's fifty-pound notes. In bundles of ten. She says: "Now, I want you to undress, not completely, just down to your underwear. That's worth five hundred. Then, if you do what I tell you, that's another five hundred. If we're pleased with you, there's a bonus. One more bundle. That's fifteen hundred pounds. No-one will touch you. Then you can leave. Do you agree?" '

Suzy paused. 'She had this really quiet, polite, voice. It was like she was asking me some special favour. Every time she said five hundred, she took another bundle out of the bag, and put it down on the table next to me. I looked at it, and I looked at it . . . You know how long it'd take me to earn that kind of money usually? Four clients. Five. A week of them mauling me about, or me jerking them off. Sometimes weeks go by, and there are no clients. I have to pay a mortgage. School fees. I like things nice. I agreed.'

'Tell me what you had to do, Suzy.'

Again that look of angry resentment passed across her face. She shrugged. 'First, I had to get bought. I think that was it. It gave her a thrill, buying me. Him too, maybe. He was watching all the time. Anyway, I did what she said. Slowly, the way she asked. I had to stand facing him, and take my clothes off. She kind of hovered around me, all the time I was doing that. It was like she wanted to touch me all the time. And she stared at me too, really stared, like she was memorizing me for some fucking identity parade. She helped undo my skirt. She even touched my hair – she said I had really beautiful hair. She stroked my breasts a few times – and that turned her on. If I'm honest, it turned me on too. I like to do it with women.' She paused, and her eyes slid across to meet Gini's. 'How about you?'

'I prefer men. Generally.'

Suzy shrugged. 'Any time you change your mind let me know. Anyway, this woman, she starts stroking my breasts, but she does it in this really weird way, standing a bit to the side, so the guy can get a really good view. It's like she's *displaying* me for his benefit, right? And she's starting to shake. Then all of a sudden, he sighs, and she gets control of herself. She tells me to sit down. Facing her friend . . . '

'She called him that?'

'Yes. Some friend. Fucking deviant. All the time she's touching me, he's got his hands in his pockets – and put it this way, he wasn't checking his wallet. Or finding his keys.'

'Fine. I get the picture. Go on.'

'Look,' Suzy shot her a hard glance, 'so far, it's not that unusual, OK? I get plenty of jerk-off merchants. The ones who want to watch. I figured, sooner or later, he'd want to watch us fuck, the blonde and me. Well, I was wrong. She might have liked the idea, but that wasn't the scenario. Not at all.

'The woman had to do all the talking,' she continued, 'all right? And I had to stay silent. She said that was the rule.'

'She used that term? "Rule"?'

'That's right. So, I sit down. She sits down – away off to my right, so she doesn't spoil his view. Then she starts giving me instructions. And she's so polite. So odd. Like a bloody robot. Like she's speaking from some script she's learned by heart.

'I'm on this upright chair,' Suzy went on, 'about twelve feet in front of him. Wearing my underwear – my professional underwear, if you want to know. It's white, ever so expensive. Stockings. A suspender belt. No bra. No panties . . . ' She hesitated and gave a tight smile. 'I've learned. Five years on the game, and you learn fast. Turn them on quick, and get it over with. I don't want hours in bed with those animals. This way, sometimes, you get lucky. You don't even fuck them. You just let them look at you. Touch your tits. Cop a feel of your fanny. Tell them they've got a big cock. Dumb bastards. Some of them are so fucking desperate, that does it. They come.'

She paused to light a cigarette, inhaled deeply, then continued. 'Anyway, I was obedient, OK? And she told me exactly what to do. So sweetly. So politely. Part your legs. Sit astride the chair. Stroke your breasts . . . Then she gave me this pair of gloves. Long black gloves. Put them on. Pinch your nipples. Feel your cunt. Touch yourself. Enjoy yourself. Look him in the eyes. Don't speak. Close your eyes when you're going to come . . . '

There was a silence. Gini rose and began to pace the room. Suzy, unconcerned, continued to smoke her cigarette. Beyond the front window, came the hum of the traffic. Looking out, to the main entrance five floors below, Gini saw a fleet of black Mercedes waiting. A party of Arab women, robed in black, their faces masked, approached them, black as crows on the wet pavement; they were carrying Harrods shopping-bags. She turned back to Suzy.

'And you did all those things?' Gini asked.

Suzy gave a smile of derision. 'Sure. Except I didn't come. I faked it. The same way I always do. Most men can't even tell when they're in up to the hilt banging

529

you. Just watching there's no way he could know.' She shrugged. 'I cheat on the deal, OK? They think they can buy me, but they can't. Collect fifteen hundred quid, goodbye, sir, and screw you . . . '

Gini ignored the bitterness of tone. She said, 'And this man – apart from that one sigh, he never moved, never spoke, all the while?'

'No. Not once. It worked for him though . . . ' Suzy shot her another glance of bitter amusement. 'The second it was over they couldn't wait to get me out of the room. The woman – her eyes were shining, her face was flushed. She was so turned on, she was shaking. She practically threw the money at me. I knew what was going to happen the second I left the room. And I was right.'

'How do you know?'

'Because I listened, outside the door. I could hear them clearly. At least I could hear her. She was all over him, asking for his cock, telling him how big he was, how hard he was. Right then she didn't sound so sweet and demure.'

'Then you left?'

'A minute or so later. I wanted to see if he'd speak. But he didn't, even then. She was going completely crazy. Then I heard him hit her really hard.'

'You're sure he didn't speak?'

'No. Not a word. Just slapped her. It sounded like he slapped her across the face, with the flat of his hand. She cried out. Then there was a thump, like she'd slumped back against the door. Then there was silence.' Suzy shrugged again. 'He was fucking her, I think. The way she asked him to, maybe. Which was up against the wall.'

There was a long silence. Gini returned to her chair. She sat for a while, looking at Suzy. Finally she said, 'Suzy, this really happened? What you've told me is true?'

'Every word.'

'I want you to think really carefully. The woman – you're sure she was blonde?'

'Totally sure.'

'Could she have been wearing a wig of some kind?'

'I don't think so. It looked like her own hair.'

'And she never removed the dark glasses?'

'No.'

'Can you describe her voice?'

'I told you. Soft. Polite. Careful – like she was reciting a part. English, very. Posh.'

'You're certain English? Not a trace of anything else? How about after you left the room?'

'No accent, unless you call rich an accent. English. Boarding-school and ponies. Upper bleeding class.'

'Anything else you can remember? About the way she was dressed, maybe? Was she wearing gloves, for instance?'

'No.'

'What rings was she wearing? An engagement ring? A wedding ring?'

'No rings. Bare hands.'

'What about the man? Can you remember anything else about him? Think, Suzy.'

'I told you. He was sitting in the shadows. Dark suit, dark overcoat, white shirt – no different from a thousand other men.'

'Was there anything in the room that struck you? A suitcase, maybe? Cigarettes, books, magazines . . .'

'Nothing. The door to the bedroom was closed. The room just looked like a posh hotel room.'

'What name were you given for the client?'

'Hastings, I think. That's right. John Hastings.'

Gini frowned. John Hawthorne; John Hamilton, McMullen's alias for his meeting with Lorna Munro; John Hastings. Again she had the feeling Pascal had described – that she was being manipulated, that a coincidence of initials was intended to imply a connection. A connection which might mislead. Opening her purse she took out three photographs. The first two were of McMullen and of Hawthorne, the third was of Lise. She passed the first two across to Suzy.

'Could either of those men be Hastings?'

Suzy looked at the picture, then shrugged. 'Either – or

531

neither. They're around the right age. They both have fair hair. So do hundreds of other men.'

'OK.' Gini passed the third picture across. 'Allowing for the difference in hair colour, obviously. Is there any resemblance to your woman there?'

The photograph of Lise, taken from the picture archives at the *News*, was in black and white. It was the most anonymous picture of Lise she could find. She was, for once, not surrounded by adulatory crowds. She had been photographed on a pavement, about to get into a car. Suzy looked at this picture for some time. When she looked up, her face was hard and suspicious.

'What is this? What's going on? I know this woman – obviously I know her. Who wouldn't? It's Mrs Hawthorne.'

'That's right. The US Ambassador's wife.'

'I know that. I'm not a fool. I've even met Mrs Hawthorne—'

'You've met her?'

'Don't sound so bloody surprised. I met her last spring. In a children's hospital ward. My youngest was very ill, last year. She nearly died. She had to have dialysis. You know who donated the money for the machine? Mrs Hawthorne. I was one of the parents there when she did her hospital tour. You ought to be bloody ashamed of yourself, you ought . . . '

Her voice had risen. She stood, and moved towards the door. 'I *talked* to her! She sat by my daughter's bed, and we talked. She's got two children of her own. She was lovely to me. Really kind. And she wasn't doing some Lady Bountiful act, either. I could tell she really cared.'

Gini knew that any confidence Suzy had placed in her was irretrievably gone. The hostility blazed from her.

'So Mrs Hawthorne and the woman in the hotel room,' she said quietly, 'they couldn't possibly have been the same woman?'

'No. They bloody well couldn't. They were nothing alike. I *told* you! The hotel woman was English. She was younger than Mrs Hawthorne. She had blond hair . . . What's fucking wrong with you? Sodding journalists. And I thought you were OK . . . I must want my head read. You're just another bleeding muck-raker, that's all.'

She opened the door and looked back with one last angry glance. 'What is it with you people? You have to do it, don't you? Drag every poor fucking sod down in the mud. And I thought *I* was the whore . . . Pay you well, do they? Well, screw you – you want to wreck an innocent person's life, you do it without my help. Just don't fucking contact me again, you understand? You or your friend!'

When Pascal returned his manner was tense and cool. Gini recounted this conversation. Pascal listened carefully.

'It's not conclusive,' he said finally. 'The man could have been Hawthorne or McMullen. The woman could have been Lise, I suppose, if she can change accents. Or more likely one of Hawthorne's blondes. What do you think? An audition of some kind? A rehearsal? It sounds like one of those.'

'Both, maybe. Some kind of preliminary to the Sunday meeting? There must be a connection, Pascal. Black gloves, silence, rules.'

'That, or we're supposed to see a connection, to imagine one.'

'I think it has to be one of Hawthorne's blondes. Going through some try-out before the Sunday assignation. This meeting was two or three days before the December Sunday, remember? Maybe Hawthorne was deciding which woman to hire – Suzy or a blonde with an upper-class accent and a two-thousand-pound Hermès bag.'

'And he opted for the more expensive product?'

'Presumably.' Gini frowned. 'It's odd though, the way Suzy described her, so sweet and polite – it made me think of Lise. I started to wonder. You remember what McMullen told us? How Hawthorne showed those pictures of blondes to Lise and asked her to choose? Maybe Hawthorne does more than just describe these events to his wife. Maybe he compels her to get involved.'

'You mean he makes her audition the girls? Gini, come on.'

'I know, I know. But the way Suzy described her, the woman was reciting a part. Something scripted. Playing a role.'

'Suzy also made it clear the woman enjoyed it,' Pascal said drily.

'That's true. But Lise's behaviour is so odd anyway, so unpredictable – and she is on medication. She takes tranquillizers. Maybe she takes other stuff as well. Maybe Hawthorne *persuades* her to take other stuff.'

'Once a month? Just prior to the Sundays he slips his wife something that transforms her into a procuress? Gini—'

'OK, OK. I agree. It's absurd.' She shrugged. 'Anyway, Suzy was definite. The blonde in the hotel wasn't Lise.'

Pascal gave a sudden dismissive gesture. 'Even that proves nothing,' he said. 'You said yourself – Lise Hawthorne is auditioning to be a saint. Well, that's how Suzy saw her, as an angel of mercy at a hospital bedside, ministering to a sick child. A heroine, if you like. People need heroes and heroines. They need to cling to their illusions.'

He paused; an edge had come into his voice. 'Speaking of which,' he added, 'you're due to see your father shortly. Gini, we should go.'

XXX

'Gini, come in,' Mary said, ushering her into the hall. They both paused in the doorway, looking down into the street outside. There, Pascal gunned the engine of his motor bike. He pulled away fast, without any gesture of farewell.

'He's coming back to collect me around eight,' Gini said. Mary sighed and closed the front door.

'One moment, Gini,' she said. 'Before you go in, there's something I want to say.'

Gini paused. The door into the studio was closed, she noted. Mary's kind features wore an expression of bewilderment. She put her hand on Gini's arm.

'Gini, I don't understand exactly what's going on. But one thing is clear: you and Pascal Lamartine have been working on an investigation, a story on John . . . ' She shook her head sadly. 'Gini, how could you deceive me in that way? You must have known, when you came to my party. You came here under false pretences. John is one of my closest friends. How could you, Gini? It's so unlike you.'

Gini's face became set. Slowly she removed her coat. 'I see,' she said. 'Then that *is* why I'm here. I might have known.'

She felt both angry and sad. Her arrival here had been preceded by another argument with Pascal. He had been very close to losing his temper, and so had she. The past hour had been one of mounting irritation between them, with both of them edging towards a confrontation, then edging away. It had left her nervous, and miserable, and this confirmation that Pascal had been correct in his assessment of her father's motives, made her feel worse. For a moment her instinct was just to walk out there and then, not to see Sam Hunter at all. Perhaps some of what she felt could be read on her face, for Mary looked at her closely, and then sighed.

'Oh Gini, what a horrible mess. Listen, never mind that now. That's not the main issue, I know. It's just that it *hurt* me, Gini and . . . Anyway,' she hesitated, 'do watch what you say. Sam's in a foul mood. He's been working himself up for hours. I've been trying to calm him down but there is a limit. He's on the second bourbon already, and you know what he's like when he drinks. I thought it was better to keep this brief. Sam has a dinner with his publisher later. I'm going too. So it'll only be an hour, darling, an hour and a half at most. But do watch your tongue. Try to stay off the subject of Pascal Lamartine, for heaven's sake.'

She broke off; her face crumpled. Gini saw that she was suddenly very close to tears. She felt a rush of affection and guilt. She put her arms around Mary and hugged her. If her father had been building up to this meeting, she could imagine what Mary had been through this afternoon.

'Oh Mary,' she said, 'I'm sorry. I will explain it all to you eventually. Don't get upset. This isn't your fault, any of it. It's not fair for you to be in the middle of it.'

'But I *am*.' Mary's hand waved a sad helpless gesture. 'I haven't been honest with you either, Gini, and I should have been. I knew about Beirut all along. I knew who Pascal was and I should have admitted it. I hate all these lies.'

'Mary, that doesn't matter. I don't mind, I'm even glad. Truly—'

She broke off. From the room beyond came the sound of movement, a chair being pushed back. Mary looked quickly at the closed door, then back at Gini. With a small agitated nod of her head she went on.

'Gini, it's not just that. Sam blames Pascal for all this, of course, and I want you to be prepared for that. But . . . '

She hesitated again. An almost guilty expression crossed her face. Gini looked at her, puzzled, then glanced back at the closed door. From beyond it came the sound of her father's voice. There was a pause, then more quietly another man replied. Gini tensed.

'Who's in there with him?' she began, in a low voice. 'Mary, he isn't alone. What's going on?'

Mary gave her a silent and unhappy look. She did not need to answer the question for at that moment there were footsteps, then the door was thrown back. Sam Hunter stood there, glowering. He had a full glass of bourbon in his hand. Beyond him, leaning against the mantelpiece was the figure of John Hawthorne.

'So,' her father glared first at Gini, then at Mary, 'are you coming in here? Or are you going to spend the rest of the goddamn evening whispering in the hall?'

He might have continued in that vein, but Mary took charge. Taking Gini by the arm, she led her past Sam, and into the room. John Hawthorne acknowledged her arrival with a brief nod, but said nothing. Mary turned, and faced Sam.

'Now, let's just get one thing clear, Sam,' she said in a quiet firm voice. 'This is my house, not yours. If you're going to start shouting and blustering, then you can leave, because I won't put up with it, you understand? This isn't easy for me, or Gini, or any of us. I agreed to all this on one condition. You say what you have to say. John says what he wants to say. You both of you give Gini a fair hearing, and then we all leave. But I will not have this degenerating into one of your brawls, Sam. So you can just sit down and calm down. If we're going to do this at all, damn it, we'll do it in a civilized way.'

Mary's tone, Gini thought, would have quelled most people, but not her father, or not her father when he had been drinking, anyway. He rounded on Mary in a belligerent way.

'Look,' he said, jabbing one finger in the air. 'Look, Mary. If you think I'm going to pretend this is some goddamn social call, forget it. It's not. I'm not here to sit around making small talk. I want to get to the bottom of this. My daughter's got some goddamn explaining to do, and the quicker we get on with it the better. I mean, Jesus Christ! I don't see her, I don't damn well lay eyes on her in two years, and then what happens? This.'

He took a deep swallow of bourbon. His eyes, which were bloodshot, ranged around the room, then fixed on Gini. 'Just get one thing straight, Gini, before we start. I blame that goddamn fucking Frenchman. But I also blame you. You're not a fifteen-year-old kid any more. Where's your judgement here?'

Both Gini and Mary began speaking then. Mary launched on some remonstrance, Gini on a quick and angry reply. Sam Hunter attempted to shout them both down, and then John Hawthorne spoke for the first time. His voice, cold, clipped and authoritative, silenced them all, including Sam.

'Sam, that's enough,' he said. 'Mary's right. There is absolutely nothing to be gained by this kind of scene. Or that kind of language. Control your temper for once, will you? Sit down. Shall we all sit down? I am the reason Gini is here tonight and since she's had the courtesy to come, I owe her a courtesy in return. I would like to explain.'

Gini said nothing. She watched her father, and she saw how easily John Hawthorne whipped him into line. It pained her to see it, but Sam capitulated at once. He gave her one last angry glance, then a truculent sigh. Turning his back on her, he moved across to the left of the fireplace, and slumped in a chair, nursing the bourbon.

Gini was shocked, and hurt, by the change in him in these last two and a half years. The continued coarsening in his appearance was now very evident. He was, as always, well dressed; he wore one of the dark suits he had tailored for him in London, and a crisp, somewhat loudly striped Paul Stuart shirt. His handmade shoes were well shined. But the thickening waistline, the ponderous bulk, the heavy jowls, the blotchy complexion of the heavy drinker – all these aspects of her father could no longer be ignored. He looked, she realized, like an aggressive, unstable and deeply unhappy man.

Quietly, she moved across to a chair opposite John Hawthorne, and sat down. Mary fussed in an uncertain way at the drinks tray for a while. She handed Gini a glass of wine, as if she would have liked to pretend this was an ordinary social occasion, then she seated herself a little behind Gini, just outside the semi-circle in front of the fire. The focal point of that half-circle was Hawthorne. He remained standing, Gini noted, despite his earlier suggestion that they all sit down.

In contrast to her father, Hawthorne looked calm and in control. He was wearing a dark, very formal suit. His manner was quiet, and when he looked at her, Gini felt there was a certain regret or possibly contempt in his eyes, as if he had expected better of her, as if he had set her some test, and she had failed.

'First of all,' he began, 'I suggest we waste no time. I don't intend to spend the next hour listening to denials and lies. So if we could just set out the parameters here. Can we all accept, please, that the *News* launched an investigation into me, and into my private life, some nine days ago, and that Gini was assigned to that story, together with a French photographer, Pascal Lamartine?'

He looked directly at Gini as he said this. Gini did not reply. Behind her, Mary gave a small sigh. Her father stirred in his chair.

'Look, Gini,' he said, leaning forward, 'John's right. Can we just cut the crap here? He knows you're working on the story. I know. We *all* damn well know. So there's no goddamn point in denying it. It just wastes time.'

'If you're so well informed,' Gini began carefully, 'then you'll also know that I was taken *off* the story, last Tuesday. By my editor. As far as I know, the story has been killed.' She hesitated. 'A few rumours had been circulating, that's all. I was asked to check them out – and for what it's worth, I got nowhere. That's one of the reasons the story was killed. The other reason, as I understand it, was that the owner of the *News* was pressured. To such an extent, I hear, that my editor's job is now on the line. What I don't quite understand,' she raised her eyes to look at Hawthorne, 'is why, when you have influence of that kind, you should now try to influence me. Why? It's pointless. I'm not even working on this any more.'

'I did suggest we avoid wasting time.' Hawthorne's reply was even, his expression cold. 'You were asked – told – to drop the story, as we're both well aware. Your editor may or may not lose his job as a result of his continuing involvement. That is Henry Melrose's decision – it has nothing whatsoever to do with me. But let's not pretend you obeyed your editor's instructions. With or without his knowledge, you have continued to work on this, and so has Lamartine. The source for this story is a man named James McMullen. You met with him two days ago, first in Regent's Park, and then in the British Museum. You have been in contact this week with his former tutor in Oxford, Dr Anthony Knowles. You've been continuing your enquiries today. You met with a friend of McMullen's today, in the Groucho Club in Soho.' He looked directly at her. 'You call that dropping the story?'

Gini met his gaze briefly. The meeting with McMullen in Oxford, she noted, was not mentioned.

'I don't know where you're getting this information.' She shrugged and looked away. 'I should double-check your sources. I met no-one at the British Museum, I went there to look at the exhibits, that's all. I had spoken to Anthony Knowles, earlier, and I called him back to tell him I was dropping the story. As for today, I had a drink at lunch-time with an old contact of mine. The meeting had nothing to do with this story at all.'

'You were with a former school-friend of McMullen's today. A man you'd never previously met.' Hawthorne gave her a cold glance. 'And in some ways when I learned that, I felt a certain relief. Presumably you're at last making some attempt to check James McMullen's credentials. It's somewhat overdue. But check him out, by all means. And make a thorough job of it when you do. McMullen is a liar and a troublemaker. I sometimes wonder if the man's entirely sane—'

'Entirely sane?' Gini's father could hold back no longer. He gave a sweeping gesture of the arm, spilling bourbon. 'That's the goddamn understatement of all time. The man's a nutcase. He's a sicko. A weirdo. He's obsessed with John, obsessed with me, he's been nursing some crazy paranoid delusion for Christ knows how long – and now he comes crawling out of the woodwork yet again, and who does he home in on? *My* goddamn daughter! You think that's some kind of an accident? Christ, Gini,' he swung around to face her, 'how long have you worked in newspapers now? Can't you recognize a crazy when you meet one? Or do you just swallow it all down, whatever stuff they feed you? *Check*, why don't you? Learn to goddamn check – and if you can't, then go back to journalism school. Better still find some other career.'

'Now wait a minute—' Gini began, but Mary interrupted her.

'Yes,' she said, 'wait, Sam, and think for once before you start throwing accusations around. You don't have the least idea of Gini's capabilities because you've never bothered to take any interest in Gini's career. Gini isn't some child, starting out. She's had a lot of experience—'

'Experience? Give me a break. Where? On some goddamn cheap sex-scandal rag.'

'She's had a lot of experience, Sam. If Gini has been working on this story, you can be quite sure she will have tried to investigate it thoroughly and properly, from day one.' Mary spoke firmly. 'If this James McMullen had been as you describe, Gini would have seen through him. It can't be as easy as that—'

'No. Mary's right.' Again it was John Hawthorne's cool tones which interjected, and silenced the others. He gave a sigh. 'It isn't as easy as that. I wish to God it were.'

He looked away as he said this, and for the first time Gini sensed the tension he was feeling. For a moment she glimpsed on his face that expression she had seen at the

541

Savoy dinner. She thought: *Beneath that calm, he is very close to despair*.

She thought that both Mary and her father sensed this too. Her father shot him a quick look, and at once altered his tone. He rose, and the belligerence lessened.

'Look, Gini,' he said, in a quieter tone, 'can you just stop and consider what's at stake here? We're talking about John's life, his reputation – you know what happens when this kind of thing gets out of control. People talk. Even if you don't publish, people *talk*, and the rumours get wilder and wilder . . . Well, I'm not about to let that happen. That's why I'm here.'

He paused, glanced at Hawthorne again, and then continued. 'Look, Gini – OK, I lost my temper just now. I do that. I've got a short fuse. But I'm not blaming you for this, not really. The way I see it, you're just way out of your depth on this whole thing. And it's not goddamn well helped by Lamartine's involvement. I'm not going to rake up the past – I don't need to. If you didn't learn your lesson about that man twelve years ago, learn it now. Just take a close look at the work Lamartine does, Gini. That's not journalism and it never will be. It's goddamn muck-raking. Lamartine's scum.'

There was a silence. Hawthorne remained staring down into the fire. Gini looked at her father, and then looked away. Behind her, Mary moved. She too rose.

'Gini,' she said in a quiet voice, 'think about what Sam says. I don't want to make a judgement on Pascal Lamartine as a person. As I told you. I quite liked him as a man. But Sam is right. You can't ignore the kind of work Pascal Lamartine does now. It's cruel and intrusive and unacceptable. You can't believe it's ethical, that work, any more than we do.' She glanced at Hawthorne, then continued. 'Gini – I think you should ask yourself, how much have you allowed your feelings for Pascal Lamartine to influence your judgement here? Would you have gone on with this the way you have if you hadn't been working with him? He's been a corrupting influence, Gini. I'm sorry, but I do believe that.'

'Mary, stop. I'm not going to discuss this. And what you've just said isn't true.'

'In that case,' Mary sighed, 'we go back to what I said before. You've been very foolish, Gini. Both you and Pascal Lamartine have been misinformed. Cleverly misinformed. If you won't listen to us, then I just hope you'll come to realize that. Very soon.'

Her voice had sharpened, and she now made no attempt to disguise her reproof. She began to turn away, and as she did so, John Hawthorne looked up and spoke.

'I'm sorry, Mary,' he said, 'but I'm not prepared to wait for Gini to see sense. I will not take that risk. Lise is involved. I will not stand by and see my family damaged by all this. I have to think of my children. God knows they've suffered enough.'

He turned away with a gesture of quiet anger and disgust. Gini stared at him. She could now see that he was deeply moved, almost unable to speak; she felt doubts begin again at the edge of her mind. There was another silence, then her father cleared his throat. He glanced at Hawthorne again, as if seeking permission.

'John?'

Hawthorne nodded.

'Very well.' Her father turned back to her, his face serious now. 'I'll say this just once, Gini. I'll keep it brief. There's no point in all this fencing around. What I have to say is between us. In confidence. It doesn't go beyond this room, you understand?'

Gini nodded.

'Very well. The truth is, for around four years now, ever since John's younger boy was so ill, Lise has been a sick woman. She's been diagnosed as manic-depressive by specialists in Washington, London and New York. She's on constant medication. She's had electric shock therapy five times. She's tried to kill herself on two occasions, once back in Washington, just before John resigned from the Senate, and a second time a month after they arrived here. She can't be left alone, unsupervised, except for very short periods. As a result, her feelings of paranoia and persecution have increased. John's done everything in his power to help her – and don't imagine it's been easy. He gave up politics for her, because she claimed she needed him there with her and the boys. He agreed to take the posting here because she was wild for him to do it, and said she wanted a bigger role. John thought it could help – a new city, a change of scene, new friends. But it hasn't helped. Her condition has deteriorated. It's been made a whole lot worse by her involvement with McMullen and the way he influences her. According to her doctors here, Lise needs urgent hospitalization and they've been saying that, Gini, since last summer. John has been fighting that. Unwisely, in my view.' His voice hardened. 'Lise is a lovely woman, Gini, but she's a very sick woman too. She can't distinguish fact from fiction. And there are a few other problems too. It's not my place to discuss those. But I'm here to bear witness to the fact that she's very ill, well-nigh schizophrenic. Mary can vouch for that as well, can't you, Mary? Yes or no?'

Gini turned to look at Mary, whose face met hers with an expression of unhappy concern.

'Yes, I can,' she said quietly. 'Gini, I told you before about the scene I witnessed. It was terribly distressing for me, and quite appalling for John. You have to understand John is in an impossible position. He has his public duties to perform. He's been trying to keep up appearances, trying to protect Lise from herself. He has to think of their sons. And he's borne all this on his own. He couldn't even discuss it, except with the doctors. Gini, just try to imagine for a moment what he's been through—'

'I'm partly to blame.' John Hawthorne spoke suddenly. He had turned back to face Gini. The pain in his eyes was now unmistakable. He passed his hand tiredly across his face. 'I have to recognize that fact. I have to live with it day and night. I should have acted sooner. I should never have allowed my sons to witness what they have witnessed. I should probably never have accepted this posting – and I should certainly have taken the doctors' advice months ago. But you see . . . ' His voice trailed off. After a moment he composed himself and continued. 'It's such a cruel disease. There are periods when Lise is almost her old self, when I start to hope again. And then there is always a relapse . . . and she turns into a person I hardly know. She'll suddenly have one of these terrible rages. Or she'll seem perfectly normal – and then she'll tell some extraordinary lie, when there's no apparent reason to lie at all.'

He looked at Gini and at Mary. 'You remember the night we came here for your party – it was Lise's birthday?'

Mary nodded. An expression of pained bewilderment now came into Hawthorne's features.

'Well, that was one of the occasions when I thought she seemed better. She was animated, almost the way she used to be. And then, when we were about to leave – you remember, Mary? She showed you her coat, and the necklace she was wearing and she said they were my birthday present to her that day?'

'I remember,' Mary replied.

'Well, that wasn't true. I gave Lise the coat and the necklace last year, back in the fall. I took her away for the weekend then, just the two of us, to the country. It was our wedding anniversary. I wanted . . . I tried.' He broke off, then controlled the emotion in his voice. 'I thought if we could just have two days, two quiet, normal days . . . And she seemed pleased with the coat, and the necklace. Then she put them away. She never wore them, not once, until the night of your party. Then she lied about when I'd given them to her. Why? Why? I can't tell whether she genuinely makes a mistake or whether it's aimed at me, as if she wanted to forget that weekend, forget our anniversary, forget our marriage. I just don't know any more . . . ' He turned away. Mary rose to her feet, and crossed to him. She put her arm around his shoulders.

'John, don't. Don't,' she said quietly. 'You're crucifying yourself over this and that doesn't help anyone, you know. It's better if you talk about it. You should learn to talk to your friends. Look. Have a drink. You're exhausted, let me get you a whisky. Don't argue. Just a small one. Come on.'

She crossed back to the drinks table, and poured the whisky. Gini looked at Hawthorne's tense figure, and a terrible sick sense of doubt welled up inside her. She thought: *What have I done? I've been wrong, totally wrong* . . .

There was a long awkward silence then. Hawthorne accepted the drink from Mary, who returned to her chair. Gini saw her father look at Hawthorne with a kind of embarrassed concern.

'Shall I go on, John? Gini might as well know it all.'

'Why not?' Hawthorne gave a bitter, dismissive gesture of the hand. 'You explain. I can't stand to talk about it any more.'

Sam turned back to Gini. He took a piece of paper from his jacket pocket, and handed it to her. 'Read that later,' he said. 'It's a copy of an article I wrote twenty-five years ago. It describes a mission John's platoon went on in Vietnam, in November nineteen sixty-eight. I was attached to his platoon. We were cut off, up country, in the jungle south of Hue, south of the 17th parallel, not far from a village called My Nuc. John's platoon was under Vietcong fire, pinned down, for over five days. Seventeen of his men died.' He paused. 'Has McMullen made allegations about what happened at My Nuc to your newspaper? Because believe me, Gini, if he hasn't yet, he will.'

Gini hesitated. She looked down at the floor. All three were now watching her closely.

'Come on, Gini,' said her father impatiently. 'We know pretty much what McMullen's been saying about John and his marriage. Has he made allegations about Vietnam as well?'

'I told you,' Gini replied, 'I've never spoken to McMullen. He's disappeared. All I was doing was checking out rumours.'

'About my marriage?' Hawthorne said sharply.

'Yes.'

546

'And about the events at My Nuc?' This time it was her father who asked the question.

Gini shrugged. 'I was told allegations had been made about what happened there. Yes.'

'Jesus Christ.' Her father shot Hawthorne an angry look. 'OK, Gini. My book on Vietnam is due out later this year – maybe that helped trigger McMullen – but let's get this straight. McMullen's raised questions about My Nuc before. He's made allegations before. Twenty goddamn years ago. Did you know that?'

Gini hesitated. 'No, I didn't,' she said.

'Well he did. Atrocities, rape, murder of non-combatants. He made them first to a US Senator, who's now dead. He took the story to two US newspapers back in nineteen seventy-two, when he spent six months in the States. They're a fabrication from beginning to end. None of it happened, Gini. *None* of it. When he tried to get newspapers interested back then, he was laughed out of town – and he didn't like that, not one little bit. Gini, I was goddamn well *there*. I was with John the entire time. The village of My Nuc had been razed before we even got there. When we reached it, everyone in it was dead including the girl McMullen claims was raped. Everything I wrote then is God's own truth. I was a goddamn eyewitness, Gini, believe that.'

There was a silence. Out of that silence, John Hawthorne spoke.

'McMullen has always claimed to know of witnesses also, Sam. I imagine Gini's heard that. There's no point in this claim and counter-claim, not twenty-five years after an event. What Gini should do is take a very close look at *when* McMullen made those accusations, and what he has done since.' He turned his eyes coldly in her direction.

'Since last July, when McMullen began on a campaign to influence my wife – knowing full-well, I believe, how ill she was – I've made it my business to have McMullen and his allegations checked out. The woman he claims was raped was not some peasant living in a tiny remote village. For a start, she was from North Vietnam, not the south. Her father and her brother were both prominent Hanoi activists. In fact, her father was on the Standing Committee of the North Vietnamese national assembly. She was twenty-five years old when she died and she'd been a political activist since the age of sixteen. She was half French and she was extremely well-educated. She had not only studied in Hanoi, but also Paris, Prague and Moscow. So I think there are some questions to be asked about what this woman was doing in My Nuc, in the south.'

'She was a fucking NLF agent, that's what she was,' Sam burst out. 'She was working with the Vietcong, Gini – have you got that?' He threw up his hands. 'Jesus, John, this is a waste of time. Gini knows nothing about that war.'

'All right.' Hawthorne showed no sign of emotion. 'Then perhaps she will understand better if I explain McMullen's situation. At the time of this woman's death he had known her, in Paris, for precisely two months. When news of her death finally reached him, he had a mental collapse – a complete breakdown. His parents tried to hush it up, but medical records exist. When British Security started checking him out last summer, at my behest, they discovered McMullen left Oxford, and spent six months in a private nursing home. It was after he left there that this obsession about My Nuc began. When my people started checking back, they found he'd even written three times to my office for information about my military record. I had never even seen those letters until now. They were filed as a routine request, dealt with by a junior secretary and forgotten.'

'He wrote to me, too,' Sam burst out. 'Twenty goddamn years ago he wrote. I put my lawyers onto him, and never heard another word. I just wrote it off, forgot it. Gini, you should know, all journalists get those kinds of letters, alleging this, alleging that. For a man like John, it's even worse. Every time he makes a speech, every time he's on TV there's some ass-hole writing in, claiming to be his long-lost son, claiming John's sending the guy personal messages over the airwaves in code – there's a lot of nuts out there. If you want to stay sane, you ignore them. Usually, they go away.'

He paused and glanced at Hawthorne, then turned back to Gini. 'Only just remember, Gini, sometimes they *don't* go away. Any American knows that. Sometimes they hole up, and they let their fantasies fester away and then, eventually, they surface. They go out one day and kill a president or slash a movie-star, or go into a playground and shoot up all the little kids.'

He paused. 'Now, I'm not saying McMullen is that kind of psychopath, but I am saying he's badly disturbed. And I am saying he's been trailing John for twenty-five years with this goddamn crazy fantasy of his.'

There was a silence.

'Trailing?' Gini said.

Hawthorne gave a sigh. 'Take a look at the pattern,' he said in a cool voice. 'McMullen pursued an active campaign on the question of My Nuc for three years. He wrote to me and to Sam. We now know that he made more direct allegations, in the same period, immediately after his breakdown, first to Senator Melville then to two American newspapers. But he did more than that. As Sam said, towards the end of this period, he spent six months in the States.'

He stopped, and looked at Gini coldly. 'Do you know who he spent those six months with? With some very distant friends of his mother's. The Grenville family. Lise is distantly related to them. I am more closely related. They are my first cousins. I visit them often. That was when I first encountered James McMullen, their pleasant young English friend who was staying with them while he recovered from a somewhat vague illness. I met him first in nineteen seventy-two, Gini, at their house. It was the same occasion on which Lise first met him. She and McMullen became close friends, and remained friends afterwards. They shared an interest in art, a passion for Italy. I always suspected McMullen was a little in love

549

with her – his devotion to her always amused Lise. She and I used to tease one another about it. He'd actually proposed to her, at some point or so she told me.'

His gaze became intent. 'I now believe there was much more to that meeting, and to McMullen's continuing contact with Lise, than I understood at the time. McMullen may well love Lise, in some strange way of his own, but he is also prepared to use her. Through Lise, he remains in close contact with me. And through Lise, and her illness, he thinks he has finally found the means of destroying me. It's taken him twenty-five years. No doubt the revenge tastes all the more sweet for the delay.'

He turned away with a curt gesture as he said this, and stared down into the fire. Gini looked at the pale tight line of his profile, and she thought: *I was right*. Hawthorne might now have given her further substantiating detail, detail McMullen had been careful to leave out, but in essence the suggestion he was now making was the one she had made to McMullen herself. It was left to her father to drive the nail home, and he did so at once.

'Come on, Gini,' he took a long swallow of bourbon then slammed the glass down on the table beside him, 'you're not that naïve. You can see the pattern here. This guy's been nursing this grievance a long time. Now my book's due out and Lise's illness, her fantasies about John – they give him the chance he's been waiting for. So, he moves in for the kill. This time, when he goes to a newspaper, he makes sure he's got a very different story to peddle. A sex scandal about an eminent man – about the one American politician I know who has a clean pair of hands in that respect. And who buys it? You do, Gini. You and that bastard Lamartine.'

He turned away with a shudder of disgust. He refilled his bourbon glass, ignoring Mary's protests. When Gini still said nothing, he threw up his hands angrily.

'You talk to her, John,' he said. 'I give up on this. Make her see sense. I can tell when she gets that goddamn mulish look on her face she's not listening to me. You try.'

'Very well.' Hawthorne put down his whisky, and turned back to look at Gini. 'I'll say this. I don't know what exact lies McMullen has been peddling this time. But I have a pretty fair idea. And he won't have invented those stories either, though he may have embellished them. He'll have gotten them from Lise. Because – and Mary's seen this – Lise is tormented with jealousy. It's tearing her apart. She imagines I have liaisons, affairs. She suspects any woman I have any dealings with in the course of my work. Nothing I say or do can reassure her – and McMullen has been working on that, to my certain knowledge, since the summer of last year.'

He gave a sudden furious gesture. 'That's the kind of man he is. He's prepared to exploit my wife's illness and I'm not going to stand for that any more. It's all lies, from beginning to end – all of it. I love my wife – and as far as McMullen's concerned, that's my one unforgivable sin. That and the fact that I married Lise, of course. Ten years after she refused – very wisely – to marry him.'

He stopped in an abrupt way, and looked Gini directly in the eyes. 'That's it,' he said. 'I won't discuss this any further. It sickens me to have to discuss Lise and our marriage in this way. Make your own judgement, Gini, but if you still intend pursuing this, despite what I've told you and what Sam's told you, just remember this: it wouldn't take a great deal to push Lise over the edge. If any of this did become public you realize she could try to kill herself again? You do understand that, do you? Because let's be quite clear – that's what's at stake here. Not my reputation, not my future. I've reached the point now where I don't give a damn about that any more. But I do care about my sons. And I do care about Lise.'

His eyes held hers. 'So, are you going to give me an answer? I think you owe me one, don't you? Do you intend pursuing this? Yes or no?'

The question was put in a peremptory way, but behind the curtness of tone, Gini could hear a plea. She looked up at Hawthorne uncertainly. There was now no doubting the strength of his emotion. She had heard his voice catch when he mentioned his children, and she could still see pain and exhaustion in his eyes. Just for a moment, one tiny instant, his expression reminded her of Pascal; he too looked this way sometimes, when he spoke of his divorce, or looked back to his years in war zones. She felt a sudden rush of sympathy for Hawthorne then, and she could tell that he sensed it. His face altered. She saw he was about to speak, or perhaps reach out for her hand.

Before he could do so, however, there was a sudden and violent reaction from her father. For him, obviously, her silence had continued too long.

'Jesus Christ, what the hell is this?' he erupted. 'You're asked a straight question, Gini, give it a straight fucking answer. Yes or no? Are you going to drop this? Because if you're not, then just take on board the consequences here. There are libel laws in this country and they're a whole lot tougher than the libel laws back home. So check your contract with the *News* or any other paper you go to very carefully. Make sure you're indemnified, sweetheart, and have your lawyer explain the fine print. No paper can cover you on a criminal libel charge anyway. You get hauled up on that one, Gini, and there's a double pay-off. In the first place, you're bankrupt and in the second, you're in jail—'

'That's enough, Sam.' Hawthorne cut him off with ill-disguised anger. 'I wanted to get through this without threats of that kind. If I have to bring an action, I'll do so. Gini will know that. She's not a fool. I don't want her to make this decision on the basis of threats. I want her to understand the human implications here. She isn't in the business of wrecking lives. Unfortunately, she's working with Lamartine, and he is. As we know.' He checked his watch. 'It's past eight now. Sam, you and Mary have to go. This has been very unfair to Gini. She's hardly had a chance to speak all evening. Why don't you two go on, we shouldn't hold you up.' He turned back to

Gini. 'It's late,' he said. 'My car's outside. Won't you let me give you a ride home?'

It was easy enough to refuse this offer the first time it was made. It was more difficult half an hour later, when there was still no sign of Pascal. Hawthorne made no attempt to leave, despite her refusal. Mary was trying to calm an increasingly irascible Sam.

'Fine,' her father said, as eight-thirty came. 'Fine. The hell with this. I'll wait too.' He began to struggle out of the overcoat he had just put on. 'I mean, what the hell? So I miss this dinner with my publisher, why should I care? It's just a minor inconvenience. We can all sit here for the next hour, why not? Let's all dance attendance on that French bastard. In fact, now that I come to think of it, I'll certainly goddamn well wait. Fuck my publishing deal. I wouldn't mind a few words with Lamartine. Why should he get off scot-free? I notice he didn't have the nerve to come in and face the music – oh no. He waltzed off into the night, and no doubt he'll waltz back if and when it suits him. Fine. Great. He and I have a whole lot of unfinished business. You wait, Gini – I wait. And while I wait, I'll have another bourbon as well.'

Mary was in the hall getting her coat. Sam, taking advantage of this, moved fast towards the drinks table, and slopped the bourbon into a glass. Gini watched him helplessly. Behind her, by the fireplace, Hawthorne watched silently; he did not say a word.

'Look, Daddy,' Gini moved forward, 'I don't want to make you late. You shouldn't miss this dinner. I asked Pascal not to come tonight – he wanted to be here. This is stupid. It was a very loose arrangement. Pascal's probably been held up.' She glanced down at her watch as she said this. Pascal had said he would return at eight. It was now eight thirty-five.

'A loose arrangement?' Her father took a hefty swallow of bourbon. 'That sounds pretty typical. Loose arrangements are rather his line. He taught you about loose arrangements before, if I remember rightly.'

'Come on, Sam. Cut it out,' Hawthorne said, in a cold voice. 'You've had more than enough to drink. You should go.'

'No. Stay out of this, John. You don't understand. Gini knows what I'm getting at.' He downed the rest of the bourbon, and reached for the bottle again.

'Look, Daddy, please . . . ' Gini tried to move the bottle out of his reach. 'Don't do this. Don't drink any more. Listen – I'll make my own way home. I'm going now.'

'You goddamn stupid fucking bitch.' He gave her a sudden hard push, picked up the bottle and refilled his glass. 'Don't you start telling me what to do and what not to do. Just sort your own life out, and don't come crying to me when you make a bloody mess of it, second time around.'

There was a silence. Gini stared at him. She began in a low, unsteady voice. 'Come crying to you? I've never come crying to you in my life. Why would I? You wouldn't listen if I did. I learned that lesson when I was three years old.'

'Oh did you just? Did you just? How about when you were fifteen years old? How about when you showed up in Beirut one morning, with all those goddamn pathetic boasts. Daddy, I want to be a journalist. I want to be a journalist, Daddy, just like you . . . '

He did a vicious impersonation of a whining child. Gini took a step back. Mary, re-entering the room, began to speak, but Sam continued, drowning her out. He fixed his eyes on Gini, took one unsteady step forward, then stopped.

'You, Gini, are just so goddamn *dumb*. You come out to a fucking war zone, this stupid arrogant kid who thinks she knows it all. You get in my way. You embarrass me in front of my friends with your goddamn inane fucking questions all the time—'

'Sam.' Mary raised her voice. 'Stop this and stop this now—'

'And then what do you do?' He lurched forward another step. 'What's your idea of being some hot-shot woman

554

journalist? You get into bed with the first ass-hole who makes a pass at you, and you spend the next fucking three weeks getting screwed. By the same fucking goddamned bastard who's screwing you now – and don't deny it, because it's written all over your face. I knew it the second you walked in that door. Well grow up, Gini. Get real. He's not just screwing you, sweetheart, he's screwing you up. And you know why? Because he's scum, and you're an idiot. You can't even see when you're being used—'

'Don't. Just don't.' Suddenly, Gini felt blind with anger. She grabbed at the glass and snatched it out of his hand. 'You drink too much. It's disgusting the way you drink. It makes me sick to watch you. I hate you for the way you drink. I hate you for the way you talk to me. You want the bourbon that badly, you have the bourbon, Daddy. Here . . . '

She tossed the rest of the bourbon in the glass at his face. As she did so, Sam made a clumsy grab for her wrist. Half the alcohol hit his shirt, the rest spilled on her blouse. Sam lurched against the drinks table. There was a crash, as bottles fell. Her father now looked blind with rage; he peered in her direction, as if he could scarcely see her, then lurched forward again. For Gini it was all a blur of movement. Mary was moving, her father was moving, John Hawthorne was moving; her father lifted his hand. The smell of bourbon was choking now.

'You bitch,' he said. 'You dumb fucking little *whore* . . . '

The arm was upraised now. Gini flinched, and then John Hawthorne was between them. She looked at the dark plain material of his suit jacket; she watched as if from a great distance, the swiftness with which he moved.

'Back off, Sam,' he said, in a voice icy with anger. He caught hold of her father's lapels and almost lifted Sam, for all his bulk, off his feet. He slammed him back hard against a chair, shook him, then pushed him into it.

'Get a hold of yourself. Sober up. That was way out of line and you know it. You get up again, Sam, and I'll knock you down.'

He stood there, looking down at her father. Sam struggled to get to his feet again, then subsided. Gini stared at them both, Hawthorne, tall, scarcely dishevelled by this tussle, his face pale with anger, and her father, slumped in the chair, breathing heavily. As she watched, he let his head fall back. His jaw went slack. He closed his eyes.

There was a silence. Hawthorne turned back to Gini. 'I'm sorry. I've provoked all this. He's been working up to it for most of the day. Are you all right?'

'I'm fine. I'm used to it. It's happened before.'

Hawthorne's mouth tightened. 'Well, you don't look fine. That's it. No more argument. I'm taking you home right now.' He hesitated. 'Mary, what shall we do with Sam? You want me to call a cab? I could send Malone around, he could get him back to his hotel . . . '

'No, John. Leave him. Really. I'm used to this as well. He'll sleep for a while now, and when he wakes up I'll give him some black coffee. Then he'll apologize. Then he'll get maudlin. Then he'll go.'

'You're sure?'

'John. I've coped with this a thousand times. Go. Take Gini home . . . ' She hesitated and Gini could see the shock on her face. She was close to tears. 'Gini, I'm so sorry. You mustn't take any notice of what he says. He doesn't mean it. It's just the bourbon talking. He does love you, in his way. He's just never had the least idea how to express it. Darling, don't cry. John's right. Let him take you home.'

In the hall, John Hawthorne helped her into her coat. He drew it around her, then took her arm. He led her down the steps and into the street. Gini looked to right and left. There was still no sign of Pascal.

'Don't worry about Lamartine.' Hawthorne opened the front passenger door of his car. 'If and when he turns up, Mary will tell him where you are.'

He helped her into her seat, then closed the door. As he slid into the driver's seat, he gave her a slight smile.

'I know. No thugs – as Mary likes to call them. Just occasionally I get to drive myself, as you see. With escort . . . ' He gestured to a black car some twenty yards behind, which pulled out behind them. 'Even so, it's a relief. I get behind the wheel of a car, and I feel human again. A private person. An ordinary person. I can't tell you how good that feels.'

At the end of the street he paused, and glanced at her again. 'Where to, Gini?'

'I'm sorry?'

He smiled. 'I don't know where you live.'

'Oh. I'm sorry. I'm not concentrating.' She hesitated. 'I live in Islington. Gibson Square. Are you sure about this? I don't want to take you out of your way. You can drop me at the tube.'

'No.' He gave her a bemused look. 'I don't think so. Not in the circumstances. I told you. I'm taking you home.'

He said nothing more, and Gini too remained silent. She kept her eyes on the road ahead. She tried to think of Pascal, and what could have happened to him. Perhaps he was still angry, she thought; perhaps he'd decided not to collect her after all, and had gone back to Hampstead on his own. But she knew that he would never do that, however much he might have resented this meeting with her father. And at that thought, her mind went into another flurry of anxiety and pain.

She heard her father say those things again, and she saw again the expression on his face when he did so. She swallowed; her whole body ached.

John Hawthorne glanced towards her. 'Shall I put some music on?' he asked. 'Would that help? I find it does, sometimes. Mozart – I like Mozart. I have *Figaro* here . . . Do you know that opera?'

'Not well.'

'It's one of my favourites. Great happiness and great pain fused together . . . ' He hesitated. 'An absurd plot, mistaken identities, heartbreak avoided by a kiss in the dark. I find it gives me hope – while the opera lasts.'

He reached forward to the CD player, and pressed the controls. Music filled the car. Mozart propelled them north, and melody ate up the distance. As the second act began, Hawthorne turned into Gibson Square, and parked the car.

He sat for a while, in silence, listening to the music, then he switched it off. He hesitated, then he reached across and took her hand.

'Are you all right?'

'Yes, I am. The Mozart does help. I've calmed down.'

'I'm glad.' He paused. 'I wish now that I had never involved Sam. The drinking's much worse than when I last saw him. If I'd foreseen what would happen . . .' He shrugged. 'I wonder. There is something I need to say to you. I couldn't discuss it in front of Mary and Sam. Could I come in with you, just for ten minutes? Would you mind?'

He released her hand as he said this, and drew back a little. Then, without waiting for her reply, he climbed out, came around and opened her door for her. As Gini stepped out, she saw the car which had followed them all this way. It had drawn in, engine running, a short way up the street. Inside it, two male figures were just discernible. Hawthorne lifted his hand, and gestured at them. The engine cut out instantly. In the silence of the square, Gini heard a faint crackle of radio static. Hawthorne led her across to her house, and she saw his eyes flick up over the dark windows. Mrs Henshaw's letter-box, Gini saw, was jammed open with mail. Two bottles of milk stood on her doorstep, proclaiming her continued absence. Gini led the way down the area steps, and fumbled for her key.

'Will you mind if I come in?' Hawthorne hung back politely. 'It will only be ten minutes. I have to get back to Lise.'

'No, no, that's fine. I'm grateful for what you did. I'll make us some coffee.' Gini bent quickly, and scooped up the pile of letters on her mat. It was obvious from their number that she had been away several days. Hawthorne gave no indication of noticing this. He followed her into her living-room, and looked about him with apparent approval. She saw his gaze take in the comfortable if shabby furnishings, the posters for art exhibitions. He looked around him, frowning.

'It's a nice place you have here, Gini. When I was your age, I always wanted to live this way. My own space . . . I guess I managed it at Yale. Never since. My father had pronounced views on how I should live, where I should live . . . even with whom.'

He turned back, and smiled at her, almost sadly. 'I told you before, we have something in common, you and I. Difficult fathers. Dominating fathers—'

'Sam doesn't dominate me,' Gini began, in her usual defensive way, then something in Hawthorne's expression stopped her.

'If he doesn't dominate you,' he said drily, 'then he certainly has a damn good try. Judging by this evening's performance, anyway . . .' He hesitated, then moved across to help her off with her coat. 'If it's any help, I was a lot older than you are before I found a way of dealing with it. And even now . . . even now my father's influence is very strong. As a child, I often hated him – but I also loved him. And it's that combination of emotions which is so hard to deal with. It's . . . incendiary.' He broke off with a shrug. 'Still, I imagine most children feel the same. Perhaps that's our problem, Gini. We still haven't severed that chain, you and I.'

He was standing quite close to her as he said this in a quiet half-mocking way. He was looking down into her face, his own expression regretful yet amused. As he had helped her off with her coat, his hand had brushed against her throat. Looking at him, Gini could still sense that brief touch of his hand against her skin. She realized that she was acutely aware of his closeness to her, and that so was he. She felt a sudden tiny pulse of attraction to him – there and then gone – and she wondered if he felt that also, or sensed her reaction, for the quality of his gaze became still and intent, then at the same moment, as if on some shared instinct, they both moved further apart.

Gini went into the kitchen, and began making coffee. She ran some water in the sink, and splashed cold water on her face and hands. She felt unsteady, not at all in control, as if all the events of this evening had thrown both her thinking and her emotions out of kilter. *It's my father*, she said to herself; *if he had not acted in that way, I'd feel perfectly calm.* But she knew it was not just her father, it was the way in which Hawthorne had defended her, it was the way in which he had spoken earlier that evening, then in his car, and now here. This Hawthorne was not the person she had taken him for, but a very different, much more complex and much more considerable man.

When she returned to her living-room with the tray, Hawthorne was standing by the window, staring out at the darkness beyond. She could see his pale reflection against the black of the window-glass. He seemed abstracted, only turning when her reflection appeared in the glass beside his own.

Then, with a smile, he made an effort to shake off his mood. He took the tray from her, drew the curtains, waited until she had lit the fire and sat down, then seated himself opposite.

'It is nice, this room,' he said, as she poured the coffee.

'It's very ordinary,' Gini replied. 'Not quite the grandeur you're used to.'

'That's probably why I like it. Grandeur's not really my style. My father's, maybe – and Lise's too, up to a point. But I've never really liked that kind of thing. Has Mary ever described to you my childhood home?' He glanced towards her. 'I'm sure she must have. Such a terrible place. A fifty-bedroom monstrosity, stuffed with the spoils of at least five generations of acquisitive Hawthornes.' He smiled. 'I hated it. I still hate it now. I go back there as little as possible, but it makes no difference. It surfaces – very often – in my dreams. I dream of walking along those endless, endless corridors. And then, of course, sometimes I can't avoid going there. I have to see my father. I go up to see him, regularly, with my boys.'

'Your father's here in England though, at the moment?'

560

Gini said. 'Someone pointed him out to me at that dinner at the Savoy.'

'Yes. He's here. He was coming over anyway for that birthday party of mine – if that ever happens, which looks increasingly unlikely. He had some business to attend to as well, so he decided to come earlier. He's staying with us. I'm afraid that hasn't eased the situation. He and Lise have never gotten along.'

He paused. 'Maybe you'll get to meet him if Lise is well enough and the party takes place. I'd like you to meet him. He's an extraordinary man.'

He looked away as he said this. He rested his gaze somewhere in the middle distance, and Gini felt that he no longer saw his surroundings, but was watching his own past. He settled back in his chair. A few minutes of silence passed. Then, as if sensing her gaze on his face, he turned back to look at her.

'You know how old I was when I first realized my father had my life all mapped out in advance?' He sighed. 'Eight years old. Can you imagine that? It was my birthday. My mother bought me a train-set – it was the year before she died. My father's idea of a present for an eight-year-old was more unusual. You know what it was?' He gave a half-smile. 'It was a clock.'

'A clock?'

'Oh, valuable, of course.' He shrugged. 'Long-case. Antique. An historic piece. Said to have belonged to Thomas Jefferson. It had a seven-day system. All these levers and pulleys and weights. Every Sunday, my father and I, we wound it up. Our special ceremony. My father liked ceremonies. Rituals. I guess he still does.'

His tone sharpened. 'You won't find this story in the clippings – for what it's worth, I kept it to myself. You know why he gave me a clock? To teach me about time. He wanted me to watch it go past, be able to measure it in the movements of cogs and pendulums and weights and counter-weights. The day he gave it to me, he said: "Forty years from now, John, you will be the president

561

of your country . . . " Then he said children couldn't imagine forty years. It was too huge. So every time I wound the clock, I had to remember. Forty years is two thousand and eighty weeks . . . '

He paused once more, still staring off into the middle distance, as if he were back in the memory, and had forgotten her presence.

'It sounds like an awfully long time, put that way,' Gini said, still watching him carefully. 'Two thousand and eighty weeks.'

'It isn't.' He jerked back to look at her. 'We're in the two thousand and seventy-ninth right now. It's my forty-eighth birthday next week.' His smile tightened. 'I'm behind schedule. As my father has already pointed out.'

His tone had now dipped towards bitterness. Gini hesitated, unwilling to break this odd and sudden confessional mood. When he said no more, she risked a quiet prompt.

'But you plan on catching up? That's what people say . . . '

'Maybe. I know I could. My father wants it.' He paused, and then turned to look at her.

'Would it surprise you if I said I had abandoned it all – all those plans, all those ambitions? I almost did. Four years ago, when my son was ill. I decided then. That's why I resigned from the Senate. There were other contributing factors – the state of my marriage for one – but that wasn't the main reason. The night my son nearly died, the night his illness reached its crisis – I spent that night, alone, by his hospital bed.' He gave a weary half-smile. 'I prayed, of course, though I have very little faith left. I looked at myself, my past life. In the end, around three in the morning, I made a deal, with God.'

He gave a shrug. 'It's the kind of thing one does, perhaps, in those circumstances. It seemed right at the time. When I looked back at my life there was a great deal I despised, and very little I liked. So I made my deal. Make my son better, and I'll give it all up. All the power and the glory and the hypocrisy and the unrest . . . ' He

562

paused. 'God was obliging. He fulfilled his side of the bargain. My son recovered. I resigned from the Senate later that week.' He glanced at her. 'You won't find that story in the clippings either. It's true, nevertheless.'

He had told her this in a strained, almost harsh way, so his tone was at odds with the actions he described. Looking at him, Gini came near to pitying him. She said gently, 'But then, you must feel – if you really made that promise – you're a Catholic born and bred – you must feel it's still binding, surely?'

'Perhaps. I look at it rather differently now.' The reply was curt; he hesitated, then said in a quieter tone, 'I can't let superstition rule my life – and that's what it is now, my religion. It's superstition. I told you, I have no faith. I have to think of my father. He's devoted half his life to his ambitions for me. He's old now, he can't have many years left to live. I'd like to give him one last gift . . . ' A brief smile crossed his face. 'And then, I'm not without abilities. In many ways I miss my former life. I miss the drive of politics. I miss having one clear goal ahead of me. After all, I lived with that goal, that one aim, for most of my life.'

'So you will return to politics, then? You haven't abandoned your presidential hopes?'

'No. I haven't abandoned them. Nor has my father, of course.'

'Do you have a timetable?'

Hawthorne smiled. 'Sure. A realistic one. A flexible one. You can't tie it down to forty years, or two thousand and eighty weeks. It depends on Lise's condition, partly. It depends on the present incumbent and his performance, just a few little considerations of that kind . . . '

He rose, in a sudden and agitated way, betraying a restlessness he had not exhibited before. He began to walk back and forth in the room. Gini watched him silently. He stopped, and swung around suddenly to look at her.

'I have tried,' he said. 'God knows I have tried to alter my life. But the agenda was set. Do you see? Even before

I was born. The inexorable rise of my family. It was never enough for me simply to be a senator. My grandfather was a senator. My father was a senator. I had to do more than that. Without that one goal ahead of me my life seems aimless, empty. Can you understand that? I've lived with that aimlessness for four years now and I've had enough. After all, what other consolations do I have, other than my sons? Take the ambition away, and there's nothing left.'

He broke off angrily. Gini had begun to speak, but he cut her off.

'I know what you're going to say. Fame? That's meaningless without power. Money? I was born with more money than any one human being could possibly want. I've already told you, I have no faith. So what's left? And don't mention my marriage. You're not as easy to deceive as either Mary or Sam. I'm sure it hasn't escaped your notice. My marriage is dead. It's been dead for at least nine of the ten years it's lasted.'

He stopped abruptly. His voice had risen, and the silence after he stopped speaking was intense. Gini could feel the room reverberate with the unsayable and the unsaid. Hawthorne's eyes now rested on her face.

She hesitated, then said quietly, 'That's not what you implied earlier this evening.'

'I know that. As you no doubt noticed, I was very careful in what I said. I told you one lie, and only one. I said that I loved my wife. I do not love Lise, and I never have loved her. As a matter of fact, I loathe her.'

There was another silence. His gaze was now intent. Gini looked at him uncertainly. The real Hawthorne, she felt, was suddenly very close, perhaps one question away. She bent her head and inched back the sleeve of her blouse, so she could just see the face of her watch. It was nine-thirty. Pascal was one hour and a half late. She felt uneasy at that, and a little afraid, but she pushed that fear aside. She looked up at Hawthorne again, and she could see the tension and the pain in his face.

'You want me to go?' he asked abruptly. 'Perhaps I should go.'

'You said you had something you wanted to say to me.' Gini hesitated. 'Was it about your marriage? About Lise?'

'Indirectly, yes.' He gave a quick defensive gesture of the hand. 'Except that I shouldn't discuss Lise. It's wrong of me . . . ' He glanced at her. 'I couldn't say this in front of your father or Mary, but those rumours you heard about me, they did concern other women, infidelities on my part, yes?'

'Yes. They did.'

The direct reply seemed to please him. He gave a wry smile.

'Then that's what I wanted to discuss with you. The other women in my life. I thought I might tell you the truth.'

'Why should you tell me of all people?'

'Why you? Well, partly because for all your denials, you've been hunting me down, and so I thought, Why not let her in, why not open the gates? Also,' he paused, and frowned, 'I like you.'

'Is that true?'

'Yes. It is.' He began to move away. 'I liked you the first time I met you, aged thirteen, with your little friend who wanted to flirt and couldn't quite manage it – you remember that? I liked you when I re-met you at Mary's. There's no point in explaining liking. Sometimes it happens, sometimes it doesn't. Maybe I don't like you or trust you and you just happen to be here at the right moment – who knows?'

He paused. He had moved across to a side table, where there was a bottle of Scotch and some glasses. He picked up the bottle and began to unscrew its cap.

'May I? Will you join me?' He was smiling, then the smile disappeared. He stood absolutely still, and Gini realized he was listening. She looked around the silent room, then she also heard the sound – footsteps passing outside in the street.

Hawthorne's expression was now alert. He still held the whisky bottle. 'Is this apartment safe?'

'Safe?'

'Is it wired?'

'I'm not sure.' She hesitated. 'It might be, yes.'

He gave a sigh, a long, slow exhaling of breath. 'You know, I don't give a damn,' he said, with an odd defiant smile. 'I don't give a damn any more one way or another. Here.'

He handed her the glass of whisky. His hand brushed hers as he passed it across. Hawthorne gave no indication of noticing this. He moved back to the chair opposite her, and sat down. He gave her a long and considering look. Again Gini felt that pulse of tension and unease.

'You remember what I said in that speech at the Savoy?' Hawthorne said. 'About accountability, about a public man's private life?'

'Yes. I do. You said if such a man had nothing to hide, he had nothing to fear.'

'Exactly so. By that rule, if my claims earlier this evening about my marriage were true, I'd have no reason to fear McMullen, yes? At best, he could start rumours, gossip. I could probably live with that. Neither he, nor you, nor anyone else would be able to supply proof.' He gave her a cool glance. 'Unfortunately, as I guess you've realized, it's not that straightforward. There have been other women, infidelities on my part. If you tried hard enough, and long enough, you'd find out about them eventually. Well, I'll save you the effort. I'll explain them myself.'

He leaned back in his chair. He gave her a long and considering look. 'You're young. You may not understand. Nevertheless, I'll tell you. This is the way it began . . .'

XXXI

It was six-thirty when Pascal pulled away from Mary's house. He looked back once, to see Gini and Mary standing in the doorway, and he knew that if he hesitated, he would change his mind, and storm back. Gini had made it angrily clear that she did not want him present, so he accelerated away fast, before he had time to waver. He gunned the bike through the dark wet streets and squares of Kensington, not caring what direction he took. Then, realizing he was riding too fast, and dangerously, he pulled into a side-street, and slammed on the brakes.

He had an hour and a half to kill. He walked up Kensington Church Street, impervious to other passers-by, or to the lighted windows of the shops, until in a side-street he saw a wine bar which advertised coffee as well as drinks. The place was half-empty. He sat down in a booth at the back, and ordered a triple espresso. Someone had left a copy of the late edition of the *Standard* on the seat beside him. He opened the pages, flicked them; the print seemed without meaning. He closed the paper, folded it in half, and stared into space.

He thought of Gini, and the argument they had had before leaving for Mary's. He replayed it in his mind: its half-truths and evasions, its suppressed resentments. There had been a moment – and they had both been aware of it – when the same unspoken panic had been felt by them both. There had been a moment when they had realized that something they both prized was now threatened. It had happened very swiftly, that sudden loss of confidence. One minute Pascal had remained obstinately convinced that the next question, the next sentence, could bridge the gap between them which he could sense was opening up – and the next minute he had seen he was wrong. The next question, the next answer, made it worse: it deepened the divide. That had frightened Pascal very much.

He had been there before, in that hinterland; he had spent much of his marriage trapped in that place. He knew that Gini had been there too, in the past: her succession of brief past affairs told him that, even if she scarcely spoke of it herself. He had, he realized now, been incautiously content in the days since Venice, and so had Gini perhaps. They had allowed themselves to inhabit a wonderful new region of amity and trust unsullied by arguments or quarrels, and he knew that it dismayed them both, to see how swiftly that amity could be impaired. Suddenly they were both back in the ordinary petty world, where two lovers did not agree, and where disagreements burgeoned with ugly speed into the shabbiness of hostility, resentment and distrust.

I will not let that happen, Pascal thought, *not to us*. And so he sat there in the bar for an hour, seeing nothing and no-one, planning what he should say and do when he rejoined Gini, and how – somehow – he would rescue them both. Quarrels were to be expected, he told himself; all lovers quarrelled and fought and disagreed. There could be purpose and egality in quarrels: they were nothing to fear, provided they did not undermine the fundamental commitment. This thought heartened him. He ordered more coffee, lit a cigarette, watched the hands of the clock on the wall move slowly towards seven forty-five. He would leave then, for Mary's house. Suddenly he was impatient to leave, could not wait to leave, to see Gini, to talk to her, to make everything between them clear again, and good.

The hands of the clock, though, seemed to move unnaturally slowly. Frustrated, impatient, he picked up the newspaper again in an effort to distract himself, and then he saw it, a tiny item on the back page, in the *Stop Press*. It was headed *Accident outside Oxford*. Pascal glanced at it, froze, read it once, then read it again.

He swore under his breath, tossed some money on the table, picked up the paper, and hurried out to the street.

It had begun to rain again, heavily. He ran back to his motor bike, mounted it, and accelerated south.

He turned into Kensington High Street. Mary's house was a few blocks off this main road, to the west. There was heavy traffic still, although the rush hour was over. Pascal began to weave in and out of other vehicles. It was urgent now to speak to Gini. He had almost forgotten about her father, and his presence at Mary's house: all he could think of was seeing Gini, and telling her this news.

All along the street, every set of traffic lights hit red as he approached. Pascal swore, and muttered to himself under his breath. There were further lights, up ahead, and they were still green. He checked his wing mirror, saw a large black Ford behind him, some twenty yards back. He increased his speed, and pulled out past a delivery truck on his left. He was now in the fast lane, with the Ford behind him. The lights ahead were still green, still green – and then he realized: the Ford had picked up speed and was now right on his rear wheel. The lights ahead were amber. He had a second to decide as he reached the intersection and they went red: brake or continue?

He thought, for one tiny instant, of a boulevard in Paris. The Ford behind was too close to allow him to brake. He increased his speed; he had just enough time he judged, to shoot the light. Neither the delivery truck nor the Ford was braking. They were still with him, on his tail and to his side, as he started across the intersection. He felt the air move as the truck skimmed alongside him. Its driver did not signal or slow. The truck cut in on him, fast, and without warning, swerving right across his front wheel.

As the bike skidded, and he started to lose control, the Ford switched its headlights to full-beam. In that long slow second of dazzle, Pascal watched the bike tilt. He watched the wet glassy surface of the road rise up to meet him. There was a grinding of metal, a screech of rubber. His spine juddered against Tarmac; he felt himself start to slide, skid, twenty feet down the road, thirty. The velocity and the pain still had a hypnotic slowness. He was not unconscious. He could see with a timeless and brilliant clarity that this was a dual-action manœuvre. The truck, having hit the bike was now speeding away, and the black Ford was heading straight at him. He was lying in the middle of the street. The Ford had all the time in the world, and all the space in the world, to make its hit.

'I don't know what story exactly McMullen fed your newspaper about my personal life,' Hawthorne was saying. 'But I do know one thing for sure – he will have concocted the story with Lise's help, and she will have lied to him. Even if she weren't ill, unable to distinguish between truth and falsehood any more, Lise would still lie where our marriage is concerned. She has never accepted the truth. Every fact has to be adjusted, so she is the innocent, the injured party . . . ' He shrugged. 'I won't get involved in that contest. There is blame on my side, I admit that.'

He paused, and Gini saw his eyes move around the room. They rested on the bookshelves by the fireplace, then on the objects on the mantelpiece – some postcards, a pottery jar and, just to the side, because she had wanted to keep it, Napoleon's collar. It was made of blue leather. It had a nameplate and a small bell attached. Gini thought Hawthorne saw none of these objects, for all he looked at them. His concentration was directed inward towards his own life.

She looked at him uncertainly. There was evil in this story, and, as Pascal had said, evil did not show in a man's face, or his gestures, or his voice. Even so she did not sense evil here: despair, yes; exhaustion, yes; bitterness, possibly – and beyond that, a desire for exactitude and for honesty which was clearly at odds with Hawthorne's reserve. Mary was right, she thought: this was not a man who liked, or found it easy, to speak openly about himself.

As he looked away, she glanced quickly down at her watch again. She was worried about Pascal, and this inexplicable delay, but she was unwilling to let Hawthorne see that. This opportunity might not come again and if she was honest with herself, it was more than a journalistic opportunity. It was not easy to remain distanced, she realized, or to remember that her function here was that of a reporter. But then, of course, Hawthorne was not addressing her as if she were a journalist. He was addressing her as if she were a friend. Was that simply a clever manœuvre on his part? It could have been – but when she looked at his expression, she thought not.

His gaze had returned to her face. He hesitated, then shrugged. 'I'm not good at this. It's something I've never discussed with anyone. But I think the problems were there right at the beginning. Lise and I married primarily for political reasons, for dynastic reasons if you like. A senator needs a wife. My father promoted the marriage, Lise herself sought it and I went along with it. There was no-one else I loved. Lise seemed sweet, very young. I thought, maybe, with time . . . But I was wrong. The marriage was a disaster, almost from the first. Within a year, both Lise and I knew we were incompatible in every possible way. Especially sexually.' He looked at Gini. 'I don't want to dwell on any of those details. But the situation deteriorated very rapidly. It became . . . painful and ugly for us both. Within six months of our marriage we were sleeping apart. Lise then seemed to expect me to lead a celibate life, except on the few occasions, the very few occasions, when we could overcome our mutual dislike and go to bed.'

He hesitated, then gave another small shrug. 'Well, that proved unworkable. I'm no different from other men. From time to time, I need sex.'

He looked at Gini intently as he said this. When she did not speak, he leaned back in his chair, and continued, still in the same even voice. 'A year and a half into our marriage, I finally did what Lise had already been accusing me of doing for months. I was away at a conference. I met a woman there who made it plain what she wanted, so I took her to bed. She was about your age. She was blond haired. She was pretty, kind, generous and inventive. We spent three nights in my hotel room, and I've never seen or heard from her since. I remain deeply grateful

571

to her. She reminded me of what sex can be between two adults. Something purely pleasurable, not part of an endless appalling bargaining process, not a power game, not a contest – and it was all of those things with my wife.' He glanced sharply at Gini. 'You disapprove?'

'I don't approve or disapprove. Adultery happens. It's not for me to judge.'

'I expect you do, one way or the other. Never mind. It doesn't matter . . . '

His gaze moved away from her face, and he looked across the room. When he continued speaking, she had the feeling that this confession was aimed particularly at her, but also beyond her, to those listening walls, perhaps, or to himself.

'It's ridiculous, isn't it?' he went on. 'For a man in my position, there's only one question that counts. Has he or has he not screwed around? If so, when, and with whom? No-one ever cares or concerns themselves with the *why* – just, did he do it, and who with?' He paused. 'Tell me something. You've met Lise. What did you think of her?'

Gini hesitated.

'Tell me the truth, Gini.'

'I thought she was afraid of you. I thought she was confused, forgetful. She kept contradicting herself. She stressed her devotion to you some of the time. She quoted you constantly . . . '

'Oh, I'm sure.' He smiled. 'And you found it convincing, did you, all that devotion?'

'I found it overstated, if you like. Sugary, perhaps.'

The term seemed to please him. 'Sugary? Honeyed? I'd agree. Lise overplays the devotion sometimes, the same way she overplays the charm. She's always done that, long before this illness. The fact is that our dislike for one another is shared. Lise detests me – but Lise is a very good actress, an exceptional actress. It was one of the reasons my father advised me to marry her. He believed – and still believes – that acting ability is essential in a future president's wife.'

He sighed, and drained his whisky. 'My father's a cynic, of course. He now views Lise as a liability. He's advising I engineer an annulment, and marry again in due course.'

'Could that be engineered?'

'Of course.' He made the statement blandly, as if it surprised him she should even ask it. 'If you have contacts at high levels in the Catholic Church, it can always be arranged. It would be difficult without Lise's co-operation, and while she remains this ill, it's an impossibility. But in the future, perhaps. If Lise could ever be persuaded that she had an identity of her own, that her fame and pre-eminence, all the things she enjoys, did not depend on her status as my wife.'

'Do you think she ever would feel that?'

'No. Probably not.' The answer was given in an offhand, almost lazy way. His gaze returned to her face. 'Of course, if I ever were free to remarry, I'd have to educate my father a little. He'd have to understand that I now require rather different qualities in a wife.'

'Such as?'

'Stamina. Discretion. Unselfishness. An ability to love. Intelligence . . . Intelligence especially. That would help.'

Gini looked away. The intensity of his gaze was now making her self-conscious. 'Lise didn't strike me as exactly stupid,' she began.

'Oh, come on.' Hawthorne rose to his feet impatiently. He moved across to the table and refilled his glass. 'Come on, Gini, you're better than that. Lise is a vain, vapid, self-obsessed woman. She's prodigiously stupid. She lives in a permanent state of anguished vanity and discontent. She has this need, this appalling inexhaustible need to be the centre of attention. Lise is the greatest egoist I ever met in my life. If cuddling sick babies in front of photographers gets her that attention, then that's what she'll do. If slashing her wrists gets her attention, she'll do that as well. Dear God, I've been married to the woman for ten years. She's the mother of my children. You think I don't know my own wife?'

There was a silence. Gini was shocked by the sudden

and impassioned vehemence with which he spoke, and Hawthorne, as if realizing that, gave a sigh and a hopeless gesture of the hand.

'I know. I'm doing exactly what I said I wouldn't do. I didn't mean to discuss Lise, or run her down. But sometimes – just for once – I'd like someone to understand what my famously perfect marriage is actually like. I've fathered two children by a woman I neither love nor respect – and if Lise is paying the consequences for that, so am I. Unlike Lise, I don't take refuge in lies, or pills. I have other remedies. Sometimes drink – just to get me through the night – and sometimes women. The drink is too addictive, too dangerous, as we saw with your father tonight. So these days I settle for something that's easier, readily available, and much less habit-forming. Women. I screw around, Gini. Yes.'

There was a pause. Gini could sense it again, that little pulse of danger in the room, and unease too.

'Are women not habit-forming, not addictive?' she said.

Hawthorne looked at her closely. 'Is that what McMullen implied? That I needed women for some kind of regular fix?' His face hardened. 'Well, if he did, it wouldn't surprise me. Lise has made that particular accusation, and variations upon it, many times. I don't think it's true. I told you. I like women. I like sex. So, yes, I've been unfaithful to my wife. I was unfaithful for the first time eighteen months into our marriage, and I've been unfaithful on many occasions since. If you want chapter and verse, in eight and a half years I've had four affairs of some duration, in each case with kind, discreet, married women. Women I liked. Women I respected. They began by mutual agreement and ended without tears the same way and . . . ' He stopped, as if considering whether to reveal the rest.

'And all right,' he went on, angrily now, 'there have been other episodes as well. One-night stands, if you like. I've slept with other women for no better reason than that I was away someplace, and I was tired, and I was lonely and sick at heart and they were *there*. So,

574

just like a million other men, I gave in to the illusion that a woman might help . . . ' He stopped again. 'I'm a politician, not a priest, Gini. Sometimes it's very simple. I just meet a woman I want to fuck.'

There was another silence, and this time Gini could sense the danger in the room acutely. He had been shifting their relationship, she realized, throughout this conversation, drawing her deeper into an area of his life where it was unwise to trespass, and now – with that one final verb – he had shifted their relationship again. This was no longer a confession, and it had long ceased to be an interview: they were now simply a man and a woman, alone in a room at night. Hawthorne might have been scrupulous up to that moment, attempting to curb his emotion, keeping his distance, but the instant he uttered that word, all that changed. The silence between them was now loaded, and it carried a sexual charge.

She was not certain if Hawthorne had planned it that way – she thought not. But she knew he could sense it as acutely as she could, and she could read it in the alteration of his face. He put down his glass, and leaned forward.

'That shocks you?' he said. 'You look shocked.'

'No. I'm not shocked. It's not a word careful politicians use too often. Maybe it's that.'

'I'm not speaking as a politician. I'm not speaking carefully. I thought you understood that.' He met her eyes. 'It's a common enough word. It's exact.'

'It is that.'

'You find it distasteful, all the same.' He half-smiled. 'Don't deny it, I can see it in your face. There . . . ' He leaned across the space dividing them, and touched her forehead very lightly, between her brows. He withdrew his hand at once. 'There. The smallest frown. And in the eyes too. I can see it. You disapprove.' He sighed. 'Why, Gini? Is it so bad? Just to want to fuck someone? Isn't it honest to admit it, at least?'

'It isn't that.' She rose hastily to her feet.

'Would you approve more if I told you I'd been looking for someone to love?' He looked up at her, still with

575

that tired half-smile, then he also rose. They were now standing very close to one another. His expression became serious.

'Would you rather hear that? Most women would.'

'No. Why should I? It makes no difference . . . '

She began to move away. Hawthorne touched her arm lightly and drew her back so she faced him. 'Wrong,' he said. 'Wrong, Gini. It makes all the difference. You know that . . . '

Gini gave a small quick defensive gesture of the hand. She had the sensation that events were moving, turning, speeding up. They were flashing past her eyes very fast, like a succession of lights on a freeway.

'Listen,' she began in a rushed way. 'It's very late. I think perhaps you should leave now, and . . . '

She stopped. Hawthorne had taken her hand in his, and raised it to his lips. At exactly the moment she felt his breath against her skin, the telephone rang on her desk. She jerked her hand quickly away and turned. She stared at the telephone.

Hawthorne said, in an even voice, 'I imagine that will be Pascal Lamartine, who is now some two and a half hours late collecting you. You'd better answer it, don't you think?'

She crossed to the desk, and picked up the receiver. There was silence at the other end; she turned to face Hawthorne, still holding the receiver. He was watching her closely.

'Pascal?' she said, into the silence. The line crackled. Then she heard not Pascal's, but another male voice, a familiar voice.

'Gini,' it whispered. 'Gini, is it you?'

She caught her breath. She felt the blood drain from her face. She realized that she was afraid, suddenly very afraid, of both these men, the one who had just kissed her hand, and the one who whispered his secret wishes in her ear. Were they alike in those wishes, or not? She froze, staring at Hawthorne. The voice whispered on. Hawthorne frowned. He moved closer, then closer still.

576

His eyes never once left her face. When he was two feet away from her, then one foot, she knew he could hear the whispers too. She saw those scratchy obscenities register in his eyes. He showed little surprise, but she saw his mouth tighten with anger. He listened for a moment or two, then held out his hand.

'Give it to me, Gini,' he said.

She handed him the receiver. He listened a moment more, then said in his clipped, cold, East Coast voice, 'Is this call being monitored? Do you know who this is?'

There was a silence. The whispering stopped.

'You call again, and you'll regret it. You've got that?' His face was now wiped of any emotion. Reaching around her, he replaced the receiver with a click.

He moved back, so he was directly in front of her once more, and Gini was backed up against her desk. He looked down into her face, and when she looked into his eyes, she could see anger in them, way back, like burning ice.

'Has that happened before?'

'Yes.'

'When? Since when have you been getting calls like that?'

'This week. I forget when they started. Tuesday. No, Monday. The day I got back from Venice—'

She broke off. That word, and that admission, had been made before she had time to think, when all she was conscious of was Hawthorne's proximity, and the pressure behind her of the edge of her desk. She saw it register in his eyes the second she said it. She crimsoned. Hawthorne gave a small sigh. She felt his whole body relax.

'Gini, Gini,' he said, in a low voice, half-amused, half-sad. 'I know you went there. I know why. It doesn't matter. Just trust me a little. A few more days. If you'd only do that. I . . . ' He broke off. 'Don't believe all the lies. Dear God . . . '

He lifted his hand, and touched her hair. 'You have amazing hair, such beautiful hair, Gini, and . . . Gini, when I look at you—'

'Don't.' She put her hands between them, and tried to push him back, but he pressed closer against her then, his hand grasping the nape of her neck, so her face was turned up to his.

'You mean that?' he said. 'You're sure you mean it? Gini, look at me. No, don't turn your face away. Yes. Like that.'

Gini became absolutely still. She looked up into his face. He was breathing more rapidly now, and she knew he was aroused. That made her very afraid. There was some desperation deep in his eyes, and a new urgency in the way he held her. He began to speak, then stopped, then began again in a low voice. He took her hand in his.

'This is what you do to me . . . You must know. It happened the first time I ever set eyes on you – and it shocked me then. It happened again, the other night, at Mary's. What were we talking about then? I can't even remember what we were talking about. I knew exactly why you were there and even that made no difference. A whole room full of other people made no difference. Tonight – when your father went to hit you. We're alike. We're kin. I know you can feel it. I can see it in your eyes. This is what they say to me – and this.'

He gripped her hand tight, and pressed it against his chest. She felt the beat of his heart through her fingertips. Then he gripped her more tightly still, and drew her hand down between their bodies. His penis was erect. He shuddered as he made her touch him.

'Gini, listen to me. Look at me . . . '

He began to press her harder, back against the desk. Gini struggled to free her hands. She wrenched her face away.

'Stop this,' she said. 'That isn't true. Get away from me. Stop this now . . . '

'Look at me and say that. You can't . . . ' he said, but when she turned her face, he bent and kissed hard on her lips. He pushed her back; he groaned, and began to caress her breasts. Gini gave a cry; he drew back just a little, and she saw his face change, become both urgent and triumphant. He twisted her arm behind her back and bent her against the desk, bearing down with his full weight so he half-straddled her, and his erection thrust against her crotch. He pulled her blouse open, ripping it. She felt the shock of his hand on her skin. His hand closed around her breast.

'Don't speak. Stop struggling. Darling – don't . . . ' He caught her hand, as she raised it to push him back. Then he was half-lifting her, one hand easing up her skirt. He pushed her down and back against the desk-top. He pushed her thighs apart, jerking her body up against his penis. Then he crushed her against him, caught her by the hair, forced her head back. She cried out again, and he pressed his mouth against hers, and pushed his tongue between her lips.

He was very strong, and these moves were swift. There was no hesitation, no suggestion that she might find his actions unwelcome or would resist. Gini fought to free her hands which were now trapped between their bodies. The pressure of his mouth was painful, and the more she struggled, the harder that pressure was. She let her body go limp, and he responded at once to that.

'Yes,' he said. 'Darling, Christ, yes . . . '

He began to kiss her throat in a frantic way. Gini freed her hands. She waited; she tensed; she thought: *When he lifts his head* . . .

'You have the most beautiful mouth,' he was saying. 'Such lovely breasts . . . '

He moved his head lower. His hands were now gripping her waist, arching her back under him. He began to kiss her breasts, more gently now, touching the nipple with his tongue and sucking it between his lips. First her right breast, then the left. A tremor ran through his body. Gini waited, waited, then he straightened.

His hands moved to the waistband of his trousers, and then – when he was half-upright, urgent, looking down at her with a blind concentration – she bunched her fist. She swung her arm, and hit him with all her strength. The blow landed in the perfect place, just on the pressure point at the side of his neck. Hawthorne gave an exclamation of pain. He released her, and stepped back.

He recovered almost immediately. He stood there, his breath coming rapidly. A look of bewilderment, then anger, passed across his face.

'I thought you understood,' he began. He took a step towards her. 'Gini—'

'Oh, I understood. I understood very well. You've been explaining all evening – I see that.'

There was a silence. His face hardened. 'Not clearly enough,' he said. 'Evidently.'

'Look – will you just get out of here now? Please?'

Gini was trying to refasten her blouse. Her hands were shaking, and she was terrified he would see this.

'You're afraid . . . '

He was staring at her. Gini stared back. She saw comprehension begin in his face.

'Your hands are shaking. I thought—' He took another step towards her. He lifted his hand, and Gini flinched. She put up her arm instinctively, to shield herself. Hawthorne stopped. His face became set.

'I see. I begin to understand. Just what in God's name have you been told about me?'

'Nothing more than you've just told me yourself. Right then.' She gestured furiously at her desk. 'If I'd had any doubts before, I don't now. You've just shown me exactly what kind of man you are—'

'Have I?' His voice had become very cold. 'I was making love to you. At least, that's what I thought.'

'Making love? You call that making love?' She turned to face him. 'You can't have thought that. I was goddamn well trying to fight you off . . . '

'Well, I expect some resistance,' he gave a slight smile, 'in the circumstances. How long would it have continued, do you think?'

'Get out of here now.' She took a step towards him. 'And don't lie. You heard me – I asked you, I told you to stop . . . '

'Ah, but did you mean it?'

'Yes and you damn well know I meant it.'

'Then I apologize.' He gave a small shrug and a cool assessing glance. 'In that case, I must have misinterpreted the signals—'

'What signals?' she said furiously. 'I never gave you one signal – not one.'

'Are you sure about that?'

'After what I'd heard about you? You think I give come-ons to men like you? Well, I don't.'

There was a long silence. Hawthorne's face had gone white. She saw her words register in his eyes like a slap in the face. He gave a sigh.

'Whatever you've been told,' he said, in a low tense voice, 'it's still possible. In this situation . . . ' He gestured at her, then at himself. 'In this situation, almost anything is possible. Any extreme. Unfortunately. As I've learned to my cost.'

He turned away, and moved across to the door, then he paused and looked back at her. 'I wasn't lying to you earlier,' he said. 'In fact, I haven't lied once since I set foot in this room – which is quite an achievement when you consider the situation. You, me – all of this. I meant it when I said I liked you. I meant some of the other things I implied – which you don't seem to have picked up. I don't expect you to believe me now. But when this is over – I hope you'll remember that, at least.'

He gave her a long steady look. 'And we were talking about sex too. Love and sex. The two subjects which most people lie about most of the time. Especially to themselves. You might think, Gini, about that . . . '

Gini looked at him uncertainly. The anger and the fear she had felt had now gone. She hesitated, then took a step towards him.

'I did not want this to happen,' she said, in a voice as quiet as his. 'You shouldn't suggest I did. I love someone. I wouldn't – couldn't – encourage anyone else. Not now. You should understand that.'

Hawthorne looked at her closely, and sadly. Then he smiled. 'You're young,' he said, in an odd, regretful way.

'When you get to my age you'll realize that even love is no protection at all. These things happen – and they get under every guard. Duty, ethics, vows – yes, even love. None is an adequate defence.' He paused. 'You say that now – but can you be sure you'd say it in six months? A year? Tomorrow? Or now – if I kissed you again now?' He took a step towards her; Gini did not move.

'It's all right. I'm not going to touch you.' He lifted his hand, then let it fall. 'You see – quite harmless.' He turned back and opened the door. 'Just remember,' he said, over his shoulder, 'I wasn't lying. And ask yourself whether you were.'

He walked out, and closed the door behind him. Gini pressed herself against it. She was shaking. She let out her breath in a shuddering sigh. She hugged her arms tight across her chest. She listened to his footsteps ascend, then cross the pavement. She heard his car engine fire, and he must have opened his car windows, because she heard music – a short fine burst of Mozart – before he pulled away, and there was silence in the street.

When he was gone, she ran across to her desk, and picked up the phone. Afterwards, looking back, she would ask herself if subsequent events might have turned out differently had Pascal not arrived back at her flat some six minutes after Hawthorne left. If the gap had been just a little longer, so she had had more time to think; if she had changed her torn blouse, washed her face, tied up her hair, removed the whisky glasses and the coffee cups – would it have been different then?

As it was, she had done none of those things. She had just sat on the floor by her desk, cradling the telephone and dialling Mary's number, again and again. She was so sure Pascal must be there, was perhaps arguing with her father even then, and it was this which explained his absence. That idea had come to her only as she heard Hawthorne drive away, and it filled her with a new agitation. She kept dialling, getting the engaged tone, then dialling again.

As she dialled, she was also listening for the sound of

his motor bike engine, but no bikes passed or stopped, just cars, just taxis. She heard one of those taxis pull up outside, but that meant nothing. Her hands would not stop shaking; she dropped the phone, picked it up again, redialled again. It was not until she heard footsteps outside, and she heard him calling her name, that she realized. She sprang to her feet, ran to the door, and opened it.

She began on some quick, joyful exclamation, clinging to him and drawing him into the light, then she stopped and gave a cry of concern. Pascal's face was white. There was a jagged cut across his temple. The leather of his jacket was ripped open from shoulder to wrist.

'Pascal, what's happened? Oh, what's happened?' she began.

She went to embrace him, and then she saw the expression on his face. She saw his eyes rest on her face and hair, then fall to her torn blouse, then fix, in turn, on the details of the room behind her: the coffee cups, the whisky glasses, the disarray of objects and papers on her desk. The chair next to her desk had been upturned, she hadn't even noticed that. Its cushion lay on the floor, together with one of her shoes. Pascal looked at these things, then looked again at her face. He was clasping her arms tightly. He looked at her mouth, and then at her neck, and she saw disbelief start way back in his eyes.

'Darling, what's happened?' he began. 'What's been happening here?'

'So many things . . . Pascal, wait, it doesn't matter now. I'll explain later. You're hurt—'

'What in hell's been happening here?'

She had been trying to put her arms around him. He gripped her wrists, and held her away from him, his eyes searching her face. The question was sharp. She saw pain and bewilderment cross his face.

Gini felt herself begin to blush. She felt the colour wash up over her neck and into her face. Were there marks on her neck? She thought perhaps there were, and they made her feel guilty. She covered them up, with her hand, and she saw Pascal's face harden into a mask of incomprehension.

'Who was here?' He walked across the room. He picked up first one whisky glass, then the other. His hands were unsteady. He turned back to look at her. 'Gini, who was here?'

'John Hawthorne was here . . . ' She made a quick movement towards him, gave a little and incoherent gesture of the hands. 'Pascal, never mind that now. When you didn't arrive – I had to leave Mary's – he gave me a ride back—'

'Are you telling me you let him in here when you were alone? Jesus Christ, what's been going on? You had that man in here? You gave him a drink?'

'Pascal, listen, you don't understand. I'll explain. It was all right.'

'It was all right?' His voice was suddenly ice-cold.

'Your blouse is torn. Your stockings are torn. Your hair – your face. *Christ* . . . ' He swung round and stared at the disorder of the room, then swung back and took her hand. 'Gini, what happened?'

'He . . . we were *talking*, Pascal, just talking, for a long time. Hours. And you didn't come back. And then the phone rang. And it was that man again, that horrible whispering voice, and then—'

'Gini, Gini . . . ' He pulled her into his arms, and pressed her tight against him. He began to stroke her hair. 'Darling, it's all right. Tell me – he didn't hurt you? Gini, what has he done?'

'Nothing.' She began to push him blindly away. 'He tried – well, it's obvious, isn't it? And then he stopped. And then he went. Pascal, I'm all right. I don't want to talk about it. Not here. And you're hurt. Your face is cut—'

'*Out.* Now . . . ' He drew back from her. He moved across the room. He picked up the desk chair. He looked at the disorder of objects knocked over on the desk, at a cushion on the floor, at her shoe lying next to that cushion. 'Get your shoe,' he said. 'Get your coat. Get any other articles of clothing that got discarded tonight—'

'Stop that.' She swung around to face him furiously. 'Just don't speak to me that way. Stop goddamn well ordering me around . . . '

'Listen.' He moved across to her fast, and caught hold of her wrist. His face was tight with fatigue. When he moved his right arm, she saw pain flash in his eyes, and he swore. 'Listen,' he said again. 'I'm not in the mood for stupid arguments. Just get your goddamn things. While you've been sitting here with Hawthorne drinking whisky, I was nearly killed. And it wasn't an accident.'

'Pascal—'

'*Listen* to me, damn it! My arm's all smashed up. I've just spent Christ knows how long with doctors and police. The bike's a write-off. When I finally get away, I go to Mary's house and there's no-one there. Then I go to Hampstead – you're not there either. I'm half-crazy with anxiety, looking for you, not knowing where you are, what's happened – and finally, I come here, and what do I find? You've spent the evening with that man. You've invited him in. You've been sitting here with him having a goddamn *drink*. Your blouse is torn. Your mouth is cut. You've got marks all over your neck . . . What in Christ's name am I supposed to think? So don't you bloody well dare start an argument now.' He broke off, and turned away. 'Just get your fucking clothes, Gini. All right?'

There was a silence. Gini did as he said. She put her shoes back on. She fetched her coat. Pascal took her arm, and pushed her outside. He slammed the door so loudly the whole house shook.

When they were back in Hampstead, the questions began again. Gini's head ached so much she could not think. She persuaded him, eventually, to remove the ripped jacket. The shirt beneath was also torn. There were cuts and grazes the length of his arm. His right shoulder was so badly bruised that it was already stained a purplish black.

'*Je m'en fiche, je m'en fiche,*' Pascal said furiously. He tried to flex the arm, and winced. 'I need to use my hands

585

tomorrow. I have to set up the cameras, use the cameras maybe. *Christ* . . . '

Gini bathed the arm, and brought him a clean shirt. Pascal became slightly calmer as she did this, but he had always hated any physical weakness on his own part, and she knew it made him furious with himself.

'I don't *know* what happened,' he said, jerking his arm away, as she tried to help him button the shirt. 'Let *me* do that. I'm not an invalid. I told you, I have to use my hands tomorrow. Fine, I'll use them now—'

'Pascal, it's hurting you. Just *rest* the arm—'

'I will not.'

'How did this happen? I still don't understand . . . .'

'I *told* you.' He moved away. 'There was the truck on my left, and a big Ford behind me, right on my rear wheel, coming up fast. The truck cut in on me – then I was off the bike. I skidded along the road. I looked up – and the Ford was coming straight at me. It had its headlights on full beam. There was nothing I could do. I could hardly move. I rolled – maybe. Just a little. Not enough. And then it missed me by this much – six inches perhaps. Maybe it was a misjudgement – but I don't think so. They could have killed me easily. But they didn't. Why didn't they do that?'

He gave another angry gesture, then a shrug. 'So, it was another warning, maybe? The last, perhaps? If so, we know now who's issuing these warnings. That's clear, at least. Look at this . . . '

He picked up his leather jacket, and from its inside pocket drew out that evening's newspaper. He tossed it across at her.

'Hawthorne *is* behind all this. He *is* responsible. You were having drinks with a murderer tonight.'

Gini looked from him to the newspaper. 'How can you know that?' she asked.

'Because there's no other candidate any more. McMullen's dead.'

'What?'

'He was killed on the railway-line just outside Oxford

– hit by a train. His body was found early this morning, around eight. He died within eight or nine hours of leaving us, Gini. I told you we were being used to find him, well there's the result. It's *there*, Gini, in the *Stop Press*.' He paused; his face became set. 'So, how was Hawthorne this evening? Clearly he was amorous. Was he also confident? More relaxed? If he was, you know why now. Most of his troubles were over before breakfast this morning, yes?'

There was a silence. Gini read the item in the paper. She bent her head over the page, and tried to think. She looked back at that long evening, that entire evening, and wondered if she had the courage now to tell Pascal what she truly thought. It would increase his anger, she knew that, and probably his hostility, but she couldn't lie, and it had to be said.

She looked up at Pascal, who was watching her closely. 'You're wrong,' she said flatly, 'Pascal – I'm sorry, but you're wrong. Hawthorne *isn't* responsible. I don't believe McMullen. I don't believe Lise. Hawthorne *isn't* the way they said.'

She was expecting another angry outburst, instead Pascal's reaction was quiet, and dangerously calm.

He moved away and sat down in a chair; he lit a cigarette. 'Fine,' he said, after a long silence. 'That seems a very surprising reaction on your part – considering what happened tonight. Obviously I don't understand what happened. Perhaps you should fill me in on all the details. I have already asked you, several times, to do that. What's changed your attitude to Hawthorne so radically, Gini?'

'Do we have to go over this now? It's late, you're in pain. It's complicated. It's a long story . . . '

'No problem,' he said icily. 'I intend to hear it. All of it, Gini. And I don't give a damn if it takes all night.'

XXXII

By two in the morning, she had already told Pascal her story twice. It had been punctuated by concern, then anger, then incomprehension on his part. Outside it was still raining heavily. Pascal's face was white and drawn, and she knew he was in pain. The more Gini said, the more she had a hopeless sense that the distance between them increased. Pascal was now looking at her as if she were a stranger, someone he did not greatly like.

'You're lying,' he said simply, when she had finally finished speaking. 'If you're not lying, you're avoiding something, leaving something out. This story doesn't explain your change of heart. The reverse.'

'Then it's because I'm not telling it the right way,' Gini said quietly. 'I wouldn't lie to you, Pascal.'

'I'm sorry.' He gestured with his hand as if warding off some hurt. He leaned forward. 'I know that, Gini, but you must see, it makes no sense. *Why* are you suddenly so convinced he's innocent? Neither he nor your father gave you any proof. All right, they told a convincing version but it's just another *version*, Gini.'

'It wasn't that. It wasn't *then*.' She hesitated, and saw him tense.

'All right. So it was later. When you were alone with Hawthorne?'

'He began to convince me at Mary's. My father too. Maybe it helped when he intervened between me and my father.'

'I would imagine so, yes. That was very convenient for him.'

Gini let this pass. She sighed. 'Pascal, I can't explain. It wasn't *what* he said to me so much, it was the *way* in which he said it. When he talked about his marriage, the other women . . . I *know* he was telling me the truth.'

'Jesus Christ, Gini.' He gave a gesture of exasperation. 'This innocent man of yours, this honourable man – what does he do when he gets you alone in your apartment?'

'I know. I know. But before that, for a long time, he just talked.'

'He talked. Fine. And what did he talk about? About women. About love. Gini, for God's sake, he fed you the oldest line in the book. How his wife failed to understand him, failed to satisfy him—'

'That's not what he said.'

'And you bought it. Gini, *think*. You're not a child. The whole conversation – it was *provocative*.'

'It wasn't.'

'You can't mean that.' He rounded on her angrily. 'Gini, he talks to you about his love affairs, his one-night stands, his *fucks*? If you can't see it, I certainly can. I *know* why men talk that way to women – I've seen men do it a thousand times. It's a goddamned come-on, you know that.'

'It didn't sound that way. It wasn't calculated. He was being honest. I believed what he said.'

'All right. All right.' Pascal threw up his hands. He rose and began to pace back and forth. She could see him fight down the anger and the impatience. He returned to his chair, leaned forward, and looked at her intently.

'OK. We go over it one last time. I don't want to. You don't want to. Still, that is what we do. Fine. I'll buy the first part of your story. It's been an emotional evening with your father. Hawthorne comes to your aid. He drives you home. He plays you Mozart, God help us. He asks to come in, and you agree. It's insane, but that's what you do. He then sits there, and he has a very proper, honest conversation with you – no undertones, no suggestivity, and you warm to him. Am I right so far?'

'I didn't warm to him exactly.' She hesitated. 'I admired him, I think.'

'What?'

'I admired him – as a person. I didn't necessarily like

589

him, or approve of him, but he was interesting. Complex. Guarded. Hurt. Honest, at some cost.'

'You were falling in love with this man? That's what it sounds like . . . Jesus Christ, Gini, I don't *understand* this.' He gave another furious gesture, then stood up. 'I need a drink. You want a drink?'

'No, I don't. I want to go to bed. I want to stop going over and over this. What's the point?'

'The point is, you've come to a totally irrational, foolish, *female* decision about this man.' He gave her a sharp glance. 'It's all instinct, intuition.'

'I don't care. I still think I'm right.'

He poured himself a brandy, and turned to look at her. 'You do realize that's no way to work on this, do you?' he said, more coldly. 'It's a totally stupid way. And I won't work like that.'

'Fine. So we take a different approach.'

'Why do you have to be so obstinate? *Why*, Gini?' He moved across, sat down, and took her hands in his. 'Darling, let's just get one thing very clear. No matter what you thought while he was talking to you, you *know* what happened next . . . '

'Do I?' She gave him an exhausted glance. 'I'm not so sure I do.'

'All right.' He sighed. 'We go through it, one last time. When did he first touch you, before the telephone call or after it?'

'After. No, before. No – I could sense what was coming before. He – well, he took my hand. He kissed my hand.'

'You never mentioned that.'

'Well, I forgot. He did. And then I asked him to leave – just after, or just before. I can't remember. Then that call came and I think it made him angry. He looked angry.'

'How did you expect him to look? Jubilant? He must have arranged those calls, Gini, come on – you *know* that.'

'I *don't* know that. And neither do you.'

'Fine. All right. So he took the call. What happened next?'

'I'm not sure. It was all very swift. He started talking.'

'Did he kiss you?'

'Yes. All right. He did.'

It was the first time she had made that admission. Pascal's face became blank. He gave a bewildered gesture.

'Are you saying you let him do that? I don't understand—'

'No. I told you. I didn't *let* him do any of it. I told him to stop. But it happened very fast. And he's strong. And I was afraid. I struggled – and then I thought maybe he liked that, maybe that made it worse. So I waited until I could hit him. When I hit him, he stopped.'

There was a silence. Pascal passed his hand wearily across his face. 'Gini,' he began, 'can you imagine how this makes me feel? To think of this happening? It makes me sick, ill. It makes me ache. I can't bear to think about it. How can you say you trust this man? He tears your blouse. He traps you against your desk. He comes very close to raping you—'

'No. Not exactly. It sounds like that. But I'm not sure it *was* like that.'

There was another silence. Pascal gave a sigh. 'So, what am I supposed to conclude? He was not forcing you? You were not resisting?'

'Yes, I was. Pascal it's not that straightforward . . .'

'Was he forcing you? Yes or no?'

'Yes.'

'Very well. Then why exonerate him now? *Why*, Gini?'

'I don't *know* why. All right, it was instinct. The things that he'd said earlier. The way he looked. The fact that he *did* stop. And afterwards . . .'

She broke off. Pascal drew back from her. His face became guarded and cold.

'Oh really? There was an afterwards? You never mentioned that. You mean there's *more* to this?'

'No, there wasn't – not in that sense. He didn't touch me again. I told you, he left almost immediately. He, well, he apologized . . .'

'That's good of him.'

'He said . . . it was a misunderstanding. He looked – I can't tell you how he looked. He looked as if he'd lost everything, and he knew he had. Pascal, it was a terrible look.'

'I don't really care,' Pascal said coldly, 'how he looked. If there's a hell – which there is – he can burn in it. I hope he does. I hope he's there right now. So don't tell me how he looked, Gini, just tell me what he said.'

'You can't divorce the two—'

'Just tell me what he said.'

'All right. He justified himself, if you like. I told you. He said it was a misunderstanding. He said he'd picked up the wrong signals from me. He implied that he'd thought I wanted all that to happen. That's what he said.'

Gini looked away, and bent her head. There was a long and painful silence. She waited for a new outburst, more anger, but it did not come. When she looked up, Pascal's face was changed, transfigured. All the anger and bewilderment and anxiety had left it. He held out his hand to her.

'Come here,' he said.

She rose and crossed to him. He took her in his arms very gently, and looked down into her face. He smiled.

'What a fool,' he said, 'to make that mistake. Gini, why didn't you tell me that before?'

'I don't know. I was ashamed. I thought you'd be angry, I expect.'

'No. Not angry – relieved. Darling, you must see now. He was lying. Giving him signals? You couldn't have done that. I know you wouldn't do that. Not you, not now. It's impossible. So he was using the cheap little excuses men like him do use to extricate themselves from situations like that . . .'

'Do you think so?'

'Darling, I *know* so. Listen, this is my fault. I shouldn't have gone on and on questioning you like this. It was just – I couldn't understand how you could defend him. But I understand now. He tried to make you feel guilty, and he succeeded. You're exhausted and confused and upset.

592

In the morning you'll see it in perspective. You'll see him for what he is . . . Darling, don't turn your face away. Look at me. I was jealous, and angry . . . Come to bed now, yes? Listen, you hear? The rain has stopped. And we have so much to do tomorrow. It's almost over, I can sense it, all of this. One more day, two – then we can leave it behind us, yes? And . . . '

'Pascal . . . '

'No more words.' He laid his fingers against her lips. 'Come and rest . . . '

When they were in bed, in the darkness, Pascal held her in his arms. There was no rain, no wind.

Pascal said: 'How still the night is.'

'I want you,' Gini said.

'You're sure?'

'Yes.'

He kissed her, very softly, and stroked her back, and her throat and her breasts. It was the slowest of love-makings and very sweet; it felt like a pledge. Afterwards, when Pascal slept, she wept, partly from happiness, partly from pleasure, and partly because despite the slowness and the sweetness and the love and the trust, the ghost of Hawthorne still returned afterwards, and all of Pascal's arguments, excellent though they were, rational though they were, still did not convince.

In the morning, Gini woke to a London transformed. Pascal was still deeply asleep. She drew back the edge of the curtain at the bedroom window, and looked out across the heath. The grass was white with hoar-frost, the sky glittering and unclouded. She quietly opened the window a fraction. The clear air was dry and bitterly cold, like an inhalation of ice.

She closed the window, and crept silently from the room. Today was Saturday; this morning they were to station themselves in that rented St John's Wood house, so that Pascal could set up his cameras well before midnight came. She sat in the kitchen, with some coffee, and looked

593

at this plan; she turned it this way and that, she wondered if she had the courage to explain to Pascal that sleep had not changed her view: she still believed in Hawthorne's statements, just as she had done the previous night.

Shortly before nine, she let herself quietly out of the house. She walked up the narrow lane that led to the summit of Holly Hill, and from there down a series of steep steps and cobbled passageways to the High Street. A newsagent's shop was open there; she bought ten newspapers – all the major dailies – and turned back up the street.

She was anxious to check the papers before she returned to Pascal, and near the summit of the hill, just above the old Hampstead graveyard, she found the perfect place. There, tucked away in a steep lane, was a tiny white-painted Catholic church. Inside, its eighteenth-century nave was warm and light. Candles burned beneath a statue of the Virgin Mary. It was deserted. She moved to the back of the side chapel, sat down in a pew, and opened the papers in turn. She scanned them all carefully, but only one carried a further report on James McMullen's death.

It was on page five of the *Daily Mail*, two inches, single column. It told her more than the brief *Stop Press* item in the *Standard* the previous day. Even so, the accident – if accident it was – had attracted little attention. McMullen had died an anonymous death.

The body later identified as his had been found on the Oxford–London railway-line, ten miles east of Oxford itself. Badly disfigured, it had been spotted from a bridge over the line, on Friday morning, by a man out walking his dog. The railway-line here was easily accessible from the bridge: death might have been accident or suicide; police enquiries were continuing. McMullen's family had been informed. The story ended with brief references to McMullen's father's work as an art historian, and to his sister's appearance, some years before, in a thrice-weekly TV soap. Gini closed the paper. An accident? A suicide? McMullen had died within ten hours of their meeting with him in Oxford. Had he looked like a man about to kill himself? No, he had not.

She sat for a while, thinking, watching the candles flicker against the blue hem of the Virgin's dress. She remembered one tiny aspect of McMullen's behaviour when they met, which had puzzled her at the time, and now struck her with renewed force.

Towards the end of their last conversation in his car, when McMullen had tried to thank them for their work, Pascal had suggested he wait until the story was concluded, and thank them then.

Ah, then . . . Of course, McMullen had replied and Gini had noticed something odd in his tone. She might not have been able to account for it then, but now she could: even then, the night before his death, McMullen had not expected ever to see them again.

Why? Had he known for certain that he was close to death? Had he perhaps expected the accident to happen to Pascal, to herself? Or was there another explanation?

She rose from her seat, and moved back into the body of the church. She stood facing the altar for a moment thinking of Hawthorne, and what he had said the previous night. She tried to imagine what it must mean to be brought up a Catholic, and then to lose your faith. Her own childhood had been godless in most respects. On an impulse, she put a coin in the box, and lit one of the votive candles. Opening the door to leave, she glanced back at it. There was a draft from the doorway; the flame of the candle wavered, guttered, but did not go out.

When she returned, Pascal was up. There was a smell of coffee brewing. He was on his knees in the sitting-room, checking his camera equipment, fitting some last small components into their cases.

He looked around, as she came in; he took her hand, and kissed her palm, then returned, absorbed, to his work. Gini stood next to him, and watched. There were two heavy aluminium camera cases. Inside them, packed into cavities cut in black latex, were the tools of

Pascal's trade: the cameras themselves, the light meters, the panoply of lenses. Two were telephoto, swollen heavy things about twenty inches long. Next to the cases, in a long black leather carrier resembling a gun-case in size and shape were the tripods.

Gini looked at the dull gleam of casings and dials, at the dark luminous eyes of the lenses. She watched Pascal's hands move, the left quickly and deftly, the right more stiffly. He flexed the injured arm, then continued. Gini thought: *Pascal's weaponry*.

She disliked cameras for their capacity to freeze time, and she understood little of their technical workings. The potential power of this arsenal disturbed her. The lenses winked, snug as jewels in their box. By this means, possibly, a truth could be fixed.

Pascal closed the cases, and snapped them shut. He looked round at her with a smile.

Gini hesitated; then, because she knew that if she was going to say this, she would have to do so at once, she said, 'Pascal. I'm not coming with you today. You don't need me. I'm going to Oxford instead.'

'What?' He straightened, and stared at her.

'I'm going to Oxford. I can't help you take photographs. You don't need me. I'm going to Oxford. I'm going to check out McMullen's death.'

'Darling, you can't possibly mean that.' He rose and took her hand. 'We must stay together now, you know that. I won't let you do that. It's pointless, and it's not safe.'

'No, Pascal. I'm going. I'll come to the St John's Wood house with you, it's on the way to the station. But then I'm going to Oxford. Someone has to check this out. You can't, so I will. We owe McMullen that much, surely?'

'Owe? Owe?' His eyes flashed with sudden anger. 'This is a story, not a crusade. We owe McMullen nothing. There's plenty of time to check his death out later – next week. For God's sake, Gini, if he's dead, he's dead. Going to Oxford won't alter anything.'

'It might.'

'I don't understand you. How can you do this? Everything we've been working towards, *everything*, has been leading up to Sunday, to this damn assignation of Hawthorne's.' He broke off. His face hardened. 'Oh, of course. I see. This has very little to do with McMullen and everything to do with John Hawthorne. Am I right? Yes?'

'Insofar as I don't believe those assignations ever happened, maybe. Yes. I don't believe you're going to see Hawthorne, or any blonde woman, let alone photograph them. They won't *be* there. It's not going to happen, Pascal.'

'How can you know that?' He rounded on her angrily. 'Is that what you thought yesterday afternoon, when you'd talked to that call-girl? No, it wasn't. Have you said that once before? No. So what's made you change your mind? That bloody man Hawthorne has made you change your mind . . . Well, enough. I'm not going over that again. I'm not arguing either. I'm going to that house, and you're coming with me. That's that.'

'No. It isn't—'

'How many times do I have to say this?' He gave her a look of desperation. 'I want you to be *safe*. Four people are now dead. Last night I was nearly killed. You're not going to Oxford without me, Gini. I won't let you do that.'

'You can't stop me, you know that. I'll be perfectly safe. It's an hour on the train to Oxford, that's all. I just want to talk to the police there – maybe Anthony Knowles, if he'll see me. Then I'll come back. I'll probably be back by early evening. I'll come straight from the station to you. Nothing can happen before midnight, anyway – if any of this is true, that's the deadline, midnight tonight. I'll be back hours before then . . . '

'No. You know I can't come with you. I have to go to that house. I have to set up the cameras. That takes time. I have to wait. Gini, I promise you, we'll go to Oxford first thing on Monday if you want. You're not going to learn anything. Why can't it wait?'

'It just can't, that's all. I feel it here.' She pressed her hand to her chest. 'And anyway, it makes sense. This way we cover twice as much ground. I deal with the McMullen question, you deal with Hawthorne. I'll be back by six—'

'No! Let's be very clear about this.' He cut her off, his voice now very cold. 'I can't work this way. Constant arguments, foolish plans, last-minute changes. You're right – I can't compel you. Very well, I *ask* you: don't do this.'

'Pascal, I have to do it. I think it's right.'

'So, you won't listen to me? My views, and my feelings, my concern for your safety mean nothing to you?'

'You know that's not true . . . '

'Do I?' He stared at her. 'I'm not sure I know you at all any more. First last night. Now this. I love you, Gini – and because I love you, I ask you one last time. Stay with me, the way we planned . . . '

'No,' Gini said. There was a long tense silence. Pascal turned away.

'Very well.' He bent, lifted the cases, and moved them to the door. 'In that case, there's no point in your hurrying back. Stay in Oxford as long as you like.' There was another silence. Gini stared at him. 'Do you mean that?' she said quietly.

'Yes, I do.'

'Those are your terms?'

'That's right.'

'Fine.' She bit her lip and forced back the tears. 'In that case, you leave me no choice. I'll come with you to the house, then I'm going to Oxford. I won't be blackmailed, Pascal.'

'How can you say that? How dare you say that? Christ . . . ' He moved towards her, and for one moment, she thought he might hit her, or embrace her. He stopped at the edge of both these actions. They stood looking at one another, both pale, both fighting back distress.

'Pascal,' she began, on a pleading note. She reached out her hand to him. 'I wouldn't do this to you. I *must* go. I told you – it's just a few hours. After that . . . '

'Be quite clear. There is no after that,' he replied, and walked out.

They reached the rented St John's Wood house at ten-thirty that morning. Pascal had not spoken to her once on the way there in the taxi, and he did not address her once they had arrived. He went straight upstairs, tight-lipped, walking past her as if she were invisible. In the back upstairs bedroom, another temple of pink brocade, he laid the cases on the bed and began to unpack them.

Gini followed him upstairs. She wanted desperately to speak to him, but none of the words flooding in her mind seemed right. Pascal did not look up when she entered the room. She gazed at him miserably, then moved to the window. She tried to concentrate, as he did, on the realities of this task. She could see that Pascal had chosen well. From this window, the Gothic villa to which Lise Hawthorne had directed them was clearly visible.

No more than fifty feet away, across an open garden, she could see both the rear windows and the entrance to the house. The villa entrance, set to the side, consisted of a flight of five steps leading up to the pointed Gothic porch. Anyone entering or leaving the house must use that route. Pascal, true to his reputation, had chosen the perfect location for spying.

She felt Pascal move behind her. He crossed to her side, and followed her gaze. He handed her a pair of binoculars.

'The magnification with the camera lens is even better,' he said, in a polite, neutral voice, as if addressing a stranger. 'Look.'

Gini looked. The porch and its approach steps were now startlingly close. She could make out the pattern on the steps' iron balustrade. She altered angle, acutely aware of Pascal's closeness, and scanned the rear of the house.

Here there were three windows, one for each of the house's three storeys. The top-most window, dormered and set into the roof, was tiny. The window below, on what must be a bedroom floor, was larger: she could just see the outline of furniture beyond its curtains. The ground-floor window afforded the best view. It was wide, and tall, opening out onto a balcony behind, with a flight of steps to the rear garden below it. The sunlight glinted on the window-panes, but even so, she could see details beyond: a pale carpet, a large white sofa, the corner of a table, a vase of flowers.

'Someone's using that house anyway,' she said, in the same neutral tone Pascal had used. 'Or they're intending to use it. There are flowers in that room.'

He took the binoculars from her, focused them briefly on the window she indicated, then moved. She saw him scan the line of gardens, back to back, that ran between their own street and the cul-de-sac beyond. She saw him survey that turning. He lowered the binoculars, and frowned.

'Strange . . . ' he said.

'What's strange?'

'It's too quiet, that's what's strange. No cars. No people.'

'Half the houses around here are second homes, I told you, you remember? They're left empty for months at a time. Besides, it's Saturday. It's still early. People sleep in . . . '

'On such a beautiful day? Take a look at it, Gini. It's like a graveyard out there.'

Gini scanned the turning. Pascal moved back to his cameras. The cul-de-sac was indeed oddly deserted. No cars were parked on its street or in its driveways. No-one was passing on foot. Gini gave a small shiver. She glanced down at her watch; she would have to leave soon.

She turned away from the window. Pascal ignored her. With careful precision he was assembling camera and telephoto lens. Gini cleared her throat. 'In daylight,' she began, and even to her own ears, her voice sounded strained and false, 'in daylight you're in the perfect position. But what if he comes at night, Pascal?'

'Well, you don't think he's going to put in an appearance

at any point, so I wouldn't worry about it, if I were you.'

'I'm just asking . . . '

'If you insist. There's no difficulty after dark. You see this?' He held up the camera. He looked through the viewfinder, and made a minute adjustment. 'We owe a lot to the military. With this, I can see in the dark. Like a cat.'

'Why the military?'

Pascal shrugged. His manner remained cold. 'I don't have time to explain. It's too technical – you wouldn't understand. Besides, you have a train to catch, remember?'

'I'd like to understand, Pascal.'

'As you like. Very well.'

He knelt back on his heels. As he spoke, he loaded the camera deftly with film. 'Much of the most recent camera technology came about through weapons research. With infrared nightsights, for instance, or a device known as an image-intensifier, a soldier armed with a rifle can now pick the enemy off from a mile away. In total darkness. He can see the man clearly. He can line him up in his sights, go for a head-shot. Before he fires, he could tell you whether the man needed a shave.' He shrugged. 'In daylight, of course, the range increases. Then he could probably hit him from a two-mile range, certainly a mile and a half. At night, well, a range of one mile – that's not bad.'

'Not bad? It's horrible.'

'Of course. It makes killing very clinical. You've heard of smart bombs? Well, there are also smart guns – and smart cameras. Here.' He held the camera out to her. 'You see how heavy this is? Its technology is similar to night-deployment weaponry. With this I can see in darkness as well as any army sniper . . . ' He paused. 'And I can also film in the dark. This is loaded with specially coated film. At this distance from that villa, with the right aperture and shutter speed I can shoot thirty to thirty-five frames in the time it takes a man to walk up those steps over there. If

Hawthorne, or anyone else, walks up those steps, or into those rear rooms I've got him.'

'Clearly?'

'Of course. When the pictures are processed, you'll be able to see every line on Hawthorne's face. You'll see the expression in his eyes, the pattern on his neck-tie . . . '

'And the blonde?'

'The blonde too. *Evidemment*.'

Pascal looked up at her as he said this. He could see the strain in her face. She was standing there awkwardly, twisting the strap of her shoulder-bag. Her mouth looked a little swollen; he could now see faint bruise marks on her throat. He thought suddenly of their night at the Oxford hotel, of the phone call received then, and of that last ugly whispered message: *Be there, Gini. Come after dark . . . be sure to wear the black dress.*

He rose quickly to his feet, and looked at her. She met his eyes miserably. With a low cry, he caught her to him, and began to kiss her face and her hair. She clung to him tightly; her mouth opened under his. He kissed her deeply. She was beginning to cry, so he kissed her tears, then her mouth again. He began to unfasten her coat, and the desire he felt for her then was blinding. She stumbled, and he pressed her hard against him. She gave a low moan. He laid his hand over the curve of her breast; he lifted back her hair and buried his face against her throat. He said, 'Darling, please stay . . . '

He felt her whole body tense at once. She tried to draw back from him, then let him kiss her once more.

'No,' she said, and reaching up, she put her fingers against his lips. She looked at him sadly. 'No, Pascal. You won't persuade me. Not even that way.'

There was a silence, then, with an abrupt gesture, he turned away. 'So be it,' he said. He bent over his camera case, took one of the cameras from it, and began to adjust the lens. His concentration on this task was intense.

'Why,' Gini began passionately. '*Why* can't you agree? It could be important, you must see that.'

'I don't care.' He looked up at her. 'I've tried – I can't

try any longer. I love you and I'm concerned for you, but you won't listen to me. I have a job to do here. I shall do it. That's all. You could help me here, as I've tried to help you ever since I began work on this. But no, you don't care about that. You're wilful and impetuous and obstinate, Gini. If you're going – go.'

'Pascal—'

'Just *go*, Gini.' He rose. He looked down at the camera, and then back at her. 'It's over. That's all.'

'I don't believe that. You wouldn't do that. Just now—'

'Forget just now. And I would do it, don't doubt that for one moment. I've cut you out of my life once, and I survived. If I have to do it a second time, I will. So choose.'

Gini stared at him. His face was set, and his voice was cold. She knew that Pascal never made idle claims or threats.

'I can't be controlled in that way. It's wrong. You said that you loved me . . . '

'Yes.' His face contracted for an instant. 'And I asked you once before to make a choice. In Beirut – you remember? I stood there in that terrible hotel room, with your father, after you'd lied to me, and I'd had to find that out from him, not you. I stood there, and in front of your damn father, I asked you to choose. I would have waited for you, and you knew that damn well. Two more years, that's all – and then he wouldn't have been able to dictate to you any more. But no. You wouldn't agree. Fine. You chose to end it then. I choose to end it now.'

Gini gave a cry. 'Pascal, that's not fair. You know that's desperately unfair. I was fifteen years old. I was scared and ashamed. My father had been arguing, for hours and hours before you came. You'd *hit* him, Pascal . . . '

'I don't *care* any more, do you understand?' he said. 'I don't want to go back over that. I don't want to hear arguments or excuses. Your father influenced you then. He's influencing you now – and so, God help us, is Hawthorne. Don't you have a mind of your own?'

'Yes, I do.' Gini became very still. 'I do have a mind of my own, Pascal. And I don't agree with *you*.'

'Then you've chosen already.' He gave a shrug. 'Fine. Go.'

Gini walked across to the door.

'My things are still at that house in Hampstead . . . '

'Here's a key.' He tossed one across. It landed on the floor beside her. Gini bent and picked it up.

'Collect them any time. I won't be there.'

'*Why* are you doing this? Why are you so hard?'

'Why?' His eyes flashed. 'Because you very nearly destroyed me once, that's why. It's not going to happen a second time . . . ' He broke off, then continued more quietly. 'This doesn't *work*, Gini, you can see that. We'd just end up destroying each other. Who knows? Maybe it's better this way. Neater, quicker, less painful all around.'

He said this in a flat, and final way. Then he bent to his camera cases, and began to assemble another set of lenses. He did not look up again. Gini stood there for a few more minutes, then she turned and quietly left the house.

XXXIII

'Time of death?'

The sergeant from the Thames Valley Police was young, short and plump. He had a punitive haircut. They were in the canteen at the Oxford division's headquarters, just outside Headington. The sergeant was eating sausage, eggs, chips and beans – a cholesterol overdose. He cut up his sausage and chewed contemplatively. Gini tried to force herself to concentrate: the story she'd spun about researching an article on modern police methods had seemed effective. The sergeant was being co-operative, but to her neither he nor the canteen seemed very real.

'Around six yesterday morning,' he went on. 'We reckon he was hit by one of the early commuter trains. We'll know more definitely when we get the results of the autopsy. You could call back later, talk to the detective inspector. He's over at the mortuary now.'

The sergeant had a slow Gloucestershire accent, and a stolid demeanour. His round blue eyes fixed themselves on Gini's face. He mopped up egg yolk and continued to chew.

'It can't have been easy to make identification then,' Gini said.

The sergeant shrugged. 'He was carrying the usual ID. His Range Rover was parked by the bridge. He had its keys in his pocket. He was wearing a signet ring, with one of those crest things on it. His father wears one just the same.'

'Did his father identify the body?'

'What was left of it. Yes. Not a pleasant job . . . '

'I'm sure. Was it suicide?'

'That's for the coroner to say.'

The sergeant munched the last of the chips. He looked at Gini and gave a sigh.

'Put it this way – where he died, the line's straight. You'd see an oncoming train from a mile away – more. Not too many people drive out into the middle of nowhere and decide to lie down on live rails.' He paused. 'On the other hand, he'd been drinking. The body reeked of booze. I'd say he was way over the limit to drive. There was an empty whisky flask in his coat pocket, and an empty Scotch bottle in the car. Plus, the night before, he'd been dining in college. Plenty of wine and port. He was well and truly oiled . . . '

'The night before? In college? Would that be Christ Church?'

'That's right.' He opened a notebook and flicked through its pages. 'I checked his movements myself. Well, it wasn't difficult. His tutor heard the reports on the local radio station. He called us straightaway . . . '

'His tutor?'

'Former tutor, I should say. Party by the name of Dr Anthony Knowles.'

The sergeant's expression became dour: Gini had the impression that he and Knowles hadn't exactly hit it off.

'I've heard of Knowles . . . '

'Who hasn't?' He glanced over his shoulder and lowered his voice. 'Twenty minutes after I saw him, we had his friend the chief constable on the phone. Telling me to get a move on. Don't quote me . . . '

'I won't quote you.'

'But they want this one sewn up nice and neat. I have to watch my p's and q's.'

Gini considered this. It surely could not be true. McMullen might have died on the railway-line early Friday morning, but he could not have been dining in Christ Church the night before. That night was the night she and Pascal had talked to him; he had dropped them off in Oxford around nine-fifteen, then returned to his hide-out above Hawthorne's estate. So Knowles had lied to the police. Interesting, too, that Knowles should claim he heard the news item on the local radio station. She herself had tuned in to that station in the hire-car she'd picked up at Oxford station. It played an unremitting blast of rock music – she wouldn't have expected that to be Knowles's taste at all.

She pushed her hair back tiredly from her face. She knew she was neither thinking nor operating very well. She could hear Pascal's voice at the back of her mind all the time. The pain of their parting was a physical ache. She could have located it exactly, have put her hand across her heart and said: *The pain is there*.

'You want a cup of coffee, love? You don't look too well, you know.'

'No, no thank you. I'm fine.' She leaned forward. 'So tell me, if McMullen dined in college on Thursday night, what happened then?'

'According to Dr Knowles, the dinner broke up late. He and McMullen went back to his rooms. They broke open a bottle of nineteen twelve port or what-have-you and talked. Knowles pushed off to bed around three in the morning. When he woke at eleven, McMullen had gone. Some life, eh? I wouldn't mind being one of those dons.'

'You mean he expected McMullen to be in college the next morning?'

'Oh yes. This McMullen had been going through a difficult patch, apparently. He'd been staying there as Knowles's guest for some while.'

'Really? In college? For how long?'

The sergeant consulted his notebook. 'Four days. In one of the college guest-rooms. Same staircase as Dr Knowles. He arrived there last Monday, and was due to leave Friday evening. Supposed to be going on from there to his parents'. They live in Shropshire. Near the border with Wales. But he'd obviously been planning something. They got a letter from him Friday morning. His father showed it to me. McMullen told them he couldn't go on.'

'Did he give a reason?'

'General depression. No job. No woman. That kind of thing.' The sergeant shrugged.

Gini frowned. So Knowles had lied to the police – and an attempt had been made to suggest suicide as plausible. Yet why should McMullen want to kill himself now? Could the man she and Pascal had been speaking to that Thursday night have then deliberately killed himself, only ten hours later? She did not believe that for an instant, not at all. She felt a sudden quickening excitement. She had been right, she thought: this death was not what it seemed. And if the police had accepted the idea that McMullen had been staying in Christ Church, they presumably knew nothing of the cottage in the woods. She leaned forward again.

'So I guess McMullen must have left all his belongings at Christ Church?'

'Not much.' The sergeant shrugged. 'One suitcase. Change of clothes.'

'You have a list of the belongings you found on his body? I'm interested, you know, in how you piece together someone's ID. It might help my story . . . '

'A list. Yes.' The sergeant sighed. 'Lists. Paperwork. Bumf. It never bloody well stops, pardon my French. Used to be forms in triplicate. It's all computers now. I can let you have a copy, I suppose. No reason why not. Come down to the DI's office now.'

In the office, the sergeant heaved his weight into a revolving chair, rummaged through some paperwork and eventually found the print-out he was looking for. He handed it across. 'This article you're doing . . . ' He looked up at her. 'Modern police methods, that's it?'

'Right.'

'Why pick this case? It's routine, love. We could set you up with a nice little homicide.' He smiled. 'Or drugs. The drug scene in Oxford is very active now. Only the other week—'

Gini interrupted him quickly. 'No, no. My editor wants a routine case. That's the whole point. So readers can understand daily policework. I wonder. I have a map here. Can you show me where it was exactly that he died?'

She passed her map across. It was a large-scale walkers'

Ordnance Survey, one inch to the mile. The sergeant scanned it for a second or two, then placed one large finger on a square ten miles to the south-east of the city. There, in an area with few villages, among open fields and woods, a solitary bridge took a minor road over the railway-line.

'There,' he said. 'See that bridge? Miles from bloody anywhere. It was right there.'

Gini re-folded the map without comment. Not miles from anywhere exactly, but close, very close to where she had been two days before with Pascal.

Outside, in her hire-car, she examined the map more closely, frowning and trying to remember the terrain. Yes, here was the church and the graveyard where she and Pascal kept watch. Here, in the valley below, was Hawthorne's house. Here, on the far side of that valley, were the woods and the cottage where McMullen had holed up. And here – a tiny square – was the cottage itself, and the track McMullen had driven.

The track continued beyond the cottage. That continuation had been invisible in the dark, but on the map its route was clear. It wound down through the woods behind the cottage. Three miles further on, it joined a minor road. That junction was fifty yards from the bridge where McMullen died.

And not just close to the bridge, either. She started the engine, stopped, checked the map one last time. On the map, the boundaries of John Hawthorne's estate were clear. McMullen had ostensibly met his death less than half a mile from the high stone wall of Hawthorne's estate. And, of course, for a man obsessed with pointing the finger at Hawthorne, that was a very suggestive place to die.

She hesitated, and looked at her watch. It was nearly two. She just had time to call Anthony Knowles, and then make it to the railway-line and to the cottage in the woods before the light failed.

She drove a short way, found a phone box, and dialled Christ Church. A polite porter informed her that Dr Knowles was unavailable. He had left that morning for a conference in Rome, and would be away for three days. No, he regretted, but they were not permitted to give out numbers.

Gini hung up the phone. She leaned her face against the cold glass of the door panels. She watched the traffic go past. It was beginning to rain again, lightly. Just two days ago, she and Pascal had walked this way, on their arrival in Oxford, filling in time before that meeting at the Paradise Café. On the corner of the street over there, just there, Pascal had looked down at her, and taken her hand. The pain was suddenly overwhelming. She felt it surge through her, and clench at her heart.

In her purse, she had the number of the rented house in St John's Wood. Taking it out, her hands trembling, she picked up the phone and dialled.

By midday, Pascal had completed his camera set-ups. Two telephoto lenses, their cameras mounted on tripods, one trained on the entrance steps to Hawthorne's villa, the other on the windows to the rear. He had pushed all the furniture in the room against the wall, so he could move fast and without hindrance in the window region, even in the dark. In addition to these, he had four other cameras, two loaded with monochrome, two with colour, all to be hand-held.

As long as he was intent on these preparations he could keep the pain at bay. The minute they were completed, it returned. He sat there, in that ugly, incongruous room, smoking cigarette after cigarette. Why had he said those things? Why had he done those things? He buried his face in his hands. He felt filled with rage and anxiety and self-hate; he thought: *I am a fool*.

He knew why he had acted as he did to some extent. He had been so desperate to prevent Gini from leaving alone that he was prepared to use almost any means to stop her. He had been convinced that if he loaded her choice in that way, he would prevent her going. The instant he realized she would *still* not be dissuaded, even if it meant ending their affair, he had been caught up in a hideous spiral of pain and anger and incomprehension and doubt. Jealousy of Hawthorne, that too; and continuing uncertainty as to what exactly could have happened between Hawthorne and Gini the previous evening. His mind had leapt from one crazy, facile conclusion to another: she could not love him; she was concealing something; she was not concealing something . . . He rose to his feet with an angry exclamation, and began to pace the room.

Pride, he thought: he was guilty of indulging wounded pride, of being obstinate, foolhardy, intemperate, incautious – and what was the result? He had thrown Gini a key. *Thrown* it, in a horrible contemptuous way, not even given it to her, and spoken to her in that vile, cold, distanced way he had perfected in the years of his marriage. He had done all these things, at a moment when all he truly wanted to do was take her in his arms – and then, not surprisingly, she had left. Walked out. She was now somewhere in Oxford. Alone. He couldn't call her, or contact her – and he knew, just knew, that she was every bit as proud and obstinate as he was, and so she would never contact him, she would not phone.

Fool, he said to himself. *Fool, fool, fool.* He stared around at the pink brocade, and suddenly it was unbearable to be there any longer. He slammed out of the house, went as far as the garden gate, then realized he had no bike, no car, no transport. What if Gini were in trouble? What if she needed him? He slammed back into the house, called the nearest car-hire company, stormed out again, remembered he had not switched on the answering machine, ran back in again, stared at it, and then started a series of frantic calls. The Thames Valley Police were helpful, but the sergeant dealing with this case was on his lunch-break. No, they couldn't say where he was, he wasn't answering his office phone. Pascal then tried Christ Church, and when he learned Dr Knowles was away, his spirits rose. Perhaps that meant Gini would give up and leave Oxford. Maybe, after all, she would come here, that evening, on her return. He left an incoherent message with the porter, switched on the answering machine.

He went straight to the car-hire company, and hired the fastest car they had available, a black Rover with a souped-up engine. Pascal hated it on sight. He drove it away from the garage, driving fast and recklessly, slamming up through the gears.

He drove around the area for a short while, trying to concentrate on the geography of this story, the geography here. He drove into Regent's Park, and past the mosque, past the ambassador's residence almost opposite it. He timed the distance from there back to the cul-de-sac. Gini had estimated it as five minutes. The way he was driving, he did it in two and a half.

He shot past the cul-de-sac entrance, did an illegal U-turn to the accompaniment of a cacophony of horns. He accelerated back the way he had come, slammed on the brakes, parked on a yellow line where parking was forbidden, got out of the car, and walked into Regent's Park. Avoiding the ambassador's residence to his right, he turned left and walked along a path between bare plane trees. It was bitterly cold. The sun shone. He passed the buildings of London Zoo on his left, and turned into the open spaces of the park itself. He came to a halt. He stared unseeingly at these acres of trees and grass. From behind him, where the zoo's animal enclosures were, came one long eddying cry. It was high in pitch. It could have been the cry of a bird or an animal. It was a prison-house cry, suggestive of hunger or desolation. It was not repeated. Pascal walked on.

He came to a halt, finally, some distance behind the ambassador's residence. He could just see its roof through the trees, and beyond it the glittering dome, the minaret of the mosque. The sky was a clear sharp blue-white. To look at it hurt his eyes. *My love*, Pascal thought; the pain was acute. He could locate it exactly: heartache was not a generalized, nor a metaphoric term – that was where the actual pain actually was: in his heart.

He turned, and walked back very fast to his car. He drove back to the rented house over-fast, and parked badly. If these actions drew attention to himself, he no longer cared. He could now not understand at all what had possessed him to leave the house. Suppose Gini had called? He ran inside. It was now one forty-five. The little red light on the answering machine was not blinking: so – Gini had not called. He felt then a sense of absolute despair. He went upstairs, and stared at his cameras. They failed to distract him or to console.

'Christ,' he said out loud, and punched the wall. He ran downstairs to the telephone again, picked it up, and dialled the number of Gini's flat in Islington. He did this, at precisely the second that Gini, in Oxford, dialled his line. As she was listening to the engaged tone, Pascal was talking to the answering machine in her flat.

'Darling,' he said, 'call me. Please call me. Call me the second you return.'

He slammed the receiver down, and tried to think. Maybe, when she returned to London, she would go to that safe cottage in Hampstead first, to collect her things. He could see her now, doing just that, letting herself in with the key he'd thrown at her. He gave a groan. He picked up the receiver, and dialled the number there. He left the same message. Then he hung up. Then he decided it was a bad message, and said all the wrong things. So he dialled both numbers again, and added a longer corollary. 'Gini, I love you. I love you with all my heart, darling. Call me the second you get home.'

He replaced the receiver. He was about to dial both numbers a third time, because he suddenly realized that he had forgotten to say he was sorry, forgotten to explain his remorse. He reached out his hand to the receiver, and at that second, it rang.

Pascal snatched it up. He said 'Gini', at exactly the same second that she said, 'Pascal'.

As he did so, a black car with tinted glass turned into the cul-de-sac behind him. From where he stood, Pascal could just see it. It turned in, drove to the end, paused outside the Gothic villa, then circled, drove out and disappeared.

'You mean it?' Gini was saying. 'I love you, Pascal. I

can't see. I can't hear. I can't think for happiness. Also, I'm crying. I don't know why. I started crying when the line was engaged. I'm sorry, Pascal. I'm so sorry. You're right. I am all those things you said I was . . . '

Pascal smiled. 'So am I, darling. I have to have you here with me. Come home.'

'The next direct train, the fast one, is at four-thirty. It gets to Paddington around five-forty. I'll get a taxi from there. I'll be with you by six, I swear.'

'Can't you get an earlier train?'

'There's no point, Pascal. The four-thirty is an express. Besides, I've talked to the police and there *is* something odd about this. I'm just going to look at the place where he died, *if* he died—'

'If?' Pascal said sharply.

'I won't explain now. But the police have been lied to. Pascal, I'll just do that then I'll go straight to the station. I promise you I'll catch that train.'

Pascal was about to burst out with another flood of arguments, another set of pleas. He stared at the wall, and forced himself to remain silent. He said, and it cost him great effort to say that little, 'You promise me, darling, you will take care?'

They talked on while Gini kept feeding coins into the slot. She told him about her conversation with the police sergeant, and she read him the list of items found on McMullen's body. Pascal copied it down. Gini searched in her purse: she had now run out of change.

'Darling,' she said, 'I'll have to go. I'm running out of money. It'll get dark very soon. I'll see you at six. That's only three hours and a bit . . . '

'It's three hours and a bit too long, Gini.' They talked a short while longer, then the call-time expired.

In Oxford, Gini walked out into an ordinary street which felt made-in-heaven. There was a made-in-heaven sky, and made-in-heaven rain. She lifted her face rapturously to the rain, and let it wash her face.

In London, Pascal, dazed, stared out at an empty cul-de-sac, and a dazzling blue-white sky. He made himself some coffee, smoked several cigarettes, listened to silence and to joy.

Later, when he was calmer, he looked down the list Gini had read to him: a wallet, credit cards, keys, money, cigarettes, a lighter, a wristwatch, a handkerchief, a signet ring. He stared at this ordinary list, very little different from the contents of his own pockets, and he saw almost immediately that if these were the objects found on McMullen's body, then something was badly wrong.

The place where McMullen had died was a bleak one. By the time Gini reached it, after losing her way twice, it was just past three, and the light was beginning to fail. She stood for a short while, shivering, on the bridge over the railway-line. The area was deserted. She was surrounded by newly ploughed fields. To her right was the track which led up to the back of McMullen's cottage. It was rutted, visible for perhaps a half-mile, then it disappeared into a dark copse of pine, and an older stand of beech trees at the crest of the steep hill.

The railway-lines below her, just as the police had said, ran as straight as a die. Rooks cawed. Two black crows were scavenging below on the line. The nearest house, an abandoned farm, was two miles further back down the road. *A fine and private place*, she thought grimly, *for a man to kill himself, or be killed.*

She scrambled down the bank from the bridge to the rails. They had been fenced off once, but the wooden palings were rotten and broken down. Rusty barbed wire looped among dead brambles and nettle stalks. In front of her the tattered remnants of the plastic strips used to cordon off the area fluttered in the wind. At the edge of the lines there was a welter of rubbish – rusty cans, plastic bags, a bicycle wheel. Directly ahead of her, the stone chippings between the rails were stained a brownish colour. She stared at this, then averted her eyes.

Suddenly, the rails thrummed with life; there was a loud palpitation in the air, a burst of deafening sound. Then, glaringly fast, came the lights. The train was on her in seconds. From three yards back, she felt its rush and its suck. The suddenness frightened her. She reeled back with a cry, slipped and fell. The train was past and gone, before she lifted her head. The air rocked. From the distance came the banshee wail of the train's hooter. The rooks rose up screeching from the trees.

Shaken, she hauled herself to her feet. Slipping and scrambling on the muddy bank, she climbed back up to the bridge. She turned and looked at the track which led up to McMullen's cottage. She thought she could get the car up it, if she was careful. She was no more than twenty minutes from Oxford, and the station: she just had time. She looked at the dark woods at the summit of the hill and hesitated. The light was now thickening. She had no great wish to venture up there in gathering darkness, but she had not come this far to lose her nerve. She thought briefly of Hawthorne, the previous evening. *Don't believe all the lies*, he had said.

She shook herself, ran back to her car, and eased it forward carefully onto the track. The going was easier, and quicker, than she had expected. She made it almost all the way to the summit. At this point, about sixty yards below the cottage itself, there was a clearing in the woods. The residue of the track was impassable. She cut her lights, switched off the engine, and climbed out of the car.

The silence was startling. The only sound was the whispering and creak of branches. Stepping quietly and cautiously, she edged her way up the overgrown track through the gloom.

She came out from the shelter of the trees into a small yard to the rear of the cottage. She stopped, and listened. There were no lights, no sounds. She began to inch her way across the flagstones of the yard, to the wall of the lean-to kitchen at the rear. There was a door here; she turned its handle, but it was locked. The boarded windows were impenetrable. Feeling her way along the walls, peering ahead of her into the shadows, she edged around to the front of the house.

She listened. Absolute silence. The wind had died down. She moved quietly to the front door, and gave a gasp of fear and surprise. The door was unlocked. As she touched it, it swung open silently on well-oiled hinges. The room beyond was black. She could see nothing at all.

She had come here without a flashlight, she realized, and silently cursed. She stood on the brink of the room. From some distance beyond, across the track, a bough creaked, and there was a tiny scuffling noise. She froze, but there was no further sound. *An animal*, she told herself, *some small animal, that's all*. She stepped into the room, shut the door behind her, pressed herself back against the wall, and reached for the light switch.

The light immediately steadied her. There was no-one here. The room was exactly as before. She looked around it quickly: the sticks of furniture, the two paperback books, the pile of newspapers, the whisky bottle and glasses, the paraffin heater.

There was something wrong though, something inching its way forward from the back of her mind. The rucksack was gone, for one thing, but it was more than that. She looked around, and then she realized. The room was not cold. When they had come before, it had been icy here. With a low exclamation, she moved quickly across the room. She touched the paraffin heater, and recoiled sharply. The metal was still warm.

She stood there rigid, her heart beating very fast. Someone had been here, and been here very recently too. She ran across silently to the kitchen. The container of gun-oil Pascal had described was gone. She darted back into the main room, crossed to that newspaper stack, and picked up the top-most paper on the pile.

It was a local paper, the *Oxford Mail*, Friday's edition. *Yesterday's* edition. She stared at the date. Dead men did not buy newspapers. How did McMullen acquire that paper, bring it here, when at six on Friday morning, he had been lying dead on the railway-lines three miles away?

Her eyes moved slowly around the room. A bottle of

Scotch, two paperbacks, three unwashed glasses, a still-warm paraffin stove; a lie to the police as to McMullen's whereabouts the night before his death.

Was he dead – or was he very much alive?

Her mouth felt dry with fear. Her skin felt shivery.

The house was silent. She made herself do it. She crossed to the stairway door, and eased up its latch. She stood for a moment, shivering, peering into the dark at the top of the stairs.

The stairs creaked as she mounted them. There was no banister, no light switch. They led straight into a single upstairs room. Above her head, high in the roof eaves, there was an unboarded skylight. She crept into the room, and pressed her back against the wall. She waited for her eyes to grow accustomed to the gloom.

Gradually, she began to discern shapes from the patches of faint light and shadow. There was no furniture. Across the room, under the skylight, there was a make-shift bed – a strip of carpeting, and the hummocky outline of a sleeping-bag. For one horrible instant, she thought the bag had an occupant; her skin crawled. Then she realized it was empty. She was looking at crumples and folds of puffy material, no pillow, no sign of any clothes, but next to the bag there were some objects on the floor.

She crept across the room to the bag, knelt down and tried to identify them by feel. An empty tin candlestick, a box of matches . . . and a package of some kind. She felt the outline of this package. It was flat and stiff, a reinforced envelope about twelve inches by eight. It had been opened; she could feel the neat slit, made with a knife.

She held it out to the thin light coming from above, and could just see that there was something written on the envelope, but she could not make out the words. She was starting to shiver again. She listened to the silence fearfully. She could feel something inside the envelope, something stiff and smooth.

She felt around on the floorboards, felt under the

sleeping-bag, but she could find nothing concealed. Clutching the envelope, she made for the stairs.

In the light of the downstairs room, she breathed more easily. She must hurry, hurry . . . She stared down at the envelope's computer-printed address: *James McMullen, C/O Dr Anthony Knowles, Christ Church, Oxford.* No stamp, so it must have been delivered by hand.

Inside there were photographic prints, masked by a sheet of thick white paper. When she saw what had been typed on the paper, she gave a low cry of astonishment. The signatory was John Hawthorne's father; the message was brief, and to the point:

Mr McMullen [it read]
You have been making some very unwise
allegations concerning blondes. I feel you should
know the truth. These photographs were taken
in the final three months of last year, in each
case on the third Sunday of those months.
Goodbye, Mr McMullen: I shall not expect
you to trouble this family again.

Gini stared at this message in confusion. She thought: *I was wrong, and Hawthorne lied.* She hesitated, unwilling to look at these pictures, then she lifted the covering letter aside. She had a sick premonition of what she might see, but she had not expected this, and she was unused to hard-core pornography. When she saw the three images, October, November, December, she gasped, and let them fall from her hand.

She bent down, and looked at each month's picture in turn. All three were in black and white. In all three the woman wore a black, tight-waisted basque, which left her breasts bare. She wore long black gloves, black stockings, and black patent leather stiletto-heeled shoes. In all three pictures, the woman was kneeling, in front of a man. Each of the men was different, though all three were young, in their late teens or early twenties, and all had blond hair. Gini recognized none of the three. Each had his hands cuffed behind his back; each of the men wore workman's clothes: overalls or dirty jeans; each had the heavy muscular build of the manual labourer. One of them had scratch marks on his face. The November man had removed his shirt to reveal heavy arms covered in tattoos. In each of the three photographs, the man's flies were opened, and his penis was exposed.

In the first picture the woman held the man's penis in her hand; in the second, she was sucking the man's penis, her eyes closed; the third picture, and the worst, was what Gini knew was called a come-shot in the trade. It had been taken the instant after the man's orgasm. The woman's uplifted face, black hair, and bared breasts were gluey with semen. Her expression was ecstatic: she appeared to be looking at someone else, perhaps the person who had taken these pictures; she was giving a glance of triumph and delight to someone not inside this frame.

Sickness welled in Gini's stomach. She picked up the photographs and the letter, and pushed them back in their envelope. She stood there, trembling with revulsion, and closed her eyes. The technical quality of the pictures was only too good, and there was no possible mistake. On the darkness of her retina, she saw gender switch, and a scenario reverse. It was a *man* who was handcuffed, a *man* who was blond. It was not John Hawthorne who liked sex with strangers once a month, it was his *wife*. The photographs were of Lise.

She felt an overpowering need, now, to be out of this house, to run back to her car, to catch that train and to rejoin Pascal. She crossed the room, and switched out the light. She had to hurry, but she still had time.

She opened the door, and peered out into the darkness outside. The wind was stronger now, the moon rising like a splinter of silver. The stars were splashed across the heavens. Low small tight clouds moved fast across the sky.

The light outside was deceptive, intermittent, giving the inanimate a deceptive wavering life. She stood on the threshold, suddenly afraid, watching shadows suggest shapes. She thought: *McMullen received those pictures; McMullen isn't dead, he's alive.* She took one step forward, and then she heard it: it might have been something, it might have been nothing. A brushing, whispering sound, the tiniest of noises, but she knew what it was. Someone else was out there, in the darkness to the side of the cottage, and something they were wearing, or carrying, had brushed against its wall.

She put her hand to her mouth to stifle any cry. She went rigid with fear. Could she hear breathing? She thought she could hear breathing. Very slowly, she inched back inside the cottage, and edged back behind the door.

She stood there, listening, listening. A rustle of dead leaves, the creak of a branch, silence.

Perhaps she had imagined that noise, she thought, and took a careful step forward. She reached out, in the darkness, towards the faint light at the edge of the half-open door. Then, without warning, out of total silence there was movement. Air rushed past her face. The pale slice of moonlight, the last light visible, vanished. Someone had slammed the door.

He was locking it, even now. She gave a low moan of fear, as she heard first one, then two locks engage. She could hear footsteps now, moving around to the back of the cottage. She felt her way towards the back kitchen, bumping painfully into the table as she passed. The backdoor was locked, but there was no key on the inside. She could hear someone clearly now, beyond those boarded windows, moving around the yard. The door to some outbuilding was dragged open then closed. The footsteps approached the backdoor. There was another noise, as if something heavy were being dragged, then lifted.

She clamped her hand across her mouth, and pressed herself against the door, listening. She could hear breathing, just through the panels.

Whoever was out there was waiting – waiting for what? – on the other side of the door.

XXXIV

Six o'clock came and went. In that pink upstairs bedroom, Pascal sat and waited. At six-fifteen, he went downstairs, and listened intently for the approach of a taxi in the street. For half an hour, three-quarters of an hour, an hour, his mind was inventive: it came up with explanation after explanation for Gini's delay. She had arrived at Paddington on time, but there were no taxis available. No, her train was delayed. He imagined some trivial delay, ten or fifteen minutes perhaps. Then he imagined a more serious hold-up. At seven-thirty, when these inventions began to fail him, he called Paddington direct. The four-thirty train from Oxford had arrived on time, he was told. Pascal felt the first symptoms of alarm. He tried to remain calm; he took down the arrival and departure times of the other Oxford–London trains that evening, and began to make calculations. If Gini had missed the first train, but taken the next, he could expect her around eight. For a while, this possibility buoyed him, then eight came and went.

He returned upstairs to the dark back bedroom, bent to his viewfinder, and scanned the cul-de-sac beyond. Still silent and deserted. Not one of the houses in the turning showed any lights. He scanned the entrance to the Gothic villa, then its rear windows. Nothing: their curtains remained undrawn; the pale rooms beyond dream-like, empty and still. It was as if they were waiting for something, as he was waiting.

If Gini had been this much delayed, she would have called, surely? It was now almost nine, which meant she had missed two trains. If she had aimed to be at Oxford station at four there were, he now realized, five missing hours to be explained. Only two further trains left Oxford for London that evening. One was due in around ten, the other shortly after midnight. He sat in the darkness, feeling time inch its way forward.

His hearing was acute, and the darkness intensified it. The cul-de-sac beyond might remain dark and silent, but he heard the tiniest sounds from his own street. A dog whining in a house two doors away; the sound of footsteps, of car doors opening and closing, the swish of tyres down the road. A normal Saturday night: people going out and returning. But no telephone call, and no taxi-cabs. He found it impossible to be still. He began to pace, then went downstairs again.

He was unwilling to use the telephone, in case Gini should be trying to contact him, but by nine-thirty, he could stand it no longer. He saw Gini in a frail hire-car, taking a corner too fast on a wet country road; he saw her wheels lock, start to skid. He called the police accident and emergency line, and a slow-voiced, calm and sensible woman ran some checks: no, she informed him, after a long and agonizing delay, there had been no road accidents in the vicinity of Oxford that night. Pascal tried the Oxford hospital casualty departments: no-one of Gini's name or description had been admitted that night. Then he had an inspiration: Gini had said she'd picked up a car from the station. Pascal called the station, found out the name of the firm, dialled that. A woman took his call, and she sounded impatient. She'd been waiting for one last customer on the London–Oxford train, she said, otherwise she'd have packed up and left an hour ago – it *was* Saturday night.

Pascal could tell she was about to hang up. He launched himself on a desperate and incoherent charm offensive. Finally she was persuaded to check, and – yes, Ms Hunter had returned her hire-car; it was parked outside right now, and the keys had been returned. No, she couldn't say exactly what time it had been returned and she herself hadn't actually seen Ms Hunter, but she thought probably in the last twenty minutes or so, because one of her colleagues had dealt with it, while she took a coffee-break. No, this colleague had now gone.

Pascal hung up. He looked at his watch. Ten-fifteen. He began to hope, began to feel relief. That meant, that surely meant, that Gini must have reached the station safely. Had she been trying to call him while he talked to hospitals and to the police? She was probably on that last train right now, for it would have left Oxford just three minutes ago, and would now be making its way slowly back to London. She would be due at midnight, she must be due at midnight, she must be safe.

For a while, this hope cheered him. He went out into the kitchen, and made himself some coffee. He sat at the table with his head in his hands. He had eaten nothing all day, and he had no appetite whatsoever. He sat there dosing himself with caffeine, but that and the cigarettes only made him more tense. He suddenly remembered the list of belongings found on McMullen's dead body. *If* McMullen had died, Gini had said.

He took the list out again now, and looked at it. If Gini had not said that, if she had not explained the discrepancies in the account of McMullen's movements given to the police, he would not have seen so quickly what was wrong with this list. But because she *had* told him all that, the two oddities leaped out at him. Looking at them now, the anxiety he felt increased.

The list was meticulous. It detailed precisely the amount of change found in the deceased's pockets. It described the crest on the signet ring worn, the make of wristwatch, the make of lighter – a Dunhill – the types of credit cards, and the exact brand of cigarettes. Silk Cut, a common enough English brand. But it was not the brand McMullen had been smoking, nor the type of cigarette. McMullen had smoked *unfiltered* cigarettes, a habit now so unusual that Pascal had noted it at once. And he had not used a lighter, either: he had used matches instead.

So, had McMullen staged his own death? Or had an attempt been made to kill him, and some stand-in, some helper, been mistakenly killed instead? Pascal tried to think. He tried to remember the details Gini had given him of her conversation at Mary's with Hawthorne the previous night.

Hawthorne had appeared to know nothing of the meeting with McMullen in Oxford, although he had known of the meetings in Regent's Park, and the British Museum. Yesterday, Pascal had been convinced that this was simply guile on Hawthorne's part, a technique for extracting information from Gini. It had seemed to Pascal so obvious: he and Gini had been followed to Oxford, just as they had been followed, and listened to, for almost two weeks. They had led McMullen's enemies to him, just as Pascal had feared – and sure enough, within hours of their leaving him, James McMullen was dead.

Hawthorne had himself been in Oxfordshire that same night. Pascal and Gini had watched him arrive, and Pascal had assumed his visit had one very obvious purpose. Hawthorne had been there to ensure that this time McMullen was silenced finally. The scenario had been clear to him, but now he began to doubt. What if McMullen were *not* dead? Could Gini conceivably have been right in her instincts? Was it possible that John Hawthorne was innocent, or partially innocent – that he was not guilty here?

At that Pascal felt a new idea and a different doubt come sidling forward from the back of his brain. It was an idea which sickened him, which made him go cold with fear. But once there, it would not go away, so he forced himself to look at it. After all, he had no way of knowing now whether Hawthorne was in London, or not. Suppose he were in Oxfordshire? Suppose Gini knew that? It would explain her insistence on going to Oxford today – and if she had met Hawthorne there, then that meeting would explain the length of this delay.

Pascal rose abruptly, and began to pace the room. No, he told himself, that was impossible: Gini would not lie to him directly. If she had known for certain that Hawthorne would be in Oxfordshire, she would have told him. On the other hand, he could imagine Gini, on impulse, contacting Hawthorne, and on discovering where he was, arranging to meet him. And then . . . Pascal gave a groan. He covered his face with his hands. He tried to control his own jealous imagination, but he could not damp it down.

It sent up little images, little tongues and darts of flame. He still did not know exactly what had happened with Hawthorne the previous evening, and he began to fear now that he never would know, or understand. He could see in his own mind Hawthorne touching her, and the ways in which he did so, or might have done so, were agony to him. He began to see that Gini might have responded to Hawthorne, and been unwilling and ashamed to admit that, to herself or to Pascal. If she had responded to him then, and then saw him this evening, might she not respond again?

He could see Gini very clearly now in another man's arms, an image lit like lightning by pain. He saw Hawthorne touch her breasts and part her thighs. He turned, with a despairing gesture, and tried to force the image out of his mind.

He knew Gini so intimately. Every part of his body knew every part of hers; it was not just his eyes and ears which recorded the ways in which she made love, but his hands, his genitals, his mouth and his heart. *Stop*, he said to himself, but his mind would not stop, there were the lightning images, one by one, the expression in her eyes before he entered her, the transfixing of her face as he did so, the lift and movement of her body against his, the slackening and opening of her mouth when he slowed their rhythms, that blind quick fierceness which he both witnessed, and shared, when he knew he had to move only once, perhaps twice, and she would come. These gestures, movements, touches, and tastes he saw as his alone, reserved for him only. He could not even glimpse those details in his mind without experiencing the sharpest, most immediate desire. For a second, turning his face to the wall, he felt and saw the damp strands of her hair, the salt taste of her breasts, and the exactitude – this was always very arousing to him – with which her grey eyes registered shock and want when he entered her, and she could feel him inside.

She had a way of moving then, a way of kissing, there were certain things which she would then say, and Pascal had always believed these his: it made no difference how many other lovers she had had, who they were, or what she had done with them. They were as shadowy, as distant, he had believed, as were any of the women he had had in his past. It had never occurred to him, not for one instant, that those past men had possessed her as he did, and as she possessed him. But now, suddenly, with an agonizing sharpness, he saw that belief as an illusion, or a failure of imagination on his part.

Now, one by one, in those lightning flashes, he saw Gini with Hawthorne yesterday, Gini with Hawthorne today, and she said the same things, gave the same things, to another man, to that man, in exactly the same way.

If this was jealousy, it was a kind he had never experienced before. It shot through his body; he felt it as a physical wounding, a knife in the heart and the groin. He was ashamed of, and appalled by these imaginings; he saw them as alien to him, as invading him, but he could not force them away. He stopped pacing, and stood in the ugly kitchen, very still. He looked unseeingly at clinical white surfaces, at shining chrome. He forced himself to note the meaningless detail in front of him, the shape of shelves and implements: this cup, this white plate, that knife, those spoons.

Gradually, he grew calmer, and he felt the jealous images recede. It seemed to him a betrayal, even to have thought in this way. He thought: *My mind is lying to me.* He thought: *Let her be on that last train.* Then, suddenly alert, he swung around, listening. He moved quickly out into the hall, and – yes – he had been right. It was eleven-twenty now, and he could hear the distinctive chug of a London taxi. It had just drawn up, its engine idling, outside.

Relief surged through him. He moved quickly to the front door, Gini's name on his lips. He was about to throw it open, when he heard the voices of strangers – a man and a woman, discussing some party they'd just left. He heard their footsteps go past this house. The dog's whining two doors away turned to a rapturous bark. A door opened and closed; silence returned. *Soon*, Pascal said to himself; *let it be soon*. He would check his cameras again, check the cul-de-sac was still empty – any action which kept his imaginings at bay.

The rooms upstairs were in darkness. Downstairs he had left one light on next to the telephone in the hall, and one in the kitchen. As he moved across to the stairs, both lights failed.

Pascal froze. He stood absolutely still in the dark, thinking fast. He moved silently to the door, and drew the bolts across. He felt his way from light switch to light switch. None operated. He edged into the kitchen, and opened the fridge door: no light. He moved quietly back into the hall, and lifted the telephone receiver: the line was dead. No telephone, no light, no power.

He moved quietly into the sitting-room, and eased the tightly drawn curtains aside a crack. Two of the houses opposite had lights in their upstairs windows; the streetlights were still functioning. Not a general power-cut then, but, as he had thought, another game, similar to the games played with Gini in her flat earlier that week. He thought: *It's beginning; someone knows I am here*.

At once he became alert, concentrated. He moved silently to the stairs, crossed the landing above, and went into the back bedroom.

The arrival had been well-timed. Sunday was now just twenty minutes away, and the Gothic villa opposite had its first visitor. Pascal could see well in the dark; he could see the man even without the aid of his viewfinder. The man was dressed in dark clothes; he had entered the driveway of the Gothic villa. As Pascal bent to his camera, he began to mount the porch steps.

Pascal bent over his viewfinder, made an adjustment, and scanned the man's face. *One of Hawthorne's security shadows*, he thought. It was not that man Malone, but it could have been Frank Romero – he certainly fitted Gini's description. He was tall, dark-haired, and thick-set. Pascal focused on his clothes. He was wearing a thick black overcoat, which was undone. Beneath it, Pascal could just glimpse the gleam of brass buttons. Then the man stamped his feet, and blew on his hands, and drew his overcoat tighter around him. His breath made white puffs in the cold air. He turned up his coat collar, frowned and gave a sigh. He stood there, making no attempt to enter the house, just waiting at the top of the steps.

Pascal fired off some shots. The man had a crude-featured, wide-planed, somewhat brutal face. Pascal could see a shaving cut on his left cheek; he could see the stitching on the man's lapels. The man glowered up at the sky, glanced towards the gardens behind him, then turned back to look down the cul-de-sac. Minutes passed. The man checked his watch.

Pascal flexed his damaged right arm, his fingers. He bent again to the viewfinder. He waited; the man waited – but the wait was not long.

The black car arrived three minutes after midnight, three minutes into Sunday. It was an anonymous car, but fast, a black Ford Scorpio. One driver, one passenger. Pascal tensed. His camera motor whirred. He fired off ten shots. The man in the black overcoat descended the steps, and approached the car, which had pulled in at their foot. He held open the driver's door, and John Hawthorne climbed out.

He paused, rested one arm on the roof of the car, and turned to look across the gardens behind. Pascal had him in close-up, full-face. He could see strain, and an odd almost bored impatience in his face. He too was wearing a black overcoat. Beneath it, Pascal could see the gleam of a white shirtfront: Hawthorne was wearing evening dress.

He frowned, moved around the front of the car, and paused. His security man slid into the driver's seat. As he did so, Hawthorne stooped and opened the car's front passenger door. For a moment, Pascal's view was blocked by the car door, and Hawthorne's shoulder, then he saw movement, brightness, a swing of long pale blond hair. He tensed; the camera motor whirred, and the woman stepped out.

As Hawthorne and the woman moved towards the steps, her face was averted. The car, security man at the wheel, backed out of the driveway, circled the end of the cul-de-sac, then accelerated out into the main road beyond. Its lights moved south against the night sky. Hawthorne and the blond-haired woman were now mounting the porch steps. Neither gave any impression of haste; there was nothing furtive in their manner. Hawthorne's arm was around the woman's waist. She too wore a black coat. Against its collar, her hair was startlingly bright. They paused on the porch steps: close, close, close. Pascal watched Hawthorne feel in his pocket for a key and draw it out. His lips moved. He turned and said something to the woman. Pascal focused on that long bright hair. 'Turn around,' he muttered to himself. 'Turn around – just once.'

The wind gusted. It lifted the pale strands of hair which lay across her shoulders and shielded her face from view. She moved her head slightly. Pascal caught a pale profile, pale lips. He tensed. He fired off a few more frames, then faltered, then stopped.

He froze. It was as if the woman had heard his thoughts. As Hawthorne inserted his key, and the door swung open, the woman looked over her shoulder – full-face at last. Her level brows contracted in a slight, almost puzzled, frown. She looked across the empty gardens, towards the house and the window where Pascal waited; she looked directly at the heart of his camera lens. Her expression was dazed, a little bewildered. She had, Pascal saw, a lovely face. But he took no pictures of it. His hands refused to function; his fingers refused to function. He stared through the viewfinder, and his heart went cold. His vision blurred. He swore, adjusted focus, stared again.

The woman was Gini. Moonlight bloomed on her skin. Darkness made her hair more silver. She was as pale and as still as an apparition. She moved a fraction, and shadows moved across the pallor of her face like water; air rippled her hair. For a second, half a second, less, her eyes held his in a long, blind, vacant look, then she turned, and her hair swung forward, screening her face. She moved into the doorway in a slow, trance-like way. Hawthorne, from the shadows of the doorway, held out one black-gloved hand to her. She clasped it, and moved into the shadows. The light of her hair was just visible, then invisible, then the door closed and she was gone.

They used the ground-floor room at the back – the room with the largest windows. It had curtains and shutters which folded back into the window recess, but they neither drew the curtains nor closed the shutters. Suddenly, from outside Pascal's field of vision, all the lights in that room came on, then Hawthorne entered. He stared towards the windows, then turned and removed his overcoat. He undid his black silk tie and loosened the top button of his evening shirt. He moved across to the windows, clasped his hands behind his back, and stood there frowning, looking out into the darkness of the garden beyond.

Gini must have followed him into the room, for the next second, she too came into frame. She walked slowly forward, head bent, like a somnambulist, or an actress on a film-set searching for her mark. Hawthorne turned, and said something over his shoulder. Gini's head jerked around to look at him; her long hair swung across her face. She gave a little shiver, turned so her back was to Pascal, and removed her coat. Pascal drew in his breath sharply. Beneath the coat she was wearing a dress Pascal recognized. It was the dress she had worn the night of Mary's party, that sliver of elegant black silk crêpe, with two knife-thin straps. Pascal saw Hawthorne speak; it seemed to be some brief question. He handed her something, which Gini took. Hawthorne spoke again, made a gesture. Gini hesitated; she turned a little aside, so she was almost out of frame. Pascal could just see the fall of her hair, her right shoulder, her right arm. Then he realized what Hawthorne had given her, and what she was doing. She was drawing on a pair of gloves, a pair of long black gloves. They fitted her exactly: Pascal saw her flex her fingers, lift her arm, and hold out her hand to Hawthorne. The black glove covered her arm from just above the elbow to fingertips.

Pascal stood there, frozen with indecision, unable to move, unable to think. A few moments before, in the brief interval after they entered the house, and before the lights in that room came on, he had started away from the cameras, out onto the landing. He had got as far as the top of the stairs when, over his shoulder, he saw the sudden blaze of light, and moved back. He hesitated now, irresolute, torn: this was possible and impossible. Hawthorne was distant one moment, then – when Pascal bent to the viewfinder again – startlingly close. Gini was close too, still just on the edge of the frame; she seemed close enough to touch.

Pascal reached out his hand and touched air. His hand was shaking. He trusted his eyes; he trusted his *vision* – his vision was his work. He saw now. So, was this Gini, or some crazy hallucination? Pascal thought: *I am watching my own imaginings; I am watching my own secret fears.*

Pascal stared, as if details could tell him whether or not to believe his own eyes. Gini would never wear those shoes, he thought – but the shoes, black, stiletto-heeled, were identical to the ones she had been sent. Pascal half-turned, turned back, looked again.

She had turned towards Hawthorne now, and they were standing close to one another, quietly. Hawthorne was looking down into her eyes. Pascal saw him speak. Lifting one hand Hawthorne drew her gently towards him. Her back was now to Pascal, and her face lifted to Hawthorne's. Hawthorne was still speaking. Pascal felt pain and incomprehension blinding his mind. To see and yet not to see, to be able to watch speech but to be unable to hear – this was a new agony. *This is not happening*, he said to himself. In the room opposite, Hawthorne had just taken Gini's hand. He lifted it slowly to his lips, and kissed it, kissed the palm of the glove, and Pascal thought: *That is what he did yesterday*. That was how he began then; that was what Gini described.

He stepped back from his cameras. The room and its two occupants were now blurred. Pascal passed his hand across his face. He felt trapped in his own suspicions, forced to watch his own worst dreams.

He stood there a moment, trapped by fear, by disbelief and guilt. Only a few seconds had passed, but each one felt an hour long. While one part of his mind was mesmerized by this replay of his own thoughts, another part was calculating, calculating. Thirty seconds to get downstairs and out of this house. Thirty seconds to cross the gardens and vault the fence. Thirty seconds to those steps, that balcony and those french doors. They looked frail; one kick would burst them open. One and a half minutes. Pascal felt paralysed. He started for the door, turned back, and bent to the viewfinder.

The man and the woman opposite were now locked in an embrace. Hawthorne's hands clasped her tightly on either side of her ribcage, then moved to stroke the curve of her spine. Both seemed very aroused. Hawthorne's hands gripped her by her narrow hips; he drew her tightly against him. The woman shuddered, then bent her head forward, and rested it against his shoulder. Her pale hair caught against the dark material of his jacket. *Look up, just once, turn around*, Pascal thought.

The woman was visibly trembling. Hawthorne slid his hands up over her body, and began to unfasten those knife-thin straps, first the left then the right. The dress slithered from her shoulders. Beneath the dress she was wearing a black basque, which lifted and bared her breasts. Hawthorne caught her against him; he closed his eyes. He began to kiss her mouth, then her throat in a frantic way. His hands cupped the weight of her breasts, and he began to caress them. The woman's hair swirled. Suddenly the tempo of their love-making had altered.

633

From being slow and dream-like, it had become hungry and fast. The woman caught Hawthorne's face between her hands, and pulled his head lower, so that his mouth was against her breasts. She half-turned, her movements jerky and hectic now, and the swirl of movement was very swift, so that for one long black quarter-second Pascal thought: *He is going to push her down onto the floor, her hair is going to spread out under him across the floor.* And then he realized Hawthorne was not responding, not kissing her breasts, and the woman turned a fraction more, and Pascal thought: *No.*

He could still not see the woman's face, which was averted, protected by her hair, but he could see her breasts, and the angle from shoulder to collar-bone, and relief surged through him. He knew Gini by touch as intimately as he knew her by sight. He knew the exact span of her throat, the exact curve of her spine and shoulder-blades. He knew the exact jut, curve and weight of her breasts. This woman was not Gini. She was not even a woman Gini's age: she was older, by perhaps a decade, a woman in her middle to late thirties, attractive, but with small childish breasts. Her nipples were small and crudely rouged, and her movements were all wrong for Gini, Pascal could see that now. Gini moved with ease and grace: this woman's movements were too jerky, too avid, too bold, too crude.

Hawthorne had moved now, a little to his left, and the woman turned to face him. She picked up something from a table on the edge of frame, and then began to massage oil into her breasts. Her skin gleamed. Her black-gloved hands moved assiduously; her nipples stiffened. She paused, looking at Hawthorne as if for approval then smiled, and hung her head.

Everything was wrong, Pascal thought. He couldn't understand, now, how his eyes and his mind could have been deceived like that. The hair, and the way it was arranged, that might be a careful copy of the way Gini wore her hair, and the dress, of course, was the same, but now that he could see this blonde, full-face and in full light, the resemblance to Gini was small – this was not his Gini, but Gini as imagined by someone else, Hawthorne presumably. At that, Pascal's mind went blank with anger; his limbs and his hands began to function again. He would fix this bastard once and for all, he thought. The camera motor whirred, and the shutter began to click.

Ten frames, fifteen, twenty exposures. Pascal's habitual cold objectivity locked into place. What was actually happening opposite became now almost an irrelevance: to him it was work, a task, a sequence of light, shade and angle. It was without nuance or emotional content, not sex witnessed, but abstract shapes. Shapes to be captured on film, given these lighting conditions, this distance, this equipment. His concentration was absolute. The only reality was the moving patterns in his viewfinder and the infinitesimal alterations in focus or shutter speed. What he saw through his viewfinder was depersonalized: it was not Hawthorne and an unknown blonde, but a series of attitudes. All that counted was to capture with technical precision the attitudes and angles which, when processed, when printed, would provide him with proof.

He stopped to change film. His injured arm ached. He extracted the used film, inserted the new one, and wound it on. He bent to the viewfinder again.

The black basque the woman wore cinched her waist viciously; it was made of some high-shine material which refracted light. Pascal made a tiny adjustment to aperture to compensate for this, and adjusted focus. While he had changed film, the couple had moved away from the window. Hawthorne, Pascal saw, was still fully dressed, and for the purposes of his pictures was now badly placed, sideways on, with his head bent, looking down at the blonde. The blonde was kneeling in front of him, looking up. Pascal fired off a few shots then waited for the moment when Hawthorne might lift his head. The woman was now beginning to fumble at Hawthorne's crotch. She ran her gloved hands up the inside of his thighs, then began to stroke his groin. It was then that Pascal began to have the uneasy sensation that all might not be as it seemed.

The woman's eagerness was evident: she was clearly aroused and Hawthorne, equally clearly, was not.

He was watching her in a cold dispassionate way; nothing in his attitude suggested response. His hands were by his sides. He made no attempt to touch the blonde, or to aid her. He lifted his face very slightly. Pascal took one shot, then another, then stopped. His mind was now beginning to work again, he could think in a more normal mode, and he could read the expression on Hawthorne's features, which was one of dislike and contempt. The woman shuddered, and rubbed her breasts against his thighs. As she reached up, as if to unfasten his trousers, Hawthorne hit her. The action was sudden, swift; the arm lifted, swung and smashed the woman across her face.

The blow was so hard that it knocked her to the ground. She fell back, half-rose, collapsed again, and then dragged herself a few feet away from him. She was now out of frame, hidden from Pascal's view by the edge of the window. At exactly that moment, just as Pascal realized he could not go on with this, Hawthorne looked up. He turned full-face to the window, full-face to the camera, and gave a tight triumphant smile.

Pascal straightened, and stepped back. He saw now what he should have seen at once. This was not – could not be – unintentional. Would any man in Hawthorne's position do this? Why stand in front of uncurtained, unshuttered windows, in full light? Why do any of those things, unless what was taking place opposite was a performance for Pascal's benefit, his very own private viewing, carefully arranged and staged by John Hawthorne himself?

Bewildered, Pascal bent to the viewfinder again. If this was intentional, it made no sense. Why should Hawthorne wish to provide him with evidence, with proof? One second later, as the woman stepped back into frame, Pascal had the answer to that question. Instinctively he had begun to shoot. He stopped.

The woman in front of him now was no longer blond-haired; her hair reached just to her shoulders, and it was black. Perhaps the blow, and the fall, had dislodged the blond hairpiece she had been wearing, perhaps she had simply decided to dispense with it. Either way, something, a departure from normal rules maybe, had made her acutely distressed.

Her face was chalk white, and she was trembling with emotion. She began to pull off the black gloves. She threw them to the ground. She launched herself at Hawthorne with a sudden ferocity, punching and clawing, as if she were trying to scratch his face. Hawthorne caught hold of her, and put her aside with an easy strength. This seemed to please her. She shuddered and swung around so she was once again full-face to Pascal's camera. She began to speak, a taunting expression on her face. Though Pascal could hear nothing, he could lip-read the words easily enough. *Hit me*, she said, once, twice, three times.

Hawthorne gave her a long, cold and considering look. In a deliberate way, he turned his back on her, crossed to the window, and began to close the shutters. Before he did so, he looked up one last time, directly towards the window where Pascal stood. There was no mistaking the small tight smile he gave, or the derision in his eyes.

That smile said: your pictures are unusable. Pascal straightened. He watched the shutters opposite close. He felt an instant's anger, then a flood of self-loathing. *Game, set and match to Hawthorne*, he thought. Of course the pictures were unusable. His pictures proved nothing beyond the fact that both the ambassador and his wife shared a taste for sexual games.

637

XXXV

It was a man outside the door, Gini was certain of that. The footsteps, punctuated by long periods of silence, were too heavy to have been a woman's, but beyond that they told her little. She could not tell always, where he was: sometimes he would sound close, so she expected the door to open at any second, then he would seem to be moving about further off. Then she would think he had left, and then – after another long and terrifying silence – she would hear him move again.

The darkness seemed to magnify sound and distort it. Was that breathing, or the wind moving through a branch? The night was filled with tiny rustling and scuffling sounds; there was an eerie intermittent whistling noise, thin and high above her, which she thought must be the wind seeping through the tiles of the roof.

She had lost all sense of time, and when she finally began to believe that the man had gone, that she might be alone, she had no idea if half an hour had passed, or more, or less. Her heart was beating painfully fast. She edged against the wall and felt for the light switch. Whether the man had gone or still remained, she could bear it no longer, she thought, this absence of light. She counted to ten, then pressed the light switch behind her. Nothing happened. She gave a low moan of fear, and slid down the wall into a crouching position. She remembered the noise of that outhouse door being opened and shut. Perhaps there was some mains switch outside, or even a generator: the power had been shut off.

She crouched there, trying to think. Then she remembered: there were other power sources in this house. There was the paraffin stove, and the gas cooker in the kitchen. If lit, both would provide some light. She had no matches, but there were matches upstairs, on the floor by the sleeping-bag. She started quickly across the kitchen, and felt her way into the living-room. She banged into the table, gave a cry, and felt for the wall. She found the door to the stairs, and the faint light in the room above gave her hope. Her hands were shaking: when she picked up the matchbox, she almost dropped it. *Slowly, slowly*, she said to herself. She opened the box: there were four matches left.

She tried the gas stove first. If it was supplied by mains gas, she felt certain that too would have been cut off. But a cottage this primitive and this remote was unlikely to be on a mains supply. There was a hissing, then at last, as she touched the match to the burner, some light.

It was bluish and wavering, but it steadied her at once. She listened. Still silence. She looked at her watch. She stared at its hands, unable to believe what they told her. It was past five. She'd been here more than an hour: more than an hour since that door had been slammed and locked. The realization made her frantic. She thought: *I must get out of this place*.

She tried the backdoor first, then the front. Both were heavy and reinforced with thick panelling, not normal old cottage doors. Why had she not noticed that? She tried pulling and pushing with all her strength: neither budged by so much as a centimetre. She edged back to the kitchen. The gas was still burning well. She opened a cupboard door next to the stove, and found the gas canister there. She looked at it fearfully, and tried to move it, but it was too heavy. It had no gauge. She had no way of telling how much gas was left.

She could not bear the thought of the gas expiring, of being without light. She began a frantic search for some other source of power – a flashlight, candles. There was none. Then she steadied herself, and forced herself to become calmer. The doors would not open, the rooflight was unreachable, the only means of exit were the windows – and the windows were boarded up.

There was a window in the kitchen, above the sink. She levered herself up onto the draining-board, and examined it. As with all the other downstairs windows – two in the living-room, the one here – the boarding-up had been carefully done. The windows were completely covered with thick chipboard, nailed into their frames on the inside. The nails were at one-inch intervals all around the frame; the chipboard itself was in one thick sheet.

She climbed back down to the floor, and drew her coat tighter around her. It was bitterly cold, and any residual heat that there had been had worn off.

She made her way back through the bluish flickering darkness to the living-room, and eyed the paraffin stove. She had never used one, and she tried to remember how McMullen had lit it the evening they came here. There had been a little door on its side, which he opened, and some mechanism for turning up the wick. She worked out how to do it, finally, and lit it.

She adjusted it, as she had seen McMullen do, so the smoky yellow flame burned a clean blue. The light in this room was now a little stronger. She searched both it and the kitchen carefully, going through every cupboard, and every drawer. She laid out the array of implements on the kitchen table: three dinner knives, three forks, one teaspoon, a can-opener – no tools of any kind.

She climbed up on the draining-board again, and tried the knives first. She was breathing hard now, trying to keep her hands steady. She found she could insert the thin blade of the knife between board and window frame – but that was all. She slid the knife back and forth to try to loosen the board, but the blade was too weak. Growing more desperate, she pushed the blade right in, then tried to lever with the handle. Nothing happened. She wrenched harder. The blade snapped.

She gave a cry, and threw the broken handle down. She tried again, with a fork this time, first inserting the prongs under the chipboard, then, when that proved useless, the thicker handle end. But she could not thrust the fork under the chipboard far enough to get any leverage. She pushed harder, growing frantic, and her hand slipped. The fork juddered, and the prongs impaled her palm. With a cry of pain, she dropped it. Blood welled, and dripped down her fingers into the sink. She slid back down to the floor, and went to run the water in the sink. She turned the tap, but there was no water: nothing came out, just a trickle, then a dry gurgling sound.

For some reason that terrified her. She stared around her, and saw these rooms now as a trap. She had no water and no food. The gas and the paraffin would last only so long. This house was remote, unused, closed up. No-one knew she was here. She could be here for days, weeks.

Panic swept into her mind, swamping any ability to think. Blood dripped from her hand into the white of the sink. The air in the room was now dry and acrid from the gas. She slumped against the sink, fighting down the fear, telling herself to be calm. She found a cloth, and wrapped it around her bleeding hand; she lowered the flame of the gas, and of the paraffin stove, so that their fuel would last longer, and she made herself think.

It wasn't true that no-one knew where she was. Pascal knew. He might not know precisely, because she had not mentioned the cottage to him, but he knew that she had been going to the railway-line below. He was expecting her in London at six. When she did not return, eventually, he would take action. He would work out where she might have gone. It was foolish to think of being trapped here for days or weeks – that was not going to happen. She would be found, and released. But she had no intention of waiting that long: she was going to get out of this place by herself.

She thought of Pascal. She saw his face and heard his voice. He felt suddenly very close, and this sense of his closeness gave her courage. She climbed back up onto the draining-board, and felt the edge of the chipboard carefully. Halfway down on the right-hand side, one of the nails was driven in at a poor angle. It was looser than the others. Slowly and carefully this time, she inserted the blade of the second knife. She began to lever it gently, back and forth, back and forth.

It took hours. For hours, she worked away at that one loose nail, that tiny section of board. She levered it just a fraction, first with the knife blade, then when the gap between board and window frame was a fraction wider, with the fork. As she worked, concentrating on that tiny section of wood, she thought carefully back over the events of that day. One by one they clicked into place. McMullen was *not* dead, she was now certain of that. He had been here. It was he who had bought that newspaper, lit the paraffin stove, and opened that envelope of photographs. It was McMullen, she thought, who had been here when she herself arrived, and McMullen who had locked her in. Now he had left – which suggested the place was of no further use to him. He had left, but where would he have gone?

She stopped her levering for a second, and stared straight ahead. Her skin went cold. He had received the photographs, and they must have been a devastating blow to him. He had left them behind, but he had taken with him both that heavy army rucksack, and the container of gun-oil.

She looked down at her watch. It was past eight o'clock. Only four hours of Saturday remained. Why would McMullen stage his own death – and she was now certain that he had done just that – unless he wanted to buy himself a little time, lull John Hawthorne into a false sense of security? Suppose, as Pascal had suggested, McMullen had decided to kill Hawthorne? When would he have the best opportunity? When everyone believed him dead. Of course, she thought, on the Sunday, on the third Sunday of the month – that date might well appeal to McMullen, and that Sunday was now just four hours away.

She levered frantically at the board again, then steadied herself. She suddenly remembered something Hawthorne had said to her, the previous evening. It was after she had mentioned Venice. *Don't believe all the lies*, Hawthorne had said. *Just give me a few more days*.

She stared at the board in front of her. When he said that, Hawthorne must have already known about that body on the railway-line, and must have assumed McMullen was dead. He must have believed that, with McMullen dead, the rest of the lies and allegations could be quickly cleared up – that was why he had felt able to speak to her as openly as he did. But if McMullen was *not* dead, then Hawthorne could be in danger: he might have not a few days, but only a few hours, left.

As she thought that, she pushed hard on the board, and at last, at last the loose nail was now dislodged; she could get more purchase on the board. She began to work at it, first with the fork, then with the can-opener, the handles of which were stronger, then – when the gap widened – with her fingers. The board creaked, resisted, cut into her hands. Gini cried out, almost fell, tugged harder, and the board split.

Even then it was still a slow, hard task. She had to break the board away from the window bit by bit. Sometimes a large chunk could be ripped away, then only a tiny sliver. But gradually she could see moonlight outside, then an angle of wall through the glass, then the flagstones. Her hands were bleeding now, and stiff with cold and exertion, but she fought with the board, hating herself for being a woman with weak muscles, bitterly aware that a man, Pascal, could have ripped this board away in minutes. She tugged and ripped and pulled and pushed: freedom felt so close. She could see the moonlit yard clearly now, and beyond it the darkness of the woods. Her car was there, just sixty yards down that slope. In another half-hour, she could be in that car and away from this place. She could find a phone, call Pascal, call Hawthorne too, yes, she must do that. Hawthorne had to be warned that McMullen was not dead.

She caught hold of the last large section of board remaining, and hauled on it with all her strength. Suddenly it buckled, and broke off in her hands. She half-fell, almost toppled to the floor, then steadied herself. The window was now clear, surrounded by a jagged edge of broken board. She grasped the catch, levered, pushed – and nothing happened. It was fastened, she saw, in three places, with security bolts.

She climbed down. Her legs and arms were shaking from her exertions. She could smash the glass, but the window – narrow and upright, with two panes of glass separated by one horizontal bar – needed to be broken open completely. The actual panes were too small to squeeze through. She would have to break the glass in both panes, and smash out the bar between them. Then, at last, she could climb out.

The gas was burning alarmingly low now. She turned it up a fraction. It sputtered and hissed. *I must be quick*, she thought, *I must be quick.*

She carried a chair from the living-room, and smashed at the glass with all her strength. One pane broke, the other cracked. She hauled herself up onto the draining-board, and began to hammer at the glass, half-sobbing, breathing hard with the effort. She wrapped the dishcloth around her hand, and began to snap off the jagged shards of glass piece by piece. She hammered the chair against the dividing bar, then rammed at it with her shoulder as hard as she could. It gave a little, but still held. She went on, fighting with the bar, fighting with the shards of glass. Her arms were trembling with the effort, and her hands were cut and bleeding. She mopped at the blood, which was making her hands slippery, and saw that her watch-face was smashed. The watch hands were jammed, unmoving. She held the watch-face close to her face and peered at it in the semi-darkness. Hours had passed – far more time had gone by than she'd realized. According to her watch, it was now half-past eleven – but how long ago had the watch stopped?

She gave a moan of anger and frustration. It could be Sunday now. She must get out of this place. She threw herself with her full weight against the dividing bar, and at last it splintered, then snapped. The sense of freedom was intoxicating. She drew in a deep breath of icy air. *Leave the heater, leave the gas, but bring the photographs*, she thought, and began to struggle through the broken window. She pulled her thick coat around her, but it caught on the jagged glass. She felt glass catch at her hair, and cut her face. Then, awkwardly, painfully, she was free. She dropped down the few feet onto the flagstones of the yard, and almost collapsed.

Her whole body ached with strain; her legs were unsteady, but she could feel a rush of exhilaration now, pumping through her body. Her car was close, very close, just ahead of her through the trees and down the slope. She ran across the yard and into the undergrowth, peering ahead of her for the track.

She ran down it, slipping, and sliding. Twice she tripped and fell full length. She heaved herself up, ran on, and reached the clearing. Then she stopped, staring around her wildly. She could feel blood running down her face; she could taste blood on her lips. It hurt her to breathe. She staggered forward a few more steps, peering into the darkness under the trees, unable to accept the obvious. She ran this way and that; she ran a little further down the track, then turned back, breathing hard. Moonlight and shadows moved around her. The car was not there. The car had been taken.

It was Sunday now, it must be Sunday, and it was a good three miles to the nearest road. *An hour*, she thought; *it takes an hour to walk three miles at an ordinary pace*. Then she turned, and half-running, half-stumbling, began to make her way down the track.

She saw the lights, and heard the noise, when she was only halfway down the track. It was coming from her left, from the valley below to her left, from the direction of John Hawthorne's house. She could not see the house from here, halfway down the hill, surrounded by pine trees, but she could hear cars, men's voices; she could glimpse lights moving beyond the trees. She hesitated, then plunged off the track to her left, making for the

645

voices, making for the lights. She ducked under branches, and felt brambles catch at her clothes. She shielded her face from the brambles, tripped on tree roots, and ran on. She came out on the slope of the hill, at the edge of the woods, and stopped.

Open fields lay between her and Hawthorne's house. That house was as bright as an hallucination. The road in front of it, the gates, the drive, the house itself were all floodlit. The buildings stood out in an unearthly greenish halogen glow, staining the sky above. And there were people – so many people. She could see police cars, and other cars slewed across the road below, parked in the driveway; she could see three, no four, long black vehicles drawn up in front of the house itself. She could see men too, moving along the road, moving across the lawns either side of the drive. She stared, and gave a low cry of panic and fear. Something had happened; something was happening. Could McMullen already have made some attempt on Hawthorne's life? Was Hawthorne here, in Oxfordshire tonight? If so, was he alive, or dead?

She began to run then, faster and faster, struggling for breath, across the ploughed fields, making for the road below. But the fields were wet and muddy from weeks of rain, and the mud sucked and pulled at her feet. She took a more indirect route, keeping close to the hedge, where the ground was firmer. Down through one field, then a second. She could see the road ahead now, and the entrance gates to Hawthorne's home. She staggered, slipped, and increased her pace.

The men in the roadway heard her approach. She was dimly aware of them turning, looking up, beginning to move towards her. She heard a voice say something sharply, and heard the sound of running footsteps, but all she could think of was the field gate straight ahead of her, the road, the entrance, and the drive beyond that.

She pushed the gate open, and half-fell into the roadway, gasping for breath. The light was now dazzling; three, no four, five dark figures were in front of her. She stared at them, and they stared at her. One of them, she realized, the one to her right, was wearing ordinary police uniform. She began to turn towards him to speak, but a man not in uniform, a man in a dark suit, moved quickly between them. He took her arm, and looked down at her face. He was very tall, heavily built, crew-cut.

'Ms Hunter, ma'am?' He was still staring at her. 'It is Ms Hunter, yes?'

Gini looked up at him. The air gusted; the road dipped and swayed. Then she recognized him. He had an alert, an intelligent face. It was the security man who had been at Mary's party, Malone. His grip on her arm tightened as she swayed. She thought the police officer to her right said something, but Malone cut him off.

'Get a car,' he said to one of the dark-suited men next to him. She saw the man move away fast, and the others bunch around her. Then the car was there, and Malone was helping her into it. He slid into the back seat beside her, and before his door was closed the car was already moving off. Through the entrance gates, into the drive of Hawthorne's house.

Gini began to speak, and with a quick gesture Malone cut her off.

'Not here, ma'am,' he said quietly and firmly. 'It's all right. Wait. Let's just get you into the house.'

XXXVI

Pascal had lost all sense of time. It could have been one in
the morning, or two, or twelve-thirty when he shot back
the bolts, and slammed out of the St John's Wood house.
He stood outside in the street, breathing in the cold night
air, staring up unseeingly at the night sky. In the Gothic
house in the cul-de-sac beyond, John Hawthorne and his
wife remained. Pascal no longer cared what they did to
each other behind closed shutters; he no longer cared
whether they remained there five minutes or the rest of
the night. Disgust washed through him, with Hawthorne,
with Lise, but above all with himself.

His immediate instinct, as Hawthorne closed the shutters with that small tight smile of derision, had been
to smash his own cameras, to lay waste to that aspect
of his life. *Never again*, Pascal said to himself, *never
again will I allow myself to do this*.

If Hawthorne had intended to teach him a lesson, he
had succeeded, he thought. He crossed furiously to his
hire-car, began to unlock it then stopped. Never had he
felt more like a voyeur. He felt tainted, sickened, by his
own actions that evening, by his own actions these last
three years of his life. He slammed his fist against the
bodywork of the car, and felt pain shoot through his
hand and arm, punishing himself for what he had done,
for continuing to take pictures tonight, even in those
few short minutes when he had still believed the woman
with Hawthorne was Gini. Even then he had continued –
how could he have done that?

*This is what I have become, this is what I have allowed
myself to become*, he thought, and his mind went black
with self-disgust, and self-hate.

He had cut his hand. He drew in a deep breath to steady himself, then another, and this time the icy air steadied him. He lifted his hand, and looked at his watch. It was past one. He stared at the hands. Past one, and Gini was not back.

He began, then, on a frantic and crazy pursuit. He drove to an almost deserted Paddington Station, and ran along the platforms, questioning porters, ticket clerks, any passer-by who would stop. The last Oxford train had arrived, on time, more than an hour before. Pascal could not let go of the conviction that Gini must have been on this train. He started searching the station, running this way, then that.

Then he saw this endeavour for the foolish thing it was. He drove back to the St John's Wood house at crazy speed, and burst through the door. His cameras were still there. His empty coffee cup was still there. But Gini was not. He ran upstairs and downstairs, then upstairs again. He saw, but did not care, that the Gothic house opposite was empty once more. The shutters in that rear room were open once more. The house was in darkness.

He ran back down the stairs, leaving all his cameras and equipment where they were. He could not bear to touch them or look at them. He stood in the hall, breathing fast. The lights here were still non-operational. The telephone was still dead.

A new mad conviction gripped him then. Gini must have returned. She must be in London, but she had gone to the Hampstead cottage, or perhaps to her Islington flat. He scrawled an incoherent message, left it in a prominent place, and ran out.

He drove at high speed, first to Hampstead, then to Islington, then back to Hampstead again. It was evident that Gini had not been to Islington: there was a pile of mail for her on the doormat. The message-light of her answering machine had been blinking but when Pascal, with shaking hands, played it back, he heard only his own voice, and the two incoherent desperate messages he had left earlier. He discovered the same in Hampstead too. He stood there, torn with indecision. In which of these three places should he wait? It was now three in the morning. He stared out at the darkness across the heath. He had just, for some stupid, hopeless reason, replayed the answering machine here too. He had already, crazily, replayed it twice.

He stood there, staring into the darkness, and listened to the mockery of his own useless and loving messages, his own former voice.

'Is John Hawthorne safe?' Gini asked.

She had asked Malone this question twice before, once in the car, once in the hall of this house; neither time had she been answered. They were now in a small sitting-room, off the main hall. Malone was standing in the doorway. Beyond him she could hear activity, voices, footsteps. Malone was watching her, she saw, and he had that security man's expression, that closed expression on his face. He glanced over his shoulder as someone passed, and said something inaudible.

Gini took a step forward. 'I asked you a question,' she said sharply. 'Is the ambassador safe?'

'Yes, ma'am.'

'Is he here? Is he here in Oxfordshire?'

She saw him hesitate, and for a moment thought he was not going to reply; then he changed his mind.

'No, ma'am. The ambassador is in London tonight. He's in London all weekend.'

Gini swung away from him. She stared around the room. It was comfortably furnished. There was a chair, a desk, bookshelves. There was no telephone.

'I have to have a phone,' she said. 'I have to use a phone . . . '

'Ma'am. I've sent for some coffee. You're . . . ' He hesitated. 'I think you should just sit down, ma'am.'

'There isn't time. I have to use a phone. There're people I need to speak to urgently.' She gave an agitated gesture, and tried to push past him.

Malone took her arm firmly. 'I'm sorry, ma'am. As you can see,' he paused, 'there's a security alert. We have a few problems here, right now, and . . .'

Gini stared at him. 'You know, don't you?' she burst out. 'You know McMullen's not dead. How do you know? Has he been seen? Is that who they're looking for out there? Well, they won't find him here – not if John Hawthorne's in London—'

She broke off. Malone, moving with that surprising swiftness she remembered, drew her back firmly into the room. He closed the door.

'Ma'am?'

'I'm not saying anything.' Gini backed away from him furiously. 'I'm not saying anything to you, or to anyone else.' She hesitated. 'The ambassador. I'll speak to him. I want to speak to him. Look, if you'll just get me a telephone. Please. It could be important – I know he'll take the call. If you tell him it's me . . .'

Malone gave her a long and considering look. He said quietly, 'If you'll wait right here, ma'am. I'll be back.'

As he left the room, another dark-suited American spoke to him briefly in a low voice. Malone looked back at her over his shoulder. He disappeared into the hall. The other man nodded politely in her direction. He left the door open, and stood blocking it. He turned his back.

Gini gave a sigh. She was still trembling, she realized, from head to foot. She turned away, and as she did so, passed a mirror hanging on the wall to her left. For an instant she thought there was someone else in this room, some strange woman – and then she realized that this strange woman was herself. She turned back to the glass, and stared at her own reflection. No wonder Malone had seemed taken aback. Her face was cut and streaked with blood; her coat was ripped; her face, hands and sleeves were covered in mud. Her hair was in wild disorder, stuck with leaves and bits of twig. Beneath the blood, and the mud, a strange white face looked back at her.

She stared at this white face with its glittering eyes, and turned away. She began to pace the room, up and down, up and down. After a short while, an expressionless Malone returned. He closed the door, plugged in the telephone he was holding and held out the receiver. As Gini took it, she heard John Hawthorne's voice.

She gave a low cry of relief, and began talking very fast, the words tumbling over one another. Hawthorne interrupted her at once.

'Gini,' he said. 'Gini, you're all right? What's happened? Where were you?'

'It's McMullen,' Gini began, speaking very fast. 'It's McMullen. He isn't dead. I'm sure he's not dead—'

'Gini, it's all right. Try to be calmer. Listen, we know that. My people know that. The results of the post-mortem came through at four p.m. today. The blood group was wrong. Gini, listen to me—'

'He isn't *here*. They're looking for him here,' Gini said. 'He *was* here earlier – at least I think he was. He has a cottage here, up in the woods on the other side of the valley opposite your house. I went there – and I think he was there too. He locked me in. But that was hours ago. At four, or maybe five. Then he left. He took my car. I think he took my car – someone did.'

'Wait.' Hawthorne's voice was suddenly very sharp. 'Just wait a minute, will you, Gini? Don't say any more on this line. Put Malone on. Will you do that?'

Malone had been watching her closely throughout this exchange. Silently, she handed him the telephone, then sank down into a chair. Malone stood next to her. She could hear the faint sound of Hawthorne, speaking rapidly; Malone said little, and his face remained expressionless throughout. After a few minutes, he nodded, then handed the telephone back to her.

'Gini,' John Hawthorne said, and he sounded much calmer, much warmer, so his voice was like a lifeline. 'Gini, I want you to listen to me very carefully. It's nearly three in the morning – did you know that? Malone says you're in shock. He says your face and hands are badly cut. This is what I want you to do. I want you to let them help you clean yourself up, and make sure you're

652

not hurt. I want you to have something to eat and drink – no, Gini, don't interrupt. Then, in about an hour, I want you to come here in the car with Malone, because I need to talk to you myself – and I can't do that on the telephone, not even this telephone. Now, do you understand that?'

'Yes, but—'

'Gini, Malone will stay with you the whole way. Door to door it's an hour at this time of night. If I can't be with you as soon as you get here to the residence – and I might not be able to be, because we have a few problems at this end as well – then I'll be with you just as soon as I can. You understand? But I have to see you, Gini, and I have to talk to you.' He paused, and dropped his voice gently. 'You remember what I said to you before, about giving me a few more days?'

'Yes. I do. But—'

'It's hours now, Gini. Hours – that's all. Now listen to me. Don't discuss this with Malone, or with anyone else. Just come straight here, you promise me?' He paused and sudden amusement lifted his voice. 'I have to tell you,' he went on, 'that you don't have a great deal of choice in the matter. I intend to make sure you're safe.'

Gini looked at Malone uncertainly. She could hear the same seductive directness in Hawthorne's tones that she had heard in her flat that Friday night. She said, 'I'll do that, but on one condition—'

'A condition? And what is that?'

'I have to call Pascal. I have to call him now.'

There was a silence, then a sigh. 'Of course,' he replied evenly. 'Put Malone back on. He won't let you near a telephone, I'm afraid, unless I give the word. I'll see you shortly. Good night.'

Gini handed the telephone once more to Malone, who again listened to his instructions with an expressionless face. When the conversation was over, he unplugged the phone without a word, left the room, and returned with a different instrument. He plugged this in, and remained by her side while she dialled. With shaking hands, Gini dialled the number for the St John's Wood house. She listened to silence, to non-connection, then redialled twice.

She tried the number twice more in the next hour, during which time she was escorted to a bathroom, where she washed her hands and face, and then escorted back to that small sitting-room, where she was given coffee, and some food she could not bring herself to eat.

Precisely one hour later, Malone rose to his feet, and checked his watch. 'We should leave now, ma'am,' he said.

Gini was allowed to try the St John's Wood number one more time. This time, to her surprise, it connected, and actually rang. An answering machine picked up. Gini was about to replace the telephone, to try her Islington number or the Hampstead number – but then she looked at Malone's face and had a quick sure instinct: he would not allow her to do that.

He was looking at his watch even now, as the answering machine at the other end fed her its pre-recorded message.

'Pascal,' Gini said quickly. 'I'm well. I'm safe. I'm returning to London now . . . '

'Ma'am . . . ' Malone took a step towards her. He shook his head.

Gini covered the mouthpiece with her hand. She looked at him. 'Can't I tell him where I'm going?'

'No, ma'am. Not in the present circumstances.'

Gini moved her hand, and spoke into the telephone again. She had to think very quickly. She had to give Pascal a message she was sure he would understand, but a message Malone – or anyone else listening in on this line – could not interpret. 'Darling,' she said quickly, 'I'll see you later today. Meantime, I'm thinking of you, and remembering . . . '

'Ma'am . . . '

'I'm thinking of Beirut, darling. And all those places we used to meet—'

The telephone went dead. Malone, who had just bent and unplugged it, straightened up. 'I'm sorry, ma'am,' he said, still in that flat voice, still with that expressionless face. 'My apologies.' He took her arm firmly. 'It's time to go.'

He said nothing more, and led her to the black car waiting outside. He opened the front passenger door for Gini, then moved around and climbed into the driver's seat.

Gini turned her face to the window. The floodlights had been cut. The house, driveway and road beyond were dark. She was feeling stronger now, calmer, and much more alert. By the time they reached the end of the drive and turned out fast into the road, her eyes were becoming accustomed to the moonlight.

As Malone swung the car right, towards the village and the motorway beyond it, she kept her head turned, looking up the hill to her left. She peered at the woods at the top of that hill, where McMullen's cottage was concealed, and the wide expanse of fields leading up to those woods. She could just see men, fanning out across those fields, making their way silently up the slope. This puzzled her, and she thought it puzzled Malone also, for he too noted the men, and frowned.

'I don't think they're going to find anything – anyone – up there,' Gini said. She glanced at Malone.

'Neither do I,' he said.

The remark was flatly made, but it surprised her, coming from a man usually so uncommunicative. He kept his eyes on the road ahead.

'Still, I guess they have to be thorough,' she said.

'The Brits are certainly trying to be thorough . . .' Malone said.

'Those are British security people up there?'

'Some of them are British. Some American. As to who's actually involved, I can't comment on that.' He increased their speed. 'I don't give instructions around here. The ambassador does.' The remark was made in a tight-lipped way. She saw him hesitate, then glance at her. 'At that cottage . . .' He paused. 'Did you actually see this man McMullen? Or anyone else?'

'No.' Gini looked at him. 'You heard me. I thought I made that clear.'

'I thought you did too.' He gave her a cool, assessing and intelligent glance. 'You also made it clear that whoever was up there left. Around eleven hours ago, right?'

'Yes.' Gini hesitated. 'Is something wrong?'

'No, no,' he replied. 'Let's just get you to London, OK?'

She knew he would say nothing more, and she was right. Malone maintained a thoughtful silence the entire way to London. Once on the motorway, he drove very fast. There was little traffic, but the route was heavily patrolled, Gini noted. They passed no less than four police cars in fifty miles. None pursued, or made any attempt to flag them down – and Gini found this lack of reaction strange.

Malone was driving at just over one hundred miles an hour. The traffic might be light, but he was exceeding the speed limit by over thirty miles an hour.

When they reached the residence, it was a few minutes before five in the morning, and still pitch dark. They turned into Regent's Park, passed the mosque, and were waved in through the residence's lodge gates.

Malone escorted her into the hall she remembered, past the pinkish drawing-room, which was empty, up some stairs, and into a small, anonymous room at the back of the house. It did not have a telephone, but Gini was not surprised to see that. Malone drew out a chair for her politely, asked her to remain there, then left the room, closing the door behind him.

The minute he left, Gini rose to her feet. She moved to the window, and lifted the curtain aside, but she could see little. Behind her was the darkness of the residence gardens, beyond that the park itself, locked at night, and beyond that the lights of London. She let the curtain fall, and looked around the room. It had two armchairs, a table with some magazines. There was an empty grate, with a large mirror over its mantel. She listened. This house, in contrast to the sense of urgency and alarm in

656

Oxfordshire, was silent. She could hear no footsteps, no voices.

She sat down in one of the chairs, listening, wondering if John Hawthorne would come to her soon, and what he would say when he did. Time passed. The silence of the room began to lull her. She felt her eyes begin to close, and realized for the first time how tired she was. She sat there for some time, half-asleep, half-awake, and then she heard a noise which jolted her upright at once.

It was a low, steady sound, somewhere between a whine and a hiss. She tensed, fully awake now, and rose to her feet. She stared at the door. The noise was louder now, she could hear it approach. A second before the door opened, she realized what it was. It was the noise of an electric wheelchair moving fast along the thickly carpeted corridor outside.

Then Frank Romero opened the door, and the wheelchair, and its occupant came into sight.

S. S. Hawthorne propelled himself into the centre of the room. He stopped the chair, swivelled it fast so he was facing her, and smiled at her in a way so like his son that Gini was shocked into silence. He held out his hand to her.

'Ms Hunter? John has been held up. He has to talk to the security people. Sit down, please. While you're waiting for John, I thought you and I might have a brief talk.'

He motioned her into a chair facing the fireplace, with its mirror above. With that low hissing whining sound, he manœuvred his chair, so he had his back to the fireplace and was facing both her and the door behind her. Gini tensed, and glanced over her shoulder. Romero, she saw, had not left the room, but was standing in front of the door, his arms folded across his chest. S. S. Hawthorne looked across at him.

'You can bring them in now, Frank,' he said, in a curt way. 'I don't want to waste time on this.'

Romero at once left the room, closing the door behind

him. Gini could feel Hawthorne's eyes on her face. She turned back to look at him. It was the first time she had seen him close up. The energy he could convey even in photographs was, at a distance of four feet, intense. It radiated from him just as it did from his son. Despite the wheelchair, despite the black rug folded neatly across his legs, despite the fact that she knew him to be paralysed from the waist downwards since the last stroke, he emanated will. She could sense it in the room; she could see it in the way his finely formed hands gripped the arms of the wheelchair, and above all, she could see it in his face.

As a younger man, she thought, he must have been at least as handsome as his son, perhaps more so. Even now, and even in a wheelchair, he could convey physical strength. Over six foot tall, she judged, upright for all his age: his back was straight, his shoulders and arms powerful. His handsome face, patrician and cold, was dominated by the strong jut of his nose, which gave him a hawk-like predatory look, and by his eyes, much lighter in colour than his son's, which were finely shaped, deep set, like splinters of blue ice. They were the coldest eyes she had ever seen, Gini thought, and their gaze was unwavering. He sat there, not troubling to speak, unashamedly giving her a hard, cold assessing stare. Literally, he looked her up and down. His eyes rested on her feet, then travelled up the length of her legs. They rested on her hips, her waist, her breasts, her neck, her hair, and her face.

He examined and assessed her in a way both sexual and oddly commercial. Gini had the sensation that he was undressing her as he looked at her, that this was his practice when looking at women, and that as he did so, he made his own valuation of what he saw, employing the same brutal dispassion with which some butcher might assess and value a side of meat.

The inspection made her acutely self-conscious. She began to wish that she were wearing different clothes – that the narrow black trousers she had on were less tight, that she was wearing a jacket over her black sweater, a jacket that could have concealed her breasts. Then her own reaction angered her. She stared back at Hawthorne in the same cold way. For some reason, this appeared to please him. He smiled.

'At times like this,' he said, 'I regret my age. I regret these useless things.' He gestured towards his legs. 'Still, I'm interested to meet you. John had prepared me to some extent. I do begin to see . . . ' He broke off. 'Ah, Frank. Thank you. On that table, I think.'

Romero walked silently across the room. He was wearing, Gini saw, the same clothes as before: dark knife-edge-crease trousers, a black blazer with brass buttons. He was carrying a small tape recorder, and several boxes of tapes. He put them down on the table next to Hawthorne, and glanced towards him.

Hawthorne nodded. 'Yes. If you'd be so good.' He looked back at Gini. 'I don't share my son's confidence in journalists, or in you, Ms Hunter. Before we go any further I'd like Frank to make some checks. Please don't interfere.'

Romero was already moving across the room. His face was impassive. He bent down and picked up Gini's bag; he began to open it.

Gini sprang to her feet. 'Just what in hell do you think you're doing?'

Hawthorne lifted his hand. 'Ms Hunter, I'm anxious not to waste time. I never speak to reporters unless I'm certain our conversation will go unrecorded. Just a little habit, I have.'

'Put that bag down, right now.'

Gini made a grab for the bag. Romero gave her a contemptuous look, and elbowed her aside. He felt inside the bag, retrieved a couple of objects, examined them, then put them back. He crossed the room, and picked up Gini's torn overcoat from the chair where she had laid it. He began to go through its pockets. Gini felt herself go white with anger. She took a step forward. Both men ignored her.

659

S. S. Hawthorne said calmly: 'The photographs, Frank?'

'They're here, Mr Hawthorne.'

'Good. I expected they would be.' He turned back to Gini. 'I'm sorry, Ms Hunter. But these pictures are not your property.'

Romero had taken the envelope of photographs from the pocket of her overcoat. He put the coat down, and laid the envelope on a table on the far side of the room. Gini bent, picked up her bag, crossed to the chair, and picked up her coat.

'Fine,' she said, tight-lipped. 'I'll leave right now—'

'No,' Hawthorne said, still in the same even voice. 'I wouldn't advise that. I know you're hot-headed – let me see, what was the exact phrase? Wilful, impetuous and obstinate, I think. But now might be the moment to curb those instincts, charming though they no doubt are in the right circumstances. Frank?'

Gini stopped dead. The three words he had just used to describe her had been used to her by Pascal the previous morning, in the back bedroom of the St John's Wood house. She felt her skin grow cold. Romero had turned to her. He met her eyes impassively.

'If you'd just lift your arms, ma'am . . . ' he said.

'Go to hell.'

'Ms Hunter, do as he says.' Hawthorne sounded bored. 'If you do, it will take him a few seconds to ensure you have no recording devices concealed on your person. If you turn this into a drama, it will take three times as long, and be a great deal more unpleasant. Just stand still and co-operate, if you'd be so good. What I have to say to you concerns my son. It concerns you and the photographer you have been working with. How long is it exactly since you last spoke to Mr Lamartine?' He glanced at his watch. 'Ah yes. Around fifteen hours ago. A great deal can happen in fifteen hours, Ms Hunter. If I were you, I'd keep still, and co-operate, don't you think?'

Gini stared at him. He might sound bored, even impatient, but he made no attempt to disguise the implicit threat. She hesitated, looked at Romero, and lifted her arms. Romero ran his hands down her body. He searched her as quickly and as impersonally as a police operative might have done. Gini averted her face. He had a shaving-cut on his cheek. She could smell his hair oil and his aftershave, and the touch of his hands made her feel sick.

'Thank you, Ms Hunter. Sit down. Frank?'

Romero had moved across to the tape recorder. Gini remained standing. Hawthorne gave a shrug.

'Ms Hunter, I have told you already. I do not want to waste time. This will be quicker if you sit down, listen, and avoid the temptation to interrupt.'

He glanced over his shoulder with a look of enquiry. Romero nodded, and picked up one of the tapes. Hawthorne smiled.

'Now, Ms Hunter. You see those tapes over there? That is just some of the tapes made these past twelve days. There are others. I felt we could save time if Frank prepared for us a composite, a selection of highlights, if you like.'

Romero inserted the tape he had in his hand. He pressed *Play*. Gini stared at the machine. The recording quality was excellent. She listened to the sound of her own voice. Her first reaction, even then, was to walk out, then she met Hawthorne's cold blue-ice gaze, and she knew that any such attempt would be unwise. She listened, although it pained her and angered her to listen. She thought: *I had better have some indication of just what he has heard, and what he has not.*

The tape had been skilfully edited, in chronological order. She and Pascal had been recorded in the car-park outside the *News* offices, immediately after leaving the briefing with Nicholas Jenkins. They had been recorded in her flat, of course. There was one little section, after the break-in there, when she and Pascal first went into her bedroom, and he showed her what had been done with her Beirut mementoes, and what had been done to her nightdress.

Hawthorne raised his hand. Romero paused the tape.

661

'My apologies,' Hawthorne said. 'Someone exceeding their duties, I'm afraid. But these things will happen, won't they, Frank?'

The two men's eyes intersected. Hawthorne nodded. Romero pressed the controls, and the recording continued. Gini listened to herself and to Pascal in Stiltskins, the restaurant where they had gone to meet Appleyard; in her flat again, the night before they left for Venice, and in Venice itself. She heard herself say: *I cannot trust my own eyes*, and Pascal reply, *I trust your eyes . . .*

Hawthorne gave a sigh. 'Trite,' he said. 'Fast-forward a little, Frank. You know the section, I think.' He turned to Gini with a smile. 'I'm sure you appreciate, Ms Hunter, that this kind of work has a tedium of its own. Any person supervising surveillance of this kind has to find a way of dealing with that tedium. They will always have their favourite sections of tape. This is one of Frank's favourite sections. Am I right, Frank?'

Romero glanced across at Gini, then away. He suppressed a smile.

'The technical quality here is good, sir, sure. That's always . . . gratifying.'

He fast-forwarded the tape, then pressed *Play*. Gini gripped the back of the chair in front of her. She listened to the most private, the most dear of sounds: her reunion with Pascal in that Venice hotel. She heard him speak words intended only for her own ears; she heard her own answer, a sigh, the sounds of two people moving closer together. She leaned forward.

'Switch that off,' she said, and the authority in her own voice surprised her, except that she knew it came from a sense of the most profound indignation, and disgust. Romero stopped the recording at once. Gini looked from Romero to Hawthorne, who had begun to smile again. He stopped smiling when he saw the expression on her face.

'Do you really think . . . ?' Gini began in a low tight voice. 'You really think I'll be beaten down, intimidated in some way by this?' She gestured contemptuously at the tapes. 'Keep your tapes. Listen to them as much as you like. I couldn't care less. As far as you are concerned, they're in a foreign language. You're despicable – both of you. No matter how long you listen, or how hard you listen, you'll never even get close. There's no way men like you could understand that.'

She began to move away to the door. Hawthorne gave another faint sigh.

'I did warn you, Ms Hunter,' he said. 'These histrionics may be good for your self-esteem, but they merely waste time. Perhaps I should make one thing very clear. If you want to see Mr Lamartine again – and judging from his performance on tape, and your own, I'm sure you will – then you will sit down, listen, and not interrupt. The final section, Frank, and then you can leave us.'

Romero pressed the controls once again, fast-forwarded, then straightened up with a slight smile. Gini stood very still. She was now listening to herself and to John Hawthorne. It was the conversation he had had with her that Friday night. It picked up at the point where he had been describing his affairs. It included the moment when her telephone rang, and it ended with those things he had said to her before he began to touch her. Gini listened, stony-faced. Romero flicked a switch, and there was silence. He looked across, towards the wheelchair, and Hawthorne nodded. Romero left the room at once.

'Now, Ms Hunter.' Hawthorne turned his wheelchair with a slight whine, a slight hiss. 'I will explain everything to you, and then we will agree you and I, as to what happens next. But before I explain, just one word about my son . . . ' He glanced away from her, his face becoming set. 'That last section of recording you listened to? I should like you to understand. My son will have suspected I had your apartment wired – indeed he mentions that possibility, though not me by name – earlier on that tape. It would not have surprised him. As I expect you know, as many people know, I have always made it my policy to know exactly what my son is doing, when, where and with whom. I have protected my investment in him from his time at Yale onward in that way. So, the conversation my son had with you in your apartment on Friday, while being very much, and quite sincerely, directed at you, Ms Hunter, was also directed at myself. He was sending a message to me, Ms Hunter, as well as communicating one more directly to you. His message to me was one of defiance. My son knows perfectly well that had it been left to me, both you and that photographer would now be dead. I do not play around, Ms Hunter, with matters of importance, as I imagine you know by now.'

Gini stared at him. 'Four people have died as a result of this investigation,' she said. 'Are you telling me you're responsible for that?'

Hawthorne gave her a cold impatient glance. 'I am responsible for the first three of those deaths, yes. I instructed that they should be carried out. The fourth, no. Whoever actually died on that railway-line in Oxford, the death had nothing to do with me. For that, we can hold this McMullen responsible. As you suggested to my son earlier tonight on the telephone, Mr McMullen, who is rather more intelligent than I had anticipated, staged his own death. I do not know whom he killed in his place, nor does it greatly concern me. My son, and his future welfare, however, do.'

He paused, sitting upright and very still now, his gaze fixed on her face. 'What I would like you to understand, before we continue, is this. When my son came to your apartment with you on Friday, when he spoke to you as he did, and acted as he did, he was directly contravening my instructions and advice.' He paused, and again looked her up and down, in that brutal assessing way. 'Now that I see you, Ms Hunter, I'm disappointed. You're pretty enough, but the world is full of pretty women, most of them obliging if one offers them enough. Personally, I cannot understand what my son sees in you. However, he sees something. He is probably influenced by the fact that as of now you are unavailable. He has always been attracted to what he cannot have. As I say, had it been up to me, you would have had a little traffic accident a week ago. There would have been a brief fuss, and then you would have been forgotten, because you are neither greatly memorable, nor greatly important.'

He paused. 'However, my son persuaded me to wait. He attempted by various means of his own, first through pressuring your paper's proprietor, then your editor, then by enlisting your father's assistance, to persuade you to drop this. He failed. Then he compounded his own foolishness by going to your apartment, and speaking to you in a very open and unguarded way.' He gave her a long, cold glittering look. 'You should understand my son's character before we continue. He is highly intelligent, very able, very ambitious, but he has two very great weaknesses, Ms Hunter, particularly where women are concerned. Here and here.' He touched his groin, then his heart.

'As he told you himself, he has a very strong sexual drive. It's perhaps rather stronger, and rather more unusual in the way in which it can manifest itself, than he admitted to you. That I understand. I have a similar drive myself. What I find less easy to understand . . .' he pressed his hand to his heart once again, 'is his occasional weakness in that area. It is, I'm glad to say, very occasional, almost bred out. So I assumed, when he interceded on your behalf that he intended to fuck you, Ms Hunter, and then to forget you. That would be the normal pattern. However, since that conversation in your apartment the other night, I have begun to see that rather more was involved. Never mind. No doubt John will come to his senses shortly. If you could be persuaded to go to bed with him, the entire thing would be over by the morning – but since I rather doubt that possibility short term, we will do it this way. I will explain, Ms Hunter . . . ' He gave her another penetrating look. 'I want your silence, obviously. Beyond that, I want you out of my son's orbit, mind and imagination. He has more important considerations than a girl such as yourself. So, I'll talk, Ms Hunter, you'll listen. And when I've finished you can tell me what your co-operation will cost.'

There was a silence. Gini looked around the room, wondering if this conversation too were being recorded, or even filmed. She looked at that large mirror above the fireplace, then at the crippled man in the wheelchair, and wondered, once this kind of insanity was begun, where it could ever stop.

She sat down in the chair opposite Hawthorne. He turned his cold gaze towards her, waited, then began to speak.

'In Venice,' he said, 'where those two degenerates were killed, you found one of Frank's buttons, I think – am I right? That was careless of him, but Frank enjoys killing, and he can get careless on occasion. Did you note the design on that button?'

'Yes, I did. It was like a garland, or a wreath.'

'I chose that device, years ago now. All my staff wear buttons of that kind on their various uniforms. It depicts the kind of garland put on the brows of . . . ' He paused. 'You know the term, victor ludorum?'

'The winner of the games. Yes.'

'The winner of the games. The victor of the games. Precisely. I have always set great store by winning games, Ms Hunter, all games, the trivial ones and the serious ones. I do not like to come second. I like to win, as does my son. Now,' he leaned forward, 'for most of my adult life I have been playing one very serious game. I want to see my son fulfil his destiny. I want to see him win the best prize of all – and I shall do that yet. There have been set-backs, delays – well, you know about those, John described them to you the other night. The illness of his own son, and so on. He faltered then. Now, however, he is back on course. Another year or so here, then a return to America – you understand, I'm sure.'

'I understand what you want for him – and for yourself. Yes.'

'Every father wants his son to go further down the road than he did,' he said sharply. 'I don't pretend altruism here. But that is what I want, and John wants, and it's what I intend to get. I don't intend to be thwarted by John's sick neurotic bitch of a wife, or by the pathetic machinations of a nobody like James McMullen, or – I should make clear – by the efforts of some paparazzo and his girlfriend reporter. Is that clear?'

'Oh, more than clear. Yes.'

'So, when John told me last summer that his problems with Lise had worsened, and when I understood that she had enlisted McMullen in her private war of attrition against John, I moved very quickly.' The icy blue eyes glittered. 'John and I came to an arrangement years ago, Ms Hunter. His hands need to be clean – mine, well, the cleanliness of mine is of no importance now. So, when he encounters problems, I deal with them. If at all possible, John knows nothing of my actions, or my techniques for dealing with those problems. He can, on occasion, have a conscience – another weakness of his – and besides, in politics, genuine ignorance is almost as good as total innocence.'

He leaned back in his chair, and folded his hands across his lap. 'So, without going into all the tedious details, I had both Lise and McMullen very closely watched. I wasn't yet quite sure just how far they intended to go. They are both unstable, especially Lise. They both believe they have a grievance against John – and I wanted to be certain in my own mind whether they intended to injure his reputation, or worse. It had occurred to me that Lise might enjoy being John's widow. She would retain her prestige, even enhance it with decorous grief. She would have sole control over their sons – or so, no doubt, she thinks. So I was interested to see, McMullen being army trained, an expert marksman, just how far she would push it, and him. I waited, Ms Hunter, and while I waited, I took out some insurance against Lise . . . '

'You mean those photographs?' Gini gestured across the room at the envelope.

'I mean those photographs, yes.' He gave her a cold smile. 'Lise has always had rather unusual sexual tastes. John is simultaneously repelled by that, and attracted by it – I think he neglected to mention that to you the other night, but it was one of the reasons he married her. In those days, Lise's little exploits were rather tamer, more predictable. She liked the milder forms of bondage, being tied up, beaten – you can imagine the kind of thing—'

'I don't want to hear these details,' Gini interrupted.

'You don't?' The cold eyes moved from her mouth to her hair. He shrugged. 'As you like. John found that erotic, briefly. Then he became bored, then repelled. From then onwards, his marriage was much as he described it to you. He sought solace elsewhere. What he did not explain to you, is that Lise did likewise, in fact, there is a slight question as to the paternity of their second son, but never mind that. In the last four years, Lise's tastes have hardened – I had once warned both her and John that they would. Those seeking satisfaction by such routes inevitably become more desperate, and more disappointed. In the last six months or so, Lise has become very desperate indeed. Hence those muscular young men.' He gestured towards the photographs. 'Lise gave a garbled account of her own tastes to McMullen, and claimed her own weaknesses were John's. McMullen, who is a fool, believed her. So, last autumn, they launched themselves on their very amateurish and feeble campaign against my son, first via that gossip columnist whose name I forget, then via your newspaper and you.' He paused, and frowned. 'To begin with, I was a little puzzled by that.'

'You were? Why?'

'Well, McMullen may be gullible where Lise is concerned, but he has had some discipline, some training – and Lise, while being profoundly stupid, as John said to you, has a certain manipulativeness, a certain cunning. It was obvious to me that their scheme would not succeed. If it advanced a little way, it could be easily dealt with,' he continued with brutal nonchalance. 'Lise would take an overdose. Simple. Quick. Lise would be no loss to the world whatsoever, and John would be free of her for good. But then I began to understand – and I wonder whether you have yet, Ms Hunter? All of this, the allegations about blondes, the approaches to newspapers, McMullen's alleged disappearance, those four parcels Lise dreamed up and he sent out – all of that was designed to give credence to Lise's story of sexual misconduct. And yet it was still only a distraction from the main event. James McMullen and Lise intended to kill my son, and that was their intention from the first.'

Gini began on a question then, but he held up his hand.

'I'll come back to that later,' he said. 'I'll explain to you how I knew, when I knew, and what their plan was. Before that there are some details I want to make clear to you. I want you to understand that from last summer onwards, *I* took action. Apart from those actions I have already described, my son did not. I arranged, first, that when Lise kept her monthly appointments with these virile young men, she would do so in a place of my choosing, where she could be clearly photographed doing so, *in flagrante*.' He glanced over his shoulder towards the fireplace and gave a narrow smile. 'She met with them in hotel rooms, and those rooms all had mirrors not so very different from this one. Frank Romero may not be a Pascal Lamartine, but put him the other side of two-way glass with the right equipment, and he can perform perfectly well.' He stopped and looked at Gini.

'Wait. I know what question you're going to ask. I'll return to that in due course. Let me continue, please, Ms Hunter, at my pace and in my way. Very well. I had my insurance, I was monitoring the situation, and I knew that after staging his disappearance, McMullen remained in contact with Lise. At that point, when Frank and his helpers were finding it difficult to keep track of McMullen, when, in fact, they lost him – you and Mr Lamartine appeared on the scene. Then I indulged myself a little, I'm afraid. I did tell you. I like games.'

He gave her a wintry smile. 'So you have me to blame, Ms Hunter, for a number of things. For the break-in at your apartment, as I mentioned before, for those additional parcels, a continuation of the four sent by

McMullen and devised by Lise. What else . . . let me think. Ah yes, the little games with the lights in your apartment, and certain telephone calls, which Frank scripted and recorded – another task he enjoyed. Sometimes I was helped, by information about you given to me by John – the touching importance you attached to events in Beirut, for instance, or the fact that you were working on a story about telephone sex lines. But before you interrupt – John knew nothing of how I used that information. And when he discovered about the calls, for instance, the other night – well, you saw. John has an unfortunate romantic streak. He was very angry indeed.' He paused. There was a silence. He leaned forward and adjusted the wheels of his chair.

'I hope you're clear,' he said, still in that same cold, clipped, East Coast voice, that voice so like his son's. 'Had I had my way, you would have been dispensed with, Ms Hunter – you and your photographer friend. I'd have wiped you out as easily as those two men in Venice, or that model in Paris. And be very sure, Ms Hunter, five minutes later I'd have forgotten you. I don't have a conscience – it's an indulgence I dispensed with years ago. I believe and I have always believed that the ends justify the means. So I would have gotten rid of you, and when I was dissuaded from doing so by my son, I decided to indulge in a little harassment campaign. A pity you didn't heed it, but there you are. I was amusing myself – and also using you, of course, as your lover duly noted. I hoped you might lead me to the elusive Mr McMullen.'

He smiled. 'It took you long enough. But in the end, my confidence in you both paid off.'

'Are you sure about that?' Gini said sharply. 'That's not the way I read it at all. I think McMullen gave you the slip. Maybe he's not quite the fool you took him for.' She met his gaze. 'You should watch yourself. You're arrogant. And arrogant people underestimate others. That can be a mistake.'

'You think so?' He appeared unruffled, almost amused.

'Well I certainly don't over-estimate you, Ms Hunter, or that lover of yours. You've been comparatively simple to deal with. As for Mr McMullen . . . ' He shrugged.

'You made things rather more difficult for Frank once you moved into that Hampstead house. But not impossible. You led me to Oxford, Ms Hunter, for which I'm grateful. By that time, both you and your photographer friend were learning. So unfortunately by the time you actually met with Mr McMullen you'd been lost . . . '

'I guess so. I'm sure that if you'd recorded my conversation with him, it would have been included on that tape you just played me. So the efficient Frank Romero blew it, right?'

'Not entirely.' He gave her a cool stare. 'As you will know, he located you again later that night. At your Oxford hotel, you recall?' He smiled. 'In any case, it was a minor inconvenience, losing you. It told us McMullen was almost certainly in the Oxford region, and sure enough, Lise finally made a mistake. She made two calls to McMullen the evening you saw him. One to his mobile phone, to tell him her husband had just left London, and a second, several hours later to his ex-tutor's rooms. Both calls were made from the same phone booth. It was one she had occasionally used before. A mistake.'

He sounded, Gini thought, not just arrogant, but also self-satisfied. It seemed to her more than possible that Lise had intended these telephone calls to be picked up, and that this device was a precursor to McMullen's staging of his own death. But it was not her purpose to assist S. S. Hawthorne, so she said nothing. She hesitated, then looked across at him.

'So, do you know where McMullen is now?'

'No. Not for certain. Not yet.' He glanced down at his watch. 'It was a mistake on his part to kill. Now even the British police have stirred themselves. My instinct is that he will have tried to leave the country, shortly after his encounter with you this evening, Ms Hunter. He may or may not have succeeded. He will have had an escape route planned.' He sighed in an impatient way. 'My main concern is that my people catch up with him before the British police, or security. They might arrest him, in fact they almost certainly would. Then there would be questions, investigations . . . '

'And you wouldn't want that?'

'Obviously not.' He smiled. 'I'm increasingly anxious for Mr McMullen to be silenced permanently. Within the next few hours, I hope.'

He frowned, and looked away from her. A thought had evidently just come to him, and it appeared to irritate him. Gini watched him become a little disconcerted; his hands plucked at his rug.

'You know when McMullen planned to kill John?' he said abruptly. 'It was discussed with Lise, in the second of their phone calls. Indirectly discussed, but their intentions were clear enough. At the party to be held for my son's forty-eighth birthday next week in Oxfordshire. After the dinner, during the firework display. The fireworks were to be timed to coincide with the actual hour of John's birth – a family tradition. Lise knows about my ambitions for John, and when I had always hoped to see them fulfilled – as do you, of course, since John discussed them with you the other night. So I imagine it was Lise who selected the date, and McMullen who saw the opportunity the celebrations would provide for a marksman.' He leaned forward. The blue ice-chip eyes met hers.

'I find that malicious, Ms Hunter. And I shall punish that malice, in due course.' He leaned back, and gave a sigh. 'Meantime, McMullen will be found and dealt with, and Lise—'

'Lise will take her overdose?' Gini said sharply. She glanced towards the door. Hawthorne smiled.

'No. Unfortunately not. My son has over-ruled me there. As he himself told you, he is concerned for his sons, and when he said that he genuinely meant it. Perhaps he would find it difficult to face his children with that on his conscience – I don't know. I sometimes suspect that there is a bond between Lise and my son that even I cannot understand, and he remains reluctant to sever it finally. Who knows? John is a very complex man. So Lise will not overdose, unless she does it by accident. No, she will be despatched to a nice quiet, secure private mental home, as the doctors have been advising for many months. She can tell her fantasies to the walls there, Ms Hunter, while receiving the most excellent care. She really is not sane. I think even you can see that my son has no choice.'

Gini looked away. If all this were true – and on the whole she believed it to be true – she could see that indeed, as far as Lise was concerned, John Hawthorne was probably making the only possible choice. She wondered how long he would succeed in protecting Lise – and she wondered, glancing back at his father, what definitions of sanity or insanity meant any more.

'So, Ms Hunter,' he leaned forward once more, 'that brings us up to date, I think. And it leaves us with just one outstanding problem. You, Ms Hunter – and your photographer friend. Now what, I wonder, should I do about that?'

There was a silence. They looked at each other. Gini met those blue ice-chip eyes.

'These are my terms,' S. S. Hawthorne said. 'First, there is no way you'll now be able to print a word of this in a British newspaper. I have too many friends. McMullen has killed once, and I have incontrovertible evidence that he was intending to kill my son. McMullen is a British army officer, with a somewhat intriguing, and impressive, military career. An attempt by such a man to kill the American Ambassador . . . ' he smiled, 'now that makes the British very nervous indeed. You try to print a word against my son in any paper in this country, and you'll get a "D" notice slapped on you and on your paper before you can move. This is now a security matter – so, here at least, I know you're foiled.'

He paused, smiling grimly. 'I'm not happy with that situation. I like to be thorough. You might talk, you might try to sell your story abroad. So listen to me very carefully, Ms Hunter. You're paying attention now, I hope? If you do that, or attempt to do that, I shall know. And I won't touch you – not immediately anyway. But I shall finish the job I began the other night with your French friend. On Friday, my driver missed him by exactly six inches. He was spared, because my son had certain plans for him which involved his remaining alive until today, until Sunday.'

Gini went white. She rose to her feet, and began speaking. Hawthorne gave a bored gesture of the hand to cut her off.

'*Listen*, Ms Hunter. Mr Lamartine has never been my primary concern. I knew he would never obtain his photographs – even he could not photograph assignations with blonde women which never took place. You worried me rather more, because – with Mr Lamartine's gallant assistance, of course – you might have come up with evidence that would damage my son. And now, unfortunately for you, John has been unwise enough actually to *present* you with evidence. However,' he paused and gave her another cold glittering look, 'my son has also won you a stay of execution. But understand this, if you give me any further problems, any at all, this is what I shall do. First, Mr Lamartine's daughter Marianne will die. Give him that message from me, if you'd be so good. Secondly, I'll have Mr Lamartine killed, and you afterwards, you understand? I shall make sure he dies in unpleasant circumstances, and I'll allow you enough time to contemplate your own responsibility for his death. Then I shall take care of you as well.' He smiled. 'Frank Romero has taken a liking to you, Ms Hunter. I know he'll find an interesting way of dealing with you.'

He looked at her closely. 'I hope you understand? I hope you don't doubt me – because I can assure you, I wouldn't hesitate. It would be like squashing some insect, some fly. Unlike my son, I do not like you, Ms Hunter. You are one of the little people – and you are getting in my way.'

There was a silence. Gini watched him. He had been speaking clearly and concisely, in the tone of voice a man might use when dictating a routine business letter. Looking at him, she felt as cold, and as exact as he evidently did. There had been, she realized, one central question behind this whole investigation: what was the true nature of John Hawthorne? The answer to that question, she thought, lay in the man now seated opposite. She looked down at the black rug covering his paralysed legs.

'I understand,' she said. 'And I don't doubt you for a moment. How long do you expect to live?'

That amused him. He laughed. 'Long enough, Ms Hunter. Long enough, I assure you. And don't imagine you'd find safety after my death. I shall operate very well from beyond the grave, Ms Hunter. My son John will see to that.'

He pressed the switch on the arm of his chair. There was a low hiss, a low whine; he began to move forward. Gini stepped in front of his chair. He stopped.

'Ms Hunter,' he said quietly, 'this interview is over. Get out of my way.'

'I will. But this interview isn't over. There are certain things you said you would tell me . . . '

'I know that.' He glanced down at his watch. 'Unfortunately, there are other matters of greater urgency than you which I have to attend to.'

'There was a question,' Gini continued, not moving. 'You said there was a question you knew I wanted to ask.'

That delayed him. He gave her a glance that was suddenly filled with both malice and contempt. He glanced over his shoulder, towards the fireplace and the mirror above it. He looked back at her, then at the door.

'My cat,' Gini said.

There was a silence. He frowned, and for one tiny second, she thought he seemed confused.

'That was your question?'

'One of them, yes. Which of your brave hit men killed my cat? I want to know.'

'I have three men here.' He shrugged. 'Any one of them. Frank Romero will have issued the instructions. But I wouldn't advise cross-examining him. His temper . . . his tastes – you understand?'

'All right. Then I have another question. What really happened in Vietnam?'

'Not what McMullen claims. The account John and your father gave you is the true one. If the question still preoccupies you, when you see him, ask my son.' He paused. He gave her an amused, considering look. '*Those* were the questions uppermost in your mind? I'm surprised.' Once again, he looked her up and down. He gave a small supercilious smile. He now seemed much less impatient to leave the room, and Gini sensed that, in his arrogance, he was beginning to enjoy himself yet again. Clearly he believed her an unworthy opponent, one whose every move and question he could second-guess. When she did not speak immediately, he gave her a complacent glance. His smile broadened.

'Come along now, Ms Hunter. Something's bothering you – which little detail do you need me to explain? I've covered most of it pretty thoroughly . . .'

'But not all of it,' Gini replied. 'The woman with the English accent, you haven't explained her. It was an Englishwoman who began all this, an Englishwoman who first telephoned that courier company—'

'And an Englishwoman who called the escort agency. A blond-haired Englishwoman who met that call-girl you interviewed at a London hotel.' He finished the question for her with a dismissive gesture of the hand. 'Come now, are you always this slow? It was Lise who made those calls, it was Lise who put that prostitute through her paces at that hotel. Ask Lise to demonstrate her English accent some time. She's a born actress. She does it astonishingly well.'

He paused, watching her closely. 'It seems to me that such petty details need hardly concern you now. Except, I see, I begin to understand.' His smile broadened. 'That's not what you really want to know, is it, Ms Hunter?'

676

'I want to know who the man was in that hotel room with the call-girl and with Lise,' Gini began. Hawthorne gave a bark of laughter.

'Of course. I might have known. These are a woman's questions, not a reporter's, Ms Hunter – aren't they? You're a whole lot more fascinated by my son than you're admitting to yourself – you realize that?'

'That's not true.'

'Oh, but I think it is. By my reckoning, Ms Hunter, John gave up too quickly the other night in your apartment. You're easier than you look. Play you the right way, and John could have you any time he chose.'

'Who was the man with Lise and that call-girl?' Gini repeated steadily. Hawthorne shot her another amused glance.

'It was my son,' he said drily. 'I did warn you, Ms Hunter.'

Gini hesitated. It was the answer she had been expecting, but it disappointed her all the same. She would have liked to believe that John Hawthorne was above and beyond such sordid encounters. She gave a small shrug, and held his father's gaze.

'In that case,' she said quietly, 'there's only one more question I want to ask. In those pictures you sent McMullen, in the third of them, the December shot . . . '

She hesitated, and remembering the details of that photograph, felt herself blush. S. S. Hawthorne noted this.

'Yes, Ms Hunter?' he prompted.

'In the December photograph, Lise is looking out of frame. There was someone else in the room with her and that man. Someone who watched her go through that whole performance . . . '

'Indeed. Lise liked to have an audience, I understand. So, yes, there was someone with her, that December, that November, that October – and on similar occasions as well.'

'Who was it?' Gini said sharply, and at once regretted the tension she betrayed.

677

S. S. Hawthorne lowered his eyes; the complacent smile still remained.

'Oh, Ms Hunter,' he said, in a half-playful, half-reproachful tone. 'I think you already know the answer to that question. If in doubt . . . '

He paused, looked down at the black rug across his lap, and adjusted it. The door was opening. In the doorway stood John Hawthorne. He looked from his father to Gini in silence. S. S. Hawthorne gave her one last amused, malicious glance, then manœuvred his chair past her towards the door. There, he looked back at Gini over his shoulder.

'Perhaps you're not quite so stupid as I thought, Ms Hunter,' he said. 'That question gets to the heart of the matter, I guess. As I say, I think you know the answer already. But if you want confirmation, don't turn to me. Ask someone you like and admire rather more, Ms Hunter. Ask my son.'

XXXVII

John Hawthorne closed the door behind his father. He leaned against it, and stood silently looking at Gini. He moved across the room, and drew back the curtains, looking out to the darkness beyond.

'What time is it?' Gini said.

'Eight. Nine. Between the two. Morning – and still not dawn.'

He turned back to face her then, and they looked in silence at one another. It was the first time she had ever seen him informally dressed, Gini realized. He was wearing a dark polo-necked sweater and black corduroy trousers, the kind of clothes Pascal might have worn. Beyond that, the alteration in him was profound. He emanated none of the energy she associated with him. His face was pale and drawn with fatigue. There was no verve or vitality. He looked like a man who had spent nights without sleep, a man who had moved into some dead zone on the other side of despair.

'How long were you speaking to my father?' he asked.

'A long time. And he did most of the speaking.'

'I see.'

'Were you listening to us? Or watching us?'

Gini gestured towards the mirror as she said this. Hawthorne glanced at the glass, then frowned. Her question seemed neither to surprise nor to annoy him.

'No, I wasn't.' He hesitated. 'I hadn't realized, that my father planned to do this.'

She saw him look at the tape recorder, and the pile of tapes. He moved across to the table, picked up the envelope of photographs, drew out the bundle with its covering letter, glanced at it, then replaced it in the envelope. He tossed it back on the table, as if it did

679

not concern him at all, then, moving slowly, crossed the room. He came to a halt a few feet in front of her. She saw him look at her hair, and her scratched face. He took her right hand in his, and examined the cuts gently, turning her hand this way and that. He released her hand, and looked at her.

'I want to say two things first,' he began, in a quiet voice. 'This evening, when you believed me to be in some danger, you tried to warn me. I'm grateful for that. In the circumstances, it was more than I had any right to expect. And secondly . . .' He paused, and looked wearily around the room, then back at her.

'Secondly, you may well not believe me – but I am sorry, truly sorry, that you became involved in this.' He gave a sigh. 'I'm sorry about a great many things – I should have dealt with this whole situation my way, and much sooner. Lise should have been hospitalized. I should not have held back. I know there's no point in apologizing but I would like you to understand. This has come very close to destroying me. These past few weeks, I came very close to wanting to die, closer than I have for many, many years. There seemed no point – no reason – in living like this.'

He moved away from her, then turned back. 'I do still want to talk to you. Will you let me do that?'

'Yes,' Gini said. She glanced over her shoulder at the mirror. 'But I don't like this room.'

Hawthorne gave a half-smile. He picked up her bag and her coat.

'We'll go to my study. It's safe, clean – if anywhere is. There's something I want to show you, in any case.'

He held the door for her, and then led the way along a corridor. In the distance, Gini could hear activity, voices, footsteps. The corridor curved towards the front of the house, and at a window there overlooking the front drive, Hawthorne paused, gestured to her to join him, and looked out.

'The ambulances are arriving,' he said.

Gini looked down. Two white unidentified ambulances were parked in the driveway, she saw. As she looked out, their doors opened. Footsteps crunched on the gravel below.

'That's partly why I couldn't join you earlier,' Hawthorne said. 'I had to finalize the arrangements for Lise. She'll be taken to the nursing home this morning. It's over. It can't go on. Now it's just a matter of formalities. I have to sign the commitment papers, which I'll do later today, once she's been admitted and examined. The doctors say I should be able to do that around noon. And then it will be finished.' He paused and glanced at her. 'Maybe then I'll feel relief.'

He went to take her arm, then drew back. 'I'm sorry. It's just through here.' He opened a door. 'I'm probably not thinking too clearly, Gini. You must forgive me. I've had Lise to deal with, and the security people – McMullen still hasn't been found . . . I haven't eaten, I haven't slept. Neither have you, I imagine. Come through and sit down. Would you like coffee? Some sandwiches? A drink?'

The room into which he led her was almost monastically plain. It had both an outer and an inner door, both of which he closed. The window blinds were raised, and the windows, Gini saw, overlooked the front gardens, the park ring road, and the mosque.

She had refused his offer of a drink. While he moved away to pour one for himself, Gini stood by this window. She looked intently at the mosque, and tried to see the road which ran between it and this house, but her view was obscured. She frowned: would Pascal have received her message, and would he have understood it, if he had? She turned back to look at Hawthorne.

'Is Pascal safe?' she asked.

Hawthorne met her eyes. 'Oh yes. Neither you nor anyone who matters to you will be harmed. I give you my word on that.'

'Where is he?'

'I don't know. My father probably does. You should have asked him.' He moved across to a desk at the far end of the room. 'However,' he picked up something,

'I do know where he was earlier – as you must understand by now. I let him take his pictures, Gini. In fact, I made it as easy for him as I could. Obviously, our opinions of Lamartine differ. I felt – put it this way – I felt I owed him that. I'm even with him now. Look.'

He moved towards her, and Gini saw that in his hands he was holding a sheaf of photographic prints.

'Lamartine won't be needing these,' he continued, in an even voice, a voice in which there was now a detectable edge. 'He cannot use them. At around one o'clock this morning, he left that house you'd rented. He left his camera equipment behind, and also his film. That was an unexpected bonus, from my point of view. I had intended to explain to you what he had done. But now I don't need to. You can see for yourself.'

He handed her the photographs, which were in black and white, still sticky from the developing process. Gini looked at a woman with Hawthorne who was almost herself; she looked at Lise with blond hair and with black. She handed the pictures back.

'Do you understand?' Hawthorne was watching her closely.

'No, not entirely. I don't.'

'Lise likes role-playing. Particularly in the context of sex.' He turned away, and tossed the pictures back on his desk. 'In fact, Lise finds sex very difficult *unless* some role-playing is involved. She has a great many scenarios, performing fellatio on rough-trade hired-help is only one of them. She also likes to believe that she can reawaken my interest in her as a woman – and her efforts to achieve that are sad. They involve her becoming someone else – someone she believes I find more attractive than I find her. Last December, when she was trying to substantiate that foolish story McMullen fed your newspaper, it was a blond-haired call-girl – you've interviewed her, I think?'

'Yes. I have.'

'The girl left me stone cold. I imagine Lise realized that.' He gave her a cool glance. 'So, this month, when she was becoming desperate, when she realized that she was finally going to have to provide you and Lamartine with some actual evidence, she decided that the best way to make sure I kept an appointment with a hired blonde was to play the woman herself. I know, I know . . . ' He gave a quick gesture of the hand.

'It couldn't possibly have worked. But Lise knows nothing of modern camera techniques, and she was not expecting to go into a room with open shutters in full light. She was probably expecting that some quick hazy shots of a blond-haired woman on a doorstep with me would suffice. Once she was actually in the room with me – well, Lise is not good at controlling her own behaviour, especially in that situation.' He looked off into the middle distance. 'In one sense, as I expect my father will have explained, that part of Lise's schemes was not of major importance in any case. If she could discredit me, well and good – it was less important than ensuring that McMullen had the time and the opportunity to kill me, widowhood being infinitely preferable to annulment or divorce.'

He looked back at Gini, and his gaze became intent. 'But apart from that, Lise had become obsessed by you – had you not realized that?'

'No, I hadn't.' Gini looked at him in surprise. 'Why was that?'

'Because her instincts are acute.' He turned away. 'Lise and I have known one another since childhood. We've been married ten years. She is attuned to me. She watched you with me, very carefully, at Mary's party. She knew at once what I felt.'

Gini stared at him. 'Are you telling me that's what provoked the scenes with her the next day – and the ones Mary witnessed?'

'That – and my decision to send my sons home. Yes.'

'But that's crazy! It was a party, we were simply talking, that's all . . . '

His mouth tightened. He turned away. 'Perhaps that was how you saw it. It was not my reaction and Lise knew that. So, after a few days of hysterics, she set about removing the threat. She did that by *becoming* you,

683

you understand? She copied your hair, talked to Mary, acquired the same dress . . . ' He broke off. His voice hardened. 'In short, I had you by proxy tonight. And if you want to know the truth, look at Lamartine's photographs. There was a short while, five minutes maybe, when the illusion nearly worked for me. I thought, if I can't have the real thing, maybe a copy will suffice . . . '

He swung around to look at her, gave a gesture of the hand, then broke off. 'Then, inevitably, the illusion wore off. Meantime – before you rush to judgement, and I can see you judging me, Gini – just remember. Your friend and lover continued to take his photographs. So, just ask yourself: whatever I am, is he so very different? Is he somehow better, or equal, or worse?'

There was a silence. Gini did not reply. She moved past Hawthorne, and looked out of the window towards the mosque. The street-lamps had been extinguished, and the sky was brightening. It was still relatively early, and today was a Sunday, of course; even so, the absence of cars on the ring road below puzzled her. She listened, but could hear nothing pass.

'The ring road is closed.' Hawthorne had moved to her side. 'They won't allow traffic through until the ambulances have left.'

'Why are there two of them?'

'Oh, standard procedure. They take different routes. There's a security alert, thanks to McMullen, as you know . . . ' She felt him glance at her. He hesitated, then touched her arm.

'It's all right, Gini,' he said quietly. 'I'm not going to elaborate on my own feelings. What I wanted to say, I've said. I said it the other night. I do know when not to press a point.'

She looked up, and met his eyes. He looked into her eyes, then touched her face lightly.

'I wonder,' he said, 'if it would have been different, in different circumstances. Probably not. So,' he moved away, 'tell me.' He picked up his glass, and took a swallow of whisky. 'Did my father do my explaining for me? He usually does.'

'Yes, he did.' Gini turned, and watched him closely. 'He exonerated you – more or less. Was that the truth?'

'Probably. It will have been factually accurate. My father's very good on facts.'

'Did you know what he was doing?'

'No. Only after the events. By which time it was too late. He's careful about that.' He took another swallow of whisky. 'Did he tell you,' he went on, in the same flat tone, 'how long he has to live?'

'I asked him that question.'

'Did you just?' A dry smile. 'That will have amused him. But he didn't tell you?'

'No. He explained it would make no difference as far as I was concerned. He was threatening me, at the time. He said he could reach out beyond the grave, and you would ensure that.'

'Is that what he said?' Hawthorne gave a small shake of the head. 'I wonder if he actually believes that. He probably does. He's wrong, Gini. And in any case he doesn't have much longer. There are the heart problems. He also has cancer, but he doesn't know that.'

A shadow passed across his face. With an odd almost defiant shrug he said, 'It could be as long as five years. It's likely to be a lot less. And just for the record, I have no intention of adopting any of his threats. If you want to expose me for what I am, Gini, you'll be able to do it with impunity in due course.' He looked at her closely. 'I wonder what you'll decide. No, don't tell me. You know most of it now. You can destroy me, or spare me. It will be your choice.'

He broke off; Gini gave a start and swung around. From a distance, muffled by walls and corridors, came the sound of a woman's scream, then silence, then a noise like shattering glass.

'Goddammit!' Hawthorne exclaimed. Then his mouth tightened. 'I'm sorry,' he said. 'Lise. There are paramedics here, nurses – she's supposed to be sedated. Excuse me a moment, will you?'

He opened both doors and went out into the corridor. Before they swung shut, Gini glimpsed the large figure of Malone. He began speaking in a low voice. She caught the word 'Italy', then the doors closed.

Gini crossed to the desk swiftly. She looked at the telephone, which she wanted to use, but knew would be unsafe. She looked at the pictures Pascal had taken the previous night, then turned away, and covered her face with her hands. She felt exhausted, drained and confused. Even if she could walk out of this house now, she thought, even if S. S. Hawthorne had made no threats and she were free to write her story, would she do it?

Despite all that had happened, John Hawthorne had protected both her and Pascal. They owed him their lives – she had believed his father when he said this, and she continued to believe it now. He had deliberately put his fate in her hands, was she now ready to condemn him to public shame and humiliation?

She turned back to the window. The activity below had increased. There was an air of agitation now: she glimpsed a male paramedic, two uniformed nurses. The doors of the ambulance were opened, a stretcher passed out; then the doors shut. She heard the sound of raised voices, then John Hawthorne saying something indistinguishable, followed by the sound of running feet.

A few more minutes passed, then the double doors were flung back, and Hawthorne walked quickly across to her. The strain on his face was even more evident.

'Gini,' he began, 'I'm sorry. It's mayhem down there. Security people, medical staff. I'm going to need your help.' He crossed swiftly to the window, and looked out.

'The British security people think they've located McMullen,' he said. 'Apparently, he flew out on a false passport from a Midlands airport around eight last night. They think he's in Rome now – at the same hotel as that ex-tutor of his, Knowles. It shouldn't be long before they catch up with him. An hour or so, maybe less.' His hand swept the room in an angry gesture.

'Meantime, two trained paramedics and two highly qualified nurses can't damn well cope with my wife. Either they failed to give her the sedatives, or what they gave her didn't work . . . I had hoped, I had *prayed*, that just this one time we could avoid a scene. I wanted Lise to leave here with some dignity. The last thing on God's earth that I wanted was this. Come with me. Look.'

He took her arm, and led her quickly out into the now-empty corridor. He halted at a window which overlooked the rear gardens of the residence, and the park beyond. 'Look,' he said. 'Look.'

Gini could see Lise clearly. She was seated in the very centre of the residence lawns, on a white-painted bench. The sunlight was strengthening now. It would be another bright day, but a bitterly cold one. Lise was wearing a thin, sleeveless, summer dress. She was shivering convulsively. Behind her, at a distance, was an anxious huddle of security men, paramedics and nurses.

'She won't come in,' Hawthorne said. 'She won't let them touch her or go near her. She won't put on a jacket or a coat. She's done this before. If they try to move her, she'll get very violent . . . Dear God! All I want, *all* I want is to avoid that. The shame and the humiliation – for Lise.' He sighed. 'For myself, too, of course, I admit that.'

He turned to look at Gini. 'It began, Gini, at that house last night. I finally closed the shutters. I could see what was happening. I didn't want anyone to witness that, least of all Lamartine.' He turned away tiredly.

'It's gone on all night. It will continue for the rest of the day if I don't do something. Will you talk to her? She's been saying she wants to talk to you since two o'clock this morning. I think, if you did, she might leave, quietly. I think she might do that.'

'If *I* talked to her?' Gini stared at him in astonishment. 'Why on earth would she want to talk to me – especially now?'

Hawthorne's face became shadowed. He shrugged hopelessly. 'Can't you guess? She thinks we slept together. Just for God's sake tell her we didn't. She won't believe me but she might believe you. Please, Gini. I may not have the right to ask any favours from you, but I am asking you to do this . . . '

'All right. If you think it will help. I'll talk to her. But I'm not going to lie.'

'I wouldn't ask you to. We've both had enough of lies.' He turned, and began to descend the stairs. Gini followed him. On the first landing, they passed a tall and very beautiful long-case clock. Gini hesitated, and looked at Hawthorne.

'Is that the clock – the one your father gave you?'

Hawthorne nodded, and hurried on down the stairs. Running footsteps passed outside. Gini looked at the clock, then turned and followed him.

On the clock-face were Roman numerals, a sun and a moon. The hands of the clock, exquisitely shaped, had just reached the ten and the twelve. As she and Hawthorne reached the hall, the clock's mechanism whirred, and it began to strike.

XXXVIII

At eight, Pascal was in Hampstead. He watched the slow dawn. At eight-fifteen, he was back in Gini's empty Islington flat. At eight-twenty, he was back outside in his car.

He drove south fast, then turned west towards St John's Wood. He felt as if he had been driving and telephoning for centuries. He had not slept or eaten. His mind felt as white as the lightening sky.

He had had all night to look at his fears. He had had all night to listen to unhelpful people with no knowledge of Gini's whereabouts, and all night to alternate between dialling Islington and this rented house he was now approaching. His mind rang with the sound of unanswered questions and unanswered telephones.

As soon as he reached the St John's Wood house, and pulled fast into its drive, he could see that the lights, like the telephone, were back on. There was a band of light just visible at the edge of the closed downstairs curtains. Pascal felt a fugitive hope. Calling Gini's name, he ran inside.

The emptiness of the house hit him at once. He could smell, feel, see, hear she was not there. Very well, he told himself, he would leave for Oxford, right now – that was what he had planned. Then, turning, feeling disbelief, he saw the flashing light on the phone.

His heart leapt. He felt a second's sweeping optimism, then a fear. It would not be Gini, he told himself – warned himself – as he pressed the playback controls. It would be another trick or warning or deception. Then he heard her voice, and the air felt bright.

He listened intently. He played back her message five times. Her voice sounded almost as usual, strong and warm: she did not sound as if she were in trouble. She told him she was well, that she was safe and returning

689

to London. Then – distinctly – Pascal heard a man's interjection. He said, *'Ma'am.'* There was a brief pause, during which something was said which Pascal could not hear. What followed was strange. Gini mentioned Beirut, the places where she used to meet him. This part of her message was abruptly cut off.

She must have been calling from outside London then, presumably from Oxfordshire. The man with her could only have been one of Hawthorne's bodyguards – who else with an American accent would address her as 'ma'am'? Pascal stared at the phone. He had no way of knowing when the message had been recorded but he was sure that Gini had been trying to communicate something to him, something she was certain only he could understand.

The places we used to meet in Beirut . . . Pascal stood there tense and alert; he listed the places one by one in his mind. Sometimes that café by the harbour, sometimes her hotel, sometimes his own room, to which he had given Gini a key that first day. Where else? Several times outside his local mosque, which was a few blocks from his room, on the edge of a shady tranquil square. He could remember seeing Gini, sitting on a bench in that square, waiting for him to arrive. Then, twice, at least twice, he had met her outside an Arab school, midway between her hotel and his room, and he could remember the voices of the children at play behind the school walls as he ran, and she ran, and he took her in his arms. Was there anywhere else – anywhere he had forgotten? He could replay the geography of those three weeks day by day. Where, where did she mean? And then it came to him: *the mosque.* There was a mosque here too, almost opposite the ambassador's residence – and driving fast it was two and a half minutes away.

He ran out to his car, reversed out into the street. He reached the park at a quarter to nine, slowed and stared. The park entrance, and its ring road, were closed.

Closed to traffic perhaps, but not to pedestrians. He drew up at the junction opposite the park gates. The gates had barriers across them, and two uniformed policemen on guard. No cars were being admitted, but as Pascal watched, a jogger and a woman with a small dog were allowed through. He turned left, then left again, and parked. He ran back towards the entrance gates. As the police came in sight, he slowed to a more inconspicuous pace; he made sure that the camera slung around his neck was inside his leather jacket, and concealed.

He walked past the two policemen who gave him a cursory glance, and turned right along the ring road. As soon as he was out of sight of the policemen he began to run fast. Ahead of him now, around a bend in the road was the mosque and the residence. Next to the residence lodge was the pedestrians' gate into the main acres of the park. Pascal slowed as he passed.

The lodge gates were firmly closed. He could see little of the residence itself as he passed it, for it was shrouded from the road by trees and thick evergreens. Through gaps in the foliage he could glimpse white vehicles. He checked himself. It was difficult to be certain, but what looked like two ambulances were drawn up outside.

Pascal quickened his pace. He jogged the sixty yards or so to the mosque the other side of the ring road. On this side, facing the park and residence, there was no entrance. A low fence divided the mosque from the road. No-one was standing there; no-one passed. He looked over the fence and saw that the area surrounding the mosque, its outbuildings and its interior courtyard, was large. To his immediate left now was the mosque itself, with its glittering dome; directly in front of him was the courtyard and the high, very high, minaret, and to his right were further buildings, all deserted, their doors closed.

The entrance to the courtyard, mosque and minaret was eighty yards ahead, fronting a main road. Pascal looked to right and left, then vaulted the dividing fence easily, and dropped down to the ground. It was a few minutes past nine when he reached the courtyard. He stood below the minaret and looked around him. There were a few pedestrians on the main road beyond. Cars passed there, and people, but the courtyard was deserted. He looked around him; he glanced up at the height of the minaret, squinting his eyes against the strengthening sun. No-one. Nothing. Did Gini really mean him to wait for her here?

He did wait, for ten or fifteen minutes. At nine-twenty, unable to stand it any longer, he crossed the courtyard again, vaulted over the fence and back into the ring road. He hesitated, then crossed the road, and went into the park.

He was now, he realized, in the place where Gini had been the day McMullen first approached her. He was standing, as he knew she had, on a small knoll, a rise of ground, under a clump of young chestnut trees. He could see both the mosque and the residence gardens clearly from here. He could see that high perimeter fence around the residence gardens, with the camouflage netting Gini described strung between its bars. He could see the gaps in the tree cover which were the results of the tree-pruning Gini had mentioned. He frowned at the fence, glanced over at the mosque behind him, moved across to a nearby bench, and sat down.

His eyes scanned the park. It would be another beautiful clear winter's day, but it was still early for a Sunday, and it was cold: the park was as yet almost empty. He could see some joggers making the circuit, several people with dogs, a couple by the boating lake, a father with two children in the small playground and beyond that, where a bridge passed over a conduit from the lake, two people, an elderly man and a woman, feeding bread to the ducks.

He could feel something edging its way forwards from the back of his mind. There was a sense here, a meaning in the apparently random views, and he was very close to it, could almost grasp it. He lit a cigarette, and began to think very hard.

James McMullen was alive – that was the first thing. He might not know it for certain, but he felt very very sure. If the dead man on the railway-line were wearing McMullen's signet ring, had been carrying McMullen's ID, then that suggested McMullen had staged his own death. But why?

If Gini had been certain he had done so by the time she placed that call, why direct Pascal here to the mosque? Was it simply that she herself was near by, in the residence, and she wanted him to know that? Or was there another reason, a hidden message?

Time was passing, passing. Pascal stared around him with infuriated despair. Joggers, a father with two children, an elderly couple, a perimeter fence, a mosque. Pascal rose, he began to pace. He looked back at the mosque, but it was still deserted. Should he go back, and try to gain admittance to the residence? He would almost certainly not be admitted – and why were those two ambulances there?

He walked deeper into the park, closer to the lake, then turned, frowning, looking back the way he had come. It was nine forty-five now, and more people were entering the park. Pascal stared back at the gate by which he had entered: he saw a group of teenagers with skateboards, a pair of lovers hand in hand, two men, one in a track suit, one in a Barbour jacket, a woman pushing a baby buggy. He thought: *At ten. I'll go to that lodge at ten, and I'll make them let me in.* But even as he thought that, he could still feel the comprehension, inching its way forwards from the back of his mind.

He began to walk back towards the gate, and the mosque, and as he did so, approaching that grove of young chestnut trees, it came to him. He stopped dead: he thought, *A knoll; rising ground.*

Little hints, little clues, which he had overlooked began to fall into place one by one. Why had McMullen taken him and Gini to that hide-out in Oxfordshire? Because it was *misleading*, that was why. It directed their attention away from London, away from *here*. This was the place where Lise had met McMullen in the past: Pascal had suspected some collusion between Lise and McMullen before – but supposing that collusion went further than he had realized? Could Lise have been planning an attempt on her husband's life with McMullen from the first, even in the days when they walked in this part of the park together? Had McMullen, when he met Gini here, had a dual purpose? Had he intended to contact Gini, and at the same time finalize his plans?

I've been an idiot, I've been a fool, Pascal thought, and he ran down from the knoll to the perimeter fence of the residence gardens. He could see nothing beyond the camouflage netting and the shrubbery, but he could hear voices in the garden beyond. He swung around, white-faced, frowning, looking at the lie of the ground. *No,* he thought; *no, it isn't possible; the ground doesn't rise sufficiently, the cover around the gardens is too thick and too high.* In the distance, a church clock tolled ten times. Pascal stood there, frozen, trying to see how McMullen might have planned this, how it might be done.

Not from inside the gardens, surely – any attempt at entry would set off a million alarms. From outside then? But from where? And how could McMullen know of a time when the ambassador would be in the gardens? Unless that was something he could arrange, for certain, using Lise. Pascal stared around him: the grass, the rising ground, the mosque, the ring road, the high white arch of the brilliant winter sky.

He understood about one minute before he saw James McMullen in the distance. He understood when he looked at that newly made gap in the garden's protective tree line, the gap Lise Hawthorne had instructed be made. He understood when, turning his eyes a few degrees further to his left, he looked at the mosque and its minaret, a minaret that was over one hundred feet high.

For one tiny instant, he travelled back to his own past. Beirut. Belfast. The snipers who could position themselves with such lethal efficiency high up, on a tall building firing down – a perfect line of fire.

At exactly that moment he saw McMullen one hundred yards away from him. He was removing his Barbour jacket; he wrapped it around something else which he had just picked up from the ground. He moved out of the gate, beyond the park hedge, and into the ring road.

Pascal began to run. He thought: *It's Sunday. It's the third Sunday in the month. That's how they planned it. It's now.*

As Hawthorne led Gini out onto the terrace at the back of the house, there was a crackle of radio static. The group of people watching Lise had now swelled: there were at least ten of them, Gini realized, as they parted to let Hawthorne through. Two nurses, a woman in a maid's uniform, who was crying, a man-servant, the paramedics, and no less than three security men. Malone was standing at the edge of the terrace, looking towards Lise. Gini saw him frown, lift his arm, and speak into the microphone in his cuff.

'Get these people inside,' Hawthorne said, in a voice icy with anger, as they passed through. Gini glanced back and saw that the command had been given to Frank Romero, who began to usher these bystanders indoors. Only one nurse and one paramedic remained, waiting. As Hawthorne led her down the steps from the terrace and onto the lawn, both Romero and Malone moved into place behind him, about twenty yards back.

'Just stay there, for Christ's sake,' Hawthorne said, swinging around, and speaking in a low voice. 'Just let me deal with this, will you? Wait there.'

Romero hesitated, Gini saw, then stopped. Malone ignored the directions. He fell back a little, halting only when Hawthorne and Gini halted. Gini saw him frown again, then scan the gardens, that perimeter fence. Following Hawthorne, she approached the white bench.

Lise did not move until both of them had walked around the bench and were facing her. She looked at them blankly for a second, then – as if she were a hostess at some embassy party – she rose to her feet. She clasped Gini's hand, with icy fingers.

'Gini,' she said, 'you're here. How lovely. Isn't it the most wonderful day? Such sun – it's quite warm here in the sun, look.'

She sat down again on the bench, motioning Gini to sit beside her. Gini looked at her uncertainly. Her face was chalk white but two patches of colour came and went in her cheeks. The sun was out, and very bright – that was true – but it was still bitterly cold. Lise looked as if she had a fever. On the side of her face, Gini saw, there was a darkening bruise. Lise stared at her closely, then gripped her hand in her thin fingers. She shivered again.

Gini hesitated. She looked closely at Lise's eyes. The pupils were huge, so large, so dilated that her eyes appeared black. What the hell is she *on*? Gini thought.

'It's cold, Lise,' she said gently. 'Would you like me to get you a coat?'

'Oh no . . . ' Lise gave a high laugh. 'I'm not cold at all. It's just such an amazing day. John – Gini and I will just sit here for a while in the sun. Why don't you fix us a drink?'

'It's ten o'clock in the morning, Lise,' he replied in a quiet voice. 'I don't think Gini wants a drink just yet.'

'Nonsense.' Her voice rose on an odd, strained, almost coquettish note. 'I'm sure she does. Champagne. A glass of champagne. You can drink champagne at any time of the day or night.'

Hawthorne frowned. He looked at Gini, who gave him a slight nod. He hesitated, seemed about to argue, then changed his mind. He turned away abruptly, and strode back across the grass. At the terrace, he stopped and beckoned to Malone. From across the lawn, Gini heard a familiar sound, half-whine, half-hiss. Lise heard it too. Her grip tightened on Gini's hand.

'Is his father there?' She shivered again.

'I think so. I can't see him. Maybe he's just inside the terrace doors.'

'We don't have long. Listen to me.' Lise fixed those black eyes on Gini's face. She stared at her very closely, frowning, as if she were finding it difficult to focus. She gave an odd little gasp.

'Tell me,' she said, 'tell me quickly. Did you sleep with him? Have you slept with him?'

'With your husband, Lise?' Gini said gently. 'No. Of course not.'

'Oh, thank Christ.' Lise tightened her grip, so her nails dug into Gini's palms. 'And you won't sleep with him, will you? You promise me? As long as you don't, you'll be safe. I think you'll be safe. He won't harm you then. He won't let his father harm you . . . ' She broke off. The black eyes narrowed. 'You are telling me the truth?'

'Yes, Lise, I am.'

'Did he try? I imagine he did,' she said with a violent shiver. 'Did he make you touch him? That's what he does – at least, he says it's what he does. He could be lying, of course. Oh, I must think. I must *think*.' She lifted her hand, bunched it into a thin fist, and suddenly struck her own forehead hard, three times.

'There. That's better.' She gave Gini a radiant smile.

'You see, I have to talk to you before they take me away. Once I get in that ambulance, that's it. He'll have me certified. All the papers are drawn up. All he has to do is come out to the hospital and sign them . . . ' Tears suddenly swam in her eyes, and spilled down her cheeks. 'Then I won't see my little boys ever again. It's so *wicked*, Gini. And no-one can help me now, not even you. Did he tell you? James is dead . . . '

She gave a low moan of distress. Gini glanced over her shoulder. Hawthorne was still on the terrace, talking to Malone.

'Lise,' she began gently, 'I don't think James is dead. I think you're wrong about that . . . '

'He is. He is. They brought him here last night. They killed him right in front of me. That animal Romero did it. They made me watch, Gini. Look. That's James's blood, here, on my dress . . . '

Gini looked down. The thin dress Lise was wearing was made of fine white linen. There was not one mark on it, of blood or anything else.

'Did he explain?' Lise said, on a sudden sharp note. 'Did he tell you lies about me? Did his father?' She clutched at Gini's hand. 'You mustn't believe him, Gini.

He lies so terribly well, he always did. John is very, very dangerous – especially for a woman. You must understand that. He can make women do things – he's made me do such terrible things, Gini, vile things, so he can watch. He doesn't love me, of course – did I explain that before? I think I did. But even so, when he gets bored with the girls, with the blondes, he always comes back to me. He humiliates me with other men. He likes that very much. I can't tell you what he makes me do to them, because it's so foul, so evil – but I don't have any choice. Gini, look . . . '

She trembled violently, and turned her face to display the heavy bruising.

'John did that to me, last night. Tell your friend – Pascal, that's it – tell Pascal. If he was taking pictures last night, it wasn't my fault. John made me do it. And after he closed the shutters, then he hurt me so badly, Gini. Listen, and I'll whisper it in your ear. I can't speak it out loud, but I have to tell you – what he did . . . '

She pulled Gini toward her and began to whisper frantically in her ear. Gini could scarcely hear her. There was a stream of muddled accusations, and four-letter words. Lise suddenly pulled away. She regarded Gini with an odd staring look.

'Will you promise me something?'

'If I can, Lise, yes.'

'Now that I've spoken to you, I don't mind leaving. I'll go away quietly, the way he wants. Maybe it would be good for me to go somewhere quiet, and have a long rest. That's what John says.' She gave a little puzzled shake of the head, then, turning away her face, she sighed.

'But if I do that, Gini, I have to know you'll be safe. You promise me you won't go to bed with him, will you, Gini? No matter what he says?'

'Look, Lise, that's not going to happen, all right? You can put it right out of your mind.'

'You mean you're not even tempted?' A sudden sly look crossed Lise's face. 'Are you sure? You're not lying to me?

Most women are tempted by John. John can be the most wonderful lover. So passionate. So strong . . . ' She gave a low laugh. 'You know that phrase, *le diable au corps*? John has that. It can be quite a ride, Gini. He takes you all the way to hell and back.'

Gini frowned, and looked at her uncertainly. Lise had suddenly sounded far less mad, and far more devious. Abruptly, she glanced over her shoulder, then turned back and snatched at Gini's arm.

'Anyway,' she went on in a low rapid voice, 'never mind that. I just want to know you'll be safe. So when I've gone . . . Gini, don't go back into the house with him, will you? Don't risk that.'

'Lise, I do have to leave here, you know. Try not to worry—'

'No. No! Listen to me. I mean it.' Colour flared in her cheeks. The black eyes fixed Gini with a beseeching look. 'Promise me. Stay in the gardens, then you can leave through the gardens. Stay where the security men can see you – where that man Malone can see you. You see that path over there? That takes you back to the front gates. Just pretend I said nothing. Oh, my God . . . He's coming back.'

Her face went rigid with terror. Gini looked at her with compassion. She was now hugging her thin arms around herself, and fiddling in a frantic way with her watch.

'Don't tell him what I said, Gini. For the love of God, don't tell him!'

Lise averted her face as Hawthorne approached. She inched away from Gini, stared vacantly around the gardens, then bent again to examine her watch. As her husband reached them, his face grey with exhaustion, she sprang to her feet.

'It's so *late*,' she cried in an animated way. 'Gini, I'm so glad we talked. John, I feel so much better now. So much stronger. Gini's made me understand – I do need a good rest. So I'm going to leave now. No silly scenes, darling, and no fuss.'

Hawthorne looked at her in a cautious way, as if this might be the prelude to a new outburst.

'The ambulance is waiting outside, Lise. And that Irish nurse, you remember, the one you like? She'll go with you. I'll come out to see you later today.'

'I know that. I know that. You think of everything. You're so good.' She gave a little smile. 'I've just been telling Gini . . . how good you are . . . Gini. Goodbye. Give my love to Mary. Will you do that?'

She bent and kissed Gini's cheek. Hawthorne held out his hand to her, and Lise ignored it. She walked around to the far side of the bench. In the distance, a radio crackled. The nurse on the terrace picked up a blanket and moved forward a few steps; she glanced at the paramedic, then nodded.

'Let me see you to the ambulance, Lise . . . ' Hawthorne said.

'No. No, don't do that.' Her voice rose.

Hawthorne hesitated. 'Are you sure, Lise? Maybe you'd prefer it if Gini—'

'No. No,' she said shrilly. 'I want to go on my *own*, John. I don't want you. I don't want anyone . . . '

'Lise—'

'Leave me alone!' She backed away a few paces. She was trembling, and beginning to pluck at her dress in a distracted way.

'All right, Lise,' Hawthorne said, gently. 'It's all right. I'll stay here, if you prefer.' He glanced away, and made a discreet signal to the nurse.

'Stay in the garden, show Gini the gardens . . . ' Lise said on a new brighter note. 'I know she'd like that. I know you'd like that. Show her our lavender walk, and the new knot garden, darling. You would like that, wouldn't you, Gini?'

'Sure,' Gini said quietly. 'Very much.'

That seemed to pacify Lise. She gave a deep sigh, turned, and walked away without another word. By the terrace, she greeted the paramedic with a smile, and the nurse with a kiss. They stationed themselves on either side of her, and disappeared into the house. Gini watched her leave, frowning. Her insistence that they remain here in the garden seemed strident, and very odd.

Hawthorne watched this departure, his face expressionless. A few minutes later, they heard the sound of the ambulances' engines starting up. On the terrace, Frank Romero lifted his hand, and spoke into his wrist-mike. Malone, to their left, thirty yards away, stood there quietly, his eyes scanning the fence. The ambulances drew away. The sound of their engines receded. From the terrace, Romero gave a small hand signal, and John Hawthorne, who had been standing as still as a statue, came back to life.

He gave a long slow sigh. He moved a few feet away from Gini, and looked up at the bright blue-white sky.

'That's it,' he said. 'It's over. It's difficult to believe – but that's it. I can begin living again . . . ' He hesitated, looking back at Gini. 'Thank you,' he said. 'You do understand, I had no choice? God, I feel as if I can breathe again.' He checked himself, then gave her a glance.

'I know what you're thinking, Gini. My problems aren't over yet? I still have to contend with this young woman reporter here, who may yet decide to be merciful, or who may not . . . ' He smiled. 'Even so. For the moment I feel . . . free, something like that. And it is the most wonderful day. So fresh. I'm too hot in this damn thing.'

He pulled off the sweater, and tossed it down onto the bench. He rolled back the sleeves of the checked shirt he wore beneath, looked up at the sky, and stretched.

'It feels like spring. Come on, Gini, shall I show you the gardens? They're not much at this time of year – and they're nothing compared to my gardens in Oxfordshire – but the knot garden is fun. I designed the pattern myself.' He held out his hand to her. When she did not take it, he checked himself.

'I'm sorry. I forget.' He gave a small gesture of the hand. 'I feel as if we're friends. And we're not friends, of course. Not yet, anyway. But . . . ' He broke off. 'You don't want to do that? Is something wrong, Gini?'

Gini's heart had gone cold. She stared at Hawthorne. It was the first time she had seen him in an open-necked shirt. As soon as he had removed the sweater, the scar could not be missed. A long, livid scratch, claw-marks, right at the base of his throat. Another mark, on his right arm, where he had rolled back his sleeve. The scars had almost healed. Gini thought: *Well, they would have by now*. Napoleon had been dead almost a week.

You bastard, she thought. He was still looking at her, an expression of puzzled concern on his face.

Mimicking his ease of manner and relaxation, she said, 'Yes, I'd love to look at the gardens. Especially the knot garden, John.'

It was the first time she had ever addressed him by his Christian name, and he seemed pleased. As he led her across the gardens, he looked down at her, then put his arm around her waist.

XXXIX

Pascal ran fast up the slope; breathing hard, he ducked under the branches of the chestnut trees, pushed past a group of children, and ran out to the ring road. McMullen had disappeared.

He glanced to his right, towards the residence. He heard first one engine, then a second, start up. He glanced to his left; a group of people were approaching the park. He ran across the road, and looked over the fence, into the mosque courtyard beyond. Still deserted. He hesitated, wondering if he could have been mistaken. Perhaps the man with the Barbour jacket had not been McMullen? How far could he have got, with a one-hundred-yard start? Not far, surely? Pascal had expected to see him in the courtyard below. He stared down, scanning the space, and the main road beyond. He looked back over his shoulder, and as he did so, the first of the ambulances passed him, driving fast. A second followed fifty yards behind. They came out from the residence, lights flashing. A second later they emerged into the main road beyond. One swung north, the other west. Pascal vaulted the fence into the mosque precincts and ran down the slope to the courtyard very fast.

There was nobody there. He looked this way and that, counting seconds. There was no sign of the man, no sign of anyone. The minaret's door was solid, and it was locked. He looked up and could see nothing, just the edge of the parapet wall around the minaret's platform, and the pillars which supported its roof canopy. He could see nothing and no-one up there. He listened. Only silence, a tight tense silence in the courtyard, a silence intensified by the hum of passing traffic beyond.

I was wrong, he thought; and then he saw it, tucked

in under the bushes at the edge of the courtyard – an old dark green rolled-up Barbour jacket. He crossed to it, moving quietly and stealthily now. The jacket was just a jacket: whatever it had been used to conceal had been removed. Quietly, Pascal laid it back down. He edged back to the foot of the minaret tower, and pressed himself against its walls. He moved around it, until he was directly beneath the side of the platform overlooking the residence gardens. He looked upwards, the sun dazzling his eyes. At first he could see nothing but stone, and beyond it white sky. Then, slowly, something appeared. He could glimpse it only when the sun glinted on its metal. From where he was standing, so far below, it was infinitesimal, but Pascal knew what it was, this thin metal object, narrow as a blade of grass.

He shouted then, loudly enough to give warning, loudly enough to spoil an aim. Nothing happened. He shouted again, McMullen's name this time, and as he shouted, he ran back to that locked door.

He hurled himself against it with his full weight. It did not move. He threw himself against it a second time, and still it did not budge. He drew in his breath. Silence sped past him. In the second before he hurled himself against the door again, he heard a minute sound from above him. It was a sound he had heard many times in the past, the click of a safety catch being released on a rifle.

'Can you make out the pattern?' Hawthorne was saying. They were fifty yards from the bench where Lise had been sitting, with the open lawn behind them, and the low, neatly clipped box hedges that made up the knot garden directly in front of them. The sky was cloudless, the sun dazzlingly bright. Hawthorne gestured to the hedges, separated by miniature paths of immaculately kept gravel. 'There are many different traditional patterns,' he went on. 'They date back to the sixteenth century and beyond. I designed this one with a dual function. The pattern is decorative, but if you look closely, you see it's also a maze. Mazes are very interesting, you know. Originally they appear as tiled patterns on church floors. Penitents had to negotiate them, on their knees. It was an allegory of the soul's search for redemption . . . ' He glanced at her with a smile. 'I like that kind of thing. I'd have fared much better in the medieval world, I sometimes think.'

'Why do you say that?' Gini asked, watching him intently.

'Oh, I don't know. The connection between morality and religion was very strong then. People had very clear beliefs – perdition, salvation. Damn.' He bent to examine one of the box plants. 'The frost has damaged some of these . . . '

He leaned forward, looking closely at the tips of the plants. Gini looked down at him. She thought: *Another minute, then I'll speak.*

'I've always been interested in gardens,' he went on. 'As were my grandfather and my father. Another inheritance, you see.' He glanced up at her. 'Shall we sit here for a while, or would you like to go in?'

He gestured to another white-painted bench, just on the edge of the lawn, overlooking the knot garden. As he looked up at her, the sun shone directly on his face. It lit his fair hair like a helmet. *A trick of the light*, Gini thought. For an instant he looked dazzlingly young and invincible, like some warrior prince.

He straightened, and moved across to the bench. Gini watched him, then glanced over her shoulder. Two of the security men, ever vigilant, had stationed themselves twenty yards back. Shading her eyes from the sun, she saw that one was Romero, the other Malone. Romero's eyes were fixed on her, Malone's gaze constantly moved. She saw him check the ambassador, scan the gardens, look back towards the house.

She followed his line of sight, taking in the lawn, the trees, the brilliant horizon. There was a gap in the screen of trees that marked the boundary between the residence and the park, no doubt the result of the pruning and felling activities she had overheard earlier that week. The day she had stood there, listening to the whine of the chain-saw and Lise Hawthorne's instructions to the workmen – that had been the day she found Napoleon dead.

She felt her throat tighten. Through the gaps in the trees she could see the glittering gold dome of the mosque; against the bright white sky rose the thin silhouette of its minaret. A beautiful view, a fine garden, a sequestered place. *The privileges of power*, she thought. She crossed to Hawthorne, and sat down next to him on the bench.

'Tell me,' she said quietly, 'there's something I don't understand. Why did you kill my cat?'

His reaction was very quick. Just a tiny and momentary hardening of the eyes, then the puzzled smile.

'I'm sorry. You've lost me. What cat, Gini? I didn't know you had a cat.'

'Oh, I think you did. And he scratched you, didn't he? I can see the marks. There, on your arm. And on your neck.'

'What, that?' He gave a gesture of bewilderment, then sighed. 'You want to know how I got these scratches?'

'Yes. I do.'

'Then ask Mary.' His voice hardened. 'She was there in the room the day Lise inflicted them. Didn't she tell you about that?'

Even then, for a moment, she very nearly believed him. It was so perfectly judged, so well timed, the tone so correct. She looked at him, and he looked back at her. She glanced down at his arm, then back at his throat.

'No woman did that,' she said quietly. She raised her eyes to his. 'You're lying.'

'Gini, I'm not. I told you – I've had enough lies to last me a lifetime.' He hesitated, then took her hand.

'Can't we move beyond this?' he went on, in a low voice. 'I thought you understood. I wouldn't lie to you. Not now. You know me too well. We've been through too much.'

'Oh, but you would lie,' she replied. 'You'd lie to me just as easily and as well as you lie to anyone else. Your wife lies too, nearly as well as you do. And your father . . .' She hesitated. 'I'm not sure how much your father lied to me. Not a great deal, maybe. You didn't tell him, did you?' She touched the scratch on his arm. 'Your father doesn't know about this.'

There was a long silence. Hawthorne continued to hold her eyes, and Gini waited. Then, at last, there was the tiniest alteration in his face, a tightening around the eyes, before he covered her hand with his.

'No,' he said. 'You're right. My father doesn't know about this and he wouldn't understand if he did.'

He released her hand then, and leaned against the back of the seat. He turned his eyes away, and looked across the gardens towards the park.

'It was Wednesday morning,' he said, in a quiet level voice. 'I had seen you at that dinner at the Savoy the previous night. I couldn't sleep. I was thinking about some of the things I'd said in that speech. I thought of you, once or twice. Early that morning, my father played me one of his damn tapes. It was you, in your apartment with Nicholas Jenkins. You agreed to drop the story on me. That didn't satisfy my father, of course, but it should have reassured me. It had the opposite effect. I wanted to see you then, very much. I wanted to tell you some of the things I finally told you last Friday – about my marriage, all that. So I went to your apartment. You weren't there, of course.'

He glanced towards her in an odd, frozen way, as if he scarcely saw her. 'I was in a very strange state. Desperate, perhaps – very pent up. I don't know why. I think I wanted you to know – who I was, what I was. I wanted *someone* to know . . . ' He produced a tight smile. 'A life-long Catholic, you see? It's been a long time since I went to confession. And I can't take communion. Maybe it was that.'

He paused. Gini said nothing. From behind them she heard the crackle of radio static. A bird began to sing in the branches to their left, then flew off. In the distance, a very long way away, a universe away from this conversation, she thought she might have heard a shout.

'When you weren't there,' Hawthorne said, 'I was appalled. I had to get into your apartment. It wasn't difficult – you have locks a child could force. When I was inside, I wanted you. I started to look for you. I went into your bedroom. I touched your clothes, and your sheets. I could smell your skin and your hair. I went through all your papers, the drawers in your desk. I thought, if you weren't there, I might find you in a letter or a diary. Then I thought that maybe I would write to you, leave you a message, or just wait, and then I looked at these things I'd found in your desk – the handcuffs, the stockings, the shoe, and I didn't know why they were there. I knew nothing about how they'd been sent. But they made me think of my wife, of things I've done with my wife, and other women too, sometimes, and that . . . excited me, I suppose, though it never feels like excitement – it feels black. I wanted you then. And one part of my mind wanted you the way you are, but another part wanted you wearing those things, even the handcuffs, especially the handcuffs, so you were just like all the other women, and I could make you do what I like . . . '

'I can't explain.' He lifted his hand then let it fall. 'It's something that happens. I have to find out what's on the other side of the worst. Sometimes I can control it, but sometimes I can't, and that day it was very intense. If you'd come in then, I'd have made you wear those things. Anything could have happened. I might have killed you. I might have killed myself. But you didn't come in, and your cat was there watching me, and I had the stocking in my hands, so I killed an animal instead. Then I put everything away. Then I got rid of all the pain and agony and want. Then I left.'

Gini gave a low cry. She rose, almost stumbled, and moved blindly away from the bench. Hawthorne came after her, and took her by the arm. He pulled her around, so she was facing him. She stared at him. Her eyes were blurred with tears but just for an instant she thought she saw light move against his face.

'That is what I am,' he said, in a low voice. 'You knew earlier anyway. You were asking my father – I heard you, your last question when I came into the room.

708

Who was with my wife once a month, last year? Who watched her with her strangers? I did. Because she liked to watch me watching her, and because that's the point I've reached. I want to know, if you go down far enough, whether you get to a place where you're really damned, where you're finally beyond reach.'

He released her and stepped back. Again something moved, glanced, against his face.

'You know it all now,' he said in a dead voice. 'All in all, for better and worse, you know me more than anyone does.' He smiled. 'Except for God, of course. If there is a God. He sees. And I don't imagine he forgives.'

There was a silence then. Gini stood very still. Hawthorne moved away from her, then moved back. Behind them, at a distance, were his two security shadows. She heard a crackle of radio static; she saw one of the men swing around, look towards the boundary, swing back. But that was far away, outside this tight little cone of silence in which she and Hawthorne stood.

'*Why*,' she began, in a low voice. '*Why* did you let this happen to you? You could have been so different. You were given so much. Who made you this way? Was it your father? Lise? Why couldn't you fight back?' She broke off. She could see it quite clearly now; something was moving on Hawthorne's face.

'Neither of them is responsible,' Hawthorne was saying. 'I made myself. I found out what I was in Vietnam. Gini, listen to me . . .'

But Gini could not listen to him. She was mesmerized by this tiny moving mark on his face. It reminded her of a game she'd played as a child with a pocket mirror, reflecting the sun's beams into a tiny patch of dazzling light, then directing them onto a friend's hand or face. Except this moving thing was not white, not dazzling. It was a small red circle, no more than a centimetre wide, moving across Hawthorne's face.

Hawthorne seemed not to be aware of it. He moved and it disappeared, then he moved again and it came back. It wavered across his cheekbones, moved up to his hair. Hawthorne was continuing to speak. He was saying something about her father, and something about My Nuc, and something about how her father had not witnessed what happened there, though he had possibly guessed.

'What?' Gini said. 'What's happening here?'

Someone behind them was moving. Hawthorne glanced away, then back. The red circle reappeared, in the centre of his forehead. He gave a sigh.

'Gini, I killed that girl,' he was saying quietly. 'She was a communist agent. Seventeen of my men were dead. She was being interrogated, inside this hut. It was hot. It wasn't the way McMullen claims. It was *war*, Gini. One woman and fifteen men who'd just watched their friends die. I was twenty-three years old. So, yes, it all went wrong and yes, she was raped, and when it was over, I killed her. She wanted to die, she died holding my hand. I shot her once in the back of the neck—'

'Wait,' Gini cried. 'Stop. Something's wrong. Your face . . . '

She stared at him. The red circle moved fractionally. Hawthorne's expression became puzzled. He frowned, and she saw his eyes take on a look of concern.

'Gini, what is it?' he said. 'Shall I take you back inside?'

He made a small movement towards her, then stopped. The red circle reappeared. His frown deepened, and time, already slow, was slowing even more, so the frown took an age to form, and the shout from twenty yards away took hours to reach them, and the fact that someone was running, both Malone and Romero were running, that too seemed to Gini to be happening very slowly and somewhere else. There was the mark, like a caste mark just between Hawthorne's brows, and as Gini stared at him and the silence lengthened, she saw him start to understand. For one tiny second, something flared in his eyes, a knowledge, perhaps even a relief. She saw his lips move. She felt him start to push her away, and then his face split.

Redness misted the air. Something red spouted, drenching her face and her hair and her clothes. She was covered in this terrible copious red liquid. Time was immensely slow now, space huge. It was *warm*, this liquid which came out of the air. It smelled of iron. When she looked down at herself, she saw she was soaked with this stuff and also something else, some vile creamy pulpy matter. She started to jerk away, to pull away. Hawthorne was reeling backwards; the wet air was filled with motion. Then she heard the crack of the rifle, the whine of an event already over.

'Get down, get down, get d—'

Malone cannoned into her. He knocked her to the ground. She lay on the damp grass, staring at a white sky.

After a while it seemed safe to turn her head, so she did turn it, just a fraction, and she could see Hawthorne. He was lying a few feet from her. Malone was crouching beside him. Frank Romero was lying half on top of Hawthorne in a tangle of limbs. He was talking over and over into his wrist-mike, his voice breaking with shock. He was saying, 'It's a hit. He's been hit. Scorpio's down.' Gini wanted to reach across and tell him that it was more than this, that Hawthorne was dead, but her limbs and her lips would not move.

Did Romero understand? She was not sure he did. Shock could affect even professionals, even killers, even ex-soldiers, and he started to do a terrible thing. He was sobbing, trying to scoop brain spillage from the grass and replace it, cram it, back inside the cranium.

Gini closed her eyes. She began to retch. She rolled away, closer to the box bushes, closer to Hawthorne's knot garden, to his penitential design.

'Get down. Leave him. Christ, get *down*!'

She heard Malone say this. Moaning, she covered her ears with her hands. There was a huge silence, then the crack of the second shot.

*　　*　　*

The door gave at last. Pascal heard the first shot as he reached the foot of the stairs. He began to run up them, up that tight endless one-hundred-foot spiral. The second shot came about forty seconds later, as Pascal reached the last turn. He cried out. He thought: *Hawthorne, and who else?* Fear clamped around his heart. He ran faster, his steps echoing on the stone stairs. There was silence above him. He thought: *Is he reloading, or doesn't he need to reload? How many will he shoot?*

He could see light above him now. When he reached the minaret platform, McMullen was standing facing him. His rifle was pointing directly at Pascal's heart.

He said, in a calm quiet voice, 'Oh, it's you. Don't move. I've no reason to kill you, but if you move, I will.'

Pascal froze. The rifle was a serious weapon, an advanced weapon. A Heckler and Koch PSG1. It had laser sights. At this point-blank range the bullet might pass straight through him, doing little damage – or it might not. It would depend on the ammunition, on luck, on God.

'Who?' he said. He could scarcely speak. 'Why did you fire twice? Who did you kill?'

McMullen looked first puzzled, then impatient. 'Hawthorne, obviously. And Frank Romero.'

'You hit them both?'

'At a seven-hundred-yard range? From this height? Of course I hit them. Hawthorne's dead. Both of them are dead. Once I had them in the centre of the garden it was an easy shot. A textbook line of fire.'

McMullen glanced over his shoulder, then back. He had heard the sound of running feet below, as had Pascal.

'If you're worried about that woman reporter friend of yours,' he said, 'she's safe. She's over there in the gardens. She was talking to Hawthorne just now.'

'*What*?' Pascal went white. 'Gini was with him – she was with him *then*?'

'Sure.' McMullen gave him a cool glance. He lowered his rifle slightly. 'She wants to cover wars, doesn't she?

That's her ambition? Well, now she knows what modern weapons do to people.'

Pascal stared at him. McMullen was slightly pale, but absolutely calm.

'How do you know that?' Pascal said. 'That was never mentioned. *How* do you know that?'

McMullen gave a slight shrug. He raised the rifle again. 'I know more than you suppose. Stand over there, would you? No, further to your right. Up against the parapet wall.'

Pascal moved. Glancing down, he could just see into the courtyard behind the mosque. Two black-clad male figures moved fast across the courtyard and took cover.

'Are they armed?' McMullen said.

'Yes.'

'Fine.' He moved towards the stairs. At the top of them, he paused.

'Did you get those photographs of Hawthorne?'

'No. Nothing that was usable.'

'He went to the house as planned?'

'Yes, he did. But it wasn't an assignation with a stranger. He went there with his wife. With Lise.'

McMullen, who had been moving, became very still. 'You mean he compelled her to go there with him?'

'I saw no signs of compulsion. The reverse. She took the initiative. She was clearly there of her own free will.'

There was a silence. McMullen moved his hand very slightly. His finger was now on the trigger of the rifle. He said, 'Are you telling me she went there to make love to him? That can't be true.'

'I can't deny what I saw,' Pascal said quietly, and waited. The odds were about sixty-forty, he thought, whether McMullen would fire, whatever answer he gave.

The silence lasted only a few seconds, but it felt to Pascal very long. In the distance, sirens began to wail.

McMullen hesitated. He took one step back, closer to the stairs. He could hear, and Pascal could hear, that there was movement below. 'You're mistaken,' he said. 'Wrong. It couldn't have happened that way.'

'I have photographs,' Pascal replied.

'Photographs? Photographs prove nothing. Hawthorne's father sent me photographs he claimed were of Lise. I wasn't taken in. They were faked. I never intended to rely on photographs, interviews, evidence. Did you realize that?'

'I realize now.'

'You can fake such pictures, can't you?' McMullen suddenly shot him an almost pleading look.

'Yes, you can,' Pascal answered truthfully. 'The only photographs I trust are my own.'

He hesitated, looking at McMullen's face. He was fighting back his doubts, Pascal could see, fighting down his emotions. More noise came from below.

'Are you intending to die for Lise?' Pascal asked quietly. 'Because if you stand here asking questions much longer that's exactly what you'll do.'

'You think so?' McMullen gave a tight smile. 'Why would I want to die now? Lise is free. She can't be certified unless Hawthorne signs the papers. He'll never sign them now. I shall be with Lise, driving her away from that hospital, two hours from now.'

'You will?' Pascal moved behind one of the platform pillars, and looked cautiously down. 'There are five men in that courtyard. You've heard the ones at the foot of the stairs. I doubt you'll get more than halfway down. Especially with a Heckler and Koch in your hands.'

'Maybe.' McMullen smiled again. 'I think you're wrong. Shall we see? You could be right about the rifle. And I won't be needing it anyway. Here.'

He tossed the rifle to Pascal. The movement was so swift and so unexpected, that Pascal reacted instinctively. He reached forward, and caught hold of the rifle stock. There was a blur of movement as it travelled through the air, and in that split second, McMullen was gone.

Pascal listened to the sound of his footsteps descending the stairs. He bent forward, and carefully placed the rifle on the stone floor, at a distance. Bending low, he approached the staircase and listened intently.

He could still hear McMullen's footsteps echoing down the stairs. He must have been running, making no attempt at caution. Pascal listened, and then he heard the car. He straightened up, pressing himself against a pillar and looked down onto the ring road below.

The car was below, engine running, doors open, one black-clad man in the driver's seat, one already out on the pavement by the opened doors. Two others must have been waiting for McMullen at the base of the stairs, because they came out with him, all three men moving fast. McMullen was clearly identifiable. Although he also wore black, he was the slightest of the three in build, the only one with his head uncovered. He was running fast between them. Pascal saw him glance back once, over his shoulder. He seemed to know the men with him.

From the base of the stairs to the car took the first of the men about fifteen seconds. He vaulted the fence, was across the pavement and into the car. As he slid into it, he shouted, 'Now.'

McMullen was no more than two seconds behind him, the second man immediately on his heels. Pascal thought afterwards that McMullen never once guessed that there was anything wrong. The man behind him shot him once, in the back, just as he reached the fence and grasped for it. McMullen slumped against it. His companions were inside the car, and it had disappeared with a screech of rubber, before McMullen twisted. He coughed up a long spurt of bright arterial blood, and fell to the ground.

Pascal moved fast. He wiped the rifle stock clean of his own prints. He removed his camera, and wound on some fifteen frames of unused film. He moved silently and very fast down the stairs. The sirens were closer now, and very loud.

It would have been timed, he knew, so the police cars arrived about a minute and a half after it was all over. He might have a gap of about thirty seconds; he needed no more than fifteen.

The door at the bottom of the stairs was open. No-one

was visible in the courtyard now. Pascal walked out, his hands raised, holding the camera above his head. Five yards from the entrance, he bent and carefully placed the camera on the ground. The sirens were very loud now, whooping and wailing. He could see the flash of blue lights in the corner of his vision, to his left, near the entrance to the park. Keeping his hands to his sides, he walked away from the lights, across the courtyard, and out into the main road beyond. He thought he was probably safe, because a dead French photographer would be an inconvenience, an unnecessary complication to whatever cover story had been planned, but even so, as he walked, he could feel vulnerability the length of his spine.

He reached the main road two seconds before the first of the police cars drew alongside. He could not see his camera from here, but he knew it would already have been removed. He began to walk away at a fast pace, heading for the rough open ground beyond the mosque and immediately opposite the residence lodge. There he vaulted the railings, ran fast across the rough grass, and crossed the road.

He reached the residence lodge a few seconds after the mayhem began. Men were running in all directions. The driveway was blocked by cars. The first of the ambulances had already arrived, white-coated men were running in the direction of the rear gardens. The air was flashing, alarms were ringing, and out of the havoc and confusion, Pascal saw the white-haired man appear. He was in a wheelchair which he was propelling along the path from the gardens. He burst through the group of paramedics, wheeled the chair around fast, began to follow them back towards the gardens, then seemed to change his mind. He wheeled to his left, then his right, then spun around to face the ambulance. He came to an abrupt halt at the edge of the drive.

He sat there in magnificent isolation amidst the running figures and the shouts and the sirens and flashing lights. His hands gripped the arms of his chair. Then two men in black blazers ran up to him. One bent over him; the other, who was weeping, knelt by his side.

A second ambulance was arriving, and a third. The gates were jammed open with vehicles and people. Pascal was about to pass through in the confusion, when a hand touched his arm. He swung around, to find Gini and that huge security man, Malone, at her side.

'Get her out of here,' Malone said. 'Get her out of here fast.'

Pascal took off his jacket, and wrapped it around her. She was drenched in blood, and scarcely able to move. As he began to guide her away, he looked back one last time through the havoc.

The man in the wheelchair had arched back, and lifted both his arms. His face was distorted with rage and grief. As Pascal watched, he began to scream abuse at the sky.

XL

The London memorial service for John Hawthorne was as Pascal had expected, perfectly stage-managed. Held at the Roman Catholic cathedral in Westminster, it was a sombre but magnificent affair.

Mary and Gini had both insisted on attending. Pascal went less willingly – he saw it as the culmination of weeks of cover-up, weeks of misinformation and lies.

'All right,' he had said to Gini angrily, in her flat the night before. 'I can see that Mary has to attend. But, darling, we don't. They gave him a hero's funeral. Now they're giving him a statesman's memorial service. I know what he truly was. You know what he truly was. Why should we participate in their lies?'

'Because I don't see it that way,' Gini had said, in the same quiet obstinate way she adopted whenever Pascal mentioned Hawthorne's name. 'You wouldn't either, not if you'd been there when Hawthorne died.'

Pascal could hear the rebuke at the back of her tone, and he had remained silent. He had given up his protests and arguments, because he could see they hurt Gini. Now, they were seated halfway down on the left-hand side of the cathedral's massive echoing nave. An organist was playing a Bach *Toccata and Fugue*. There must be, Pascal estimated, some seven or eight hundred people attending this ceremony, which was due to begin in ten minutes. As yet, the seats in the nave were three-quarters taken, groups of people still arrived. In front of him, towards the high altar, was an array of famous faces; he could recognize many distinguished men here – British politicians and diplomats, including the Prime Minister, and most of the Cabinet. Men who might have been senior civil servants, or captains of industry, a number of army and naval officers, three newspaper proprietors, including Hawthorne's friend, Henry Melrose, several newspaper editors, familiar faces from broadcasting, and groupings of other celebrities, writers, film-makers, a conductor, an opera singer, who were, Pascal knew, family friends.

Pascal glanced towards Gini and Mary. Both were wearing black. Gini's face was tight and pale; Mary was close to tears. He looked down at his order of service, which he saw was to include readings from both the Bible and Shakespeare, and the *Sanctus* from Mozart's *Requiem*. His mouth tightened as he thought: *All the best strings will be pulled.*

The very front row of seats to the right of the nave were still empty: the family, Pascal knew, would sit there. He thought of the funeral Hawthorne had been given at Washington's Arlington cemetery, which he had watched on CNN. That had been dominated by the presence of Hawthorne's father, in his wheelchair at the graveside, and by the frail, veiled, black-clad figure of Lise, who had stood beside her father-in-law, her black-gloved hands on the shoulders of her two blond-haired sons. She had been escorted, on that occasion, by Hawthorne's younger brother Prescott, and flanked by his sisters and their children. He wondered now how many of that family group would have flown over, and would be here.

He had the answer to his question shortly afterwards. Beneath the magnificence of the music, there was not complete silence in the cathedral but a decorous, just audible hum as this distinguished congregation exchanged low whispered comments: there was a feeling, despite the music, the incense, the quiet ministrations of ushers, subsidiary priests and security men, that this was theatre as well as a religious service; the atmosphere was akin to that in a theatre auditorium, in the split second when the audience realizes the curtain is about to rise. Abruptly, that background whispering stilled.

The Roman Catholic archbishop conducting the service began to move forward up the aisle; he was followed by attendant priests, by a boy carrying a gold crucifix, and behind this slowly moving group, by Hawthorne's immediate family. Pascal saw Prescott, with a pale Lise on his arm; Hawthorne's two young sons, various sisters; then, last of all, with a faint hiss and a faint whine, the wheelchair in which S. S. Hawthorne was seated, flanked by two black-suited security men.

When she heard that wheelchair, Gini averted her eyes. Pascal saw her stare straight ahead, into the high dark echoing spaces behind and above the altar. The music swelled and beat around his head. A few minutes later, the prayers and psalms began.

Pascal could see that both Gini and Mary found the procedures confusing; neither was quite sure when to kneel, when to sit or stand. It was many years since Pascal had attended mass, and the last occasion on which he had done so had been in a tiny village church in Provence. He found that a gap of some twenty years made little difference. These rituals and responses were in his bones. He knew them from his earliest childhood onwards, and to his own surprise he found they retained a power over him.

He found that he was deeply moved. He thought back to the time before he lapsed. He considered the fact that, in the eyes of his Church, he had lived in a state of sin for many years. The Church of his childhood did not recognize his civil marriage, or his divorce, or the Anglican baptism upon which Helen had insisted for Marianne.

His unease intensified as each minute passed. Was he justified in judging and condemning John Hawthorne? Before entering the church, he would not have hesitated to do so; now, suddenly, he felt less sure. On an impulse, he rose abruptly to his feet. He was in an aisle seat, and could leave quietly without attracting attention. Suddenly he felt he had to leave: it felt unbearable to be here.

Gini glanced towards him as he rose, then looked away. Mary had already begun to cry. Pascal turned, and walked out. He stood on the steps outside the cathedral. It was a sunny cold March day. He began to pace back and forth in an agitated way. Traffic passed. It was a day very like the one on which Hawthorne had died. Pascal thought and thought. He stared up at the small tight clouds which raced across the sky.

When, exactly, had he realized for the first time that none of them had seen the full extent of this story – not Gini, not himself, not John Hawthorne or his father, not even James McMullen and Lise? He had begun to understand, he thought, when he realized that McMullen, standing on that high platform with his rifle in his hand, had *expected* those black-clad figures to be below them in the courtyard. He had suspected the truth then, and he had known it for certain when he watched McMullen make his escape with men he believed to be aiding him, believed were his friends. Pascal thought: *When they shot him in the back, I knew then.*

It angered him that he had not seen any indication earlier. He had enough experience, after all. He had seen this kind of covert operation carried out elsewhere in the world. He had seen it in the Falklands, in Beirut; it was commonplace in Belfast. Why had he not guessed that McMullen was not simply a lone assassin, but a man who was being used, a man who would inevitably be dispensed with, once that usefulness came to an end?

So who had been using McMullen, and who had determined that John Hawthorne had to die? The CIA, or British Security – or some unholy alliance between the two? Pascal could see that Hawthorne, with his pro-Israeli stance, would have made powerful Middle Eastern enemies; he could also see that vested interests in America – party political, nationalistic or even military – might have viewed Hawthorne as an embarrassment best removed, for with Hawthorne, of course, died the truth about an incident in Vietnam.

There were numerous candidates, and Pascal – suspicious of conspiracy theories, that twentieth-century disease – was unwilling to select one, unwilling to enter that particular maze. Whoever had masterminded these events, they were efficient, as were most of their kind. Even as he led Gini away from Regent's Park that day, he had known what they would find when they returned to the houses they had been using: no evidence – that was what they would find.

He had warned Gini, who had not believed him, and who, in any case, was in a state of shock so deep she could not care. And he had been right. In St John's Wood, in Hampstead, in Islington, there was no film, no tapes, no notebooks, no disks, no handcuffs, shoes, stockings, wrapping paper. Every single fragment of evidence had been painstakingly removed.

'None of it happened,' he had said to Gini later. 'None of it. That's the effect they're after, darling – can you not see? They've taken the last two weeks, and they've made them a fiction, a dream.'

So were these shadows who had decided the time had come for John Hawthorne to be surgically removed governmental or extra-governmental? Pascal suspected that both the Americans and the British were involved, and that whoever gave the final order was highly placed. That suspicion was confirmed when, as the myth-spinners and the news-novelists got busy with the headlines, and the authorized version of John Hawthorne's murder began to appear, the first discreet pressure was applied.

Within twenty-four hours of Hawthorne's death, a meeting was arranged. It took place, on the morning following Hawthorne's killing, in an anonymous block of flats in Whitehall. Present were Gini and Pascal, an Englishman whose name was never used, an American who said little but listened professionally, and that security man drafted in from Washington, Malone.

The Englishman wore an unlikely tweed suit, and looked as if he had just wandered in from some country estate in the shires. This was deceptive. He asked a great many questions to which Pascal was certain he already knew the answers. He had a chill manner and highly intelligent, highly alert eyes. When he paused, the quiet American took over. He concentrated on Gini,

Pascal noted. The manner he adopted was sympathetic and warm.

It went on for over two hours. Pascal adopted the procedure which had served him well enough in the past. He simply denied everything. He had been nowhere, seen nothing, and had nothing to report. This, he could see, did not please them. The Englishman, in particular, was riled by his increasingly insolent tone.

'M. Lamartine,' he said, leaning forward, 'could we stop this pretence, and stop it now? If you have no story, were not working on any story, and therefore have no intention of trying to publish your non-existent story, why did you telephone two American magazines yesterday evening? And this morning why did you contact *Paris Jour*?'

'Routine.' Pascal shrugged. 'I work for those editors all the time.'

'Look.' It was Gini who spoke, making Pascal start. She had, so far, said very little, and her answers though more polite than Pascal's had been noncommittal.

'Look,' she said again, quietly, her voice very firm. 'Why don't we *all* stop this pretence? Pascal and I know very well why we're here. He has no film, no photographs. I have no notes and no tapes. You needn't have bothered to organize this kind of clean-up operation. I discovered very little about John Hawthorne, and what I did discover, I have no intention of publishing. I am not going to write this story. And I'm leaving here right now.'

The quiet American and the tweed-suited Englishman exchanged a tiny glance. The American nodded. Malone rose and moved towards the door. As she and Pascal were leaving, Gini stopped and looked at Malone closely; she said: 'Did you know?'

Malone had honest eyes, Pascal thought – insofar as anyone in his profession did. His gaze met Gini's without wavering.

'No, ma'am,' he said. 'I give you my word.'

'Considering how he was betrayed by everyone else,' Gini replied, 'I hope that's so.'

That view, that Hawthorne, however guilty, had been betrayed, and that she would never write this story, anywhere or in any form, was one from which Pascal could not shift her, although he tried to do so very hard.

'No,' she would say, whenever he raised the subject. 'No. In the first place, I can't prove anything, and in the second, I prefer the authorized version. Let them spin their myths. I don't want to disillusion Hawthorne's sons. Let them grow up believing in him. I don't want to disillusion Mary. What's the point in destroying his reputation now? He's dead. I won't do that, Pascal.'

'OK. What about his father?'

'His father is a dying man. A broken man now, too.'

'All right, what about Lise? She's every bit as responsible for Hawthorne's death as McMullen was. She's halfway insane. And now she has custody of their sons.'

'I know all that. And I can't prove it, any more than you can. Besides . . . ' she hesitated, 'I think Lise will be punished sooner or later, for sure.'

'You mean that overdose will be arranged?'

'Possibly. I think it's much more likely that Lise won't need any assistance. She'll go right over the edge on her own.'

And then she would always turn away from him, and refuse to continue this argument. Once or twice Pascal suspected that there was one last thing which Gini was not telling him, but even of that he could not be sure.

And so, with Gini immovable and himself unable to act, the weeks had passed. John Hawthorne's death held the headlines for four days. Then there was another IRA bombing, further outrages in Yugoslavia. The matter was relegated to the inside pages, then disappeared. James McMullen was depicted as a lone killer, a man with a history of mental instability, someone who, after leaving the Army, had become progressively reclusive, obsessive and deranged. Although very few details of his military career emerged, some material was leaked which suggested links with and sympathy for Arab activists, dating back to contacts he'd made when serving in Oman.

John Hawthorne's reputation, as a politician of exceptional promise, as a servant of his country, as a father and as a husband, remained unimpaired. Some of the most laudatory articles about him were published in Gini's own paper, the *News*: Pascal believed that was easily explained. Nicholas Jenkins, far from being fired, had been just recently promoted. He was now executive editor of the entire group of Lord Melrose's newspapers in Britain, and had been awarded a seat on the board.

Pascal tried to push these recent events from his mind. He began to pace the cathedral steps again. From behind him, through the thick doors, he could now hear music, and the voices of the choir. The service was almost over.

He leaned up against the doors, and listened to the music. It quietened the angry resentment he still felt at the ways of his profession, and the ways of the world. Perhaps Gini was right, he thought; perhaps some of his own motivation was both personal and jealous. Perhaps, indeed, Hawthorne might be better left in peace, and this story be better left untold.

Within the cathedral, the choir's voices rose. Mary was weeping openly. Gini stared straight ahead of her. She felt as if she saw John Hawthorne through the music. In its cadences she could sense his paradox – the frailty and the good in the man.

Her interpretation might be judged wrong by others, but she felt it to be true; indeed, from the mesh of deceptions here, the claims and counter-claims, it was the one certainty she retained. If she could not condone his actions, neither could she condemn the man. As the music drew to a close, she shut her eyes. She knew that she had made the right decision in remaining silent, and she believed that, with time, Pascal would come to believe that too. She had told him, these past weeks, every detail of what had happened to her that weekend, as he had told her of his experiences. She had left out only one detail; although she had told him about S. S. Hawthorne's threats to him and to herself, she had not mentioned the threats against Marianne. It was better, she thought, to shield Pascal from that fear, as she was certain now that Hawthorne's father could never present a serious danger to them or to anyone else. She wondered, glancing across at him now, if he might have suffered a second stroke. She thought: *He too has been punished; he will not live very long.*

The choir were singing the Mozart *Sanctus* now. It seemed to Gini as she listened that both she and Pascal had learned and gained from this story, as well as experiencing doubt and pain. Pascal had found the strength now to abandon the type of work which had occupied him these past three years; she knew he would never undertake it again, and she thought that among the other types of work he would turn to, he would almost certainly return to the thing he had always done best, the coverage of wars.

And she herself had learned too: somewhere in these past weeks, she had lost her dependency on her father. She had seen, by way of example, the destructiveness of Hawthorne's father's influence on him; her meeting with Sam had been a final reckoning; a burden long carried had been lifted: she no longer felt like a daughter; she felt she was her own woman now. She had little wish to see her father again; if she did, she knew she would have no illusions and make no excuses. *It's over*, she thought; *I'm free.*

As the *Sanctus* reached its close, the service ended and the congregation rose. Hawthorne's family left first, proceeding slowly down the centre aisle. As S. S. Hawthorne came closer, she could see clearly that these eight weeks and the loss of his elder son had affected him like the passing of twenty years. He sat hunched in his chair, which was pushed for him. His hands were trembling uncontrollably. He looked like a lost and frightened old man.

Lise, walking beside Hawthorne's brother Prescott, clutched tightly at his arm. Her white face wore a dazed expression, as if she did not understand where she was, or what her purpose was here. She walked stiffly down the aisle, staring straight ahead of her, like a woman in a trance. Her two small sons, Gini saw, had been detached from their mother – and she suspected that this arrangement was likely to continue in a more formalized way. Behind Lise, the rest of Hawthorne's family bunched: they gave the impression of a clan. Hawthorne's two boys now walked with his eldest sister, flanked by her sons. Both Hawthorne's father, and his wife, Gini realized, were the outsiders here as the rest of the family closed ranks, defending his reputation, and his children. Gini looked at the pale set faces of the two young boys; the elder, in particular, was very like his father. She looked away, and let the music from the organist calm her. Mozart. She thought of John Hawthorne, playing her a Mozart opera in his car. *The music gives me hope, while it lasts.*

Turning, she took Mary's arm. Mary was wiping her eyes. Gini put her arm around her.

'Pascal will be waiting for us outside, Mary,' she said. 'We'll take you home.'

'What I believe, what I truly believe,' Mary said, 'is that John's father was to blame. You remember that story I once told you, Gini – about how John struck his father, when he was only a child?'

She gave a little sad gesture; Gini said nothing. That story could be interpreted in more than one way, but she had no intention of hurting Mary by saying this.

Mary gave a sigh. 'I always hated John's father,' she went on. 'Still, I shouldn't judge him, perhaps. If he made John suffer, he must be suffering himself now . . . '

She bent towards the fire, stroked Dog, and gave him a chocolate biscuit. Pascal and Gini exchanged a quiet glance: Mary knew some of what had happened, but by no means all.

'What I do know,' Mary continued in a firmer voice, 'is that I have lost a friend. All those people who still imply John was arrogant, cold, manipulative. That wasn't the John I knew. He was a good man, a kind man, a fine

727

man . . . ' She sighed. 'I hate it now, watching all these petty little people, picking over his soul. And as for that McMullen – I know I shouldn't say this, but I can't regret that police marksmen shot him. He can't have been sane, but even so – the malice of the man! Even before all this, Gini, when Sam was here and he and John explained all those allegations, McMullen had been making – it was so desperately perverse. John was an idealist. He was harder on himself than anyone I know. He hated to fall short of his own ideals. It tormented him to fail. *How* could that man spread such malicious rumours about John's marriage, about his service in Vietnam?' She shook her head. 'It's so desperately unfair. You have an American president who gets pilloried because he didn't fight, and didn't believe in that war, and then you get a politician like John, who *did* fight, who was decorated, nearly killed – and that's not acceptable either. Someone like McMullen comes along and starts querying every incident. You can't *do* that. Surely in a war no soldier can be entirely blameless or innocent. Am I not right, Pascal?'

'Possibly,' Pascal said, in cautious tones. 'It's certainly very difficult for an outsider to judge. Particularly twenty-five years later.'

'I suppose so. I suppose so.' Mary gave an unhappy shake of the head, then made an attempt to push these events away. She gave a little sigh, looked at her watch, then smiled.

'Anyway,' she went on, in a brighter voice, 'there's no point in going over the past. I don't want to make you late for the airport. Do you want to ring for a taxi from here?'

'No.' Pascal rose. 'I'll flag one down in the street. It will be quicker.' He hesitated, then glanced at Gini, who gave him a tiny nod. 'In fact, if you like, I'll just go out and see if I can get one now.'

When he had left the room, Mary and Gini looked at one another. There was a silence, then they both rose. Mary took Gini in her arms.

'Oh, Gini,' she said, 'don't look at me that way. I do like him. I'm sure I'll come to like him more, when I know him better. It's just . . . at the moment, I can't quite forgive him for all that business with John. I still feel that if he hadn't influenced you—'

'You're wrong, Mary.' Gini looked down into her kind face, and anxious eyes. 'I promise you, you're wrong. I would have acted the same way whoever I was working with. It had nothing to do with Pascal.' She hesitated. 'He does influence me – you're right. And I hope he goes on influencing me. Mary, when you know him better, you'll see. Pascal's good. He's a rare man.'

Mary smiled. 'Well, well,' she said. 'Spoken from the heart. All right. I'll reserve judgement. You can tell your Pascal, he can come to dinner with you when you get back, but he needn't think I'm a pushover, I'm not easily won over you know.'

'Yes, Mary, you are.'

'Well, maybe a little bit. I'm soft-hearted. A sentimentalist. And he does have very nice eyes . . . ' She smiled, and drew Gini towards the door. 'You won't tell me where you're going?'

'No, Mary. It's a secret. Just for now. We'll tell you when we get back.'

'Not even a little hint? Oh, very well, very well . . . ' She opened her front door. Pascal, who possessed an uncanny ability to find taxis in most major cities around the globe, even in torrential rain, even in the rush hour, had found one now. It had pulled in at the foot of the steps. Pascal was standing beside it, explaining a route he knew to Heathrow which avoided all traffic jams. He did this with some verve.

Mary watched this tall, dark-haired young man. He made some Gallic gestures; he was speaking very fast. She glanced at Gini, and gave her a little push. 'I do see,' she said. 'I do see, Gini. Was he like that when you first met him?'

'All that impetuosity and vitality – and impatience?' Gini smiled. 'Yes, he was.'

'Then you'd better not keep him waiting. Call me the second you both get home. And have a lovely time,' she added, 'in that mysterious place, wherever it is. He's waiting for you, Gini. Go on . . . '

Gini ran down the steps. In the taxi, Pascal took her hand. He was looking anxious.

'It's an hour ahead there,' he said. 'I wanted us to arrive in sunlight but we won't. It will be dark.'

'That's fine.' Gini rested her head on his shoulder. 'I'll see it in twilight. Then tomorrow, we'll get up very early—'

'Possibly. We might not want to.'

'Well, one day we could. We could get up early one of the days, Pascal, and see it at dawn.'

It was not a very lengthy journey. With a change of planes it took just over two hours. While they were on the second plane, Pascal talked at great length, very fast. He explained when his ex-wife was moving to England, and so when and how he was planning for Gini to meet Marianne. He was full of ideas as to where he and Gini might live in London, and how often they might spend time in France. He had a million plans for how he would work, and she would work, and how and where they might work together, and when Gini said that she also had one or two plans in this respect, he gave her a glance of delight: fine, he said, they would, of course, incorporate her plans as well.

'Don't you think, Pascal,' Gini said contentedly, 'that all these plans of ours might take up a long time? Years and years. We'll never get through them all, you know.'

'So?' He gave her a sidelong smile. 'I don't want to be through with these plans. I intend to spread them out and keep you busy. I intend them to last us a very very long time.'

'Some of those plans are quite dangerous.'

'So? I like danger. And so do you.'

He drank a glass of champagne very fast. He said, 'I've rediscovered who I am. For that I have you to thank, Gini. I think I shall kiss you. I think I shall kiss you for a long time, right now.'

'On a plane? In front of the stewardesses?' Gini smiled.

'The hell with the stewardesses. The hell with the rest of the passengers. Lean a little bit this way. No, a bit more, darling. Excellent. Now.'

By the time they landed, Gini felt dazed. She looked at the airport where they landed, and she saw the woman at the car-hire desk, and she saw the streets of the town through which Pascal drove them, surely and fast. She saw all these things, and the narrower, steeper roads which they came to eventually, but they were blurred and made imprecise by the happiness she felt. She leaned back in her seat, and watched the light over the hills around them turn silvery, then mauve. She had waited a long time to come here, and now that she had, it felt momentous but welcoming. She knew this place with her mind. To come here felt like coming home.

'When we get there – it's only a few kilometres more,' Pascal said, 'I want you to close your eyes when I tell you, and then open them when I tell you . . . ' He broke off and gave her an anxious glance. 'Maybe you'll be disappointed . . . '

'I won't be disappointed, Pascal.'

He drove on, the narrow road winding upwards. Ahead of them, through the gathering darkness, Gini could see the outlines of buildings, a small church, a farm. She wound down the window, and breathed in the scents of the air. Pascal slowed. She could hear faint music in the distance. To her left, a pale hunting owl swept over the hills.

'Now you must close your eyes,' Pascal said, stopping the car. So she did. Pascal came around, and took her arm. He led her quietly and carefully a short way. Gini could feel cobbles underfoot, and hear voices. The past weeks slipped away. It felt so good, so immensely good to be alive, to be with Pascal, to be here.

'It's just around this next corner,' Pascal said. 'And then you can open your eyes.'

He led her on a short way. The voices were a little louder now, and they were accompanied by other noises – music, the clink of glasses, footsteps, the laughter of children.

The air smelled of open country and cooking and red wine and the promise of long summer evenings. When Pascal stopped, and told her she might look now, she opened her eyes. She saw trees with their trunks lime-washed white, and their still-bare branches strung with lights. She saw two cafés facing one another on either side of his square. She saw the houses he had described to her, and the small church he'd worshipped in as a boy. She saw a priest in a soutane, and two men who might have been farmers, and a mother with a small child. She saw, on the far side of the square, the village's one hotel, which was where he had promised her they would stay, and she saw the shuttered window on the top floor, which would have a view over the hills, and which he had told her would be theirs.

It was very ordinary and very extraordinary; it was as he had described it and much more than he had described it. Pascal looked at her face, then up at the night sky which was patterned with the most brilliant stars. He kissed her, then he led her across to one of the cafés, where he was recognized at once, and where together with the priest who had confirmed him, and the two farmers who had been taught by his father, they drank *marc*. Pascal was teased, and she was teased, and Pascal took this in good part.

When he had had enough of the teasing, he rose, and took her into the hotel, whose owner had been his mother's cousin. She showed them, with pride, to her room with the best view, on the top floor. And they both looked at that view, which was very beautiful, the next morning. But as Pascal had predicted, they did so long after dawn.

THE END

NOTE

All the characters in this novel are fictional: they bear no relation to any politicians, journalists or diplomats, alive or dead. All the locations, however, are real, although details such as names and street numbers have been changed. Appleyard's apartment building exists, and is just as described. There is a palazzo very like the Palazzo Ossorio in Venice, though it does not go by that name. In particular, the details concerning the residence of the US Ambassador in London's Regent's Park and the buildings adjacent to it are exact; apart from tree-felling activities, this area is as described.

SB, 1993

DESTINY
by Sally Beauman

'The most talked about novel in years' *Daily Mail*

One evening in Paris, Edouard de Chavigny becomes a man obsessed. A wealthy, notorious womaniser, he is captivated by the mysterious young English woman, Hélèn Craig, and knows that she is the woman he has been searching for all his life.

But Hélèn is not what she seems. While Edouard offers her wealth, freedom and passion, she must weigh these attractions against the demands of her own secret life and her determination to exact revenge for the destruction of her childhood world. What neither she nor Edouard know is that their lives are already linked, and that ahead of them lie years of public glamour and private pain.

'A compelling and gripping read' *Elle*

A Bantam Paperback

0 553 17352 9

DARK ANGEL
by Sally Beauman

'A rich and engrossing read' *Evening Standard*

Halley's Comet night at Winterscombe in 1910 ends with a violent death which throws a giant shadow over three generations of the Cavendish dynasty.

At the centre of events is the beautiful and dangerous Constance, who casts a spell – which may be a curse – on all the sons of the family.

Following the destruction of two World Wars – and the passions, deceits and hatreds of the intervening peace – it is the coruscating power of Constance's personality, and the sinister secret at the heart of her life, which will determine if Victoria, last of the Cavendishes, is to inherit happiness or misery.

'Unputdownable' *Company*

A Bantam Paperback

0 553 17632 3

A SELECTION OF FINE NOVELS
AVAILABLE FROM BANTAM BOOKS

☐ 17632 2	DARK ANGEL	Sally Beauman	£4.99
☐ 17352 9	DESTINY	Sally Beauman	£4.99
☐ 40427 X	BELGRAVIA	Charlotte Bingham	£3.99
☐ 40163 7	THE BUSINESS	Charlotte Bingham	£4.99
☐ 40428 8	COUNTRY LIFE	Charlotte Bingham	£3.99
☐ 40296 X	IN SUNSHINE OR IN SHADOW	Charlotte Bingham	£4.99
☐ 40496 2	NANNY	Charlotte Bingham	£4.99
☐ 40171 8	STARDUST	Charlotte Bingham	£4.99
☐ 17635 8	TO HEAR A NIGHTINGALE	Charlotte Bingham	£4.99
☐ 40072 X	MAGGIE JORDAN	Emma Blair	£4.99
☐ 40298 6	SCARLET RIBBONS	Emma Blair	£4.99
☐ 40372 9	THE WATER MEADOWS	Emma Blair	£4.99
☐ 40321 4	AN INCONVENIENT WOMAN	Dominick Dunne	£4.99
☐ 17676 5	PEOPLE LIKE US	Dominick Dunne	£3.99
☐ 17189 5	THE TWO MRS GRENVILLES	Dominick Dunne	£3.50
☐ 40364 8	A SPARROW DOESN'T FALL	June Francis	£3.99
☐ 40407 5	THE GREEN OF SPRING	Jane Gurney	£4.99
☐ 17207 7	FACES	Johanna Kingsley	£4.99
☐ 17539 4	TREASURES	Johanna Kingsley	£4.99
☐ 17504 1	DAZZLE	Judith Krantz	£4.99
☐ 17242 5	I'LL TAKE MANHATTAN	Judith Krantz	£4.99
☐ 17174 7	MISTRAL'S DAUGHTER	Judith Krantz	£2.95
☐ 17389 8	PRINCESS DAISY	Judith Krantz	£4.99
☐ 17505 X	SCRUPLES TWO	Judith Krantz	£4.99
☐ 17503 3	TILL WE MEET AGAIN	Judith Krantz	£4.99
☐ 40206 4	FAST FRIENDS	Jill Mansell	£3.99
☐ 40361 3	KISS	Jill Mansell	£4.99
☐ 40360 5	SOLO	Jill Mansell	£3.99
☐ 40720 1	MALINA	Penny Perrick	£4.99
☐ 40363 X	RICH MAN'S FLOWERS	Madeleine Polland	£4.99
☐ 17209 3	THE CLASS	Erich Segal	£2.95
☐ 17630 7	DOCTORS	Erich Segal	£3.99
☐ 40262 5	FAMILY FORTUNES	Sarah Shears	£3.99
☐ 40261 7	THE VILLAGE	Sarah Shears	£3.99
☐ 40263 3	THE YOUNG GENERATION	Sarah Shears	£3.99
☐ 40264 1	RETURN TO RUSSETS	Sarah Shears	£3.99
☐ 40582 9	THE SISTERS	Sarah Shears	£4.99